PROTECT AND DEFEND

Also by Eric L. Harry

Arc Light
Society of the Mind

PROTECT AND DEFEND

Eric L. Harry

Hodder & Stoughton

Copyright © 1997 by Eric L. Harry

First published in Great Britain in 1997
by Hodder and Stoughton
A division of Hodder Headline PLC

The right of Eric L. Harry to be identified as the Author of
the Work has been asserted by him in accordance with the
Copyright, Designs and Patents Act 1988.

10 9 8 7 6 5 4 3 2 1

A CIP catalogue record for this title
is available from the British Library

ISBN 0 340 64891 0

Typeset by Hewer Text Composition Services, Edinburgh
Printed and bound in Great Britain by
Mackays of Chatham PLC, Chatham, Kent

Hodder and Stoughton
A division of Hodder Headline PLC
338 Euston Road
London NW1 3BH

Table of Contents

PART III

Chapter Nine

Chapter Ten

Chapter Eleven

Chapter Twelve

Chapter Fifteen

Chapter Sixteen

PART IV

Chapter Twenty

PART V

Chapter Twenty-Three

Chapter Twenty-Four

'Our first work must be the annihilation of everything as it now exists.'

Mikhail A. Bakunin
Dieu et l'État (1882)

Prologue

OUTSIDE TOMSK, SIBERIA
August 15, 1030 GMT (2030 Local)

The only signs of man were the huge black pipes running undefended from horizon to horizon. The man atop the shaggy native horse turned his collar up against the chill. Nightfall came slowly in that northern clime, but the wind began to bite long before dark. He eyed the featureless dark blue sky. It seemed to weigh down on the earth, pressing the horizons below their accustomed positions. He had never seen true wilderness before. The sky there seemed to assume a greater prominence in the order of things.

With a gentle prod of his heels the horse started forward. Its rider had been awkward at first. He'd dug his heels into the horse's flanks then yanked back on the reins to slow the beast. Over the weeks of his trek to this remote spot, however, horse and rider had become one. He now sat comfortably in his saddle – his body attuned to the gentle sway of the animal's motions. A slight tug on the reins pulled the horse to a stop, and he climbed down.

He paused beside the horse to listen. The jet-black cluster of pipes and a few others like it supplied the homes and factories of Western

1

Europe with almost half their energy needs. The massive volumes of natural gas rushing across the Eurasian plain made no sound. But as he moved nearer to the pipe, he could feel the heat.

Friction, he thought. *It's in there*. He untied the faded blue bedroll lying across his horse's rump and laid it on the ground with a faint clanking sound. When the coarse blanket was unrolled, the tools of his new trade lay spread before him as if on a surgeon's tray.

The emptiness swallowed the few sounds he made in the same way that it swallowed his thoughts. His mind wandered. The swiftly flowing stream he'd crossed a few kilometers back. The view of the night sky from a dozen camps in as many days. The perfect stillness of the deep woods on a windless evening.

The crisp, clean air of Siberia constantly bathed him with its ebb and flow. He breathed of it deeply, filling his lungs through his dry nose. The weather had cooperated. He'd never seen a more beautiful day than the one that was just ending.

The man forced himself to concentrate when he came to the delicate part of his long-practiced routine. Time passed – not quickly, but without notice of its passage. All the while memories made fleeting forays into the periphery of his consciousness. The bath he'd taken in a frigid stream. He had emerged to dry on the bank. The sun was hot on his bare skin. His horse had wandered out into the water, pausing to lap the cool liquid and then darting through the shallow stream every so often with surprising vigor, chasing and chased by the dragon flies. He would miss the horse, the summer nights.

As he had lain on the bank with the sun shining red through closed eyelids, other memories had come. Each roused him from his slumber with a start. That night they had come again. He had awoken in a full sweat – shivering from the cold. He had clutched his blanket to his chin – staring out with pounding pulse at the blackness that surrounded the small bubble of light from his campfire.

He took a deep breath and paused to look up at the sky. He felt drawn to the reddish hues of the setting sun. Maybe here, in the great nothingness, he could change. He would remain in the wild, live off the land, suffer the immense hardships of a winter, maybe two. When he emerged, he would be a new man. Maybe the harshness – the sheer dominion of Siberia over all creatures great and small – would kill the old human and give birth to a new one. A new man cleansed of all that had passed.

It was at that moment he realized the truth. That no matter where he was or how far his travels took him, he would carry with him the baggage of all that had passed. All he had done. It was the punishment of God or of nature; it made no difference which.

He mounted the horse – the effort made greater by the burden of his memories – and rode a short distance alongside the pipeline. He pulled a crinkled piece of paper from his pocket and wearily climbed down. He opened a small can of thick white paint with his knife. He held the paper in one hand and a brush in the other, carefully copying the words from the paper onto the pipe.

Rising again to his saddle, he spurred the horse and slowly ascended a low hill. There he waited. He caught himself looking on instinct to all corners of the horizon. A habit born of life in the other world. The world of humankind. He saw nothing, of course; nobody.

A chill passed over him as the last sliver of blood-red sun sank into the West, and he wrapped his arms around himself, shivering. The cold would come early that night.

Four small charges popped within milliseconds of one another. Natural gas gushed from the torn pipes in phenomenal volumes. The tiny explosions had depleted the nearby atmosphere of oxygen. But when the heated and compressed gas jetting from the pipes found air, a mammoth fireball erupted. Like a giant can-opener, the burning gases expanded and split the pipe for a hundred meters in each direction.

The jarring boom rolled over the barren landscape and startled the horse.

'Spokoyno,' the man murmured. He patted the horse's hard neck that lay just beneath the short bristles of its coat. There were no echoes on the tabletop-flat terrain. After the first concussive shock wave had passed, the only sound was from the burning gas. It filled the normally quiet world with a sonorous roar like that of a speeding train. A pall of black smoke rose high above the conflagration and blotted out the darkening blue sky.

The man scanned the now devastated length of black pipe. For a hundred meters in each direction, it was twisted and split and broken. But the large block letters he'd scrawled lay undisturbed just beyond the limit of the explosion's violence. The paint ran like white blood beneath the words. 'Destruction is the mother of all creation!' he mumbled out loud as he read. A single ear of the agitated horse twitched to take in the sound of his voice.

He spurred the animal on. He was from nowhere, and it was to nowhere that he returned.

PART I

'The first two laws of thermodynamics can be summarized thusly: the natural course of the universe is to go from a state of order to a state of disorder. Those laws also describe systems built by man.'

Valentin Kartsev (posthumously)
'The Laws of Human History'
Moscow, Russia

Chapter One

RED SQUARE, MOSCOW
August 15, 2300 GMT (0100 Local)

'Anarchy, anarchy, anarchy,' Kate Dunn said into the brilliant lights of Woody's mini-cam. Just behind her, the sustained roar of a hundred thousand voices echoed across Red Square. Her night vision was spoiled by the camera's lights, but she could see the demonstrators' fists pumping in air. The throng fell silent to await the speaker's next cue.

'Sound is good,' Woody said with his eye glued to the mini-cam's eyepiece. 'But the light ain't worth shit. We won't pick up more than the first few people in the crowd down there.' He plugged his headphones in. 'Gimme some more sound,' he directed.

'This is Kate Dunn, reporting to you for NBC News,' Kate said. 'How's that?'

'Fine.' Woody's fingers tapped at the camera's controls. It was all automatic, but for some reason he always overrode the computer's settings with his own manual tweaks. Kate looked out over the crowd. She felt a flutter in her chest at the excitement of the moment. From her vantage atop the abandoned police van she could see the mob's

7

leader in the distance, bathed in harsh footlights from the speaker's platform. The angry man spat out another stream of invective. The sound truck's speakers were at maximum volume. It distorted the rabble-rouser's voice. Again the crowd roared. Their clenched fists shook at the Kremlin walls, on which danced shadows from the flickering light of bonfires and thousands of torches.

Kate felt goose bumps ripple across her skin. 'This is prime-time footage, Woody. I can feel it.'

'Uh-huh,' he replied. He worked the knobs on top of the tripod. His face was glued to the eyepiece. The scene around her was awe-inspiring, but she forced herself to close her eyes and go over her report. Not the words – she knew those cold – but the mood, the inflection, the calm of the veteran reporter's voice conveying in measured tones the excitement of dramatic events. She had watched foreign correspondents do it all her life. Her lips moved and she nodded her head in time with the crowd's chanted slogans.

'Show time!' Woody said. Kate opened her eyes, totally calm.

Woody's fingers counted down from five, but when he hit zero and pointed, she waited. She waited for the perfect moment. A thunderous shout rose from the hundred thousand angry Russians. They waved the black flags of the Anarchists in figure eights. In the quiet that followed the roar, she began.

'Anarchy,' she said – thinking, *slowly, slowly* – 'All current values are baseless. No political system known today works. Life as we have lived it is meaningless.'

The roar rose up again, then the crowd fell silent. Kate was in rhythm with them. 'These Russian Anarchists want to improve their "spiritual condition" through destruction of all existing social order. "From destruction, creation arises!" This is the slogan of a new generation.'

A sustained cheer erupted, and Kate half turned to witness the spectacle. It was one of history's turning points, she could feel it. In the capital of a great power. Revolution sweeping the course of mankind down a hundred-year tributary. And she was there . . . reporting it all to a fascinated world.

'Among the ideologies considered to be of continuing significance,' she said into the blinding lights of the camera, 'Anarchism alone has never been tried. That it still attracts fervent adherents such as those here tonight is testimony to its intellectual credibility. Single-minded obsession with individual liberty and skepticism of government, it seems, are as alive today as they were in the nineteenth century. Now, here, in this land of great social experimentation, we may soon learn whether Anarchism is utopia, or whether it will lead down yet another detour through hell on earth.'

A roar erupted just as she completed the sentence. *This is it!* she thought in the torrent of noise. *Don't screw it up now!*

'But what sort of idea *would* you expect to flourish in a Russia that has lost all hope?' Kate continued as fiery words were spat in Russian from distant loudspeakers. 'In a Russia that has tried everything, and failed? What *sort* of ideology would take root in the minds of a hundred million lost souls?'

'*Anarchi-i-i-a-a!*' the crowd roared in stirring unison. Kate was almost overcome by a wave of emotion as her mind's eye viewed the scene from the camera's perspective. *Perfection, sheer perfection.*

'Anarchy. A rejection of everything, every ideology. When you can't create, *destroy!* "To think is to say no!" A mean, uncompromising idea to vent the pent-up energy and frustration of a nation of the idle. An idea that captures the imagination and fires the empty bellies of a long-suffering people. The black flags, the feverish rhetoric,' she paused, 'and the violence.

'With the world's attention focused on student protests in Beijing, the violence in Siberia earlier today came as a complete surprise. There, saboteurs launched concerted attacks on the system of natural-gas pipelines that supply much of Western Europe's energy needs. Spokesmen for western oil companies said late today that the sabotage, if the reports were accurate, would cripple the entire supply system due to the remote locations of the damage.' Another roar went up, and Kate raised her voice and shouted into the microphone. 'They further pointed out that no repair crews would be sent until the Russian government could guarantee their safety from terrorists.' The crowd quieted in the repetitive pattern of exhortation and response. 'As the gas pressure in the system steadily falls, prices on world energy markets are going through the roof. North Sea crude and other alternate sources of European energy rose more than forty percent by market close with no sign that . . .'

A stunning flash of light barely preceded a deafening boom that reverberated among the buildings enclosing Red Square. Kate ducked involuntarily at the stupendous sound. A hundred thousand people in Red Square flinched in unison. 'Over there,' Kate shouted. She pointed for Woody to turn the camera. Smoke billowed into the air from the end of the square in front of St Basil's – from where army troops had gathered but stood idle. The chants quickly degenerated into random shouts from a multitude of shrill voices.

The crackle of machine-gun fire began the terror.

It was as if everyone panicked at once. 'It appears that the Army has opened fire!' Kate managed over the din. Woody moved to shoot the scene from close behind her shoulder. The heat of the bright lamp glowed warmly against her face. Objects hissed through the air all around, and Woody turned out the lights and lowered the camera.

'What are you *doing?*' Kate shouted over the noise of the crowd, which had turned as one and was streaming away from the guns. 'Aren't you *getting* this?'

The 'z-z-z-i-i-i-p' of what Kate suddenly realized were bullets and the rocking of the van under their feet sent the first jolt of fear through her system. Woody pulled Kate down to the flat metal roof as the steady, deeper rattle of heavy guns settled into a rhythm of machine-like killing. 'We gotta split, Kate!' he yelled, pushing her toward the edge of the van's roof.

'Hey!' she shouted before tumbling through air onto the heads and shoulders of the fleeing crowd. Kate fell in the darkness through the sea of tightly packed bodies, barely managing to gain her feet at the last second. She looked up in horror to see the force of the horde topple the van onto its side. Woody leapt feet first – camera in hand – into the human tide on the opposite side.

All around her was a crushing press of grunting, snorting panic. Growls and brief shouts burst forth. The men – much taller than her five foot three inches – elbowed and jostled their way toward the narrow exits a half-step at a time.

Kate was terrified. The breath was pressed from her lungs in the crush. Her face was pinned between bodies and she couldn't even turn her head. There were arms clutching at her legs as screaming people were being trampled under foot.

The bullets splitting the air all around and the booming explosions were now just background noise; a secondary concern. Her life depended upon footing. Upon tiny patches of cobblestone on which to place her next step. For to fall, she knew, was to die.

Kate began to claw and scratch for small openings in the mob. She grabbed onto lapels and sleeves and eventually hair as the crowd lurched this way and that. She maintained her balance as much by the grip of her hands as the placement of her feet. Suddenly, the sea of humanity surged in an unexpected direction. Kate had guessed wrong. She fought for a toehold amid a tangle of legs. She was falling. She fought to grab onto something. An elbow smacked her squarely in the nose – blinding her with a white flash of pain.

Kate screamed as she slipped beyond the point of no return into the darkness of churning knees. The sea swallowed her up in slow motion, and the sounds of the explosions and the gunfire grew distant. There were different sounds down there, underneath the surface. The wails of the dying who lay on the stone pavement echoed amid the forest of stamping boots.

I'm going to die. The thought hit her with the physical effect of a body blow as her knees landed on cold paving stones and the flow of the bodies threatened to press her flat. All her senses abandoned Kate in that moment, the prickly grip of fear consuming her. She pounded her fists against the headless bodies that kicked her ever lower toward the oblivion of the earth. Pain shot unexpectedly through her ribs and she screamed long and loud – her eyes forced shut by the effort.

The pain in her ribs came from a tight grip. Fresh air bathed her face as she twisted and shouted and scratched her way up, up to the surface. To the air. Kate had been pulled from the depths. Someone had lifted her up from the grave. She couldn't see who it was. She didn't care. She fought viciously now. She would not fall again. Her jaw was clenched in a sneer. Everybody around her was an enemy, to be pushed and slapped and scratched if advantage could be gained. Everybody but the man behind her. His two hands remained fixed on her ribs.

Slowly, the crushing force of bodies began to wane. As the pressure of the packed crowd fell, the pace of the crowd's flight picked up. The crackle of gunfire could still be heard in the distance as the demonstrators streamed toward the exits. Kate was swept along. The fighting and jostling of the crowd fell with the lessening pressure of the crush. Still, however, the hands held her.

Kate stopped and turned. A tall man, in his late thirties or early forties, looked down at her in the semi-darkness. He had tired eyes set in a handsome, pale face. His hair was pitch black. He said nothing, turned and disappeared into the masses before Kate could say a word. He wore the black garb of the Russian anarchists.

Huge red flames boiled into the air over their heads as another stunning boom caused all to duck and turn. A second ball of fire shot skyward, and another boom rolled over the square.

The flames from the explosions rose into the air from behind the Kremlin walls – from *inside* the Kremlin! And then so did a helicopter. In the light from the blazing fires Kate could see the white, blue and red tricolors of the Russian Republic painted on its sides. It was the Russian President's helicopter. As it wheeled onto its side and hurtled away through the caverns of downtown Moscow, the night was lit by hundreds of burning tracer rounds fired past the fleeing aircraft at tremendous velocities.

BETHESDA, MARYLAND
August 16, 0000 GMT (1900 Local)

'It's anarchy, Elaine,' Gordon Davis said to his wife. The local news reported the downtown killings as a 'crime.' But the appropriate words were anarchist atrocity. 'They have no rules. They're incapable of feeling empathy for their victims. They're totally unsocialized. We'll *never* go back to the way we were. We're just going to have to live our lives in a country with wild animals running loose on the streets.'

'I *know* you don't believe that,' Elaine Davis said into her mirror. 'I know what you really believe, Gordon. You're a totally hopeless idealist.'

'We interrupt your programming to bring you this ABC News Bulletin.'

They both turned to the small television in their master bath. 'This just in to ABC News,' the deep-voiced anchor said. 'A major riot is reported to have taken place in Red Square in central Moscow.'

Gordon saw his wife return to her make-up. *Another food riot*, he thought, knotting his tie.

'Western journalists on the scene report that anarchist demonstrators defied Russian Army orders to vacate the square by nightfall. Although it is unknown who fired the first shots, regular army troops had begun taking over barricades from Interior Ministry riot police earlier in the day, and by sunset were massed in the thousands. Estimates vary as to the number of demonstrators present, with some sources putting the number as high as two hundred thousand.'

'Those poor people,' Elaine said as she carefully drew a faint line under her eye with a pencil. Gordon had to look away. That process always made him nervous.

'At this hour, the violence appears to be spreading outward from Red Square, and now seems to have consumed most of Moscow's center.' Those words drew Gordon's and Elaine's attention, not to the television but to each other. 'Experts have kept a close eye on the situation in the Russian capital in recent days amid rumors of impending upheaval and worsening political instability. There are numerous *un*confirmed reports from Moscow tonight of widespread fighting between security troops and Russian anarchists, but ABC News must reiterate that those reports remain as yet unconfirmed. Please stay tuned to ABC for further word on this breaking story as it develops. We now return you to your local programming, already in progress.'

As the 'Special Bulletin' screen replaced the picture of the ABC anchorman, Elaine said, 'You think Greer will call the Armed Forces Committee back into session?'

'No-o-o. Everything these days is China, China, China. Plus, everybody's down at the Convention.'

'Are you guys decent?' their older daughter Celeste interrupted from the bedroom door.

'Come on in,' Elaine said as she powdered her nose at her vanity.

'Ta da!' Celeste announced, smiling and holding her hands up to present her younger sister – Janet – who wore her new cheerleader uniform. Janet shook the pom-poms and kicked. 'Doesn't she look like a complete dweeb?' Celeste asked. Janet shook a pom-pom in her sister's face.

'You were a cheerleader once *too*, Celeste,' Elaine noted. 'Just because you're "way cool" now that you're going off to college doesn't mean you should spoil your sister's fun.'

'That's right!' Janet shouted, again shaking the pom-pom in her older sister's face as she headed out. Celeste slapped it away and followed, an argument breaking out.

'The victim,' the local news anchorwoman read, 'age eleven, had a record of minor criminal activity and school suspensions. Eyewitnesses said that the boy pulled a knife in the stairwell of the school and was shot to death by the accused, also age eleven. School officials deny there is a security problem in the building's stairwells although students claim assaults are common in the cramped and windowless

13

space, where lights are repeatedly broken by gangs seeking to cloak their planned attacks in the darkness.'

'My *God*,' Elaine said, stroking her eyelashes delicately with her mascara brush. 'I don't know what I'd do if the girls had to go to public school. I'd never get a moment's rest I'd be so worried.'

'It's horrible,' Gordon agreed. The story of yet another murder played on their television, complete with a bloody sheet covering the corpse being loaded into an ambulance. The crowd gathering in the lights around the crime scene was entirely black, as was, Gordon felt sure, the victim. This crime was simply a garden variety drug killing, not one of the more sensational reports.

'What are you going to talk about tonight?' Elaine asked.

Gordon straightened the top edge of his crisply starched collar. 'Take a wild guess.'

'Oh, Gordon!' Elaine said, turning to look at him. 'Not at your daughter's *pep* rally, for goodness' sake!'

'Well, crime and violence is what's on everybody's mind!' he said, holding his hand out to the television. 'Somebody's got to talk about it. We've got to get those people off the streets. I don't care how many cops, how many courts, how many prisons, how many electric chairs it takes, or whatever the cost. This country is in a major state of decline, and it's primarily due to crime and violence.'

'Just who are "those people", Gordon?'

'Jesus Christ, Elaine!' he snapped, and she shushed him – looking at the door where the girls had been. 'You and I both know who I'm talking about,' he said in a lowered but still urgent voice. 'People are leaving this country, Elaine! Native-born citizens just up and checking out of Hotel America. You saw that *Newsweek* article about Vancouver and Toronto. If the trends continue, half the damn urban population of Canada will be former Americans by the middle of the next century.'

'I thought you said we'd all just have to get used to things. What can you possibly say? What can anybody do about the problem?' Gordon slumped and frowned. 'Plus, I don't think now's the time to launch any bold new initiatives,' Elaine said, nodding at the news coverage of the Republican Convention. The Republican National Committee had asked that Gordon delay his arrival at the convention until the last day. The entire Davis family was scheduled to catch a flight for Atlanta at six o'clock in the morning. '*And*,' Elaine continued, 'are you so sure that it's crime and violence that are the problem? Maybe they're just symptoms of something else that's wrong.'

'Oh, now you sound like Daryl! It's just "the situation"?' Gordon said sarcastically. They both let the subject drop, and Gordon checked his watch. 'Let's not stay too late tonight, okay?'

'Did you give them the school's telephone number?' Elaine asked, clearly trying to act nonchalant.

'Yeah,' Gordon replied, not needing to ask who 'they' were. 'And Daryl has it too. He promised to call if he heard anything – even rumors – from the convention hall.'

Elaine stood, and Gordon wrapped his arms around her. He could see her smile in the bathroom mirrors. 'Just relax,' he said. 'We'll know soon enough.'

'You know, what if . . .' she began, and Gordon's mind bolted ahead. He felt a rush of excitement at the wild speculation he had denied himself. 'What if nobody calls?' she finished. His mood crashed. 'We've really built this up, and if . . .'

'They're going to call,' Gordon said with more certainty than he felt and a note of irritation in his voice. The signs were all there. They'd done a full-blown background check. Gordon had had good talks with all the right people.

'You know what I think?' Elaine said – pulling back and smiling up at him. 'I think there's a cabinet post with your name on it.' Elaine shook him playfully from side to side.

'Sh-h-h! Don't jinx it,' he shot back, kissing her to hide the grin that forced its way onto his face. 'Besides, the President is still way up in the polls. Bristol has a lot of ground to make up by November before he can offer me anything.'

'There's plenty of time for something to happen,' Elaine said, sinking to Gordon's chest. 'Life's a funny thing. I mean really, sweetie. Who ever thought you'd be a Senator? You never know what's going to happen next. You just never know.'

'We all think we're safe behind these walls,' Senator Gordon Davis said, spreading his hands to encompass the ivy-covered gymnasium of his daughter's private school. The bleary-eyed parents sat impassively, waiting, Gordon imagined, for the blow-hard politician to finish his spiel. 'But we're not. We fool ourselves into thinking we can insulate.

15

Isolate. Escape the violence out there that is eating away at the fabric of our country.'

The silence was deafening. 'It is a delusion. Like a cancer, anarchy is a disease attacking the cells of America – its citizens. Most of us here, the parents whose children attend this fine school, think ourselves immune from the disease. But let me remind you, ladies and gentlemen, that we live in a society. A collection of citizens. A nation. And if that host nation grows *sick*, then *all* the cells that make that nation up are at risk, the *healthy* as well as the *diseased*. Thank you.'

Polite applause filled the gym. Gordon was an appointee who'd filled an unexpired term of a Senator who had been driven from office in disgrace. He'd never been an inspiring speaker. He left the podium to rejoin Elaine. It was the prep school's first gathering of the year – a pep rally to introduce the athletes and cheerleaders. Elaine cast her husband a forced and, he knew, disapproving smile. Worse yet was the scowl Janet aimed at him from the front rank of the cheerleading squad.

'Senator Davis, you have a telephone call,' a school administrator whispered to him as the headmaster stepped up to the microphone to introduce the football team.

Maybe this is it, Elaine said through her smile and gentle squeeze of his arm. The band struck up a march – the sounds of their blaring and discordant instruments painfully loud in the enclosed space. Gordon followed the woman off the stage to a tunnel leading through the bleachers. Only Daryl Shavers, the chief of his Senate staff, and the Republican National Committee staffers knew of his plans to be at the school that night. Only they had been given the phone number.

His heart began to pound. He tried for the hundredth time to deflate his expectations, not wanting to be disappointed. The Republicans were trailing President Marshall's Democratic ticket by eighteen points in the pre-convention polls. The economy was humming along. Governor Bristol, the Republican nominee, was making no headway with his neo-conservative, social activist platform. *NBD*, Gordon thought to calm himself – using one of Janet's many acronyms. '*No Big Deal*.'

The woman led Gordon into an office. He swallowed the lump in his throat. *But a cabinet post*, he thought. He was a born appointee.

'Hello?' he said.

'Senator Davis?' came the breaking voice of a kid.

'Who is this?' Gordon demanded – deeply disappointed.

16

'You gotta get out of that gym right now, sir. I'm sorry! I think I really screwed up. I've . . . I've already called the police.'

'What are you talking about?' Gordon asked as another phone chirped and the woman picked it up.

'Just trust me, sir. Please! Go! Right now!' There was a click as the boy hung up.

The woman held up the other phone. 'They said it's urgent.'

Gordon raised the other receiver to his ear. 'Gordon Davis.'

'Sir, my name is Carl Jaffe. I'm Deputy Director of the Secret Service. We'd like you to get your family and head to the school's security office. We have some agents en route and they'll meet you . . .'

Long rips of automatic weapons fire erupted inside the gymnasium. The woman next to him jumped with a start then stared at the glass door, her mouth agape. The first screams rose but were drowned out by still more shooting. Gordon dropped the phone and rushed for the door. A torrent of booming gunfire assaulted his ears as he headed out of the office into a full-blown war.

Well-dressed parents, wild-eyed with panic, streamed out of the gymnasium with young children in their arms or being pushed along by firm grips on their shoulders. Some had lost all control and screamed wildly as Gordon waded into the flood of people fleeing the terror inside. The going was slow against the human tide. The rapid-fire bursts of the guns were brief and selective now. Shoulders and elbows pummeled Gordon in mindless flight from the terrible noise, some people bent over to run in a stoop. When Gordon reached the tunnel that led into the gym, he saw the first blood. It streamed down the face of a stunned middle-aged woman from beneath neatly groomed blonde hair, coating her white silk blouse in remarkably brilliant crimson.

The next burst of gunfire was long and jarring, emanating from just inside the gym. Its horrendous noise made Gordon pause, and it easily drowned out the horrible wails of the panic-stricken. A great wave of humanity gushed into the tunnel – their vigor renewed by the now incessant sounds of several guns. Gordon was battered by blows so great that he was being swept with them – away from his wife and daughters. With all the strength he could muster he tore at the crowd, parting the men, women and children with rough shoves as he barely maintained his footing.

Another long tear of fire – closer and much louder than before –

caused people to throw themselves to the ground all around, clearing the tunnel momentarily.

Gordon slammed into a man who dashed out of the gym looking over his shoulder. The man turned, and he and Gordon stared at each other for a moment – each stunned. The man wore a calf-length black overcoat. His blond hair was shorn short, mere bristles. His blue eyes shone in stark contrast to his tanned face. They were in that instant all alone.

The man stepped back and raised a smoking machine pistol. The muzzle of the ugly black gun traced a line up Gordon's body that he could almost feel as a prickly itch along its aim point. A shiver that began as a tingle in his groin rippled across Gordon's body as the man's blue eyes smiled and the gun steadied on Gordon's chest.

'No!' Gordon yelled just as a bullet smashed into the metal stands right beside the gunman. The blond man flinched and twisted, the muzzle of his gun spitting flame. Gordon felt the weapon's hot breath, but the sting of bullets did not follow. He darted under the sloping bleachers to his right, the blazing gun swinging to follow him but the bullets miraculously striking a thick concrete pillar in between. Stooped over and hurling himself into the darkness beneath the stands as fast as his feet would carry him, Gordon felt jabs of pain in his ears from the sounds of the machine pistol's fire. When the shooting stopped a second or two later, Gordon looked back and saw through the maze of supports and columns. A school security guard lay in the tunnel in a pool of blood. In his hand he still clutched his pistol.

A stunning blow struck the side of Gordon's head. He reached out into the semi-darkness and felt his way around the concrete support with which he'd collided. His head was throbbing in pain, but his attention returned to the blue-eyed gunman who peered after him from the well-lit tunnel. He was slapping another long magazine into his weapon.

Flame erupted from the gun, and Gordon slid around the thick pillar to the opposite side. Bullets cut through the air all around and thumped into the concrete at his back. The trusses and girders and concrete pillars under the stands were lit in the strobe of the flaming muzzle.

The gun fell silent, but Gordon's ears still rang. 'Come out, come out, wherever you are,' the man's lilting voice came. It had a strangely resonant quality to it in the steel hollows under the stands. He had

18

trilled his Rs deep in the back of his throat. He was foreign. Another long rip of fire clanged off the girders ahead of Gordon, sending great showers of sparks through the air.

Gordon took off running, heading deeper and deeper under the stands. He dodged the increasingly thick forest of obstacles visible in the blazing light from the killer's gun. Sparks rained down on him from clanging ricochets, and fierce spitting sounds tore open the air just inches from his body. Sprays of splattered concrete stung his face and hands as he ran dodging and weaving through the erector-set maze.

The gun fell silent again, and Gordon slowed and stooped over low to the ground in a crouch. His breath came in shallow pants and his heart thumped against his chest so hard he added it to his list of worries. Darkness descended on the ever-lower stands around the curved end of the basketball arena. Gordon felt his way into the deepest, darkest regions – his face covered with a thin gauze of spider webs. The clacking sounds of another magazine being popped into the machine pistol presaged another storm of lead.

'You can run, but you cannot hide,' the thickly accented voice tormented Gordon, who probed now through the near-total darkness. He held his hands in front like antennae, his fingers jamming into the hard obstacles just ahead of his body.

A burst lit the way ahead for just an instant, and Gordon dropped to his knees to crawl into the recesses of the stone and steel cavern.

Gordon dragged himself through the heavy coating of dust still covering the floor from the gym's construction. He squeezed his body as far as it would go into the wedge formed by the lowest row in the stands and pressed his back between two heavy girders that rose at an angle to the sides. Inside the gym above him, the shooting had stopped. But the shrieks and shouts and the vibrations of stamping feet against the steel at Gordon's back told a story of unspeakable horror. His wife. His two precious daughters. Tears welled up in his eyes, which he jammed closed to shut out the picture that flashed through his head. *Oh, God, no!*

'Sounds like some sort of *distu-u-urbance* up there, ya?' the man asked coolly – trilling his R deep in his throat in a thickly Germanic accent. 'Maybe you are worried about Mrs Davis, eh?' He knew Gordon's name! 'Maybe your delicious young daughters, ya?'

He was close. In the hard, enclosed space, every sound was sharp.

It focused Gordon's mind, shutting out the background commotion from the bleachers above.

'Maybe you and I, ve could go find out, ya? Find out if your family is safe?' The man was cool, his manner almost serene. Gordon saw him now, creeping forward in the darkness – the dim profile of his pistol leading the way. He was moving slowly past Gordon, who lay totally still – curled in a fetal position and breathing slowly, quietly, through his parched mouth.

The gunman stopped, not ten feet in front of Gordon. He was fumbling with something. There was a sound like the tearing of paper. Then a snapping sound.

A brilliant flare seared the darkness with bright light, leaving an orange spot on Gordon's eyelids as his eyes shut involuntarily. When he opened them, the man was looking down at him – the flare in one hand, the machine pistol in the other. The light from below his chin cast long shadows up his face, forming dark crevasses in the creases of flesh around his smiling mouth.

'Ah, there you are,' he said, carefully placing the flare on the ground in front of him and rising to near full height just under the sloping ceiling of their world. 'Behold, Senator Davis, ze end of your vorld.'

He raised the gun with both hands. A swastika was carved sloppily onto his knuckles.

The stunning booms of automatic weapons in the cave-like environs threw Gordon into shock. His whole body clenched in a grip of fear so great that he could feel nothing. He opened his eyes to see the blond man lying on the ground next to the flare. Gordon stared at him, waiting for him to move. More shots rang out – these in a series of single but still rapid booms. His pursuer – his tormentor – jerked with each plug of a bullet. Sprays flew from his lifeless corpse in time with booms and flashes. Gordon watched black blood fill a small depression beside his body.

Gordon's throat was pinched so tight with terror that he gagged, unable to draw a breath. Three men in dark suits appeared, stubby Uzis barely larger than a pistol held extended in two hands. They fanned out, combat style, ready. One crawled up to the coughing Gordon.

'Are you hit, sir?' the tense man asked. Gordon managed to shake his head, but then turned and vomited into the dust beside him. Gordon felt hands poke and press his body, lifting his jacket and patting him down as if for a weapon. 'He's good,' Gordon heard. He watched smoke from the man's gun barrel rise in the dying light from the flare. 'Are there any more of them down here?' Gordon's savior asked. Gordon was transfixed by the darkening, reddish hue. The man's hand shook Gordon's arm gently. 'Sir? Can you answer me?'

'No,' Gordon croaked, wiping his mouth and twisting his way through the dust toward open space. Toward the air that he suddenly craved. 'I mean, no, there aren't any more. Just . . . that one.' He coughed on the choking stench of gunsmoke.

The three men each produced a small flashlight. The one next to Gordon pulled the lapel of his suit to his lips. 'Big Top, Big Top, this is Red Leader,' he said. 'The package is secure. I say again. The package is secure.' Gordon's head was still swimming as he looked up at the man. A wire ran into an earphone like a hearing aid. The man's pinstriped suit was immaculate. He wore a pin, an American flag, on his lapel – the universal badge of the Secret Service.

'Copy that,' he said, then motioned toward one of the other two agents. 'Skinner. You go.' The agent took off for the tunnel without further instructions. He too had an earphone. The third agent turned the body of the terrorist onto his back.

It was then that Gordon's pounding heart and paralyzed mind calmed just enough to admit the 'background' sounds from above. The flare burned itself out, leaving only the two agents' flashlights to light their world in narrow beams. They discussed the body. 'That one got him,' one said – the harsh white glow from his flashlight pointing under the dead man's overcoat.

'Jesus,' the other said. 'Look at that. Must be ten mags sewn in there.'

Gordon's mind drifted off, away from the dark world filled with the acrid smell of smoke.

'Oh, God!' a woman wailed. *'Why?'* The words were barely audible over the ringing in Gordon's ears. But the woman's cries rose in tone and anguish above the shouts of pain and despair of others in the gym above. Tearful, shattered sounds. There were families in the gym, nothing but families. Like Gordon's family.

'I've got to go,' he said, rising to his knees.

The agents and their flashlights turned his way. 'You'd better stay here, sir.'

'I'm sorry, but I've got to . . .'

'Somebody is checking, sir. On your family.'

They didn't know. They had to check. Alive or dead. Gordon sank back down into the dirt. Alive or dead. The weight that held him there was heavier than the steel and concrete above his head.

Sounds of commotion. Sirens. 'I need a doctor!' someone yelled.

The two agents both grew still, listening. Something was coming over their earphones. Gordon was focused so completely on the agent nearest him that the sensation was almost physical. 'Red Leader copies.'

Gordon gasped for air. 'What?' he asked – tears filling his eyes. Which way was his life headed?

'They're all right,' the man said, then lifted his lapel again in the dim light and said, 'Copy that. We're coming out.'

'You mean, my wife and daughters . . . I have two . . . they're all safe?'

'Yes, sir. They weren't harmed. We've got them under our protection.' The two Secret Service agents stood. One helped Gordon to his feet, saying 'Watch your head,' just as Gordon smashed it into the stands above. He was so drained, so exhausted, that he stumbled along in their grasp.

The two agents held onto Gordon's elbows as if he were an invalid, solicitous of every beam overhead and sweeping the cobwebs from his path with their Uzis.

Gordon stopped and turned to the head agent. 'Were they after me?' Gordon asked. He could see in the growing light from the tunnel the nodding head of the agent. 'Why? Why me?'

The man stared at Gordon for a moment as the other agent looked on. 'You don't know?' he asked quietly, almost whispering. Gordon shook his head. The agent explained. 'Some kid phoned in a tip about an assassination attempt to the Bethesda police. They contacted the Secret Service. The Deputy Director called the RNC and the kid's story checked out. You were lucky, sir. Very lucky. We'd just rotated off duty at Camp David and were heading back to D.C. We were on the Beltway about six miles from here when we got the call.'

'What . . . what story? What was the kid's story that you checked out?'

There was a pause. The man considered not answering, Gordon guessed. The two agents exchanged glances. 'Senator Davis, sir, you're about to become the Republican nominee for Vice President of the United States.'

22

Gordon's head swam on hearing the words. *Vice President*, he thought. The two agents grabbed his elbows and ushered him on like a prisoner. Through the dizziness, the sirens, the shouting – the news somehow managed to sink in. Gordon once again halted the men, this time on the very edge of darkness which he knew would cloak the look on his face. *Vice President of the United States*, he thought, holding onto a steel girder. *The first African-American nominee for Vice President in American history.*

CAMP DAVID, MARYLAND
August 16, 0423 GMT (2323 Local)

Thomas Marshall – President of the United States – awoke in a sweat to thoughts of war. In the confused moment before alertness came, he felt a sickening guilt over the awful tragedy of it all. In his nightmare there had unfolded a relentless march of errors.

There was a shout from outside his window. He opened his eyes, fully conscious now in a room lit only by the light from the digital alarm clock. Not yet eleven thirty. He and the First Lady had only just fallen asleep.

Marshall thought he heard another shout, and he propped himself up on his elbows. He'd had briefing after briefing on the student sit-ins at Beijing University. Several had come on the golf course as the Chinese government threatened force. His muscles were sore from the thirty-six holes he'd gotten in that day. The Camp David relaxation was just part of the ritual. Disappear during the Republican Convention. Let them have their day in the sun before kicking their butts up and down the campaign trail.

His mind was leaden. The wine he'd drunk to relax himself for sleep had done the trick.

An engine – deep and heavy like that of a truck – groaned to life outside. There was another shout before the engine revved and tires squealed. Deep male voices shouted urgently to one another. A string of firecrackers went off, then another, and another, punctuated by a sharp explosion. Marshall spun his feet to the floor and groped in the plush carpet for his slippers. His wife stirred and mumbled, 'What?'

Marshall padded over to the window and pulled the heavy curtain aside. There was a fire of some sort in the distance. From the direction of the main road. From the main guardhouse. The 'firecrackers' were gunfire, he realized, and they came from there also.

A sharp boom rattled the windows and rocked him back a step in surprise. Flame boiled into the sky from along the road between the gate and the President's lodge.

'What was that?' his wife muttered from the bed. The door to his bedroom burst open. He turned in time to see a dark figure rushing at him – profiled in the light from the sitting room. The large man tackled Marshall in a jarring collision. The curtains were still clutched in the President's hand, and the curtain rods fell onto the two men in a heap.

'Tom?' the First Lady shouted from bed.

'Stay out of the window, sir!' the man on top of the President said. Marshall watched as the ceiling was bathed in the flash from yet another explosion. The popping guns of a firefight were slowly being drowned out by the whine of a helicopter's engines.

'Let's go!' another Secret Service agent shouted from the door. The President was amazed to see a man appear wearing a dark suit carrying an M-16 rifle.

Marshall crawled beneath the window alongside the man who had tackled him. Marshall heard the First Lady grunt. An agent had forcibly bent her over and draped a bulletproof vest over her nightgown.

At the door, an agent helped Marshall slip his pajama-clad arms through his own body armor. Strong hands then pushed him down the darkened hallway toward the service stairs at the end.

'Let's go! Go! Go! Go!' an agent was shouting as the entourage practically ran down the hall.

When the President reached the stairway door, he paused to look at the two men at the hallway's end. Their hair was clipped short. Marines, he could tell, even though they wore only T-shirts and boxer shorts. They were setting up a machine-gun in the open hall window amid the draperies the First Lady had picked out earlier that summer. A long belt of bullets was being pulled from a metal box.

Down the stairway they ran. The President joined the First Lady just inside the door to the rear lawn. The large form of a blacked-out Marine One helicopter sat on the pad forty yards from the house. Its engines drowned out all sounds of the fighting. The stairs behind them were now crowded with Secret Service agents talking excitedly into their radios. The flash of an explosion lit up the dozen or so Marines crowded around the door just outside. One was bare-chested but wore dog tags and combat boots and carried a shotgun.

'Hit it!' someone yelled, and out they rushed. The Secret Service agents and Marines formed a human shield around the President and First Lady. Their weapons were raised and their gaze peeled in a phalanx of flesh that protected their charges from all directions.

'What's going on?' the President shouted as they rushed across the lawn.

'I don't know, sir!' the distracted agent next to him yelled over the helicopter's noise. In seconds they were aboard, and the aircraft took off with the door still open. Pressed into a seat by helping hands, the President felt his seatbelt being fastened for him and he looked out the window. Brilliant white flares dropped from the helicopter's belly, illuminating the now scattering group of escorts on the lawn below. Fires rose into the air from the guardhouse and in a string along the main road. Marshall caught sight of tracer rounds flying in both directions in the dark woods by the gate.

The thin treetops of the Maryland countryside scraped against the belly of the twisting, turning Marine One.

MCLEAN, VIRGINIA
August 16, 0455 GMT (2355 Local)

'Hey, dad!' Nate Clark's teenage son appeared at the door of his study. 'Come take a look at this on TV.' Jeffrey Clark disappeared just as quickly as he'd appeared.

'What about the American Express?' Nate asked his wife as he rose.

'Paid it,' Lydia answered. Her legs were slung over the side of a padded leather sofa. She was gently kicking her feet while reading a catalog. 'What do you think about this?' Lydia asked, holding the catalog up to him just as Jeffrey shouted '*Da*-ad!'

'Pretty,' Nate mumbled mechanically before joining the boys in the family room. 'Look!' said Paul, his younger son – pointing at the announcer on television. It was CNN. 'This Just In' read a graphic in the background. 'We have no independent confirmation of any of this just yet,' the anchorwoman said. 'If something like this were to be true, it would be absolutely unprecedented.' She hesitated, distracted, then said, 'I'm being told we have Elizabeth Crane on the line from the Maryland Highway Patrol. Ms Crane, can you hear me?'

'Yes.'

'You're on the air.'

The woman cleared her throat. 'Well, about fifteen minutes ago, we received a call from the Presidential compound at Camp David requesting back-up units and stating that there was a "firefight" – that was the word he used – under way. Two units responded and reported that there were flames at the main guardhouse and at various places inside the compound, and that gunfire could be heard from the surrounding woods.'

'Wait, let me get this straight,' the anchorwoman interrupted. 'Are you saying that there was some sort of battle at Camp David? That there was gunfire and . . . and a "firefight," as you said?'

'The units reported casualties at the gate, and the initial call to dispatch was from a Marine guard on a cellular phone. The dispatcher also reported that the sounds of gunfire could be heard over the phone.'

'Do you know whether the President was still there at the time of the attack? My producer is telling me that President Marshall was reported there as late as this afternoon.'

'We don't know anything more. We're advising all motorists who don't have to be out to avoid the area, and we're cordoning off all roads into and out of Camp David with road blocks.'

Nate headed for the telephone in the study. It began ringing before he got there.

'It's a Captain Fairs?' Lydia said, shrugging at the unfamiliar name.

'Hello,' Nate said as he powered the television up.

'General Clark?'

'Speaking.'

'Sir, this is Captain Fairs. I work for the Chief of Staff's office. We're sending a man from the protective service by a few homes, and yours is on the list. And I've also got a message that General Dekker has requested you be in his office at zero nine hundred.'

26

'All right, I'll be there. What's the security for, captain?'

Lydia shot him a look of concern.

'Just a precaution, sir. We're calling in extra security personnel here at the Pentagon. And there was some trouble at the SecDef's home – an alarm went off – but there was nobody there.'

Lydia was already up and staring at the television. Nate couldn't hear the anchorwoman, but the pictures were from Chicago. Flashing police lights filled a city street slick with an evening rain. In the distance, several cars burned. The street was strewn with sparkling debris.

Nate hung up.

'What is it?' Lydia asked.

'I don't know. Terrorists. Get the boys and let's go.'

Lost in thought he heard, *'Nate?'*

He turned to her. 'It's just a precaution,' he said. 'Someone also hit the Secretary of Defense's home. That's all.'

Lydia headed for the family room in a daze. 'Oh,' Nate called out to her, 'and send Jeff back.'

Jeffrey appeared just as Nate pulled a 9-mm Beretta from the locked drawer. The seventeen-year-old's eyes widened. Nate slapped a magazine into the butt and pulled the slide, chambering a bullet. He carefully lowered the hammer and slipped the pistol into his waistband, but Jeffrey's eyes followed his father's hands. Nate put three full magazines into his blue jeans pockets.

'Come on, son,' he said as he headed for the hall closet. He reached up and took the dark green canvas bag from the top shelf. He extracted the engraved silver shotgun in two pieces. In seconds, he had it together and loaded two shells into the side-by-side double-barrel twelve gauge.

'Be careful with this,' he told Jeffrey – catching his eye to confirm the boy understood. Nate closed the shotgun and held it out to his first-born. The boy looked at the gun respectfully for a moment before he gingerly took it from his father.

They joined Lydia and Paul at the garage door. 'Lydia, you drive. Jeff, in the front seat.' Nate turned and headed for the back door, grabbing a cordless phone from the kitchen counter.

'What about me?' Paul asked – his fourteen-year-old's voice breaking.

'Get in the back and keep your head down.' He turned to Lydia. 'I'm gonna go around the side of the house to check out the drive. I'll call if the coast is clear and climb in with

27

you out on the driveway. Don't open the garage until I say so.'

Nate slipped out the side door. It was dark and hot outside. Crickets chirped from the nearby pasture. The sound of the pistol's hammer locking back seemed overly loud.

He felt a surge of alertness – an unpleasant rush of hyper-attentiveness. It caused a flutter in his chest that left him drawing shallow breaths. The pistol was at eye level, its butt and the heel of his right hand supported by the palm of his left. He forced himself to blink. *Calm down*, he told himself. He took deep, slow breaths. It had been a long time, but he remembered the physical sensations all too well. The sickening anxiety just when you most needed calm.

With his eyes now adjusted to the dim light and his heart pounding, Nate headed up the walk with the pistol leading the way. The pebbles crunched under his first step, and he suddenly felt exposed. He had to fight the urge to drop and crawl. *Jesus, Nate!* he thought, swallowing and forcing himself to stand more erect. To calm himself. His shoulder muscles already ached, and he unclenched his cramping stomach. He stepped off the gravel walk and onto the grass.

There were too many dark places. The bushes, the garbage cans, the treeline. The treeline worried him most. He checked his rear, turning his entire body in order to keep his right eye in line with the pistol's sights.

He shouldn't have done it that way! Blind. He should be covered. Riflemen on the bushes and trash cans. A machine-gun on the treeline. He forced himself to concentrate. At the side of the garage, he felt a jab of pain in his left side. The sensation was so sharp he had to drop a hand from the pistol to probe the spot. Only when he didn't feel any moisture was he convinced there was no wound. At least, not a new wound. It was there that the bullet had entered. In the decades since, he'd felt the pain return in random jolts. It was as if the nerve endings retained some memory of the agony they'd transmitted that day.

By the time he'd inched his way down the hedge that bordered the drive all the way to the quiet street and then back again to the house – checking for wires across the narrow strip of pavement the whole way – Nate was exhausted. He pulled the cordless phone from his pocket and dialed his Range Rover.

The faint hiss of static as he waited for the ring brought back the crystalline image of a single moment in his life, long, long ago. Lying

28

on the dirt, the pain was so great that all he felt was varying degrees of it. It was at once icy cold and searing heat. All he recalled was the tug on his skin of the suture . . . and the steady hiss of white noise on the radio. Clark had clung to the sound of the static. His life had depended on it.

He heard the ring over the phone and from the garage. Lydia picked up the car phone immediately. 'Come on out,' Nate said, then he sagged against the wall. The garage door opened slowly, noisily.

He hadn't only been wounded on that patrol, he'd lost four men. Five, in fact, only one didn't die until he was on the operating table. Nate had held his hand out and touched the boy on the flight back to the aid station. Sky-high on morphine by then, Nate remembered the warmth of the boy's chest which slowly grew cold as air whipped through the open doors of the helicopter and life bled from his body more quickly than the IV could replenish it.

The car appeared. Nate carefully lowered the hammer on the pistol and climbed in the back with Paul. Lydia wasted no time backing down the driveway.

'What's wrong, dad?' Paul asked.

'Nothing,' he said. 'Let's just . . . just drive.'

Lydia headed off as Jeffrey manually searched the radio for the fast-breaking news stories.

Nate had lain in the dirt all day long. Then night had offered a respite from the heat. But when darkness fell, the North Vietnamese had poured it on. Bullets cut through the dry grass just inches over Nate's face. The casualties streamed in, dragged for the most part by men who were wounded but returned to the fighting.

Everyone was pressed low. He had been so thirsty . . . so thirsty.

'You're sweating, dad,' Paul said in a quiet voice. Lydia looked at Nate through the rear view mirror.

'Leave your dad alone, Paul,' Lydia said softly.

The static in between radio stations cut through Nate's fog. 'Romeo India Two Three, I read you, over,' the distant voice had said just after a burst of static. Nate felt moisture fill his eyes. All day long he'd waited for those words. But all he'd heard was the crack of rifles. The smacking sound of bullets through the brush. The whimpers of men with bloody bandages pressed to their ravaged bodies. All day long he'd listened to the static. Waiting. Hoping. Praying. Thinking only of his life and how

29

much it meant to him now that it seemed to be slipping away at age twenty-two.

'It's okay, dad,' Paul said. He put his arm out to pat Nate's back awkwardly.

Lt General Nate Clark reached out and pulled the boy into his arms, hugging him. Hiding his face in the boy's hair. *Why me?* he thought for the thousandth time. *Why did I live, and the others die?*

Chapter Two

THE KREMLIN, MOSCOW, RUSSIA
August 16, 0455 GMT (0655 Local)

Colonel Pyotr Andreev, commander of the Russian Presidential Guard, climbed the last metal rungs of the bomb shelter's air shaft. His dozen surviving security troops trailed just behind. Andreev's arms, shoulders, back and lungs burned from the thirty minutes of strenuous ascent. But the broad, slatted vents that would close on the flash of a nuclear burst were now within reach. Andreev and two of his men began to pry open with bayonets the screen that prevented birds from entering the shaft. It was painstaking effort, for any noise would mean certain death.

Andreev squeezed out of the vent into the dim light of dawn; he crouched amid the hedges that concealed the air shaft from view. He breathed heavily. Sweat soaked the dark trousers and white dress shirt that he wore under the ballistic vest and bandoliers full of ammunition. He peered through the bushes. Russian army troops were forming into ranks in the headlamps of armored fighting vehicles whose hatches were thrown wide open. The lick of flame from a doorway and from the wrecks of a couple of cars were the only evidence of the fierce fighting that had raged across the old fortress's grounds.

The sound of gunfire beyond the Kremlin walls, however, could be heard from all directions. The commander of the motorized rifle regiment sent to relieve the beleaguered Kremlin defenders had radioed that they had been ambushed by anti-tank missiles on Gorky Street. Andreev's men all looked at each other in silence – jaws agape as the ferocious, ripping sounds of firefights filled the fresh early-morning air. The Kremlin was roughly in the center of Moscow, and it seemed as if the entire city was engulfed in war. It was a sound that meant only one thing – the end of the Republic of Russia.

Andreev found their best route through the darkness to the ancient stone wall and the relative safety that lay beyond. The wall there appeared to be lightly defended. The dark forms of only two soldiers were profiled against the city lights. One was walking slowly along the wall away from them with his rifle slung over his shoulder. The other was peering intently through binoculars into the distance. Andreev led his men in a quiet dash across an open road just under the crest of a hill that shielded them from the busy main Kremlin square.

Andreev crept up the steps toward the soldier with the binoculars. His men were close behind with weapons raised. When he reached the top, he saw that the second soldier had rounded one of the towers that dotted the high walls and was now out of sight.

'Don't move,' Andreev said in a low voice. The soldier's binoculars sagged, but otherwise he stood stock-still. He wore the blue-striped shirt of a 'Desantnik' – a paratrooper – under his full combat gear. Andreev's men quickly disarmed the frightened soldier, then dropped a rope over the wall to the park-like grounds below. The soldier was forced to kneel and put his hands on his head. He stared down Andreev's rifle through wide eyes set in a face blackened with grease paint.

'What unit are you with?' Andreev asked as his men rappeled one-by-one down the wall.

When he didn't answer, a grizzled sergeant in Andreev's security force pulled a knife from its scabbard. Its menacing, serrated edge drew a darting look from the frightened paratrooper. '104th,' he answered.

'From Omsk?' Andreev asked, and the man nodded. They had come all the way from Siberia. That meant Air Force transport. *That* meant the rebellion was widespread and coordinated. 'Why?' Andreev asked without thinking. The private's mouth hung open. He clearly didn't know how to reply. 'What did your officers tell you your mission was?'

He closed his mouth and swallowed, taking one more look at the large blade before replying. 'They . . . they said we would save Russia.'

The rope shook – slapping at the stone. All of the men were now safely on the ground, and they were anxious for Andreev to join them.

'Get down to the men,' he ordered the sergeant.

As the sergeant rappeled down the wall, bright lights lit the tops of trees. Andreev dropped to one knee behind the low stone wall. Across the open central square that had been their brief battleground, a five-car motorcade pulled up – their brilliant headlamps lit. They were unconcerned with security now. They were in complete control. Emerging from the black limousine in the center was a lone figure.

Andreev instantly recognized the short, balding man in the blazing headlights. He wore a broad smile on his face and shook hands with a tall officer in full combat gear. They both then strode briskly toward the Palace of People's Deputies. The civilian's round glasses – like those worn by academics – gave him away. It was Valentin Kartsev, former general in the KGB and now the acknowledged 'leader' of the Anarchists.

That son of a bitch, Andreev thought. *So he's behind this.*

Andreev raised his rifle. Resting the barrel on the stone in front of him, he brought the fixed iron sight onto Kartsev's mid-section. At just over a hundred meters, Andreev knew he wouldn't miss, even in the poor light. *Die, you little piece of shit.*

The rope slapped at the wall again. Andreev's men would be holding the rope stiff at the bottom of the wall – standing there exposed while they dutifully waited for him.

His job was done. The President had fled God knew where. Andreev had other things to think about. His young wife Olga. Their two little girls. Kartsev's back was to him now, and Andreev's aim had moved unconsciously to follow his target. Staring down the rifle at the man, he felt the tension in his finger hard against the trigger. The slightest pressure now would loose the sear, and the single bullet would shatter the bastard's back.

It was his chance. Andreev knew Kartsev. The man deserved to die.

The rope slapped the stone again.

Andreev closed his eyes and took a deep breath, carefully easing the tension on the trigger. He rose to a stoop, leaned over the young Desantnik and raised his finger to his lips. The boy nodded.

Andreev rappeled quickly down the rope to the grass at the base of the wall.

I had the shot, the thought nagged him. *I had the shot.*

HEATHROW AIRPORT, LONDON
August 16, 0500 GMT (0500 Local)

'I've got the lights,' the co-pilot said out of habit.

The flight computer flew the huge A-400 Airbus in for its automated landing. The pilot kept his hands lightly on the wheel – also out of habit – as the computer trimmed the plane for its near-perfect descent onto the well-lit runway seven miles ahead. The night was clear. Often the autopiloted landings on calm nights like this were so soft the passengers had to be awakened from their slumber at the gate. The flight from Hong Kong had been uneventful.

But not so their departure from Hong Kong. Several Hong Kong newspapers had openly sided with protesting students in Beijing. Armed troops had shut them down a few days before. On board the flight was Great Britain's Foreign Secretary, who was returning from a well-publicized protest. The airport's tarmac had been lined with chanting anti-western demonstrators.

The engines throttled up just slightly, and then up a little more – noticeably louder.

'Must be some headwind,' the pilot commented.

'Airspeed two twenty,' the co-pilot replied. The sound of the engines rose a little more, and the pilot could clearly feel the acceleration press his back into the seat. 'Two thirty-five,' the co-pilot announced.

That was too fast, and their airspeed was climbing.

'Flight Niner-Two-Niner,' the control tower said, 'you're above the glide path. Please reduce speed to two ten.'

'Roger that,' the pilot replied. 'I'm disengaging the autopilot.'

The 'fly-by-wire' flight controls were responsive to even the lightest touch. The flight crew had to be extremely careful not to brush the wheel during normal autopiloted flight. The computer interpreted any movement of the yoke by the pilot or co-pilot as a manual override.

The pilot pulled back on the wheel and the throttle in a smooth, coordinated motion.

Nothing happened.

'Speed two forty-*eight*,' the co-pilot said.

The pilot jerked the wheel. Nothing. Even the lumbering airbus should have lurched at that much control pressure. He looked at the altimeter. Five hundred meters.

'Tower, this is British Airways Flight Niner-Two-Niner. I'm going around.'

He pulled the wheel back toward his chest.

'No *response*?' the co-pilot asked.

The pilot turned the wheel from side to side. The co-pilot stared at him in terror.

'State your problem, Niner-Two-Niner,' the tower called.

'Heathrow Tower,' the pilot said, his voice flat despite the rising fear, 'BA Niner-Two-Niner is declaring an emergency. I'm having problems with the autopilot disengage.'

The engines rose to a new plateau of sound, and the nose pitched down just slightly, still heading toward the lights at the end of the runway.

'Jesus!' the co-pilot said, pulling the throttles back all the way to reverse thrust, and then forward again. Nothing. No change in the whining engine sound. 'Airspeed is two ninety. Altitude four hundred.'

'Reset the computer,' the pilot said to his seatmate.

'Christ, James! It'll take six or seven seconds for . . .'

'*Reset* it!' the pilot yelled as the engines increased power again, and the aircraft pitched forward. The nose was aimed right at the touchdown marks on the runway.

The co-pilot flipped a protective cover up, then pressed the button over and over. 'It won't reset!'

A buzzer sounded – the ground collision avoidance alert. It was the sound that signaled to the human crew that they should take over. That something was wrong. The pilot thrashed the wheel about wildly, cursing it and kicking at the rudder pedals.

The engines wound up to full power.

'Oh, mother of God!' the co-pilot shouted.

'Flight Niner-Two-Niner,' a new voice came over the radio from the tower – a supervisor. 'Please advise situation, over.'

'Airspeed three fifty and climbing!' the pilot shouted over the cockpit noise. From the First Class cabin in back he could hear screams. 'Altimeter three hundred and falling! Controls totally nonresponsive!'

The whining wind past the windshield made a sound like a dive bomber in an old war movie. 'Shut it down!' he shouted to the co-pilot, and they both reached up to start throwing circuit breakers on the panels above their heads. The avionics of the advanced cockpit began to fall dark one instrument at a time.

'Airspeed four forty. Altitude two hundred.'

The nose dipped down again. From the carnival-ride feeling of free fall the pilot got in his groin he knew it was too late. He and the co-pilot, strapped in their seats in the nose of the mammoth aircraft, hurtled toward the hard concrete runway.

The investigators listened over and over to a shout on the cockpit voice recorders. Finally, one investigator thought to check the pilot's personnel records. It was his wife's name, but it was nearly instantly drowned out by the sound of the wrenching force that tore the life from all two hundred aboard.

OVAL OFFICE, THE WHITE HOUSE
August 16, 0700 GMT (0200 Local)

The sound of the ringing telephone filled the Oval Office. The principals of the National Security Council and the heads of the nation's law enforcement agencies listened – waiting.

There was no answer.

'Try his dacha,' Marshall finally said, and his aide called the Russian President's home outside Moscow. The phone rang and rang. Secretary of State Hugh Jensen looked at his watch and shook his head. 'Tom,' Jensen said in a low tone, 'it's just after nine o'clock on a Friday morning in Moscow. We've tried all the telephone numbers we keep on file for President Krestyanov. One of them – their military command net number – is supposed to rove and guarantee contact twenty-four hours a day.' He was hunched over his elbows. 'There's nobody there.'

In the background, the sound of the ringing telephone droned on.

*   *   *

President Marshall read the *Chicago Tribune* at his desk in the Oval Office. 'The Terror Continues' a banner headline proclaimed. Marshall sighed as he skimmed. More lurid details of violence. 'Chinese Crush Student Protest,' read a 'below-the-fold' article. What would have been the top story – hundreds of democratic protesters feared killed – was relegated to second-class news. An article toward the bottom of the page caught his eye. 'Bold VP Nomination Changes Race.' Marshall smiled at the presumably unintended pun. '*Changes Race*,' he thought. He rocked back and put his stockinged feet on the desk to read the story about Gordon Davis.

The first flash poll following the close of the Republican Convention was out already. Marshall's lead had fallen from eighteen to eleven points. The *Tribune*'s political analyst attributed it to a masterstroke by Governor Bristol. 'Bullshit,' Marshall whispered, snorting. 'Just post-Convention bounce,' he mumbled.

The intercom buzzed. Marshall lowered the paper. 'Yes?' he said.

'Sir, the Swedish Prime Minister is on line three for you from Stockholm.'

Marshall made a face. He'd met the man only once. *What the hell could he want?* Marshall had his secretary summon his chief of staff, and then he pressed line three. 'Prime *Minister?*' he said in an energetic, vibrant tone – his public voice. 'To what do I owe this pleasure?'

'Mr President,' came the deep and heavily accented voice, 'I have news of some significance of which you should be made aware.' The President's chief of staff walked in, carrying his coffee mug and nodding jovially at Marshall's secretary. 'Approximately one hour ago, there was an unauthorized landing by a Russian aircraft on a runway outside Kiruna in the far north of our country.'

'Who is that?' Marshall's chief of staff mouthed, pointing down at the phone. He placed his cup on a coaster and sat across the desk from Marshall.

'Swedish PM,' Marshall whispered.

'In that aircraft,' the slow voice came over the background hiss of the transatlantic connection, 'was the President of Russia, the Russian Prime Minister, several members of the cabinet, and their families.' The President rocked forward. The White House chief of staff leaned over the desk closer to the phone. 'They are all seeking political asylum.'

'Jesus Christ,' Marshall whispered.

NATIONAL AIRPORT, WASHINGTON, D.C.
August 16, 1300 GMT (0800 Local)

'It's about Goddamn time!' Daryl Shavers exclaimed. He was craning his neck to look out the small round window of the business jet.

'Daryl!' Elaine Davis said as Celeste and Janet looked at each other and giggled.

Daryl looked around at the girls and apologized. They had been waiting on the cramped jet for forty-five minutes, and the plane was now sweltering despite the early hour.

A tanned and well-groomed man boarded the jet. The single flight attendant closed the door behind him. 'Senator Davis,' the new arrival said, 'my name is Arthur Fein. I'm the head of Governor Bristol's Vice Presidential Team.'

Gordon rose and shook his hand. 'I'd like you to meet Elaine, my wife.' They shook hands. 'And my two daughters . . .'

'You must be Celeste!' Fein said. The jet the Republican Party had leased fired up its engines. 'And you're Janet.' The two girls smiled. 'Look at you two! You're both very pretty.'

Gordon marveled at how quickly the girls had recovered from the horror of the night before. It had to be the novelty of the limos and the press and the jet that had snapped them out of it. *And they're young*, he thought. Gordon looked at Elaine. He saw only the blank, bland expression she'd worn since their drive home from the gym. It worried him. She hadn't yet recovered from the shock.

The jet began to taxi. Gordon turned to introduce Daryl – his chief of staff, right-hand man and best friend. Fein instead greeted the two Secret Service agents who sat quietly in the front. 'Hey, I know you!' he said, shaking the hand of one of the agents with a flourish. 'You were on the Bush detail, right?' The man nodded. 'Coffee, black, with two Equals, right?' Fein said, smiling and pointing at the man's face. 'Am I *right?*'

'That's right, Mr Fein,' the man said – smiling for the first time. He then introduced his unsmiling younger partner.

Daryl sat down and buckled up as the jet turned onto the runway.

Fein sat across from Gordon. The noise of the engines on take-off was too great to introduce Daryl. Gordon waited in Fein's fixed gaze. The man took in Gordon with a placid expression on his face. A study in comfort with his foot on the low coffee table and his hands – protruding from crisp white cuffs studded with gold cuff links – clasped in his lap. His suit was Savile Row – broad pin stripes down thick, heavy fabric despite the summer weather. His red tie matched the kerchief sticking jauntily out of his breast pocket. His blue shirt was topped with a starched white collar pinched together with a nearly hidden gold collar pin.

Gordon averted his eyes self-consciously from Fein's stare. Daryl was looking at Fein also. The look on his face was one of seething anger. Elaine looked down at the table, uninterested in any of it.

The moment the engine noise dropped, Fein unexpectedly turned and said, 'You must be Daryl Shavers.' He held his hand over the table to shake Daryl's – a pleasant smile on his face.

Fein's hand hung in air for a moment, and Fein waited. Gordon looked over at Daryl, who finally shook hands without comment. Fein was unfazed. 'Dear?' he said – turning to catch the flight attendant's attention. 'Sparkling water, please. Chilled, no ice.' He then pulled a slim briefcase up and laid it on the table. 'I hope you don't mind if we jump right in. We're going to be pretty busy when we touch down, so this might be our best opportunity to get down to the nitty-gritty.'

'I absolutely agree,' Gordon said. Daryl extracted a legal pad filled with notes from an expandable folder that served as his briefcase. 'There's a lot we need to discuss. What will our statement on the terrorism be? On the Chinese crackdown in Beijing? You know I've got a strong record on crime. And the anarchy that's sweeping this country is really just a variant of . . .'

Gordon fell silent when Fein made a big production of laying a single sheet of paper on the table. 'Okay,' Fein said in a businesslike tone. 'Day one. "Hi, my name is Gordon Davis. I'm a young, handsome, conservative, well-groomed, well-spoken, well-educated African-American male with an equally attractive, perfectly functional and loving wife and family. I'm a Norman Rockwell wet dream for the 1990s. I'm the great hope that we might all just possibly end up getting along together after all."' He held his index finger up. 'Day one.'

Gordon stared back at him. In the silence that followed, Daryl rolled his eyes. Elaine was looking out the window.

'Any questions so far?' Fein asked, ignoring Daryl completely.

Gordon shrugged. 'Go on,' he said.

'That's it. The substantive part, that is.'

Daryl snorted and turned his head toward the window. 'Sh-shit,' he muttered.

'Now,' Fein continued, smiling as if at his own humor, 'for the next couple of hours, I'd like to work with you on a few things . . . with your permission.'

'Absolutely,' Gordon said. He leaned forward and rested his elbows on his knees. 'I have a lot of questions, obviously.'

'Good! Let's have them.'

'Well, first off, what is Governor Bristol's position on the latest wave of terrorism? If it turns out that it's tied directly to the Russian anarchists, will we propose any direct action?'

Fein wore the same pleasant smile. It was part of his ensemble. 'I haven't the foggiest idea.'

Gordon screwed up his face. 'I don't understand. I was told that you were being sent to handle the press.' Fein pursed his lips and arched his eyebrows, nodding amiably. 'Well,' Gordon said, looking over at Daryl, who was grinning ear-to-ear, 'what am I supposed to say when I'm asked questions in Atlanta?'

Fein slid the single sheet of paper across the table to Gordon.

Gordon picked it up. 'Hi, my name is Gordon Davis,' he read in silence. 'I'm a young, handsome, conservative, well-groomed, well-spoken, well-educated African-American male with an equally attractive, perfectly functional and loving wife and family.'

'That's really quite a lot to cram into one day, you understand,' Fein said.

'What . . .?' The words hung in Gordon's mouth. He was at a loss.

'Okay, now,' Fein said, leaning forward. 'A few additional points. First,' he began, speaking earnestly now, 'you need to work on what I call "white space."' He smiled at Elaine for no reason, Gordon thought, other than to politely 'touch base' with her. She stared back at him – expressionless. 'Pauses in your speech. They're very effective for stressing emphasis. Slow it down. You have a tendency to try to jam as much content as you can into any given period of time. What we need to do is work on your sound bites. To get sound bites, you need emphasis. For emphasis, you've got to learn that pauses are very important. So is voice modulation. No monotone. We *want* to capture some . . . of . . . that . . . *passion!*' he said by way of example – his voice rising and falling. His words stressed merely by the pacing of his speech.

40

Gordon was impressed. Daryl said, 'Jesus Christ!' disgustedly.

'Give it a try,' Fein suggested. He sat back and ignored Daryl completely.

Gordon stared at him for a second. 'What? Now?' he asked. Fein nodded, folding his arms and waiting. 'What do I say?'

'That doesn't really matter,' Fein said – his words spoken slowly, spaced, intentionally filled with emphasis.

'*That* is something I feel very strongly about,' Gordon said slowly.

'Even slower,' Fein corrected.

Gordon repeated the words with an unnaturally slow pacing, watching himself in the mirror.

'There. See?' Gordon saw Fein's reflection in the tiny lavatory's mirror. 'Now, what I want you to do is lean forward a little.' He pressed Gordon in the center of his back. 'Go on.' Gordon leaned forward just slightly. 'There. Leaning forward creates intensity. Next, empty one pocket and put your hand in it.'

Gordon looked at him in the mirror. 'Which one?'

'It doesn't matter.' Gordon put his left hand in his pocket and pulled his handkerchief and breath mints out and put them on the sink. He slid his hand into the empty pocket. 'All right,' Fein continued, 'chop the air with your right hand for even more emphasis.' Fein made a motion like he was breaking a board with a karate chop. 'Try it. Pick any word and emphasize it with a chop.'

Gordon watched himself in the mirror. 'That is something I feel very *strongly* about,' he said – chopping on the word 'strongly.' The delivery gave the word more punch. It worked.

'Pick a different word,' Fein said.

'What?'

'Pick a different word and chop. Give it a try.'

Gordon looked back into the mirror. '*That* is something I feel very strongly about.' The context changed meaning with the gesture. 'That is something *I*,' he stressed and chopped, 'feel very strongly about.' Gordon had to smile.

'You see? What did I tell you? And the beauty of it is you can take any word in the human language and make people think you

41

feel *passionately*,' he said – grabbing the air with both hands and yanking down – 'about any subject just by body language.' Fein slapped Gordon on the back. 'Can you remember all that?' Gordon nodded. 'Let me hear it. Let's go over it again.'

'Move,' Gordon repeated. 'Forward and back, never side-to-side. Lavaliere mikes, not stick mikes. Never raise your hands above your head. Smile. Leaning forward emphasizes, leaning back de-emphasizes. Eye contact. Modulate your voice. Speak slowly with lots of pauses.'

'Then you can speed it up later in the speech to create excitement. Okay. Any questions?'

Gordon looked down at his handkerchief. 'Why did I empty my pocket?'

'So all that stuff doesn't go flying when you take your hand out. As a matter of fact, you shouldn't carry anything in your pockets. Your wallet ruins the line of your suit.' Fein pulled up on the shoulders of Gordon's jacket like a tailor.

'What do I do with it?'

'We'll have somebody carry it for you.'

'My handkerchief?'

'Put it in your jacket pocket. Whatever works for you. Now. Are you ready? You're gonna kill 'em, Gordy. You're gonna knock 'em dead.' Gordon smiled. 'If you want to go through it one more time I could get the pilot to circle.'

'No,' Gordon replied, trying to turn but finding the lavatory too cramped. Fein stepped out into the narrow hallway. 'I'm a policy wonk by nature,' Gordon said. 'This just isn't my thing.'

'But it *can* be!' Fein said – barring Gordon in the doorway with hands on both walls. 'I've got a product. It's a product the American people will buy, I can *feel* it. My job is to put that product in an attractive package – a package that will sell. That's all. If you'll do what I say, Gordy,' he leaned forward and lowered his voice, 'I'll put you one heartbeat away from policymaker heaven.' He arched his eyebrows, waiting for a response.

Gordon said nothing, and Fein lowered his arms. He was all smiles as he returned to the cabin.

But Daryl wasn't. He spun into the short hallway to block Gordon's path. 'Can we talk?' Fein didn't bother to look back as he sat next to a glum-looking Elaine.

Daryl guided Gordon back into the lavatory. He pressed Gordon in and closed the door behind them. 'What the hell are you doing?' Gordon asked.

'I was going to ask you the same question.' Daryl's jaw was set, and there was venom in his voice.

'Look,' Gordon whispered, 'he's a jerk. But he's . . .' The words stuck in Gordon's throat.

'The first string? And I'm what?'

'You're my chief of staff.' Daryl glared at him, then turned to open the door. Gordon pushed the door closed. 'I meant that you're my principal adviser. But listen, Daryl. These guys are pros at what they do.'

'Which is what?'

'Which is getting people into the White House!' Daryl looked down at the sink. 'We're in this all the way, Daryl. For Christ's sake, we're on our way to the convention to accept the nomination for Vice President of the United States!'

'No, *you* are on *your* way.'

'Come on,' Gordon said, lowering his voice. 'I need you.' Daryl began to interrupt, but Gordon said, 'I know what you're thinking. You're thinking I'm drifting. That I've changed. Well, I *am* more conservative than I was when we got out of school, but I'm *also* seventeen years *older*. It's not drift. I know exactly where I am, and I'm heading straight down my center line.'

Daryl wouldn't look up at Gordon. 'Don't forget your breath mints,' he said.

'Come on, Daryl. It's just like makin' sausage, you said it yourself. It isn't any prettier on the Hill.'

Daryl nodded. 'Okay, but no promises. I won't take any of their bullshit. And if you expect me to keep my mouth shut and just go along if . . .'

'Open the door, and let's get out of here,' Gordon interrupted – grinning.

They headed out, but Daryl stopped suddenly and Gordon bumped into him. Daryl looked at him with an intense gaze. 'What?' Gordon asked.

'Just don't forget.'

'Forget what?'

'Who you are. What you believe in.'

43

THE PENTAGON, WASHINGTON, D.C.
August 16, 1300 GMT (0800 Local)

Lieutenant General Nate Clark passed the normally dark operations room. Junior officers from all four combat services were scurrying around, arranging piles of paper on the large map table in the center. The Navy officers far outnumbered those of the Army, Air Force and Marine Corps.

'What's going on down there?' Clark asked a young officer who milled about outside an office.

The man stiffened. 'They're PACOM, sir,' one said. 'I don't know what's up, but they were in there this morning when I got in.'

'Does it have something to do with the protests outside our bases in Japan?' Clark asked. The officer shrugged.

Men and women hurried in and out of the room in brisk fashion. Clark was destined for command of U.S. Forces Korea, and Pacific Command would only indirectly affect Clark's theater. Still, his curiosity was piqued and he returned to the room.

When he stepped inside, several of the officers stood erect, but no command was typically given to come to attention inside the Pentagon.

'What's up, gentlemen . . . ladies?'

'Nothing much, sir,' a Navy Captain said. 'Purely precautionary.' Two Petty Officers entered carrying boxes filled with files, which they placed in a row of similarly numbered cardboard boxes along the walls around the table. 'There were some assassination attempts in Beijing last night. And there's rioting this morning in Harbin, but it's probably nothing.'

At the end of the room two Navy lieutenants were pulling a large folded map out of one of the boxes. 'Are you telling me PACOM convened a crisis action team on China?'

'Just a precaution, sir.'

'But *everybody's* got problems with terrorists today. Moscow, Berlin, Seoul, Tokyo – everywhere.'

'Yes, sir, but not everybody put their armed forces on full alert. Call-up orders are going out every hour on the half-hour over radio and television. And the PLA has been holding maneuvers just across the Taiwan Straits. The CNO's putting a carrier battle group in the East China Sea.'

Clark nodded and wandered out of the room. *China?* he thought, leaning his back against the wall just outside the door. From inside the room he could hear the routine workings of the PACOM team. *That's not your show*, he kept telling himself.

'Who the hell was that?' he heard someone ask.

'Clark. Word is he's gonna get Korea.'

Nate smiled. Korea was the prize of his career. It was the culmination of all his hard work. Few theater commands got the attention, or were expected to be as combat-ready, as U.S. Forces Korea.

'He's a tall son-of-a-bitch,' the first man said. 'What's he like to work for?'

'He's *infantry*,' came a new voice. 'Got passed over in Europe 'cause he wasn't a tank driver.' Clark arched his eyebrows in amusement, having forgotten how gossipy these inter-service teams could get. 'He's a fuckin' case, though. Wife's Chinese.' The smile left Clark's face. 'Some sorta professor or something.'

'You mean she's like, *Chinese* Chinese?'

'No o! Chinese-American. Anyway, like I said, watch out, 'cause he's infantry. Everybody thinks they're big teddy bears 'cause they never yell at the troops. But behind closed doors they'll chew you a new asshole if they think you didn't take good enough care of your men. "*Why didn't they get three squares yesterday?*" the talker said in imitation of a shout. "*What the hell were they doin' standin' around in the sun? Didn't you see that shade a hundred meters away?*"

'All right, listen up!' Clark heard – the loud voice of the Navy Captain with whom he'd spoken. 'We've got one hour to get this room in ship-shape for our first briefing. Let's get that map going.'

Someone asked, 'What color should the Chinese Army be? Red?'

'Yeah, whatever,' came the answer.

'Should I use blue for the Russians?' the same man then asked.

'Use green,' someone replied. 'Always save blue for the good guys.'

On hearing the man's words, Clark's mood changed subtly. *Save the blue grease pencils for the good guys*, he thought. But there was no chance of that. There was no chance of any friendly units appearing on those maps.

'All right, first unit,' the captain said loudly from inside. 'Chicom – 411th Infantry Division, eighty-five percent strength, Jiamusi.'

Clark headed down the corridor, repeating to himself over and over, *'That's not your show. That's not your show.'*

From the moment Nate Clark walked into the large office, he knew something was wrong. Clark was ready for broad smiles, warm handshakes and a slap on the back. Instead he was ushered in relative silence to a semicircle of chairs that faced the desk of General Dekker – Chief of Staff of the U.S. Army. Although he got smiles, they were of the polite variety. By the time he'd finished shaking hands with the half-dozen senior officers present, Clark's own demeanor matched theirs. He was ready for bad news.

'Have a seat, Nate,' General Dekker said. The two- and three-star generals all sat on invitation of the four-star. Everyone was so somber that Clark was forced to confront the possibility that had, until then, seemed an impossibility – no command at all. Retirement. He'd gone as far as he was going to go. From the furthest corner of his mind, a voice screamed *Why?*

'Nate,' Dekker began, and Clark subtly stiffened his back – determined to greet the indignity of his professional failure like a man – 'I know the scuttlebutt around these halls has been that you were in for U.S. Forces Korea. I've heard it myself, and, quite frankly, did nothing to squelch the rumor because, until very recently, that was the plan. That was your command.'

Clark's jaw was set and his face a blank. But in his head he searched for any possible error he might have committed. Any impolitic remark that he or Lydia might have made in the final round of socializing. But whatever it was, he decided, it was going to come as a complete surprise.

'Nate, the final decision is you're instead going to command U.S. Army Pacific.'

Clark swallowed as he held Dekker's gaze. Dekker paused, waiting for a response. Clark spoke slowly to better control what he said. 'That command is up for decommissioning.' He looked at the row of faces in the chairs to his left, and then turned to take in the officers to his right. All looked at him with discomfort.

'We've been fighting to keep it, Nate, you know that,' Dekker said.

'It's a two-star billet.'

'Not technically. We've had a major general in there for the last

46

nine months while the Armed Services Committee did their force levels review. But technically it's a three-star command. And it *is* a command. You'll have Ninth Corps under you.'

Clark swallowed, inhaling and exhaling slowly, calmly. 'Ninth Corps only has one division attached,' he said, then began to wonder where he was headed. They knew all that. It was done. He needed to start the process of accepting his fate – or decline and resign here and now. Those were his choices. He tried to run through his mind what they were asking him to command. 'It's a light-infantry division – the 25th,' came out of his mouth.

Dekker nodded slowly. 'Not much, I know that, Nate. But nobody has as much as we need or would want these days. We can maintain two and a half LIDs for every heavy mech or armored division because of the . . . because their equipment tables are so . . . light.' Clark ground his teeth, and Dekker's eyes drifted down to his desk. '*Light*,' Clark thought. *Good word. So is 'inadequate.'* Dekker finally looked up, a hardness now in his eyes. 'It's what we've got for you, Nate.'

'Who gets Korea?' Clark asked.

'Tim Stanton,' the Army's head of personnel said from Clark's left.

He was a classmate of Clark's from West Point. *At least he's not from a class behind*, Clark thought, then took a deep breath. 'He's a good man.'

'So are you, Nate,' Dekker said – able finally to look Clark in the eye. 'Some would say – some of us here – that you're the very best we've got.' Clark didn't look, but he caught sight of nodding heads from his left and right out of the corners of his eyes. Clark's gaze remained fixed, however, on Dekker. *So why the hell didn't I get Korea?* he thought. He unclenched his jaw and swallowed to be able to speak, when necessary, with a natural voice. 'That's why,' Dekker continued, 'you've been given USARPAC.' He pronounced the acronym as if it were a word.

Clark had to take a deep breath now, and then loosen the cramping muscles of his neck by stretching back against his hard, starched collar. His green jacket was decked out with row after row of ribbons and badges. His officer record brief was filled. Every step on the ladder from platoon to Corps commands formed the perfect Army résumé. His was a career to be capped, quite possibly, by Dekker's job a few years hence. He'd even spent the better part of the last year since returning from

Europe kissing butts all over the greater Washington area – until then the one base he hadn't tagged. And now, after all that, he was going to be given a backwater command, probably to furl its colors while on his watch, and almost certainly thereafter to be retired at Lieutenant General. He had thought he could take it stoically, quietly, the way he'd always been taught to take adversity. But the cheap words of praise from Dekker just then seemed too much to bear.

'Excuse me, sir, for saying so, but might I respectfully suggest that all sounds like a load of shit.'

Dekker wasn't pleased by Clark's comment, and he picked up and restacked some papers on his desk. The blue stone of Dekker's West Point ring glinted in the light of his desk lamp. Dekker had been a fourth-year at the Point – Clark's company commander when Clark was a lowly plebe. Despite being close in age – Dekker at fifty-five, Clark at fifty-two – Dekker had always been one grade ahead of Clark throughout their careers. Both were accustomed to the deference of Clark, the junior officer, to Dekker, the senior.

'You are going to go to Ft. Shafer and assume that command, General Clark. You are going to kick their lazy butts off those Hawaiian golf courses and out of those nice warm winter barracks up in Alaska and turn USARPAC into a fighting command.' Dekker looked at Clark now without any trace of consolation. 'That is an order. What *we're* going to do – and I pledge this to you right here and now – is to lobby Congress to get you some extra muscle out there. To at least give you a readiness budget that'll allow you to get Ninth Corps and the 25th into fighting trim, and hopefully to attach an independent brigade or two and maybe an armored cav regiment from FORCECOM.'

'What about the decommissioning of USARPAC?' Clark asked.

'It's not going to happen.'

'Is Congress on board with that decision?'

Dekker nodded. 'The leadership of the Committee has quietly agreed to set aside any further discussion of the subject, but I expect you to keep that under your hat.' The first sign of a smile twinkled in his eyes. 'You can tell Liddy, of course, assuming she hasn't already heard it through the wives' grapevine.'

Clark still wasn't ready to play the good soldier and smile at Dekker's attempt at humor. 'Might I ask the reason for the Committee's change of heart?'

'Geography,' Dekker said curtly. 'Korea gets the 2nd Infantry and all the attention, Nate. But let's not forget that USARPAC is responsible for the defense of U.S. interests and allies from the Ural Mountains to the California coast and from the North to the South Pole – *ex*-clusive of the Korean peninsula.'

'What else is there but Korea, sir?' Clark replied.

There was a long pause, and Clark sensed the heads of the officers swiveling between Clark and Dekker.

The Army Chief of Staff spoke in deep and slow tones. 'You are not to utter one word of this discussion, Nate. *This* part of it, anyway. Not even to Liddy.' Dekker looked one at a time then at the faces of the senior officers gathered around his desk. 'This conversation didn't happen, is that understood? If it ever got out that we even *breathed* a word of this here, I'd have the State Department and the White House probing my lower intestines with a hot poker.'

There was muted laughter, but not from Clark.

'We do have a potential threat in the theater,' Dekker said. 'You know who I'm talking about?'

'I'd like you to say it, sir. I don't want any misunderstanding, not on something like this.'

Dekker took a deep breath. 'China, Nate.' There was dead silence around the room. 'They've been modernizing their military for over a decade. And they're wetting their pants to bust out of the straitjacket they're in all along their borders. If they go south, no problem. That's Vietnam's fight. If they go west, that's India. Still fine. If they go north, let the Russians take care of it. But if they go east – Korea, Japan, Taiwan, the Philippines – they run into us. *You*, specifically, with the exception of Korea. That's why we're sending you to Oahu. What I'm saying, Nate, is that if this country goes to war with the People's Republic of China, it'll be your war. I want that command ready. I need you to make it happen.'

THE GEORGIA DOME, ATLANTA
August 17, 0230 GMT (2130 Local)

It was growing late. Gordon Davis and his family were exhausted.

The door opened. The roar of the crowd poured into the small but well-appointed waiting room. The noise extinguished the small talk

between the Davises and the Bristols. A man with a clipboard and a
headset entered. In the concrete corridor outside there lurked large,
stony-faced Secret Service agents.

'All right,' said the man with the headset. 'Governor Bristol, Senator
Davis, we've got about five minutes before the Chair sends it back to
the Connecticut delegation. Your home state passed earlier, Senator
Davis, so they can put you over the top. Right after they vote, the
Chair is going to suspend the roll call and request a nomination by
acclamation. Then the standard stuff. Balloons, bands, yatta yatta. Now
let's run through real quickly what you're gonna do. First, we'll cue you
to head out by yourself. It's twenty-two normal-length paces to your
mark, which is number eighty-four. It's printed on some tape stuck
onto the stage floor just to your left of the podium. The stage manager
will have a diagram when you get up there. If it's covered in confetti,
just remember twenty-two paces to the left of the podium. Okay?'

Gordon nodded.

'Raise your arms up like this,' the man said, holding his arms up
and out, waving with both hands at the imaginary crowd.

'Skip that,' Arthur Fein said from the corner. 'It'll bunch up his
shoulders and his jacket'll ride up. Too Nixonesque.'

'All right,' the man with the headset said, scratching something off
his clipboard.

'Wave with one hand in the general direction of the floor,' Fein said
to Gordon. 'Every once in a while point with that same hand to one
spot or another. You can wink if you feel comfortable, but above all
smile, smile, smile.'

'We've got about three minutes planned for the ovation,' the man
with the headset said. 'Three minutes and twelve seconds for the song
"Proud to be an American." Then we cut to your family. Mrs Davis,
you bring the girls out one on each side, the little one between you
and the crowd.'

'I don't want them on stage,' Gordon said. All eyes turned to him,
including his family's. 'I'd just rather not, after last night.'

The man with the headset said, 'Senator Davis, let me assure you that
security is extraordinarily tight. I've done dozens of stadium events in
my life and I've never seen anything like this. The Secret Service even
has sharpshooters up in the press boxes.'

Arthur Fein stepped in and took Gordon's elbow. Off to the side
of the room, Fein said, 'Gordy, this is a prime time, command

performance. The networks tell us we might break records for the last day of a convention. Remember what I told you today's message was? Ten or fifteen minutes on stage tonight will put it out to a forty share.'

'But I'm not even going to *say* anything,' Gordon protested.

'All the better. We've got you and your lovely wife and daughters all standing amid an adoring throng. Balloons, confetti, rousing music on nationwide television!'

'Two minutes,' the man with the headset said.

'Gordy,' Fein said, squeezing Gordon's elbow. Gordon gently pulled it free. 'We're gonna get all four anchormen talking how, in a day when deep divisions fragment our society and . . .'

'Okay, okay,' Gordon said. The words meant nothing to Fein. They were bullshit that scored points in the polls. Gordon turned to the coordinator. 'If you can guarantee my family's safety . . .' The man nodded distractedly.

On television, the Governor of Connecticut repeated over and over, 'La-a-adies and gentlemen, ladies and gentlemen.'

'Let's go,' the coordinator said. Gordon and his family were swept from the room with one last slap on Gordon's back by Philip Bristol. The Davis kids passed awkwardly by their opposites from the Bristol family. They smiled but had nothing to say.

'Gordon,' Daryl Shavers said. He ran to catch up with the entourage. 'Gordon, we've gotta talk.' He squeezed into the mass of handlers. They bumped and jostled their way past party workers who applauded as Gordon passed. 'They're gonna play "We Shall Overcome",' Daryl said.

'What?' Gordon snapped. He turned and halted. The coordinator nervously glanced down at his watch. '"We Shall Overcome"?' Gordon asked the coordinator.

'What?' the man said. 'I don't get it.'

'No, you don't,' Gordon said. 'I want the song out.'

A burst of air was all that came from the exasperated coordinator. He was smiling but shaking his head. 'That's impossible! It'd screw everything up. That's a live band out there. They've got sheet music. The timing is . . .' He held the boom mike from the headset to his lips. 'Tell Connecticut to stretch! Just *stretch* it!'

Gordon and his family were swept along. They barely made it to the edge of the stage before another man with a headset grabbed Gordon by the arm.

'. . . the next Vice President of the United States of America,' the loudspeakers boomed, 'Senator Gordon Davis!'

Gordon eyed the bare wood and exposed wires on the rear of the stage wall. On the public side, all was seamless blue. But the view from the inside revealed the flimsy façade.

Gordon felt a gentle push on the back. He walked free of the escort's grip into the bright lights. The already raucous stadium roared in a spectacle for which Gordon was unprepared. Tens of thousands cheered wildly. They waved thousands of banners and signs. Gordon smiled and began to count his steps.

The Chairman shook his hand as they passed. But he kept up his count until he found some tape. Gordon smiled and waved, smiled and waved, smiled and waved. The whole time his skin crawled. With every flash of a camera, with every shout that rose above the others, with every rush of movement in the crowd, Gordon tensed. When his family joined him, the feeling of dread redoubled. Twenty-eight agonizing minutes later – after 'Proud to be an American' and 'We Shall Overcome' and the last of the balloons had fallen – it was over.

Walking off the stage now crowded with party luminaries, Gordon remembered he hadn't pointed or winked. He spotted a comical woman in the front ranks wearing a red hat and vest covered with campaign buttons. Gordon smiled, pointed and winked as he made the shape of a gun with his hand and pulled the trigger. A hundred cameras flashed at once. The next morning, the picture was on the cover of almost every newspaper in the country.

Chapter Three

FINAL APPROACH, JFK AIRPORT
August 17, 0700 GMT (0200 Local)

'Papa, smotri!' the high-pitched voice chimed, Masha's finger pointed through the window at the New York City skyline.

'Only English, Mashenka,' Pyotr Andreev whispered into his three-year-old's ear. 'Remember what mama and papa said. Only English. It's a game, all right?'

'Okay,' she said. Pyotr kissed her smiling face.

His wife Olga and five-year-old daughter Oksana sat quietly. Their escape from the collapsing Russia had, in fact, worked perfectly. One last hurdle remained. No one said another word as they landed, deplaned and queued up at customs.

The security was extraordinary. There were uniformed officers with rifles along the walls. Every bag was opened and inspected carefully. Even the dog in the cage ahead of the Andreevs was removed. It yapped and kicked its short legs excitedly as another customs officer waved a long wand inside the cage, sniffing for explosives. The barking of the dog grated on Pyotr's nerves, but little Masha enjoyed it immensely. She looked back and forth between Pyotr and the noisy pet. Pyotr kept her hand in his, ready to administer a painful squeeze if she lapsed into Russian.

His throat was dry when their turn came. The officer looked at their Swiss passports, down at their pictures, up at their faces, back down again – repeating the process over and over. It reminded him of the old Soviet Union. Things had changed since the last time he'd visited America.

'You're Swiss?' the officer asked, unzipping a bag with a tearing sound.

'Yes,' Pyotr replied. His heart pounded as he wondered whether they'd found all of the tags and cardboard inserts that came with their new luggage. On a quick trip to the bank in Zurich they'd gotten money and passports from the safe deposit box. They'd bought western clothes and toiletries.

He glanced down at the girls. Oksana's eyes were wide, but she was deathly quiet. Masha was waving at the dog, who had been returned to his cage. His sniveling nose was pressed to the small, grated window.

'And you are here on vacation, Mr Hoffman?'

'Yes. We are going to Disneyworld.'

'Do you have tickets to California?' the customs officer asked casually as he probed through their clothing with hands covered by white Latex gloves.

'Florida,' Pyotr corrected. He pulled his ticket from his jacket pocket. 'Orlando. We are going to Disney-*world*, not Disneyland.' The man looked at the Delta Airlines folder. He didn't reach for it, and Pyotr put it back into his jacket pocket. It really did have tickets to Orlando in it. The Andreevs, however, had no intention of using them.

Pyotr felt dampness under his armpits. It took incredible concentration to look so at ease – feigning a German accent while speaking English. Uvular trills when pronouncing the letter 'r,' not trills off the tip of the tongue as in Russian. 'Ch' sounds from the front of the mouth – almost like a hiss of air – not the Russian gargle from deep within the throat.

'Gaf! Gaf-gaf-gaf!' Masha's tiny voice came with a giggle as the dog barked back at her. Pyotr swallowed and he squeezed her hand, but she just smiled up at him. It was the sound Russian kids made to imitate a barking dog. He had no idea what sound dogs made in German or English. Slowly, Pyotr looked back up at the customs officers. *Had they noticed?* The loud snarl of a zipper being run down the soft bag's side indicated they were through.

Pyotr awkwardly wheeled a luggage cart down the concourse. The wheels turned this way and that. Just ahead of them, a man whose hands were thrust deep in his windbreaker stopped to get a drink of water. It was strange. An August day, the sun was hot. And the man wore a jacket. Not a sport coat or some other item of apparel more fashion than function, but a windbreaker.

Pyotr had to consciously avoid turning to look back over his shoulder as they passed the man. He stopped a couple of times to readjust the baggage on the cart. He saw nothing, but he felt it. That undefined sense of being followed.

OUTSIDE INTERIOR MINISTRY, MOSCOW
August 18, 1730 GMT (1930 Local)

The crowd chanted in unison. 'Authority is oppression!' one of the Anarchists on the street below had translated.

'How's the light?' Kate asked from in front of Woody's camera.

''Bout fifteen minutes left,' he said as he carefully adjusted the focus.

Kate stood with her back to the railing of a second-floor balcony. Down below, the front ranks of a mob were taunting lines of riot police who ringed the Interior Ministry headquarters. 'I don't really want to use the spots,' she said. She was still spooked from the Red Square stampede on the first day of the fighting. Doubly spooked by the anonymous tip on her cellular phone that had led them to the Interior Ministry.

'No arguments from me,' Woody said. 'Batteries are low anyway.'

Kate peered down over the railing of the sleazy hotel's dining room. They had bribed one of the kitchen workers with a one million ruble note, which at the day's closing exchange rate was worth ten cents. By tomorrow it would probably be worthless.

On the street, three lines of white-helmeted riot police nervously stood their ground holding clear plexiglass shields and raised truncheons. They made occasional forays out to the ragged front ranks of the angry mob, raining blows onto someone's head or spraying long streams of pepper gas into faces before retreating. In return, the crowd was pulling up paving stones and lobbing them into police ranks.

'Okay, ready when you are,' Woody said.

Kate tugged at her navy blue jacket and then reached under it to pull down on her white silk blouse. It would only be a head shot, so she wore blue jeans and running shoes beneath. She took one last look in a small mirror and arranged her hair, then cleared her throat loudly for several seconds.

'Give me some sound,' Woody said.

Kate fixed a serious expression on her face. 'The Russian government collapses, but first a word from Purina cat chow.'

'Your teeth are too damn white,' Woody groused, fiddling with buttons. 'Ever consider getting 'em capped?' She made a face. He held up his hand – five fingers spread out. Kate wiggled her shoulders and rolled her neck. Woody counted down with his fingers. When his last finger curled down, the red light came on and Kate began.

'The situation in Moscow hangs in the balance as darkness descends on the capital. Lines of troops loyal to the Russian President ring the Interior Ministry behind me, having retreated from one pitched battle with demonstrators after another in bloody street fighting during the afternoon. The whereabouts of the Interior Minister and his top lieutenants is as yet unknown, although sources at the Duma – the lower house of the Russian parliament – indicate that he has fled to the Ural mountains east of the city.'

'Okay,' Woody said. He checked some readings. 'Batteries are almost gone.'

'And those are your last ones?'

'Yep.' He looked up. 'Okay, now's where we'll splice in the scenes of the shit we got caught in on the bridge and over by the embassy. Voice over, voice over, voice over. Now,' he lowered his eye to the camera, and he again repeated the countdown. Woody was milking every ounce of juice out of his precious batteries he could. Normally he'd just start taping and Kate would begin when she was ready. Kate tried to nail the next part of the report on her first try.

'In scenes reminiscent of 1917, angry mobs have taken to the streets while most ordinary Russians cower behind locked doors. We spoke of the fighting in Moscow with one family earlier today.'

Woody rolled his index finger in the air. They would splice the interview in right there.

'Concerns such as those expressed by the Semyonovs,' Kate continued without missing a beat, 'must be on the minds of most Russians as night falls on a city of eleven million lit only by the fires of overturned vehicles and by the first torches, which I can see now, carried by the crowd on the street below.' Kate squinted at the sight of the approaching group, who held torches high above their heads. They wore black, from head to toe.

'Woody,' Kate said, pointing at the large group of black-clad men who pushed their way down the crowded street toward the Interior Ministry. Woody swung the camera toward the approaching phalanx and rolled his finger to keep her talking.

'There appears to be a group of Anarchist "Black Shirts" approaching. That is what they have come to be known as because of their distinctive black shirts and leather jackets. Each time a group of men such as this has arrived, the scene has erupted in violence. Each time the Black Shirts have attacked the police, the police have retreated. This time, however, there is no retreat for the beleaguered Russian security troops. This time their backs are literally to the wall of their headquarters building.'

Kate backhanded Woody and he glanced at her without moving his head away from the camera. She pointed for him to get a shot at the lines of police toward which the Black Shirts pressed. He complied, but then returned to the shot now just below their balcony. In the long shadows cast by the buildings, the flickering torchlight would be dramatic. Kate let Woody get the shot he wanted. He had roamed the earth for twenty years to cover wars and famines and civil unrest, and she trusted that he knew what he was doing.

A dark orange light on the top of the camera began to blink. 'The Black Shirts are headed straight for the ministry building now, and the crowd has begun to stir. Many of the demonstrators who have been here for some time are starting to take cover, and the general disturbance seems to have passed right into the lines of the police, who are looking around and craning their necks to see into the crowd they face. I don't think they've spotted the Black Shirts yet, but it's just a matter of seconds before . . .'

There was a beep and then a clicking sound as the tape mechanism shut down.

'Shit!' Woody said. He lowered the camera and slapped the Jamaican reefer decal on its side with his hand. 'I can't fuckin' believe this, man!' Kate's eyes were trained on the now scurrying demonstrators, who had opened up a path for the Black Shirts. The 'thonk' of tear-gas canisters lobbed into the Black Shirts presaged the choking gas to come.

Ripping bursts of machine-gun fire broke open the night. Woody and Kate lowered themselves onto the floor of the balcony. Popping sounds filled the air. Kate watched the growing confusion as police began to fall. Most of the rest threw their shields and truncheons down and ran. The flashing muzzles came not from the police, but from the Black Shirts who charged their lines.

Shots rang out from the upper windows of the ministry building. But the disciplined Black Shirts surged into the building. Gunfire rose from floor to floor as Kate and Woody watched. By the time an explosion blew out the top-floor windows, the glass landed in a tinkling rain on empty streets.

It was then that Kate realized what had just happened. There were no police, no security troops, no sign of the army. There was no more government to speak of left in Moscow. There was a complete absence of power. An end to all social order. Anarchy.

THE WHITE HOUSE SITUATION ROOM
August 19, 0100 GMT (2000 Local)

President Marshall watched the television screens in the underground Situation Room. Around him sat his National Security Council – the Vice President, the Secretaries of Defense and State, General Dekker, Chairman of the Joint Chiefs of Staff, and the Directors of the CIA and National Security Agency.

'Is the mysterious Valentin Kartsev behind the Anarchist violence that's sweeping the world?' reported NBC correspondent Kate Dunn. 'As Russia slides toward its third day of chaos, signs increasingly point to the growing power of one man – Valentin Kartsev, former professor of political science, former KGB general, Russian millionaire, mafioso kingpin, and chief Anarchist ideologue.'

President Marshall and his senior national security advisors sat transfixed by the images. Solid masses of black-shirted men standing shoulder-to-shoulder in closed ranks and rushing toward their objective. Crowds of people running in great swirls of motion this way and that as swaths fell before orange bursts of flame from automatic weapons. The smoke from explosions soon obscured the picture, and after the report concluded the screen cut to color test bars.

'That was the unedited, raw feed off the satellite from Moscow,' the Director of the NSA said. 'We've got some other feeds from around Russia if you'd like, Mr President, but this one is the first that purports to have some sort of inside information from the anarchist movement.'

'Where did that reporter get her info on this guy Kartsev?' Marshall asked.

'We talked to her producers in New York. They said she got an anonymous phone call on her cell phone – her second tip in as many days.'

'So,' Marshall said, 'is this man Kartsev behind it all?'

The Director of the CIA leaned forward. His shoulders hunched as he rested his elbows heavily on the conference table. 'Things are such a mess over there right now, Mr President, it's hard to say. The *real* player is the army, which our sources say could enter the fray full force any time now. The problem, however, is that the same fissures that run through society run through the military as well. That raises some obvious risks.'

'What would happen if the army split?' Marshall asked. 'What are we looking at?'

Heads turned from one to another. There was a reluctance to take a position. Finally, Secretary of State Jensen ventured a response. 'I think the consensus, Tom, is that things will get worse before they get better.'

Marshall exploded. 'Jesus Christ, I *know* they'll get worse if there's a Goddamned civil *war* in *Russia*!'

'What I mean,' Jensen said, 'is that . . . that the situation won't improve much before *November*. There's real pressure building in the EC for some sort of action. The Europeans are scrambling for alternate sources of energy. With Siberian gas off the market, oil's up to fifty-five dollars a barrel.'

'What the hell kind of "action" are they talking about?' Marshall asked.

Jensen shrugged. 'Intervention,' he said simply.

The room stirred all at once. 'Inter*vention*?' Marshall exclaimed. 'In a Russian civil *war*?'

Jensen held his hands up as if to fend off the President's verbal blows. 'I'm totally opposed to it, Tom. *Totally* opposed. But there has been some talk about the feasibility of a peacekeeping mission *if* the U.N. can garner the support of the local Russian army commanders in Siberia where the oilfields are. The violence out there has been limited, mainly directed against those gas pipelines. There's been very little civil or military disorder in the east.'

'They're too worried about China,' the Secretary of Defense suggested.

Marshall leaned back and rubbed his pounding temples. '*Who lost Russia?*' Marshall could already hear the Republicans asking. 'What do we know about this Kartsev?'

The CIA Director pulled open a file.

'Kartsev, Valentin Konstantinovich. Born 1949 in Novgorod. Educated at the pedagogical institute in Moscow. Believed to be KGB informant on faculty of Moscow State University Marxism/Leninism Department until assuming rank of lieutenant colonel in the KGB at their Dzerzhinsky Square headquarters in 1984.'

'Lieutenant colonel at age, what, thirty-five?' the Director of the FBI asked. 'That's a pretty fast track, especially for someone who'd just been informing on a bunch of professors.'

'He was one of Andropov's protégés,' the CIA Director replied. 'Andropov was an intellectual. Widely read. Bookish sort. Before he died, he collected a coterie of similarly cerebral types with whom he'd spend hours spinning ideas. Kartsev, in his later years at the University, was among that inner circle.'

'What about since 1984?' Marshall asked.

The CIA Director again read from his file. 'Liaison to the GRU – military intelligence. During the worst of the Afghanistan war – when intelligence about Russian atrocities, booby-trapped toys, torture, assassination and the like were being picked up by the press – we got a "walk-in." A Russian army officer assigned to their embassy in Karachi approached our station chief and fed us reports of "excessive measures" by a renegade KGB unit that was responsible for all those operations. It was pretty clear to us at the time that he was simply feeding us straight from the

Russian Army's High Command, and so we took it all with a grain of salt.'

'What do you mean?'

The Director shrugged. 'We figured it was just the army trying to keep its skirts clean by blaming the KGB. But some of the intelligence did prove up. Kartsev's liaison unit – and their Afghan proxies – were operational in Afghanistan.'

'What happened to the officer who fed us the information?' Marshall asked. 'Maybe we can talk to him.'

'He was recalled to Moscow for a briefing. He was shot in KGB prison three months later.'

Marshall arched his eyebrows. 'Nice people. What else does your file say about Kartsev?'

'He fled to Kirgizia when Gorbachev returned after the failed August Coup of 1991. Severed his relations with the KGB . . . we think. He disappeared for a few years until his name started showing up on DEA and ATF intelligence reports for trafficking in drugs and weapons out of the former Soviet Union. The only other cross-references to Kartsev we've got in our database come from a variety of western businessmen who have been offered partnerships – some of them lucrative – in deals with Kartsev or his affiliates. A couple did their deals, made a fair amount of money and then were cut out by Kartsev. They just let it drop. One – a Dutch gentleman in the business of giving seminars on western management techniques – apparently spurned Kartsev and went it alone in Moscow. He was found dead in his Moscow apartment with thirteen bullet wounds to the back of the head. Small caliber weapon. Neighbors heard nothing. No suspects.'

'Okay,' Marshall said, glancing at his watch. He had a campaign finance meeting. 'So Kartsev's a bad guy. He's behind the Anarchists. The Anarchists are fanatical terrorists who're spreading violence around the world. The Europeans are inclined to go in there and root 'em out,' Marshall rose. 'I say more power to them. Good luck, and God speed.'

'The Chinese aren't going to like it,' Jensen said. 'A U.N. force that doesn't include Asian troops being deployed on their border?'

'We're sitting this one out,' Marshall said – ending the meeting. 'Let the Europeans worry about the Chinese. I can't see how it concerns us.'

SEOUL, SOUTH KOREA
August 19, 0444 GMT (1444 Local)

The mid-afternoon sun streamed through the windows. The South Korean President raised the large spoon to his lips. The soup was hot, and he blew on it as his mouth salivated at the faint aroma of garlic. He had stolen away to his private dining room from all-day meetings on the Chinese mobilization, and his stomach was growling noisily.

He touched the soup gently to his lips, testing its temperature. A 12.7-mm projectile traveling at the speed of sound punched cleanly through the window. Before the force it imparted could rip the entire pane of glass from its frame, the bullet cleaved the President's head off above the line of his ears. It was thirty minutes before the President's aides discovered the effects of the single shot.

LOS ANGELES, CALIFORNIA
August 20, 0715 GMT (2315 Local)

LAPD officer Paul Maxwell returned the steely gaze of the black Muslim bodyguards. Maxwell was assigned to the security detail of the minister – a fiery civil rights leader scheduled to speak inside the old movie theater at Maxwell's back. But from the hard stares that the uniformed policemen attracted from the black men in the bow ties, Maxwell had no doubt who their enemy was.

A large crowd had gathered across the street. It began to roar with cheers when a limousine carrying the Muslim minister pulled swiftly up to the kerb. Maxwell carefully scanned the cameramen, who began to lean out over the yellow tape for a better shot. The bright lights of the mini-cams bathed the car door. The brilliant strobes from the still photographers lit the night like silent gunfire.

'Behind the tape!' Maxwell ordered – his voice lost amid the noise of the throng. He pushed several members of the local media back from the red-carpeted walk to the theater's entrance.

The limo door opened. A bodyguard wearing dark sunglasses emerged from the car. Behind him came the stern-faced reverend, attired in a dark, conservative business suit.

A loud blast from overhead caused Maxwell to nearly jump out of his skin. He distinctly heard whirring and popping sounds as the car was riddled with holes. Maxwell dropped to one knee and pulled his 9-mm – his heart racing as he looked all around.

A surreal quiet fell over the crowd, but it quickly gave way to rising cries of pain and fear. Great swaths of people lay on the pavement all around. They were bloody and writhing and beginning to moan. Smoke billowed from atop the marquee under which Maxwell knelt safe and sound.

Maxwell's radio was filled with reports of an anti-personnel mine going off at the theater. Maxwell rose and rushed toward the popular firebrand, who lay slumped in the car door – a pulpy red mess. Holes riddled the car's doors and side panels. The windows were completely shattered.

A bodyguard shoved Maxwell in the chest with both hands. The bodyguards dragged the minister back into the car, pulled the dead driver to the street beside it, and tore off – running over the legs of one of the fallen supporters.

What happened next was totally unexpected. The voices of fear turned to outrage. The cries for help became shouts of anger. Fists were raised and shaken. The crowd surged onto the street through thin lines of uniformed police. The officers were knocked to the ground – their hats flying off their heads.

There was a shot from down the street. Then rapid firing from a handgun. Then a shotgun.

Maxwell retreated toward the theater – firing his first shots into the onrushing crowd as he backed into the doorway.

WHITE HOUSE, WASHINGTON, D.C.
August 20, 1000 GMT (0500 Local)

'Mr President? Mr President?'

Thomas Marshall opened his eyes. He lay in bed in his darkened bedroom. 'Hm. What?'

'I'm very sorry, sir. But you have a phone call. It's Governor Bristol. He says it's urgent.'

'Bristol?' Marshall croaked. He cleared his throat. 'Phil Bristol?'

The aide nodded. 'What the hell would he . . .?' Marshall rose, still pondering his unfinished question as he padded into the adjoining sitting room. *What would he want to talk to me about?*

A different aide handed Marshall the phone. He cleared his throat again. 'Hello, Phil! What has you up so early?'

'Not early, Tom. It's late out here on the West Coast. I apologize for having to disturb you like this.'

'If you're calling to throw in the towel and announce you're going to support the Democratic ticket during these troubled times, there's no need to apologize.' Marshall was awake now. He winked at his grinning aides as Bristol politely chuckled.

'I'm afraid, Tom, this doesn't have to do with the campaign. I've got some official business to discuss with you. I've just called up a goodly portion of the California Army National Guard to deal with a situation we've got down in L.A. I wanted to tell you personally what I was doing with them.'

Marshall's guard was up. 'What "situation" is this you're talking about, Phil?'

'We've got a full-blown riot in progress. It looks like the Rodney King thing all over again.'

'Good God, Phil. What the hell happened?'

Bristol told the President about the civil rights leader's assassination.

'The pot's been simmering down there ever since the mayor cracked down on crime,' Bristol said. The President's political antennae tingled. It was Marshall who'd been hammering the 'get tough on crime' theme ever since the first night of the terrorist attacks. 'Apparently,' his Republican challenger continued, 'the L.A.P.D. community relations people had been warning the mayor about it. It seems the feeling on the streets was that your anti-terrorism campaign had succeeded mainly in netting a large number of arrests from minority communities.'

Marshall's jaw was set firmly, now. Bristol thought he already had his points up on the scoreboard. He was wrong. 'So how bad is it?' Marshall asked.

'The looting and arson is spreading all through South Central. The fire department reports twenty-six structures ablaze – most they can't get to because of sniping. I'm worried particularly about the Koreans. Since the last riots there's been a mini-arms race among the store owners. The police have already stopped carloads of grocers and their families heading in to protect their property, all of 'em armed to the teeth. I'm determined not to let this get out of hand, so on my authority as Governor of California I'm calling up the Guard to put a stop to it.'

Marshall could already see the Republican media spin in his mind's eye. Bristol's private army crushing the chaos – the 'anarchists' – on the streets of L.A. Lots of clean-cut citizen-soldiers responding to Bristol's strong, decisive leadership.

'Phil,' Marshall said, 'I agree with you one hundred percent. What's more, if things are *that* bad, I'm going to look into sending regular army troops in there to help you out.'

'I appreciate that, Tom, but I don't think that'll be . . .'

'Nonsense! I'm not going to leave you out there all by yourself to deal with the situation. This damn' business with the terrorists isn't a local problem, it's a national one. You're going to get every bit of help you need and more – no ifs, ands, or buts. I'll have my people get on this right now.'

'Listen, Tom. I don't want to crowd your plate at a time like this. You've got enough to worry about with the international crisis. Why don't we just wait and see where we are this time tomorrow and . . .'

'I won't *hear* of that kind of talk, Phil. Unless you seceded while I was catching up on my beauty rest,' Marshall said jovially, 'California still *is* a part of the United States, and I'm still the President. I'll call after we've had time to check what assets we have available and do our own assessment of the situation. We'll talk soon. Goodbye, Phil.'

There was a momentary pause. 'Goodbye, Tom.' Marshall hung up.

An aide took the phone, and Marshall grabbed the man's arm. 'Get me the Secretary of Defense.' He waited, chewing on the inside of his cheek. The aide handed the phone back to him. 'Have you heard what Bristol is doing?'

'Yes, sir,' the Secretary of Defense replied. 'I just got word.'

'I want you to federalize the California Army National Guard. Call them up.'

There was a long silence as the political gears spun in the man's head. 'Just the California Guard, sir? I mean . . . that would be a little . . .' He let the sentence trail off unfinished.

Marshall understood. A little too obvious. 'I want a nationwide call-up to deal with domestic unrest.'

'How large a call-up do you want?'

'How the hell should *I* know? You tell me. But I want it big enough to put men on the streets nationwide,' Marshall said as the idea grew on him.

'Well, say . . . about six brigades?'

'Sounds fine. And I want a full National Security Council meeting in three hours.' Marshall hung up – pleased at having seized the opportunity presented him.

BETHESDA, MARYLAND
August 21, 1300 GMT (0800 Local)

Daryl Shavers entered the Davises' bedroom. Gordon nodded at his chief of staff, who joined him at the television. Fires still raged in the early morning sky over Los Angeles. 'Did you hear that Marshall federalized the California Guard? Governor Bristol's lawyers tell him that Marshall can't even *use* the troops now. Once they're part of the U.S. Army, the Posse Comitatus Act prevents them from helping out the local police! It was a *blatantly* political act! Bristol plans on slamming him in a news conference this morning. We've got to be ready to join in. We're just waiting on Fein so we can get started working up the right tone.'

'Fein's already here,' Daryl said. He laid his ratty folders crammed with protruding papers on Gordon's desk. 'His car's out front.'

Elaine stuck her head out of the bathroom. She was putting the finishing touches on her make-up. 'Where the hell is he?' Gordon asked. 'This is *huge!* Campaigns *turn* on things like this!'

Daryl looked tired. Gordon knew he'd been working – fighting one-man turf battles with the massive staff of the Republican National Committee.

Gordon took off in anger for the stairs. Elaine and Daryl followed. Fein was in the dining room. The two girls were seated at the table. Celeste wore jeans and a sweatshirt. Janet was still in pajamas and robe. Laid out on the half of the table covered with a linen tablecloth was the Davises' silver service and their finest china and crystal. A woman whom Gordon had never seen before – wearing pearls at eight o'clock in the morning – hovered over Celeste. She was straightening the already orderly placement of the several forks on her right.

'Now,' the woman said with a proper British accent, 'the finger bowl arrives with dessert. But you don't use it until after you've finished. You should gingerly grasp the bowl with both hands and place it beside the upper left edge of the dish. Then take the doily from the plate and fold it carefully.'

The girls giggled as they began to follow the instructions. Janet pinched her lips in imitation of a doughty matron.

'*Excuse* me,' Elaine said. She stormed past Gordon into the dining room.

'Good morning, Elaine,' Fein said, smiling. 'Gordon! Trust you slept well.' There was a pause. 'Daryl,' Fein said, nodding.

'Just *what* is going on here?' Elaine burst out.

'Mr Fein's teaching us what to do at a state dinner,' Celeste said. She smiled broadly to affect the role of the gracious host. When she realized Elaine was furious, Celeste muttered 'Mo-*ther*,' in a lilting voice – her lips curled in a frozen smile of decorum.

The dam of Elaine's outrage held. Gordon could see her breathing deeply. Fein jumped in. 'Elaine, this is Mrs Agnes Fillmore, formerly of the White House protocol office.'

'How do you do, Mrs Davis?' the woman said, smiling. 'It's a pleasure to meet you. And I really *must* commend you. Your girls have truly impeccable manners.'

Janet cleared her throat and wiggled in her seat – her back now ramrod-straight. She raised her empty teacup to her lips. 'Oh dear,' Mrs Fillmore said with mock sadness in her voice. She tilted her head at Janet. 'You really shouldn't stick your pinky out like that. Backstairs manners and all.'

'She was just playing,' Elaine snarled. 'She knows better than that.'

'Of course she does,' the ever-gracious woman said graciously.

Finally convinced that Elaine wouldn't break the peace, Gordon said, 'Arthur, I think we really ought to get down to business.' He turned to clear a path to the door. Daryl stepped outside to make way.

Fein looked surprised. 'Oh, all right.' Turning to the girls at the table, he said with evident good humor, 'I want to see you properly distinguish between the meat fork and the fish fork before you leave this table, young ladies.' He winked as he passed Gordon on the way out.

Gordon closed the dining room door behind him. Fein stood beside Daryl. But there was nothing in Fein's body language to indicate any acknowledgment whatsoever of Daryl's presence. 'What might I do for you, Gordon?' Fein asked pleasantly.

Gordon's mouth hung open before he finally blurted out, 'The riots! We've got to . . . to jump on this. Marshall's get-tough policies went too far.' Gordon lowered his voice. 'He stepped on his dick, and we should be all over him for it!'

Fein's expression never changed. He blinked once or twice, but Gordon's words seemed not to impress him in the least.

'What's Bristol's position?' Daryl asked – filling the silence.

Fein looked at Daryl, then turned back to Gordon. 'This is a difficult time for the nation,' Fein said slowly. 'Terrorists attacking government officials such as yourself, new dangers abroad, and now lawlessness on the streets of our cities. It's as if anarchy is eating away at the fabric of society. At times like these, we must show *strength*,' he lightly tapped his clenched fist into an open palm, 'a *resolve* in the face of our enemies, foreign *and* domestic.'

It was a sound bite. Gordon got the distinct impression that he was to memorize the position statement verbatim. Were it not for the mocking roll of Daryl's eyes, Gordon would have asked Fein to repeat the response . . . more slowly, this time.

The dining room door opened. Elaine emerged with a frown on her face as Mrs Fillmore was saying, 'No, you push with your knife. You pile the food onto the fork. Never *spear* the meat like you're harpooning a whale.'

Elaine closed the door behind her. Gordon eyed his wife cautiously. The fact that she had allowed Mrs Fillmore's lesson to continue must only mean, Gordon thought, that she grudgingly accepted the woman's abilities. 'What's going on? What's the plan?' Elaine asked, turning her attention – her need to act – back to the campaign. It was a good sign, Gordon thought. She was getting over the trauma of the attack.

'I've taken the liberty,' Fein said, 'of jotting down a few notes.' He handed Elaine a single, typewritten sheet. 'I'm sorry for the delay, but Gordon's selection came so suddenly that I only had time to focus on him. But I hope you'll find those tips helpful.'

Elaine was reading the paper in silence.

Daryl was already smiling. 'You wanna share some of those "tips" with us, Elaine?' he asked.

After a few moments, she read in a wooden tone without looking up. 'One. Control emotion. No tears or anger unless we talk first.

Two. Eye make-up is most important. Go light on the lipstick. But don't skimp on hairdressers or facials – once or twice per week. Three. Muted shades of clothing are better than sharp colors. Lots of soft blouses with long sleeves. Elegant scarves are good accessories. Four. In public, cross your ankles not your knees. No scratching, twitching or squirming. Better to . . .' she swallowed and moistened her lips with the tip of her tongue. 'Better to listen than to speak. Always look interested in what the other person is telling you. Be prepared for stupid questions. Five. Keep smiling and smiling and smiling, and if all else fails . . .' she looked up, 'smile.'

'*Well*,' Daryl said – satisfied. 'Too bad you just missed the fine *speech* that was outlined for Gordon. It appears that "we" have foreign *and* domestic enemies.' His voice oozed venom. 'I know who those "domestic *enemies*" are. My only question is, who's the "*we*" that Fein's talking about?'

Fein's eyes never left Gordon, who could also feel the heat of Daryl's stare. Elaine appeared concerned as well, but her voice would be heard later. They would argue. He would defend Fein and the RNC and the campaign's natural political decision to play hardball with the rioters. Behind closed doors, she would strike back. They would each move toward the other's position until they were again reconciled.

She folded Fein's notes neatly and held onto them.

Gordon looked over at Daryl. A fire burned in his eyes. Gordon could never reconcile himself with Daryl. He could never muster that level of anger.

TAMAN DIVISION BARRACKS, MOSCOW
August 22, 2000 GMT (2200 Local)

Kate Dunn lay on the ground in the fetal position next to Woody. Her hands were clamped over her ringing ears. She'd never been so terrified in her life.

The night air around the small ditch in which they lay was filled with all manner of speeding projectiles. They whipped close by their unprotected bodies with vicious cutting sounds, or streaked through the dark sky overhead in burning trails. Cement chips flew off the concrete abutment against which they cowered. Kate realized in horror that the hulking armored vehicles which rumbled along the road above them were drawing and returning furious fire.

Her world exploded as flame shot over her from the long, thick barrel of a tank. She was afraid even to lift her head to follow the quickly passing main gun. She saw instead a brilliant flare of light erupt from the upper floor of a building. From it emerged the wiggling and fiery trail of a rocket. The missile quickly locked onto its course. But before she could tell where it was headed . . .

She jammed her eyes shut in expectation of an enormous explosion as the missile streaked by. Nothing happened. When she opened her eyes, she saw two shiny wires over the earthen ditch. The missile had missed its target – one of the armored vehicles which roared past.

Next up in Kate's nightmare were the dark forms of men diving into the ditch with loud grunts. Soon, the slit was filled with over a dozen Russian soldiers. It had been another anonymous tip that had sent Kate and Woody to the tense Army base. There had been no other journalists on the base. Another scoop, Kate had thought as she and Woody had set up on the road just overhead. Woody had warned her. They were on the main road from the front gate. If the caller was right and there was going to be fighting . . . But Kate was energized by the prospect of the air time they would get. She had shamed him into cooperating with joking comments about his manhood. It had never occurred to her that maybe the other foreign journalists weren't at the base because they knew better than she what was coming.

The Russian soldiers in the ditch around them rose to charge barracks full of other Russian soldiers. They didn't get far before a brilliant explosion hurled several bodies into the air. Kate had felt the earth shake beneath her. Tanks attacked with infantry across the green lawns of the base. Other tanks raced out from the buildings and fired. She watched in horror as geysers of pyrotechnics gushed from dozens of vehicles. All the men and vehicles looked identical. The Russian Army was fighting itself.

The attack faltered. Men sprinted back across the tabletop-flat lawn in ones and twos. Their hands pumped furiously as they fled in panic. Most had discarded their weapons.

'How do you feel fighting other soldiers in your own army?' Kate shouted over the noise of battle.

The one Russian soldier who could speak broken English opened his mouth to reply. The low-light lens on Woody's camera recorded the faint green images of the soldier and of Kate's microphone to the soldier's mouth.

'Wery bad! I am . . . uh, not so much like it! When I,' he raised his empty hands in the air like he was holding his rifle – his finger bent like it was around a trigger – 'shootit my, uhm, gun, I . . .!' He raised his imaginary Kalashnikov to aim into the air.

'You try to miss on purpose?' Kate asked.

'Yeah, yeah! I shootit the air!'

'Ask him which side he's on,' Woody whispered – his eye pressed to the camera.

Kate was annoyed with him feeding her questions, but asked anyway. The soldier cocked his head and looked confused. Kate tried to rephrase the question so he would understand the words she used. 'You are fighting for one side – one part of the army – and the men whose base you attacked were fighting for another! Which side are you on? Who do you support?'

Still the man looked confused. One of his buddies who was huddled close by in the ditch began discussing the question in Russian. 'Why are you fighting?' Kate tried again.

'Ah!' the soldier said – comprehending her question at last. 'Because zey tell us to.'

WHITE HOUSE SITUATION ROOM
August 24, 2200 GMT (1700 Local)

'Do you think it's a trick?' President Marshall asked as he leaned toward the speakerphone on the conference table.

After the momentary delay, the ambassador replied over the secure link from Moscow. 'We can never know with any certainty, Mr President. On its face, the General's offer appears entirely responsible. The Russians obviously have no interest in seeing the disorder spread to control of their nuclear arsenal. International supervision over the weapons is an imminently reasonable suggestion.'

'May I get something straight, here?' General Dekker interrupted. All eyes turned to him. 'Are we talking about deploying *U.S.* troops? To *Russia?*'

The ambassador answered. 'To the eastern provinces only. To Siberia. The General assured me that the Defense Ministry has absolute control over the nuclear forces in European Russia.'

Dekker sat with his forearms resting heavily on the polished wood table. 'And just what are they supposed to do if the fighting spreads out that way?'

'Their mission would be limited,' the White House Chief of Staff chimed in. Marshall noted the heads of the Joint Chiefs turn to look at the civilian. The political animal who was the object of their loathing, however, was focused on his boss. 'This is a low-risk, high-return plan.'

'What returns are those, might I ask?' came from Dekker.

The two men then locked eyes. 'Preservation of our national security, of course.' Everyone there knew, however, that there were also political returns. That Marshall had been beaten up by Bristol for failing to counter Russian terrorism.

The President drew a deep breath, and with it the attention of his national security team. 'Would NATO go in there with us?' he asked – turning to the Secretary of Defense.

'Great Britain, Germany and France are all clearly behind the plan, which should bring in Belgium, the Netherlands and Denmark. Bonn is only a day or two away from agreeing with Paris on a deployment into Ukraine, which they see as a strategic buffer between Russia and the West. They would view a Siberian deployment as a logical extension of their policy to the east. *And* it would allow them to secure Siberian gas supplies all the way back to the wellhead.'

'It's a mistake,' Marshall heard – the words spoken softly. He turned to see Secretary of State Jensen sitting slumped in his chair with his arms folded over his chest.

'You care to elaborate?' Marshall asked testily.

Without looking up, Jensen said, 'We're being sucked into a power vacuum. The collapse of the Soviet Union left an enormous geostrategic void over the entire Eurasian landmass. It's been pulling us eastward ever since the Bosnian deployment and the expansion of NATO into Poland, the Czech Republic and Hungary. Now, it's drawing NATO troops into Ukraine and Siberia.'

Marshall huffed, then rubbed his eyes. 'That's a fine subject for a *Foreign Affairs Quarterly* article.' He slammed his hand down, startling several at the table. 'But *God*-dammit this is the real world, and we've got real issues to deal with!' He turned to Dekker. 'I'd like you to draw up some contingency plans. Figure out how many men it would take to secure those missile sites and nuclear weapons depots. Keep it simple. Use a minimalist approach. As long as we have the Russians' full cooperation, I wouldn't think we'd be talking about too large an undertaking.' Marshall stifled a yawn – wanting to get to the end of it. 'What about the Japanese?'

The Secretary of Defense nodded at Jensen, who remained silent. 'We've worked out some arrangements – roughly the same payment terms as the Gulf War.'

'I'm not talking about *payment*,' Marshall said. 'I want them in there *with* us.'

Jensen looked up. The Secretary of Defense licked his lips. 'On the ground?' he asked – clearly uncomfortable with the suggestion. 'That might be highly unpopular in Japan.'

'We could offer them the Kuriles back,' Marshall said. No one else spoke. 'That should win over the nationalist vote.'

Marshall liked the idea, but everyone else squirmed.

'They'd have to amend their Constitution to allow foreign deployment,' the Secretary of Defense remarked.

'It's about damn time they *did!*' Marshall snapped.

General Dekker spoke up even though it was clear Marshall wanted to leave. 'Sir, if I might suggest, Japan is most useful for support. The POL – petroleum, oil, lubricant – either comes from Japan, or from a long way away. And if the Army can't stage massively in Japan, its alternatives are Forts Richardson and Lewis in Alaska and Washington. That's a *hell*uva long way away for a divisional supply train, sir. And we'd need more than logistical support, too, sir. If it should ever come to it, we'd need them for medical support and for strategic air projection.'

'Well,' Marshall said as he rocked back in his chair. 'It doesn't seem that we're in disagreement then. They can pay their share,' he counted off with his thumb, 'by meeting the petroleum needs of the deployment and by allowing full use of all bases and airfields.'

'What about the Chinese?' Jensen asked in a faraway tone.

'*Fuck* the Chinese!' Marshall said as he headed out the door.

Chapter Four

MCLEAN, VIRGINIA
August 25, 0900 GMT (0400 Local)

Nate and Lydia Clark sat cross-legged on the kitchen floor in their jeans. Nate held in his hands the front page of the *Washington Post*. A photograph of charred bodies lying beside an infantry fighting vehicle on the streets of St Petersburg dominated the page. He crumpled it loudly and stuffed it into a tall water glass, which he laid in the cardboard box with all the other plates and glasses. One room per day, that was the way they had always done it. Korea, Japan, Panama, Frankfurt, Kansas, Washington – wherever Nate's career had taken them.

'Did Jeff tell his girlfriend we're moving yet?' Nate asked.

Lydia rolled her eyes. 'Not yet.'

'You're kidding!' He laughed. 'That's pretty shitty.'

'He's in *lu-u-uve!* He just can't bring himself to tell her.'

'Is he taking it hard . . . the move, I mean?'

Lydia looked at him with a knitted brow. 'Nate, he's seventeen years old and has a girlfriend. He has to pull up stakes again and move thousands of miles away. Do you think he cares one *whit* that you didn't get the Korean command?'

'I didn't *mean* that.'

'*Yes*, you did.'

'No, I *didn't!*' Nate lied. He avoided her face so as not to see the annoying grin that he knew she had fixed there. 'Well,' Nate said, 'he'll be fine in two weeks. I mean, *Hawaii*, for Christ's sake! Once he gets a load of the girls on those beaches we're gonna have to chain him to the bumper of the car.'

Lydia leaned over the box and kissed him. She looped her hands around his neck and pressed her forehead to his. It was always like this. The disruptions to their domestic routine that each new posting had brought were immense. But always they'd greeted the change with a sense of excitement. Always before, Nate thought, they had been on the way up. He gently prised her hands loose and resumed his packing.

Lydia left him to his thoughts for a while. Finally, she casually said, 'What do you think about the China thing?'

'I don't know,' Nate mumbled. The repetitive motions of packing served to wash away the grievances. A hundred times he had replayed in his mind the meeting with Ed Dekker. Each time, he'd improved upon the complaints he had failed to raise. Nate looked up at Lydia. 'What China thing?'

'You know,' she said innocently. 'I mean the possibility of going to war with China.'

Nate sat back on his heels. 'What the hell are you talking about? Have those bridge club biddies over in Arlington been gossiping about . . .?'

'About you and your professional slight?' she confronted head-on, but lightheartedly. 'Nate, really. They're much more interested in who's been sleeping with whom. Which of the young colonels on their husbands' staffs married beneath himself. Important things like that.'

'Then what are you talking about? Where do you get that kind of nonsense about war with China?'

'Why, from you, dear, of course!' she said, still smiling. She was toying with him.

'I never said anything about . . . about that.'

'Darling,' Lydia said in a tone reserved for the dim-witted, 'you've been talking about China this and China that for a week now. You've had the "C" volume from the Encyclopedia on our nightstand since the day you came home from your big meeting. The television is droning

76

on in the background and all of a sudden your newspaper flies out of your face so you can watch a story about riots in Beijing. Do you think I'm an *idiot*? Do you have no respect for me whatsoever?'

Nate was a little disappointed that it hadn't been something more. That the risks from an economically burgeoning China which was rapidly mobilizing its armed forces wasn't the talk of the town.

'Besides,' Lydia said – leaning over to cup his cheek with her cool, soft hand – 'why else would the Army take their very best general and put him in command of the whole Pacific?'

'I'm not "in command of" the Pacific. I report to PACOM, and that's a *Navy* billet, for God's sake! I'll be reporting to an *Admiral*.'

Lydia sighed noisily. 'Good thing you're not into all this political infighting crap. Just wanta do your duty for God and your country.' Nate tilted his head and frowned. 'Well, *really!* You were the one who had to be dragged kicking and screaming back to a desk job in Washington last year. I could've sworn you were having an affair with that tank you crawled all over in your dress uniform after your send-off.'

'I didn't know if I'd ever get another command!' Nate shot back with more vehemence than he'd intended. He softened his tone as a means of apology. 'I agreed to brown-nose my way through those offices and cocktail parties because that was the only way I'd ever get another one. Hell, I've practically crawled up the lower intestines of half a dozen joint staff officers.'

'Don't be crude,' she said in a purely perfunctory manner. 'Besides, you *got* one! A command! And a deployment to Siberia! As perverse as it may be, I'd think you'd be *excited* about that. What's there to bitch about?'

He looked straight at her now. 'It's probably my last command, you know. No matter what Dekker says, USARPAC is a graveyard. I'm off the track. This time next year I guess we're moving to some golfing community down in Florida, just waiting to die.'

'Jesus Christ, Nate! You're fifty-two years old. If you want to work, *work!*'

'Doing what? A glorified sales rep for some defense contractor? Pawning off overpriced toilet seats to O-6s over in Procurement?'

'This time next year, who knows what the world will look like, Nate.' He looked up at her, waiting for her to put together the broken pieces of his dreams. 'You may know all kinds of facts and statistics about

China from your encyclopedias and those files you keep locked in the safe upstairs. But there's one thing *I* know that you don't. *I* know what Chinese think about their place in the world.'

Nate sat back and took a deep breath, his gaze drifting off.

'You listen to me, dammit!' she snapped

Nate turned quickly to face her. 'I'm sorry, Liddy.' From her tone he knew this wasn't Lydia-the-personal-therapist applying a verbal balm to Nate's slowly healing bruises. This was the Lydia whom he'd met while getting his Masters in History at Berkeley – a degree being one of the better career tickets to get punched when there wasn't a war on.

'We Chinese had civil service exams a thousand years before Rome was built. We had masterpieces of art and literature long before the Greeks. When Ghengis Khan and his Golden Horde tore out of Mongolia to take over the earth, he made it all the way to Austria until the death of his father the king brought everybody home for the funeral. But in the twenty years of war against China – his neighbor just to the south – how far did he get? He only took over the northern half. And two hundred years later, the Mongols were so inbred they were *Chinese*.'

'I know,' Nate said, but he listened.

'So . . . you run along to your new command in Siberia. You want a worthy enemy to worry about, just look south.'

'This Siberian deployment is just what I always *dreamed* of,' Nate said in a sarcastic tone. 'You know what the manuals call these things? "Operations other than war,"' he said in disgust.

'You'd prefer *war*?' she asked.

'*No-o-o*. It's just . . . I didn't put this uniform on to command blue helmets. I'm trained for war, Lydia, not humanitarian relief missions, or peacekeeping, or counterterrorism.'

Her head hung low. Her hair covered her face. 'Be careful what you wish for,' she mumbled.

'What?'

'Maybe you should *know* something about the place,' she said – changing the subject and tone. She cleared her throat and wrapped another dish. '*So*, there were no Russians in Siberia till the mid-1600s,' she said – beginning her lecture. 'They "discovered" the Bering Strait in 1648. The first clashes with the Chinese were two years later, but the Chinese held onto their territory. Russia and China signed the Treaty of Nerchinsk in 1689. It gave the Amur River basin to China, but the Russians kept pressing east – as far as Fort Ross, California, by 1812.'

She packed another plate. Nate waited in silence – listening.

'The-e-en,' she resumed in an airy voice, 'China disintegrated. The British, French, Dutch, Germans – they all feasted on the carcass. But less *noticeably* in the north, the *Russians* pushed down the Amur and Ussuri Rivers and planted the flag at Vladivostok in 1860. The British finally stopped them, but the Russians hung onto Manchuria, which they industrialized.'

'Then the yang,' Nate said. He didn't know the history, but he knew his wife.

'*Then* came the yang – the Japanese. The Russians were the preeminent power in the Far East. Then the Japanese won the Chinese-Japanese War in 1895 and the Russo-Japanese War in 1905. Then, the *yin*,' she said – her head swaying in time with her story – 'when the Russians again seized Manchuria at the end of World War Two and infected China with Communism. Communism practically killed the philosophy of Confucius, but now Communism is itself dead. China's really a post-Communist, socialist country. Nobody believes in Marxism-Leninism any more. And the Chinese nationalists are taking advantage of the crisis in faith. They're filling the ideological void with charges that western countries are stifling China's emergence as a great power. Interfering with internal Chinese affairs in Tibet and Taiwan. Practicing moral superiority in human rights that's especially repugnant in light of Britain's opium trade and the wars it fought to protect it.'

'You realize, of course, that I wrote a Command and General Staff School *paper* on the rise of nationalism in . . .'

'You know the *dates* and the *facts* and the *names*. But what you *don't* know is the *mind* set. That's because you're Western. You're a hopeless Eurocentric, Nate Clark.'

Nate rolled his eyes. 'And you're *not* European to the bone – culturally, I mean?'

'No! Not completely. *You* see China as this overpopulated country that once, a lo-o-ong time ago, used to be a big deal. Then, the West hit their stride and developed steam engines and the riding lawnmower, and *boom* . . . China's a third world country. But the Chinese see things *completely* differently! Europeans see things in nice straight lines. Linear progress. You start at A, then with hard work you advance and you get

79

to B and then to C. But the Eastern way of thinking – the Chinese way – is the yin and the yang.'

'I *know* all that,' Nate said.

'No, you don't! You think the West has passed the East through technological and social progress, and that's the end of it. But Chinese view history as cyclical, like a pendulum, swinging from one side but always coming back 'round to the other. The yin and the yang. They see that despite the recent scribblings of Western historians, China is the true center of the world – "The Middle Kingdom." "Foreigner" and "barbarian" are the same word – someone whom they saw as equal parts human – meaning Chinese – and *ape*. The point is that the Chinese have been down for a few hundred years. But they believe that sooner or later they're going to be back on *top* for a few hundred years. And it's what they *believe* that's important.'

'But you aren't denying that there's such a thing as "progress," are you?'

'No, of course not! The point is that the West has such a short history, really, and it's completely ethnocentric. What Europe sees is the rise of a truly superior people that will, presumably, forever outpace the lesser peoples of the rest of the world. But the *Chinese* see Europe as yet another pretender. Another temporary challenge like the Mongols to be overcome in due time. The yin, for which there will most certainly be a yang.'

'Meaning what – specifically?'

'*Meaning*,' Lydia said, 'that the Chinese, at the end of the second millennium of the Western calendar – but well into the fourth by the Chinese – might well be thinking it's about time for the yang. That the power of the Russians who occupied Asia to the north and called it "Siberia" might be on the wane. And that China might just be on the rise. Ready to join the Asian Tigers on the Pacific Rim. Can you imagine, Nate, the economic might of one and a quarter *billion* Chinese if they attained the per capita GNP of the Japanese? Or even that of the Koreans or Taiwanese? The Chinese economy has been growing at double digits for a decade, and what have they been doing with that economic might?'

Nate's gaze was unfocused, but he was totally transfixed by Lydia's words. 'Buying weapons . . . from the Russians, mainly.'

'And so now they're mobilizing. Millions and millions of men – their biggest asset.'

'They're just getting the glut of trouble-making teenagers off the streets,' Nate protested. 'What was it Lin Hoa said in that speech he gave in Beijing? That Chinese youth are "besotted by the drunkenness of prosperity." The old Communist octogenarians are trying to dry out a population they think is too spoiled by Coca-Cola and blue jeans. That call-up is their way of giving this generation a little discipline.'

Lydia was nodding through all of what Nate said. This time, it was her eyes drifting off into space. Her lips parted, and with a nod she grabbed Nate's hands. 'You're *right*, Nate. This is just like the Cultural Revolution in the Sixties. A blooding of the young. A revival of the spirit of hard combat. The unity forged by fighting against the odds. They want discipline. Discipline to begin the new century. To assert themselves. To make the Twenty-*first* Century the Chinese Century like the Twentieth was the American. Don't you see? They want discipline, Nate – the discipline of war.'

NORTH LAKE TAHOE, CALIFORNIA
August 27, 0425 GMT (2025 Local)

The Secretary of Defense slowed the Range Rover as he approached the road construction signs. The signs hadn't been there that morning when he and the German Defense Minister had left the isolated lodge for a half-day of fly fishing.

'You understand,' the Secretary of Defense said, 'that we expect our NATO allies to carry most of the burden in Siberia. The President feels very strongly that's fair since you have the most to gain from starting up the flow in their gas pipelines.'

The Defense Minister looked at him. 'Your President has much to gain also, yes? In November?'

The Secretary glanced his way. 'Or to lose.'

The headlights of the Bronco behind them came on. In it rode German and American bodyguards, redoubled because of the terrorism. The Secretary turned on his own headlights in the growing darkness and slowly bumped his way over the uneven cut in the road.

'Look at that sunset,' the stout German bureaucrat said. The Secretary looked out the passenger window at the blood-red sun setting over the blue lake.

The heavy Range Rover was lifted straight into the air by the blast. It turned and fell off the road's shoulder – rolling over and over down the hill. Back on the road behind the now toppled construction signs, the hundreds of rounds of ammunition in the flaming Bronco began to cook off from the heat of the truck's fire.

FORT SHAFER, OAHU, HAWAII
August 27, 0700 GMT (1700 Local)

Nate pulled up to the Headquarters entrance and parked where he found 'Lt. Gen. Clark, CINCUSARPAC' stencilled on the curb. The front steps were bustling with soldiers in camouflage. The U.S. Army of the Pacific had obviously responded to Nate's first official order. Full battledress uniforms would be worn till further notice. He got out and was saluted repeatedly by the crowd bottlenecked at the door. An armed detail was checking IDs, but the sea parted and Nate walked through. An MP captain led Nate to his office and turned the overhead light on but remained in the hall.

Nate entered the most spacious office of his Army career. It was twenty by thirty feet. Carpeted wall-to-wall with a map of the Pacific theater. Lined with cherry bookshelves, glass display cases, and flag stands. His personal effects were neatly arranged. Pictures of his family. Books and bookends. Framed field maps with unit positions from Vietnam. Nate would use the office for barely more than a week. Another one was being prepared for him in Siberia.

A man at the door cleared his throat and Nate turned. The deeply tanned officer stiffened. 'Major Reed, sir,' he reported – saluting.

'Yes, of course,' Nate said. 'I remember you from SHAFE.' His return salute went straight to a handshake. 'You were on operations staff, right?'

Reed laughed. 'If you can say a captain at Supreme Headquarters Europe was on operations staff, then yes, sir. But I *am* on operations staff now. I was *also* tasked to deliver your orientation briefing.' Nate waited. '*And*,' he finally continued – not looking Nate in the eye – 'there was one other thing. The thought was I'd deploy with you . . . to Siberia.' This time he made eye contact. 'You see I've . . .

I've been in the Pacific for eight of the last twelve years – counting Korea. I know my way around the other services.'

Nate noticed the man's hair was just recently shorn. He had a dark tan, and the distinct line showed his hair had been longer before. 'I guess you and your counterparts in the other services play tennis and golf – or is it maybe surf, since this is Hawaii?'

He shrugged. 'I run. There are a good number of us who run before second mess. Some classmates of mine.' Nate glanced down to see the man's West Point ring.

Clark nodded and put his files on the desk. 'As for you deploying with my staff, I could use someone with your familiarity with the command and the theater.'

'I consider it a privilege, General Clark,' Reed replied. 'A real honor!' Nate looked up at the suddenly buoyant man. 'You know, sir,' Reed said, 'my father was a classmate of *yours*.' Nate arched an eyebrow. 'I'm Chuck Reed . . . Jr.'

Nate tried not to register the shock. He held out his hand. Reed shook it again. Nate was surprised to find how dry his mouth was. He licked his lips, saying, 'Last time I saw you – your picture, I mean – you were . . .' Nate held up his hands in the approximate size of a baby.

They laughed. Nate recalled many things from Vietnam with clarity. The crumpled photo of the pretty wife and newborn child was one of them. Cadet Chuck Reed had gotten married, as allowed, in their last week at the Point. It had been a big affair at the campus chapel with crossed sabers and hurled rice. He'd left for Vietnam with his wife seven months pregnant. It was late in the war. He could have gotten out of it. But that wasn't what brand-new second lieutenants did. The picture of the baby had arrived in Vietnam with the first mail. The homesick twenty-two-year-old carried it with him everywhere. When he got plowed on R&R, it was shoved in faces.

Chuck Reed and Nate Clark had been fellow platoon leaders in the same infantry company. It was the first and only tour for both of them. Nate would recover from his wounds. Chuck would die from his.

'We got your letter,' Chuck Reed's son said. 'It was all we really knew about how it happened. My mother still has it.' Nate had written. He nodded, hanging his head. He'd always meant to visit. 'We also got some letters from my father,' Reed said. Nate's mind was far away. It had been over thirty years since his last deployment to the Pacific. His memories were of heat and dirt. 'My father wrote us about the Vinh Phuoc River.' Nate's gaze rose. 'That was your first action, right?' Nate nodded. 'He wrote my mother that you saved his ass.'

Nate still had trouble accepting that Chuck Reed's son was a grown man. His own boys were products of a late marriage and years of unsuccessful attempts. Reed waited. 'Your father's platoon was all alone on the far side of the river when the NVA struck,' Nate said slowly. 'He'd been covering the company's crossing after the bridge was blown.'

'And you crossed back over the river and pulled his nuts out of the fire,' Reed filled in.

It had been a bad situation for two green platoon leaders to be in. Nate looked up at the framed maps on the wall. Swirling greens and browns of jungles. Contour lines. Grids for artillery. His map of the Vinh Phuoc didn't survive to become office decor. It didn't survive its several immersions in the brisk, cold stream.

'We both lost men that day,' Nate said, almost without thinking. He took a deep breath and looked up at Reed. He thought, but didn't say, *'Your father died two months later trying to return the favor.'*

Reed looked at his watch. 'Well, it's time for your briefing, General Clark.' He ushered a quiet and thoughtful Nate through the busy headquarters building.

The two dozen colonels, one-stars and two-stars, all stood in unison. Nate knew many of them. He rounded the long table shaking hands. 'Welcome to USARPAC,' and 'It's a pleasure, sir,' were the typical greetings. They were introduced by name, rank and job. His heads of Personnel, Intelligence and Logistics – the J-1, J-2 and J-4 – were all brigadier generals, as were the Corps and Divisional Deputy Commanders. The two-stars – major generals one rank beneath Nate – were the J-3 in charge of USARPAC Operations and the commander of the 25th Light Infantry Division. The various colonels were the flag officers' assistants and commanders of miscellaneous subordinate commands.

When Nate completed his circuit and sat, everyone settled in immediately. They were all aware of the news, he felt certain. All eyes were fixed on him.

'A little over two hours ago,' Nate began, 'the Secretary of Defense was killed in a terrorist bombing in California.' There was no stir. But none of the officers' rigid backs touched the padded cushions of their chairs. 'It's too early to tell, but all signs obviously point to Russian Anarchists. You've all been working hard, I know, on the details of Operation Eastern Order. So let me take this opportunity to make an observation about how our mission furthers the national security of our country. We are headed into the base of operations of the Russian Anarchists – Siberia. We know from national intelligence sources that they are trained there. That they stage for their operations there. And that they return there – if they survive their missions. While Security Council Resolution 919 pursuant to which we will deploy establishes as our objectives humanitarian relief, peacekeeping and securing Russian nuclear weaponry, our rules of engagement allow us to seek out and destroy any Anarchist facilities within our areas of operations.'

Nate looked into the faces of each of the men in slow succession. He wanted to make certain they understood the White House's unspoken objective communicated to him directly by General Dekker.

'Very well,' Nate said – turning to Reed. 'I understand you've got a briefing for me before we move on to the deployment plans.'

The young major strode to a large wall map depicting half the earth centered on the Pacific Ocean. When Reed spoke, he spoke to Clark. 'The U.S. Army of the Pacific has an area of responsibility extending from the east coast of Africa to the west coast of the Americas and from pole to pole. That 100-million-square-mile AOR contains more than fifty nations and more than half the earth's population, which makes USARPAC the largest of the unified commands. Within that AOR also are the seven largest armed forces on Earth with over ten million ground troops under arms.'

Reed's pointer fell squarely on the People's Republic of China. Although his eyes remained on Clark, the pointer's placement clearly wasn't accidental.

'USARPAC fills the ground role of U.S. Pacific Command, whose commander-in-chief is Admiral Furguson. Our major subordinate command is U.S. Army, Japan, whose operational arm is IX Corps headquartered in Camp Zama, Japan. USARJ's 10th and 17th Area Support Groups at Torii Station, Okinawa and Zama also provide logistical support to Korea by serving as managers of theater war reserve stocks. The two ASGs will constitute primary support for our deployment into Siberia.'

'Who's on the ground in Siberia now?' Clark asked – unable to wait patiently.

Reed had no need to resort to notes. 'Elements of the Military Traffic Management Command are in Vladivostok and Khabarovsk, and the 45th Support Group out of Pearl has a transportation company at the port of Vanin further up the Russian coast. Advance teams from the 1106th Signal Brigade and the 500th Military Intelligence Brigade are going into Khabarovsk today for command, control and intell.'

'What security do those men have?' Clark asked.

'They're carrying personal weapons at all times and will not stray from areas secured by Russian military support teams. We also have units from the Law Enforcement Command going in tomorrow to provide military police combat support and installation law enforcement. They could muster company-sized MP units if necessary to respond to local situations.'

'When do the first combat troops go in?'

'In about seven days,' Reed replied.

'Make that two days,' Clark said, and his officers scribbled notes. 'I know this is officially a host-country operation, but I want a contingency plan in place if we have to provide our own security. Let's not forget that the Russian Army in European Russia split and is engaged in a very hot civil war right now.'

'Might I suggest, General Clark,' his head of USARPAC Operations said, 'that we accelerate the insertion of the 1st Battalion, 1st Special Forces Group out of Okinawa.' He looked across the table at the commander of the 4th Special Operations Support Command, who nodded once.

'USARPAC's standing major combat formations,' Reed continued, 'consist of the 25th Light Infantry Division and 29th Infantry Brigade (Separate) here in Hawaii. The 25th 'Tropic Lightning' Division is the theater's rapid-deployment force. It will begin rotating battalions north to Forts Richardson and Wainwright for acclimatization training, which will be supported by the U.S. Army Garrison, Alaska. It and the 29th Infantry Brigade are designated as theater reserve. For deployment to Siberia we will receive the 10th Mountain Division from Fort Drum. We're also moving the 1st Battalion, 501st Infantry (Airborne) to Zama in Japan. They're USARPAC's only unit with true forced entry capabilities. USARPAC has initiated its force reconstitution plan. We'll augment our combat strength through mobilization of designated reserves. The U.S. Army Readiness Group, Pacific, and IX Corps (Reinforcement) have given action orders to the Alaska National Guard's 207th Infantry Group (Scout), and the 731st and 368th Military Police Companies – which are ARNG and USAR units, respectively, based on Guam. We've also called up the 29th Infantry Brigade's USAR round-out battalion based here in Hawaii – the 100th Battalion, 442nd Infantry.'

'The "Go For Broke" Battalion,' Clark said, drawing smiles from the men who knew their Army history. 'What about Stateside reserves?'

'Only the 205th Infantry Brigade (Light) has been called up so far, sir,' Reed said. There were frowns from many of the senior officers. 'The Two-Oh-Five is from the Minnesota National Guard and therefore has good cold-weather skills. They're the round-out brigade for the 25th. But we've also talked – informally – to the commanders of the 73rd Infantry Brigade of the Ohio National Guard, which would go to Alaska Command, and the 844th Engineer Battalion of the Tennessee Army Reserve. They've pledged to increase their pace of training – again on an informal, voluntary basis. We've also called up personnel assigned to the staffs of Tripler Army Medical Center here in Hawaii, and Bassett Army Hospital up in Alaska . . . just in case, sir. We've done it quietly.'

Clark nodded once. Reed moved on to the next map. Although as large as the map of the USARPAC area of responsibility, it depicted only the Russian Pacific coast to the east and Mongolia to the west. To the north was the endless wilderness of the Siberian plains. To the south – the People's Republic of China.

'Under the terms of the Russian Army's invitation, the United Nations Forces, Russia, or "UNRUSFOR",' he said – pronouncing the acronym as one word – 'may operate no further west than Chita, Siberia, and no further north than the Lena River. By similar invitations, German, French and British forces will secure and maintain the Trans-Siberian Railway to the *west* of Chita all the way to the European rail grid. All European forces will deploy by rail directly from Europe and will come under UNRUSFOR command at Chita. All U.S. forces will arrive by air or by sea at Russian Pacific ports and will be under UNRUSFOR operational command upon debarkation.'

Reed's pointer slapped the map. It landed on the Chinese border. 'The principal geographic features in the UNRUSFOR theater of operations are the Amur River and the Trans-Siberian Railroad. The

Amur – which the Chinese call the "River of the Black Dragon" – is the border between Russia and China and flows west-to-east. Sovereignty over the Amur River basin has historically been contested . . . militarily.' Reed and most of the other officers looked at Clark, who nodded. 'The Amur River,' Reed continued, 'is the principal north-eastern waterway on the Asian continent. It turns north at Khabarovsk and empties into the Sea of Okhotsk. It broadens in some places into what is almost an inland sea. In other areas, it snakes through steep gorges and spreads fingers out through cuts in very rough terrain. The Amur joins the Ussuri River at Khabarovsk, where the Russian Far East Army Command will make room for UNRUSFOR's headquarters. The Ussuri runs south-to-north and forms the border between Russia's Maritime Provinces and China. At the southern tip of the Maritime Provinces is the only year-round port – Vladivostok. Further north, the port of Vanin will be available to us till it freezes over for the winter in November.'

'What about the defense infrastructure in that part of Siberia?' Clark asked.

Reed's briefing seamlessly transitioned. 'During the peak tensions between the Soviets and Chinese in the late 1960s, the Russians built a series of "voenny gorodoks" all along the border. They're self-contained military bases complete with concrete bunkers, hardened radar sites, et cetera. Most have fallen into disrepair, but we plan to improve and man them during the second stage of our deployment in December.'

'But aren't those bases arrayed in such a way as to refuse the Chinese border?' Clark asked.

'Yes, sir,' Clark's J-3 replied. 'The Russian Strategic Rocket Forces dispersed their missile silos in rights-of-way all along the Trans-Siberian Railroad. The International Atomic Energy Commission people are gonna need security to go onto those missile bases and secure the warheads. The voenny gorodoks are spaced very conveniently along the railway.'

'I understand, but what's this going to look like to the Chinese?' Clark asked. No one had an answer. He motioned for Reed to continue.

'The Trans-Siberian Railway is the other principal geographic feature in theater. The southern branch hugs the border. The northern branch runs from the port of Vanin through the military industrial complex in Komsomolsk-na-Amur to points west. Both are double-tracked for simultaneous east-west traffic. They're Russian wide-gauge, so we'll have to use local rolling stock. But rail is virtually the only means of ground transportation other than special-purpose military roads connecting the defense infrastructure.'

Reed faced Clark full on. 'The importance of the Trans-Siberian Railway cannot be emphasized strongly enough. There are *no* roads connecting European Russia with the Far East. Whoever controls the Trans-Siberian Railway . . . controls Siberia. It's as simple as that.'

Nate was quickly growing to appreciate Reed's abilities as a briefer. He now viewed the slender rail lines running east and west across the large map of Eurasia in the appropriate perspective. Their importance and the myriad of problems incumbent in their defense assumed greater significance in his quiet thoughts. 'Tell me a little more about the terrain,' Nate said to the major.

Again, the pointer went to the map. 'From Beijing to the Arctic Ocean, and from the Gobi Desert and Mongolian steppe in the east to the Pacific ocean, the terrain is best described by the Russian word "taiga" – dense, virgin, evergreen forests covered in thick brush. The trees are primarily large oaks, cedars, pines, linden and birch. They're typically overgrown with liana and wild grape or creeping brush and subbrush. Thickets with spines as long as fingers and sharp needles fill most of the spaces between trees. The topography is mostly rugged and broken north of the Amur. To the south of the Amur in Manchuria and between the Ussuri and the Pacific coast in the Russian Maritime Provinces major mountain chains run north and south. The mountains rise from foothills that are cut through with narrow, overgrown ravines formed by creeks that turn into muddy swamps in the short summers.'

'How the hell does the local population get through all that with no roads?' Clark asked.

'There are roads all throughout Manchuria connecting villages to towns to cities . . .' Reed began.

'No,' Clark interrupted. 'I mean on the *Russian* side of the border.'

'There are only a few small cities in Siberia,' Reed replied, 'and they're connected by rail. Out in the boonies, there is no "local population" to speak of. Only a few huts used by trappers and hunters during the summer that are connected by narrow footpaths.'

Clark squinted to read the legend – studying the scale of the map. The distances were enormous. 'Just what *is* the population in-theater?'

Reed turned back to the map, which was roughly evenly split by the Amur – China to the south and Russia to the north. 'There are less than two million Russians in UNRUSFOR's theater of operations. And that number is dropping rapidly because people are packing up and fleeing to the west.'

'Straight into the civil war?' Clark asked. Reed nodded. *Fleeing what?* Clark thought. His eyes drifted south across the Amur River. 'What's the population of northern China just across the border?'

Reed didn't take his eyes off his boss. 'Approximately one hundred million people, General Clark.'

KANSAS CITY, MISSOURI
August 29, 1800 GMT (1200 Local)

'And in conclusion,' Gordon Davis read from the teleprompter, chopping his hand in the air for emphasis and counting to five silently, 'let me say *this* to any Anarchists who think Americans are easily intimidated.' The gathering of union workers listened quietly. 'If you continue to sow your seeds of violence about this great and peace-loving nation, you will soon reap a *bitter* harvest from a just but mighty people!'

Yells and thunderous applause reverberated through the mammoth I.B.E.W. hall. A high school marching band struck up a very loud rendition of 'The Battle Hymn of the Republic.' Gordon smiled, Elaine joined him and they both smiled. Everyone was on their feet. Even though Gordon knew it was all staged for the cameras, whose lenses roamed the podium and euphoric crowd, he couldn't help but feel enthused.

His press had been good. He was cast as a compromise candidate – a healer of the nation's many divisions. Allegations of tokenism on the Republican ticket were not as forceful or as frequent as he had feared. But part of the reason, he felt certain, was the preoccupation of the media with the continuing wave of assassinations.

As he and Elaine left the stage, a cordon of over two dozen Secret Service agents held back the throng. Gordon raised his hand again to wave, feeling the downward tug of the body armor underneath his dress shirt. Backstage, Fein rushed right up to him, taking his elbow and shouting over the noise, 'Perfect timing! You hit it just right!'

Gordon felt pleased to have the man's approval. Over and over Fein had proven his prowess. In the evenings after their grueling days of campaigning, Fein, Gordon and Daryl sat down to watch videotaped coverage of Gordon's various appearances. They were spun by the media just as Fein had predicted they would be. Fein's sound bites were served up as planned, and Gordon's campaign looked just like all the others. That was comforting to Gordon. It was an appearance of professionalism in which he took pride.

They headed out of the union hall through the kitchen. In the short distance from the exit to the limousine, a hundred reporters stood shouting questions from behind barricades.

'Senator Davis!' Gordon felt Fein's hand on his elbow – guiding him toward the car. 'Is it true, sir, that you smoked pot in college?' The lenses of half a dozen TV cameras focused on him.

'Yes, I did,' Gordon replied calmly.

There was a pause before another reporter asked, 'Did you inhale?'

Everyone broke out laughing at once. The hand gripping Gordon's elbow fell away. 'Next question,' Gordon replied. Again there was laughter.

'The Republican platform is very conservative,' another reporter shouted, 'but your voting record seems a bit mixed. Would you call yourself a liberal, or a conservative?'

'Those are just labels,' Gordon heard Fein mutter from behind him.

'I hold conservative views on matters of national defense and the economy, and liberal views on certain social issues.'

'*Which* social issues?' exploded from several mouths at once, but another, more insistent voice carried above all others. 'What about the article you published in the *Dartmouth Review* criticizing affirmative action and minority set-asides? Do you today find them to be, as you wrote, "mere windfalls for the black middle and upper-middle class that tend to diminish the hard, honest work of black students and businessmen by casting doubt on the means by which their success is obtained"?'

Fein couldn't help him there. A voice from deep inside Gordon screamed that he didn't need help – that he *shouldn't* need help –

because these were the questions that should be asked and answered. Another part of him – a larger and growing part of the public animal that he was becoming – sensed danger. 'I do not remember my exact words from that article.'

Fein stepped in now, smiling apologetically and holding up his watch to Gordon. 'Sorry, folks,' he said loudly, stepping between Gordon and the press and ushering Gordon to the open limousine door. The questions erupted from behind him. 'Are you against any other civil rights laws?'

When the door slammed closed, the noise level dropped to utter silence. Gordon, Fein and Daryl sat in back by themselves as the car pulled past the mob of reporters.

'Well,' Fein said, 'I think we need to talk.' Fein's eyes remained fixed on Gordon's.

'I thought you were some media guru,' Daryl jumped in. 'Some *expert* who never lets things get out of *control*.' Gordon frowned – feeling himself to be at fault. He hadn't let Fein do his job. He'd made Fein look bad and might have done himself some harm in the process. 'Did you know, Gordon,' Daryl continued, 'that Arthur here used to be a marketing executive at Pepsico? That's right, isn't it, Arty? Before you started selling people, you sold soda pop?'

'I was Vice President of Marketing at Pepsico,' Fein confirmed – not taking his eyes off Gordon.

'And that makes him eminently *qualified*, don't you think? I mean, soft drinks – Vice President of the United States – what's the difference?'

'What kind of damage are we looking at?' Gordon asked Fein. Daryl fell silent – stung.

'From the pot thing – nothing,' Fein answered. Daryl shoved papers into his file folder and turned to stare out the window. 'From the *Dartmouth Review* piece . . .?' Fein began, then shrugged.

'Did you know about it? About me smoking pot? About the article?'

Fein just smiled, then leaned forward. 'You're a complicated package. Usually, with the Veep, we just want one dimension. People get overloaded with too many messages, so we want one solid, consistent image coming out of the lower half of the ticket so as not to overburden the electorate with detail.'

'Jesus, Gordon!' Daryl snapped. 'Are you listening to this shit? Are you hearing the same bullshit I'm hearing? "Overburden the electorate with detail." That means talking about the fucking issues! God forbid you do *that!*'

'In your case, however,' Fein continued without so much as a glance at Daryl, 'you are obviously a ticket balancer. The Party has a conservative platform. We've nailed down the right wing of the electoral spectrum. Now, we can't let Governor Bristol creep too far toward the left . . .'

'Toward the fucking *center!*' Daryl interjected bitterly.

'. . . without risking alienation of our core. They won't vote for Marshall, but they could just stay home. And that core represents not only votes, of course, but probably a hundred million dollars or so in campaign contributions that we expect to roll in between now and the election. But *you* give us a very interesting opportunity. It's really never been tried before. We've got some computer models which project that for every right-wing voter we lose with you, we pick up two, and some models even project three or more black or liberal voters. Now that's within certain ranges of tolerance. We can't move you too far to the left for risk of engendering internal dissension in our camp. But what we're trying to do is to poach some of the Democrats' traditional base by positioning you – within limits – to the left of Bristol. It requires delicacy, but it promises a potential two- or three-to-one payoff.'

'Is *this* what you want, Gordon?' Daryl asked calmly. 'Poaching, positioning, trading off one voter for another?' He leaned forward. 'What about the things that you really believe in? Ask him what you're supposed to do about *those*. Where do they fit in? Are they inside the program's parameters or not?'

Gordon already knew the answer. Fein had been up front with him from the beginning. In a campaign, it doesn't matter what he truly believes. What matters is winning the election. Then he could act on those beliefs from high office.

'So you're saying the pot thing could actually *help?*' Gordon asked. 'We might lose the redneck vote – assuming they'd vote for a black man anyway – but it could make me appeal to the baby boomers who make up the more populous center?' Fein nodded sagely – a twinkle in his eye. Daryl sank deeper into the plush leather seat. 'But what about the affirmative action article?'

Fein shrugged. 'That's what makes this an art, not a science. It's impossible to predict. But I do know one thing. If we let this become

93

a big issue – set you up as the anti-civil rights candidate – we'd be hounded straight to the gates of hell by the very people whose votes we're after.'

'What are you suggesting?' Gordon asked.

'That article was written before your appointment to the Senate,' Fein replied. 'You were a relatively young man. You've learned a lot of things since entering national politics.' He shrugged again.

'Oh, for Christ's sake, Gordon!' Daryl burst out. 'Just disavow the whole Goddamn article.' He leaned forward. 'Oh! Oh! I've got it!' He held his hands out to keep everyone quiet and looked back and forth between Gordon and Fein. 'We can tell them you were stoned when you wrote the article.' He clapped his hands together and sat back – crossing his arms and smiling in a sarcastic pantomime. 'Isn't this great? You're too Goddamned *conservative* for the Republican Party! Don't you get it?' he said – backhanding Gordon's knee. 'You're not just their token *black*, you're their token *liberal* too! A two-fer!'

Gordon stared at Daryl in silence. He wasn't angry – as he should have been – but sad. For he realized now what had to be done. What *he* had to do. It would be the hardest thing he'd ever done in his life. Daryl was his best friend. They'd made every step together. Every step but this last one.

Out of the corner of his eye, Gordon could sense Fein looking at him. He turned to Fein. There was a hardness in his eyes. He knew what Gordon was thinking, and the Party approved.

MOSCOW, RUSSIA
August 30, 1600 GMT (1800 Local)

There was a loud rapping at the door of Kate Dunn's apartment. She and Woody looked at each other over the early dinner he'd brought with him from the central television studios. The loud tapping of knuckles quickly turned to a closed fist pounding on the door. It stopped.

A violent crash sent wood splinters flying across the room. The door flew open to admit a half-dozen men in dark suits. Woody grabbed his film bag. They headed straight for Kate. She tried to dodge their outstretched arms and weave past them for the door. But she ran headlong into the clutches of a burly man with a meaty and close-shaven head. The man wore a well-tailored suit, but he smelled of days-old sweat.

'Let *go!*' she screeched as she was hustled to the door. The intruders never said a word, but Kate could hear Woody protesting loudly. 'I'm an American!' she shouted. 'A correspondent!' With two men holding her arms roughly, she was taken to the stairs. She jerked her body to try to free herself – kicking and screaming all three flights down to the street.

A long black limousine waited at the curb. Two more large men in dark suits stood by the open door.

'*No-o-o!*' Kate shouted – twisting and digging her heels into the pavement. Fear turned to icy dread and then to outright panic as she was shoved roughly into the car. The door slammed shut behind her.

A small man sat impassively across from Kate.

The door wouldn't open. The car gunned its engine. Turning to the lone man, Kate's first impression was of a police inspector. He regarded her with a pleasant smile. Facing backwards Kate saw two cars following. They were jammed, she assumed, with the brutes who had broken into her apartment. She twisted around to see through the thick glass screen that another man sat in front beside the driver.

Kate's throat was pinched tight, and no words would come out of her mouth. She tried her best to calm her jangled nerves. The man opposite her wore an expensive pinstriped suit and patent leather formal shoes at the ends of short legs crossed in feminine fashion. His most distinctive feature was his round, black-rimmed eyeglasses which stood perched on his bald head. On second thought, the man looked less like a policeman and more like a professor. She swallowed and cleared her throat. 'Who are you?' Kate asked finally through a throat dry with fright.

The man chuckled. There were gaps in his front teeth that gave him a faintly unpolished look. His manner was altogether unthreatening. 'You are a good reporter, Miss Dunn. Don't you know who I am?'

Had Kate not already been in a state of semi-shock, her realization would have terrified her. 'Valentin Kartsev?' she said quietly.

'It's a pleasure to meet you.'

Kate dug her elbows into her sides to ward off the chill from the air conditioning. 'What do you want from me?'

'We each have our interests. And I believe that our interests in one subject just happen to coincide.'

'What . . . subject is that?' she asked as the motorcade sped down the empty road.

'Me. Or, more aptly stated, your reportage on me.'

He spoke English well – his accent mild and his manner cultured. Kate drew a deep breath before speaking, then blurted out, 'Where are you taking me?'

'On a tour of the most interesting country in the world,' Kartsev replied. His eyes turned to the window. The passing landscape reflected off the round lenses of his glasses as if projected onto a screen before his eyes. 'You do think that, don't you? That Russia is the most interesting country in the world?'

Kate was too concerned with drawing air into her lungs to respond. But she turned to look at the dreary Stalin-era apartment complexes that rose from the bare soil around Moscow like mushrooms. They were dirty and dingy. Bed linen and drying laundry hung from open windows and crumbling balconies. The buildings rose high into the air, despite being surrounded by empty, unused land, in a seemingly intentionally haphazard manner. Here and there the cars passed black clumps of charred vehicles. They stood like monuments to the savage fighting now radiating outward from Moscow. She turned her mind to Kartsev's question – trying to shut out her fears and worries.

'This is the world's kitchen. Or, perhaps better put, its laboratory. We Russians are not the Japanese. We've never been content merely to copy the West. We have always seen it to be our destiny to improve upon your ways. Perhaps it is that we knew deep down we could never really surpass you by mere imitation. Or perhaps it is a hopelessly romantic, Quixotic vision of ourselves as social pioneers. Regardless, we Russians have always thought we were destined for great things. An incubator for grand strains of revolutionary social thought.'

'You're talking about the past now, right? About Communism?'

Kartsev shrugged, looking out through the fleeting images reflected off his glasses. 'The past, the future . . . I'm really just talking about Russia. Or, more precisely, Rus-*sians*. Do you see that?' He waggled a bony finger back and forth – pointing. 'That little village?'

Kate looked down the hill beside the empty highway along which the limousine raced. There was a small collection of shacks. Faded and peeling blue and green paint adorned the otherwise pitiful structures. '"Izbas" we call those little houses in Russian. One room kept warm by a single woodburning stove.' The main boulevard through the middle of the village was twin ruts in the dirt. 'Here we are, not twenty kilometers outside of the capital of Russia, and those people know nothing of what is happening in Moscow's streets.'

An old babushka switched at a horse to drive it alongside the paved highway. She wore a black dress and a shawl over her head. Her lips sank in around a toothless, wrinkled mouth. The horse pulled up the hill a flat-bed cart that looked as if it could've been built centuries earlier but for its big rubber tires.

'The czars came and went. The Revolution, Civil War, collectivization, the purges. I know that little village down there. Hitler's troops were stopped right there. Those little houses were in "No Man's Land" between two great armies. And there they stand fifty years later following the collapse of the Soviet Union. Democracy. Free markets. Hyperinflation. Industrial collapse. Mass unemployment. The interesting thing is that none of that changed those people at all. The Great Patriotic War rolled fire and death over their little izbas. Their men were drafted into the Army and killed. But none of it fundamentally altered the lives of those villagers one iota.' He smiled and shook his head. 'It's truly remarkable, Miss Dunn.' Kate shrugged. 'And this village is just outside Moscow. What do you think it's like over the great expanses of our country? Far, far away from the two great cities of Moscow and St Petersburg?'

She didn't answer. 'Do you think your Anarchist Movement will be different? It will somehow affect the Russian people like those down there?'

'No.' The answer was not what Kate had expected. 'It is in the cities where anarchy's effects will be felt. And not just the cities of Russia.'

'So . . . how? How will an anarchist society work?' Kate asked.

'Miss Dunn,' Kartsev said with a brief laugh, 'asking how an anarchist society will work is a very "archist" question. Archism esteems control as its highest value. *An*archism is not an ideology or a prescribed set of values. We are to the state as atheists are to God. We are simply "anti-archist."'

'But what is it that your movement stands for? What are you trying to accomplish?'

'If you want programs and platforms, Miss Dunn, you should interview a Republican or a Democrat. We are engaged in an *experiment*. We are attempting to establish the world's first advanced, non-statist society. We reject all the various claims to governmental legitimacy. Mandates from heaven. The will of the majority. Racial superiority. Government arises from a voluntary communal exchange of autonomy for order People trade their freedom for punctual railroads. The government they get in return is invariably based on coercion and force. If you don't believe me, just try disobeying the government. Quit paying your taxes. Build a walled compound and tell the sheriff to go away when he comes calling. The government you've spurned will not only take your property away. They will attack with paramilitary force, lock you up, kill you – even in your country. *We* simply reject the historical social trade which gave rise to government in the first place. We claim autonomy and a relief from that threat of governmental violence in exchange for the social disorder that will necessarily ensue.'

'So who is "we" – exactly?' Kate asked.

'We anarchists. We are a collection of individuals who oppose institutions that enforce order by infringing upon liberty. We are anti-technologists, laissez-fairists, syndicalists, individualists, pacifists, vanguardists. We are punk rockers, squatters, far left Libertarians, atheists, radical ecologists, tax resisters, draft resisters, resisters of every sort. We are united not by what we are for, but by what we are against, which is any form of coerced social organization.'

'But what about criminals?' Kate asked. 'It's those same "social organizations" that get murderers off the streets so they don't kill again.'

'Which, do you suppose, would kill more people – murderers running rampant on anarchistic streets, or national armies fighting territorial wars across continents?'

'So you are out to destroy every nation on earth?'

'We *must*,' Kartsev replied. 'If any archist institutions survive at all they will sprout order, and hierarchy, and power-mongering. Society will organize around them like crystals form in a liquid solution.'

'But what about peoples' rights? Don't people have the *right* to choose their form of government?'

'"Rights" are an archist concept. Rights are only important when you are confronted with superior power. Rights are what is left to the people after the government has taken what it wants. Your country's Bill of Rights, for example, defines your cherished freedoms by limiting the legal power of government to encroach upon them. But all those rights may still be overridden by the government in certain circumstances, and guess who it is that retains the power to interpret when? The state. What we Anarchists say is there is no need for rights when there is no state to encroach upon your freedom.'

Kate opened her mouth for another question, but Kartsev said, 'Oh! We're here.' The car slowed and turned through a gate. Two guards in long black overcoats stood at the gate with assault rifles dangling from slings over their shoulders. The private drive then wound through a park-like forest.

'Where are we?' Kate asked. Her voice quivered slightly.

'My dacha.'

Kate had last been to a dacha one month before to do a story about how ordinary Russians spent their leisure time. The one she'd been shown was an unimpressive little cottage crammed together with other similar shanties on a poorly maintained dirt road. Kartsev's enormous manor came slowly into view. They pulled up to the front steps. More guards with assault rifles descended the steps from the house.

The car stopped, and they got out. Instead of heading toward the 'dacha', Kartsev led her along a path of neatly brushed mulch into the thin woods that surrounded the mansion. Kartsev seemed content to stroll without talking. Kate spent her time watching for dangers and trying to conclude why it was everything would turn out all right.

It was an overcast day – slightly cool, slightly humid. The sound of their footsteps crunching in unison and those of the two guards who followed was the only sound Kate heard. The path ended at the edge of the Russian forest. The slender white birch trees were widely spaced. The ground was nearly clear of brush. It was a young forest, she thought. The trees were not very tall. Kartsev looked out of place in his expensive dark suit. He walked with his hands clasped behind him. Kate's eyes were level with his, which meant he wasn't much over five foot four.

'So, what do you think of my country home?' Kartsev asked.

Kate shrugged. 'Seems a bit remote. Lonely.'

'Oh, but we're not alone.' Kartsev stopped. He held his arms out to the empty woods around them. 'We are surrounded, you see, by the social scientists from Russia's past. Fellow Russians,' he said as he looked around at the thin trees and bare forest floor, 'who launched their own grand experiments in the past. Like *their* work, the project in which *I* am engaged will be a great service to mankind. It will expand our knowledge base, and all knowledge is, of course, good. I intend to keep accurate records – journals – for posterity as well as for my own analysis, unlike the less scientific of my predecessors.'

Again he looked around as if he were speaking of people whom he thought were present. Kate felt nervousness fray the calm she'd managed to attain. A sudden sense of uncertainty on finding herself in the presence of madness. 'Mr Kartsev,' she said calmly, quietly, 'there's nobody else here.'

'But that's where you're wrong, Miss Dunn. You are very wrong indeed. You see, when I looked for a place to build my dacha this site seemed perfect. A great tract of completely unspoiled government land.' He looked around the beautiful woods with a smile of satisfaction. 'They had been trying to privatize the parcel for some time, but had gotten no takers. There were rumors of environmental problems – of chemical or radiological wastes which are commonplace concerns in Russia these days. One local rumor even had it that there had been a chemical weapons plant located behind the barbed wire fences. But I had an advantage, you see. I was with the KGB . . . or I had been in my earlier days. You never really quite leave, you understand. So, I knew the true story behind this parcel, and the more I thought about it, the more the idea of building here appealed to me. The more appropriate it seemed, in fact.'

'Well . . . what *was* here?' Kate asked. The serene woods betrayed no signs of the secrets they held.

'This was the main Moscow burial ground first of the NKVD, and then of its successor – my own KGB. You are standing, right now, atop the final resting place of almost a million of my fellow countrymen. They were brought here by the truckload for decade upon decade. Here lie the great experimenters of the past. My brethren in the quest for social knowledge and advancement.' He beamed from ear to ear.

Kate halted and turned to face him. 'What do you want with me?'

'I want you to spread the word.'

'What word?'

'Anarchy.' His lips still retained their curl from his earlier smile, but his eyes – magnified slightly by thick lenses – seemed devoid of humor. 'You in the Western media are my trigger. I want you to spread the word of our grand experiment. My country is filled with the failed structures of seventy years of Communism. They are holding it back. We have maintained a social safety net and haven't allowed Russia to fall hard enough or far enough to break those institutions and organizations into pieces so that new ones can sprout up from their rubble. "Destruction is the mother of creation."'

'So that's what you propose to do? Let everything fall apart so new "structures" can replace them?'

'No. I don't plan to let them fall at all. I plan to quite actively tear those structures apart. In a few months' time, Russia will be a country with nothing left but people. No government to speak of. No large employers. No political parties. No religions or organizations or associations of any kind.'

Kate stared at him in disbelief, then laughed nervously. 'You're kidding, right? I mean that's just . . . rhetoric.' The mild-mannered Kartsev smiled. 'Do you realize what that would mean?' she asked.

He spread his hands and shrugged. 'Anarchy.'

'And . . . death. Disruption. Homelessness. Disease. *Ruin!* People will *starve* to death!'

'Oh, it will be much worse than you can even imagine. Packs of people, roaming the streets for something to eat. Anything. Anybody. Funeral pyres will light the night, Miss Dunn.'

'But . . . the army will never let that happen!'

'The army, my dear, is the first target. Have you not wondered where they are? Why they have not put down my Black Shirts? They are experiencing entropy. The first signs of that decay will be seen quite soon now. Quite soon. The army is an institution, after all, and one that is very rigid. Its discipline threatens to maintain some semblance of order in society at large. A skeletal structure from which the sagging flesh of state will hang. We cannot allow that. Oh, no! Not at all.'

'Why are you telling me all this?' Kate asked – almost whispering despite the fact that the bodyguards were well out of earshot.

'Because I want you, Miss Dunn, to spread the word. I want you to watch it happen, and to tell our story.' He held out his hands as if to include his predecessors buried under the dark soil. 'Anarchy, you see, is an idea. A thought. I want to do nothing more than spread that thought – the seeds of that idea – far and wide. When the seed lands on fertile soil, it will sprout shoots and grow. That's all. I don't even know what it will grow into, but there are minds out there that are ripe for this idea.'

'Like National Socialism in 1930s Germany?' she asked – sneering.

'Exactly!' he said. 'I spread the idea of anarchy to the four corners of the earth and see if it grows. Consider it my small contribution to the social sciences.'

'I don't know how much good I'm going to do for your cause, Mr Kartsev. I'm sorry to tell you this, but even with the deployment of U.S. troops to Siberia what's going on in Russia isn't going to get much air time when there are terrorist attacks and riots in American cities.'

'But they're all part of a single process,' Kartsev replied.

Kate stared at him. 'How long have you been watching me?' she asked without knowing why.

'For a while. You're very good at what you do.'

'And you've been feeding me anonymous tips so that I can scoop the other correspondents?'

'Simply do your job, Miss Dunn, and report the news as you see it. If it is in my interest to assist you, then, well . . . it's a free country,' Kartsev said with a wry grin.

'I will *not* be manipulated.'

'You would not be alive if it were not for the helping hands of a random stranger who caught you during the Red Square massacre,' Kartsev said. He stared back at her – letting what he'd said sink in. 'I need your skill, your insights, your way with words. Plus, you have a high "Q" factor, I believe the networks call it. You're an attractive, appealing messenger. Viewers like you.'

'So you want me to incite the restive inner-city underclass with stirring reports of anarchist violence so they will storm into the streets and get slaughtered by tanks?'

'No, no. That's not what I want at all. The audience I have in mind for your reports is that great middle class of your country. I need for you to scare the hell out of them. It's easy, you see, for those rioters to pour out onto the streets and get slaughtered. It's far more difficult, however, to motivate the people who actually *do* the slaughtering.'

PART II

'"For every action, there is an opposite and equal reaction" – Newton's Third Law of Motion. The behavioral sciences have laws as well. "For every action, there is an opposite and unequal overreaction" – Kartsev's First Law of Man.'

Valentin Kartsev (posthumously)
'The Laws of Human History'
Moscow, Russia

Chapter Five

THE BRONX, NEW YORK
September 1, 0130 GMT (2030 Local)

The shot was so easy he didn't even need the night vision device. From the light of street lamps and two burning cars, the mounted policeman's chest filled the crosshairs of the optical sniper scope. The horse underneath the cop was the only problem.

The animal was spooked by the noisy crowd and the occasional stone hurled over the police barricades. It stepped this way and that – taking its rider in and out of the sights. 'Chyort vozmi!' the sniper cursed under his breath from the rooftop four blocks away from the demonstration.

At that range, the angry shouts of the residents who protested the beating of three high school students sounded more like the distant roar of a stadium crowd.

The next time the horse took a few nervous steps, the mounted cop steadied the animal with a firm tug on the reins. The sniper exhaled half a breath. The rider lay squarely behind the crosshairs. He squeezed the trigger almost involuntarily.

A single crack echoed among the buildings. The sniper quickly cycled the bolt, chambering a fresh round. But when he surveyed the scene, he saw what he had hoped for. The horse was out of control now – its rider barely hanging on and probably mortally wounded from the high-velocity round. He found another officer who'd turned his back to the mob to look at the commotion. His riot shield was out of place. Another squeeze, and another sharp recoil and crack.

The officer went down like a sack of potatoes. The bolt clacked again, but a third shot proved unnecessary. Someone in the police line opened fire. Then one of the rioters returned fire. Within seconds, blazing muzzles began to pop like flash bulbs from both sides. Before the man had packed his rifle, a war had consumed the street.

THE BRONX, NEW YORK
September 2, 1730 GMT (1230 Local)

Evelyn Faulk and her son Andre trudged their way to the south through the noise and commotion. The light was dim under the thick smoke rising from hundreds of fires all around the Bronx. It was two dozen blocks to the police lines. Neither the subway nor the buses were running. The few other people out that day headed furtively down sidewalks toward Manhattan like refugees from a war zone.

Evelyn's legs and back ached. It was slow going. Every few intersections they had to zig one block over or zag back the other way to avoid the unopposed looting of the city.

'Where we *goin'*?' Andre asked again.

'Just you *shush*!' she snapped back. She was doubly, triply angry. Angry at the thieves that ran loose like animals on the streets around her home. Angry at the police for running away and hiding behind barricades that did little more than protect rich whites from poor blacks. And angry at her own son. When the sun had risen after a sleepless night of shouts and gunfire, Evelyn had seen the look of anticipation in the eighteen-year-old's eyes. He was dressed and ready to hook up with his 'crew' – children who'd grown up to be called a gang. She had seen all in Andre's eyes. To him, this was an exciting new world filled with adventure. To her, it was that trip to the morgue she lay awake imagining during the hours her son was on the street.

106

'Look at *that*,' Andre said.

Evelyn followed Andre's outstretched finger. There was trash strewn all about the entrance to Mr Cantu's bodega. Empty soda cans, boxes of donuts only half eaten . . . but no people. Evelyn and Andre crossed the street to peer inside.

The power was off all over the Bronx, and the store was dark. All they could see from the doorway was disarray. Flies buzzed about the spoiling food. The tiny bodega had been ransacked. Everything was overpriced, but the residents of Evelyn's neighborhood nevertheless cherished the store because its brave owners had not been chased away by crime. They had put bars on the windows and had guns behind the counter and . . .

'Come on, momma!' Andre said suddenly – stepping outside. He tugged her back out onto the sidewalk.

'Let's go,' he said. Evelyn pulled her arm from his grip and headed back inside. She nearly tripped over the man who lay on the floor in a white butcher's apron. It was stained with three black splotches. His eyes were wide. His mouth gaped underneath his bushy mustache. Mr Cantu was covered in flies.

Evelyn felt like screaming, but she didn't panic. She marched out of the store and grabbed Andre's arm. She towed him straight down the block to the south. Her walk was purposeful, and it forced Andre to break his long-practiced saunter just to keep up with her pace. His hundred-dollar hightops flopped all about – their laces untied as was the fashion.

'Where we *goin'*, momma?'

'Hush up, I said!'

By the time they got down to 96th, people were out in the streets like it was a holiday. There was no sense of danger, just an air of excitement, an energy. Everyone was talking and laughing and pointing at the smoke. There were sirens of every sort near and far. But Evelyn hadn't yet seen any police cars or fire trucks.

Except up ahead. They stopped at the sight of it. Lights flashed through the gaps in the crowd. It looked like a riot, but she couldn't see or hear any signs of a disturbance. With tentative, wary steps, they waded into the mass of people. 'Excuse me. Excuse me,' Evelyn repeated over and over as the mostly indifferent crowd let her pass. They seemed to have gathered only to gawk at whatever lurid crime

ERIC L. HARRY

had been committed. After a minute or so, Evelyn and Andre reached
the front ranks.

It was an amazing sight. New York City police cars were parked
bumper-to-bumper all along 95th Street from east to west for as
far as the eye could see. The lights on their roofs were all flashing.
Evelyn grasped the brightly colored wooden barricades erected a few
feet short of the cars. There was another barricade running along the
opposite side of the street.

'What's going on?' Evelyn asked the woman next to her.

She looked Evelyn up and down and said, 'They're not lettin''
anybody cross down from Harlem.'

Evelyn looked at the barricades. It was like a wall had descended
across the city. But a few yards to her left, the wooden barriers opened
into a corridor through the new border. A gauntlet of uniformed police
officers with dogs lined the passage which led from the anarchy of the
blighted northern borough.

'Excuse me!' Evelyn began again . . . but loudly. She pushed her
way for the opening with Andre in tow. Police on horseback inside
No Man's Land kept watch deep into the crowd from Harlem. Tired
men milled about in full riot gear – their helmets' visors raised. Clear
plastic shields leaned against police cars, and long black truncheons
lay on the pavement next to them.

A man wearing a black bulletproof vest and holding a large shotgun
propped on his hips stood asking questions at the entrance to the
crossing. Evelyn and Andre got in line and waited.

'This is America!' a man shouted up at the head of the line. An
argument ensued. The man finally turned back in anger.

Next up was a woman wearing a white nurse's dress under a dark
sweater. She got through with no hassles, but she had to lift her large
purse high above her head as snivelling police dogs strained at their
leashes on both sides.

'I'm a maintenance engineer at the Garden,' the next man said.

'What does that mean?' asked the cop with the shotgun. 'You clean
up elephant shit when the circus is in town?' There was silence. 'Go
o-o-on,' the cop barked.

Finally, it was Evelyn's and Andre's turn. 'Where you headed?' the
tall white cop asked – addressing Evelyn but eyeing Andre. He ran a
hand-held metal detector over their bodies – raising a Latex-covered
finger and spinning to indicate that they should turn around. Evelyn

108

complied, but Andre just stared back at the man. Evelyn backhanded the boy. 'What's the matter?' the cop asked. 'Them looters steal your tongue?'

'Downtown,' Evelyn said quietly.

'Oh, yeah? What ya doin' down there today?'

'I got me some business to take care of,' Evelyn said softly. Her eyes were cast down toward the cop's shiny buttons.

'Whoa-hoa! Some *business*, ya say? I suppose you gotta deal with your stocks and bonds and shit.' Evelyn looked up. Through the open corridor ahead she saw taxis and people and activity. Life. 'Go on!' the cop growled – a grin on his meaty face.

Evelyn and Andre headed through. A German Shepherd reared up on its hind legs as it lunged. It was stopped by its leash, but not before its nose left saliva on Evelyn's good coat.

It was like crossing a border into a foreign country, Andre thought, although he had never seen a border before. Once they were across, they were free to roam the streets of the United States.

But the people on those streets shied away from Andre. Purses were clutched to sides or switched to the opposite shoulder. Conversations were halted until they were safely past. Eyes were kept warily fixed on him, Andre noticed, even by the well-dressed black businessmen. He smiled, thinking all he needed was to yell 'boo' and they'd hand him their wallets.

They walked block after block. Andre finally said, 'Where the hell are we *goin'*, momma?' She said nothing. She just limped along with her head held high and her eyes fixed straight ahead. People passing in the opposite direction clutched purses and grabbed for children's hands.

'We're here,' she said finally. She grabbed Andre by the jacket and pulled him toward a nondescript door. There were pictures like travel posters in the windows. 'U.S. Army Recruiting Center,' the sign said over the door.

'What the hell is this, momma?'

'You can read!'

'Yeah, I know what it say, but . . .'

'Your daddy died on these streets.' Andre hung his head. 'It was Friday, and he'd been paid. He just couldn't give up that money. He'd worked *too* hard just to give it up. I will *not* lose you too, Andre. You *hear* me?'

109

Andre still avoided her eyes. 'But the *Army*?'

'Your daddy was in the Army. I *married* him when he was in the Army.'

'I know all *about* that, *momma*! And I know he got sent to a *war*, too!'

'He was a boy just like you when he went off. He was a man when he came back from that desert.' Andre frowned. 'What you gonna do now that school's over, huh? I gave you all summer to think it over 'cause you done so good graduating, but what you gonna do now?'

Andre shrugged. 'Get a job,' he muttered.

'Doin' what? Loadin' trucks? Diggin' up streets on cold winter days? Honey, the *Army* don't take no one without that degree. It *means* somethin' to them. And the Army teaches you special things like computers. It'll teach you to get along with different people.' Andre rared back. 'Ain't *nothin'* wrong with actin' a certain way if it helps you get ahead.'

'Puttin' on is what it is,' Andre mumbled.

'*What*?' she snapped sharply. 'You're a man, now, Andre. My oldest. Time to start actin' like one.'

'Momma, if I'm a *man*, I can make my *own* decisions!'

She nodded, then nodded again. 'Yes. Yes you can.' She sniffed. Her eyes moistened. It was killing Andre. He couldn't stand seeing her give up on him.

She waited outside for an hour.

PHILADELPHIA, PENNSYLVANIA
September 4, 1500 GMT (1000 Local)

'They're everywhere,' Olga Andreeva said. She held her hands over her mouth as they watched the buildings burn in Los Angeles.

'Nobody has said that Kartsev's people started this,' Pyotr said, trying to calm his panic-stricken wife despite his own suspicions.

'Don't be naive! Of course they did this. Why else would it happen now? Just coincidence?'

'The police are being more aggressive. They just pushed the black people over the edge.'

'Oh, you're so ignorant about such things. You think like a man. Everything must be straightforward or you miss it entirely.'

The pictures on television now were of bodies strewn about one particularly devastated block. Andreev got his wallet from the kitchen counter and headed for the door.

'Where are you going?'

'Out,' he said, standing in the door and looking both ways down the hall. 'I'll be back soon.'

'No, sir, we don't sell any German guns,' the sales clerk said to Andreev.

'How about Uzis?'

The two men behind the counter looked at each other and laughed. The clerk standing in front of Andreev ran his hand down the glass-topped counter. 'We got Colts, Smith & Wessons, Rugers, Berettas . . .'

'What kind of Berettas?' Andreev interrupted. '9Ps?'

'Yep. They're seven fifty new. Or I got some mint, like new-in-box, for five fifty.'

The salesman pulled one of the new Berettas from the display and pulled the slide back, locking it open. He lay it on a beat-up rubber mat atop the glass. Andreev picked the pistol up and released the slide. It snapped forward with a crisp 'clack.' He opened it again and stuck his thumb into the chamber, peering down the barrel which was lit with reflected light. The interior of the barrel looked smooth, and there was no wear on the gentle grooves which twisted down the barrel toward his eye.

'That one there's seven hundred and fifty dollars.'

Andreev checked the tension in the trigger and worked the slide again.

'Can I ask what you're lookin' to use it for?' the man behind the counter asked.

Andreev was testing the heft of the weapon by lifting it to his line of sight and resting the butt in the palm of his left hand. 'Target shooting.'

He lined up the sights, which were well-designed and crafted.

The salesman leaned all the way down to the bottom shelf and came back up with a huge, nickel-plated automatic. 'Well, this here is an American gun – a Smith & Wesson. *Ten*-millimeter.' He pulled out

two boxes containing ammunition of different calibers. The salesman
pulled one bullet from one box, and a noticeably larger bullet from
the other. 'Now this one here is a nine-millimeter Parabellum, like
the army uses in those Berettas. *This* one,' he said, placing the much
larger, thicker bullet down beside the first, 'is a *ten*-millimeter. The
Smith & Wesson 10-mm automatic was developed for the FBI. It's got
a thirteen-round combat capacity, twelve in a double-stack magazine
and one in the chamber. It's heavy. It kicks like hell. But it'll knock
the holy shit out of your "*targets*".' He and his grinning co-worker
laughed.

'I'll take it,' Andreev said, looking at the beautiful weapon without
even lifting it from the mat.

'It's a thousand bucks.'

It had the right look about it. Businesslike. And the business of
a pistol was killing human beings. Andreev handed over a fistful of
one-hundred-dollar bills. He had been paid well to protect the Russian
President. Now that money bought protection for Andreev.

'You gotta fill these out,' the salesman said. He laid a set of forms
on the counter. 'Then we run a check. There's a seven-day waiting
period.'

'What?'

'It's the law But if you're worried about crime . . .' He lifted a huge
pump shotgun – black metal overlaid with ribbed plastic – and held
the heavy weapon by its pistol grip. The maw of the huge muzzle was
gaping. Menacing. 'You might try this ten-gauge pump. Holds five
rounds. I'd recommend a mix of shot and slugs. It's a mother, this
ole pump. And there ain't no waitin' period on the shotgun.'

Andreev looked at the huge weapon. The bell at the door jingled,
and he looked back over his shoulder with a start. It was a young couple,
and they sheepishly made their way to the gun counter. They huddled
together, whispering and pointing at the few remaining guns. It was
only then that Andreev noticed the gaps on the display shelves.

'I'll take it,' Andreev said.

Pyotr and Olga sat glued to the TV news. The knock at the door
made them jump. They knew no one in America. Pyotr got the
shotgun and headed for the front door. He risked pressing his eye
to the peephole.

There was a small gathering of people in the corridor outside – mostly old men and women. He put the large gun aside before opening the door. Olga joined him.

'Oh, hello,' a kindly-looking old lady said – smiling. 'We've never really introduced ourselves. We're all from the building.' Several people from the mostly male group nodded or waved at Pyotr. He nodded back. 'I had noticed your children on the playground. They're beautiful little darlings.' Olga's face lit up with a smile.

'We're forming a neighborhood watch,' an old codger said from off to the side. 'We were wonderin' if you'd like to join up.'

'A "neighborhood watch"?' Pyotr asked.

He was met with stony stares. The talkative old woman in the center finally said, 'That's a beautiful accent. Where are you from?'

'Switzerland,' Pyotr said, and the group eased up. 'What is this "watch" group?'

'A *neighborhood watch*,' the old man repeated more loudly as if Pyotr had a hearing problem. 'You know, a patrol.'

Pyotr and Olga exchanged looks. She was equally perplexed.

'It's a group of us from the building,' a younger man said from the back. 'We patrol the apartments and look for any signs of trouble.'

'What kind of trouble?' Pyotr asked.

'With the blacks,' the old codger blurted out. Several people chastised him loudly.

The smiling woman in front said, 'There's just so much crime these days. And with what's going on in California, we just decided to make sure our homes stayed safe. We're going to patrol every night in shifts. We have radios,' she said, holding up a cheap plastic children's toy.

Pyotr looked at Olga. She had been scared of street crime in Moscow, but she was terrified of what they had found in America. 'All right. I will join.'

They all welcomed him. 'Oh,' the old lady said, 'there is one more thing. Do you have a gun?'

'What?' Pyotr asked. He couldn't believe they were talking about armed patrols.

The woman stuck her hand inside her purse. 'A *gun*,' she said loudly – pulling a small revolver out. She held the weapon in her frail, bony arm – her finger on the trigger.

Pyotr was stunned, but he nodded. 'Yes. Yes, I have one.'

'Wonderful,' the woman said – smiling and returning her pistol to the purse. 'Then welcome to the watch. Oh, and welcome to America!'

ERIC L. HARRY

UNITED NATIONS BUILDING, NEW YORK
September 6, 1500 GMT (1000 Local)

The Security Council meeting took a surprising turn. Angela Leighton
– U.S. Ambassador to the United Nations – leaned over to her aide
as they waited for the Chinese handout to reach them. 'What's this
all about?' she whispered.

The man shuffled papers and shook his head. 'It wasn't on the
agenda.'

The red folder was handed to Leighton. She opened it and saw a
map of Asia. 'Chinese Territories Taken by Imperialism in the Old
Democratic Revolutionary Era (1840–1919).' She felt her jaw slacken,
and she clenched her teeth. People were watching. On the map, the
borders of China were clearly marked. But another set of lines bulged
into neighboring countries. Huge tracts of China's neighbors were
blotted out by cross-hatched shading of different styles. And nowhere
was the shaded area larger than in Siberia.

'What the hell *is* this?' Leighton whispered. Other staffers gathered
around the folder. The buzz of urgent conversations slowly filled the
Security Council chamber. Legends written in Chinese, English and
French were cross-referenced to numbers on the map. The Russian Far
East bore the number one. '1689 – the Treaty of Nerchinsk. Russians
cede Amur River basin to China. China rules area for 150 years. In
1858 and 1860, Russian Army forces regional Chinese authorities to
sign Treaties of Aigun and Peking, giving Russians north bank of
Amur and east bank of Ussuri. Central Chinese authorities promptly
repudiate both Treaties.'

'Oh, my God,' Leighton whispered.

As the disturbance radiated outward from the chamber, the Chinese
ambassador began his presentation. Leighton sent a senior aide out to
alert State and the White House of the crisis. The British ambassador
leaned over and said, 'We need to talk.' Leighton nodded as she
donned her earpiece. Simultaneous English translation was being read
by an edgy UN translator.

'. . . at a time in our history when China was weak and Russia was
strong,' the Chinese ambassador read from his prepared text. 'No
Chinese government has ever acknowledged the legitimacy of those
seizures. And now, that balance of power has shifted.' The sixty-year-old

114

diplomat – young, by Chinese standards, and quite reasonable – looked up. He awaited the translation of his carefully spoken words into over a dozen languages. The room was astir with aides rushing out and staffers beginning to fill the gallery behind the circular table. 'Asia is rightfully the territory of Asians. But as you can see from the map we have just handed out, rapacious Western powers seized the indicated regions by force or by proxy.'

'It's not just Russian territory they're after,' Leighton's aide whispered into her ear. His finger traced the cross-hatched areas spilling over China's borders to the west and south. 'It looks like basically they're claiming every region that at one time or another paid some form of tribute to Beijing.'

In addition to Tibet and Mongolia, Leighton observed, the Chinese were laying legal claim of a sort to Nepal, Sikkim, Bhutan and Assam along the Indian frontier. And in Indochina to Myanmar, Malaya, Thailand, Vietnam, and Laos. In East Asia to Taiwan, Okinawa, and Korea. And, from the territory of the old Soviet Union, the Pamirs, Sakhalin Island, Kazakhstan, Kirghizia, Tajikistan . . . and the Amur and Ussuri River basins in Siberia.

She turned the page. In each of Chinese, English and French there was a resolution. She didn't need to read far. 'Whereas, the former Republic of Russia unlawfully seized the territories of Greater China by military force, specifically 650,000 square kilometers of Siberia ceded by the Treaty of Aigun and 400,000 square kilometers ceded by the Treaty of Peking . . .'

'Get me the President,' Leighton whispered to her aide.

Angela Leighton could tell from the President's tone that he wasn't taking the development seriously enough. She sat in a small conference room in the UN trying to decide how to brief him properly. 'What could they possibly seek to gain out of perfecting some theoretical legal claim to all that territory?' Marshall asked.

She had to decide quickly how to begin. What to say in her five minutes in private. 'Mr President, may I take a step back for a moment and address the bigger picture. If you look at a map, China's present territory *seems* large enough, even given their enormous population. But only two-thirds of their land is under cultivation, and most of that not intensively. A lot of the territory they managed to hang onto during the imperial expansions is mountain or desert that can't support even modest populations. Manchuria and Inner Mongolia, for example, have both been heavily populated only in the last hundred years and contribute little to food production. The result is that the fertile central regions of China are all hugely *over*populated. But just across their borders to the north, Central Asia, Mongolia and Siberia are one of the *least* populated regions on earth. Mongolia is half the size of the continent of Europe, but has a population of only one million people. Yakutia – which spreads across northern Siberia to the Bering Strait – is approximately the land area of the United States but has a population of 365,000! Sure, most of that land isn't arable, but the exception lies in the Maritime Provinces well inside the "Greater Northeast Area" that was ceded to the Russians in the nineteenth century.'

'Wait a minute, Angela,' Marshall said in an angry tone. 'Are you suggesting that the Chinese are demanding a return of that territory to them?'

'Yes, sir. And that would give them strategic control of all of Asia east of the Ural Mountains.'

'But . . . that's *insane*! That sounds like some sort of . . . of "Chinese *Lebensraum*"!' Marshall shouted. Leighton held the phone hard to her ear, but said nothing. 'There's no *way* I'm going to be their Neville Chamberlain! Fuck that! This is a Goddamn *election* year!' Leighton closed her eyes as the President ranted. It was the only way she could manage the incredible tension she felt building.

KHABAROVSK, SIBERIA
September 7, 0000 GMT (1000 Local)

Nate Clark and Major Reed walked down the sloping ramp of the transport. Nate stopped short of the waiting entourage from his forward headquarters to watch troops standing in loose formation at the rear of the giant C-17. The morning was cold. The bright sunlight falling on his Arctic white field jacket did nothing to warm him.

'Weapons in the *a-a-air!*' the platoon sergeant shouted. The infantrymen with whom he had flown in raised the muzzles of their rifles, squad automatic weapons, and machine-guns toward the sky. Like Clark, they wore all white except for their helmets, which were covered in the blue cloth of U.N. forces. Heavy white packs lay to their sides. Other platoons filed down the ramp and formed up in similar fashion.

'Safeties *o-on!*' the platoon sergeant yelled. Faint clicking sounds could be heard by the dozen. 'Okay, ladies!' the sergeant said to the all-male combat unit. 'Lock and load!'

There were clacks and tapping sounds of metal against metal as magazines and belts of ammo were seated in weapons. The most common sight was of soldiers pulling the charging handles of their M-16s to the rear – chambering a round.

'Grenadiers,' the platoon sergeant shouted next, 'load frags!'

The men with grenade launchers mounted under the barrels of their M-16s inserted stubby 40-mm bullet-shaped grenades into the launchers' breeches.

'Check your safeties! *Safeties* on!' The men all looked at their weapons, which were still pointed away from their comrades. 'All right, ladies! You now hold in your sweet little hands a *loaded* weapon! If it discharges a round, *someone* will die! It's up to *you* to make sure that someone is a very *bad* person and not the guy standin' in formation next to you!'

They headed off in two files. *Just like that?* Clark found himself thinking. Right off the airplane – with a hundred and ten pounds of equipment on their backs – they marched past huge piles of gray and muddy brown snow that had been bulldozed to the edge of the tarmac. They disappeared into the dense forests Clark had seen slide by beneath their plane on final approach. No questions asked. No idea what lay ahead.

It had been hot as shit when he had landed at Danang. They had ridden off in trucks beneath the smelly canvas. It had been two weeks before they first went into the field. Two days into their first battalion operation, Chuck Reed, Sr., had been left on the north bank of the Vinh Phuoc River. Three months later, he'd been killed and Nate grievously wounded.

'Sir?' Clark heard – nearly jumping as Chuck Reed, Jr., tapped him on the shoulder. 'Sorry, sir,' the major said quietly. Clark realized that a Humvee had pulled up. He climbed into the heated armored car for the drive to his new command.

* * *

Nate walked into the crowded, windowless conference room. Senior officers from half a dozen allied armies rose. 'I'd like to introduce,' Major Reed said in a loud voice, 'Lieutenant General Nate Clark, United States Army, Commanding General United Nations Russian Forces.' Nate made his rounds – meeting his staff. Instead of the 'J' designations of USARPAC, the officers he met had been given jobs beginning with 'G'.

'I am your G-3 – Operations – sir,' the British general said before saluting. Nate returned the salute and shook hands.

The staff was entirely mixed European and American, but the senior officers under Nate were all European. The British got the real plum – Operations. The G-1 – Personnel/Administration – went to a Dutch officer whom Clark knew well from his tour at NATO Headquarters. The impressive man was fluent in all major European languages. The G-2 – Intelligence – was French. Clark had never met the General before. And the G-4 – Logistics – was German. It was the G-4 who provided Clark's amusement for the morning.

The German general pulled Clark aside. He spoke thickly accented English. 'Excuse me, General Clark,' he said – pronouncing the 'G' in 'General' as in the word 'gun.' 'I wanted to discuss something, please.' Clark nodded. 'We might have a small misunderstanding. I was told that I would be responsible for theater logistics, but I overheard a member of your staff saying that *you* would run the railroad. I have substantial experience in the area of rail maintenance. Many of my reservists work on German rail lines in their civilian jobs. It seems to me that . . .'

Clark was already laughing. He explained to the confused officer what the expression 'run the railroad' meant and sent him away with assurances that he was indeed in charge of rail logistics.

Major Reed had waited at a distance, but from the twinkle in his eye he'd clearly heard the exchange. The officer's smile disappeared, however, when Nate spoke to him in deadly earnest.

'We're going to have to learn how to fight in coalition,' Nate said. 'Amusing ambiguities in language like that can turn into rows of bags filled with dead men and women. Our allies are providing to us not only highly competent officers. They're sending men who are almost totally fluent in *our* language. Almost. The official language of this coalition is English, but I want every American soldier from private to general to understand that if an order is garbled in communication, it's *their* fault. I want them sensitized to the nuances of idiomatic speech. I want them to be patient, but not patronizing. To define, to repeat, to speak slowly and use common words with precise meanings, not slang or jargon or colloquial expressions. It's a matter of life and death, Major Reed. You draft the memo. I'll sign it.'

DETROIT, MICHIGAN
September 9, 1500 GMT (0900 Local)

Daryl got into the limousine and looked around. 'Hey!' he said to Gordon. 'Not only do I get to ride at the front of the bus, I get you alone for the first time in two days.'

Gordon felt awful. He'd been dreading this moment since Fein first cleared the time on his schedule with the advance men the night before last.

'I made some notes on the draft of your speech to the workers at the hospital emergency room,' Daryl said as he rummaged through the shiny new leather briefcase his wife had just bought him. He handed a sheaf of papers over. 'I apologize that I didn't have time to type 'em up.' He laughed. 'I guess you can read my handwriting after all these years, though.' Daryl stared back at Gordon. His smile slowly grew stale.

'The speech was canceled,' Gordon said.

Daryl's face betrayed momentary embarrassment before turning to the inevitable anger. 'Now when the hell did they do that? That was going to be a major address on the health-care crisis! What was it? Too many sick people for the nightly news's taste?'

'It was security,' Gordon said. 'The FBI arrested some terrorists in Chicago. They had hospital scrubs in their bags.'

Gordon looked out the window and ran his hand over his face. His skin felt different. He still wasn't used to the base make-up they applied in the hotel every morning.

'Something's the matter,' Daryl said – almost whispering.

'We've gotta talk.' From the change that passed over Daryl's face, he clearly understood just then what was happening. Gordon could tell from Daryl's eyes just before he looked away. Daryl was stunned – reeling. Gordon felt his eyes water. 'I'm sorry.' Daryl was looking out the window now at the passing landscape. It was a blur of empty roadside. The motorcade was traveling at high speed, and their route had been unannounced.

Gordon took a deep breath. 'It isn't working out,' he heard himself say.

Daryl looked at Gordon. He appeared so deeply, so profoundly hurt that he eyed Gordon not in anger, but warily. On guard. As if he didn't know what it was Gordon would do or say to him next to hurt him more. Or at least that was what Gordon thought.

'I need you back on the Hill to handle things for me there,' Gordon said. 'To take care of my office.' Daryl's eyes sagged shut – a wince of pain at Gordon's words. 'You will stay on, won't you?' Daryl was staring down at the three black television screens in the console opposite his seat. His eyes were unfocused. 'Daryl, if we make it – if we get elected – I want you on my staff.'

'Stop the car,' Daryl said. He didn't bother to look at Gordon. 'You can do that without asking Fein, can't you? You *can* stop the fucking car?'

'Daryl . . .'

'Stop the fucking car!'

'Daryl, you've got to be reasonable. We're out in the middle of nowhere.' Gordon gestured out the window. The first low buildings – abandoned and boarded up – flew by on the way into the city. 'I can't just stop this whole motorcade and let you out.'

'Gordon, if you have a single shred of humanity left in you – if you have one last ounce of friendship for me – you won't make me get out of this car at a crowded campaign stop. You won't make me see Fein or any of his people again. Jesus Christ, Gordon! Don't you realize that I *see* now? That I realize they all knew? How long? How long ago did you decide to can me? I know what all those looks meant now. All those conversations that were stopped when I walked in. Why it was that I didn't seem to know what was going on any more. Why I couldn't get anybody to . . . to help me . . .' He was losing it. 'I stayed up till *two* a.m. last night making copies of the campaign budget figures. But when I put them in your chair before going to sleep on the sofa in my fucking *office*, I saw *another* folder there! It had this real pretty plastic cover. And when I looked inside, I find this new, *revised* budget that I hadn't ever *seen* before!'

Gordon felt so totally sympathetic toward Daryl's plight – so completely on Daryl's side – that it jarred him to remember that he himself was the enemy. That he had done this to his best friend – his longest political associate – just days after his nomination. But it had to be done, he told himself. Daryl just wouldn't drop the 'angry young man' bullshit. He was constantly quarreling with the other members of the campaign staff. There had even been some press rumblings that all wasn't well inside Gordon's team. Worse yet, the implication had been that the lines were drawn on the basis of race!

'Stop the car, Gordon,' Daryl said – composed.

Gordon picked up the phone and said, 'Stop the car.' The agent with the phone to his ear looked back through the soundproof glass. 'I said, stop the car, right now. Right here.'

The man hesitated, then said, 'Yes, sir,' and hung up. He made several phone calls. All the while the motorcade hurtled toward the city. They were in the blighted slums now. The glittering buildings downtown toward which the Vice Presidential party was headed loomed high over low-rent apartments. Every third building was boarded up. Some were burned out. Men congregated in empty trash- and rubble-strewn lots. Daryl didn't say a word. He just stared out the window.

Finally, the motorcade slowed to a stop. It had taken quite a long time to arrange the unscheduled maneuver. It was as if the inertia of the dozen cars, trucks and vans had resisted the effort. Agents poured out of their vehicles. Shabbily-attired pedestrians stopped and stared at the well-armed, well-dressed security forces. Daryl opened his door.

'Daryl!' Gordon called out. When Gordon could think of nothing to say, Daryl slammed the door. He looked totally out of place in his dark gray suit and starched white shirt. He walked up to an unshaven man on the sidewalk. The brim of the man's stained hat hung limply down around the gray stubble of a scraggly beard. The man raised a bony arm and pointed up the street. Daryl took off walking, his stride confident.

The limo's phone buzzed. Gordon picked it up. 'Can we get going, Senator Davis?' the agent in front asked.

The effort of speaking was almost too much. 'Yes.'

The agents piled back into their vehicles as Gordon watched Daryl recede up the street until he was out of sight. Finally, the motorcade took off again. Gordon kept his eyes peeled along the sidewalk as they picked up speed. He never saw Daryl, but he spotted Daryl's new briefcase. It was sitting incongruously upright in an open mesh trash can.

ZAVITINSK MISSILE BASE, SIBERIA
September 11, 0000 GMT (1000 Local)

The crewman slid open the helicopter door. Nate Clark felt sub-zero air fill the warm cabin. As raw as the weather in Alaska had been during his brief acclimatization training, Clark felt instantly that the cold of Siberia was of a different order. And it was not yet technically autumn. The worry of what was coming that winter was with him constantly.

After fleeing the downdraft of the rotor, Clark was met by a civilian who introduced himself as an employee of the International Atomic Energy Commission. He led Nate to a nearby missile silo. Russian officers from the Strategic Rocket Forces milled about the heavy blast door. It had been swung open on its hinges. A crane slowly raised a jet-black cone from the silo. In it, Nate knew, was a thermonuclear warhead.

He couldn't help but look around at the nearby hills. They stood in the open. The exposed crane operator was now lowering his delicate cargo into a heavy armored container mounted on a flat-bed truck. His civilian host described their progress in removing Russian nuclear weapons for safekeeping. But Nate's eyes roamed the treeline. The skyline of the surrounding ridges. The swale that fell away from the flat, bulldozed missile pad.

On a nearby hill, Nate saw the regular string of dots for which he was looking. He thanked the civilian for the tour, then led Major Reed and the small security detail toward the firebase.

As they neared the base of the hill, men shouted in German from above. Clark and the others froze. German soldiers wove their way down the slope. The Germans saluted – wide-eyed on seeing the three black stars on Nate's collar – and led the entourage through their defenses. They kept repeating 'Minen' as they pointed all around. The mines were all marked with thin sticks to which were tied colorful strips of cloth.

At the top of the first steep grade Nate was met by an officer. The man removed his glove to salute. He then shook Clark's hand and rammed his fingers back into his glove before introducing himself in English.

'Welcome to Firebase Zavitinsk, General Clark,' the man said.

The German paratroopers were camped at the edge of the Zavitinsk Missile Base. At sunset, Clark knew, the IAEC technicians all returned to warm quarters. But in their outpost just north of the Amur River, the two hundred Germans hunkered down for the night. From his vantage on the hill, Nate's eyes followed the twin tracks of the Trans-Siberian Railway into the haze to the east and west. After days spent organizing his staff, he had chosen these men for his first inspection tour.

They were the closest forces he had to the Chinese border.

'Sorry for the unannounced visit,' Clark said. He zipped his parka up to his chin and tugged the knit cap he wore under his helmet over his chilled ear lobes. 'How are your men adjusting to this weather?'

'This?' the handsome German colonel asked. His bright white teeth and eyes were set in a red and weathered face. 'The weather is not a problem today. There is sun.'

'I meant the cold,' Clark said as he followed the man down steps into an icy cut in the earth. His chin quivered with the first chatter of his teeth.

'Ah!' The colonel shook his head. 'You must do what you must do, *ja?*'

They stood upright but still remained behind cover. The trench had been dug about three feet deep. An equally high mound of sandbags was piled around the lip. 'These sandbags must give a pretty good fix on your positions,' Clark commented. 'Shouldn't you deepen your trenches?'

The German shrugged, then kicked the toe of his boot into the dirt at the floor of the trench. 'We dug until the first freeze. Now . . .?' He shrugged again. 'We could blast it out with explosives, but we don't have enough yet. Our supplies are . . . are not so *gut*.' His smile was gone.

Clark looked around at the soldiers. One thing that would degrade a unit faster than cold would be empty bellies. 'We'll fix that,' Clark said.

'Besides,' Clark's host continued, 'when the snow comes, it will cover everything.' The colonel held out his hand toward a dark bunker that opened off the trench. 'Come, General Clark.' Nate stooped and entered. His eyes stung immediately from the fumes of small chemical heaters. Clark was so uncomfortable bent over at the waist in the low room that he knelt on one knee. His escort knelt beside him.

'We keep living quarters separate from fighting positions by fifty meters,' the German whispered. As Clark's eyes adjusted, he realized that the dark rolls covering the floor around him were men. Nothing but their faces protruded from black sleeping bags that fitted around their heads like the hoods of parkas. 'Separating the two areas make less casualties from artillery.'

Clark looked at him at the mention of artillery. The only potentially hostile artillery in the area was Chinese.

'Artillery is a *problem*, yes,' the colonel said, 'when you do not control the surrounding area. If it got bad, we would push the perimeter out. That would allow us to conceal and disperse our fighting positions. It would also give us some security against surprise attack. But we have good command and control in concentrated positions, and the soldiers fight better when they are together.'

'I can imagine that your men wouldn't be too ecstatic about leaving these trenches,' Nate said.

When the silence dragged on, Nate looked the German officer in the eye. 'My men are not trench soldiers, General Clark. They would attack if I order it.'

'I'm sorry. I didn't mean to suggest that they wouldn't.'

Nate looked around the bunker. Interspersed with the bags full of sleeping men – who presumably had been on duty the night before – were machine-guns, anti-tank missile launchers and automatic grenade launchers.

'Why are all these crew-served weapons in here?'

'We keep them in the living quarters during the day to keep them warm. At night, we keep all crew-served weapons and half the riflemen in their fighting positions.'

Clark nodded again, and they rose to leave. Although it was relatively warm in the bunker – Clark guessed it was slightly above freezing – he still relished the crisp, clean air under the blue sky outside. The colonel led Clark down a narrow trench.

'The living quarters are connected to the fighting positions by slit trenches.' When they passed men, they had to edge by sideways. Empty machine-gun revetments would be filled at nightfall. They stopped at a small, covered hole dug out of the side of the wall. 'We have bombardment shelters every twenty meters. On top we put three sandbags,' the colonel said, patting the three green sacks filled with dirt. 'Half a meter overhead gives us protection from indirect fire, but we have trouble finding loose fill for the bags.' He again kicked the toe of his boot into the frozen floor of the trench with a scraping sound.

They moved on. The narrow slit trench eventually opened into a much roomier main trench. There, a squad lounged around the floor – eating, cleaning weapons, writing letters. They all dropped what they were doing and rose to rigid attention.

'As you were,' Clark said, but they remained ramrod-straight. 'At ease.'

The colonel issued his own order in German, and the men relaxed but still remained standing. Clark shook the half-dozen men's hands. His nods were returned with a crisp bow of the soldiers' heads. Clark and the colonel then climbed up to fighting positions that had been carved into the forward walls of the trench.

The gently sloping hill had been cleared. The few stumps that remained wouldn't severely restrict their fire. 'I noticed your mines are still flagged,' Clark said.

'Ah, yes, sir. We keep them out for the nighttime. When the snow falls, we will dig them up. The trouble with landmines is the pressure of the snow. Heavy snowfall will trigger them, *ja*?'

'What about tripwires?'

'We could lay tripwires. But you have to leave slack. When metal wire grows cold, it contracts. If you don't leave slack, it will set off the landmine. But if you leave too much, the wire just lies on the ground. *Und* all of it will be covered with snow soon. Plus the ground is frozen. We could just lay the mines on top, but the Anarchists might take them in the night. *Und* even if we have the mines out there, the snow will smother the blast. So, mines are not that effective, *ja*?'

Clark nodded, having already concluded two things. First, the man knew what he was doing. Secondly, Clark did not. He had a lot to learn. From then on, it was less an inspection tour of a forward post than a field trip with an able teacher.

The young colonel led Clark through another maze to a round, heavily sandbagged junction. Men fell silent and shot to attention. Clark again shook hands. 'These troops are for our "*Gegenstösse*" – our hasty counterattack. Our positions can be fought from every direction. We plan to let the enemy troops penetrate our weak points. Then, before they can consolidate their gains, we attack with these troops in a *Gegenstösse*. A hasty counterattack by a platoon is better than a "*Gegenangriffe*" – a deliberate counterattack – by an entire battalion the next day. But these men . . . they must attack over open terrain.' The colonel peered out over the sandbags. Clark followed his gaze into the thick woods. The trees would protect these men as they dashed into the gaps in the lines. 'Mobility is the key, *ja*? When the deep snow comes, we will pack it down in lanes with our snowshoes for them to go fast.'

'You tramp down paths?'

'*Ja*? "Tramping." We tramp along axes of our counterattacks this way,' he chopped at the air with the blade of one hand, '*und* that way,' he chopped again along a different bearing. 'These men,' the colonel said, turning to face the soldiers, 'they are our very best, *ja*? Our most *daring*.' Clark looked from face to face. They were all young. 'They have to be – ya-*a-a* – for zis job?'

Clark nodded again. 'Where are their weapons?' he asked.

'Ah, here!' The colonel stooped and picked up a small blanket at the feet of one of the men. He unwrapped the fabric and removed a small black machine pistol – a Heckler & Koch MP-5. 'The teams are armed for close combat. Machine pistols *und* hand grenades only.' He unzipped one of the men's white parkas. Hand grenades were affixed to bandoliers under the thick winter jacket.

They wound up the tour with a look at the artillery emplacements. Before Clark boarded the warm helicopter for the return to the warm command post in Khabarovsk, he mounted the sandbagged roof of a German bunker. From that vantage, he took in the panorama – the look, and feel, and smells, and sounds of a firebase. How many years had it been since his last? Since Vietnam?

Was it different, or the same? he wondered. Men worked all about the base. In Vietnam, they would have been stripped to their waists, soaked in sweat. Here, they were thick white shapes, moving about the altered landscape of the well-prepared defenses like men in spacesuits on the moon. But it was the same, Clark felt certain. It was all the same . . . all the same.

Chapter Six

WEMBLEY STADIUM, LONDON
September 12, 2000 GMT (2000 Local)

This is going to be easy, he thought as he squeezed his way through the crowd of young rowdies. A cyclone fence ran through the cheap seats from the soccer field to the top of the stands. It divided the visiting fans from the locals. He picked his mark and headed straight for him.

The singing fans were jammed shoulder-to-shoulder on both sides of the fence. All looked to be working-class or unemployed. Despite the ban on alcohol, they all held cans of beer or bottles of liquor. The air reeked of pot and hash. Many of the young men sported outrageous dangles of looped earrings from their ears. Their hair was shorn short. There was the occasional tattoo on their ruddy necks. Ratty leather jackets, black denim pants, and black boots tied with silver chains were de rigueur.

The man he had chosen as his mark was a 'bull moose' – a huge man who was the center of attention among his friends on the London side of the fence. The fence drooped low right where the big man stood. A single wooden support was snapped in the middle. It looked like an oft-used crossing point between sections . . . or perhaps a flashpoint of battles past. He stopped beside the mangled fence and turned to watch the action.

The stadium was packed. The fans sang lilting and rhythmic chants as the London midfielders passed the ball conservatively back and forth. They never ventured too long a pass – moving the ball from side to side or safely back to a defender but never advancing it too far into Liverpool's end. London led one goal to nil, and the players were taking no chances.

'Fucking *pussies*!' he shouted in English at the top of his lungs to the Liverpudlians around him. They laughed boisterously. Several voiced their concurrence. 'Fucking big *hairy* pussies!'

'Bugger off, faggot!' the mark shouted from across the sagging fence. Laughter rose from the crowd on the London side.

He turned to the mark – a large, ruddy-faced redhead. He reached into the lining of his coat and pulled the now-warm beer from a pocket. The bull moose was smiling through twisted, yellow teeth. The up-and-down shaking motion of the bottle drew the attention of the street toughs on both sides. The anger of the London supporters rose in anticipation of the affront to come. Smiles of amusement at the slow-motion act lit the faces of the Liverpudlians.

He opened the bottle but plugged the eruption with his thumb. Everyone stared as he held the bottle up and pointed it at the face of the bull moose. A spray of white foam spewed straight across the fence. He slewed the geyser back and forth, shaking the bottle still more as the laughter and shouts from the respective sides rose up.

A bottle was thrown, but he ducked. 'Shit!' the man behind him shouted, reaching up to feel the bloody slit in his forehead. More bottles began to fly, passing over the flimsy fence and spilling their contents in a fine rain of alcohol. He made for the exit.

By the time he made it to the aisle, the fans had forgotten the game. They were lobbing projectiles over the fence in high trajectories. By the time he reached the exit the game had been stopped. The sounds of a stampede were under way. The crush of the crowd grew as people streamed both toward the fighting and away from it, compressing those caught in the middle into a human traffic jam. It took an elbow here or a knee there or an unexpected stomp of his boot to make his way out of the stadium.

When he finally broke into the relative calm, the riot was in full swing. Bobbies were gathering in large numbers on the field. Over the tops of heads he could see wildly swinging fists and flailing arms. The fence was nowhere in sight underneath the trampling feet. Men were being pulled off into the sea of enemy fans. The lone victims kicked and twisted. Their jackets were half torn from their arms. They slowly disappeared beneath the pummeling blows. It was a drunken frenzy, and the first spinning canisters of tear gas did little to tame the beasts.

FORT BENNING, GEORGIA
September 15, 1300 GMT (0800 Local)

Gay and Roger Stempel sat in the front seat of their Mercedes as they drove Harold into the fort. 'I still just can't believe he did this,' Gay said for the hundredth time – the tissue wrapped around her finger and permanently pressed under her nose. 'I *just* can't believe this.' Harold's dad was silent. He'd given up replying. 'You should've called a lawyer, Roger,' she sniped – her anger turned on her husband.

'He's eighteen years old, Gay,' Roger said. The car wound through the sun-baked Georgia base.

'Harold!' she burst out – turning and shaking her head. 'What . . . what pos-*sessed* you to,' she looked out the window, 'to join the *Army*?' Harold looked at the sculpted green lawns – ignoring a question he'd tried vainly to answer. 'I know you were upset being wait-listed at Harvard when all your classmates got early admission, but you *got* in! That's the important point,' she said insincerely.

'The Worths!' she suddenly blurted out, turning to Harold's dad. 'We have reservations for dinner with the Worths in Boston!'

'I'll call Harry Worth and explain,' he replied.

Gay Stempel rolled her eyes and groaned at the ceiling. She turned back to Harold. 'Their son is an upperclassman. It's important for you to network from the very first day. We set this dinner up to get you off on the right foot. It's the early days when friendships are formed, when everybody's new. Your father and I have told you over and over how much those friendships can mean to you later in life when you're trying to get ahead in your career and in society. And it's not as easy as it used to be. Everything is getting more and more competitive. Some of the better clubs require not just one, but two or *three* members to sponsor admission. Some even require four! *Four*, Harold!'

Harold ignored her as best he could. Just a few more minutes of this and he'd be free of them. Of her.

'Roger,' she said, 'maybe if he was on drugs, he couldn't have known what he was doing. Some sort of legal way out.'

'That's probably the place,' Harold said. He tapped his father on the shoulder and pointed to the gathering of green Army buses whose former occupants filled the streets all around.

Gay growled in frustration and anger, flipping the sun visor down and lifting the small mirror. By the time they found a parking space, her face was freshly powdered. The large sunglasses took care of her puffy eyes.

The three doors all opened at once.

'Your *other* right, *maggot*!' shouted a disembodied voice from the other side of a bus. Harold tried not to look at his mother, but his father rounded the car to take her arm.

'I'm all right,' she said, and shook off his attempt to help her. 'No, I'm all right.' She straightened her back and headed off toward the noise made by the hundreds of others gathered on the steaming concrete. 'It is so *hot*!' Gay said, fanning herself with the tissue as she disappeared around the bus.

Harold and his father hurried after her. Rounding the bus, they encountered a sea of people in loose groupings. It was a motley crowd, wearing clothes of different colors and styles. They had long hair and short hair. They wore shorts and jeans. One poor soul had chosen to wear a suit. Black, white, Hispanic, Asian – everybody stood around waiting.

Harold's mother was nowhere to be seen.

'Uh, son,' Roger Stempel said, looking down at the ground and shuffling his feet, 'this is a big step in your life. You know, your mother and I obviously had different plans for your next few years, but sometimes these things happen. You need some time to find yourself, so . . .' He shrugged. Harold looked at him, but his father's gaze was toward the masses of recruits.

'It'll all work out,' Harold said. 'It's only two years.'

'That's the attitude, son.' His father put his hand on Harold's shoulder. A rare feeling of closeness seemed to bond them. 'All I wanted to say was, your mother and I understand how anxious you're going to be to get on with your education and the rest of your life when you come out. Despite all the words we might've had in the heat of the moment, we're still your parents, and I wanted,' he paused, reaching into his pocket, '*we* wanted you to have this.'

He brought Harold's hand up to his. 'It's a gold card. It has a twelve-thousand-dollar limit, not the two thousand like on the VISA card you had before. If you ever get into any trouble – *any* trouble at all – this card will get you out. We'll take care of it, no questions asked.' His father sniffed and looked away – his eyes watery. He cleared his throat. 'Now, let's go find your mother.'

Harold slipped the card into his pocket and waded into the amorphous clusters of men and women. As he watched people joke and chat casually amongst themselves, he again regretted not coming by himself and meeting people on the buses from Atlanta. Instead, he had acceded to his mother's wish that they drive down from New York. *It's gonna be just like Dalton*, he thought with growing anger. *I miss the first week of school because of mother's fittings in Paris, and by the time I get to school everybody's already made all their friends.*

'Oh, yes ma'am,' the tall black man in the Smokey the Bear hat said. He nodded as he looked down at Harold's mother. 'Uh-huh, uh-huh,' he said. The broad brim of his hat bounced up and down as he stood there with his arms crossed, listening intently.

'Now, I've written down a few of the foods that upset his stomach,' she said. Then she saw Harold and her husband. 'Oh, over here! Over here!' she shouted, waving her Kleenex.

She introduced her husband, and then said, 'Sergeant Giles, I would like to present Harold Stempel. Harold, this is Sergeant Giles.' Harold nodded. 'Shake his hand, dear.' Harold and the sergeant obeyed. 'Sergeant Giles will be one of your Instructors here at the fort.'

'Drill Instructor, ma'am,' he said pleasantly, and she nodded. 'He'll instruct you about *drills*, dear.' She turned to the tall man. 'I think you'll find Harold is an excellent student.' Looking around and lowering her voice to a whisper, she said, 'He tested in the top seventh percentile on his SATs.'

'Don't say?' the man exclaimed.

After a moment of awkward silence, Gay blurted out. 'Well, he's all yours, then! Take care of my little boy.'

Harold hugged his mother and shook his father's hand.

'Now I *mean* it! You take care of him, Sergeant Giles,' she said good-naturedly – shaking her finger at him in mock warning.

'Oh, yes, ma'am,' the DI replied – grinning. 'We'll take care of ole Harol', all right. You can count on that.'

With another hug and a kiss from mother, Harold's parents were finally gone. Harold and Sergeant Giles stood side-by-side . . . waving. Harold heard the Sergeant laugh one more time, and he couldn't help but share the humor of his basket-case mom.

'You a fuckin' momma's boy, ain't you, Stempel?' Giles said quietly.

Harold felt agitated suddenly. He looked up at the man. Giles smiled and waved once more as Harold's mother peeked out from around a bus before being pulled on by his father. The grin was still frozen on his face.

'You a pussy? Huh?' he asked. He didn't bother to even look down at Harold. 'Do I got me a Grade A pussy for thirteen weeks, Stempel?' Harold pondered his response. But before he could think of one, the sergeant asked another question. 'You know what happens to pussies, don't you, Harol' ole chap?' It was a rhetorical question, Harold understood, demanding no response. As the intended meaning of the jibe sank in, Harold's lips curled in amusement at the wordplay. He nearly jumped out of his skin at the next sound – shot out of the DI's chest through his mouth like from a cannon.

'*Answer me when I ask you a question, Private!*'

Thus began Private Stempel's boot camp.

'*What are you lookin' at?*' was screamed straight into Stempel's right ear. Stempel concentrated on an imaginary dot straight in front of him. '*Answer me!*' came the tearing screech.

'Nothing, sergeant!' Stempel yelled. His shout was lost amid the screaming NCOs who roamed up and down the line of recruits. Stempel kept in line behind the red-headed guy ahead of him. An electric razor came up the side of the recruit's head. Great masses of red hair fell to the floor in heaps.

'*What are you lookin' at now?*' a DI shouted. Stempel winced at the pain in his right ear.

'What is this piece of shit?' came a new voice from Stempel's left ear.

'It's the Goddamn fuck-up!' the sergeant at his right ear responded. Stereo drill instructors. 'Every platoon has one!'

The last shock of the red hair fell to the cold concrete floor. The air conditioning had frozen Stempel into a block of ice. He stepped forward in his briefs – walking barefoot through thick mounds of hair.

The hot metal of the loudly buzzing razor dug roughly into the side of his head. The barber's free hand grabbed Stempel's chin, holding his head still. Stempel's hair was gone in seconds.

Stempel followed the barking shouts, all of which seemed to be directed at him. It was particularly bad when the line was delayed at the counter where soldiers handed out camouflaged uniforms. 'Thumbs along your trousers!' someone shouted even though Stempel was wearing only jockey shorts. 'Stand up straight!' He stiffened, bowing his chest out and tucking his chin in. His hands were sweating profusely. 'Close your mouth! You'll let *flies* in!' His mouth was dry. He was so thirsty.

A man with a tape measure wrapped it around his waist then down his legs. Folded uniform trousers and blouse were piled in his arms. He followed the bald redhead. Socks, boots and underwear were laid on top of his other clothes. '*Get into your uniforms!*' thundered from somewhere. 'You're *soldiers* now!'

It took Stempel the longest to get dressed. The room was empty and the shouts receding as he finished buttoning his blouse. One DI remained with him – leaning patiently against the wall. He clutched a clipboard to his crotch. His eyes were barely visible under the wide, sharp brim of his green hat. Harold tensed as the man walked over toward him.

'F-finished, sergeant!' Harold shouted out, but the man blocked his way. Stempel came to attention. Their chests and faces were only inches apart. Stempel was prepared for the worst.

'Do you know what you're doin' here, recruit?' His words were so unexpectedly soft that Stempel didn't know how to answer. He couldn't tell what the man wanted him to say. 'Do you understand what *we're* doin' here today – me and you?'

'Yes, sergeant!' Harold said loudly, but without shouting.

'Look at me now, but I don't ever wanta see your eyes again.' Harold looked up into the man's face. It was Sergeant Giles from the parking lot. 'You gotta do this, son. You gotta do this, no matter how hard it gets. If I can break you here, I'll be takin' your manhood from you.

I'm not sayin' we gonna make you a man. We *cain't* do that here. But if you quit, you'll be passin' up on maybe your one chance to be a man among men. To stand tall. To be a soldier. You catch my drift there, son?'

Harold swallowed but didn't trust his voice. He nodded, and Giles stepped out of his way. Harold broke into a run down the hall – batting his eyes to dry the moisture. A sign was posted over the door. 'Victory Starts Here,' it read.

TOMSK, RUSSIA
September 19, 2230 GMT (0830 Local)

Clark waited in the French base's icy command bunker – the telephone receiver to his ear. The ever-pleasant White House operators had put him on hold. Even though he was at the most far-flung outpost in the most remote place on earth, the small satellite dish on the roof allowed direct dialing to any phone in the world. After briefing General Dekker on the attack, the Army Chief of Staff had transferred Clark's call to the White House on express directions from the President.

There was a click, and then Clark heard, 'Hello? General Clark?'

Although he'd never spoken to the man, his voice was instantly familiar. 'Hello, Mr President.' The heads of the captains and lieutenants who filled the low-ceilinged room shot up in unison. 'What happened out there?' President Marshall asked.

'A French legionnaire base was raided, sir. Fifteen dead, another forty wounded.'

'Who did it?' the reply finally came. The satellite delay was now quite familiar.

'Well, sir, they didn't leave any casualties, and we didn't take any prisoners, so we can't tell. But the guess is the Russian army. The attack was coordinated. They used mortars. It was a professional job, not the sort you'd expect from irregulars.'

'I think you might be underestimating the Anarchists,' the President replied. 'They've been showing some pretty impressive organizational skills in their terrorist attacks.' Clark began to object, but the President kept speaking. 'What do you plan to do to prevent future attacks like the one last night?'

'There's not too much we can do, sir . . . with what we have here now. As you know, I'm sure, our European allies have siphoned off some of their troop commitments because of trouble along the Trans-Siberian Railway further west. We've only got enough men to deploy to isolated positions at the missile bases and weapons depots. They're not mutually supporting, and they're not *self*-supporting. We can't do any patrolling in strength, which means ceding the countryside to whatever bands of renegade army or Anarchist groups lurk out there.'

'Is that a roundabout way of asking for more men? Because if it is, you're wasting your breath. More men only means more targets. We're going to keep this operation simple and quick. You're there only to secure those nuclear weapons, not to start policing the countryside. Once the Russian army gets things under control, you'll furl the colors and head home – you understand?'

Nate took a deep breath, then said, 'Yes, sir. I understand. I understand completely.'

WHITE HOUSE OVAL OFFICE
September 19, 2230 GMT (1530 Local)

President Marshall's Chief of Staff punched the button to disconnect the call.

'Well,' Marshall said, 'it doesn't sound like our man on the ground there is too happy.'

'They always want more,' his Chief of Staff replied. 'More tanks, more troops, more jets. And you know what that leads to. Commitment. It's quicksand. We can't start throwing people in there like it's some sort of invasion. The Chinese would go ape shit! Besides, I thought we already acceded to Clark's remarks when we gave him that extra brigade.'

'But still,' Marshall said. 'What if it was the Russian army? What if there's more of it to come, and we've sent those men and women out there without enough support?'

'It was Anarchist terrorists,' his trusted advisor insisted, 'and they got lucky. We should retaliate to let them know we won't be messed with, and to assure the electorate that we're not letting them push us around.' Marshall winced on mention of the political ramifications. 'You can't overlook the campaign! Those were French troops, and the French don't really give a damn about them. But if those body bags were filled with *our* people, there'd be hell to pay. We'd have to react strongly or take hits for coddling the Anarchists.'

'React in what way?' Marshall asked.

With a shrug, the Chief of Staff suggested, 'An Executive Order.'

Marshall raised an eyebrow in surprise. 'Are you suggesting that I authorize an assassination?' His question was met with another shrug. 'And just whose death would you propose that I sanction in signing an Executive Order?'

The man was clearly waffling, but he replied nonetheless. 'This guy Kartsev.' Marshall frowned. 'He's got *plenty* of blood on his hands if the reports we get are true!'

'That's hardly due process. Could we convict him in a court of law on what we know for a fact?'

'But we're not talking about trying him in *court*!' Marshall's Chief of Staff replied. 'I'm talking about fighting fire with fire.'

'You're talking about being *seen* fighting fire with fire. You're talking about the boost we'd get in the polls if one day Kartsev woke up dead. The media has demonized the guy – setting him up as the one man behind all the terrorism.'

'But he *is* behind the terrorism. I *know* you think that.'

'But *I'm* not a judge or a jury!'

'Oh, yes, *sir*. You *are*. That's why we've *got* Executive Orders. You sign it, and everything's legal.'

Marshall smiled and shook his head. 'Legal, sure. But is it moral?'

It was his advisor's turn to smile. 'What the hell does *that* have to do with anything? Kartsev is fucking *evil*! There's no *question* that what he's doing in those Siberian training camps is depraved and immoral. It's practically medieval! Young girls disappearing from local villages! Aerial photos of mass graves! The man tried to kill you and your wife. He's killed your Secretary of Defense and world leaders all across the world. And he killed those fifteen French soldiers last night.'

'I'm not signing any Executive Orders.'

'Okay, okay. So you don't sign anything. So maybe you just pick up the phone and call the Pentagon. Every so often we get a Kartsev sighting out of the CIA. Maybe next time we do, he's somewhere out in the boonies. If it makes you feel any better, we don't "assassinate" the guy with a bullet, we just have the Air Force drop bombs all around and maybe one lands on his head, okay? It's nice and neat and doesn't have any paper trail. If we miss, we just make sure what we *do* blow up has some military value.'

Marshall stared back in silence. Heaving a deep sigh, Marshall finally picked up the phone and said, 'Get me General Dekker.'

OVER TYUMEN OBLAST, SIBERIA, RUSSIA
September 23, 2000 GMT (0600 Local)

Kate Dunn had simply left a note for Woody, gone to the Kremlin, and requested an interview with Kartsev. To her amazement, the black-clad guards at the gate led her straight in. Kartsev had sat in an ornate, high-ceilinged room, sipping tea.

She had asked. He had answered. He had also checked his wristwatch repeatedly.

After ten minutes, Kartsev had risen in mid-sentence. The interview wasn't over, he'd assured her, but they had to leave. Just outside the room, they'd passed heavily-armed Black Shirts. Her repeated calls of 'Mr Kartsev' had drawn no more than a smile over his shoulder. She had followed – blindly. The collapse of Russia was the biggest assignment she'd ever had, and he was her source, her guide . . . her protector.

Kate, Kartsev and an entourage of armed escorts had descended several flights of stairs. The walls had grown bare and dingy. The halls had narrowed, and the Black Shirts had pressed in all around. Kartsev never gave an order. He never even exchanged a look.

The Anarchist soldiers were all dressed the same. Nylon, zippers, boots, leggings and gloves – all black. But the men who wore the gear were each distinct in some way. One had short hair to go under his black helmet, but a bushy beard hanging from his face. Another was shaved clean of all hair – his face deeply pock-marked and his unsmiling eyes black. There were compact men, tall men – Caucasian, Asian, black.

None had entered the large service elevator with Kartsev and Kate.

'Where the hell are we going?' she'd asked.

'To Siberia,' he'd replied – smiling. 'The last refuge of scoundrels.' She had peppered him with more questions, and he had always politely replied. He had not, however, answered. They'd left the Kremlin through a special subway car – the only people on the highspeed train. When they'd emerged, they were at an airbase somewhere outside of town. The only light on the runway had come from the open door of an unmarked business jet.

Thunder had rolled across the wooded hills. They'd paused on the tarmac to listen. Again Kartsev had looked at his watch. 'Punctilious,' was all he'd said.

The darkening sky above the treeline had flickered with man-made flashes.

'What's going on?' she'd asked.

'They're attacking the Kremlin,' he'd informed her as the jet's door had been slammed closed behind Kate. 'To kill me,' he'd said as they sat. 'The last scene of Act One,' Kartsev had said, but never explained.

He had talked, however – non-stop, for hours. Never in direct reply to Kate's questions. Instead, he'd told her stories. The history of ancient dynasties of which she'd never heard. He was brimming with obscure details about the darkest eras of man.

Kate had fallen into a fitful sleep.

The change in the engines' tone caused Kate to awaken with a start. 'Where are we?' she asked as she looked out the small window.

'Tyumen Oblast, just east of the Urals,' Kartsev replied.

The jet descended between two strips of parallel lights. The tires squealed. They slowed and stopped, not turning off the runway. The door was opened from the outside. Kartsev rose.

The engines wound down to a low whine. Kate stared out through the window at the runway lights. In the few moments before they fell dark she saw the dark outline of a limousine. Then they were replaced by the reflection of her face in the glass.

She followed Kartsev into chilly blackness. The sky overhead was clear and filled with stars. Wind whipped at her in the short walk to the car. They took the same seats as they'd had on the jet – facing each other. An aide climbed into the limousine's rear in a crouch. The man lowered small blinds over the windows by their strings. He then slammed the doors, and they were alone again.

Always alone. Kartsev never seemed to have people around.

The roads were deplorable. The car rocked back and forth as they periodically traversed major potholes or ruts. There would be no paving in this part of the world. They were hundreds of miles from anywhere. They might as well have been millions.

Kate's eyelids began to droop. The swaying motion, the warmth of the heater, the late hour – all conspired to leave her craving rest. Craving respite from her worries. Refuge from the sickening sense of danger that she felt.

She said nothing lest her voice quiver. Self-assured people, she'd always thought, were less likely to make stupid mistakes. *Like pretending to let Woody talk her out of going to the Kremlin,* she thought, *then going straight there when he was out scrounging up food. Stupid mistakes like following a madman into the middle of nowhere!* she tortured herself behind closed eyelids.

Her head fell back. She awoke with a start. Kartsev was watching her.

She was instantly alert.

'We're going to visit the training camps,' he said – answering the question she'd repeatedly asked.

'Wha-*at?*' she blurted out. She sat upright. 'To the *terrorist* training camps?' Kartsev nodded. *Calm,* she thought to herself. *Calm-calm-calm-calm.* 'I *assume,*' she began in an even but too-high tone, 'you're going to show me the . . . the standard stuff.' She had no idea what that was. 'You know, rifle ranges, obstacle courses, that sort of thing?'

Kartsev shrugged. 'If you'd like. But I thought you'd be more interested in the . . . *psychological* dimension.'

She swallowed – twice – then asked, 'Where are we – exactly?'

'For your own protection, Miss Dunn, it's really best if you don't know. Let's just call this . . . "the end of the earth".' Kate felt her lower lip twitch – the beginning of a quiver. She smiled reflexively and ducked her chin to hide it. She tucked her cold hands under the seat of her blue jeans. 'You won't be *harmed,*' Kartsev said in what sounded almost like alarm. 'I can assure you of that.' She looked up. He stared at her openly – wearing a concerned expression. 'You can go whenever you wish. You're . . . free.'

Kate took a deep breath and broke eye contact. But he kept staring, she could feel it. Everything about his manner was unobjectionable. He kept a distance from the ugliness. It was a luxury – a perk of his high station.

'What . . . psychological dimension?' she asked without looking up.

'Do you know who these terrorists are?' Kartsev asked. 'These men who do unspeakable things?' She stared into her lap and shook her head. 'They are Armenian Fidayeen from Nagorno-Karabakh, their Azeri enemies, Afghan Mujahedeen, Hamas, Hezbollah and IRA. Tamil rebels from Sri Lanka, Khmer Rouge from Kampuchea, Philippine Communists, Angolan UNITA rebels, Bosnian Serbs and Bosnian Muslims, Georgians, Kurds, Tajiks, Lebanese, even *gang* members from your own country. They're freedom fighters and bandits and criminals. They come from every mountain pass and urban alley which lies just beyond the edge of civilization. They're erratic primitives with shifting allegiances. They're habituated to violence. They have no stake in civil order.'

Kate heard the rustle of his jacket as he leaned forward. Her eyes remained fixed on her knees.

'The primary function of civilization, you know, is to restrain man from horrible excess. We're not the children of Rousseau, Miss Dunn. It isn't the evil government which keeps us from living in peace and harmony together like some Benetton advertisement. *Homo sapiens* are killing animals. We organize into the disciplinary structures of civilization out of fear of the alternative. With your Western social conditioning, you probably have little insight into the sullen world of our recruits. They live in very dark places. I'm going to give you a glimpse of the alternative to civilization, Miss Dunn. A peek into an anarchic world. I couldn't possibly make you believe with mere words what you're about to see with your own eyes. They're in the middle of their night, now.'

She looked up at him then. She closed her dry mouth and swallowed. For the first time, questions did not fill her head. There was nothing more that she wanted to know.

'The one thing, Miss Dunn, that all these men have in common is that they're impossible to reconcile to civilized order. For them, peace is not a desirable state of affairs. They were pathetic misfits before their wars. But when their societies collapsed, they led fantasy lives as action superheros as they killed women, children and old men. So what do you think such men *do* when their war comes to an end? Their broken countries offer them no assistance. Would they get a laborer's job for minimum wage? These are men who rousted villagers from their beds to dig latrines, and then shot them because it was more convenient than returning them home. They murdered the men who'd slighted them before the war. They plundered from the weak what they could never have owned. They raped the women who'd spurned them. Unlike the soldiers in the great armies, Miss Dunn, who experience only war's sacrifices, these men developed a taste for the spoils. Imagine . . . for the very first time growing to *like* life amid the world's greatest horrors. While whole societies immolate themselves in ethnic, nationalistic or religious civil war, these men's talent for violence blossoms.'

She steadied herself by thinking of a question. This was an interview. She should lead Kartsev. She was in control. 'So, you provide a home for all the heros of ethnic cleansing?'

'Ethnic cleansing works very well, Miss Dunn. Roman legionnaires dispersed troublesome Jews. The U.S. Army virtually exterminated the Plains Indians. After World War One, ethnic Greeks were kicked out of Anatolia. After World War Two, ethnic Germans were brutally expelled from East Prussia, Pomerania, Silesia and Czechoslovakia – killing millions. In each case, the violence was very effective in stabilizing an ethnically volatile region.'

'So,' Kate said – snorting in disgust – 'you search the world for the best ethnic cleansers, do you?'

He shook his head. 'No. They come to us. I estimate the pool of potential recruits to number well over ten million. We couldn't possibly use them all. We don't accept, for instance, some who might have led productive lives had war not destroyed their schools, formal worship systems, communities and families during the formative years of their youth. They're too readily gathered back into the civilizing structures of society. We also reject the patriots – men who fought for ethnic or religious causes, believers in national superiority or endangerment, people who suffered tragic losses of family and loved ones. They're the easiest of all to reintegrate into society, especially if their experience with violence was brief. They're also the most individualized psychologically, which complicates our handling of them.'

'So . . . who *do* you accept?' Kate asked.

'Two types, really. The largest group is from the underclass. No education,' he bent his fingers back as he counted their characteristics, 'no earning power, no abiding attractiveness to women, no future. For them, the half-understood rhetoric of a cause gives them some pretense of personal dignity. But – even more importantly – the end of the fighting for these men means the end of good times. It's really

141

a "Catch-22" for them, because the longer the fighting continues, the more irredeemable they become.

'But men of the second type are the most dangerous of all,' Kartsev said – again leaning forward. 'Dispossessed military men. Cashiered officers. Soldiers with failed careers. They bring with them the military art. Their skills heighten the level of the killing to a different order of magnitude. Their only problem is that many have been inoculated with the moral and behavioral codes of Euro-American armies. They've learned a highly stylized, almost ritualistic form of warfare with rules and customs and traditions. Soldiers are trained to fight other soldiers. They learn to expect and deliver a symmetrical response. We teach them to respond *a*-symmetrically. To confound organized soldieries and police with unorthodox methods. It's like the British Redcoats fighting American Indians. Or American Rangers in the streets of Mogadishu. They snipe, ambush, mislead and betray. It's quite amazing what just a few thousand of such men can do. The science of complexity offers a scientific demonstration of how seemingly inconsequential variables can spark immensely disproportionate reactions.'

'Meaning what?'

'Meaning it doesn't take that much violence to change the course of history.'

Kate's gaze rose to him now. 'Are we still talking about terrorists' training? Or . . . or are you talking about something else?'

Kartsev just smiled. 'I believe we are entering a new age. An age of shattered belief systems like what last occurred in the sixteenth century. That sociopolitical earthquake led directly to the Thirty Years' War – the greatest trauma of modern Europe. It annihilated an entire moral and social order. For a generation after, the remnants of disbanded imperial armies spread syphilis and banditry across continental Europe.'

Kate swallowed again. 'What is it you're taking me to see?' she asked in a quiet voice.

He grimaced, slightly. 'We let these men live the way they want. We feed them . . . in whatever way they want to be fed. And what they need most is not bullets, or drugs, or food, but the raw material they value most – people. Women, mostly, but . . . whatever. In their world, they reign supreme. They do . . .'

'Stop it!' Kate said finally – clamping her hands over her ears.

When she raised her head, he apologized. 'But, you see,' he said softly, 'it serves a purpose.'

'Sure! You *feed* human beings to these ... *monsters!* It's like a Club Med for the sick and depraved! No wonder they beat a path to your door!'

'You're missing the psychological dimension entirely. Even the most depraved of these men still has an identity, a self, an ego. A fantasy about who he *really* is. That self is what these camps are designed to destroy. You see, once you so betray that idealized image of who you are, that self stands like the grand inquisitor – constantly tormenting you with accusations. "And you say you're so brave!"' Kartsev mimicked in a theatrical voice. '"You think you're irresistible to women? You're made of superior stuff? But you're *none* of those things! You're a *thug!* A *punk!* The *slime* of the earth! *Look* what you did! *Look* at it! *Look* at it!"'

Kate felt carsick.

'You become "self-destructive",' he said – smiling in amusement at his turn of phrase. 'In these camps, the trainees do things that their fantasy "selves" would never do. Things so hideous – so far beyond the pale – that their behavior cannot *possibly* be rationalized. We take their souls, and in the end they readily go off on their missions. It puts an end to their mental torment, you see. We have quite a lot of "spoilage," I call it. Suicide rates run as high as fifteen percent.'

'You're evil,' Kate said in a low voice.

The car pulled to a stop.

'Ah!' Kartsev said. 'We're here.'

He opened the door. Outside was a dimly-lit building. The cinder block walls were painted white. They were unbroken by windows or doors.

Kate didn't budge, leaving Kartsev poised in the open door. 'Well then, Miss Dunn,' he said – holding out his hand – 'I guess this is goodbye, then. The car will take you back to the airstrip, and the jet back to Moscow.'

Kate looked down at his outstretched hand but didn't move. 'Till we meet again then, Miss Dunn.' After two crunching steps in gravel, the door was closed in her face. Kartsev said something to the driver in Russian. Kate opened the door on the opposite side and vomited onto the ground.

When the limousine pulled off the road abruptly, Kate thought her worst fears were coming true. She could hear the car doors open.

143

The horror ran wild through her imagination. But then she heard something more . . . thunder. Flashes of lightning pulsed through the blinds.

Despite the tension of the moment – or perhaps because of it – Kate sensed that something was amiss. The men from the front of the car were talking. *The night was totally clear!* Kate realized. There wasn't a cloud in the starry Siberian sky. And, there was something more. The lightning came in regular strings of popping lights, and the noise was less a rumble than a series of distant booms.

The doors closed again, and the car tore off at high speed.

DALLAS, TEXAS
September 24, 1300 GMT (0700 Local)

Elaine Davis sat at the breakfast table of the plush hotel suite – staring at the newspaper in which Gordon had buried his face. 'Fifteen French Soldiers Killed' the *New York Times* headline read. Underneath was a picture of President Marshall warning the Anarchists against such perfidies.

'What do you think he's going to do?' Elaine asked. It was rare that they got any time together other than late at night when they were both tired to the bone.

'I don't know,' Gordon mumbled, reading an article about their rise in the polls. *Eight points back*, he thought. *That's still in landslide territory for the Democrats unless Undecideds break our way four-to-one.*

'What would *you* do?' Elaine asked, not minding that her mouth was half full.

Gordon looked up. It was precisely the type of exchange that he and Daryl Shavers used to have. Gordon would be preoccupied with something else, and Daryl would challenge him on an issue he hadn't considered. It had sharpened Gordon's views. Gordon looked at Elaine and shrugged. He moved on to another story. It was the silence that alerted Gordon he might be in trouble. He lowered the newspaper, and found Elaine staring at him.

'You know, Gordon, one day you may have to make a hard decision. If you do, you'd better already know who it is you are and what it is you believe in. Because you wouldn't have the time to figure those things out in a crisis. You know?'

Gordon opened his mouth to protest. He wasn't the President. He wasn't even the *nominee* for President. He was just the Vice-Presidential nominee on the challenger's ticket, and they were eleven – or now eight – points down with only five weeks to go.

Although he returned to his paper without answering, Elaine's question increasingly bothered him. *I know what I believe in*, Gordon thought as he moved on to the next article. 'Russian Armed Forces Split,' the headline read, and underneath it in smaller type was 'Fighting reported heavy in Western Russia.' But instead of concentrating on the names, the places, the figures, he held a running dialogue with himself. He believed in a government that was just, and honest, and fair. He believed that people had the right to walk down safe streets. He believed that stopping the spread of anarchy was absolutely essential to both.

FORT BENNING, GEORGIA
September 28, 2000 GMT (1500 Local)

Every muscle in Andre Faulk's body ached, but the white kid next to him looked half dead.

'Listen up, gentlemen!' shouted the weapons instructor – a lieutenant wearing thick-rimmed shatterproof black glasses. 'This is your weapon.' He raised a black assault rifle in the air, and despite Andre's general misery a smile broke out on his face. The gun was a motherfucker.

Andre looked over with rising excitement at the sagging white kid. He was all red in the face like he was sick. His eyes were half closed, and his mouth hung open. Andre looked around, but nobody else in their training platoon dared take their eyes off the instructor with DIs roaming the perimeter of the group.

'This weapon is the most *important* thing,' the lieutenant continued, 'you'll get to touch in boot camp since we don't allow masturbation.' The recruits all laughed nervously. 'This is also the most *dangerous* thing we let you near, 'cause this rifle don't know from Adam. It just kills. Wherever it's pointed when the sear releases – whoever is standing there at that exact moment – will take a 5.56-mm round going twenty-eight hundred feet per second. *This weapon*, gentlemen, will go off if you drop it!'

Andre felt the white guy lean against his shoulder. He was sagging against him in a stupor. Andre pushed the guy away, saying, 'Hey.'

The kid opened his eyes and sat up.

'You some kinda troublemaker, Faulk?' a DI shouted, but after a moment the lecture resumed.

Out of the corner of his eye, Andre saw the sick guy slowly weirding out again – swaying this way and that with drooping eyelids. *He's fuckin' fallin' asleep!* Andre realized. *That motherfucker is fallin' asleep and they bust* my *ass!* It was practically the only time he'd spoken to another recruit, and it had gotten him in trouble. Andre decided to shut up and keep his head low.

'How about you, recruit?' the lieutenant said. He was pointing at the sleeping white guy. Andre smiled.

'*Stempel!*' rang out like a shot, and so did a burst of laughter from the group. The recruit's eyes were wide open now. 'You stupid shit!' the DI shouted. He stepped high over men sitting crosslegged and stood over the poor bastard. 'Did we not give you enough sleep last night, Stempel? Is that what it is? So you just decided to nap your way through the most important fucking lecture you've ever gotten *in your short and miserable life?*'

Everyone laughed again.

'*What the hell are you laughing about?*' the DI shouted – spinning around and glaring at the forty or so men seated in the semicircle. Coiled and ready, the sergeant menaced the now unsmiling platoon. 'Don't you realize you're a *unit*, and this poor bastard's *in it?* Have you somehow failed to appreciate that those friendly casualties the lieutenant is talking about is *you?* You see humor in the fact that Stempel here won't know anything about fundamental safety procedures when dealing with a high-powered military assault rifle?'

Everyone now looked at the scrawny kid.

'Twenty push-ups!' the DI boomed. Stempel started to assume the push-up position, but the DI shouted, 'Not *you*, Stempel! Everybody else! Gimme twenty! Count 'em!'

'One!' Andre yelled amid the other forty-odd voices as he pressed his chest to the dirt.

'*Now*, Stempel,' the DI announced loudly, 'I want *you* to laugh!'

'Two!'

'*Laugh, Goddamnit!*'

'Three!'

Stempel started to laugh insincerely. 'Heh, heh, heh.'

'*Louder!*'

With Stempel laughing, his fellow recruits did twenty push-ups. Many barely completed their last few, and others gathered around them to shout encouragement. The DIs took it all in – obviously approving of the camaderie of the men. Andre finished and sat quietly – waiting.

When the last were done, Stempel was ordered to stand.

'Now, recruit,' the lieutenant asked – sounding satisfied by the punishment although he'd played absolutely no part in it. 'Why don't you give me the nomenclature of the M-16A1 rifle?'

Although still looking as sickly as ever, if not worse, Stempel belted out the words. 'Sir, the M-16A1 assault rifle, sir, is . . . is a 5.56-mm, magazine-fed, shoulder-fired, gas-operated, assault rifle capable of semiautomatic fire or three-round bursts through use of a selector switch . . . *sir!*'

'Very well, then. Sit down and listen up.' There were glares from the other men when Stempel sat. He looked at Andre with a pathetic expression on his face. *Shit*, Andre thought. *What's he lookin' at me for?* 'I'm only gonna do this twice!' the lieutenant shouted. 'Once at regular speed, once more slowly.' He put the rifle onto a metal table. 'To field strip the M-16 rifle, you remove the magazine.' The empty black box dropped into the instructor's hand. 'Release the charging handle. Pull the charging handle to the rear.' He slid a black metal piece of the rifle toward the butt. 'Remove the charging handle by pulling down and to rear.' It came off in his hand and he laid it down. 'Push out the retaining pin,' he held the tiniest of metal pieces, virtually invisible to the recruits, 'and drop out the firing pin.' A single dart-shaped object came out of the black weapon. 'Rotate the bolt to the right until the cam pin is clear of the bolt-carrier key.'

The instructor lost Andre completely. From the looks of some of the other recruits he had lost them too. Still, the lieutenant went on. 'Rotate the cam pin one quarter-turn and remove. Pull the bolt from the bolt-carrier.' The pieces of the weapon – some large, others minute – were piling up all over the table. 'Hold the extractor down to control spring tension. Carefully push out the extractor pin and remove the extractor.' A long spring – coiled so tightly that the lieutenant handled it with care – slid out with a piece of metal stuck in it. Each part had a name. The lieutenant went on and on.

Andre was looking at the faces of the others for reassurance that no one else understood the lieutenant when he saw Stempel's eyes. They were thick with moisture and his nose was running.

Chapter Seven

LONDON, ENGLAND
October 2, 2100 GMT (2100 Local)

He pulled the van up to the manhole cover on the side street. He carefully lined the vehicle up with minute turns of the wheel and releases of the brake. When the spot was just right, he put the van in park and applied the handbrake. He twisted around and rapped on the wall with his knuckles. The narrow street was deserted. There had only been nine attacks in London proper since the 'go' order had been given, including the Wembley Stadium job he himself had done. But people were still staying home at night.

A single thud vibrated through the floorboards of the old Volkswagen. After a few seconds, a distant boom broke the peace of the evening. 'Down ten, left twenty,' the words came quickly over the radio in Russian. In back, his partners had to turn two knobs on the mortars' aiming mechanisms to adjust the fire – one click of the elevation knob, two of the azimuth. Another thud shook the vehicle. He heard the first wails of a siren in the distance.

Another boom jarred the night. 'Fire for effect,' came the radio call from the spotter. The back of the van came alive with thuds as the mortarmen began firing through the open roof. These were not the light 60- and 80-mm hand-carried mortars. They were huge 120-mm tubes and projectiles. The rounds would be penetrating the roof of No. 10 Downing street and exploding on the lower floors of the Prime Minister's residence.

Through the windshield he saw a bobby stop at the corner, then take off running. He cursed, threw open his door, and raced down the street. When he rounded the corner, the policeman was nowhere to be seen. He slowed to a walk down the deserted city street. The front stoops of the row houses jutted out onto the sidewalk. He passed the first set of stairs with great care. The shadows on the opposite side were empty. He passed another. Nobody.

As he reached the third, he stopped. He had a feeling – an internal estimate of the distance a fleeing man could have run. He raised the machine pistol, holding it one-handed into the air with his elbow bent.

He edged his way around the stoop. A dark figure squatted in the shadows. The bobby raised his head and then his useless billy club. He wasn't one of the new special squads. He had no gun.

Even as he lowered his machine pistol, a wave of disgust washed over him. The bobby shied away, his back pressing against the painted bricks behind him.

I could let the man go.

The thought surprised him. It had come from nowhere. The two of them remained there – motionless, silent – as he turned the thought around and around in his head. He inspected it from all angles.

But why? came the response every time.

Fire blazed from the end of the machine pistol – lighting the darkness and sending the bobby sprawling.

JFK AIRPORT, NEW YORK
October 6, 1500 GMT (1000 Local)

'Hey, Kate,' Woody said, gently shaking her. Kate Dunn opened her eyes. Bright sunshine streamed through the plane's window. They were parked on the airport tarmac. She was lying on her side and curled up in her window seat under a blanket. She felt a rush of excitement on arriving back in the States.

'We're home,' she said sleepily – turning to face Woody. The plane was empty save for two men in dark suits who stood over them. Woody sat there with his blanket pulled up under his chin.

'Looks like we've got some kind of official welcoming committee from Uncle Sam,' Woody said. His eyes were puffy. He'd obviously slept through the landing too. He looked up at the two men. 'I have nothing to declare.'

'Would you two please come with us,' one of the men said. He flashed a badge in a leather folder perfectly – the folder flopping open and then closing in one motion.

'Hey, hey!' Woody said. 'Not so fast. Lemme see that again.'

The dour man's face showed a hint of a frown as he retrieved the wallet from his jacket. He flicked it open again and lowered it to Woody's face. Woody perused the FBI. ID then turned to Kate. 'Looks real to me.'

They rose and collected their things. 'Look, I've been through this before,' Woody said as he pulled his camera bags from the overhead compartment. They were plastered with bright green decals in the shape of marijuana leaves. 'I knew Jimmy Hoffa, *okay*? We had a little falling out, that's all. But those garbage bags I dumped in the Gulf of Mexico were just some animal carcasses I'd picked up on the highway. I had nothing to do with any CIA contract killing, okay? Not that I'm saying the CIA killed him, mind you.'

'Woody,' Kate chided, but it did no good. Woody was having too much fun.

'Say,' Woody said – motioning the agent closer. 'Is it true what I heard about Jay Edgar Hoover?' he whispered. 'That he was partial to dark, solid colors and the layered look because of his weight problem?' The two agents eyed each other – apparently vying to see who could appear more indifferent. 'I mean, sure, I understand that when he foofed up for parties and things that he'd make a statement with some florals or, like, a hot pink one-piece thing. But, you know, for business I bet he was pretty conservative. Flats, no heels, right?' He grinned and nodded his head – pointing at the agent. 'Am I right?'

'Let's go,' was all the man said.

*   *   *

151

Woody kept up the running barbs on the private jet all the way to Washington. The agents had told them nothing other than their destination and that they just wanted to ask them some questions. 'Man,' Woody said – eyeing the small, well-appointed jet. 'Your tax dollars at work. Does this thing have a bidet?'

Kate tried her best just to tune him out, but grew more and more annoyed as the flight wore on. She knew it was his way of dealing with power. She had seen him try the same shit with Russian police, to varying degrees of success. When confronted with authority figures who robbed him of control, Woody just peppered them with comments – pin-pricks in the elephant's hide. He was convinced that, sooner or later, he would gain the upper hand by so annoying them that they lost their cool.

'You know, you really shouldn't wear navy with,' he nodded and made a face, 'you know,' he nodded again and then leaned forward, 'your dandruff problem,' he whispered. The two agents sat stony-faced across a coffee table, facing Kate and Woody. The agent to whom Woody spoke smirked. But sure enough he shortly stole a quick glance at his shoulder. Woody tapped the side of Kate's leg with his knuckles. He thought he was getting somewhere now.

'Man, it's been a long time since I've been to D.C.,' Woody said to Kate, then turned back to the agents – grinning. 'It was back during the Iran-Contra hearings. I got some photos with a telephoto lens of Oliver North watering his lawn. He was wearing a T-shirt that had an American flag on it and the words, "These colors don't run".' He grinned at the two men. 'Get it? "These *colors* don't *run*"?'

'I get it,' the agent said. The flatness of his voice and his completely stern look signaled to Kate that he was ready to take offense.

'Pretty witty, don't ya think? Double entendre.' Woody was grinning his stupid smile. 'That's French.'

'I know what it is.'

'Do you speak foreign languages?' The man said nothing. Woody maintained a broad smile on a tanned face framed with long, graying hair tied in a pony tail. The government agent – many years younger – had short hair, pale skin, and no smile. 'You don't, do you?' Woody asked. 'That's really pretty provincial of you. I mean, it kind of makes you, like, the ugly American.'

'Woody,' Kate said.

'But, I mean,' he objected – holding out his hand palm up to display the agent for Kate's inspection – '*look* at him. He went to some podunk community college. Took English Lit courses he should've taken in high school and they give him a degree. Gets a gun courtesy of the U.S. government. Buys a three-hundred-dollar suit from some warehouse outlet. Thinks he's hit the big time. But he doesn't even speak any foreign languages.'

'Leave him alone,' Kate urged.

'You wouldn't even know what somebody said to you in a foreign language, would you? Could be "Gee, Mr Officer, you look swell today." Or could be something else. Like . . . "*Yob tvoyu mat*".'

The agent's leg uncrossed and he leaned forward. The other agent backhanded the man's chest to restrain him.

Woody was grinning ear-to-ear now. He leaned over to Kate, his eyes still on the angry agent. 'They're not FBI. They're CIA. They're taking us to Langley, I'll bet you a hundred bucks.'

'What the hell are you talking about?' Kate asked.

'It's an old trick. The CIA. is prohibited by law from operating in the States, so they gin up these FBI badges and keep right on going.'

'Jesus, Woody. You've got this paranoid conspiracy crap oozing out your ears.'

'Or, they might be FBI – technically – but they're really CIA.'

'Where in the world are you getting this shit?'

'They speak Russian, Kate,' he said, finally turning to her. 'The guy got pissed when I said "Fuck your mother" in Russian. Now how many run-of-the-mill, gumshoe G-men do you think take all that time and effort to learn Russian, huh? You mark my words, we're headin' straight for Langley.'

The nondescript government car pulled up to the main gate at the CIA Headquarters in Langley, Virginia. Instead of heading for the front door, however, they pulled around to an underground parking garage.

Woody looked like the cat who ate the canary. He had turned toward Kate and arched his eyebrows at every turn the car had made on their trip out to Langley. He'd backhanded her repeatedly and pointed as the highway signs led ever closer. She had finally withdrawn her shoulder and said, 'Cut it *out!*' Now he just sat there, loving every minute of what he viewed as a triumph over 'The Man.'

They were whisked inside the building and into a long antiseptic corridor. There were no names on the doors. No signs directing people to different departments. 'Where do you do all those LSD experiments?' Woody asked as they went through a set of double doors. They opened automatically like in a hospital, and the small group entered another featureless hallway. 'You know, when I read about those experiments I sent an application to you guys volunteering for the program, but I never heard back.'

They reached a T-shaped intersection. Sets of closed double doors led off in opposite directions.

'This way, please,' one of the agents said. He took Kate by the elbow and headed to the right.

The other agent was taking Woody to the left.

'Don't tell them anything, comrade!' Woody called out to Kate as their respective doors opened. 'Long live the Party!' The doors closed behind them.

The 'FBI agent' who escorted Kate did, she noticed, seem to know his way through the maze of corridors in the basement. He stopped at a door with the number '141' on it and knocked – waiting a moment before opening it.

She had expected a bare, concrete room with a single metal table, two chairs, and a harsh, bright light overhead. Instead, several men and two women rose from the sofas and chairs around the carpeted room. It looked more like the 'Green Room' at a network television studio than an interrogation cell. There were even hors d'oeuvres on the coffee table and a small bar/kitchenette off to the side.

'Hello, Miss Dunn,' a middle-aged woman wearing a business suit said as she held out her hand to shake Kate's. Most of the men and women wore plastic IDs pinned to their lapels. Some did not. 'My name is Eve Fitzgerald,' she said. 'I'll be your liaison during your visit to Langley, which we really don't expect will take more than a few hours.' She began the introductions. 'Mr So-and-so' from 'State.' 'Ms What's-her-name' from the White House. The names went in one ear and out the other, but Kate saw their names were all conveniently printed in large letters on their shiny 'Visitor' IDs.

The introductions did not include the several men who wore no IDs. And none of the people other than Eve were introduced as being from the CIA. Kate was having fun, now. It was like a movie.

They poured Kate the tea she requested, and she settled onto a sofa. 'You understand, Ms Dunn,' Eve said, 'that our conversations will be recorded.' Kate nodded. 'And you consent to that recording?'

Kate chuckled. 'This sounds like you're reading me my Miranda rights or something.'

Eve smiled graciously. 'Nothing you say here, I assure you, can legally be used by the U.S. government in any court. As a matter of fact,' she said, smiling, 'if you want to establish immunity from prosecution for failure to pay income taxes or something, you should go ahead and blurt it out now.'

Several of the people in the room laughed, and it broke the ice somewhat. 'I hope you don't give Woody the same opportunity,' Kate said with a smile. 'We could be here several days while he confesses.' There was more laughter. 'But, in answer to your question, I consent to the taping or whatever.'

'Wonderful. And let me take this opportunity to thank you for your cooperation. I know you must be tired, but we appreciate your agreeing to meet with us on such short notice.'

Kate decided to let the comment pass. She could only imagine what kind of time Woody was giving them.

'Can I ask you, if you don't mind,' Kate said, 'just what it is I'm doing here?'

'Certainly, Ms Dunn,' a man seated directly across the coffee table from her replied. 'There's really nothing all that secret about this, although we would like to get your agreement that everything that we ask you – the entire fact of your visit here – be held in confidence. That, I should say, *would* be a legally binding agreement.'

He was so polite – they were all so friendly – that Kate almost reciprocated, but she hesitated. 'Well, I'm not . . . I'm not sure I want to do that,' she said. They stared at her in silence, now. She felt their disappointment – their disapproval. They were being so nice, but she wasn't returning the courtesy.

The man with no name tag seated across from her nodded. 'Very well. That is your right.' He looked at another man – also anonymous – in the chair next to him.

The new mystery man said, 'Ms Dunn, we have all followed your reporting from Moscow with interest. The quality of it, let me say first off, is excellent. You seem to possess a rare blend – an ability to fact-find, together with a grasp of the broader perspective on the events unfolding around you. You are to be commended, and that comes from people who have spent a lifetime of judging the quality of information content.'

Heads nodded all around, but no one else spoke. 'Thank you,' Kate said.

'Of particular interest, obviously, given what's going on in Russia today, have been your reports on the Anarchists. Especially your reports on a . . . Valentin Kartsev.' Kate nodded. That would make sense. Still, on hearing Kartsev's name she felt a slight chill. 'Can we get you something?' the obviously attentive interrogator asked.

'No,' Kate said – embarrassed at being so transparent. 'I'm fine.'

The man cleared his throat. Kate looked for – but couldn't find – the camera. 'We're going to ask you a series of questions. Most of them will be very innocuous – minor things about Mr Kartsev that you may find amusing because of their seeming insignificance. And most will, quite honestly, be unimportant. But we ask them anyway because you never know when some little piece will fit and be useful. You understand?' Kate nodded. 'But first, since most of the people present here are not going to stay long, I'm going to call your attention to the trip you took with Mr Kartsev to the Siberian training camp.' Kate nodded again, swallowing the lump in her throat. 'We are all familiar with your report on that trip. What we're interested in is this. When you left for your return to Moscow, was Mr Kartsev still there at the camp?'

All eyes were on Kate now. She shrugged and nodded. 'I never got out of the car. Kartsev got out, said something to the driver, and then the car left him there to take me back to the airfield.'

'Excuse me,' someone said from off to the side. 'Is this the car?' he asked. He rounded the sofa and showed Kate a photo of the black limousine. It had been taken from directly overhead. 'It could be, yes.'

The man returned to the wings, and Kate's questioner continued. 'What was Mr Kartsev doing when you last saw him? Did you see where he headed after you parted?'

Kate shook her head – as much to rid herself of her recollection of that unpleasant night as in reply to the question.

Another glossy eight-by-ten photograph was presented to her. The shot was also from directly overhead. It showed a complex of nondescript buildings visible through the canopy of trees. 'Can you tell where the car was when Kartsev got out?' her interrogator asked.

She grasped the edge of the photograph, squinting as she searched for some landmark. There was a gravel road and a white windowless building.

'That building,' she said – pointing for the man holding the photo. 'That one right there.'

'C nineteen,' he said to her questioner. The man excused himself and joined a small group of people at the bar. They all leaned over a sheaf of papers.

The room was nearly empty of people within minutes. All politely bade her farewell. Her 'liaison' and two others remained. They asked her question after question for hours.

It was all very odd. The next few questions all centered on the flash and thunder of the attack. They were trying to gauge how far she had traveled when the bombs had fallen – how much time had elapsed since Kartsev had been let out.

'You think he's dead, don't you?' Kate finally asked. 'Your bombs hit that building, and you think you killed him.'

They didn't say a word.

PHILADELPHIA, PENNSYLVANIA
October 10, 0000 GMT (1900 Local)

There was a knock at the door. Pyotr Andreev saw that it was one of the men from the neighborhood watch and opened the door.

'Pete! We got trouble, and the police ain't here yet. There's three guys in the parking garage wearing all that black get-up. Anarchists!'

Pyotr handed the pistol to a frightened Olga and took the shotgun. 'Jesus,' the man said as he stared at the pump. The two men wound their way through the building. The ground floor of the three-level garage seemed quiet. 'They were on the second floor,' the man whispered. Pyotr led the way to the stairwell.

'Oh, there they are!' the old woman who organized the group called out. Pyotr cringed on hearing her loud voice. She approached, waving at Pyotr who was crouched at the bottom of the steps. 'Marge!' Pyotr's partner hissed. 'Sh-h-h! For God's sake!' Pyotr sighed.

Before the others arrived, Pyotr whispered, 'You stay here. Make sure nobody goes down or comes up.' Pyotr headed up the rusty metal stairs. His running shoes made no sound at all. A car alarm suddenly went off. He hurried up the last few steps – his progress masked by the strident alarm.

The three 'Anarchists' were breaking into a sports car. Two black youths were crammed into the front seat – the third was keeping watch. As Pyotr crept his way in a crouch toward the three men, the alarm fell silent. Bumper by bumper Pyotr closed on the car. He took one final check of the scene, then rose. The shotgun was on his shoulder and aimed at the lone sentry's chest. When the young man saw the ten gauge's muzzle, his eyes widened in holy terror. 'Hey! Hey!' he shouted, holding up his hands and revolver in plea.

'*Freeze!*' Pyotr shouted. 'If you move, I will kill you!' The other two black youths rose up from the car. 'Freeze! Freeze! Freeze!' Pyotr shouted repeatedly – trying to get control through intimidation.

They ignored him to raise their hands in the air. They wore black, like Anarchists. Black overcoats. *But why were they breaking into a car?* Pyotr wondered.

'Hey, man, just be cool,' one of the boys said. Their coats splayed out around them like capes.

'Move away from the car! Move! Move! Move!' Pyotr shouted.

'Yeah-yeah!' one kid said – his posture more relaxed after seeing that Pyotr was all alone. 'Anything you say, man.' His arms sagged, and he ignored Pyotr's order to move.

'Get out here!' Pyotr shouted again.

'Yeah, man, sure,' the kid said, casually edging closer to Andreev. 'Say, man . . .' he began.

'Stop! Don't move!'

'Listen, blood,' the guy said, slowly lowering his arms – a friendly grin spread wide on his face. He drew closer and closer. Pyotr considered one last warning, but a quick check revealed the other two slowly lowering their arms.

Pyotr squeezed the trigger. With a thunderous roar the shotgun hammered his shoulder. The shot caught the boy squarely in the chest. He was blown backwards onto the hood of the sports car. As Pyotr pumped the shotgun, the boom echoed through the concrete garage. When Pyotr spun the gun to the other two, he saw that they stood frozen with their arms stretched to full extension.

The door to the police station's interrogation room opened. A graying officer in a well-pressed business suit interrupted the questioning.

'All right,' he said, 'you can go.'

The detective who had been interviewing Pyotr said, 'But I'm not through here yet.'

'He's outta here. The investigation's closed.'

'What the hell does that . . .?'

'It's *closed*, Kozlowsky!' The detective sat silently for a moment, then slammed his notebook shut. His chair scraped noisily across the floor. The two men eyed each other before the detective headed out, leaving Pyotr alone with the older man. 'You can go, cowboy,' he said – not a trace of civility in his voice.

'Is that all?' Pyotr asked. 'I am free?'

'You can *go*, so *go*!'

When Pyotr headed out the door, the cop grabbed his arm roughly. Through gritting teeth he muttered, 'Don't kill anybody else in this town, you hear?' The grip was painfully tight. The cop sent him on his way with a push.

As Pyotr walked through the open room filled with plainclothesmen, eyes followed him surreptitiously. The buzz of activity quieted a bit as Andreev passed.

Olga and the girls wrapped themselves around him. Olga cried inside his hug, and the girls squealed in joy at the return of their father. Pyotr's eyes, however, scanned the uniformed officers behind the counter. Several averted their gaze. Something was up.

FORT BENNING, GEORGIA
October 14, 2030 GMT (1530 Local)

'*Come on, Stempel!*' Harold heard from a dozen voices. He tried desperately to recover as he dangled under the taut rope by his hands and locked heels. He had crawled half-way across the water obstacle, and now he was in dire trouble.

'*You can do it, come on!*' urged the fellow recruits in his Training Platoon.

Stempel struggled with all his might. But his arms – already aching from the exercise – were quivering. His heels slipped out of their clench. Now it was all he could do to keep the toes of his boots over the rope.

'*Stem-p-e-e-l!*' came the unmistakable voice of Staff Sergeant Giles. 'Git over here! You're holdin' up the whole Goddamn platoon!'

Stempel's toes both gave way. He swung down and barely hung on by his fingers. The rope was swinging and shaking. Another recruit behind him was holding onto the rope for dear life.

'Stempel! What the hell're you doin'?' Giles screamed. 'Jesus H. Christ, son!'

Harold knew all was lost now. His arms squeezed his head. He couldn't draw enough air, and he began to grow faint. The yelling continued, but through his popping ears all he could hear was a droning noise of unintelligible shouts.

He tried one last time – not with the thought of succeeding, but to show he had made the effort. Bringing his knees up and dropping them, he began to rock and bicycle-kick through mid-air. His grip on the rope was down to the last joints of his fingers, and they were frozen in icy pain.

'*A-a-ah!*' he grunted as he kicked one heel upwards toward the rope. He floated as he spun through air. A stunning crash of water engulfed him. It rushed in a burning flood up his nose. He fought to regain his equilibrium. He opened his eyes underwater and saw light between his knees. He spun and propelled himself for the surface.

Bursting out of the water, he spluttered and gasped for air. His back stung terribly from the flop. He thrashed at the water for balance.

'Stempel, git the hell over here!' the DI shouted.

Harold lowered his head and swam. In desperation his hands clawed at the mud. With his next breath he took in a watery gulp. He coughed and spat and coughed. A yank on his blouse tugged him onto dry land.

Sergeant Giles stood in the knee-deep water. 'Stempel! *Git on yer fuckin' feet!*' Stempel rose in utter exhaustion. 'Hands on yer head!'

Stempel complied, still fighting the dizziness. His platoon was urging the next man to shore. But some of the fire had gone out of their shouts. By falling, Stempel had lost the tight race with a rival platoon. They paid Harold no attention whatsoever.

Sergeant Giles stepped in front of Harold. With his face close and his voice low, he said, 'You quit on me, boy.'

'N-no, Sergeant! No!' Stempel spluttered – his hands still on his head.

'You quit on yer buddies, Stempel. That makes you a quitter. You know what quitters are when they're in the Army, Recruit? Yella-bellies. They run out and leave their buddies to die so they can save their own hides. They're cowards, Private Stempel. Cowards.' The tears welled up from Stempel's chest, and he tried desperately to stem the tide. His lips grew strained and his jaw quivered. He fought to maintain some semblance of composure, but his body betrayed him. 'You let yer buddies down,' the DI continued. 'You're dead now. You're no good to yer country, you're no good to the Army, but most importantly, Stempel, you ain't no good to yer buddies no more. You let 'em down. Go on back and change yer gear, Stempel. Hell, take the whole day off and think about it awhile.'

Stempel hesitated.

'Go *on*!' Giles barked.

Stempel turned and trotted off with his hands locked over his head like a prisoner – glad to be free of the DI. Tears poured down his face. Looking back, he saw the rest of his platoon race on to the next obstacle – a tall wall over which hung a rope. They would all make it over the way they were trained – as a team, each helping the others. As much as Stempel hated every second of every day of training, he hated one thing more. He hated the thought of sitting on his bunk in the barracks all day waiting for the doors to burst open upon his platoon's return. He wasn't a part of them. They could cut it, but he couldn't.

'Faulk! Git over here!' Sergeant Giles boomed.

The remainder of his platoon filed into the barracks. Andre hustled over to the Drill Instructor. The sun was setting, and this was the only fifteen minutes of the day they had to themselves. Every bone in his body ached, but he braced himself for another physically demanding waste of time.

'You and Stempel are both from New York, aren't you?' the sergeant asked in a strangely civil tone.

'Uh – I dunno, Staff Sergeant!' Faulk shouted.

'You don't know where you're from?'

'No, Staff Sergeant! I mean, I don't know where Private Stempel is from, Staff Sergeant!'

'Well, apparently you're both from New York City, so I'm gonna buddy you two up.' He looked up at Andre, measuring his reaction. 'You know what that means?'

'No, Staff Sergeant!'

'That means I'm makin' you responsible for gettin' Stempel through basic.' He again paused – again studying Andre's face. Andre sensed that Giles was waiting, and searched his mind for some response. Giles wasn't asking him to take care of Stempel. He was ordering him to.

'Yes, Staff Sergeant!'

Giles nodded. 'All right, then. Get on in there and get cleaned up. Dismissed.'

Andre took a step back, did a crisp about face, and ran toward the old wooden steps of the barracks. It was only after he got inside – passing the line of men standing naked or wrapped in a towel in line for the showers – that he began to get pissed about the order. By the time he passed Stempel's bunk, he was totally outraged. What the hell did the DI expect? What the hell could Andre do?

Stempel was filthy. He sat on the floor so as not to soil the tightly tucked white sheets of his bunk. He must have been there for hours. He picked lethargically at the knotted laces on his boots. He seemed resigned to being trapped forever inside the waterlogged footgear. He slowly looked up at Andre. On catching his eyes he lowered his gaze and wrapped his arms around his knees – hugging them to his chest.

Andre knelt and patiently unraveled the knot.

CINCINNATI, OHIO
October 18, 1900 GMT (1400 Local)

'As this Administration has shown,' President Marshall shouted in a rousing climax, 'we will *not* tolerate lawlessness in our streets! We will put a *stop* to that violence, no matter where the mission takes us, and no matter how hard that mission is! God bless the United States!' With a wave, he stepped down from the podium and into the open arms of an aide.

'I'm sorry to disturb you, sir!' the man yelled over the cheers and the marching band. Marshall held up a finger for the man to wait and stepped back up to give another wave. The roar of the crowd rose higher again. 'Sir! I've got a message from the Secretary of State.' Marshall followed him through some cloth partitions. 'Secretary Jensen just got a communication from Beijing! The Chinese ambassador paid a visit to the Secretary of State on very short notice and delivered it verbally!'

The scene was a hubbub of noise and activity, and Marshall was totally distracted. He smiled and winked at the VIPs who still applauded as they watched him from the dais. 'Sir!' the junior national security staffer called out. 'The ambassador demanded that UNRUSFOR get out of Siberia in thirty days!'

Marshall turned back to him and cupped his ear. '*What*?' Marshall was incensed. 'Well, *fuck* them! I hope Jensen kicked their butts right out of the fucking building!' The staffer shrugged. 'He *did* tell them to go to hell, didn't he?'

'I think, sir, the Secretary wanted to speak to you before replying.'

Marshall snorted, shaking his head as he felt the anger well up to new dimensions. His Secretary of State was a gutless bastard. *I've got to fire his ass!* Marshall decided. He ached to do it right away. To pick up the phone, unload on the son-of-a-bitch, and be done with it. But it wouldn't look good. He'd have to wait till after the Election.

'Secretary Jensen *did* say that there was something stilted, formal in the Ambassador's manner! He was communicating something with the utmost care and precision! The entire delegation appeared uncomfortable – like they were apologetic! Secretary Jensen thinks they may be signalling something about Taiwan!'

'What in the *hell* makes him think *that*?'

'The Chinese Ambassador and his aides were wearing morning suits, sir, with tails, top hat, everything.'

Marshall sat by the speakerphone in his hotel suite. He was surrounded by campaign staffers who were fascinated by the excitement of the conference call but had absolutely nothing to contribute.

'Our best analysis,' Secretary of State Jensen said, 'is that it's part of a power struggle in Beijing. Some faction is trying to garner support from the nationalists by talking tough on our Siberian deployment. And let's not forget how this plays among the Chinese populace. It's an authoritarian regime, but the faction that can claim popular support for their policies has an advantage in the political infighting.'

'Okay,' Marshall interrupted. 'Just who is it we're dealing with over there?'

'It's really impossible to know,' Jensen replied. Marshall rolled his eyes to the amusement of his campaign aides. 'The preeminent power in China remains Lin Tso-chang. In early August, several dailies across China reported that Mr Lin's title would be elevated from its current "Paramount Leader," to the exalted "Chairman." That, of course, is closely associated with Chairman *Mao*, who remains almost a deity in China. But, after the articles appeared, nothing more was heard. Since then, our official contacts we have still referred to Mr Lin as "*Paramount* Leader."'

Marshall waited. Finally, he said, 'And . . .?' to still more amusement in his hotel suite.

'Well, obviously it was a trial balloon that didn't fly. While Mr Lin is hardly a liberal reformer, he was associated with a series of – quote, unquote – "liberal" decisions with respect to Hong Kong. The decision to allow opposition newspapers to reopen. An end to censorship of the local movie theaters. Withdrawal of those proposed restrictions on foreign travel by Hong Kong residents that sent such a scare through the population.'

One of Marshall's senior staffers tapped his wristwatch. He had a photo op at a day-care center run by a consortium of local businesses with no federal government help. Then a swing by an American-owned local factory making digital video disks. Then a fundraiser for a struggling Democratic Congressman – one of the two dinners he had planned for the evening.

'Okay, Hugh, let's cut to the chase. In ten words or less, who are we dealing with, and what do they want?'

'Well, there's Lin Tso-chang, who's head of state, commander-in-chief of the military, and General Secretary of the Communist Party. He's clearly the most powerful man in government, but he's in his mid-eighties and in failing health. Arrayed against him is just about everyone else in the "younger" generation – men in their late sixties. There's the chief of the "State Council" – their Prime Minister – who runs the government day-to-day. He's gone on record calling for a new "Cultural Revolution" to rid China of western pornography and materialism. There's also the chairman of the National People's Congress – their speaker of the house – who's just to the right of Ghengis Khan. Then there's the President – Mr Lin's chosen successor. He personally ordered the riot police to Beijing University during the protests in August, killing sixty students. All those men are trying to outdo one another to establish their reactionary credentials to the seven-member Politburo and the much larger Central Committee and, through them, the fifty-million-member Communist Party. Every five years they hold Party Congresses. The 16th is only two years away, so it's the beginning of their campaign season. They have a very complex political system that we get little insight into. For instance, the party bosses in Beijing, Shanghai and Hong Kong all have extensive power and . . .'

'Okay, Hugh,' Marshall said – cutting him short. 'Boil it all down for me. What's going on in Beijing?'

'It's probably a power play by nationalists, who want to be seen as righting the wrongs committed against a weak China by a stronger West. They view Mr Lin and his supporters as vulnerable on the issue, and that's why this is dangerous, Mr President. Mr Lin will have to steal the wind from their sails by adopting even more nationalistic policies.' The pollsters, briefers, speechwriters and spin men in the room around Marshall were all nodding. 'He'll have to take a harder line, or we'll be staring across the table at dyed-in-the-wool hardliners.'

'So you're saying there's a risk of an international political confrontation,' Marshall recapped, 'solely as a result of *domestic* political developments in China.'

'All politics is local, Mr President.'

KHABAROVSK, SIBERIA
October 22, 1430 GMT (0430 Local)

'General Clark.'

Nate Clark opened his eyes and rolled his boots to the floor. He slept in his fatigues even in his headquarters. It didn't feel right otherwise. He clicked on the lamp next to his bed. Major Reed stood beside his cot.

'What is it?' Nate asked.

'It's the Chinese, sir. I think you'd better come down to the Op Center.'

'We've been monitoring these broadcasts for several hours,' Clark's intelligence officer said. The British colonel and Clark stood over a short-wave radio. The bulky green device emitted the whiny and distant voice of a Chinese broadcaster speaking in a shrill and strident tone. 'They've been blitzing the airwaves with propaganda about the evils of capitalism – Hong Kong and Taiwan-style. Then, a short while ago, all the television and radio stations broadcasting out of Hong Kong either switched to patriotic music or went off the air. The intelligence consensus appears to be that they are planning some sort of move. It may already have started.'

Clark locked his gaze on the man. 'Are they coming our way?'

A look of concern settled on his face. 'They've certainly been building. Latest force strength estimates put the front line units in Manchuria at eighty percent, up from sixty-five. But,' he shook his head, 'my guess is no. They've only got thirty days' war stocks in the north, and their transport in-theater wouldn't allow for any large-scale operations without unacceptably lengthy halts for resupply.'

'So what, then?' Clark asked.

The man shrugged. 'Something else.'

Clark headed straight for his office, closed the door, and got on the secure phone. When General Dekker finally answered, Clark could tell that he'd been asleep. 'I need one heavy division at Khabarovsk,' Clark demanded, 'and one Marine division at Vladivostok. I need two air wings *on* the ground in Siberia – not four hours away in Japan. And I need your *personal* pledge to me that if the PLA begins to stage in north China, you'll back me to the hilt when I request either *three* times that many men, or that we pull out of Siberia altogether.'

There was a long delay – much longer than necessary for the satellite relay. When Dekker replied, he didn't ask for an explanation. He had obviously been watching things in the Far East closely.

'You got it, Nate. I'll call in the staff tonight and take it to Himself in the morning. I'll get you the Big Red One – 1st Infantry Division – and the 3rd Marine from Okinawa. We won't leave you out there by yourself. You've got my word on that.'

When Clark hung up, he sat there in the quiet of the former Soviet military base ten thousand miles from home. His mind's eye roamed the frigid wastes of Asia. The tiny pockets of humanity that were his troops were scattered, isolated, vulnerable. They were no match even for random mortar attacks, much less for . . . what? For the Chinese?

Would two additional divisions do the trick? Six? Sixteen?

He hit the intercom button. 'Get me Major Reed,' he said to the man.

*   *   *

Nate Clark had led a mechanized infantry division into combat in the Persian Gulf. Of all the briefings, planning sessions, and operations and logistics reviews that led up to their attack into Iraq, none had been like this one. An oppressive weight hung over the large conference table around which were gathered senior officers of half a dozen nations.

Major Chuck Reed, Jr., rose. He was easily two pay grades the junior of any other officer in the room. He was also the best briefer Clark had ever run across. 'The People's Liberation Army,' Reed began, 'is trained to hold fire and fight close-in. That reduces the advantages of superior enemy weapons and brings to bear the Chinese advantage in numbers. But the Chinese tactics require the extreme confidence and courage of their troops. They are an infantry army. Their spirit – their willingness to fight, to sacrifice, to die – is the key to their effectiveness. Lin Piao – Mao's defense minister – used to say that at ranges under two hundred meters, the PLA was the equal of any army in the world. To defeat the PLA, therefore, UNRUSFOR would have to win the war beyond two hundred meters. We would have to shatter the confidence, the courage, the morale of their troops before they get into range of small-arms fire, or risk being overwhelmed by an attack in the main.'

The attention of the room was riveted on the junior officer. The normal order of a briefing – 'METT' – had noticeably skipped the first subject, 'Mission.' That was left to the defense ministries in Europe and North America, and defining UNRUSFOR's mission was looming as a monumental task.

'The PLA has three million men under arms,' Reed continued. 'They also have a militia variously estimated between seven and twelve million and fifteen special border divisions. They have infantry capability but little integral heavy weapons or transport. The most recent battles fought in the theater began on March 2nd, 1969 along the Ussuri River.' Reed's silver-tipped pointer went to the map. It ran north and south along the border between Vladivostok and Khabarovsk. On the Russian side there were strung tiny beads of blue – company- and battalion-sized units of German and Belgian paratroopers and American Marines and support troops. 'The first two battles on March 2nd and 4th were Chinese victories, killing almost a hundred Russian soldiers in small border outposts. On March 15th, however, the Russians moved heavy missile forces forward and fired across the border on a town deep inside

China. The town was destroyed and several hundred Chinese civilians died. In total, the PLA lost approximately four thousand killed in combat.'

Heads were turned at the numbers of casualties incurred in such a low-intensity border skirmish.

'The PLA has two direct avenues of approach into the Russian Far East,' Reed went on. 'Both would stage at Harbin. Both would have a single Main Supply Route up the central valley. One turns east through the Manchurian highlands. It crosses the border in the Ussuri River valley north of Vladivostok. It chokes off nicely at some mountain tunnels east of Suifenho. It's the lesser threat. The other route is more difficult to interdict. It continues north through the Lesser Khingan Range. It crosses the Amur to the west of Khabarovsk. There are enormous distances to defend.'

He waited as senior officers sketched their own maps. But he knew what they experienced emotionally. He'd lived it on nights, after duty hours . . . for months and months. He knew their study of Siberian maps. It was the study of distance. Of thinning lines. The resources stretched due to nothing more than empty space. Their next question was universal, he was sure. *Are my people in harm's way?*

It was an attitude that would ensure defeat.

'Rates of advance?' Nate asked Reed. 'What are they?' He'd already heard Reed's answer and agreed.

'A mechanized army with good engineering support – one hundred kilometers per day. Except during severe winter conditions or the summer thaw and flooding. The *Chinese* troops, however, are only motorized. They're transported by truck and dismount to fight. But those trucks are very soft targets. They'd be slowed by their poor engineering support. It's based primarily on a large number of backs. Attrition could reduce them to cross-country foot-slogging. Maybe supplied only by pack animals. Three kilometers per day. And without survivable tanks, they'd have no way to rapidly reduce fortified positions.'

'Point one,' Nate interrupted, 'for you to take back up your chains of command. We need engineers. As many units as you can get out here. And I know that means call-ups. We'll call the entire Army Reserve and National Guard. You know we won't lose Nine Corps. We don't lose corps. So we need engineers to prepare positions. To map terrain obstacles. To build and maintain our road/rail network. For engineering reconnaissance of the Chinese.'

'Without engineering,' Reed said, 'the *Chinese* would be canalized. Single echelons down a limited number of routes. With the exception of Lake Khanka – which is more trafficable – the infantry would have to chop those supply lines out of the forest. And vehicular traffic over makeshift roads would degrade them till they're impassable. Maintenance would tax engineering resources. When forward resupply grew infrequent, their momentum would be gone.'

'What about *our* engineering?' Clark asked.

'We need extensive surveying. But the most difficult engineering problems would be bridging. Bridging rivers between Vladivostok and Khabarovsk. So instead we'll use airmobile. We'll organize battalion or even brigade raids. We'll choose the timing and stay till we win. Then we'll pull back and choose another mission. The *Chinese* would be open trails twenty meters wide . . . with manpower. In the dead of winter. With total air supremacy by the enemy.'

Most kept their head down. Their thoughts were of the death. But not the air chiefs.

'The air mission is total victory,' Reed said. 'Not a single Chinese plane flying in theater, in fifteen days.'

The talk went on. Commanders taking more control. Mixed accents but a common vocabulary. Easily understood talk of engineering maintenance. Elaborate directional aids for drivers sent through trackless forests. On routes open day and night. Through blizzards that would leave ten-foot snow drifts. In the deep woods, the engineers proposed, they could build corduroy roads out of lumber. The armored people said no way. A battalion of tracks would destroy it completely. Better that their fighting vehicles knock down saplings. The engineers could improve from behind. But neither the Amur nor the Ussuri was fordable, the engineers reminded. Plus their men weren't infantry fillers.

'The watercourses freeze in winter,' Nate said. 'The thickness supports vehicular traffic – even armored. That fact alone changes all our terrain analysis. In winter those water obstacles turn into supply routes paved in ice. It's in winter that we're vulnerable to attack.'

ERIC L. HARRY

WHITE HOUSE SITUATION ROOM
October 22, 1930 GMT (1430 Local)

Marshall had been awakened with the news. Thirteen Chinese missiles had struck Taiwan. Islands were being shelled. Plus Chinese soldiers were swarming all over Hong Kong. Beijing was silent as the troops went out of control. All the deals made with the city were being broken.

The president and junior staffers waited in the underground conference room.

'Why didn't we get some kind of warning?' Marshall asked. The junior staffers from the Military Office were mute. 'Or at least the British. The Prime Minister assured me they still had good intelligence.'

One of the junior Army officers ventured an answer. 'We checked with the British, sir. The Chinese were in the middle of a rotation. Their special garrison was mainly kept in barracks. They were hand-picked anyway. Of the highest quality. So the first warning the Brits got was when trucks came across from Shenzhen filled with ordinary infantry. They were armed and in combat gear.'

'First video is in, sir,' a Naval officer announced as he entered. He turned on the room's four screens. 'We picked it up off Japanese TV.'

Soldiers were smashing store windows with rifles. It didn't look to Marshall organized so much as mass. Boxes carted out of stores. Confiscated on authority of the army. Wheeled armored vehicles belching smoke on city streets. Civilians shaking fists from doorways. Large helicopters sweeping in low over the sea. The video came to an end abruptly. It was replaced by color test bars.

Secretary of State Jensen arrived at the door

'Can you believe this shit?' Marshall asked angrily.

'Could we clear the room?' Jensen asked.

The junior aides were all caught by surprise. Jensen and Marshall stared at each other in silence. When the door closed, Jensen took a deep breath. 'We should get out of Siberia right now,' he said. 'Announce it. Step back. And if you don't agree, I'm going to have to tender my resignation.'

Marshall was boiling. But he didn't so much as flinch. 'Are you sure you mean that?' he asked.

170

'I've thought a lot about where things are headed. I no longer feel I can head up your Department of State, sir.'

I'm resigning, Marshall understood him to say. 'Just where *are* we headed, Hugh?'

'War!' Jensen blurted out. 'We're headed for *war*, Tom. It's as plain as the nose on your face!'

'No, we're *not*, Hugh. I'll pull the plug. That was the plan all along. We're not there to fight for Russia's border. A few more months, that's all.'

'This is our last warning from the Chinese,' Hugh Jensen said calmly.

'The *Chinese*,' Marshall replied loudly, 'are kicking in *store* windows in Hong *Kong!* We'll condemn *looting*, Hugh, but by *God* we won't go to *war* over it. Hong Kong is *theirs*, for Christ's sake! What the hell can *I* do about it?'

Jensen looked up at the president. He wore a peculiar expression. 'Tom, have you been briefed yet?'

'I've watched Japanese video from downtown Hong Kong with my own two *eyes*. What more do I need to . . . ?'

'No, I mean about Taiwan?'

Marshall stared back at him. 'The missiles.'

Jensen rested his arms heavily on the table. It was as if he were physically exhausted.

'They've invaded, Tom. They've invaded Taiwan.'

Chapter Eight

USS *LABOON*, STRAITS OF TAIWAN
October 23, 1730 GMT (0730 Local)

The scene was tense in the windowless Combat Information Center. But only a familiar eye could note the change to the darkened compartment. The sweat-soaked brow of the radarman. The sonarman whose hands pressed earphones to his head. The fire control coordinator hunched over his screen. The dark blue circle under the arm of the Seaman First, who raised his flourescent pen to draw targets on Lucite.

Lieutenant Commander Richards felt all the ship's systems. As the captain they were his second skin. Situational awareness, it was called. Reports of F-14s swatting down MiGs by the dozen. Noisy subs that were minutes from death. Silkworm missiles exploded harmlessly miles away.

But his mind was focused on a large round screen. The surface radar. It was there the danger lay. The real danger, Richards knew, was in his ever-shortening range to the Chinese invasion fleet. The first landing the day before had drawn the Taiwanese army to the west coast. This second and much larger force was circling the island to the northeast. It was aimed straight at the Taiwanese capital – Taipei.

173

'Any visual contact?' Richards asked his fire control coordinator.

'Negative, sir. We've got a whole screen full of radar targets, though.'

At the center of the monitor was the *Laboon*. To the port and starboard a few miles away steamed its sister ships – the *John McCain* and *John Paul Jones*. Up ahead were hundreds of green blips. Chinese coastal patrol and fast attack boats. Minesweepers, training ships and support and supply craft. Salvage ships and repair ships and even survey ships. There were barges being towed by ocean-going tugs. Only a fraction of the craft were true landing ships. But all were packed to the gunwales – a makeshift invasion fleet carrying seventy thousand men.

The *Laboon* had seen her first action in the darkness of early morning. She'd fired a dozen TASMs at targets leaving Xiamen. She'd then fired Tomahawk cruise missiles at the port itself. But now the orders were to go guns and torps. It was old-fashioned surface warfare. But it was coordinated with an all-out aerial assault. And six attack submarines would strike from the south simultaneously. They had to stop the fleet in the Straits. They had to dump seventy thousand men into flaming water.

Richards shook the thought from his head. It was a scale of human tragedy beyond all comparison. But he had a job to do.

'Communication from Task Force, sir,' came from the communications officer.

'Put it on.'

'. . . to the *Laboon*, you are approaching the destroyer screen. Repeat. You are approaching Chinese destroyer screen.'

The three American destroyers were vastly superior ships. But the Chinese combatants carried lethal weapons. Over a dozen Taiwanese ships had already attacked. They'd smashed into the Chinese flotilla an hour before. The *Huei Yang* and *Lo Yang* had been sunk. They were old USN hull numbers DD-696 and -746 – the former USS *English* and USS *Taussig*.

'We've got radar targets inside twelve nautical miles,' the fire controller reported. They could engage at any time.

'Hold fire till we get a visual,' Richards repeated. The CIC was cooled to seventy degrees. But the radarman in front of Richards was sweating profusely. 'Listen up,' Richards announced loudly. 'There are Taiwanese warships out there mixing it up. Destroyers and frigates plus corvettes and fast attack boats. I don't want any friendly-fire casualties. Our rules of engagement require visual contact. We've got over ten miles of visibility. We're gonna do this slow and steady, you read me? I want positive ID before we fire.'

'Aye, sir,' replied the fire controller. He was a twenty-something lieutenant junior grade.

Rather than easing Richards's nerves, the man's reply had put him on edge. That his crew would follow his orders was a given. That the captain was responsible for his ship was an immutable law.

The *Laboon* was not built to slug it out. The Arleigh Burke-class was made of steel, not aluminum. And it was reinforced with over seventy tons of Kevlar. But even three-point-nine-inch shells from Chinese guns would make short work of her. And every hit by guns or missiles meant deaths.

'What's our speed?' Richards asked.

'Thirty-three knots, sir. Engines all ahead full. Course one eight six.'

Richards could feel the vibration of the deck. Four gas turbines turning two shafts. Two hundred thousand horsepower each. And the churning screws put the destroyer on a hundred screens. Every sonarman from the Philippines to the Ryukyu Islands could hear the noise.

'Range to nearest surface contact?' Richards asked.

'Eleven point two,' the fire controller replied.

'Any visuals yet?'

'Negative, sir. There's a lot of smoke that's adding to the haze. But there should be any second.'

Richards felt those seconds' passage. Visual contact wouldn't lessen the danger. It would raise it. If the *Laboon* could see the Chinese . . . the Chinese could see the *Laboon*.

'LAMPS is low on fuel, sir,' the air controller reported. 'Requests permission to land.'

The destroyer carried an anti-submarine helicopter. It was returning from its sweep of the ship's rear. It was there the sonic wake of its propellers created a blind spot.

'Permission denied,' Richards said. 'Divert it to the *Eisenhower*.'

'Radar contact bearing one nine five – range eleven point one – turning to port.' Richards looked at his fire control officer. 'She's maneuvering toward the *McCain*. Now tracking a new bearing. Bearing constant. Bearing constant. She's steadied up. Range ten point eight. Tracking bearing three-four . . .'

'Vampire! Vampire!' called the air defense center. 'I got *one* missile! Range *ten* miles. Bearing one *seven* nine! Bearing constant! Range decreasing! It's coming at us!'

'Begin evasive maneuvers!' Richards ordered. 'Fire chaff and IR flares at four miles.' The deck began to heave under their feet. 'Unsafe the Phalanxes. Put 'em on Auto.' Richards steadied himself on the nearest console. 'I'm going to the bridge.'

Richards left the CIC. He was thrown from wall to wall along the short corridor. The ship was heaving wildly at top speed. The armored hatch was dogged tight. Richards opened it into bright daylight.

'Cap'n's on the bridge!' a seaman announced.

'Mr Lawrence,' Richards said. 'I've got the bridge.' Instead of climbing into his tall chair, Richards grabbed his binoculars. He walked to the angled glass overlooking the ship's single gun. The helmsman spun the wheel in the opposite direction. The deck heaved. 'Put the CIC on the speaker,' Richards ordered. He raised the binoculars.

Tinny reports of inbound missiles filled the bridge. 'Five miles. Speed six twenty.'

A new voice – his fire control coordinator – suddenly called out, '*Visual* contact! It's a frigate. She's got empty missile rails.'

Richards raised the handmike. 'Fire control, this is the captain. Do we have ID?'

The thudding booms of the chaff dispensers drowned out the first part of the man's reply. '. . . Hull. No. 508. It's the frigate *Xichang*, sir! Definitely Chinese hostile. Range nine point seven.'

'Fire two Harpoons,' Richards ordered. 'Engage with guns.'

'Aye, sir! Engaging.'

'I got it!' one of the lookouts shouted. 'Eleven o'clock. It's a sea-skimmer!'

Richards saw the missile just off the port bow. White foam flew into the air with each swell. It obscured the missile. But in between he could see the small, round nose. And the smudge of heat blurring the sky in its wake.

'Constant bearing, decreasing range!' the lookout reported. 'Missile inbound! Missile inbound!'

It was zeroed right in on the *Laboon*.

The ship shuddered. It fired a Harpoon. Then a second. Chaff dispensers boomed. All of a sudden the five-inch gun opened up. The bridge's window was filled with gunsmoke. The sea breeze blew the windows clear and there was the missile.

'Hard-a-starboard!' Richards ordered the helmsman. 'Bring her to two seven five! Continue evasive maneuvers!' He was turning broadsides. Presenting a fat target. But it was also bringing both of the six-barreled Vulcan cannon into action. If he'd maintained course, only the forward gun could have fired. Now both would lock on radar image. When they got one, that was. The five-inch gun below the bridge fired again. Its automatic loader filled the breech every three seconds.

Richards opened the hatch and went out onto the port watch deck. Cold wind rushed by. The five-incher boomed again. He fixed his binoculars on the enemy ship. The seventy-pound shell struck the superstructure. The flash ripped through the radar mast. The frigate belched boiling white smoke.

Richards searched the sky for the inbound missile.

The missile popped up into the air a mile away from the *Laboon*. Richards looked not at the missile but at the nearest gun. The six-barreled weapon sat atop its white metal body. *Fire!* Richards silently urged. Both of the Vulcan cannon opened up. Computers unleashing two hundred shells a second.

The 'Flying Dragon' missile arced skyward. It nosed over. It headed straight down for the *Laboon*'s aluminum funnels.

The two six-barreled cannon sounded like buzz saws. The air was filled with their explosive shells. The missile burst in a bright orange fireball. Cheers rose up from the lookouts. Richards watched the rain of debris just off the port beam. He started to breathe the air he'd denied himself.

'Incoming!' yelled the lookouts in unison. A shrill whistle barely preceded hot tongues of fire. Richards felt the thunder of a near miss. A tower of water collapsed on itself.

'*Xichang*'s been hit!' someone shouted from the bridge. He raised his binoculars. The frigate that had fired the almost deadly missile was listing and low. She was smoking from a direct hit amidships. Her guns had not yet fallen silent. But she was turning in fear of capsizing.

Two Harpoons in succession flew straight into the hull just above the water line. An orange explosion threw a geyser high into the air. The *Laboon* sailed straight through it. It was the *Xichang*'s final miss – its closest yet. Water rained down on the bow. Mist coated the lenses of his binoculars. The *Xichang* lit the hazy day with pyrotechnics. Her main magazine went off in a mini-mushroom cloud.

New visual targets were being called out, and Richards returned to the bridge and fired the remainder of his six Harpoons. The five-incher's twenty-round-a-minute rating was put to the test. The results were one more Chinese frigate set ablaze, and a destroyer turned turtle amid a pool of burning oil.

'We're through the screen!' came the report from the CIC. The calls of ship-sightings now changed. 'Hull Number 928! Landing Ship Tank. Range four point two!'

'Engage with ASROC,' Richards ordered, calmer this time.

'Aye-aye, captain,' came the excited reply of the fire control coordinator.

A moment later, an enormous burst of white smoke obscured the windows of the bridge. A huge torpedo lifted out of its armored canister mounted flush with the deck. It rode the belching white thrust of its booster. More sightings led to more anti-submarine rockets – regular torpedoes flown to the enemy vessels by powerful rockets. Richards followed the flight of the first ASROC.

It splashed almost anti-climactically into the sea. It was three-quarters of a mile from the jam-packed landing ship. It was surreal. Richards counted off the seconds. A torpedo could make forty knots.

The Chinese LST broke in half. The ship's midsection literally rose into the air. The flat-bottomed ship slipped into the sea at the bow and stern. Crates and light vehicles splashed into the water all around. The view through the windows of the turning ship was constantly changing. Smoke rose into the air from horizon to horizon. Richards conserved his anti-ship missiles. A couple of five-inch shells or a single ASROC was all it took. They even turned broadsides to fire regular torps from the six tubes on the stern. In thirty minutes the Taiwan Straits were a flaming graveyard.

AUSTIN, TEXAS
October 26, 1500 GMT (0900 Local)

'In the battleground state of Texas,' Kate read – her stopwatch running – 'the election appears to be up for grabs. The latest NBC News/*Wall Street Journal* poll shows President Marshall and Governor Bristol running neck-and-neck both nationally and here in the Lone Star State. The results of that poll were borne out by an unscientific survey we conducted of voters on their way to work.' She hit the watch's stop button – confirming that the voiceover would correspond roughly in length with the taped footage. Kate swivelled her chair and hit 'Play' to watch the man-on-the-street interviews. She then switched to a second player to see her taped conclusion.

The unedited tape began with Kate wiggling her shoulders to loosen up. Her heavier-than-normal make-up wasn't obvious. She watched herself brush her bangs back. The navy blue cloth overcoat was a good choice. She cleared her throat and looked into the camera.

'The voters seem to be asking two questions.' Kate held the stick mike in her gloved hand. A small but distracting wisp of hair blew loose across her forehead. 'First, how could the Marshall administration allow tensions with China to escalate into a shooting war? Although the invasion of Taiwan was repulsed, Governor Bristol spent much of the day hammering the Democratic ticket with the bitter remarks to *Newsweek* magazine made by former Secretary of State Jensen.' *Too long*, Kate thought. 'Governor Bristol's finest moment came when he suggested the time for a show of U.S. strength was *before* our ally was attacked – not after.' *Should have used the sound bite*, she thought. 'But far more ominous for the President is the question many voters raise about the risks to American troops now stationed along the Chinese border in Siberia. With the World Court having agreed to consider China's claim to much of eastern Siberia . . .'

She stopped the tape. Woody – if he would ever show up – would splice in video from the port of Vladivostok as Kate's report continued. She turned to another tape deck. Maybe she should cut instead to the Japanese story. 'Shit,' she whispered, then played the tape from where it was cued.

'. . . J-j-a-apanese constitutional amendment would allow the military to deploy overseas. Parliamentary proponents argue for easing the

179

World War II-era restrictions due to skyrocketing tensions in the region. And the first act that the Diet should take – Japanese opinion polls suggest – should be to rename the "Self-Defense Forces." The leading candidate is simply the "*Armed* Forces," but even those words are fraught with significance in an Asia still wary of Japanese militarism. Meanwhile war stocks pour into Japanese harbors from American ports. But they're all property of the United States military. And now that South Korea has gone on general alert, the East Asian rim of the Pacific Ocean is alive with instability. Urgent issues are debated nightly in Tokyo – both in posh clubs and along riot lines. Public officials here have quietly complained of America treating Japan like another aircraft carrier – once a taboo topic, now merely sexy.'

'Damn!' Kate said – stopping the tape. Did she want to take the time to edit the word "sexy" out?

She instead turned back to the first tape player.

'The U.N. operation in eastern Russia is now entering its second month, and the Pentagon today announced the deployment of one additional Army and one Marine division to Siberia. Department of Defense spokesmen denied that the deployment was in any way connected to the Chinese attack on Taiwan and its ruthless suppression of Hong Kong. But the President's Chief of Staff made it clear that no such aggression would be tolerated in Siberia. In a *separate* story, President Marshall requested today that Congress approve a Pentagon call-up in excess of the president's 200,000-man limit. The current resolution would allow reserve activations to go as high as 500,000 men and women, although Administration officials refused to rule out requests for more. The Pentagon also announced that the six brigades of National Guardsmen previously deployed to the riot-torn areas would be formed into three new Army divisions.'

Then cut back to me, Kate thought. She looked at her watch and leaned toward the open door. '*Woody-y-y!*' she shouted – then hit 'Play.'

'In responding to Republican attacks, administration officials point to their success in calming Anarchist violence worldwide. Confirming earlier rumors, a CIA spokeswoman today announced for the first time that they believe that Valentin Kartsev was killed in a bombing of Anarchist training camps shortly after my interview with him last month.'

Kate winced. She'd told Woody that the reference to her interview would ring hollow. They would now have to reshoot the entire piece.

'In a race most thought would turn on the domestic issues of the economy, terrorism and civil unrest, it is foreign affairs that now looms as the deciding factor. In the photo finish for which President Marshall and Governor Bristol seem headed, the question analysts are asking is – will the boost that incumbents expect during periods of international crisis be offset by the perceived mishandling of Chinese aggression by the administration? And are there any more surprises in store for the candidates in the one week remaining before the election? This is Kate Dunn, NBC News, reporting from the campaign trail in Austin, Texas.'

Her toes were wiggling in her shoes. Her teeth were grinding despite warnings from her dentist. She willed herself to stop both.

'Woody-y, would you *please* . . .!' she shouted.

He suddenly appeared in the doorway.

'Oh . . . Hey,' she said. 'Look, we've got a lot of editing to do before . . .'

'You've got a phone call,' Woody interrupted. He held her cellular phone out to her. He'd borrowed it to order pizza. Woody couldn't quite suppress his grin.

'Who is it?' she asked.

He shrugged. 'Russian. Genocidal nut who controls worldwide Anarchist terrorism. He's about five-foot-four, bald.'

She grabbed the small phone and held it to her ear. There was a hiss connection.

'Miss Dunn, how wonderful to hear your *breathing*.'

Kate felt her skin crawl. 'Mr . . . *Kartsev*?' she asked, almost whispering.

'Yes, and I'm alive and well contrary to all rumors.'

Kate was stunned. 'Where have you been?' she asked, suddenly unsettled, insecure . . . as if he were with her.

'Staying out of harm's way, mostly. Doing a lot of writing as well. I have greatly enjoyed watching events on the world scene develop, as you can imagine.'

Kate finally came out of her trance when Woody handed her a small rubber ring. A wire with a jack at the end was attached to the ring. It was a microphone. She plugged the jack into a tape recorder and placed the ring around the earpiece of the phone. The red light indicated the recorder was taping. 'I've made substantial progress on my manuscript,' he continued. 'I hope it's going to be a work of some importance. It should spell out my thoughts and conclusions about what's happening currently.'

'And so you've concluded what?' she asked.

'That it's difficult to control things as complex as world events. But it's surprisingly easy to "get the ball rolling", I believe the expression is. To be a catalyst. A bullet here, a bomb there, a computer virus or two and . . . voilà! It's analogous to plate tectonics theory. Only the forces are not geological, they're social. They lie pent up. All they need is a triggering event to release them.'

Kate checked the red 'Taping' light. She held her hand out to Woody for a 'high five.' She was already composing the story she would do. Her report might even make it on before the first commercial.

'May I ask why you called me, Mr Kartsev?'

'Two reasons. I missed your company. It's the middle of the night, and I was having a bout of writer's block.' Kate looked at her watch and wrote the time on a notepad. Quickly doing the calculations, she realized that he was somewhere in Siberia. 'But secondly, I had thought you might want a story, and so I thought I would do you the courtesy of giving you one.'

Her heart was pounding in anticipation. 'What story?'

Kartsev cleared his throat. 'Very well. Are you ready?'

CHICAGO, ILLINOIS
October 26, 2330 GMT (1730 Local)

A dozen people were clustered around the television in Gordon Davis's hotel suite.

'. . . at precisely fourteen hundred hours Greenwich Mean Time tomorrow,' came the voice of Valentin Kartsev, 'all units of the Russian Army on both sides of the current Civil War will lay down their arms. All soldiers and officers of the armed forces of Russia will immediately, as of that time, be discharged from further service and be free to return to their homes. No authority or other privileges will, after such time, be afforded any citizen of the Russian Republic by virtue of his former service in or rank with the armed forces.'

'What will happen with the army's weapons?' the female correspondent with NBC News asked.

'They will be left in place.'

'What about nuclear weapons?'

'They too will be left in place. We are relying upon the presence of U.N. forces to monitor the safekeeping of all weapons of mass destruction.'

'Why is this happening? Why is the army disbanding like this?'

'It was by agreement of the warring parties. Both sides were suffering terribly from battle losses, and even worse from desertions. Furthermore, as you are quite aware, I am sure, from your news reports, supply problems are so extreme in many parts of our country that military units have been reduced to marauding bands, terrorizing the populace in search of food. And military production has come to a complete standstill. It was in that state of exhaustion that the two sides met and agreed to desist from further hostilities.'

'Will there be an amnesty granted to soldiers of the White Army?'

There was a laugh. 'Miss Dunn. You seem to be missing the point. There will be no amnesty, because there is no one to grant that amnesty. Government in Russia in any form will, as of fourteen hundred hours GMT tomorrow, simply cease to exist.'

'Ho-o-oly *shit*!' someone in the crowd gathered around Gordon Davis exclaimed.

The NBC News anchorman began his interview of the female reporter who had broken the Kartsev story.

'It was definitely Valentin Kartsev. There was one recorded interview with him by a Dutch independent film crew, and NBC had the voiceprints compared and found them to be an exact match. In addition, I asked the man several questions about details of our previous meetings which I believe could only have been known by Mr Kartsev, and all were answered correctly.'

'Then the next question, Kate, is – was Kartsev telling the truth? Will the Russian army just up and disband at nine o'clock Eastern Time tomorrow morning – election day in this country?'

'There is no way of knowing the answer until that time, but I found in my earlier dealings with Mr Kartsev that he was totally candid and straightforward. He wasn't given to bluffing or grandstanding.'

'Thank you, Kate,' the anchorman said. The camera zoomed in on him as he stacked a sheaf of papers. 'Well then, in a little over fourteen hours we'll learn whether the anarchist revolution that has swept over Russia will achieve its final victory and leave that massive country completely ungoverned. To repeat this breaking news, what is known is that Valentin Kartsev – long claimed by unnamed White

House sources to have been killed in bombing raids ordered by President Marshall – has surfaced and dropped what can only be described as a bombshell of his own on President Marshall.'

There were cheers in Gordon's suite which he quickly hushed. The anchorman turned and the camera zoomed out to reveal a guest seated beside him. Behind them was a map of the United States. The studio was all set for election night coverage. 'I have with me Bill Luck, our political commentator. Bill, it looks like the gang that couldn't shoot straight on Pennsylvania Avenue has managed to wing their collective feet once again. Will there be any fallout to this, or is the election pretty much decided by now one way or the other?'

'It definitely does *not* appear to have been decided yet. The election eve polls are almost evenly split, and all of those polls are well within the margins of error inherent in the polling methods used. What the numbers *do* tell us, however, is that this election is going to be decided by which way a very small percentage of swing voters break between now and about twenty-eight hours from now when the last polls close in Hawaii.'

'Almost a year of campaigning and billions of dollars of campaign spending,' the anchorman commented with a grin and a shake of his head. 'After all the debates and speeches and position statements, this country's president is going to be chosen by a very tiny fraction of the electorate which hasn't yet made up its mind.'

'Well, it *has* been a very newsworthy year, to say the least,' the analyst added. 'With all the fumbling and bumbling that contributed to President Marshall's slide in the polls, we in my business couldn't have been any busier if Congress had enacted a Political Commentator Full Employment Act. So it's probably fitting, I suppose, that this election go right down to the wire just to keep people like me talking.'

'If you had to call it, Bill, which way do you think it will go?'

The commentator shrugged. 'If I had to take a wild guess, I'd say this last bit of news from Kartsev was the straw that broke the camel's back. I'd have to guess that the Republicans are going to be moving back into the White House come next January.'

Raucous cheers erupted from the campaign staffers. Gordon was too stunned to react. For the first time he realized that it really might happen after all. That he might become Vice President of the United States.

'*What would you do?*' came Elaine's question in his mind. It haunted Gordon.

FORT BENNING, GEORGIA
October 28, 0800 GMT (0300 Local)

Andre Faulk felt something hard probing at his side. He opened his eyes to see the barrel of a gun. Standing above him was a man wearing night-vision goggles under his helmet. His face was blackened with grease paint. The man held his fingers to his lips to shush Andre, just as another man roused Stempel from his slumber. Stempel was supposed to have been on watch. But he was sound asleep in the fighting hole beside Andre.

'Huh?' Stempel said with a start – kicking Andre in the process. Andre kicked him back as Stempel stared up at the M-16's muzzle. The orange metal hood that would harmlessly deflect the blanks' wads was just inches from Stempel's chest.

The grease-painted man in front of Andre raised a rubber knife and swiped it slowly across Andre's neck. He pointed with it then toward Stempel. 'You two are dead,' he whispered, then again raised his finger to his lips.

From the bushes all around them there emerged over a dozen black-clad attackers. The dark forms advanced up the hillside toward their sleeping platoon. Stempel's head was darting this way and that. They both watched the 'OPFOR' – the Opposition Force composed of instructors – rush unopposed through their defenses. That was all he and Stempel could do. They were dead.

Andre punched Stempel hard on the arm. 'Hey!' Stempel hissed. That drew a sharp 'Sh-h-h,' from an 'enemy' soldier carrying a machine-gun right past them into the heart of their position. 'What'd you do that for?' Stempel whispered, barely audible.

'You fuckin' fell *asleep*, that's why! God-*damn*, man! *Shit!*'

Stempel sagged back into the hole – a desperate, sick look on his face.

They both jumped as the roar of gunfire shattered the quiet. Harold turned to see the dark hillside above light up. A dozen muzzles blazed. It sounded like ten strings of firecrackers lit off at once, only a hundred times louder. Harold clamped his hands over his ears, but lowered them when he saw Faulk staring at him in disgust.

Just as quickly as it had started, it was over.

From the darkness, Andre heard a skidding sound through the dirt.

185

A man appeared out of nowhere. The hot muzzle of an M-16 was stuck in Andre's side.

'Get up!' the man yelled as Andre recoiled from the burning metal.

They were prodded roughly with the muzzle up the hill. At their camp they came upon a confusing scene. The rest of their training platoon knelt under the swaying beams of half a dozen flashlights.

'Kneel down!' was shouted right in Andre's ear.

Andre and Stempel knelt beside each other, and their captors roughly pulled their hands up onto their heads.

There followed several long seconds of silence. Then Andre heard the familiar voice of Staff Sergeant Giles – their drill instructor. 'The Chinese don't take no pris'ners!'

With that as Andre's warning, there was a single boom from a rifle. A hot strobe gave Andre the start of his life. His profile lit the ground in front of him for an instant – kneeling, hands on head, helpless.

'Mrs Faulk!' Giles shouted. 'The U.S. Army regrets to inform you your son is *dead*!'

Andre was shoved roughly onto his face. His hands barely came down in time to partially cushion his fall.

There was another shot, and Stempel landed roughly on his chest with a thudding grunt.

'Mrs Stempel! The U.S. Army regrets to inform you *your* son is dead!'

'Good riddance,' somebody mumbled from behind.

The process was repeated for each of the forty recruits.

Sergeant Giles took Faulk and Stempel apart from the others. The dim light of dawn turned everything gray. 'All right. What I want to know is, which one of you pieces of shit was on watch? Which one of you assholes fell asleep and let your entire unit get massacred?'

Stempel's head was hanging. His eyes were closed. He was shaking. He was crying, Andre realized.

'It was me, Staff Sergeant,' Andre said.

Giles's eyes were already drilling holes in Stempel. He was slow to turn to Andre. When he did, he said in a calm voice, 'You realize that even though this is training, you could be court martialed for falling asleep on sentry duty?'

'Yes, Staff Sergeant!' Andre replied.

'And if it was during war, you could be shot?'

'Yes, Staff Sergeant!'

'But since I can't shoot you, I'm gonna have to do the next worst thing I can think of, whatever that is.'

'Yes, Staff Sergeant!'

'He wasn't on watch, Staff Sergeant!' Stempel yelled all of a sudden – his voice thick with tears. 'It was me, Staff Sergeant!'

Giles turned his attention back to Stempel. 'Well, well, well,' Giles said. ''Pears to me that one of you is lyin'. Now that's a *awful* serious offense.' He looked back and forth between the two of them. 'I cain't figure no way of tellin' which one is lyin', and which one is tellin' the truth. But it don't really matter much, since one of ya is lyin', and the other fell asleep on watch. So it looks like you're both fucked.'

Andre caught a hint of a smile in his wrinkled eyes.

OFFICERS' BARRACKS, SHENYANG, CHINA
October 29, 1300 GMT (2300 Local)

Lieutenant Chin couldn't sleep. For three hours he had lain in his bunk tossing and turning, every muscle sore from the day's work. Snores filled the long, open barracks as the other junior officers slept soundly. But Chin spent his time trying to trick his mind. Soothing images of his family's farm. But it didn't work. They had given way to new images. Images of disgrace. The sight from earlier that day of the young lieutenant who, like Chin, was from a peasant family. During the morning's field exercise, he'd failed to follow water purification procedures before drinking from a river. He and his entire platoon had fallen ill. The Regimental Commander himself had stood the young officer up on the reviewing platform and shouted at him for over an hour. The entire Regiment stood at attention below.

During the long tirade, Chin could see the young man wince repeatedly. Not from the occasional blow on his legs or butt by the short swagger stick the Regimental Commander carried, but from the shouting – the words. 'You can't *read*, can you? *Read this! Read it!*' All that Chin could hear from the young man were his sobs. Chin spun his legs to the floor in anger. Anxious. Wondering what it was

187

in written manuals that he should know but didn't. He knew his job. He'd been taught everything important in classrooms and in the field. And he *could* read. He knew all two thousand characters. It was just sometimes he didn't understand.

He got up and walked the length of the darkened barracks to the lavatory. When he got there, he heard whispering from the mop closet. He groped along the wall for the switch. When he had found it, he opened the closet door and twisted the switch until it clicked – flooding the small area with light.

In the glare Chin saw four men squatting in a circle. Mops and brooms hung from the walls all around. One of the men rushed toward Chin and turned the lights off.

They were all officers in Chin's infantry battalion. To his great relief they appeared to just be talking.

'Come here,' someone said in the darkness. He took Chin's arm and pulled him into the room. Chin squatted down to join the rest of them.

'Lieutenant Hung?' Chin asked – thinking he recognized the voice of a fellow platoon leader from his company.

'What are you doing?' a different voice whispered – ignoring his query.

'Getting a drink of water,' Chin answered. His own voice was lowered to a whisper. 'What's going on?'

There was silence from all sides.

'Who the hell is he?' someone else asked.

'Some ox driver from nowhere,' replied Lieutenant Hung, Chin was certain.

'You go to school, ox driver?' Chin was asked.

'Yeah. Sure,' Chin replied, immediately defensive. 'Beijing Polytechnic.'

There were laughs. 'From ox driver to tractor driver,' someone remarked.

'Your family buy your way into Officer Training, tractor boy?' Chin said nothing. The man poked right at his most sensitive core. 'I bet you've never been more than twenty kilometers from your momma till school. Just out there with mud between your toes raking in all that farm money, selling to . . .?'

He fell silent. Chin now understood what was going on. His anger was stored up after months of similar abuse from classmates during

Officer Training. He and all the other boys from farming families always caught shit from these university snots. But they gave as good as they took in Chin's estimation – taking rickshaws and eating at restaurants when on leave in the city. The farmers had money. The city kids were poor. That poverty bred jealousy.

'Selling to who?' Chin asked in the silence. *Go on – say it!* Chin thought hotly. *Selling to the Block Committees. Selling to the Goddamn party officials. Say it!*

'Look, Chin, we didn't mean anything by it, okay?' Hung said. 'Honestly. We were just giving you shit. No hard feelings?'

Chin knew he had them now. One mention of this little meeting and they'd all learn how heavy your legs get behind an ox team when mud gets caked up to your waist. Chin hadn't been farther than the market before the polytechnic, but it had been far enough to see the local re-education camp along their route. It was filled with college pukes like them.

'Hey, come on, Chin. What about it?' another voice asked.

'Fuck you all,' Chin said as he got up and left the closet. *Let* them *lose sleep tonight*, he thought. He waited by the door to the lavatory, straining his ears to hear their insults. One word – even an obnoxious inflection in their voice – and he was going straight to the Company Commander.

But they didn't mention him again. They spoke in low tones. The wobbling beam of a flashlight could be seen under the door. 'All right,' someone said. 'Look this one up.' The next word spoken was in a foreign language. '*Un-al-ien-a-ble.*'

After a few seconds, someone read, '"Not capable of being transferred."'

'Ah,' Chin heard several voices say at the same time. 'That makes sense,' someone whispered. 'Read it again.'

It was in English, Chin was almost positive. '*We hold these truths to be self-evident, that all Men are created equal, that they are endowed by their Creator with certain unalienable rights, that among these are Life, Liberty, and the Pursuit of Happiness . . .*'

Chin listened, but he understood none of it. None of it but the word '*unalienable*' – 'not capable of being transferred.' He went to bed wondering. What was it that was '*unalienable*'? What could not be transferred? Whatever it was, it was dangerous. Those college pukes were taking huge risks to read it.

His mind wandered as he lay there. What was it that couldn't be transferred? He thought and thought, finally drifting off to sleep.

FORT RICHARDSON, ALASKA
October 30, 0900 GMT (1700 Local)

Clark sat inside the Humvee – the radio-telephone to his ear. The steady 'swish-swish' of the windshield wiper cleared the steadily falling snow. The driver idled the engine and the heater kept the vehicle warm. Clark worried at the rate that fuel was being expended. His was a mechanized army. During alerts, engines were run for several hours on cold days solely to ensure the vehicles would start when needed. It added up to consumption of enormous quantities of . . .

The clicking over the phone drew his attention. He'd failed all afternoon to get the President through ordinary channels, but there was always one line that remained open continuously.

'National Military Command Center,' the male operator said from "The Tank" on the third floor of the Pentagon.

'This is General Clark, Commander-in-Chief USARPAC. Get me the President.'

'One moment, sir.'

'Hello?' Clark heard a moment later.

'This is General Clark,' he repeated. 'I need to speak to the President.'

'He's at a rally. He can't come to the phone.'

'Who is this?' Clark asked quietly.

'I'm the FEMA communications officer. We're parked in the van outside the Alamodome.'

'And isn't your job to keep the President in constant communication with the national military command system?'

'Yes. Yes, sir.'

'And do you know who I am?' Clark asked calmly.

'You're CINCUSARPAC?'

'That's right,' Clark said, almost whispering now to control his anger. 'Now, just stay with me on this. Check your manuals if you have to. There are only eight Major Commands. Is USARPAC one of them?'

'Yessir, it is. I mean, I don't have the list right in front of me, but I'm sure it's on it.'

'Good. Now what's the significance of USARPAC being a Major Command and me being its commander?'

'You . . . you can get me in a lotta *trouble?*'

Clark ground his teeth. 'I have direct access to the President, and I want it now.'

There was a clicking sound, then the phone began to ring. On the third ring, Clark heard '*Hello?*' shouted over a blaring band.

'This is General Clark. I need to . . .'

'*What? Could you speak up?*'

The Humvee's driver glanced over his shoulder. Clark took a deep, steadying breath. '*This is General Nate Clark! Get me President Marshall!*'

'He can't come to the phone right now! Can I take a message?'

That was too much. Clark had left half a dozen urgent messages. '*You get me the President, or I'll have your Goddamn ass! You read me?*'

'You're the General Clark who has been faxing all those memos, right? Listen, has anything changed? They haven't come across the border, have they?'

'What? *No*, they haven't come across!'

'Good!'

There was a long pause.

'Are you saying the President got my reports?' Clark asked.

'Of *course* he got your reports. He even read most of 'em.'

'Well? What about my requests?'

'What? For more troops? I'm afraid that's not gonna happen tonight, General.'

It all suddenly seemed absurd. The whole fate of UNRUSFOR – of two hundred thousand soldiers – and perhaps the Asian continent for generations to come was hanging on the whim of a boy who would at most command a platoon in Clark's army.

'Does the President realize . . .?' Clark hesitated, then started over. 'There's something called the Shenyang Army Group. They have three hundred and fifty thousand combat troops, and they're moving into staging areas near the Russian border. And the *Beijing* Army Group has been moving north since . . .'

'The President has taken care of it, general!' the staffer interrupted.

'He sent a cable to Beijing. Now tomorrow is Election Day, for Christ's sake! You've gotta understand! Okay?'

Clark understood.

The connection clicked and the line fell silent. The hardware had worked perfectly – just as designed. But the human link in the system had failed. Something always failed. War was never the result of a series of successes.

Clark wanted the native Alaskan scouts he was seeing. He needed them in Siberia. It was freezing out, but they went about their business. The unit's commander lectured Clark as they walked. 'Artillery, mortars, landmines, hand grenades – they're ineffective in deep snow. They don't explode. Or they're smothered. Or lateral fragmentation is zero. Command-detonated mines in the upper branches of trees work, though.' Clark absorbed all the facts he could. 'Artillery rates of fire fall way off. Even with cold-resistant grease and oil, mechanisms get sticky and sluggish. Strikers and springs break like glass. Ammunition areas get covered in snow.'

Barrels of weapons protruded from well-concealed fighting positions.

'Snow and ice get in your sights and barrel. You can't take your gloves off to clean the weapon. But if you take it inside, you gotta strip it completely. It's covered in condensation. It'll freeze up when you go back out.'

'Your men seem to handle this weather easily,' Clark commented. 'Is it because you're from the north? You've lived up here?'

'No, sir. There's a big difference between growing up where there's cold weather, and never bein' able to get out of it. Same goes for those northern Chinese. When bad weather comes through, they go to barracks. And in severe cold, they'll die in thirty minutes if you don't rotate them.'

A Kiowa scout helicopter swooped low overhead. It disappeared into the falling snow. Clark had suspended peacetime operating minimums. He wanted pilots flying in dangerous shit.

'You gotta check your people constantly,' the colonel said. 'Change socks. Wash your feet. Use foot powder. People get numbed by the cold. They'll take a nap out in the open and die. They'll get snow blindness 'cause they forgot their sunglasses. And you gotta exercise 'em. Stamp your feet. Clench and unclench. Wiggle your toes. Knee bends. It can keep you from losing an appendage. You gotta check the snow flower after they urinate. If it's dark yellow they're dyin' of dehydration. And you can't let 'em drink liquor. We had a master sergeant up here on an exercise. He took a swig from a bottle of Jack Black he'd left outside overnight. Alcohol doesn't freeze, so what poured down his throat was at minus twenty degrees. Burned him so bad he almost couldn't breathe.'

Casualties. Nate's war had been hot. He asked.

'Sleds. Two men on the flats. Three in the mountains. Just pile blankets on top. Casualties are low on defense. And the intensity of the combat slows in winter. You spend so much time just in self-preservation. If temperatures go down to minus twenty, vehicles require five times as much maintenance. At minus forty, forget large-scale operations. Siberia gets even colder. Plus there's wind chill. You can feel it just walking. Open vehicles and helicopter downdrafts are dangerous. Storms kill massively. Add a twenty-knot wind to minus twenty degrees and the wind chill is minus sixty-five. It'd then take maximum effort to do even the simplest task out in the open. Exposed flesh would freeze in thirty seconds. Your men go under canvas and your vehicles in laager. You survive. A ten-man Arctic tent and a Yukon stove will get you by . . . but just barely.'

Two squads silently trudged past. Clark wanted to know everything.

'You still gotta send people out. Patrols for the sake of morale. You got two enemies – the opposing army, and the cold. And the cold is always there. Men get down. The only cure is activity. You can't just stand sentry. You get all bundled up cocoon-like in your hood. You look *out* . . . but you don't see. You withdraw. It's dangerous – psychologically. You gotta patrol. Draw 'em out. Make 'em think about livin'. *Care* about it.'

They proceeded into an ever-stiffening breeze.

'You can't go far or fast. Twenty inches slows foot marches to half a mile an hour. Any deeper and men risk sweating. Thick woods and high crests are best. Snow doesn't accumulate. Frozen watercourses and lakes are fine. Make good LZs – even airfields. But sound-ranging teams with seismological gear can fix you. Ambushers can conceal themselves very well in snow. You gotta look for shadows. Either that or hope they've frozen to death during the wait.'

Nate's thighs were beginning to burn from less than ten inches of snow.

'Skis are good for long-range recon. You can tow a squad behind a Humvee. You can break a trail – tramp a path. But you gotta take 'em off to fight. And you lose 'em every time. You can't carry heavy loads. And for the *deep* stuff – bushland, draws, ditches – you gotta use over-snow equipment. Snowshoes. Just hope it crusts over enough to hold your weight. And hard-frozen snow is noisy as hell. Sound travels a *lo*-ong way on a cold night. The question boils down to how much you can leave behind and still survive? Hundred-pound loads are cut to forty – thirty for ski troops. Every squad's gotta carry two radios because small-unit tactics predominate. And you'd be surprised how much water you've got to carry. And large quantities of high-energy foods like fats, breads and sugars. You burn calories like a runner just keepin' your body warm. And of course you carry automatic weapons. Fighting is at close range in the Arctic. High cyclic rates of fire predominate. You'd rather have one machine-gun with a thousand rounds, than a thousand men with one round.'

On the hill below there was an attack. The infantry looked to be stuck in molasses.

'You can't mount a classic attack,' the colonel continued. 'You crawl forward, digging in as you go. Don't plan on taking advantage of artillery prep. You can't move fast enough. The enemy is heads up before you even make it to the killing zone. And if your attack bogs down . . . withdraw. Sweating men will freeze to death in the open. Or you could try infiltration. Dress up in captured outer gear. All bundled up you can merge with returning patrols. In extended formation you can slip inside the perimeter. We always have somebody with an M-60 doin' a head count at the wire.'

They talked for half an hour. Of windproof parkas for patrols. Of Gore-Tex for sweat-prone ski troops. Of fur overcoats for sentries and drivers. Of saunas that toughened the body, built resistance, cut down on illness, and helped morale. And of dogs to hunt for casualties in the snow.

'Snow covers irregularities. In Arctic whites, prone, in flat light – you can't see 'em. And it's like somebody fallin' overboard in cold water. They don't last long. Ten, fifteen minutes. The Arctic gives pilots a helluva time with navigation. You can't see coastlines if there's ice. Flat vapor layers hang over the ground like still fog. They're impossible to tell from snow. Landing in a chopper can be kinda chancy.'

But it was something toward the end of their talk that Clark remembered most. It was what stood out most in his memory. It was a simple statement made by the colonel. But it crystallized in Clark's mind and in his plans.

'Defenders win the battles in winter.'

PHILADELPHIA, PENNSYLVANIA
November 2, 0500 GMT (2400 Local)

Pyotr and Olga Andreev were curled up on the sofa under a blanket. Pyotr's shotgun was propped against the wall beside them. They were bleary-eyed from the election coverage, but they were glued to the flickering light of the television.

'I've got to go to the bathroom,' Olga said. She climbed out from under the blanket.

Pyotr watched a bewildering succession of election results from all across America. He knew nothing about anything but the presidential race, but he found himself gripped by the numerous tight contests. There was the governorship of South Dakota up for grabs. And a bitter fight for a congressional seat from southern Florida. The tallies – like those in the presidential race – swung back and forth. Sometimes they were separated by only a few hundred votes.

Behind the network anchorman a map of the United States was evenly divided. The southern and western states were dark Republican red. The northern tier of states was bright Democratic blue. It was a dead heat for the White House – as fascinating as any soccer match he'd ever watched.

'Did I miss anything?' Olga asked as she buttoned the top button of her blue jeans.

'Santos has pulled back ahead of Dickson in Florida.'

'*Again?*'

'By under two hundred votes. They have over ninety percent counted, but they still can't . . .'

'Oh, *look!* Look, look, look!' Olga said, pointing at the screen. When Pyotr saw they had brought up a map of California, he fumbled with the remote control to raise the volume.

'I am now being told,' the anchorman said, holding the earphone in place and pausing, 'yes, I'm being told that ABC News is ready

195

to make a projection for California, which has a sufficient number of electoral votes to decide the presidential contest.' Olga clutched Pyotr in excitement, and he felt the tension of the moment.

There was a loud rap on the door. 'With just three percent of the precincts reporting . . .' the anchorman said as Pyotr muted the television and grabbed the shotgun. He headed for the door. Olga cowered behind him and then ducked into the hallway to the girls' bedroom. Pyotr looked through the peephole, then turned to Olga. 'It's just Fred.'

Pyotr opened the door.

'Your watch, Pete,' the man said. 'All's quiet, but the lady in 304-D asked us to check on her every four hours or so. She's diabetic and needs to take some juice.'

Pyotr turned back to Olga, and she handed him his jacket. 'Would you like to step inside for a second?' Pyotr asked. 'They were just announcing the winner of the election.'

'Oh, who gives a shit,' Fred said. 'Nothin's gonna change. They're a-a-all the same. When they get in office, they forget their promises before the balloons hit the floor, and start linin' up votes for next time. Haven't had a decent president in this country since Abraham Lincoln, if you ask me. The place is goin' to hell in a handbasket, and who do we get to choose from – Marshall and Bristol! No-o, I don't even vote any more. What's the point? We're spent. *Kaput*, I guess they'd say in your country. Yep, by this time next century, the world will belong to the slope heads.'

'The who?'

'You kno-ow.' The man pulled the corners of his eyes back. 'The Japs and Chinese. Too bad ole Honest Abe's not around any more. You know much about Lincoln?' Andreev zipped up his jacket and shook his head. 'Yeah, well . . . That was back when we were really somethin', ya know. A helluva country. Now,' Fred shook his head slowly, 'we're just coastin' down the hill built up by all that hard work. By the time we're old men, Pete,' he laughed, backhanding Pyotr's chest with a sad grin, 'we'll be talkin' about way back when like them old Britishers in movies after their Empire went *poof.*' He shook his head one more time. 'But, boy, this place was somethin', it really was. We thought we had somethin' goin' here. It's just a damn shame there ain't no Abe Lincoln left in us somewhere. It's just a da-a-amn shame.'

PART III

'"Does the flap of a butterfly's wings in Brazil set off a tornado in Texas?" In systems like the weather, small perturbations cascade upward, and predictability gives way to randomness. Such is the problem with influencing the course of human events. You can change the direction of history, but you cannot know where that change will lead.'

Valentin Kartsev (posthumously)
'The Laws of Human History'
Moscow, Russia

Chapter Nine

BETHESDA, MARYLAND
January 16, 1330 GMT (0830 Local)

'If you're going to get that driveway clear, Gordon,' Elaine said as she cleared the dishes from the breakfast table, 'you'd better get started.'

'Just a minute,' Gordon mumbled. He was right in the middle of a three-part series in the *Washington Post* on life in the U.N. forces in Siberia. 'Did you know,' Gordon said, raising his voice, 'it gets so cold in Siberia that your breath freezes? When you exhale, it freezes right in front of your face and falls to the ground.'

From the center of his newspaper came a loud crumpling noise. Elaine stared at him with one eyebrow raised – her hand atop the paper. 'Did you know it gets so cold in Maryland that water freezes and falls right onto peoples' driveways?'

Gordon heaved a sigh and put the paper aside. 'You're not supposed to shovel snow first thing in the morning,' he mumbled as he climbed into his overshoes. 'People get heart attacks.'

'Not people with five-thousand-dollar Sharper Image snowblowers,' she said as she headed off.

'It was nine hundred dollars!' he shouted after her.

'You were the one who wanted that thing,' she replied from the kitchen. 'It takes up half the garage, Gordon. Do you know how many times,' she said, returning for more dishes, 'we could have gotten our driveway shoveled if we had paid a neighbor's kid nine hundred dollars?'

Gordon was shaking his head. He had her on that one. 'That's just the point. Neighbors' kids aren't reliable.'

'And *you* are?'

Gordon let out a long, sustained huff. He rose to don his coat. The garage was dark, but the light came on when he hit the opener. The door made its noisy ascent, revealing a driveway covered with four inches of snow.

Gordon smiled. He clapped his gloved hands together and put his goggles over his eyes. The snowblower had a Kawasaki engine in it. He stretched his muscles and touched his toes before he began the effort of yanking the starter cord. Five hard pulls later, the cold engine showed no signs of life. Gordon stood and breathed deeply – gathering his strength for another assault. *Man's work*, he thought. Still, he should have gotten the top-of-the-line model. It was another two hundred dollars, but it had a patented 'quick-start' ignition.

He began pulling again and again and again. There were some sputtering sounds of life, but the engine didn't catch. 'Need some help, sir?' the man said from just outside the garage. He wore dark sunglasses and a dark suit. An Uzi was slung over his shoulder as casually as a tourist would tote a camera bag.

'Nope! Almost got it,' Gordon said, breathing heavily. He pulled and pulled until finally the motor kicked in. He revved it up and looked at the agent with a smile. 'Purrs like a kitten!' he shouted. The agent turned back to the front yard and circled his finger in the air.

Gordon headed out of the garage into the bright sunlight. The engine made so much noise that he almost couldn't hear the shouted commands of the senior agent right by his side. The handle of the snowblower vibrated as he revved it up once again. 'Look out!' he shouted to the two men along his property line to the right of the drive. They didn't turn to acknowledge him. Their eyes were peeled and their fingers on the triggers of their own Uzis.

After the warning, Gordon began to blow snow. It shot out of the side of the blower in a geyser of white – pelting the backs of the unperturbed agents some distance away. A second agent took up position behind Gordon on his right opposite the senior agent to Gordon's left. They liked symmetry, Gordon had noticed. A third man walked directly in front, his head on a swivel.

The 180-degree turn at the end of the driveway was a little unwieldy. More agents stood around two Broncos parked on the street. Some had long rifles and scopes. Down the street just inside the police barricades, two vans blocked access to Gordon's small stretch of Spring River Drive. One was filled with members of the local SWAT Team. The other had satellite antennae raised above it. His entourage had to switch positions around him.

Gordon saw his neighbor two houses down out with his own snowblower. Two agents shadowed the man within easy pistol range. Gordon gave the guy a big wave, which was returned with a broad grin matching Gordon's.

'Sorry!' Gordon shouted to the agent standing guard at the side door. He was removing his sunglasses to wipe the slush from his face. He made sure he powered the baby down before he made his next turn and headed back down the drive. 'Beautiful day, isn't it?' he shouted over the noise to the man in the right rear position. The man said nothing. The small earphone's wire trailed down into the agent's jacket.

When Gordon had finished both the drive and the sidewalk, he shut the engine off just outside the garage and took a deep breath of the refreshing air. It was foul with gasoline fumes from the snowblower, but it was cool and dry. Gordon didn't want to go inside right away. He waited while the body heat he'd generated from the exertion dissipated. His wrists were sore from the vibrations of the handle. 'It's a pretty day,' he said to the senior agent. 'Maybe I should go knock on doors and try to pocket a few extra bucks clearing driveways.' The man's smile reminded Gordon of the Mona Lisa.

The man looked over his shoulder at the street just past the barricades. Moments later, a car that Gordon recognized as belonging to one of his neighbors appeared. The senior agent seemed distracted by something being said to him over the radio. All the agents now faced the approaching menace – a Volvo station wagon filled with groceries. When it turned into its driveway and a woman got out with her two small children, the men eased.

'Are you going to work the Inauguration?' Gordon asked.

'Yes, sir.'

He turned again and looked around. Gordon could see nothing. *What was it?* he wondered. '*Yellow dog. Range two hundred meters. No tags.*'

Elaine stepped out onto the porch. The unexpected appearance of another member of the 'secure package' sent several agents scurrying for new positions across the front lawn.

'Gordon!' she yelled. 'It's time to come in and get dressed!'

'Just a *mi-i*-inute!' he replied. She tapped her wristwatch with both brows raised, then disappeared back inside the house. Gordon turned to the agent and frowned. 'I've gotta go to this . . . *reception* thing being given by Capital Hill *spouses*.'

The agent nodded, then turned to look down the street. A man in his pajamas and robe was just exiting his house with a white garbage bag. Range: one fifty.

SHENYANG, CHINA
January 17, 0500 GMT (1500 Local)

Chin couldn't decide whether to remain in his seat by the open flap at the rear of the truck, or to wade up into the sea of men to sit under the canvas away from the brutal cold.

The truck hit a huge pothole or slid into a rut every few meters. It threw everyone into the men seated around them. The column crawled along at a few miles per hour. They could have marched faster given all the starts and stops, but Chin was not about to turn down the ride.

The next time the truck's brakes squealed, they came to a complete stop. Chin climbed over the rear gate. The dirt road through the mountains was frozen solid. He walked around to the front of the truck and ordered the private out of the passenger seat. His experiment with riding with his troops was over. The men hadn't said a word to Chin, or Chin to them. The cabin was nice and warm, unlike the back.

They started moving again. Chin peered out the frosty, fog-smeared windshield. The road ahead curved to the left as it hugged the ridge line. It was jammed full of canvas-covered trucks under a thick and overcast sky.

He didn't know where they were. He was only a junior lieutenant. Such information was reserved for officers of much higher rank than him. Officers with maps and binoculars who rode in jeeps. Chin didn't even know where they were going or what awaited them. Like the millions of others on the move that day, he just went in the direction in which he was pointed. There were no questions asked, and none expected.

KHABAROVSK, SIBERIA
January 17, 2200 GMT (0800 Local)

Nate Clark shut his eyes and rubbed his forehead. The phone was jammed hard against his ear. He was sunk deep into his chair. UNRUSFOR now occupied the entire former military headquarters of the Russian Far East Army Command. General Dekker – Chief of Staff of the Army – was on the secure line to the Pentagon.

'Ed,' Nate said, 'the *entire* Shenyang Army Group is heading north. Five armored divisions, twenty-three infantry divisions – 350,000 men. And the Beijing Army Group is clearly staging. That's another four armored and twenty-five infantry divisions – 375,000 *more* troops – as a follow-on.'

'A *potential* follow-on, Nate,' Ed Dekker corrected. But there was no vigor in his voice. He made the point solely as a matter of form.

'It's not just the satellite photos, Ed,' Nate said – trying a new tack. 'Or the electronic intercepts, or the human intell, or the warnings through diplomatic contacts. There's . . . *something* – all my unit commanders say they can feel it in their gut. It's in the air, in the woods, in the shadows at night. It's been there for days, Ed – for *weeks*.'

'What the hell are you talking about?' Dekker replied testily.

'The Chinese – they're coming across. They've been infiltrating in force since days ago . . .'

'Where's your *proof* of that, Nate?'

'My *proof* is those fifteen Chinese bodies that German patrol stacked up two days ago!'

'*Fifteen* soldiers, Nate!' Dekker shot back. 'That's not coming across "in force."'

'For *Go-od's* sake, Ed! Don't tell me *you* are gonna give me the same . . .!'

'Okay!' Dekker snapped – stopping Nate cold. Nate knew he wasn't just crossing the line with a superior. He was trampling it. 'I took it up, and they weren't persuaded. Maybe if they'd taken a prisoner who talked.'

'The Chinese soldiers were all sappers,' Nate said dejectedly. 'They killed themselves right after the firefight got started.' Dekker said nothing. He knew all the details. 'How high did you take it?'

'All the way to Himself,' Dekker replied – meaning President Marshall.

Nate pressed down on his sore eyes with his fingertips. 'Ed, they could be all over the place. They could be ringing every firebase we got. There's so much Goddamn real estate out here – most of it covered in forest . . . I've been patrolling as much as I dare, but I'm terrified, Ed – absolutely *terrified* – at what those patrols might find. That's how that German airborne company found those Chinese sappers – on a long-range patrol. And those Chinese were carrying twenty kilos of C4 *apiece*. That wasn't a recon unit, Ed. They were gonna blow some things up.'

'Nate, I'm shooting straight with you. No bullshit. I've pushed as hard as I can. We're not going to get any reinforcements out of President Marshall.'

'How about the Second Infantry?' Nate asked.

'What?' Dekker shot back. 'Just invite North Korea into Seoul?'

'We could deploy them to Vladivostok. From there they could hit North Korea from the Russian border if the North attacks the South.'

Dekker sighed audibly. 'There's only three days till the Inauguration. Governor Bristol's people tell me he's "fully apprised of the situation" and "is sympathetic to our plight." There's nothing he can do right now.'

'That's bullshit. He could get together with Marshall and Congress and . . .'

'I *know* that, Nate! We're in a transition period between administrations. From November to January we're in lame duck limbo. You're not getting any more troops until after the Inauguration. I can't get you more troops. But I'll do anything within my power to help. What else can I do for you, Nate?'

Clark filled his lungs and let the air out slowly. 'Just tell me why I'm here, Ed. What I'm supposed to be doing? When I can come home?'

There was dead silence on the phone now.

'I'm ordering my troops to take off their blue helmet covers and put on white camo,' Nate said. He hung up and gave the order.

It was a purely symbolic act. But changing from 'blue hats' to Arctic white at least was something. An act he could take to prepare for war. For blue hats meant humanitarian peacekeepers. Arctic white meant concealment in war. The significance of the change was lost on no one in his headquarters. The mood changed. The pace of work quickened. Commanding generals, privates in snow holes – all braced for the shock that was coming.

FORT BENNING, GEORGIA
January 18, 1900 GMT (1400 Local)

Andre Faulk read his posting from behind the glass-covered bulletin board. After two months of Basic Training and two more of Advanced Individual Training at Infantry School, the recruits were being sent to the swelling ranks. Andre's smile drained from him upon finding his name. Others were shouting and slapping backs. Andre had to look up the strange number he'd found next to his name on the listings of Military Occupation Specialties.

'Andre!' Stempel shouted.

Before he could join up with Faulk, a burly, tanned recruit from California grabbed Stempel. He squeezed his neck and rubbed his knuckles through Stempel's short hair. 'Did you hear what billet Fuck-Up landed in?' the muscular beach bum shouted. He let Stempel raise his head just enough to tell Andre himself.

'11B!' Stempel said – beaming. Infantry. 'The 25th Light Infantry Division.'

'Hawa-ii,' the surfer added – using the native pronunciation. 'Hey, Stemp, it's possible even *you* might get laid there, troopuh!' He pushed Stempel nearly to the ground. Harold was grinning from ear to ear. He'd been posted to one of the combat arms like all the others. He'd made it.

Men from their training platoon were gathering around.

'What about you, Andre?' Stempel asked. Everyone waited.

Faulk mumbled, '2nd Infantry.'

'Aw ri-i-ight!' the surfer said. He punched Faulk on the arm. 'They're good to *go*, man. Most combat-ready unit in the army outside the airborne.'

'What MOS?' Stempel asked, just like Andre knew he would.

'71L,' Andre answered. The laughter and noise slowly ended.

'What's that?' came the expected question – again from Stempel.

'Admin Specialist.'

The hulking beach boy snorted a laugh. 'You're kidding, right?'

Faulk turned and walked away. It was Stempel who ran after him. He fell into place at his side. He seemed at a loss as to what to say. After walking like a puppy halfway back to the barracks – glancing every few steps at Andre's face – Stempel finally said, 'You're still on for dinner with my parents, right?' Andre frowned. 'Oh, come on, man! You promised. It'll be some real good chow. They're payin'.'

'All right,' Andre said. He watched their boots. They now walked in step out of habit.

'How long you got off before you gotta show up for duty?'

''Bout ten days.'

'Cool. I only got a week. My mom's gonna be pissed 'cause she wanted to take a cruise or somethin'. We'll pro'bly just park ourselves in some condo on the beach. How 'bout you? You headin' home to New York?' Faulk shook his head. 'Why not? Ten days is plenty of time.'

Faulk stopped and turned angrily to Stempel. '*Look*. I got some things to do, okay?'

Stempel looked hurt. 'Hey, man,' he said almost in a whisper, 'if it's that Admin Specialist thing, that don't matter. Shit! We all know you're the best soldier in the platoon! The Army's just fucked up. They send you to be a clerk and me to be an infantryman. How stupid is that?' Stempel softly backhanded Andre's shoulder. 'Look, Andre,' he said, conspiratorially, 'you could use that letter Sergeant Giles got for you.'

'Sh-h-i-i. I joined the army, but I didn't say I'd go jumpin' outa airplanes.'

'But that must be what *happened!* Stempel exclaimed. 'They had a slot open for you in Airborne School. When you told Sergeant Giles you didn't wanta go, all the combat arms slots were *filled!* That's it! So why don't you just go! You can give that letter to your new CO!

It's supposed to get you in if you change your mind!' Stempel could tell something was wrong. 'What is it?' he asked.

Andre was petrified of heights. He always had been. He couldn't even get close enough to look out the windows of his mother's apartment. He turned and took off.

'I'd never have made it without you,' Stempel said from behind. 'Thanks!' Andre kept walking. He reached up and wiped away the tears.

VLADIVOSTOK, SIBERIA
January 19, 2200 GMT (1000 Local)

'B-r-r-r-r,' Kate Dunn said. She and Woody descended the stairs from the airliner's door to the tarmac. Kate quickly buttoned up her parka all the way to the top and then put on her gloves, but she was still cold. 'J-e-e-ez,' she said through clenched teeth. Her jaw quivered as they walked into the stiff wind that blew across the concrete. 'It is *co-o-o-old!*'

Woody seemed completely comfortable. 'Like I said, you need a hat.' Kate turned her entire torso to him to avoid exposing any more of her bare skin. One hand clenched the top of her parka closed under her chin. The other was pressed tight against her side. Woody wore the most stupid-looking fur hat Kate had ever seen. 'They must've had to k-kill twenty or thirty rats to m-make that thing,' Kate said.

'It's rabbit,' Woody said proudly.

'Wood-man!' they heard. The call came from behind a roped-off area where the departing passengers waited. The flight they'd just taken from Anchorage to Vladivostok had been nearly empty. Business was booming, however, on the return trip.

'O-la!' Woody yelled. Kate followed him over to the rope. A waiting man had half a dozen cameras dangling from his body. Woody gave him a soul shake. 'Que pasa, hombre!'

'How many times do I have to tell you I'm not Spanish?' the man said with a distinct Irish accent. His white teeth shone through a dark beard flecked with gray. His ruddy face had been turned leathery by the elements.

'But you've got the *soul* of a Spaniard, man. That's what counts!

Hey, I'd like to introduce you to Kate Dunn, cub reporter.' Kate shook the man's gloved hand with a smirk. She quickly grabbed her collar as the cold air poured in like icewater. But it did little good. The chill seemed to have sunk straight through her Orvis cold-weather gear. 'Mick here is black Irish. His people were washed up on the shore of Ireland by the great storm that sunk the Spanish Armada.'

'Pleased to meet you,' the man said. A gust of wind immersed Kate in the frigid air. She dug her elbows in her sides and pressed her legs close together.

'We'd better let him g-go,' Kate managed.

'You need a hat,' Woody's friend said.

'I *told* her that, man,' Woody said.

Kate rolled her eyes and nodded toward the terminal building. The Russian gate agent – wearing a greatcoat so thick that he looked like a bear – opened the roped-off area. The departing passengers stampeded toward the plane, which hadn't even turned off its engines.

Mick grabbed Woody and whispered into his ear. The Irishman was looking at Kate. He and Woody laughed loudly. 'He-*hey!*' Woody exclaimed. 'Always good to *see* ya, compadre!' They parted. Kate practically ran to the terminal and, once inside, went straight over to an old radiator. There she shed the parka and gloves, which had themselves become the source of the cold.

'O-o-o-oh,' Kate moaned. She sagged in exhaustion as she held her blue fingers to the hot iron. '*God!*'

'I *told* you it'd be cold,' Woody said. 'Next time, I'd appreciate it if you didn't ask for me by name.'

'I fought my ass off for this assignment, Woody,' she said. Her teeth remained clenched as she toasted each side of her hands before turning to warm her rear. 'You're the very best cameraman there is, and . . .'

'Yeah, well . . .' he interrupted, then fell silent. 'Anyway, *look* at you. I mean, we just like walked from the plane to the terminal, and you're already frozen solid.'

'I'll be *fine!* That jerk in San Francisco just didn't know what he was *talking* about. "Gore-Tex" this and "polymer" that. My ass!' Woody was distracted. He kept looking around the concourse. 'Trying to spot some more old friends like that leering bastard out there?'

'Hey, if he leered any, it's because of his Spanish blood.'

'Well, what about that macho male lewd shit he was whispering to you about me.'

Woody rocked his head back – feigning shock. 'You think that was what it was? Wait here.' He headed for the men's room.

Kate began the process of putting her Arctic gear on again. The parka was so cold that she held it over the radiator. Then she remembered the salesman's warning that the high-tech fabric might melt. 'Gore-Tex my ass,' she grumbled as she slipped the parka on.

When Woody returned he had a shit-eating grin on his face. 'Hee, hee-hee, hee-hee, hee-hee.'

'*What* is *wrong* with you?' she said. 'Has that rat hat made you go mental?'

He pulled open his massive overcoat. A large plastic baggy protruded from an inner pocket. In it was an enormous quantity of pot.

'Jesus, Woody!' Kate whispered. She stepped closer to him and looked all around. The terminal was deserted now. 'Where the hell did you get that?'

'Mick-a-roono! He wasn't talking about yer bod, Kate. He was tellin' me where he'd stashed his *sensimillia*!'

'Oh,' she said. 'Well, what the hell are you gonna *do* with it, Woody?' she whispered. 'What about Customs?'

He laughed, holding out his arms and looking from one side of the empty building to the other. 'This is Russia, Kate. No government. No customs. *Anarchy*, man. You can do anything you want here!'

'No, you can't,' Kate said. 'You can't call me "man". Now come on,' she said. She headed for the empty baggage claim.

ATLANTA, GEORGIA
January 20, 0030 GMT (1930 Local)

'Are you ready to order, Andre?' Mrs Stempel asked.

'You go 'head, ma'am,' he said.

He was still studying the bewildering array of foods on the menu. She ordered things he'd never heard of. Four different things. His eyes darted all about the menu. Harold too ordered several things. Andre's eyes were drawn not to the food, but the prices. His momma could have fed the whole family a fine meal for the price of any one of the things on that menu.

'And for you, sir?' the waiter asked.

'I'll have the same as him,' Andre replied – indicating Harold.

Even though he'd been clear enough, the waiter seemed surprised. Everybody acted funny. They dabbed at their mouths with napkins.

After Mr Stempel ordered, they all sat there quietly and waited. It wasn't like a real dinner table. Stempel's folks talked, but one at a time like some kind of talk show on TV.

'Andre comes from New York too,' Harold said.

'Is that right?' Mr Stempel said – smiling. 'What part?'

'The Bronx, sir.'

He nodded and arched his eyebrows. He couldn't think of anything to say.

'What are you going to be doing now that you graduated, Andre?' Mrs Stempel asked.

A small dish filled with food in tiny portions was laid in front of them.

Andre wondered whether it could get any worse. 'Postal detachment, ma'am.'

'Now, you see, Harold,' she said. 'Why is it you didn't get something that might better prepare you for the future? You've had a computer since the day you were born. There have to be plenty of jobs in the Army that use computers. Maybe you could ask for a transfer.'

And that's the way it went, all the way through four lousy courses. The steak was fine, but he'd had better. Only the dessert tasted like it was worth the money.

'Are you sure you don't want us to drive you to the airport, Andre?' Mr Stempel asked after the ordeal was finally over.

'No, sir. Tha's all right.'

'Where are you headed if you're not going home?' Mrs Stempel asked.

'Korea.'

'Oh,' the two elder Stempels said almost in unison.

'Thanks for dinner,' Andre mumbled. He put his cap on his head and pulled away . . . free.

'Hey, 'Dre!' Harold shouted. He ran after Andre. 'Good luck, man.'

'You too, Stemp.'

They shook hands. Harold held Andre's hand longer than was normal.

OVAL OFFICE, THE WHITE HOUSE
January 20, 0230 GMT (2130 Local)

President Marshall already felt like an outsider. All of the Marshalls' belongings in the residential quarters had been packed a week before. Marshall toyed with the pens and pencils on the desk. His staff had already packed up his files. No one expected him to work on a Saturday. The day before the Inauguration.

Bristol would be hopping from balls and bashes all across town. They'd be picking up steam and heading into the wee hours of the morning. Looking around the office – stripped bare of anything personal of Marshall's – he saw he was leaving it in good shape for his successor. He wished he could say the same for the world situation. Marshall shook his head and frowned. So much left undone.

The door burst open and the sound of two busy men followed just behind. When they saw him there, they froze. Marshall didn't recognize their faces.

'Oh. I'm sorry, sir,' one of the men said. 'We didn't know . . .' They held in their hands stacks of files . . . for the new President.

'No, no. Come on in,' Marshall said. He swept his arm across the desk – turning it over to them with a gracious smile.

They looked at each other before tentatively proceeding. Marshall walked along the walls of the office with his hands shoved deep in his pockets. There were portraits of his predecessors. He'd never studied the artwork before. There had always seemed like there'd be time later.

'No, put that one on top. The ones with the red labels go on top.'

Marshall looked back around at them and smiled. 'You boys aren't out at the parties?'

The one giving the orders and doing the talking shrugged. 'We've been spending all our time down in the Situation Room.'

'Oh, you're national security?' Marshall asked. The man nodded. 'I didn't know . . .' he began. He stopped himself. He didn't know the national security staffs had already made the transition. He turned away. 'I didn't know there was anybody down in the Situation Room tonight.' He moved on to the portrait of Washington.

'There was a crisis action team convened, Mr President,' the man

211

said. When Marshall looked up at him, the man stood there awkwardly. He didn't know what to say. 'It's a *joint* team. Some of . . . of the *outgoing* staff is down there too.'

Marshall nodded, resuming his inventory of the dead presidents. 'What's the topic du jour?' he asked.

'Oh . . . China, sir.'

'Anything new?'

The man cleared his throat. 'Some more troop movements. Closer to the border. And . . . and some patriotic broadcasts have replaced normal programming. Old documentaries about the Long March on TV. Classical music on the radio. That sort of thing. We thought at first that somebody in the leadership had died.'

'Wouldn't be surprised,' Marshall said. His hands were now clasped behind his back. His eyes roamed the walls. 'The youngest one of 'em must be in his nineties.' The two men laughed more loudly than was appropriate. They were excited. This was a beginning for them.

'Oh!' the staffer added. 'And there was a . . . an order that came down last night from Beijing. Every single soldier from general to private was ordered to shave his head.' Marshall turned to look at the man, who was smiling at the humor of it. 'Almost three million haircuts. Imagine all that hair.' The man wilted under Marshall's worried gaze. 'They . . . they have had problems with head lice, NSA said. They think. In the army. The Chinese Army.'

Marshall headed for the door. He intended to go directly down to the Situation Room. But he stopped. He looked at the two junior aides standing behind his desk. *Bristol's desk*, Marshall thought. He left the Oval Office for the last time and headed off to a guest bedroom. His late-night snack awaited him . . . as usual.

THE KREMLIN, MOSCOW, RUSSIA
January 20, 0425 GMT (0625 Local)

Kartsev had awoken early to watch the coverage of the Inaugural Eve gala on C-SPAN. He sat in his office in front of the television. It was the night of his experiment's final catalyst. The last brisk stir of the sociopolitical pot. His few remaining assets had been lying low. Most, in fact, had perished during the extended period of inactivity.

Drug overdoses. Violent accidents. Men condemned to Schedule A for risking operational security. Plus suicide was already ten percent a month.

The television cast the room's only light. On it, a great hall had been turned into a crowded ballroom floor. Kartsev had muted the announcers' running commentary. Only the occasional close-up drew his passing attention. The party-goers were obscure political dignitaries. Kartsev didn't recognize any of the names shown as the camera zoomed in.

When the scene switched to the motorcade pulling into an underground garage, Kartsev turned the volume back up. With it rose his excitement.

'. . . have just arrived under heavy police and Secret Service protection. This Inauguration will be marked by the tightest security in history after the wave of political terror that flashed across this country last year.'

'Excuse me, Tim,' another voice interrupted as the President-elect emerged from a limousine. 'Governor Bristol is just now arriving.' They went on to identify each of the other passengers as they gathered. They all smiled and waved to the cameras campaign-style. When the Bristol and Davis families were assembled, they headed through the cordon of security officers toward the service elevator. Kartsev watched and listened now with rapt attention. His heart pounded in his chest.

THE WILLARD HOTEL, WASHINGTON, D.C.
January 20, 0430 GMT (2330 Local)

The air that rushed through the sheet-metal duct was hot. He was sweating profusely from the exertion of crawling a painstaking pace of a meter or two per minute. Every point of contact with the ducting had to be planned. A hand there – by the jagged rivet he could feel in the darkness. A knee where he estimated the last strap support to be. The noise now poured in through the grating at the end. He inched his way toward it.

The sheet metal had already given three times. Each time it made a loud bang like he'd slammed his fist down. The duct was a meter wide and high. It was suspended above the grand ballroom by black

213

fabric belts looped around it that hung from the ceiling. He could feel the entire thing swaying gently with each movement he made. Each time his weight tested the metal, he cringed in anticipation. Not that he feared death. He would die that night regardless. And he wasn't indifferent to death. He was sickened by the prospect of it. It had been a long run, however. Most of the others from his class were dead already. Siberia, The Bronx, Wembley Stadium, and No. 10 Downing Street – he should by all rights be dead. He had faced the void before . . . just never with quite the same certainty.

The metal enclosure resounded again with a bang. It was so loud it sounded like a gunshot. There was none. It was the duct's floor popping back into position after he'd moved on. But the noise of the band and the buzz of the room were too loud. Once again they'd missed a sound for which four dozen pairs of ears were intently listening.

He tried to imagine whether he'd left dents that might tip his opponents off. Each time the swinging of the duct became excessive, he froze in place and waited for the motion to dampen. It took an hour and a half to crawl sixty feet.

Finally, he reached the grate. He rubbed his eyes clear of the sweat and peered through. He couldn't see the stage! Enormous nets filled with red, white and blue balloons hung just in front.

But the balloons will come down, he decided. He took a vise grip and went to work on two neighboring slats. He pried and twisted the thin metal until a hole opened up. That would do for the muzzle. He spread another space several inches above. The bands had stopped and the speeches had begun. He'd barely finished in time.

He replaced the tools in their pouches on his vest. He pulled the rifle off his back where it had been securely strapped. The magazine was already loaded. A bullet was already chambered. The scope was even focused correctly for the range.

The band played 'America the Beautiful' as he shouldered the rifle. The muzzle protruded slightly through the hole in the bottom slat. And when he looked into the eyepiece he could see blurry balloons. The upper hole in the slats had been made for the scope. He rested his thumb on the power switch to the laser sight.

Now he waited. The cheers of the throng rose several decibels, and then rose again to a sustained roar. The nets opened up. The balloons began to drop past his scope. His field of view at high magnification was very narrow. All he could see was a falling mass of colorful spheres.

All at once, the net was empty and the podium came into focus. He flicked on the laser aimpoint.

Like circus performers Bristol held Gordon's hand aloft. It was clenched in his own as the adoring mass of black ties and sequins cheered. Fifteen, twenty minutes here, tops, before they moved on to the next gathering. Each party was a step up the ladder. At the last stop were the largest contributors.

Gordon waved awkwardly with his left hand as Bristol held his right captive. Every so often he pointed at a face in the crowd. People jumped to punch balloons into the air. The cheering went on and on. Bristol – the consummate campaigner – held Gordon in that pose far longer than Gordon felt comfortable. The grin was frozen on his face and felt unnatural. He looked over to see that Bristol's grin looked the same as always – never quite natural, never obviously staged.

A small red dot wiggled on Bristol's bunched-up jacket. It took a moment for Gordon to realize what he saw. In that moment the dot settled squarely on Bristol's chest. Gordon hurled himself into the larger man.

The boom of a rifle shot sounded almost instantaneously. Gordon's momentum carried the two men to the hard floor. They landed in a heap – Gordon on top of Bristol. He rolled off. Screams rose up from the crowd. They were behind the podium. Milliseconds seemed like an eternity. 'No,' Bristol said just before the podium began to shatter into pieces. Gordon felt the hot daggers in his face, neck, and pelvis. Holes exploded through the podium one at a time. Brilliant footlights shone brightly through each. Bristol's body shook and lurched against Gordon. Searing pain shot through Gordon's chest.

Lights hung from the ceiling over the stage. They were hidden from view by short curtains. Like the bottom of his parents' dining room table. Like the raw wood underneath the bright polish.

Strings of firecrackers like Chinese New Year in long bursts. '*Cease fire! Cease fire!*' a half-dozen men shouted.

The man on top of Gordon rose. None too soon because his weight had crushed the breath out of him. The cool air washed across his soaking chest. Gordon tried but couldn't draw any of it in. He needed the breath for the words he so desperately wanted to speak. Instead, he just mouthed them over and over and over again. 'I've been shot. I've been shot. I've been shot.'

Chapter Ten

BETHESDA NAVAL HOSPITAL
January 23, 1500 GMT (1000 Local)

The snippets of sound and fleeting images whirled around the spinning, sweat-soaked bed. Gordon Davis was so nauseous and drained that he couldn't quite regain consciousness. It was as if he'd tumbled into dark water. He didn't know which way was up. But he saw the anguished face of Elaine. How she gasped for breath as she sobbed like a child. He felt the plastic mask on his face. He heard voices calling out to him from the surface.

'Can you hear me?' a man asked over and over. His voice was deep. He was so close Gordon could feel the man's breath. There was an awful, steely taste in Gordon's mouth when he swallowed. His eyes were pried open and a painfully bright light appeared.

It was dark again when he lifted his head. Pain split his skull in two. It fell back into the cold, sweaty pillow. Fleeting images of ghostly forms rushed to his bedside in his dreams.

'Can you hear me?' someone asked. Gordon's eyes drifted open. It was a man – a silver-haired man – in a dark suit. Gordon stared at the ceiling tiles in the brightly-lit room. He swallowed the fiery

217

bile that threatened to erupt in a gush from his stomach. 'I concur,' he heard several times amid a confusing jumble of words. They came from different people and different places scattered around Gordon's bed. He tried to lift his head, but pain burst from his abdomen like a tearing of tissues. He collapsed in agony – his eyes jammed closed. But not before he saw the curtain of men in suits that ringed his bed.

Questions. He was being questioned by someone. Prompted. With his eyes closed, he tried his best to croak out the reply the silver-haired man expected. Mere fragments were all he caught. Words that he just repeated. He swallowed over and over to wet his parched mouth. 'Swear . . . solemnly swear' . . . something. And 'protect and defend.' He remembered those words. 'Protect and defend.'

Gordon opened his eyes. Sunlight streamed in through open curtains. 'He's up!' Gordon heard a man shout. It was followed by the rustling sound of a newspaper and the sudden appearance of several men in suits.

'Ex-*cu-u-use* me,' a nurse said – elbowing her way through the crowd.

'Get everybody in here,' one of the men whom Gordon didn't recognize ordered. 'Now!'

'Good morning!' the nurse said. She fiddled with the drip hanging over his bed and checked her watch. 'How do you feel?'

Her voice had the casual sound of a day at work. Gordon realized he was in a hospital.

'Terr'ble,' Gordon mumbled. He licked his lips with a dry tongue. The nurse knew exactly what he wanted. She held up a cup with a lid like the one they'd used for the girls when they were toddlers. She let him have only the tiniest sip before pulling it away.

'Ah-ah-*a-a-h!*' she said. 'Not too much.'

Behind her grew a wall of men – none of whom Gordon recognized. The door opened and closed repeatedly as the bed-side continued to fill. He saw Fein. He saw Bristol's campaign manager.

He saw Elaine, for whom the crowd parted. She was crying. But there was a smile on her face as she leaned over and hugged him. Gordon felt the wet tears on his cheeks. It was only when he felt a strange tug that he realized some kind of tube was stuck down his nose. His own eyes filled with moisture.

'Go-o-ordon,' Elaine cooed. 'Oh, my sweet darling husband. Gordon, I love you so much.'

'Elaine,' Gordon managed. 'I've . . . I've been *shot.*'

'I know, honey. I know all about it. And you're gonna be fine. Everything's gonna be all right!' She stared at him through tears and a smile, then lowered her head to his shoulder. 'Oh, Gordon,' she whispered, 'I was so scared. I was so, so scared.' The floodgates opened now. He could feel her shaking against him. He cried too, but few tears materialized.

When she rose, she smiled and sniffed. She wiped her cheeks clean with two swipes of her hand. She didn't, however, take the other hand from where she'd lain it flat on Gordon's chest underneath his gown.

'The girls?' Gordon asked.

'They're outside,' Elaine said. She turned to the crowd – now four or five deep all around. Gordon looked at them too. 'But . . . there's some business these people need to attend to first, Gordon.'

She looked back down. She must have sensed something in his face. She bent over to whisper in his ear – her cool hand rising to cup his cheek. 'Do you remember what happened, Gordon?'

'I . . . I was on a stage.'

'No, I mean after that? Last night.' He thought for a moment, then shook his head. She spoke softly. Calmly. Clearly. 'Phil Bristol is dead, Gordon. He was shot too, don't you remember? You tried to save him, but it was too late.' He shook his head again. He now realized what she was saying. 'You're the President, Gordon. The President of the United States. You were sworn in last night. You took the oath, can't you remember?' He shook his head. 'But there was a competency vote. The Speaker of the House is the acting President. These men are here to take another vote. They're here to vote whether you're competent now to assume office.'

Gordon panned the faces around his bed. President Marshall's outgoing cabinet. Would-be nominees for the same posts in Bristol's Administration. *My Administration*, he thought. His head spun with the unbelievable truth of it.

'Where's President Marshall?' Gordon asked – slurring the words drunkenly.

'He was killed, sir,' replied the silver-haired Chief Justice of the Supreme Court. 'He was poisoned in the White House the night

219

you were shot.' Gordon closed his eyes. 'Are you ready to proceed, Mr President?' Marshall looked up and nodded. 'Can you state your name, sir?'

'Gordon Davis.'

'Your full name, if you please?'

'Gordon Eugene Davis.'

'Thank you. Now, sir, can you tell me where and when you were born?'

'Jackson, Tennessee. March 17th, 1945.'

The silver head bowed in acknowledgment of Gordon's answer. 'And can you give me the names and ages of your children?'

'Celeste, she's . . .' He had to think. 'She's eighteen. Janet is fourteen.'

Again the Chief Justice nodded. Gordon was doing well. 'Now, sir, can you tell me what you know or understand has happened since the night of January 20th? Since you received your wounds?'

'Well, I was . . . I was shot.' The Chief Justice nodded, coaching now. 'And so was Phil Bristol, only Phil . . . he . . . didn't make it. And I remember the ambulance. Elaine,' he said, turning to her, 'you were there.' She nodded – forcing a smile onto her face. 'Then not much.' Heads turned. 'The oath,' Gordon quickly added. The Chief Justice's eyes remained locked on Gordon. The same deep voice had spoken the words – protect and defend. 'I took the oath,' Gordon said. 'You administered it.'

That seemed to break the tension. The Chief Justice had a muted conversation with the Speaker of the House, who nodded.

'I'm going to take the poll now,' the Chief Justice said to the gathering. 'The question before you is whether Gordon Eugene Davis is competent to assume the office of the President of the United States.' He began with Marshall's acting Secretary of Defense. 'I believe that he is,' came the man's reply. 'I certify him competent,' said the acting Secretary of State. The other cabinet secretaries all replied in succession. Gordon, for his part, struggled to keep it all straight in his head. Piercing shots of pain purged his mind of all thoughts. Brief respites were swamped by sickening waves of nausea.

Elaine squeezed his arm. 'You did great, darling,' she whispered into his ear.

It was quiet now. The room had grown warm, the air stale from so many bodies crammed into it. Arthur Fein stepped through the crowd to stand beside Elaine. He held in his hand a leather portfolio which he opened.

There was a legal document inside in duplicate. 'This is a written declaration, sir,' Fein said, 'that no inability to discharge the powers and duties of the office of President of the United States exists. If you sign these two copies, sir, and I transmit them to the Speaker of the House and the President pro tempore, you will immediately assume the powers and duties of the President.'

A sea of faces watched him. Somber men and women. The most powerful people on earth. And by signing those papers, he would become their boss. The leader of the free world. He looked at Elaine. She winked. Gordon saw now that Celeste and Janet had been ushered to the foot of his bed. They grinned and waved, but were inhibited by all the people. Tears filled his eyes. A movie camera and two television minicams parted the crowd for a better vantage. A boom mike extended high over the bed.

The proffered pen was thick and expensive. Cameras flashed as he scribbled his signature. Elaine kept the pen. Fein squeezed his way to the end of the bed. The Speaker and President pro tempore accepted the portfolio. When they'd finished reading, the Speaker said, 'Congratulations, Mr President.'

The crowd suddenly burst into applause. Cameras recorded it all. Lights flashed. The girls made it to the head of the bed. They hugged Gordon's neck. Their faces were cool – wet with tears. The camera lights fell dark. The applause died out. The room began to clear. Congratulations drifted through his daughters' hair. The sweet smell was what he registered most.

Gordon thought for a moment they were going to leave him alone with his family. But in place of the men in suits came men in uniforms. Rows of ribbons on their chests. Stars on their shoulder boards.

'Come on,' Elaine said to the girls. 'We've got to let your dad do some work.' They each hugged him again. Janet started crying and hugging him. Celeste shook her and said, 'Let's *go-o*,' in a menacing whisper. Gordon smiled.

Elaine kissed him. She then admonished the gathering generals and admirals not to keep him long. Behind them easels were being set up. Maps were pulled from large, flat cases sealed with combination locks. The soldiers carrying them wore sidearms.

'You need to go potty?' the nurse asked. She was holding a

stainless-steel bed pan. Gordon looked at the waiting crowd – their big production ready to roll. He shook his head. She shrugged and showed him the button with which to call her.

Gordon's agony was more or less constant. 'What about some pain medication?' he asked.

'Try to cut back. If you really need it, you ask. But we took you off the heavy stuff last night. That's why you're so *chipper* today. But it's going to hurt, Mr President. For a long time. You're going to have to get used to it.'

A trickle of cold sweat ran down his neck. When she left, a Secret Service agent locked the door behind her. Gordon was all alone now with men he barely knew. The Joint Chiefs of Staff. Bristol's proposed nominees for State and Defense. The Director of the CIA. A host of others who might be important.

'Mr President,' began Bob Hartwig, Marshall's nominee for Secretary of Defense, 'I'm sorry to have to hit you with this, but we've been paralyzed for the last three days. And the situation is getting worse and more dangerous by the hour.'

General Dekker – Chairman of the Joint Chiefs – appeared. He was followed by a large map. It was walked under the brighter lights at the bedside. Two men tilted it down toward Gordon. 'Eleven hours after the assassinations,' Dekker said, 'three days ago, the army of the People's Republic of China crossed the border into Mongolia.' Dekker held a pointer to the map. Mongolia was almost completely filled with red crosshatched lines. 'It was a massive invasion. There was very little resistance. The occupation is nearly complete.'

Gordon's eyes roamed the map of Siberia further to the north. Small islands of blue marked the American and other U.N. forces.

'Mr President,' Bob Hartwig said. Gordon opened his eyes wide. He had no idea how long he'd slept. He tried to clear the fog. 'Mr President,' Hartwig continued, 'I'm afraid the news gets worse.'

'About twelve hours ago,' Dekker continued, 'the Chinese crossed the Amur River into the former Republic of Russia.'

'That's when we had the doctors cut your medication,' Hartwig said. 'Mrs Davis okayed the decision.'

Gordon said, 'Can't see the map.'

The map was held closer. Hartwig and the Chief of Naval Operations raised Gordon's head. Put another pillow under it. The pain was almost too great. From the sources of the pain, he knew there were multiple wounds. They must have been life-threatening.

Dekker was talking.

Gordon looked up. Red lines slopped over an irregular border. The 'former Republic of Russia.' The map looked like a child's coloring book. Drawn by an unrestrained pre-schooler. Gordon had no military experience. But he saw red lines of advancing Chinese. They extended from North Korea all the way to Mongolia. That left little possibility of mistake. This was no tentative probe meant to take America's measure. This was a war. War. Gordon felt the word for the first time. It mixed completely with his unrelenting pain.

He focused on Dekker's finger. At the blue unit nearest the invading red. It wouldn't be long until they met.

'We've been in contact in the air but not on the ground,' Dekker said.

An Air Force general said, 'We've been knocking down MiGs and Tupelovs for hours. But most of our intercepts are well inside Russian airspace.'

Gordon filled his lungs. The process was painful. 'Have we warned the Chinese to get out?' he managed.

'Yes, sir,' said Horton Cates – Marshall's acting Secretary of State. 'They claimed to have warned former Secretary Jensen what would happen if western troops didn't clear out.'

'Ask Jensen to come here,' Gordon requested.

Cates looked at Hartwig, then down at Gordon. 'Hugh Jensen was found dead this morning, Mr President.'

Gordon sighed with a hiss. 'Terr'rists?'

Cates shook his head. 'Shot himself . . . after news of the border crossings.'

The extent of the tragedy took shape. Proportion. Gordon looked back at the map. He struggled to keep his eyes open. He tried but abandoned the effort to draw another deep breath. 'All right,' he said. His voice was weak. Each syllable sounded like his last utterance. He looked at Dekker. 'What do we do?'

Dekker cleared his throat and shifted his weight. 'Well, sir, that's not really . . . It's a call that's over my pay grade, sir.'

'You're still Chairman of the Joint Chiefs, right?' Gordon asked.

'Well, yes, sir. But whether to pull out or go to war is a purely political question, sir.'

'Wait,' Gordon croaked. He coughed. Pain wracked him. He had to breathe. In. Out. He slowly regained the strength to speak. 'I'm not asking you . . .' he continued in a raspy voice, 'whether we go to war.' He was swimming over great swells of agony. With each dizzying fall his head swam. 'How do we stop the Chinese?' He closed his eyes to listen. He opened them every so often to look at a map. To let them know he was still paying attention to their plans.

OAHU INTERNATIONAL AIRPORT, HAWAII
January 24, 0100 GMT (1500 Local)

Harold Stempel descended the stairs to the tarmac. He stared at the masses of soldiers dressed in white. There had to be thousands of them in ranks and files. They were loading onto a hodgepodge of dark green military transports and brightly painted civilian airliners.

'Aloha,' a woman in a grass skirt said at the bottom of the steps. She hung a lei around Harold's neck and kissed both his cheeks. He smiled at the pretty woman with long straight hair and olive skin. 'Aloha,' she said to the paunchy man behind Harold. She kissed his cheeks as well.

'Pardon me,' Harold said. She seemed surprised he was still there. 'But who are they?' Harold asked – pointing at the troops.

She looked over her bare shoulder. 'They're soldiers. Been here all day. Aloha,' she said, smiling to the next passenger.

Harold headed toward the men in uniform through curiosity. It felt good to walk. To unlimber his tight muscles after so many hours of travel. The cruise ship had docked in San Juan. After hours in the airport with his parents, they'd said their goodbyes and he had flown to Orlando. From there to L.A. Then on to Hawaii. He had slept on each of the flights. He was only just now waking up.

Two MPs slouched next to their Humvee. They noticed his approach, but were uninterested.

'Pardon me,' Harold said.

With a bored look one said, 'Yeah?'

'Sorry to bother you, but what unit is this?'

They both turned his way. Both wore sidearms. 'Who the hell're you?'

Harold stiffened. 'Stempel, Harold, Private, U.S. Army, serial number . . .'

'He *me-eans*,' the other man said, 'who the fuck do you think you are, askin' military secrets, fuckhead?'

'I . . . I'm headed for the 25th. I thought, maybe, you know.'

'Lemme see yer orders.'

Stempel rummaged through his bag. They looked over the orders, then handed them back. They ushered Stempel into the staging area of the 25th Infantry Division (Light).

'You have a will?' the woman asked without looking up from her table.

'No, staff sergeant.'

Name. Name of beneficiaries. Stempel signed. 'Over there,' she said. She jerked her thumb over her shoulder.

A man wore a lab coat with camouflaged fatigues underneath. He held what looked like a staple gun from which a long hose protruded. He lifted Stempel's left sleeve and dabbed some cold alcohol on his arm. 'I already had my shots. I just got out of basic . . .'

With a hiss of air Stempel felt the sting. The man repeated the process three more times with three different injectors, never saying a word. It was over in seconds. When Stempel picked up his carry-on, he had to switch it to the right arm because of the pain.

'Name and serial number,' a man asked at another table. Stempel answered. Everybody seemed tired. The hangar was nearly empty. But there were row after row of tables. 'You're done. Head out.' He pointed at the lone plane that sat on the tarmac. A short line of soldiers ascended the stairs.

'What about my bags? They're still in baggage claim.'

The man seemed pissed. But he got Harold's flight number and baggage claim checks. 'Hurry up, man! Your plane's leaving.'

Stempel ran across the concrete. The contents of his carry-on jangled noisily. The door of the plane was being closed. The engines started up. A man began to pull the stairs away. 'Hey!' Stempel yelled – waving. He had to bang on the airliner's door. It opened. He was in.

The lavatory on the airliner was tiny. Harold barely got the door closed. He held an armload of gear scavenged off other soldiers. He couldn't believe it. He just couldn't believe it. He dropped everything and sat on the commode. He grabbed his head. The bristles folded first one way, then the other as he ran his palms across his scalp.

Yesterday, he was having a rum swizzle with his parents at a shipboard bar – ignoring them while eyeing the girl in the pink bikini by the pool. Today, he was on a plane headed for war in Siberia. He'd asked every man he'd spoken with what was happening. The privates and PFCs had just shrugged.

'Oh, ma-an,' Harold moaned. He rocked forward and clamped his hands between his knees. He tried to control his breathing. *I'm ready for this*, he told himself over and over. *I made it. I'm a soldier now just like everybody else on this plane.*

He decided to put on his uniform. Maybe if he got out of his jeans and into a uniform like all the others he'd settle down. It was a chore in the tight quarters. He stripped down to his jockey shorts and T-shirt. Printed on the shirt was the torso of a bronzed bodybuilder. Harold's head stuck out at the top. Around his neck was his plastic lei.

He began to shiver. The men were in winter battle dress so the cabin was kept chilly. Harold shoved the lei into the first pocket he found in the pile of clothing. He hurried into the loose, oversized long-johns and single pair of cushion-sole socks. Then, he donned mottled green-and-brown camouflage BDUs. Next, he found the white winter-combat boots. They were insulated, rubber-lined and waterproof. He put them on and bloused his trousers over them. A woodland camo field jacket with its liner zipped in place completed the standard battle dress.

From there he had to follow the platoon sergeant's instructions. Scissors-type braces over the field jacket. Baggy wool trousers hooked to braces. Loose wool shirt over everything. It was all a size too large. But the sergeant had told him to expect that. Something about circulation. Stempel climbed into the Arctic white nylon shell. He found the hole in the large cargo pockets on the thighs. In it was tape, which he tied around his thigh. 'Prevents the material from rubbing and making noise,' he'd been told. He pulled the shell's drawstring tight around his boots and slipped into the white Arctic overshoes. The solid white parka came next. There was a drawstring at his waist. Its tail was split. He tied each side separately around his thighs. He put on his cold-weather cap. His white, cloth-covered helmet went on over it. The parka's hood fit over the helmet. He pulled a drawstring, leaving only his face exposed. At the edge of the hood was a fur ruff, and inside it there was a pliable wire that he bent so the fur covered his face.

Stempel felt sweat forming at his brow. In the small mirror he looked twice his normal size. He had cotton, anti-contact gloves for working on 'cold-soaked' equipment – whatever that was. But he put them in his pocket and pulled out the black mittens. An 'Arctic Mitten System,' the sergeant had called them. They had thick wool inserts. Pile backs for warming your cheeks and nose. A strap for hanging them over your neck. Snaps to connect them behind your back. A gauntlet to go over your sleeves and an adjustment strap to pull them tight. And a single little sleeve for when you needed to use your trigger finger.

The one spare piece of equipment they didn't have was a weapon. Everyone else had one. But unlike clothing that could be scrounged up to make a kit for the new guy, there were no surplus weapons. It bothered him.

Someone banged on the door and Harold jumped. He began pulling the gear off – embarrassed at having been caught playing dress-up. 'Quit pullin' yer pud and clear out!' came the muffled voice of one of Harold's new comrades. He gathered his gear and opened the door. He apologized to the man outside. He then looked for a place to sit.

The plane was packed. He couldn't find the platoon sergeant. All the seats were taken. People looked at him. 'Do you know where . . .' Harold began. But he didn't know anyone's name. He moved on. Bags and gear were crammed into every space. The aisle was cluttered with overflow. He stepped from hole to hole apologizing – smashing his large Arctic Bag into faces accidentally. Even when he reached the galley, people still glared down the aisle after him. No one talked. But no one slept.

A flight attendant finally directed him to a fold-down seat. It was in the back beside the lavatories and behind the galley. He settled in with his gear at his feet in heaps.

Harold sat there alone for the duration of the flight – writing his name on his gear. He carefully printed 'Stempel, Harold' on his parka's label. *Just in case*, he thought. Since no one knew his name.

KHABAROVSK, RUSSIA
January 24, 0200 GMT (1200 Local)

'I called this meeting for two reasons,' Clark began. He sat at the head of a long table. Aides stood at maps all around. Before him sat the commanders of each of the coalition's contingents – large and small. Each had his own agenda. 'First, I wanted to inform you of my government's intentions with respect to the Chinese invasion. Secondly, I am going to ask you what *your* governments' intentions are.'

Heads swivelled. Discomfort was evident.

'First, *my* orders.' Most all knew through diplomatic channels what he was going to say. They must also have known that Clark's worst nightmare was playing out right before his eyes. 'I have been ordered by the President to repel from Russia – by military force – the People's Liberation Army.'

Everywhere Clark looked they stared back at him. It took willpower to survey each and every face. He was searching for signs. Who's in? Who's out?

'What are our rules of engagement?' asked General Sir Arthur Howard. The British commander's businesslike tone seemed to lift the oppressive weight that had hung over the meeting. Junior British and American officers began to chatter in good-natured whispers.

'Conventional weapons only,' Clark replied. The room fell silent.

'Do the Chinese understand that?' Clark's first clear ally asked. He'd chosen his words carefully.

'They have been informed of the consequences,' Clark said. 'I've seen the transcripts of the meeting. The Chinese ambassador asked for and received clarification in both English and Mandarin. We sent the same message in a telephone call from the Secretary of Defense to the Chinese Minister of Defense.' Clark leaned forward. 'One *hint* of chemical, biological or nuclear weapons and we respond *dis*proportionately, massively, and without targeting limitation.'

Howard's back remained erect – not resting against the chair. His hands were clasped before him, but he kept his elbows off the table as if at dinner. 'Was there any discussion of . . . of the current hostilities? Any conditions? Demands?'

'We demanded that the Chinese withdraw immediately. They reiterated their claims to large parts of Siberia.'

Protect and Defend

There came a new voice – the French. 'Have you already begun the fight?' the general asked.

'The Space Defense Command has downed all seven Chinese recon satellites. Anything they put up, we'll knock down. They'll be totally blind. The embargo imposed by the U.S. Navy after Taiwan is now a blockade. Notices have gone out. We'll sink any blockade runners . . . no matter what the flag. The Chinese Navy hasn't put any surface forces to sea. We're sinking them in port. The eleven diesel-electric subs at sea were being tailed. Our attack subs confirmed eleven kills in twenty-seven minutes. The blockade will cut their exports and their access to hard currency. With no way to pay for war materials, their overland imports should be limited. We'll wage unrestricted air war along the coast to a depth of two hundred kilometers . . . and as far south as the Fortieth Parallel.'

'But not *south* of the Fortieth?' the French general asked.

'We've got enough targets without including downtown Beijing,' Clark replied. 'The Fortieth gets us to the suburbs. And it covers all of Manchuria.'

Every member of the German contingent had written '40 degrees' on their pads, Clark noted.

'But that doesn't include any action against the Deng Feng missile fields?' the French general asked unexpectedly. The Chinese 'East Wind' ICBMs had a 9,000-mile range. They were the only Chinese nuclear weapons capable of hitting the West Coast of America.

'There will be no action taken against Chinese nuclear delivery systems,' Clark answered.

'And you will inform us – well in advance – if those rules of engagement change?' It was not a question. It was a condition to French participation.

'Of course,' Clark replied – wondering how many other conditions there were. 'I *will* tell you, however, that I *have* ordered a full-scale air interdiction campaign. I intend to begin the total destruction of their lines of communication. In addition to air suppression, we'll go after troop marshaling yards, rail lines, supply warehouses. In about one hour, six hundred aircraft from Air Force bases in the U.S. and Japan and from carriers in the Yellow Sea and Sea of Japan are going in with raids as deep as Shenyang.'

'Will you hit their Army Headquarters – North-east?' General Howard asked.

229

'We're underground.' Clark held his arms out to the bare concrete room. 'I want them to be.'

'Why were we not informed of these raids?' the commander of French forces asked.

'You are being informed of them now.'

'I do not consider this adequate notice. These strikes have not been authorized by the Security Council.'

'The forces are not part of UNRUSFOR. I called for the strikes in my capacity as commander-in-chief of U.S. Army Pacific.'

'Let's not quibble over the details,' the British commander broke in. The German commander made a gruff noise and nodded. 'Like it or not – and I expect *not* – we have the better part of seventy Chinese divisions bearing down on us. Now this is General Clark's meeting. We should hear what he has to say.'

Clark nodded to him in thanks. 'We of course already have the 10th Mountain, 1st Infantry and 3rd Marine Divisions in the field. The 82nd Airborne Division is en route to us here. We're projecting brigade strength in the field within twenty-four hours. We'll use them initially to join the 10th and form hasty defenses around Khabarovsk.' Heads were bowed along both sides of the table. The battles were being fought in their minds. A hundred-thousand-man sledgehammer against thin lines of light infantry and paratroopers. 'In addition,' Clark resumed but had to clear his throat, 'the 25th Light Infantry Division is en route from Hawaii. We plan on placing them in a screen of strong points just south of Khabarovsk along the Trans-Siberian Railway.'

'What about more armor?' the German general asked.

'The 2nd Infantry Division will begin immediate transhipment to the port of Vladivostok. Plus, the U.S. Marine Corps has a Marine Amphibious Unit offshore. Within ten days, they'll have another half-dozen landing ships giving us a reinforced brigade as a ready reserve. The next forces to arrive will be the Eighteenth Airborne Corps with the 101st Airmobile and 24th Mechanized Infantry Divisions. I also expect an additional four tactical fighter wings inside of thirty days to add to the two that are currently engaged. Plans are also for heavy bombers from the Strategic Projection Force based in the continental United States to begin bombing 'round the clock, with aircrews to turn the planes around out of South Korea and Japan.'

'Will your Congress make a formal declaration?' the French commander asked.

'Whatever legal and constitutional requirements,' Clark recited carefully, 'required to authorize our commitment will be undertaken at the appropriate times.' *God*, he thought after parroting the script dictated by the White House lawyer. 'Okay,' Clark said. 'I have now told you the intentions of the United States. I propose that we move on to the second item on our agenda – a declaration of the intentions of your governments with respect to the Chinese invasion.' His pulse was racing. He thought it could go either way. He turned first to his most stalwart ally. 'Arthur?'

The British general sat forward as if he were ready to answer. 'I'm afraid I'm going to have to beg off, for the moment, Nate. The parliament is meeting in closed session. I'm sure it shouldn't be *too* much longer.'

Nate was devastated. He tried not to show it. 'What about your forces?' he asked the Bundeswehr general.

'I also am awaiting my orders,' he said simply. A heavy silence hung over the table. The German seemed most discomfited of all. 'My troops do have authority to fire in self-defense, but,' he shrugged, 'we are not currently in positions nearing contact.'

Clark turned reluctantly to the French officer. The last of the big three. 'General?'

The Frenchman's lower lip protruded from his mouth in a caricature either of a pout or a scowl – Clark couldn't decide which. 'I received instructions from Paris while en route here this morning.' Clark braced himself. 'If the United States is committed to the fight, so is France. I am personally highly opposed to that decision, but I await your command, General Clark.' He bowed his head like a courtier.

Clark's forces on-hand were now doubled. Just as he had tried not to show disappointment, he tried now not to grin like a schoolboy. He moved on to the Belgians, who fell in line with the French. The exceptions were the Finns, who answered simply that they would fight, and the Danish, whose sole contribution was a medical contingent that would be bolstered to treat war casualties. All of the others deferred until orders were received from home.

Despite that, however, Clark was buoyed. After all, no one had actually backed out. And the French were in and – when Clark asked – seemed ready to send more troops. It was at that point the meeting was interrupted. The commander of a Belgian firebase was on the radio. The call was patched into the meeting. Clark lamented the fact that he didn't speak French as the commander delivered his report. The faces of the officers who did, however, grew increasingly long. The occasional background burst didn't sound like an artillery barrage. He realized suddenly what it was. The Chinese were busting bunkers one at a time . . . with demolitions. They were mopping up the Belgians.

The slow and calm report of the officer on the radio took on in Clark's mind a funereal quality. The sudden burst of noise over the radio ended in static.

No trace of Clark's smile now remained.

NORTH OF AMUR RIVER, SIBERIA
January 24, 2130 GMT (0730 Local)

The rolling landscape slid beneath the helicopter gunship. Warrant Officer Hector Jiminez sat atop the Apache's chin gun. His head was level with the knees of the pilot. The higher elevation gave the pilot a clear view of the snowy forests ahead. Sitting low gave Jiminez the feel of the gun.

Airspeed, altitude and heading lit Jiminez's visor. As copilot/gunner he wore the Integrated Helmet and Display Sighting System. He listened constantly for the sound of threat warning tones.

'There's the river,' Hector heard over the helmet's headphones. It was the familiar voice of the pilot – fellow Warrant Officer Steve Tipton.

Up ahead snaked a flat, white highway. Hector felt the aircraft decelerate through the armored seat of the AH-64. Their flight of bug-like gunships all pitched nose-up in unison. They maintained their stagger – strung out to the right of the flight leader's stubby winglet. The airspeed displayed in Hector's visor fell from 160 to near zero. The frozen Amur River – the border between Russia and China – disappeared from view. The helicopters all settled below a ridge into a hover a few feet above the treetops. Snow was lashed off the branches of the twisting evergreens in the narrow valley below.

They waited. Hector looked at the Apaches to his left and to his right. The cross-hairs on his visor traversed the snow-covered hill just in front. The other gunners were doing the same, he could tell. He watched the 30-mm chain guns under their feet slew from side-to-side.

They were slaved to the sighting systems, which traversed and slewed in sync with the copilots' helmets. The long, single-barreled cannon turned this way and that – their gunners nervous and ready.

Underneath the helicopters' short wings were four pylons. They would normally be filled with Hellfire missiles – sixteen in all – which could knock out even the most heavily armored main battle tanks. This mission, however, was against soft targets – trucks and dismounted infantry. They instead carried four fat, round rocket launchers. Each held nineteen 2.75-inch rockets – seventy-six rockets in total. Each Apache packed the equivalent of a two-minute barrage by an artillery battery. There were eight Apaches in all.

'Victor Sierra five three, this is Victor Sierra one one,' came clearly through the earphones. 'Objective in sight. Mounted and dismounted infantry. RWR is negative. Repeat, RWR is negative. Out.'

RWR is negative, Hector thought. He took a deep breath and relaxed a bit. No Chinese guns or missiles had lit up the Kiowa Scout's Radar Warning Receiver.

'All units, this is Victor Sierra five three,' came a new and familiar voice – their flight leader. 'Weapons hot. On my lead. Tallyho.'

The chin-mounted guns all swivelled left as the gunners looked at the lead Apache. It banked left and dipped its nose. The other seven gunships did the same. From a line abreast they turned into a single file. They followed in a long line through the valley – twisting and turning around icy outcroppings.

Jiminez could feel the acceleration in his back. The noise and vibration rose until they shook the cockpit controls. At full military power they roared out of the valley. Speed one hundred and ten. Altitude thirty feet and falling.

They heeled over hard – turning sharply over the Amur. The frozen river snaked through white hills. Tipton rolled the Apache from side-to-side to follow it. To the right was Russia. To the left – China.

Hector's hand firmly gripped the joystick. His finger was ready to pull the chain gun's stiff trigger. The pilots of the gunships now increased their spacing. The Apache they followed was over two hundred meters ahead. Hector could no longer see their flight leader's aircraft.

'Engaging!' came the lead's shout. The loud rattle of his chain gun was clearly audible in the background. The river turned sharply to the left just ahead.

'Here we go!' Tipton yelled.

They banked hard around the river bend, then flew straight into the drifting smoke. The gunship ahead of theirs opened fire. It belched orange flame nearly straight toward the ground. Hector saw the first Chinese.

The river was brown from one side to the other. The Chinese had poured dirt to improve the vehicles' traction. Half a dozen narrow lanes traversed the white ice of the Amur. Each was choked with trucks and scattering infantrymen.

'Goin' *rockets!*' Tipton shouted at a range of two miles. A half-dozen rockets *whooshed* from their tubes. Tipton wove wildly through the wide river valley as the rockets raced off in straight, smoking trails. Red fireballs burst all along the Amur. Trucks filled with fuel and ammunition added towering secondary explosions.

Hector shut the sights and sounds from his mind. He lined up a group of scurrying infantrymen and squeezed off a short burst. The gun thrummed through the floorboard into his feet. Small orange flames lit the frozen surface, felling men. A truck pulled out around a burning hulk. Hector laid the crosshairs directly atop the fleeing vehicle. He steadied the aim as Tipton rolled the gunship again. A squeeze of the pistol grip let loose a dozen rounds in a single second. Troops tumbled out of the back of the smoking truck. Fire began licking at the green canvas top.

They were fifteen feet over the battlefield flying at 150 miles per hour. Hector aimed and squeezed as fast as he could. The gun gyrated wildly. Shells exploded in orange strings along the white ice.

A crashing blow knocked the aircraft sideways. Hector's breath froze solid in his lungs. His eyes shot to the instrument console. There were no red warning lights. When Tipton fired more rockets, Hector assumed the aircraft could still fly. Red-glowing tracers stretched across the flat, open river. He saw flashes in the trees on the riverbank. He trained the crosshairs on the flaming muzzles and held the trigger down. His 1,100 rounds remaining dropped quickly to under a thousand. The woods were on fire. The Chinese anti-aircraft gun fell silent.

The helicopter burst out of the smoke and flame of the battlefield. There were no more targets in the windshield. Hector saw the flight leader's rotor over a hill to the north of the river.

'Five three's at two o'clock!' he called out. 'Circling back.' Tipton followed the river then banked. Two helicopters hovered on the far side of the hill. They rose in unison above the crest and fired. Their wings belched fire as they expended rockets from the safety of a mile's distance.

Tipton flew up to the ridge beside them. Once in a hover, they began to rise. They peeked out over the rocky spine of the hill. The frozen river lay before them, smoking. The last of the Apaches was weaving its way across the valley. Brilliant flares spat from its tail.

'Better pull on up clear of the . . .' Hector began to say to Tipton, but it was too late. The *whoosh* of a rocket and blinding flash of an explosion was followed instantly by shrapnel. The 2.75-inch rockets had flown only thirty feet before impacting the hill.

'Auto-*rotating!*' Tipton shrieked. Hector hung on. The Kevlar main rotor hit the rocks. The canopy shattered. Hector was riddled with shards. By the time the helicopter came to rest in the snow drifts on the valley floor, Hector didn't have long to live. Leaking fuel cut the process short. The fireball lit the surrounding hills.

PHILADELPHIA, PENNSYLVANIA
January 25, 1300 GMT (0800 Local)

Pyotr Andreev sat glued to the television.

'The White House, Pentagon and Pacific Command in Hawaii all declined to comment on the reports coming out of Paris. But other news agencies in Europe confirmed them. To repeat, Agence Presse reported today that U.S. aircraft in Siberia *have* engaged Chinese air and ground forces violating the border of the former Republic of Russia. And in Beijing, the Foreign Ministry reiterated its demand that UN troops withdraw from Siberia. "The claims of the former Republic of Russia to Asia," the Foreign Ministry said, "have never been accepted by the People's Republic of China and have no legitimate basis in law or in fact."'

'Aren't you going to eat your *bweakfast*, daddy?' Masha asked.

It was in such flawless English that Pyotr and Olga both turned. Olga beamed as she dished out pancakes. The girls already spoke to each other exclusively in English. And they had met American friends and adopted American ways. All the trouble seemed so far away.

'Satellite photographs,' the news continued, 'apparently show mass

235

graves just on the outskirts of Moscow. The State Department was unable to speculate whether the deaths were from starvation or disease – which have grown to crisis proportions in Moscow – or from political repression by the Anarchists.'

The television went dark. 'Come, eat,' Olga said. She laid the remote control on the table. She wouldn't look him in the face. His eyes were drawn repeatedly to the darkened television screen.

Chapter Eleven

SOUTH OF BIROBIDZHAN, SIBERIA
January 26, 0300 GMT (1300 Local)

The C-130 revved its engines. Stempel looked back over his shoulder at the noise. Snow flew off the one-lane road behind the engines. The aircraft had just dropped him and his new platoon in Siberia. Others like it had offloaded the rest of 2nd Battalion, 263rd Infantry. They had flown them in from Japan via Vladivostok. Now they were leaving. Stempel shivered when the backblast washed over the ranks. The stubby, dark green aircraft sped away. It lifted easily into the air. It was empty.

'2nd *Platoo-o-on*,' the lieutenant called out, 'lock 'n *load!*' Men busied themselves all around Stempel. They worked on weapons. It reinforced the nakedness he felt at having no weapon. It was like one of those dreams that you had, showing up at school with no pants. Only it wasn't a dream.

His bulging white Arctic Bag was strapped onto his back. Mountain Bag for sleeping. Air mattress. He'd read the instructions on the plane. You laced the water-repellent Arctic Bag onto the sleeping bag. It had a quick release zipper for emergency exits.

The platoon sergeant decided Stempel's load was too light. He hung four ammo belts for the platoon's two M-60s around his neck. 'Stick close to the LT,' he said. Stempel was an unknown quantity. An outsider. Dead weight.

'Don't you got a pocket knife or anything, man?' someone asked. Everyone laughed. It was the jittery laughter of nervousness.

Stempel looked at the sky. The transports were gone. All was quiet. Even the men moving off the road seemed to make no noise. The warmth of his Arctic gear seeped out. It was replaced by the same cold that scraped at his cheeks with each breeze. The sky was clear. The sun was still high in the early afternoon sky. But it seemed to emit no heat.

Their platoon spread out in a skirmish line – three squads abreast. The platoon sergeant kept increasing their spacing. Stempel remained in the center with the platoon leader. With a machine gun. He could barely see the platoon's flanks. They covered a 400-meter front. Fifteen meters of separation.

Each ten-man squad sent a scout out a hundred meters. They moved out. Stempel followed the small platoon headquarters section. They were about thirty meters behind the main line. Everyone seemed to know what they were doing. The crackle of conversations from the radio carried on the back of the lieutenant's RTO were reassuring. They reached the treeline and headed into the woods.

The going grew more difficult. The ground was scrubby. Deep drifts had gathered around every clump of brush. When Stempel sank up to his knees, they had to pull him out. Their progress slowed. It grew noticeably darker. Quieter. The deep woods were still. Frozen.

Stempel's thighs began to burn. He felt the first trickle of sweat underneath his got gear. He unzipped his parka. Took his hood off. The tiny hairs on his face were crusted with ice, but he was sweating.

The LT's hand went up – 'Halt.' A quick radio call. The LT put the map in his teeth and jabbed at the ground with his finger. The men dropped their packs and began to dig in the snowy cathedral.

Stempel delivered the extra belts of ammunition to the machine-gunner, then waited for orders. 'Dig a Goddamn snow hole, buttfuck!' the machine-gunner cursed. Stempel followed the man's finger. He dropped his pack onto the snow. Using his folding metal shovel, he dug and dug and dug. The white, powdery snow formed a high mound in front of the hole. He struck hard black soil at the bottom. While the other men set up their weapons and worked out their angles of fire with their squad or fire team leaders, Stempel dug.

The earth was frozen solid. He dug outwards. When it seemed suitably wide, he began to even out the breastwork of snow in front until it was a uniform height of about two feet, and about two feet thick at the base.

'That ain't gonna stop bullets,' the machine-gunner called out from the hole about ten meters to his left. Again the sound carried with amazing clarity.

'Knock it off!' the LT snapped.

Stempel was done. He looked down at the little fort he'd built, then back up at the machine-gunner. A hundred-round belt of shiny brass hung from his M-60. The gun pointed through gaps in the line into the trackless woods ahead. The gunner lay behind it. His ammo bearer lay beside him ready to keep the hungry gun fed. About fifteen meters to the other side of Stempel's hole, the LT held his radio-telephone handset under his helmet. The gloved fingers of his free hand were pressed hard against his exposed ear.

Stempel heard the pounding of his heart. He felt the artery in his neck pulse against his clothing. He sat down behind his wall of snow and stared out into the trees ahead. The widely spread positions on the platoon's thin line were barely visible. Men wearing white parkas and helmets lay in cottony snow.

The cool and collected platoon sergeant strode along their line. He barked out curt commands through teeth holding a stubby, unlit cigar. He left steady, organized soldiers in his wake.

Stempel was again in the world of the familiar. He drew a deep breath and relaxed. These were good soldiers. Real soldiers. They were ready.

'Heads down!' the LT shouted. 'Splash over!'

There was a faint crackling sound in the sky overhead. The platoon sergeant lay prone on the snow. The LT was now low in his hole. Only the top of his helmet was visible.

A stunning boom rattled Stempel's insides. The shock wave that pounded his ears had a solid feel to it. Snow drifted from the heavily laden limbs of a thousand trees.

Are we shelling them? he wondered. *Or are they shelling us?*

He closed his now dry mouth and swallowed. When he heard the faint crackle of another round, he curled up at the bottom of his hole. He felt the thump through the ground a split-second before he heard the boom. Again there was silence. He looked up. There was no blackened crater. No fallen trees. No smoke drifting on the wind.

He took a deep breath to soothe his ragged nerves. Sergeant Giles's warnings about the ferocity of artillery must've been exaggerated. Again came the tell-tale screech of incoming fire. The thump. The stunning boom.

'Where's that fire, over?' the LT shouted. Stempel stuck his head up. The platoon leader was peering over the front edge of his hole. '*Bull*shit, sir!' he yelled into the handset. Another shell crackled overhead, but the LT didn't duck and so neither did Stempel. The boom shook the trees again and drowned out the LT's shouts. '. . . expect us to hold this position? We need fire support, Goddamnit! What about air? Over!'

Stempel glanced over at the machine-gun crew to his left. Their heads were raised also – watching the lieutenant. From the forests up ahead Stempel saw small groups of men hustling back toward their lines. They were shouting both parts of the sign-countersign combination. Their voices sounded panicked.

'Hold your fire!' men ordered up and down the line. One returning group headed straight for the platoon headquarters.

The LT hurled the handset into the snow. His radio-telephone operator looked petrified. Stempel began to shiver from the cold as he watched the lieutenant. The platoon leader settled back into his hole. His wide and unblinking eyes looked haunted. Stempel's next breath caught in his throat. He exhaled in similarly awkward fits.

The two men from the observation post slid to the ground beside the lieutenant. Their backs were to Stempel, but their report was easily heard.

'God Aw-mighty, LT,' the large black sergeant said. He gasped for breath. 'There's gotta be a whole Goddamn *regiment* comin' this way! Fo' hun'erd meters away! Christ, sir!' He pulled his helmet and cap off his head. Steam rose from his bare scalp. 'We gotta call that arty in on them fuckers right *now!* Them spotter rounds was bang on! Tell 'em to fire for *effect!*' The lieutenant muttered something. '*What?*' the sergeant shot back. 'That didn't do *shit!* Five Goddamn *rounds?* For the love of *God*, LT, they're gonna . . .' He regained control and lowered his voice to an angry whisper. 'The woods is fuckin' crawlin' with 'em, LT!' 'We gotta pull back! They jus' ain't no fuckin' way, LT! *No* way!'

Again Stempel couldn't hear what the lieutenant said. But the two men began a string of cursing that continued all the way to Stempel's hole. 'Shit!' the Private First Class said. He slid in beside Stempel, who was forced to the far end of his fortress. The sergeant piled in after him.

They paid no attention to Stempel at all.

'What's goin' on, man?' the machine-gunner to Stempel's left called to them.

'We 'bout ready to git fucked *up*,' the sergeant replied. '*Tha's* what's goin' on!' He began to pull every magazine and grenade he had out. He laid them at the front of the hole. 'They's a whole Goddamn regiment comin' right at us. This is it, man. Those rear area mother-*fuckers* jus' sent us here to *die*, man. Jus' sent us here to *die*.'

'Pardon me,' Stempel said. His voice trembled. The two men glanced up at him. 'Could I maybe have a grenade or something?'

'Say *what?*'

'He ain't got no weapon,' the PFC said. His breath stank with fear. 'Stupid son-of-a-bitch is straight outa boot camp!'

'You a cherry, Snow White?'

'Yes, sergeant.'

He laughed bitterly – shaking his head. He picked up one of his half a dozen grenades. 'You gonna use this?'

'Yes. Yes, I will.'

'Here,' he said – tossing it to Stempel. He was now armed.

'Look at that!' someone shouted from the line ahead.

Out of the woods – darting and weaving and leaping into the air – came first one, then ten, then nearly thirty deer. They ran and hopped like gazelles, changing course at each clump of snowy brush. In utter amazement, Stempel and the others watched the deer. They raced through the American fighting positions and kept going. They were fleeing in fright. Something massive was approaching.

There were two sharp blasts from a Chinese whistle. The shrill commands were repeated from a dozen other whistles to the left, right and front. Stempel felt as though he would vomit. His mouth was as dry as dust. All was quiet save for a great scraping noise. It sounded like ice breaking. Or an avalanche of falling snow.

'What's that?' the machine gunner whispered urgently.

'It's them,' the sergeant beside Stempel replied. 'They're coming.'

'Knock it off!' the LT snapped.

That left only the sound of a thousand – ten thousand footsteps approaching through snow. Growing louder. Growing nearer. A bitter pit of bile was forming in Stempel's stomach. He felt it rise toward his esophagus. To the sound of crunching snow was now added a chant. A single voice raised high in words Stempel couldn't make out. It was rhythmic Chinese – called out in time, he felt sure, with their pace.

A thousand voices responded as one – the roar of a solid wall of men directly to their front. The white helmets of the U.S. troops twisted and spun in their line of holes ahead. Terrified men – catching each other's gaze. Measuring the size of gaps between the holes.

A loud '*Hu-u-h!*' erupted from deep in the attackers' diaphragms. The sound was jarring in contrast to the high-pitched voice which led them. Stempel wondered whether they chanted to build their own courage, or to sap the nerves of the defenders.

He was freezing. He was shaking like a leaf. He jammed his gloved hands into his armpits but still it did no good. The white shell he wore vibrated. Even the sergeant noticed, but said nothing. Stempel could do nothing to stop it. His teeth were chattering. His abdomen was clenched so tight that his bowels churned. He suddenly felt an overpowering need to urinate.

The crunching and chanting were suddenly drowned out by a fusillade of gunfire off to their right. Units quickly engaged on both sides. But everyone was still in his platoon. Waiting. The LT had his M-16 raised to his shoulder. He was just a simple rifleman, now.

In the next few seconds, a layer of ice coated Stempel. A lens descended over his eyes. The time did nothing to prepare him. Stempel could never have been ready for what happened next. No one could have been ready for that.

The few Claymore mines they'd strung up with tripwires blew almost simultaneously. That set off a cacophonous bleating of whistles, bugles and shepherd's horns. The Chinese all began to shout at once.

The line of American riflemen in front of Stempel's hole opened fire. Their rifles were deafening in the enclosure of the forest. Stempel couldn't even see the Chinese until they opened fire. Then, the bright orange flashes lit the woods. The machine-gun to Stempel's left opened up. Then the two men in the hole with Stempel began to fire.

Stempel was peering out of his hole when the first bullets sent sprays of snow into the air. He ducked his head . . . and vomited. The world spun dizzily in between spasms. The two soldiers beside him hunched low under the hail of bullets. They rose up to fire hurriedly aimed bursts despite the tremendous risk. Another bout of vomiting overcame Stempel. He clenched his grenade tightly to his fiery stomach. The snow beneath him filled with foul-smelling bile.

When nothing more would come up, Stempel tried to lift his head into the storm of bullets. Cringing with each inch his helmet rose, Stempel heard the 'z-z-z-z-i-i-p' of bullets passing by. Inches away. Each caused Stempel to pause. With his eyes jammed almost completely shut and his jaw clenched, he forced his head up.

Smoke filled the woods. Hundreds upon hundreds of men ran in a crouch. Their knees sent heavy coats flapping. Their weapons blazed. They had gleaming bayonets fixed to the ends of their rifles. Fifteen meters behind the first line was a second. Fifteen meters behind that – a third.

Buzzing sounds sent Stempel back to the depths of the hole. He shivered in fright. The air forced past his vocal cords sounded like moans. The PFC flew backwards. He sprawled against the rear wall of the hole before he tumbled on top of Stempel.

The dead weight of the man crushed Stempel. Grenades went off all around like firecrackers. They rained down in showers. Stempel could see them hit the upper branches of the trees. Some burst in the air. Others dropped straight to the ground, which shook with the pounding they delivered almost instantly. One grenade bounced off the rear lip of the hole right beside Stempel and kept going. Stempel cringed, but it didn't explode – a dud!

Boom! The blow stunned him.

The sergeant dropped his rifle and grabbed Stempel's entrenching shovel. He swung baseball-style at the grenades. Fire filled the air. A shower of snow half-filled the hole.

Everywhere men screamed, 'I'm hit! I'm hit!' Some even shouted, 'I'm hit again!' in utter terror. Branches shorn from trees crashed to the ground. Explosions created a drizzle of twigs.

'Grab his rifle, private!' Stempel heard. It was the sergeant. Stempel's stomach began dry heaving over and over. 'Sweet Je-e-ezus!' Stempel heard screamed. Bullets split the snow walls all around. Stempel began to sob.

Grenades burst everywhere. Hot fire preceded an avalanche of snow as the walls collapsed. Stempel's eyes were filled with the icy slush. To the heavy weight of the PFC's body was added that of the sergeant's. Stempel lay still at the bloody bottom of it all.

TONGDUCHON, SOUTH KOREA
January 26, 0330 GMT (1330 Local)

Andre Faulk hauled the mail bag across the bustling base into the barracks of 3rd platoon, Charlie Company, 2nd Battalion. Everyone on base was packing. Cleaning weapons. Filling packs and pouches with combat loads.

'Mail call!' Andre announced just inside the door. That usually began a stampede.

'Sh-h-h!' he heard from the opposite end of a long corridor. A large group of men in camouflaged fatigues were clustered around an open door. All were intent and quiet.

Faulk dropped the bag and slowly approached the gathering. He passed rooms in various states of disorder. New Arctic gear lay piled on bunks. The closer he got to the end of the hall, the louder the wavering whine of the radio grew.

Andre stood on his tiptoes to look over the shoulders of the silent men. A soldier sat on his bunk and leaned over a field radio. His hand constantly tuned the frequency knob. A distant voice pierced random white noise. It was so distorted he could make out nothing. But as Andre listened, the signal rapidly grew stronger. The voice grew louder and sharper. The words were being shouted, Andre realized.

'. . . zero niner niner Echo! Fire for effect! I say again, fire . . .' The signal strength waned.

A new voice cut through – much clearer than the first. 'Negative, negative, November Echo Seven Two. This is Bravo India Three Niner. That grid coordinate is friendly – I say again *friendly* – unit position. I countermand that fire order. Over.'

Next came a vehement string of unrecognizable electromagnetic squeals. They were clearly shouts from the unit calling for fire. Again the signal strength grew. The desperate voice was warped into a drifting howl. '. . . left! They're a-a-all gone – all gone! The Chinese are pouring through their position right at u-u-us! Fire for effect! Fi-i-ire for e-e-effect!'

'Charlie Foxtrot Seven Seven?' came the much louder voice of the fire controller. 'Can you confirm that grid coordinate has been overrun, over?'

The signal was dying out. Swallowed by the distance. 'Fire for effect! Fire for effect!' shouted the fading man.

'Charlie Foxtrot Seven Seven, do you read, over?' There was no response. 'Charlie Foxtrot, *do you read*, over?' Again nothing. Through the swirling electronic noise they heard, 'Charlie Foxtrot Seven Seven, fire for effect at last coordinates.' They couldn't understand the garbled response. But the fire controller could. 'Fire for effect, Goddamnit! On my authority! Out!'

The sign-off broke the spell cast over the room. The radio fell silent with a click. It was an ordinary field radio carried on a backpack. Like the one the man screaming for fire was probably using. People began to clear out.

'Weird atmospherics,' someone muttered on passing Andre.

Andre grabbed the man by the arm. 'Who was that?'

'I dunno,' he said. 'Somebody in the shit.'

'It's the 25th,' another man said.

Men edged past Andre, who sagged against the wall.

'Hey, man? You gonna hand out the mail?' someone yelled from down the hall.

Andre couldn't move. *Stempel's in the 25th*. He shook his head. *No*. Stempel was back in Hawaii. Or still on some ship with his parents. He headed down the hall to the mail bag. But still he couldn't shake the unsettling feeling. If it wasn't Stempel, it was somebody else. It was thousands of people just like him. All in the shit. The deep, deep shit.

'Are you gonna hand out the fuckin' mail or what?' one of the soldiers said, reaching for Andre's bag.

'Hey-hey-*hey!*' Andre warned. He jerked the bag out of his reach. There were complaints from all around. Andre smiled. 'Now this *is* 3rd platoon, Charlie Company, 2nd Battalion, ain't it?'

'Come on, fuckhead!'

'*Wait*, now. We in the Postal Detachment got us a pro-*cedure!*' He reached into the bag and pulled out the stack of envelopes and small packages. All were battered and crushed. Two thick rubber bands held everything together. Andre cleared his throat theatrically, again rousing the men's obscenities. 'Is there an "Aguire" here?'

245

'Yo!'

Andre tossed him his letter. 'Okay,' he said, intentionally taking his time. He fended off an impatient grab at the mail. It was the same every day. He cleared his throat again. 'How about an "Alvarez"?' Alvarez got his package. 'So far, so good,' Andre continued. He held the next letter up as if he were farsighted. 'Next we got us a "Be-", "Bej-" . . . Jesus Christ!'

'Bejgrowicz!' several shouted all at once. One man grabbed the letter and tossed it high into the air. Bejgrowicz went to retrieve it. Thus it went until 'Wolfson' walked away with the padded envelope which clearly held a videotape. Nearly half of 3rd Platoon, Charlie Company, 2nd Battalion were still waiting to see if something had been sorted out of alphabetical order.

AMUR RIVER, RUSSO-CHINESE BORDER
January 26, 1400 GMT (0400 Local)

Every day since NATO first attacked China, Lieutenant Chin had heard the distant rumble. For the first hour or two, he had looked for storm clouds. Chin didn't remember the exact moment that he realized what the deep drumbeats really were. He just remembered the feeling. The sinking sensation from somewhere inside. Like when he feared he'd caught leprosy during an outbreak in his province. It had turned out to be a rash, but until the fear had been dispelled by a visiting doctor it had eaten away at him like a psychological rot.

It wasn't fear. It was melancholy. The thunder of the NATO bombing was fate. It was drawing nearer to him, and he to it.

At the top of the last ridge he finally saw it. The River of the Black Dragon. He knew it was their destination even though they'd been told nothing. They climbed down from the trucks. The road that descended to the riverbank was clogged with burned-out hulks of trucks. More trucks would meet them on the far side of the river, they were told. Chin and his platoon headed down. The river snaked through the hills. They followed its track with their eyes in silence.

The bank was rocky. The river was frozen solid. Men traversed it in long lines of tiny specks. Chin stepped out onto the flat surface. His platoon trailed single file. There were at least half a dozen such columns visible before the twists of the river bent the ivory highway beyond sight.

Chin was nearly halfway across when he saw the first wounded men. One helped the other as they limped to the south. The taller man leaned on a long, crooked branch. His leg was wrapped in bloody bandages. His shorter comrade's bandages covered his face and head. His arm rested on his buddy's shoulder. Their progress was slow, but it had purpose. It was homeward bound.

Chin passed the lucky pair. Their faces were drawn and pallid. They were surely in no mood to accept the congratulations of Chin – a healthy man. Perhaps they wouldn't even understand why he would congratulate them.

But Chin understood. He'd understood for days. Ever since he first heard the rumble. When they reached the Russian side of the river, there were no trucks.

KHABAROVSK, SIBERIA
January 26, 0730 GMT (1730 Local)

Nate Clark stood before a bank of radios. But he was too exhausted to remain there any longer. They still couldn't raise the 2/263.

He stumbled through the busy room. He passed men and women from various nations without seeing them. He sank heavily into his chair. His head, his limbs – they seemed heavy. Like he was on the surface of a huge planet.

Clark picked up the telephone. 'Get me General Dekker.' He waited through a series of clicks and hisses – ever more distant connections. The telecommunications net patched him into the Pentagon some seconds later.

'Nate?' Dekker said. No words came out. 'General Clark? Are you there?'

'I'm here, Ed. I got some bad news.' He took a deep breath. 'Second Battalion, 263rd Infantry Regiment's been overrun by the Chinese.'

'How bad are the casualties?'

Clark closed his eyes. 'I said they were overrun, Ed. They met and engaged advancing Chinese infantry from hastily prepared positions.

They were overrun as were their rear areas. Brigadier General Merrill
– commander of the 2nd Brigade – needed a screening force to buy
him time to organize defenses around the airbase at Birobidzhan. The
2nd of the 263rd was that screen.'

'Oh, God, Nate,' Dekker said. '*Squads* disappear without a trace,
Nate! Sometimes *platoons!* But never an entire *battalion*, for Christ's
sake! And you're tellin' me Merrill just sacrificed five hundred
Goddamn *GIs*?'

'I don't know, sir. But are you ready for the rest?' Dekker said
nothing. 'We're not going to be able to withdraw Merrill's brigade
from Birobidzhan to Khabarovsk. The road was cut by Chinese who'd
infiltrated undetected to set up blocking positions.'

'Can't they push on through?' Dekker asked. 'What's the Chinese
strength?'

'We don't know. We got only sporadic radio reports from some of
the transportation units that were ambushed. Aerial recon shows over
a hundred vehicles – mostly trucks – destroyed and burning on the
road with no sign of their crews.'

'Jesus Christ,' Dekker muttered. 'This is a disaster of the first
magnitude.'

'General Merrill had three battalions at Birobidzhan,' Nate continued. 'On my orders he was packed up to leave. All their supplies
were sitting in crates and pallets on the side of the runway. One mortar
round would've set 'em off. They would've been reduced to what they
were humping in their *field* packs. Merrill had a fourth battalion that
was inbound. It was diverted to a road about twelve clicks to the
south. I don't know what expectations he had about that battalion,
Ed. But they've already fended off three major tries at the airbase's
perimeter. They lost a C-130 *with* crew on the ground to a Goddamn
RPG. That battalion bought them a few hours. If they make it, those
few hours could be the difference. There's no way they'd have gotten
their defenses organized if the Chinese hadn't been slowed. But I'll
know more when I get over to Birobidzhan later tonight.'

'When you do *what*? Oh, no you're not, general. You can't get
yourself tied up in a brigade-level action like that. The damn airbase is
surrounded! Do you know what the propaganda value of your capture
or death would be to the Chinese? That's one of the most selfish acts
I've ever heard proposed. What's gotten into you, Nate?'

Clark's head was spinning from lack of sleep. 'Goddamnit, Ed. What the hell use am I here? I don't have the horses to fight this war. I might as well grab a fuckin' M-16 and lend a hand.'

'Nate, you get your shit together, that's an order. I'll bust your ass right outta the Army if you crap out on me like this. As it stands now, there are gonna be some long Goddamned knives out when word of this massacre gets around.' Clark rubbed his sore eyes. Through blurred vision he saw Major Reed holding a message slip. Clark wiggled his fingers and held out his hand. It was a short message. 'I might be able to limit the damage to Merrill. But any more debacles like this and they may stick *my* head on the White House gate.'

'Merrill's dead.'

Dekker's reply was abnormally delayed. 'Say again.'

Clark read, '"General Merrill killed in action by sniper fire."' His voice trailed off. 'So . . .' He had nothing more to say.

After they signed off, Clark tossed the crumpled message in the trash. He looked at the papers on his desk. He'd read them all hours before. The maps were unchanged. He rocked his chair forward and back and forward. He fished all of the pens and pencils from his desk and lined them up for quick access.

Reed appeared. 'Did you tell General Dekker?' he asked.

Clark nodded. 'Get me a helicopter,' he said.

'Birobidzhan?' Reed asked. Another nod. 'May I go?'

SOUTH OF BIROBIDZHAN, SIBERIA
January 26, 0800 GMT (1800 Local)

Stempel was lying in a shallow, snowy grave. He'd carefully rummaged through his pockets, still holding his grenade. He'd been looking for the candy bar they'd handed out. He'd found instead the plastic lei hung around his neck in Hawaii. He dug deeper. The credit card his father had given him before boot camp. *If you ever get into any trouble*, he'd said, *any trouble at all – this card will get you out.*

He lay under two dead bodies. He was covered in their blood and gore. He didn't know where he was. He was all alone. He was waiting to die. How long it would take he had no idea. Water, you need water. You'd die in four days, he'd once read, without water. He then spent a while trying to decide whether the cold would kill him first.

He'd heard nothing for a long time. Before that . . . He jammed his eyes shut. He held in the scream of mental pain. He ground his teeth. He forced the images from his mind by mere negation. *No, no, no, no, no!* was his mantra. It had a remarkably soothing effect. It calmed him. He could again coolly contemplate his demise.

The shallow hiss of his breathing was the only sound. The trees overhead were growing dark. With surprising urgency the need to act – to move – came over him. He had to force himself to remain still. Will himself not to sit bolt upright and peer at the landscape around him.

Slowly, he raised his arm and looked at the black sports watch he wore outside his sleeve. '*This is Siberia!*' the platoon sergeant had shouted on exiting the transport plane. 'Local time is fourteen fifty hours – one four five zero!' That was all Stempel knew of the world into which he'd been deposited. His rough position on a continent, and the correct local time.

Which was now eighteen hundred hours. He shook his head and lay back. Three hours since . . . A lifetime. A huge cloud billowed out of his mouth. He exhaled again to test the phenomenon. It seemed as if the entire contents of his lungs turned white. He didn't remember that from before. There had been the typical fogging of his breath, but not a thick cloud. He tried one more time, with a similar result.

It was growing dark, and the temperature was dropping. He swallowed, but his mouth was bone dry. 'The canteens'll freeze if you don't keep 'em close to yer bodies!' the platoon sergeant had shouted. Harold was thirsty. Their platoon's only drinking water was kept warm by body heat. All their canteens would be freezing soon. The cold, calculating part of his brain returned to work. He had a canteen. But it wouldn't last long. He could rummage through the gear of the others . . .

The conscious, feeling part of his brain came alive unexpectedly. Stempel had grown accustomed to the weight pressing down on his body. But they were corpses – the sergeant and the PFC. He began to wriggle out from under them reflexively. With his first movement – the first shifting of their weight – the sense of revulsion rose to unmanageable proportions. The workmanlike rise became panicked flight.

Grunts and gasps escaped Stempel's mouth with whining cries. He climbed out of the hole and lay on his back . . . fully exposed.

All around him lay the detritus of war. Still. Lifeless. Chinese dead were strewn about the forest floor in great numbers. But it was the American dead that sent Stempel into shock. He had known, of course, that they were all dead. He had heard them die. The pleas of surrendering men. The merciless executions. Rifle shots in hole after hole . . . coming closer. The flaming muzzle. The gore that oozed from the corpses' new wounds. But seeing them there – half naked in the snow – just about sent him back into his hole. The Chinese had stripped most of them right down to their underwear. The sight of men lying bare-skinned in the snow was appalling. 'Oh, God,' he said. He looked up at the sky. An arm – severed at the shoulder – hung from a branch.

If I leave here, he realized, *they'll never find my body*. The Army would send people after the war. If he walked even a short distance away from the battlefield he'd forever be 'Missing In Action.' He'd never have a funeral. Or a grave where his mother could come and be with him.

'Hey!' he heard. He jerked his head around. A man in snowy white Arctic gear crouched beside a tree. There were others – also in uniform – vaguely visible in the snow. All had rifles raised.

I'm alive, Harold thought as he climbed to his feet. He began a slow run toward the men through deep drifts. When he noticed the man's strenuous gestures he stopped in confusion. The man was motioning for him to get down. Harold plopped onto the snow. He didn't take his eyes off the others. He'd never let them out of his sight.

Slowly, cautiously, the man made his way toward Stempel. He advanced a few steps at a time, then dropped. His head was on a swivel. He looked in every direction before continuing on. With a great crunching through the crust that had formed, he dropped next to Stempel – out of breath.

He looked Stempel over. 'Are you hit?' he asked. Stempel shook his head. His eyes roamed the woods again. 'You heard anything?' he whispered. Great puffs of smoke emanated from his mouth.

'Not in a while,' Stempel replied. The man was a sergeant, Stempel saw from the three chevrons on the front of his helmet.

'Anybody else in your area make it?' Stempel shook his head. He girded himself for the next question – *Why aren't you dead?* 'Okay, you fall in with us. *No noise!*' he whispered through clenched teeth. They rose. Stempel's white parka was drenched in blood. The deep brownish-red was almost black. His dirty secret was clear for all to see.

251

'Where's your weapon?' the sergeant asked. Stempel felt tears well up in his eyes. 'Never mind,' the sergeant said. 'There's gear lyin' around. We'll scrounge one up.'

Stempel followed the man and joined the others. Sure enough, they found the battlefield rich in equipment. The unit had been fresh from barracks, and each man had carried a full load. The Chinese must have been in a hurry. Some of the bodies were picked clean. But others still wore full existence loads in blood-splattered packs and pouches.

They scavenged everything they needed, and finally found the most prized possession of all. Beside a fighting hole, one of Stempel's new comrades reached down into the snow. He pulled up the black barrel of an M-16. Like a paleontologist, he carefully brushed away the snow and ice. Stempel watched as the man looked the weapon over. Satisfied, he handed the rifle to Stempel.

Stempel made no sound. He gave no outward sign. But inwardly, silently, where it counts, he vowed he would never put the weapon down. He would die with it pressed firmly into his shoulder. He would raise his head up into the storm. *Just like the PFC and the sergeant*, he told himself. *Just like the PFC and the sergeant.*

VLADIVOSTOK, SIBERIA
January 26, 0930 GMT (1930 Local)

'This is the most stupid idea you've ever had,' Kate whispered to Woody. They sat huddled together at a table in the center of the dark barroom. Gold-toothed Russians and a smattering of rough-looking foreign oil workers occupied all the other tables. They sat there staring at Kate – the only woman not working the place – and getting more and more drunk.

Woody slammed down a shot of vodka with a backward toss of his head. The fifty-dollar bottle had been their price of admission to the bar. He exhaled, winced, and wiped his lips with his hand. 'Nope,' he replied. 'The *stupidest* idea was to try to *sneak* our way up to the front.'

'But the army hasn't taken the press pool anywhere *near* the fighting, Woody,' she whispered.

'Yeah, well, did you ever think there might be a *reason* for that?'

Kate rocked back against the huge, thick Russian fur that she'd draped over the back of the chair. It made her look more like a bear than a fashion model, but it was warm. It also stank. 'I can't believe *you*, of all people, would kowtow to the military like that.' Woody poured another shot and threw it back. 'Don't you think you've had enough to drink?' Kate asked. Woody was the veteran at these things – her navigator through a dangerous world. They had bought a dilapidated Russian car for a hundred bucks from a former officer in the Russian army. Woody had smoked a joint as thick as her thumb on their drive through town in search of the seediest bar in Russia. Now he downed vodka like it was water.

'Actually,' he said – pouring another shot in the dirty glass – 'I have not yet begun to drink.'

He raised the glass to his lips, but Kate's hand pressed his wrist firmly down. 'Woody, please,' she whispered. He sniffed loudly, but left the glass on the table.

Ascending the staircase behind Woody was a hairy, pot-bellied Russian. He grinned lasciviously at two women. His hand firmly grasped their pudgy rears. He kissed one with a disgusting, sloppily open mouth. Kate winced and looked away as the other woman reached to rub crudely at his fly.

'So,' Woody said in an argumentative tone, 'you want to get to the *front*, as you call it. *I* happen to call it the onrushing Chinese *army*. But let's just use the word "front" for the sake of convenience. Now, the suits at NBC News say they can't get permission through the Pentagon. *And*, you might have noticed, they pointedly did *not* exactly *send* us there. Why do you think there were so many lawyers on the speakerphone? Why'd they use such hyper-careful language when you told them about getting up to the action? They were doing some fast legal maneuvering – that's why – so they don't get sued by our heirs when we get our butts killed.'

'Come on, Woody. Watergate was a long time ago. Give it a rest, okay?'

Woody giggled. 'Okay. Paranoia. Fine.' He sniffed again. 'The Army says it's too dangerous.'

'Well, that's just bullshit!' she replied. She looked around. Everywhere men tried to catch her eye. Brutish men, unshaven and unclean, with bad teeth. 'They're just saying that,' she continued in a whisper, 'because they must have something to *hide*. They screwed something up. Now, they're trying to *cover* it up.'

'Who's spinning conspiracy theories now?' He had slumped down into his chair. He looked tired.

'What is it with you?' she asked.

'Nothing,' he replied, but she pressed him. 'Look!' he finally snapped. 'I think it's a fucking *stupid* idea. This isn't the bush leagues, Katie, it's the big show. People die. All the time. The camera and the official U.N.-accredited press badges don't *stop* bullets!'

'I *know* that, Woody! I know it's a dangerous job. But it's a job that *I'm* still trying to *do!*'

Her last jibe deflated him. He was slumped even lower than before. A door beside the bar opened. The noise of a tiny, smoke-filled casino poured in. There was no law any more. No police. The British patrolled the streets. They occasionally responded to impassioned pleas for help from foreigners or from Russians who spoke English. Most of the British soldiers, however, trod warily down both sides of darkened streets. Armored cars rolled down the middle at foot pace. The last man in each file of troops periodically spun around to walk backwards a step or two – the 'Ulster twist.'

'If we can't get there officially,' Kate said – repeating her earlier logic – 'then places like this are the best for making alternate arrangements.'

The door to the street opened. Everyone in the bar fell quiet and looked attentively at the new arrival. It was yet another natural resource of Siberia that seemed in virtually inexhaustible supply – scary-looking men. The bar's patrons resumed their silent drinking. They accepted the presumably suitable newcomer into their fold. When the bartender pointed at Kate and Woody, however, Kate grew frightened. 'This is who we were *waiting* for?' she whispered – incredulous.

'The bartender said he could help us,' Woody replied.

The man pulled up a chair from the table next to them. He turned it around and straddled it – seated backwards. His hands rested on the high wood back. His chin rested on his hands. He let out a noisy gush of air through his nostrils like a beast of burden. He looked at Woody briefly. Then he ran his bloodshot eyes over Kate from toe to head – especially at points in between. The certainly large but otherwise indeterminable contours of the man's body were hidden from view by a fur coat. Its rough quality made Kate's look like it was straight off a hanger at Saks. He even smelled like a mastodon – completing the image in Kate's mind.

He turned to Woody after finishing his inventory of Kate. 'Speak

English?' he asked in a thick Russian accent. Woody nodded. 'American?' Woody nodded again. 'You want to go places?'

'We want to go to the front,' Kate said.

The man turned to her. His beard thinned raggedly at the tops of his cheeks revealing pock-marked skin every bit as red as his eyes. He didn't *grow* the beard, Kate thought. He simply never shaved.

'Hah!' he belched. It took Kate a moment to realize he'd laughed. The man rose at the same lethargic speed with which he had sat. He was easily three feet across at his widest point, Kate thought. He leaned over the table – eclipsing the long bar with its row of stools. He picked up Woody's shot glass and threw the vodka back just as Woody had done. He shook the glass to drain every drop into his open and waiting mouth. His thick tongue darted inside the glass like a frog. Kate cringed. Woody stared up at him. He didn't seem scared of the man. He appeared more in awe, the way humans tend to be on seeing wonders of the animal kingdom.

The woolly beast ambled away.

Woody raised the bottle of vodka and took a swig. His face contorted in pain. A shudder rippled down from his head to his shoulders. 'I don't think he wants to go to the front, Katie.' He wiped his mouth with the back of his hand. 'Too damn bad!' He was beginning to slur. '*Pro*-bably a *pos*-thumous *Puh*-ulitzer *Puh*-rize, too!' His stupid grin threatened to crack open his chapped face.

MOSCOW, RUSSIA
January 17, 0600 GMT (0800 Local)

'Schedule A,' Valentin Kartsev said. 'Next?'

'Victor Afanaseyev,' the young aide read in a matter-of-fact tone. Their limousine raced down the center lane of the broad boulevard. 'He snorted, kind of like a laugh, when Program 412B was mentioned at a dinner party.'

'What Program is that?'

'The aborted plan to retrain steel workers for the lumber industry.'

'Oh,' Kartsev chuckled. Through the curtains he could see lines of people waiting for something – patient as always. *Food*, he guessed.

'That one was a real fiasco,' Kartsev said. *Who would've guessed that steelworkers didn't want to be lumberjacks?*

The aide waited – staring at him. It made Kartsev highly uncomfortable. He loathed the dreary administrative work, but especially this. 'Schedule A. Next?'

There was a second's pause before the young aide returned to his list. Kartsev kept his eyes on the man. Surely there was a better way.

'Lyudmila Vavarov,' the man read.

'Who is she?'

'She's a substitute secretary in the typing pool.' Kartsev shrugged, not recognizing the name. 'She was working on a sensitive typing job. Each secretary got a different page. She took hers up to hand it in, but she stopped and talked to another secretary. When she left the other secretary's desk, she picked up the sheet her friend had just finished typing. She said it was a mistake.'

'Did she have a chance to read it?'

The aide shrugged.

'What were they typing?'

'This report doesn't say.'

The young man's eyes now studied Kartsev. Kartsev stared back at him. The aide looked away. Kartsev made a mental note to consider computerizing this particular process. He really shouldn't risk so much contact with people anyway. And things would get worse before they got better.

'You know,' Kartsev said, 'power – the accumulation of power – is the ultimate achievement of man. Everything else – fame, fortune, political office – it's all just a means of attaining the real goal of all humans, which is power over others. The ultimate power is the power to make each and every human being do *what* you want, *when* you want it done. That requires a close attention to every detail and the willpower to act when you know in your heart what is necessary.'

His aide's eyes betrayed no hint of anything. Such was the extent of his fear of Kartsev . . . which was good. Kartsev lost interest and sighed. 'One more for Schedule A,' he said, feeling fatigued. *One more bullet to the back of the head.*

Chapter Twelve

BIROBIDZHAN AIR BASE, SIBERIA
January 27, 0900 GMT (1900 Local)

Clark watched their approach through the windshield of the Blackhawk helicopter. Night was falling slowly. But even in the waning light he saw the ring of smoke that rose around the airbase. Guns on both sides contributed to the haze that defined the perimeter defenses. But most of the fires were from the massive, round-the-clock air raids. They churned the earth just beyond the last string of wire.

Clark stood braced in a wide stance. Trees slid under the helicopter's belly at astonishing speed. He gripped the crew's seats as they weaved to avoid small arms fire. The corridor down which they flew was particularly smoky. The area had been marked for intense 'preparation' like a single spoke from the wheel of the airbase. All the traffic to and from the besieged base would fly down that corridor. In a couple of hours, they'd prepare another spoke.

Choppers headed in with special forces. They were Clark's only ready reserve. The same choppers headed outbound filled with wounded. Clark had seen casualties unloaded before he and the dozen Green Berets climbed aboard.

Out of the upper left-hand corner of the windshield roared an inbound C-130. Painted white, the transport plane blotted out the sky momentarily. It passed close overhead. The turbulence buffeted the smaller helicopter. Clark watched a massive parachute blossom behind the transport. It pulled a pallet down the open rear ramp. Securely strapped crates fell twenty feet to the ground. They burst open and scattered their contents over the near end of the runway.

Clark was momentarily distracted by a single clang. A bullet struck somewhere in back. When he looked back, the C-130 was practically scraping the runway's pavement. Parachute after parachute popped open. The pallets now had less than ten feet to fall. They skidded to a halt – braked by the parachute and the friction. It was a race – prodigious rates of fire versus mammoth payloads. Maybe three thousand men and women firing their weapons more or less continuously. It was the greatest test the U.S. Air Mobility Command had ever faced.

The helicopter neared the base perimeter. It was a scarred zone of felled trees and thick black smoke. A barrage of orange flame boiled from the trees. Streaking tracers lit the growing darkness. It was remarkable, ferocious fighting. There must have been an attack under way that very moment. Several more bullets clanged off the helicopter. Clark turned to look into the crowded but still cabin. He remembered the flailing arms of a man swatting at the burning tracer in his body like at a bee. The coughing splutter from the old Huey's single engine.

They burst out over the airbase and dropped still lower. The Blackhawk banked steeply. Clark feared their rotors would strike the earth. Clark's knees buckled. The nose rose. The G-forces ended with a jarring thud. The landing threw Clark forward. Pain shot through his ribs. When he tried to breathe he could draw no air. Pain spread hot fingers across his chest. He couldn't straighten up.

The side door slid open behind Clark. The roar of the rotors' downblast poured in. The engines still whined at high pitch. Reed helped him stumble to the door. The cabin was empty. The first litter was being loaded aboard. On it was a man covered in bloody bandages. Clark leapt to the ground. A searing jolt of pain nearly felled him. The Green Berets with whom he'd arrived reached up for him. He fell heavily to the ground.

Tiny holes appeared out of nowhere in the helicopter's fuselage. Sprays of glass exploded from its windshield. It was slow, methodical sniper fire. It was unreal. The noise from churning rotors masked the sounds of the bullets' impacts. The pilots sat motionless at their controls. They were fully exposed inside their plexiglass canopy. They watched the loading of their increasingly bullet-riddled aircraft. Clark imagined their tremendous anxiety. Their desire to get airborne. To pitch and weave their vehicle as taught. But they sat there . . . waiting.

The helicopter lurched into the air. A man standing just inside was almost thrown to the ground. The aircraft headed back into the wall of smoke from whence they'd come.

Clark now heard the full roar of the massive firefight. The popping, bursting, crackling noise came from every direction. He heard also the tell-tale splitting sounds of bullets through air. The twelve-man Special Forces team was spread out in a rough semicircle. Their weapons were raised to their shoulders. Two female medics lay inside the tiny perimeter. So did Clark's group of two officers and two riflemen. All were volunteers.

The first Green Berets rose to rush toward the piles of sandbags around nearby artillery emplacements. Bullets cut through the air overhead. The two soldiers dropped, but appeared unharmed.

'That sniper's got us zeroed in!' Major Reed shouted. But there was nothing they could do to fight back. That was the frustrating thing about snipers. Clark remembered the afternoon he'd spent hugging the embankment of a rice paddy. He'd been soaked waist-high in muddy water. His entire forty-man platoon had been pinned down by a lone man with a bolt-action rifle.

But this war was different. You had no choice but to take your chances. No choice but to accept casualties. 'All right, listen up!' Clark shouted. 'We'll all make a run for it at the same time!' The effort sent sharp stabs of pain through his torso.

The Captain who commanded the special forces A Team counted down.

Everyone rose at once and began their labored run toward the sandbags. The Green Berets weaved this way and that. But Clark knew it was wasted effort. At extreme distance, snipers aimed only at the area. It was luck – the law of averages – on which they counted. Since snipers had a slow rate of fire, going all at once would lessen the number of shots he'd get off.

Each time Clark's boots hit the hard earth, pain shot through his side. He'd busted a rib, he knew it. His anger at himself made him momentarily forget the sniper. The singing 'z-z-z-i-p' by his left ear, however, refocused his attention. He ran straight toward the booming artillery pieces as fast as he could. The others ran faster. It wasn't just that Nate couldn't draw a deep breath. He felt like an old man.

They all made it safely to the cover of the sandbagged walls. Every few seconds the self-propelled 155-mm gun fired – its barrel at maximum elevation. The high-angle fire meant the Chinese were close. The guns were firing at their shortest possible range.

An artilleryman led them to the brigade command post. The Green Berets were all sent to the most critical sector of the defenses. Stairs made of railroad ties led down into an enormous mound of sandbags. The snow covering it was blackened and pitted from mortars. The last vestiges of what must have been camouflage netting hung in tatters from poles and spreaders.

Inside he found a wounded colonel – Brigadier General Merrill's successor in command. He was sitting at an awkward angle – leaning against a large map table over which hung the best light in the bunker. He was in too much pain to answer Clark's questions coherently. Clark understood, however, that Merrill had led two battalions out to try to reinforce the 2/263rd. But they'd been hit hard on the way. They'd barely fought their way back to the base. Merrill was dead.

It was a quiet story given by a man in great agony. Clark had seen it before. Pain had turned him pasty. Nauseous. Sweaty. He ordered the man to the aid station. The colonel didn't have the energy to argue.

Clark looked up to see that everyone at brigade headquarters was staring at him. Bare bulbs hung intermittently from the low ceiling by strings of wire. Clark removed his outer garments and gear. Reed at his side did the same. At least twenty people were crammed together amid banks of radios and tables with laptops. They lived in the perpetual darkness of the bunker.

'Call 'em to attention,' Clark said to Reed.

'Ten-*shun*!' Reed barked.

The weary men and women stood and straightened. Everyone but a radio operator. She stooped at her small table because the wire to her headphones was too short.

'Listen up!' Clark bellowed. 'My name is Lieutenant General Nate Clark! I am the commander of UNRUSFOR, USARPAC, and now – temporarily – 2nd Brigade, 25th Infantry Division!'

Clark was astounded at the sudden burst of applause and cheers. Paper

260

flew into the air like confetti. When he saw the genuine excitement on their faces, however, he realized instantly what it was. It was a lesson he'd learned long before – first in books, then in the field. It was a lesson he now learned anew as he watched the suddenly energized soldiers await their first orders.

'*You can't lead from the rear*,' Clark remembered, then went to work.

The brigade staff was gathering. Clark and Reed pored over unit markings on the map – Reed whispered comments and rough headcounts. When all were present, Clark shook their hands briskly.

'All right,' Nate said before he'd even finished shaking hands. 'Our objective' – he turned to the map – 'is to defend as large a piece of ground as possible with limited resources against an unimaginably large enemy force. That means we're going to have to consolidate our position. Tighten our perimeter. Give *up* ground we want and are fighting to hold right now. Ground we'll have to take back in a week at heavy cost to be able to operate this airfield.'

He paused. Not to invite comment. But to get them to think. To consider their situation. He picked up a blue pencil and drew a circle around the cleared airfield. Its radius was about two kilometers. It was well inside the sagging lines of their current heavily dented perimeter.

'Even after the consolidation, we still won't have enough people to man a continuous defensive perimeter. So I want an intelligence assessment by twenty-four hundred hours telling me what the most likely Chinese objectives are. We'll defend those, and cover the undefended areas with artillery fire only. That means our lines are going to be porous. Chinese sappers, stragglers, even whole units are going to get through. So I want all the service and support units in the rear to put pickets out at night. They'll also need to form provisional infantry platoons to sweep designated sectors clear of infiltrators after every attack. And if the Chinese get through the lines in force, they'll have to defend their own positions against direct assault. And since we've given up these dominating heights around the airfield,' he said – drawing red 'Xs' on three hills – 'we'll be under direct fire from those hills round the clock.' They all stared down at the 'Xs'. 'So I want those hills under air and artillery attack round the clock, too. I want every Chinese soldier up there either heads-down or killed-in-action.'

The enthusiasm they'd shown upon his arrival was gone.

'We'll *also* have to draft men from the service and support units for infantry fillers,' Nate continued. 'We'll form them into provisional infantry companies. We need at least one infantry battalion as the brigade reserve. We can add line crossers from units out in the field who make it back inside the perimeter.

'The provisionals in the brigade reserve will counterattack to plug breaches. They'll go three ways as three separate companies, or all together against one point of attack – whichever I say.'

No one seemed particularly happy with Clark's plan. A lieutenant colonel – the operations officer – was the first of his staff to speak up. 'Sir . . . those provisionals are clerks and cooks and mechanics, not infantrymen. They can clear out a few holes. But to maneuver against an enemy under fire they need time to organize.'

'They're soldiers, colonel. They wear the same uniform as you and I.'

'Just keep their tactics simple,' Reed jumped in. 'Nothing complicated. Just single-line, massed frontal assaults for sweeping operations.' He turned to Clark. 'I could put the battalion together,' he said.

And command it, he knew Reed to be proposing. But it would be an awful job. Clark worried that losing so many men might ruin him. You'd never convince him it wasn't his fault . . . if he lived.

But Reed was good. Those men deserved him. Clark nodded. 'Take off,' he said.

Reed flew out the door still climbing into his parka.

The group waited for Clark, who still stared at the exit. When he turned back, he said, 'Okay. What's our current fire support plan?'

The operations officer pointed at the artillery symbols – hand-drawn rectangular boxes with a single cannon ball in the center. 'We've got a collection of about three battalion-strength artillery units. They're all firing 155s, which helps with supply. One is American, one British, and one French. They're each covering the areas defended by their nation's contingents.'

'Who directs them?'

'They're under the control of the three different commands.'

Clark stood upright. 'You mean to tell me their fire control isn't integrated?'

'We didn't want forward observers controlling fire-direction centers they hadn't worked with. Plus, there's the language barrier. And the different national commanders all wanted their own people available to *them* in case . . .'

'And *un*available to everybody *else*!' Clark exploded. He tried to rein his temper in. But it was a critical mistake. He was sure men were dying – right at that moment – because of it. 'I want centralized fire direction. I want a single, integrated fire plan for every mortar, rocket, and artillery tube on this base. I want to be able to lay pre-registered fire – from *every* gun on this base – *wherever* the Chinese mass for an attack. But only *I* will have authority to release all *three* battalions' guns to a single forward observer.' He leaned out into the light. His hands pressed heavily on the table. 'We *own* the terrain inside those guns' ranges. They will *stop* the Chinese – *dead* in their tracks – if used properly. If used *intensely*. If *concentrated*. Search and traverse – box patterns – poured out as fast as those crews can cycle their guns. *Forget* what happened with the 2/263rd. Those guns will cut exposed infantry down. They'll *butcher* them. It can be *made* to work. It *has* to be made to work . . . if we're gonna hold this base.'

He gave his staff the opportunity to tell him that it couldn't be done. No one took that opportunity. If they had, Nate would have quietly taken him aside and reassigned him to different duties.

'Do we have any Firefinder radars?' Clark asked.

'They're packed up and ready to move out,' replied his chastened operations officer.

'Unpack them. I want counterbattery fire laid against any guns before they get off a second shot.' Clark looked down at the map. 'Now, why is this artillery unit here,' he said – pointing – 'deployed so close to the perimeter?'

'They're still providing fire support for units strung out along the road to Khabarovsk. Those units are at the extremity of the guns' ranges, sir. If we pull them back, they won't be able to support . . .'

'Pull them back, colonel,' Clark said. He got looks that verged on contempt. Clark resented it. They didn't have to make the hard decisions. 'I'll authorize all the unrecoverable units to surrender. We can't risk those tubes that far forward. Pull them back safely inside the perimeter.' He ran his finger back and forth across the map. 'And make some sense of these deployments. If it takes moving gun emplacements, then move them. If it takes blasting and bulldozing new positions for every last gun, then do that. I want those guns protected, and rationally dispersed. I want them interlocked and capable of responding to calls from every fire-direction center on this base no matter what nationality. And I want it by twenty-four hundred hours.'

Their faces were set in grim masks.

'Now, do we have an inventory of exactly who is on this base?' Clark asked.

'Not exactly, no, sir,' the operations officer replied. 'We've spent the last forty-eight hours collecting units from smaller firebases all around. We were also a transit point for units moving down the road to Khabarovsk before it was cut. Some units we thought were here had already headed on toward Khabarovsk. Others we thought were gone fought their way back down the road to us. There are plenty of others I'm sure we don't know about – bits and pieces, some of them smashed, from a half-dozen different nationalities.'

'I want an inventory by twenty-four hundred,' Clark ordered.

The man nodded.

'And I want everyone else digging,' Clark said.

At first it was if they hadn't heard him.

'*Digging*,' he repeated. 'Get engineers to blow the topsoil with shaped charges. You'll be amazed how good an entrencher men with long-handled shovels can be. Men properly organized. Well led . . . by *you*.' He had their attention now. 'You *structure* their lives for them. They'll be getting no sleep, so their minds will be mush. We will do their thinking *for* them. We tell them *what* to do. *When* to do it. *How* to do it. We'll *motivate* them to keep going. Give them a direction to head in – an objective. And if that objective is directly related to holding this base . . . you've done your job. And they have done theirs. *That's* all they want out of you right now. That's all you can ask of them.'

'Should we . . .' the operations officer began, then shrugged. 'Pass any words of encouragement down to the troops?'

'You tell them we're going to hold for the night. Then tomorrow you tell them again. And the next day – again. If they haven't taken us in three days, they never will.' Clark looked each of them in the eye, then straightened. 'Twenty-five percent strength in fighting positions till dusk. All patrols in before dark. Starting at dusk, I want automatic weapons moved to alternate weapons pits and test-fired every hour to prevent freezing. We go to fifty percent strength on the line from dusk till twenty-two hundred hours. Seventy-five percent till oh four hundred. Then one hundred percent through the dawn attacks.

Afterwards, we'll send out patrols – *combat* patrols. We'll take the fight to the enemy. It'll police the battlefield. It'll keep the Chinese from digging in within small-arms' range of our lines. And it'll build morale. Everyone not on patrol or in their fighting posts . . . digs. Every day. Every night. Till I say stop.'

'Excuse me.' A soldier approached Clark in the brigade CP. He wore no insignia.

'Yes?' Clark replied.

'Can I have a few moments of your time?'

'Who are you?'

'Jim DeSilva, *Newsweek* magazine.'

Clark chuckled. 'Boy, what'd you do to get this assignment? Hit on your editor's daughter?' The journalist laughed. 'And no, you can't have any of my time. Check with me after the war . . . if anybody gives a shit about what I have to say then.'

There was a stir at the entrance to the bunker. A small crowd gathered around a man in Arctic whites. A staffer led the man – a captain – up to Clark's small desk. Everyone wore grim faces.

The captain was carrying a white towel on a stick.

'Sir,' the haggard, unshaven man said. 'I've been sent as an intermediary from the Chinese. Captain Lawrence, sir. Bravo Company, 2/263rd.' Clark offered the man his seat and ordered hot food brought in on the double. 'I was captured when they overran us,' he said – his voice breaking. He licked his chapped lips and coughed. 'They're promising good treatment of prisoners and to turn the wounded over to friendly lines. But they're demanding the immediate surrender of Birobidzhan.'

The food was brought in on a metal mess tray. The captain ate it in huge bites.

'I want him debriefed,' Clark said to his S-2 – the brigade intelligence officer. 'Chinese troop strengths and deployments. Numbers of friendly prisoners of war. Names or descriptions of all he can remember.'

'Are you sending him back to the Chinese?' the S-2 asked in an incredulous tone.

The captain looked sick from stress, from exposure, from lack of sleep. Lawrence looked at the intelligence officer. 'They'll kill men if I don't go back. They've got about thirty or so that I've seen.'

'You go on back,' Clark said. The man nodded. 'You can write a letter home, if you want, before you leave. We'll give you a list of units along the road to Khabarovsk that will surrender. You take it back to the Chinese' Clark turned to his operations officer. 'Tell those unit commanders to begin destroying their weapons once they've made contact with local Chinese commanders.' Clark turned back to the captain. 'And as for this base, you tell the Chinese that the only way they're gonna get it is to come in here and take it.' The captain raised his head to face Clark. 'Use whatever words you want, but you understand what I'm saying, don't you?'

Captain Lawrence nodded. He wrote a letter to his wife and children at Clark's desk, and then returned to Chinese lines with Clark's answer.

SOUTH OF BIROBIDZHAN, SIBERIA
January 27, 1245 GMT (2245 Local)

Stempel's small band had followed the sound of the fighting all through the night. Every time they'd stopped moving, numbness spread up his limbs from his extremities. Every time they had resumed their march, he'd regained some feeling . . . but not all.

At the only road they crossed, they saw Chinese. The sergeant – a pair of binoculars to his eyes – had said there were trucks being unloaded on the road's shoulder. It was dark, and they had crossed the road at a dead run – all together. The Chinese obviously had no night-vision goggles because the crossing had been uneventful. After that, however, their rate of progress toward the ever-increasing noise of battle slowed, and their caution grew. There had to be Chinese in the woods.

On one of their pauses they had watched while the flickering light of flares burst in the sky and fell, visible only briefly through the treetops. It sounded from the distance as if a giant fireworks factory had blown up and was slowly cooking off its wares. But the sounds of the fighting seemed never to diminish. They fell sometimes for several minutes, then grew again in just seconds to a fever pitch. The closer they got, the more awesome the sound became. The more frequently they looked at each other with significant arches of their brows – their only permitted manner of communication.

Stempel felt an odd kinship with the men. He had spoken only once – his first brief exchange with the sergeant. But he felt a bond with them that was hard to describe. He knew their ranks from the black plastic insignia mounted on the fronts of their helmets. They were mostly privates, like himself. But there were two PFCs, a Spec Three, and the sergeant. The names Stempel ascribed to them for personal reference began with those ranks. There was 'The Sergeant' and 'The Spec Three,' of course. Then 'The PFC With the Grenade Launcher' and 'The PFC Without the Grenade Launcher.' Next came 'The Large Black Private' and 'The Skinny Black Private.' 'The Private With the Bloody Face.' 'The Private With the Dead Radio.' And 'The Private With the Leg Wound,' who had to be helped along by two others on a rotating basis – one on each shoulder. The others Stempel had had no reason to name.

The Sergeant gathered everyone around as the night sky crackled. It was an unprecedented gathering. Stempel got the sense that something momentous loomed. When The Sergeant began to whisper to the huddled group, Stempel found it both unfamiliar and dangerous. He and the others kept looking around even though the volume of The Sergeant's voice was barely audible three feet away.

'That's the airbase,' he said – nodding toward the sound of the fighting. Stempel knew nothing about any airbase. The noise rose several decibels as a flight of jets roared in. A string of thudding explosions sounded in their wake. 'The fighting, too. We're gonna have to wait. It'll be light soon. We gotta spread out. Dig in. Don't mess the snow up. We want concealment, not cover.'

'What about our bootprints?' The Spec Three asked. 'If we stop here, they may lead the Chinks straight to us.'

'Shit,' The Sergeant replied. 'Okay, listen up. You know that little stream that we passed? It's iced over. There's not much snow on the ice. We'll double back. Keep to our old tracks. Then we'll head down the streambed a ways and dig in on the bank. Everybody okay with that?'

After a moment, one of the privates with no name said, 'I cain't feel my toes.' There was a depth of fear in his trembling voice that led Stempel to share his worry – both for the private with no name, and for his own numb extremities.

'There ain't nothin' we can do but git into that airbase,' The Sergeant replied. 'And we can't do that till the fightin' dies down. Now let's move out. It'll be sun-up soon.'

267

They all rose and began to follow the bootprints back toward the streambed. They took high, awkward steps. Their boots squeaked as they descended through the same holes in the snow as before. Someone grabbed Stempel's arm in the darkness. It was the private with no name from before. Stempel could see in the starlight that the man's brow was deeply furrowed. 'I cain't feel my toes!' he whispered. There was an angry shush from up front.

Stempel could only shrug. He tried to wear a sympathetic expression. He watched the man head on. His steps were even more awkward than the others. The guy's feet dropped down through the snow in an ungainly plop. Stempel wondered whether the problem wasn't worse than just numb toes. Thereafter, Stempel had a name for the man with the dark eyes and deep furrow in his brow. He became The Private Who Couldn't Feel His Feet.

BETHESDA NAVAL HOSPITAL, MARYLAND
January 27, 1430 GMT (0930 Local)

'How are you feeling this morning?' a smiling Elaine asked.

'I hurt all over,' Gordon said.

She kissed him – careful not to lean on the mattress. 'Do you need anything?'

'A new kidney. Maybe a new hip.'

'I mean painkillers. Do you want me to get you some?'

'Can't.' He took a deep breath and winced. Gordon didn't waste words any more. He only had about an hour per day of alertness. The rest of the time, he was either asleep or adrift in a sea of nausea and pain through which he wished he could sleep. Any more painkillers and he wouldn't be alert enough to listen to the five-minute updates on the war. The reports were almost universally bad. But they were so couched in bureaucratese that Gordon could only guess how bad the situation really was. And he was too weak to ask pointed questions, or to press for a more complete briefing. 'Got an NSC meeting,' he said. 'Then Congressional leadership.'

'I know. I saw them all gathered out in the hall – arguing.'

'About what?'

Her gaze dropped. 'This war, Gordon. It's awful.'

'*All* wars are awful!'

She immediately placed her hand on his chest. 'I know, Gordon. I know. It's just . . . why *this* war? Why are we there? Don't you think maybe we bit off a little more than we can chew?'

'"We" who?' he croaked

Elaine reached for the cup and gave him a drink. 'I mean America,' she said softly. 'Honey, those early reports sound terrible. Three thousand dead – most of those Americans. And the numbers of *Chinese* killed . . . ! Can that be right? Forty-five thousand in just four days?'

Gordon lay back. There was so much he wanted to say. Impassioned arguments he wanted to make. The Europeans were committing their troops. They would provide half the manpower. But America was the glue that held the coalition together. Gordon's resolve was its most crucial manifestation. America had been leader of the free world since World War II. Was it ready to slough off that mantle because the burden had grown too great? To allow the balance of world power to shift to China? Totalitarian rule to dominate the Asian land mass? The future was being decided.

But the most compelling reason for war was completely unrelated to geopolitics. It was simple, to Gordon. To capitulate in the face of naked aggression would be humiliation. Not just for Gordon. He could beg for a cease-fire, get everyone out, then tender his resignation for reasons of health. His footnote in the history books would be kind. But he'd leave his countrymen utterly defeated. That would deal a blow to their self-image. Their self-respect. It would mar the psyche of a generation. The so-called 'Vietnam Syndrome' would be nothing compared to what would follow. It would mean isolationism instead of leadership. It would mean the end of the 'American Century,' and the beginning of the Chinese one.

Character, he thought. The nation would lose some element of its character. And it was character that had made America great. It was the engine of the most powerful country in history. It had been forged in the crucible of war. It could be shattered by a cowardly retreat. War carried a terrible price. But Gordon was not willing to allow *his* weakness to put at risk his country's greatest asset.

Gordon had all those thoughts. But all he had the strength to say to Elaine was, 'We'll win.' His head felt light. She came into and out of focus . . . talking. Soothing.

'The tree of liberty . . .' he remembered.

'What?' Elaine asked.

He'd read it once. The tree of liberty must be refreshed from time to time with the blood of patriots and tyrants. *Thomas Jefferson* . . .

'Mr President,' said the minority leader of the Senate. Gordon opened his eyes. How long had he been asleep? He was in the middle of a meeting. 'There's going to be a resolution on the floor of the House to cut off funding for the war at ninety days.' He paused to let Gordon digest the terrible news.

'Will it carry the Senate?' Gordon asked.

His former colleague shrugged. It was a gesture of defeat. 'Gordon, I'm gonna just lay it out for you, okay?' Gordon nodded. 'Nobody wants this war. Nobody. Not in Europe. Not on the Hill. Not even in your own Administration. Ninety percent of the American people oppose it. This is shaping up to be *the* most unpopular war in our country's history – the Civil War *included*. Everybody on the Hill is getting bombarded with faxes and letters and calls and e-mails.'

'That's not the people.'

The Senator smiled. 'No. You're right. But I guess you haven't been reading the papers, either.'

'Can't hold 'em up,' Gordon croaked.

'Well, according to the front page of the *New York Times*, there are over two thousand AWOLs reported. And the number may be going way, way up. And there have already been the first demonstrations.'

'So you're pulling the rug out from under me?' Gordon asked. He turned to the leadership. They were clearly uncomfortable.

'I'm sorry, Gordon,' the Speaker of the House said finally. 'The measure will pass. You've got three months to bring our people home.'

They waited, but Gordon said nothing. He couldn't. He was too angry. Too busy planning. When the room was cleared of all but a sheepish Fein, Gordon knew what he was going to do. He gave Fein his orders.

'Get me Daryl Shavers.'

BIROBIDZHAN AIRBASE, SIBERIA
January 27, 2000 GMT (0600 Local)

The winter sun had yet to rise into the misty sky. But flames lit the breach in the lines they'd just closed. Reed and Clark stood staring as the already frozen Chinese bodies were stacked like cord wood. 'They completely shattered the single platoon manning the perimeter,' the dazed Reed said. 'They broke clean through. They had broken field running ahead of 'em.' He shook his head. 'But they stopped here.'

Men were pulling bodies out of the tattered rags of the mess tent. Huge, gleaming pots still steamed where the starving Chinese had stopped to fill their stomachs after overrunning a battalion field kitchen. Major Reed's provisionals had counterattacked – pouring fire and grenades onto the absurdly exposed Chinese. Over a hundred Chinese soldiers – crammed inside the mess tent – died amid the pots and pans. Some were covered in now frozen soup. All had removed their gloves to gobble down the hot food.

Clark's radio crackled. His radioman announced that another Chinese attack was coming. Clark asked where, then tensely awaited the radioman's reply. 'Southern perimeter,' the man repeated as he listened to the radio. 'In the gap between the U.S. and Belgian positions.' A wave of relief washed over him. It was just as and where he'd expected. He ordered the pre-arranged call to go out to the air commander. Pilots sitting in their jets on the runways of Khabarovsk a hundred and ten miles away would be there in ten minutes on afterburners.

Before departing, he shook hands with Reed. 'Good job,' Clark said tersely.

Reed held Clark's gloved hand. The major looked back at Clark through puffy, bloodshot eyes. The two men were surrounded with growing mounds of the dead. Twisted, contorted, grossly disfigured. Men Reed had ordered slaughtered as they desperately filled their starving bellies.

'You did what you were supposed to do, Major.' Reed opened his mouth to speak. Clark squeezed his hand tight. *Not now*, Clark thought. *Don't start asking the questions.* 'You did what you were *supposed* to do, Major,' Clark repeated. 'Now get your provisionals ready for another counterattack.'

271

Clark headed for the perimeter.

The Chinese were going for the lone rise on the base to the south of the airfield. Clark had dug in a half-dozen .50 calibers near the crest. The heavy machine-guns were awesomely destructive. They had devastated the light probes they'd sent in the night for the sole purpose of mapping the positions of the guns. Now, they'd come back to root the weapons out. The fire support plan was ready. All forty-eight tubes – too close to be brought to bear on the battlefield – would begin firing at extreme elevations onto the immediate rear of the attacking Chinese. But the support on which Clark pinned his hopes would be orbiting above the clouds – unbeknownst to the Chinese – with wing pylons heavily laden with high explosives. Clark stopped to look at his watch. All forty fighter-bombers should be on station in fifteen minutes.

Clark edged his way through the narrow slit in the earth. He was bent in a stoop just below the snowy surface. The slit trench connected the defensive perimeter with the command and aid posts to the rear. It would soon be jam-packed with traffic. Ammo and fast reaction teams would move outward. The dead and wounded would be evacuated to the rear. Bugles and whistles began to blow just as Clark got to the deeper and wider main fighting trench. His radioman and two-man security team followed close behind.

The soldiers all sat or stood with their backs pressed to the outer wall. Their heads hung down. They eyed Clark with bleary eyes sunk deep into their sockets as he moved down their ranks. 'How's it goin'?' Clark asked. He slapped men's shoulders and shook hands on passing. They were so weary that it took time for Clark's presence to register. But in his wake the men stirred and came to life. An officer stood on a step carved out of the wall. He peered at No Man's Land through periscope binoculars. By the time Clark got to the young platoon leader, his men were doing a double-take. They thought they'd seen it all in the last seventy-two hours. But this was something new.

'What'cha see, lieutenant?' Clark asked in a loud voice.

'More fuckin' Chinese,' he said. He then took his face uncertainly from the binoculars. His feet slipped off his precarious step. 'S-s-sir?' he said. He saluted awkwardly.

'No saluting, lieutenant. No sense giving those snipers a target.'

'Yes, sir!' he replied.

'Where's the nearest gap in the lines?' Clark asked.

'About a hundred fifty meters that way,' the young man replied –

pointing toward their right. 'We've turned back the last platoon on the line along that flank. It's about a two-hundred-meter gap to a Belgian company on the opposite side that's turned back its left flank. We're planning on plugging the hole with 4.2-inch mortars and some heavy machine-guns on the hill behind us.'

'Sounds like a plan,' Clark remarked. 'You mind?' he asked – nodding at the binoculars but not waiting for a reply. He stepped up onto the perch. The binoculars had mirrors inside that allowed the viewer to remain safely below the lip of the trench. Its massive lenses were pointed at the wire. When Clark adjusted the focus slightly he saw the Chinese sappers stealthily creeping forward. The cleared killing field had been tortured and blackened by the awful violence of modern war. 'What's the range to the treeline from here?' Clark asked. 'Treeline' was hardly descriptive. They were shattered and blackened trunks pointing skyward.

'Two hundred meters, sir,' he answered.

Clark whistled. 'Pretty tight quarters. You got any Claymores out?'

'We blew the last ones about zero three hundred. We haven't been able to get back out there 'cause of the snipers.' The Chinese soldiers moved slowly. They never rose much above a squat. Their moves were unhurried. They held their old AKS rifles – a Chinese derivative of the ubiquitous AK-47 – high and in front like they expected imminent hand-to-hand combat. *They're all about to die*, Clark thought.

'Can I ask you a question, sir?'

'Sure,' Clark replied. He panned the binoculars to the left. The picture was the same all up and down the wire.

'Who are you?'

Clark looked around at the man and held out his hand. 'Lieutenant General Nate Clark.'

A small crowd had gathered. Clark shook everyone's hands.

'You're the commander of . . . of the whole thing, right?' the lieutenant asked. 'Of the whole UNRUSFOR?'

Clark nodded. 'Yep. That and fifty cents'll buy me a cup o'coffee,' he said. The tired old line drew laughter from the exhausted men.

'Well, uhm,' the lieutenant began, 'wh-what're you doin' *here*?'

Clark laughed, and they all joined in. Clark considered making a joke – '*I was beginning to wonder the same thing*.' Or maybe bravado – '*Brushin' up on my target practice*.' But men had died there, he realized. In a dirty trench that smelled of urine. There was blood on the icy floor. A crimson bandage on one man's neck. An arm in a sling. An NCO who'd lost part of a foot. It was a hallowed place. Consecrated by these men and their dead friends.

'I'm here to fight,' Clark replied simply.

The smiles remained on some of the grimy faces. On others, there were different emotions displayed. All, however, were alert and alive. Clark and his small entourage moved on. They followed the winding trench to the right. Toward the gap. He pressed the flesh on the way like a politician. After passing what had to be over two hundred defenders in the already reinforced sector, the sky lit up with trip flares.

Nate decided he'd fight from right there. 'How far out are the flares, lieutenant?' he asked the platoon leader. He then checked his M-16. He had a full magazine – twenty rounds.

'Three hundred meters, sir,' the nervous twenty-something replied.

'You lay any mines?'

'No, sir. But we strung some booby traps between the trees on a wire. Grenades with the pins pulled, in tin cans.'

The grenades started to go off. The Chinese ran into the wire in the darkness, spilling the grenades to the ground. Freed of the confines of the cans, the grenades' handles flew off. They popped by the dozens.

'How far out are the booby traps?' Nate asked.

'Two fifty, sir.'

Then came the first shouts of 'Rifle grena-ades!' from the trench's observation posts.

Everyone pressed themselves low to the front wall. The rifle grenades came arcing down from the mist on long smoking tails. They were slow enough for Clark to watch before ducking his head. The explosions rippled up and down the line. The closest shook ice loose from the sandbags. Poor man's artillery.

The American guns opened up. 'Commence firing!' the platoon leader yelled. The men all climbed up to their firing posts. Brass rained down onto the trench floor from all manner of infantry weapons. The M-60 crews had sandbagged roofs built over their nests. But the soldiers with SAWs and M-16s had to duck with each bursting grenade.

Clark climbed up onto the earthen step of an empty firing post. Peering over the sandbags he saw two things. Hundreds upon hundreds of running, weaving Chinese, each of whom would have to be killed.

And caked black blood that ran down the sandbag just in front. The post was empty for a reason.

He glanced at his watch. The fighter-bombers were just a couple of minutes out, he guessed.

Clark raised his M-16 and lined up the nearest Chinese infantryman. He flicked the selector switch to 'Semi' and gripped the trigger firmly with his index finger. When it came time for him to fire, Clark found it remarkably difficult. At first he thought maybe he'd left the safety on and the trigger wouldn't pull. But it wasn't the rifle's mechanism that prevented him from firing. It had been a long time since he'd killed a man.

Clark jerked the trigger – releasing a round just to get it over with. The rifle bucked. The boom of the round's release rung in his ear. All was as he expected. Even the thin swirl of smoke from the muzzle was as it should be. Clark centered the next shot on a man's chest and squeezed. The rifle bucked and boomed and smoked. This time his target fell. Prostrate. Unmoving. Dead.

He had forgotten how hard it was to kill a man. How much it took out of you emotionally. The men firing weapons all around him weren't exhausted from lack of sleep. They had been deprived for too long of something else. Mercy, kindness, forgiveness – all those things man calls 'humanity.' Clark fired again, and missed. He fired again. This time a hit. The man he'd shot writhed on the ground. He thrashed about in pain from a high-velocity round that had just shattered bones, jellied tissue.

Clark pulled his eye back from his sights. The Chinese were dying in numbers Clark had never before witnessed first-hand. Some of the grizzled old vets in 'Nam had told stories of the human waves in Korea. But words could never do the scene justice. When men fell and died by the thousands, individual targets quickly lost their significance. There were so many they just became a part of a whole. Clark was killing a platoon, a company, a regiment. Whether one at a time by the pull of a trigger, or en masse by issuing orders from his CP. The targets weren't individual human beings. They had no face. No family. No past. That would've been too much. The scale of the slaughter forced him to wall his mind up. To shut out reality.

His two riflemen and even his radiomen were on the wall now. They all fired across the two-hundred-meter shooting gallery. The smell of the gunsmoke made Clark vaguely nauseous. Still the Chinese came.

A fresh wave appeared in the broken trees even before the last of the ranks before them had fallen. *What were the Chinese commanders doing?* Clark wondered in sudden confusion. *Entire regiments hurled against well-prepared positions? How could they possibly be expending men's lives in such a coldly calculated fashion?* Then Clark remembered Brigadier General Merrill. You did what you had to do.

The depleted front ranks of the onrushing infantrymen were at one hundred meters. Clark began to fire three-round bursts. He quickly ran through two magazines. He then grabbed three more from a man who carried a rucksack up and down the trench line. A new wave of attackers leaped over the flattened razor wire in the killing zone.

He turned to his radioman and shouted, '*Find out what's keeping that air!*' He then returned to his rapidly fired bursts. The sandbag on which he steadied his aim jerked and split open. It leaked its contents just like a human body would.

Another shot whizzed by his head. Clark caught himself feeling momentarily amazed. He then raised his rifle almost in reflex. He had been a green second lieutenant three decades ago. Somehow the greenness had grown back.

The air was now filled with the enemy's return fire. Out of the corner of his eye Clark saw the first man fall. The ragged but still charging line was now seventy-five meters away. He glanced back at the fallen, writhing man. Most wounds in the trench would be like his, he realized. Head wounds. A medic was trying to pry the man's hands away from his face without success. He was screaming. It was just like before. It was every bit as awful as he remembered.

'Tango Lima One Niner, this is X-ray Yankee Five Eight, do you read me, *over!*' the radioman shouted. He got no response. He was sitting at the bottom of the trench – repeating, '*Tango Lima One Niner . . .!*'

Every shot counted now. The men nearest the trench were hurling hand grenades in volleys. Just before Clark and all the others dropped, he saw a fresh line of Chinese emerge from the smoky forest.

The spinning grenades rained down all around. The earth shook with several dozen explosions. Fire and smoke shot down the trench from around the bend. A grenade had dropped home on the unlucky squad. Grenades fell end over smoking end from the sky. But an NCO shouted, 'Everybody *u-u-up!*'

'*Tango Lima One Niner . . .!*'

When Clark stepped back onto his fighting post he felt fear shoot up his spine. He didn't have time to wonder what had gone wrong. He didn't have time to rage at the forward air controller. He had time only to fire his rifle. The first Chinese were only fifty meters away. This time he jerked at the trigger. Still his targets fell at nearly every pull. They were right at the end of his front sight, impossible to miss. The searing heat of grenades licked at his skin. Their thunderous booms frayed his nerves to a jangled mess. Violence raged around him. Grenades burst in and all around the trench. Bullets ripped through the air at supersonic speed. Clark killed without thinking.

'*Tango Lima One Niner, do-you-read-me-ove-e-e-r?*'

Clark dropped down and ejected an empty magazine. He could hear the full-throated shouts of the massed Chinese. Suddenly, the world erupted in fire. The air at the bottom of the trench shook. Choking dust rose. Snow cascaded from walls onto his helmet and shoulders. Everybody had fallen from their posts and lay now on the icy floor. Men leapt down into the trench or onto the far wall just as another earth-shattering roar shook the darkening sky. Flame shot out of rifles, lighting the trench with flashes as men killed other men. All was noise and confusion and death. Soldiers of both armies clawed at the walls to escape. Another thunderous vibration filled the air with falling and burning debris.

The fighting inside the trench was over. The survivors hugged the walls for their lives. The staggering, earth-shattering, end-of-the-world violence was near constant now. Clark rolled himself into a fetal ball. He didn't know if they had won or lost. The bombers had arrived out of nowhere to begin the apocalypse. They were the enemy now. Their bombs were the greater risk.

His heart was still pounding when he realized the worst had passed. The intense bombing was farther away. 'Come on!' someone shouted before choking on the smoke and coughing. 'Sweep the trench!' Clark rose back up to the wall. The misty morning sky was now obscured by a pall of black smoke. A shroud over the countless dead. Crackling fires burned near and far. No one moved. Nothing lived. The battle was won.

'I know where the hell you are!' General Dekker shouted over the satellite phone. 'God*dam*mit, Nate. We've soldiered together for years. But you disobeyed an express order. I don't need to tell you where I'm headed with this. You put the commander in chief of *all* forces in theater into a *surrounded* airbase under *imminent* threat of overrun! You're risking getting yourself killed in a *sideshow*, Nate! A fuckin' *sideshow*! *Jesus* Christ!' Dekker's sigh sounded like a gale wind blowing into the mouthpiece. 'Why'd you do it? Why'd you disobey my order and go in there?'

'I'm sending men off to die, Ed.' Clark's voice quivered. 'A lot of men. You should see them. You'd be proud of 'em. All these years and I still don't know what makes 'em lace up their boots and head out into that shit. I swear to *God* it amazes me more today than it did back when we were their age. They don't have a clue why the hell they're here. They just . . .' He choked. 'They just . . .' Clark shook his head. Goose bumps rose on his arms as he spoke, 'By *God*, they're fine soldiers, Ed. Every last one of 'em. I don't care what they did before or what they'll do if they make it home. Nothing can take away the fact that right here, right now, they're the best Goddamn army that's ever taken to the field.'

Dekker was silent. When he finally spoke, he sounded drained of his earlier anger. 'You know I should yank your Goddamned command. I should bust you down two grades and retire your ass on half pension. But if that base holds, they'll pro'bly pin a fuckin' DSM on your chest.'

'I won't take it. As far as I'm concerned, my visit here didn't happen. It's off the record. This base is gonna hold, I can feel it. We're gonna start sending out combat patrols to clear the snipers. These guys've got the starch to hold the place, and it doesn't have *anything* to do with me.'

'Tell that to *Newsweek* magazine,' Dekker said. 'They've already called. Your picture's gonna be on the Goddamn *cover* – 'Come and take it!' printed in big letters. I can't fire you now, Nate. You're a *hero*. But if you *ever* disobey another order that I give you – I don't care *how* trivial – I'll stand you up against a wall and make your Goddamn death wish come true! *You* read me?'

'Yes, sir,' Clark replied.

Dekker slammed the phone down.

A man was waiting with a radio message. It was from an unrecoverable unit on the road to Khabarovsk. Nate had personally decided it was unrecoverable. 'Ammo is gone. All weapons destroyed. No sign of relief. Will surrender my unit as ordered. Am destroying radio. Please pray for us. Out.'

Chapter Thirteen

SOUTH OF BIROBIDZHAN, SIBERIA
January 27, 2100 GMT (0700 Local)

Things had grown worse and worse as the night wore on. Columns of Chinese had come close to Stempel's small band. There had to be thousands of them – tens of thousands of them – all moving toward the airbase. Finally, one long file of men walked straight through the middle of their dispersed hiding places. Lying under his blanket of snow, Stempel didn't even breathe for fear of exhaling a white vapor that would begin the killing. But no one saw them. From the frightened looks on the faces of the passing Chinese soldiers, they were too concerned with what lay ahead to pay any attention to their immediate surroundings.

By dawn, the last waves of Chinese had passed, and the battle had begun. So many Chinese had passed that Stempel couldn't imagine how the airbase could've held. The sounds of fighting were intense, but they were nothing when compared with what was to come next.

The woods exploded. That was what it seemed like to Stempel. Wave after wave of concussions. A flight of four jets screamed overhead. In their wake, a storm of fire rolled through the forest. The last bomb in the string was barely a hundred meters away. The ground vibrated under Stempel's back. Then came the stampeding Chinese. They ran like wild animals. Leaping fallen logs. Darting this way and that. Crashing through limbs that hung low with their weight of snow – falling and being half covered by the avalanche. Stempel feared the retreating infantry. But he feared death from the sky the most. The thick drifts of snow beside the streambed had been a natural place to hide. But the streambed also offered pilots a break in the thick forest's canopy.

Gunships flew straight down the narrow stream. Their chopping rotors and whining engines changed pitch as they twisted and turned in the air. Fleeing Chinese who crossed the stream were mowed down. The Apaches' chin guns stripped branches and even felled whole trees. Thick ice was thrown up in great sheets. The earth shuddered with hundreds of blows. Chinese caught in the open simply disintegrated. Desperate mobs – heedless of the sounds of the airborne predators – crossed the ten-meter cut through the woods. Turbines whined. Rotors hacked at air above the agile birds of prey. Snow and ice exploded.

It was impossible to count the dead. The constituent parts of their bodies littered the landscape. Gunships cut great swaths through masses of men. Others ran on unharmed. Life and death were reduced to a senseless, random lottery. And in the background – far, far away – there was thunder. The deep, hellish sound of heavy bombing. *B-52s*, Harold thought. It had to be. Every thirty-second rumble reminded Stempel that if death sought him out, there was no place on earth to hide.

When the last of the surviving Chinese were gone, the whines of the engines diminished until all was quiet. Even the wails and moans of the wounded quickly fell silent.

The Sergeant rose up. Snow cascaded from his Arctic gear. With vigorous arm signals he waved everyone to their feet. Six of the men got up. Three didn't.

The Private Who Couldn't Feel His Feet and two others remained stuck in their banks of snow. During the stillness of their hours in hiding, they had lost all feeling in their lower extremities. The Sergeant took a look at them in the dim light – peeling back their clothes and prodding and probing.

He moved away to exchange urgent whispers with the Spec Three. Stempel heard everything.

'They got frostbite bad,' the sergeant said.

'Should we try rubbin' snow on their skin?' the Spec Three asked.

'Naw. They're frozen too deep. Don't rub or massage 'em. Don't even try to bend 'em. They're gonna lose them toes and fingers. They'll be lucky not to lose their hands and feet.'

'Can they walk at all?'

'No way.'

That started Stempel on his own calculations. There were six of them who could walk. But one was The Private With The Leg Wound. There weren't enough healthy guys to go around.

'Everybody down!' the Sergeant suddenly hissed. All those who had risen returned to their spots and covered themselves back up. Stempel had barely finished the last flicks of his gloved hands when he caught sight of movement. A point man profiled against the light. Not stooped over, but with his rifle at the ready. Stempel let the man pass before burying his arms and hands, finding the hard grips of his rifle under the snow.

Stempel kept his eyes right on the rounded shape of the helmet. The man wearing it was clearly watching him, also.

'All right,' The Sergeant said in a normal tone of voice. 'Nobody move. You got that flag?' The Spec Three showed him the white towel. The Sergeant nodded. 'Okay. Lift it up slowly – *slo-o-owly* – and wave it over your head.'

The Spec Three spun the white towel in lazy figure eights. Time passed. Stempel shivered in the quiet of the frozen woods. He waited to die. He gripped his rifle so firmly with numb hands that his forearms cramped. His gaze remained fixed on the round, white helmet.

'Freeze!' someone shouted. The towel hung limply from the Spec Three's upraised arm. 'American soldier! Identify yourself!'

Stempel couldn't believe it. The Sergeant had a grin on his face. The Spec Three was laughing. The Private Who Couldn't Feel His Feet cried. It was true. Stempel's eyes drooped shut.

'Second of the 263rd!' the joyous Sergeant replied.

Stempel opened his eyes. They sunk closed. He heard the crunching of snow. His eyes opened just long enough to see GIs with M-16s. They closed again.

'You guys really from 2nd Battalion?' he heard. Stempel forced his eyelids open. Several heads nodded. 'Is there anybody else?' he asked. Puffs of smoke shot from his mouth and nose.

Their vow of silence seemed to have taken hold completely. No answer to his question was given. Stempel's eyes again closed.

PHILADELPHIA, PENNSYLVANIA
January 27, 1830 GMT (2330 Local)

Pyotr Andreev trailed Olga through the Safeway. He positioned himself at the end of an aisle. He stayed between the shopping cart filled with his girls and the suspicious-looking man. As his family turned into the next aisle, the man approached Pyotr slowly. He appeared overly preoccupied by the shelves of goods. Pyotr checked his family's aisle, then stepped back around to watch the man.

He wore a long coat. It wasn't black – and his hair was bushy, not shaved – but he was large. Muscular. Menacing. He lingered. He stopped at every new brand to study its package. *Diapers!* Pyotr thought. *What's a* man *doing shopping for* diapers? He quickly checked Olga's aisle again. She was reading labels – slowly approaching a spot directly opposite the man. Only the thin metal shelving separated the two.

Pyotr stepped back to the diaper aisle. His hand reached into his jacket. He seized the butt of the automatic. The man's hair was unkempt – sticking up all around. His eyes were red and puffy. *Drugs!* The man reached into his pocket!

Pyotr yanked the pistol out. The man pulled a crinkled piece of yellow paper from his overcoat.

'*Frank?*' Pyotr heard. The man turned. The pistol was already back in Pyotr's pocket. 'Frank Bradley! How's that *ba-aby* doing?'

Pyotr disappeared behind a display of fat-free cookies. It was then that he heard Olga calling out his name. He charged into her aisle toward the basket. His hand again grabbed the pistol butt. There appeared to be no danger on Aisle Five. '*What?*' Pyotr snapped – checking both ends of the empty aisle.

'What is wrong with you?' Olga asked. She wore a look of concern.

'You called for help!' Pyotr responded. His heart was pounding.

'I wanted to know if it was Prego or Ragu that we had at the Hall's for dinner?' She stood there holding the competing brands of spaghetti sauce.

Pyotr closed his eyes. He took a deep breath, stuck his chin in the air, and stretched his clenched and cramping neck muscles.

'Papa's sweating,' one of the girls said.

'Pyotr?' Olga said. *'V chyom delo?'* she whispered.

He loosed a ragged breath. 'Nothing.'

'No. It's not "nothing". Something's wrong.'

The guy with the long coat wheeled his basket full of diapers and formula onto their aisle.

He looked at her. 'I almost shot that man,' he whispered.

She looked back and forth between Pyotr and the new father – her jaw drooping. *'Why?'*

Pyotr was still so agitated that he blew his top. 'Because he was buying diapers!' The girls giggled. Pyotr again closed his eyes and leaned against the shelves. Olga's cool hand found his face.

'You're too upright.'

'"Up-tight",' Pyotr corrected. Her hand pulled back. He opened his eyes. An elderly woman was passing, looking his way nervously. He let her pass, then said, 'I'm sorry.'

'Nobody is looking for us, Pyotr. We are safe. Everything is good here.' She turned to look over her left shoulder. 'Tfu-tfu-tfu,' she said, pretending to spit – to ward off the bad luck that comes with congratulating good fortune. 'We have nothing to fear from . . . *Kartsev.*'

Pyotr didn't argue. But it wasn't lost on him that she couldn't say the man's name above a whisper.

Olga continued her maddeningly slow perusal of goods. Pyotr concentrated on calming himself. But mention of Kartsev had changed his mood from agitated to bitter. By the time they got to the dairy products, he was gritting his teeth in anger. Olga read the labels on five different types of cream cheese. Pyotr slammed his palm on a shelf. A row of small yoghurt containers collapsed onto the floor.

Olga just looked at him. He turned away.

I had the shot, he kept saying to himself. *I had the shot.*

VLADIVOSTOK, SIBERIA
January 28, 0400 GMT (1400 Local)

Kate Dunn watched the press pool footage with growing frustration. The scenes were dramatic, but her job was not. 'There!' she said, pointing. The image froze. Woody rewound and placed an index mark on the clip before rolling the tape forward. 'Stop,' Kate said. She rolled her finger in air slowly until Woody found exactly the place. 'There.' He marked the end of the video clip. 'How long is that?' she asked.

'Eight point two seconds,' Woody said. 'That gets us up to a total of . . . one minute, twenty-nine point seven seconds. That should do it!' Kate drew a deep breath in through her nose and held the air in her full lungs. 'You ready?' Woody asked.

Kate raised her microphone and tested the sound. Woody gave her the 'okay' sign. She cleared her throat, waited for the taping light, and began. The video ran silently in the background while she read. 'As the Battle of Birobidzhan enters its third day, all signs point to an Allied victory. Chinese forces have suffered major losses, some estimates running as high as twenty thousand dead. But the price has not been cheap. Defense Department sources put the number of U.S. killed, or missing and presumed killed or captured, at seven hundred and fifty-nine, with an additional four hundred wounded, many seriously. UNRUSFOR spokesmen here in Vladivostok have downplayed the importance of this opening battle. *Newsweek* magazine, however, is reporting that Lieutenant General Nate Clark – supreme Allied commander in Russia – personally flew to Birobidzhan to take charge of the bastion's defenses.

'Elsewhere along the thousand-mile front, however, the Chinese Army continues its seemingly inexorable advance.' The pictures now were from Iranian television footage. Their quality was poor. But they showed rugged, mountainous terrain touched here and there with patches of ice and snow. A narrow dirt road wound its way up the rocky slopes of a ridge. Long columns of white-clad soldiers – four abreast – were broken only by the empty space between units. The camera panned. Horses, mules, two-wheeled trailers pulled by porters – the procession out of the Chinese heartland seemed endless. 'Round-the-clock bombing by U.S. and European air forces has reduced the rate of advance to only the foot speed of individual infantrymen. This slow-motion tsunami of men and materiel, however, is pouring into Siberia at the rate of one division every three hours. Meanwhile, allied firebases that dot the thin defensive line just south of the Trans-Siberian Railway brace themselves for an onslaught that many military experts believe can have only one result – massive bloodletting, followed by inevitable Chinese overrun.'

The images switched to rusty Russian cranes offloading armored fighting vehicles in the port of Vladivostok. Kate made a mental note to superimpose a graphic identifying the site of the footage. 'While American and European reinforcements are being rushed to Siberia from Western Europe, Japan, Korea and the United States, estimates are that it will take upwards of thirty to forty-five days before those forces will be ready to mount large-scale operations in the brutal winter conditions. So the race is on. Allied ships, planes and trains rush toward Siberia from the far corners of the earth. And Chinese foot soldiers slog their way ever northward – straight for the outmanned westerners whose guns lie in waiting. This is Kate Dunn, NBC News, Vladivostok.'

The last shot was of an American soldier who couldn't have been more than eighteen. He was looking out over the snow-covered lip of his trench from under his white helmet. He held a single black M-16 in his hands. She flicked the switch to end the taping.

'Timing's great,' Woody said. 'Now, wanta do it for real?'

'What do you mean? That *was* for real.'

'It sounded like you were reading last week's *grocery* list. Jeeze, Kate, there's a huge, bloody war on and you seem bored by the whole thing. That wouldn't get on the air on a *slow* news day. And business is booming back at network. So what gives?'

Kate frowned. Her shoulders slumped. 'I'm not bored, Woody. I'm *pissed off!* This isn't the way to cover a war! The most *dramatic* part of our day is elbowing our way to the front of the line to get the raw footage from the news pool!'

'You know,' Woody said, 'I've been wondering for a while whether you weren't some kind of thrill freak. High threshold level of excitement. You have to push the envelope to get any kind of rush at all. I mean, you did say you were into bunji jumping.'

'I did it *once!* And my top came off!'

'How about base jumping? Maybe some of that freefall parachuting with a snowboard?' Kate rolled her eyes and gave him the finger, but Woody was just getting started. 'Which would you find more stimulating?' he said in a mock examiner voice. 'A: The perfect performance of Pachelbel's Canon played at dusk in the shadow of the Parthenon? B: A ninety-nine-yard run from scrimmage to win the game with no time left on the clock? Or C: Walking along the edge of a precipice?'

'Fuck you, Woody.' She swiped her hair back off her forehead. 'We gotta go out there and get some news.'

'You mean "make" some news, don't you?' He held his hands in air to hang the block type of a headline. '"NBC News Crew Missing", followed by "NBC News Crew Found Dead; Woman Thought Strangled by Cameraman."'

She ignored him. 'It's our job, Woody. We're not editorialists. We're not supposed to sit back and rehash somebody else's story. We're supposed to be out there getting first-hand accounts. Talking to the soldiers and the commanders. Witnessing the battles with our own eyes. Feeling what it's really like for the poor bastards who're stuck in this mess.'

Woody shrugged. 'Okay.'

'What?'

'Okay. Let's head out there.'

Kate hesitated, fighting her inclination to argue the other side. Wary that Woody might just be baiting her into some stupid joke. But he just raised his eyebrows and waited. 'How?' she asked.

'Kiss some officer's ass. Hitch a ride with one of the units that are unloading down at the port.'

'But the Public Affairs Officers only allow press pools to go out.'

'*Fuck* the PAOs. Everything's so screwed up that those guys getting off the boats don't know the rules. You may have to ask a dozen officers before you find one who says okay. But these military types lord over their units like little fiefdoms. Promise to interview them. Somebody somewhere'll jump at the chance. Imagine – getting your handsome face all over the airwaves back home where your mom and the guy who stole your girl in high school can see it. All dressed up in your combat gear heading off to war.' Kate's back was straight as a board. She was hardly able to remain seated there even a moment longer. 'A free ticket to hell, Katie,' Woody said, staring at her – unsmiling.

Kate avoided his eyes. She rose. She began to plan out loud where they would start. What her pitch would be. She started to climb into her cold weather gear in the cramped editing room. Woody reminded her about retaping the voiceover, and she removed the gear and sat down. This time, she nailed the taping first try. Woody put the tape in the queue for transmission to New York. Kate got dressed again – talking non-stop. After a few moments, Woody quietly began to put his own woolly coat on. His motions were slow and lethargic.

PORT OF VLADIVOSTOK, SIBERIA
January 29, 0200 GMT (1200 Local)

Andre Faulk was exhausted from two days at sea. The smelly, rusty freighter was crammed with all the low-priority shipments. It had been pitched and tossed in the winter seas. Andre hadn't been able to hold down any food since he had first vomited six hours into the voyage. They had been packed like cattle – like captives on an old slave ship from Africa – deep in the musty holds of the wreck. The whole way the men and women of the Division Postal Detachment had seethed over their poor treatment. And they'd been up all night while their Navy escorts spent hours pounding the sea with explosives.

The combat units had flown over on luxury airliners.

He walked down the rickety gangplank carefully. The cold air cut right through Andre's loosely hanging parka, but he breathed deeply. Ahead was land, and fresh air, and open space – the end to the miserable voyage. He fell into formation with the others from his unit – a motley crowd of the overweight and the slight-of-build. They dressed right – holding their left arms out to the next man's shoulder to ensure uniformity of spacing.

Andre knew everyone thought him to be a moron. He could tell it by the jobs that they gave him. And they spoke slowly and used different words with the same meaning when they thought he couldn't understand. He was black and from the inner city. He had a heavy accent, he now realized. And he was by far the most physically fit. So why else would he be thrown in among the army's basket cases? On the first day, his section leader – a sergeant with thick, coke-bottle glasses – had asked if he 'felt comfortable' delivering the mail to the units. When Andre didn't catch his drift, he said, 'You know, reading all the names out.'

287

He felt himself sway slightly from one foot to the other. He was on the concrete wharf of a harbor, but *still* the experience of his one and only ocean voyage tormented him. Still he felt nauseous.

'Listen up!' the lieutenant yelled as he approached the formation. In the heavy winter gear he looked almost athletic. But Andre had seen him in the gym back in Korea. He was almost six feet tall, but maybe weighed one forty. 'You are now in the city of Vladivostok, Russia! I don't know how close you've been following the news, but there *is* no Russian government left! It's collapsed! This whole area out here is under military government by UNRUSFOR! That stands for "United Nations Russian Forces"! You should consider yourselves in hostile territory any time you're outside a secure military compound! There haven't been any reports of Chinese attacks inside the city, but they're on the way! The real problem we've got is with lawlessness! There may still be Anarchist terrorists out there! Plus the civilian population is hungry, so they'll do lots of crazy things like slit your throat to get at your food or your wallets! That means standing orders are *no fraternization!*'

A groan went up. 'Now I *mean* it, guys!' the lieutenant shouted in a high-pitched voice. He was really cracking down now they were in a war zone. Andre rolled his eyes. 'Okay! What we're gonna be doin' is processing and sorting at *two* different stations! One here at the port for the bulk mail and packages. One at the airport for first-class and all priority courier services! But given the distances involved in getting to the front, there's only gonna be one truck goin' out per day, and it's gonna have to pick up at *both* stations! It's a real mess over here right now, guys! I know we haven't trained to split up the sorting to two stations, but we're all strained to the max and are gonna have to buckle down and get it done!' His fist pumped the air in front for emphasis. 'All *right*, then!' he shouted as if they had all just responded. They hadn't. 'First mail goes out tomorrow morning, so let's get cracking!'

Andre picked up his camouflaged duffle bag and rifle. When he stood up he saw that the ship berthed next to the rust bucket on which they'd arrived was disgorging Bradley armored fighting vehicles. They'd all been freshly painted white in the Division's barns back at Tongduchon. Andre watched a Bradley descend a ramp to the dock. He wondered where Stempel was.

'Oh!' someone said as he ran into Andre from behind. 'Sorry.' He straightened his helmet and almost dropped his rifle to the concrete. 'Jeeze! Whew!'

Andre headed off with the rest – disgusted.

BIROBIDZHAN FIREBASE, SIBERIA
January 29, 1000 GMT (2000 Local)

Harold Stempel had been awakened not by the thumping explosions – more felt through the floor of the warm bunker than heard. He'd grown used to them. But he couldn't sleep through the shouts of the staff sergeant, who'd rousted everyone who could walk out of their sleeping bags. *More digging*, he thought. He was dead tired. He'd slept most of the first day on the airbase. He'd spent most of his second day digging trenches. Their labor detachments would take cover behind walls. Explosive charges would roar through the trench. The men would then shovel the blasted soil into wheelbarrows.

Before crawling into his gear he took two codeine. They'd given them to him to dull his aches and pains. But he hadn't gone to the bathroom in two days.

When Stempel had climbed back into his blood-coated Arctic shell, the sergeant had asked if he was wounded. Stempel replied that he wasn't, but it really wasn't truthful. He was wounded, you just couldn't see the wounds. But he could feel them. The unexpected shivering. The panic and paranoia that seized him out of nowhere. The nightmares and sweats during the night. He'd twice woken with a shout.

In the day and night since he'd made it inside the perimeter, everyone had left him alone. No fighting. 'Excused duty.' He'd slept all day and all night, but still he was tired. Every time he had settled into that bliss of deep sleep something had awakened him. Not bombs and the firecracker sounds of a firefight, but something in his head. A sudden wakefulness – a fear of imminent danger – that had each time ruined the quality of his sleep.

The sergeant led Stempel and a dozen others out into the cold, night air. The fighting sounded low-level and sporadic. Occasional rips of automatic fire that died down quickly. A grenade. A single shot. Despite the apparent calm, the staff sergeant was bent over at the waist. His rifle was held out in front of him at port arms as he

289

crept through the slit trench – alert to danger. Stempel took his cue from the man. He flicked the selector switch of his M-16 to 'Burst' and slipped his trigger finger into its sleeve.

They arrived at a bunker that opened off the slit trench. It was open to the freezing air outside. The staff sergeant poked his head in and asked, 'How many you need?' One more, came the reply. The staff sergeant turned to Stempel and said, 'You.' He nodded with his head toward the dark and icy entrance.

The bunker was filled with noxious fumes from the single gas stove. Stempel coughed. In the light of a single kerosene lantern, Stempel could make out the large, warmly-clad shapes of nine other men. Eight of them faced the ninth, who held a piece of paper and a ball-point pen awkwardly next to the lantern.

'Take a seat,' he said to Stempel. Harold just sank between two men. Their parkas rubbed together noisily. Everyone looked at Stempel. At the caked brown blood coating his parka. 'You're now in 1st Squad, 3rd Platoon, 1st Provisional Infantry Company.' The man's eyes darted from Harold's face to the dried blood. 'My name is Harper – Specialist Five. I'm your squad leader.'

'Stempel, Harold, Private,' Harold reported.

The squad leader wrote his particulars on his paper. 'Okay, what about you?' he asked one of the others – obviously resuming what Stempel's arrival had interrupted. The man gave him his name and serial number, which the squad leader wrote down. He was having trouble both with the pen, and with his writing surface – his knee. As he shook the pen, he said 'MOS?'

'82C,' the man replied. 'Field Artillery Surveyor.'

The Spec Five wrote the reply on his makeshift roster. He then moved on to the next soldier.

'31M – Multichannel Communications Systems Operator.'

It suddenly dawned on the dazed and still sleepy Stempel what was happening. They were forming a squad. He was being added to a squad. *To do what?* he wondered.

'63B,' came a woman's voice. Stempel's gaze shot to the dim profile in the corner. 'Light Wheeled Vehicle Maintenance,' the African-American woman supplied. Her chin rested on an M-16's front sight.

The Spec Five continued his inventory of Stempel's new squadmates.

'88M – Motor Transportation Operator,' came the quivering voice of the man next to Stempel. He was Stempel's age. He wore thick, shatterproof glasses.

'457XB,' came the next person.

'What the hell's *that?*' the Spec Five asked – his upper lip curled in confusion.

'Airlift Aircraft Maintenance/C-5,' the guy replied. 'I'm Air Force, not Army.'

'Gre-e-eat,' somebody mumbled.

The Spec Five was himself incredulous. 'Is there anybody *else* here who's Air Force?' he asked. The rubbing sounds of fabric drew the bunker's attention to two others. They'd both raised their hands. 'Ah, sh-*sh-shit!*' the Spec Five cursed. He got the first Air Force guy to repeat his MOS, then asked the next two for theirs. 551XO-Pavements Maintenance, and 703XO-Administrative/Reprographic were the replies.

The Spec Five huffed loudly as he finished writing. 'We got any Navy?' he asked. 'Coast Guard? Boy Scouts of America?' There were chuckles. 'Okay, Army! Who have I missed?' Again a rubbing sound from the darkness. 'Speak up!' the Spec Five barked in irritation.

'Well, m-m-my *official* specialty is 02B, sir . . . sarge . . . But, well, I was called up as a 92B – Medical Laboratory Specialist – which is my civilian job.'

'You're Army Reserves?' the Spec Five asked.

'National Guard,' the guy replied.

There were groans.

'Shut the fuck up!' the Spec Five snapped. As he wrote, he asked, 'What's an 02B?'

'Uhm,' the guy chuckled nervously. Stempel could see his helmet turning from the woman on one side to the man on the other. 'It's actually,' he laughed, 'you're gonna get a kick outa . . .'

'What the fuck is it?' the Spec Five said – ready to write.

'Cornet. I'm a Cornet player. 02B is for Cornet and Trumpet players.'

'Oh-oh-oh,' somebody groaned in the darkness. 'We're dead meat, man.'

'Shut the fuck up!' the Spec Five shouted. 'Nobody says another Goddamn word unless I tell him to . . . or her!' He turned to Stempel. Again he glanced at the blood of the sergeant and PFC from the fighting hole. 'What about you?' he asked in an almost deferential tone.

'11B – Infantryman,' Harold replied. The man next to him sighed in a show of relief. Another shook Stempel's hand in a Sixties-style soul shake.

As the Spec Five wrote, a question came from the darkness. 'What about you?'

The Spec Five looked up – realizing it was directed at him. He busied himself with a recount of the ten names on the list. 'OOJ,' came his reply.

'What's an OOJ?' came from a different man.

The Spec Five's patience was again exhausted. 'Club Activities Manager, *okay?*'

No one groaned, or sighed, or said a word. The only sound came from outside. From high-powered assault rifles popping away in the night.

'What are we supposed to do?' the woman driver asked.

'I'm gonna *tell* you. But first I've got to hand in this roster.'

He left them there.

'Oh, man,' the guy next to Stempel said. 'This is some shit, huh?' Harold just nodded. 'Guess you've already seen some action, though.' Harold nodded again. 'Who were you with?'

'Second of the two-six-three.'

No one seemed to know what to say. Harold saw something in that reaction. A different perspective on what he'd been through. It had been Hell. Harold appreciated that fact only after seeing their faces. He'd walled it up so tight he hardly knew what had happened.

He felt guilty. A wave of self-pity washed over him. Nobody should have to go through something like that. It was a miracle that he'd survived! The guilt tugged down on him like undertow. He wouldn't have lived through it . . . if he'd fought. The thought kicked him in the gut. He felt sick. But if he'd grabbed a rifle – if he'd thrown his grenade – they'd have killed him. Stripped him naked in the snow like all the rest.

In the silence of the bunker, Harold poked at the feeling. Hiding under the bodies was nothing, he concluded. A mere detail. One he so far had managed to tell no one. He jammed his eyes shut. The mental agony was total now.

The Spec Five returned with an officer. Both men carried heavy sacks.

'My name is Lieutenant Dawes,' the officer said. He seemed confident. Stempel clung to that. 'We've got to go clean out some Chinese. They smashed through the perimeter, but they're pretty much pinned down. We're gonna counterattack and reestablish the line.'

Up until then, Harold thought, everyone was with the man. His use of the word counterattack, however, brought home what they were about to do.

'We're not infantrymen, sir,' one of the airmen said.

'I know that,' Dawes replied. 'But we gotta do this. We're gonna do this real straightforward. You and Second Squad are gonna do a simple leapfrog. Sergeant Brunner is gonna take Second Squad. I'll take you guys. We'll form a single line. Five meters of spacing between us. We'll advance ten meters, drop and lay down covering fire. Then, Second Squad will advance. That's the drill. No fallin' behind. And listen. You're gonna have to maneuver under fire, understand? I'm sorry, but you're just gonna have to do it.'

In the silence Harold could sense the sickened reactions of his squadmates. Dawes dragged a sack out in front. 'Everybody take five grenades.' The Motor Transportation Operator next to Stempel unexpectedly gulped air and coughed. He put his hand on Harold's shoulder as if to rise, but he never got off his knees. Dawes told him to drink some water. Harold thought he was going to vomit, but he didn't.

'Fire at their muzzle flashes,' Dawes said as the heavy bags were dragged around. 'That'll keep their heads down. When we get in grenade range I'll tell ya. Just go to ground and start tossing.'

'And they'll be tossing them back at us,' someone pointed out.

'Probably not. They're runnin' outta grenades and ammo pretty quick. We just gotta get that line squared away before they come again.'

'How do we know we're not shootin' our own lines up?' came a question.

'I'll get you to the right line of departure and keep you pointed in the right direction, okay? Now, let's go. Single file.'

They filed out into the slit trench one by one.

Dawes put everyone in their places along the wall of a slit trench. When all was set, he waved his arm and they climbed up onto the snow.

The staccato pops of Chinese guns began immediately. Bullets whooshed through the air overhead. It was a sound Stempel still heard in his nightmares. They'd been spotted. They were being fired on by prepared troops. Stempel pressed low to the crusty, windblown snow. He looked left and right to confirm that the rest of his squad had joined him.

'First Squad,' Lieutenant Dawes shouted from the right, 'pick a target and prepare to fire!'

Stempel raised his rifle to his shoulder. The snow-covered ground was uneven. It rose and fell just enough to obscure all but one blazing Chinese gun. He aimed at the bright muzzle flashes and flicked the selector to 'Semi.'

'Second Squad,' he heard called out from their left, 'prepare to advance in line!' There was a moment's pause. Stempel centered the popping muzzle on his front post's sight. '*Second* Squad . . . let's *go!*'

'First Squad open *fi-i-ire!*' Dawes shouted.

Stempel squeezed the trigger, and his M-16 recoiled hard against his shoulder. It was the same rifle he'd fished out of the snow. He'd cleaned it once in the bunker. It functioned perfectly. All of a sudden, the field ahead came alive with Chinese guns. Each was marked by its flashing muzzle. Just like Stempel's position would be fixed with his every shot. He fired rapidly in the general direction of the new targets – moving from gun to gun and squeezing his trigger as fast as he could take aim.

The snow around him began to spray into the air. Out of the corner of his eye he saw Second Squad all drop to the ground at once.

'*First Squad,*' Dawes shouted over the roar, '*advance twenty meters!*'

Stempel and his squadmates rose. Moving forward, Stempel heard the angry bees that buzzed by him. To stay on his feet required the complete abandonment of reason and sanity. Every rational thought screamed at him to dive to the ground. He shut them from his head. He detached his mind from his body. His body might at any second be torn to shreds. Cored by a hot steel bullet. But his mind was above the fray. It focused on such minutiae as staying in line. Not falling behind. And switching the selector to 'Burst.'

He got off a three-round burst before he heard, 'First Squad *down!*'

Stempel hit the snow hard – knees first. His face was covered in icy crystals.

'Fire at the *gu-u-uns!*' Dawes yelled.

Stempel spat the cold grit from his mouth. He wiped the back of his glove across his face. Second Squad was leapfrogging ahead. He fired a three-round burst at the now closer muzzles. The blazing gun was extinguished. Stempel smiled in surprise and fired at the next hole. His second burst knocked out that gun, but his bolt remained open. His magazine was empty. He ejected it.

'First Squad ad*va-ance!*' Dawes shouted.

Stempel rose slowly. He fumbled with the snap on his ammo pouch. He ran forward as the guns from Second Squad roared. He was behind, but he couldn't get the Goddamn plastic *snap* open on the Goddamn *pouch!* He stumbled through the drifts. The air around him was filled with zips and zings. Death. He got the pouch open and reached inside.

He snagged his parka on a tree limb. It jerked his sleeve around. 'First Squad *down!*' Dawes shouted. When Stempel raised the new magazine, he saw the hole through his parka and realized two things. There were no trees on that field. And he was hit.

The scratch became a sting, then a throbbing ache. A bullet had passed between his biceps and his chest. When he probed inside, he saw blood on his glove.

A grenade burst up ahead. Then another. They illuminated the sixty or so meters that now separated the two sides. It was table-top flat and covered in a blanket of sparkling snow. He fired and fired again.

'First Squad *u-u-up!*' Dawes screeched.

It took all the will Stempel could muster to rise. To abandon the soft snow for the hail of bullets and sprays of shrapnel. Gone was the pain from his arm. Gone was the shockingly cold snow that had found its way inside his collar on his hard fall. He stood up and almost instantly thought he would die.

The random streaks of passing bullets became a constant stream. He zig-zagged. '*You're a dead man if you run straight!*' he remembered the DI's shout. To his right and his left men fell. Screams now joined the zips of bullets and pops of Chinese rifles. Stempel willed himself onward step by step. But the gale grew particularly heavy. He cringed, then ducked, then dropped.

A stunning blast of hot fire dazed Stempel. He was stunned. He felt like someone had kicked his helmet and slapped open palms on his ears . . . all at once. Somebody was shouting, '*Grena-a-ades!*' at

295

the top of his lungs. They were bursting everywhere. Snow and flame shot skyward.

Stempel suddenly remembered that he too had grenades. He patted his cargo pockets and fished out a steel pineapple. Another explosion almost knocked the wind from him. The ground underneath him bucked. Only after the violent blast did he register its heat on his exposed face. Then snow fell all around him. Huge gobs came first, then a fine, frozen mist.

Harold looked down and saw his left index finger in the metal ring. He twisted and pulled and twisted and . . . The ring came out. He held the grenade and handle in his right hand. Another blast peppered his neck and face with ice. It stung terribly. His eyes watered.

Yet another grenade burst nearby. It forced a realization. Harold looked around through tears but saw no one. Those grenades were hurled not at his squad . . . but at him and him alone. He was in grenade range. All by himself. They were trying to kill him.

He rose to one knee. Drew the grenade back to his right ear. Pointed with his left hand at a group of flashing muzzles. And hurled the grenade with a grunt. He dropped down. The effort had wrenched his shoulder painfully. The air above him filled with lead.

By the time his grenade went off, he was pulling a second pin. He reared up – heedless of the terrible danger – and threw at a different cluster of flashes. He pressed himself flat into the snow. The buzzing bees above him had never been angrier. His parka jerked – tugged by a passing bullet. Another bullet stung his boot. Pain shot through his ankle. He contorted his body to look down. A piece of rubber had been peeled off the sole of the thick, insulated boots. His ankle must have been twisted by the force.

Twack! A jarring blow to Stempel's helmet simultaneously hurt his ears and his neck. It gave him an intense headache. A bullet had glanced off his helmet. More skittered through the snow. Buzzed by his ears. The pain meant nothing. He had to save his life.

He got a third grenade, frantically pulled the pin, and set his teeth in a clench. He rose up into that death and threw with all his might. '*A-a-ah!*' he shouted with the effort.

A black object disappeared into the snow in front of him. He dropped back down. He felt like he was inside the explosion. Everything was a blur. He could make no sense of the battlefield. He found his rifle but as if in a dream couldn't clear his head enough to use it. He was still patiently brushing ice from the M-16 when he felt a hand grab his parka and shake.

'Charge those holes!' Lieutenant Dawes shouted. He was pointing.

'You're bleeding, sir,' Stempel said. There was a huge gash along his jaw line.

'Come *on*, soldier!' Dawes shouted. Blood that hung from his chin fell in large, black drops.

Stempel rose – rifle in hand – and charged. He sprinted in the direction Dawes had pointed. He ran straight at the Chinese guns. When he zigged, he saw no friendly troops. He zagged. He was all alone.

He ran like a maniac straight toward the enemy.

Chinese guns fired on either side. But in the center – where he'd thrown his grenades – it was dark. He headed for the target of his first toss. It was a round mortar pit. The last few steps took forever. He was so, so exposed. The pit was ringed with a low wall of sandbags. The air was filled with smoke. The dark hole looked still. But it had been filled with flaming muzzles.

Grenades went off all around. They sounded like a string of thunderous firecrackers. These, he realized, were American grenades. They were thrown forward . . . *toward* him! He leapt over the sandbags and fell through the air into the mortar pit. Behind him, the night erupted in flame. He landed feet first, but it did little good. He tumbled and crashed onto the icy ground.

And onto warm bodies. The dark pit was full of them. He could see them with every burst. Chinese soldiers. It was still. But they weren't all dead. He didn't know why he felt sure. Someone was hiding under the bodies. He raised his rifle. His finger on the trigger. Tense. Ready to fire. He threw himself backwards against the wall. With his back to the sandbags, he traversed the pit with his muzzle. The weapon to his shoulder. The sight to his eye.

A man scampered over the wall in a shower of snow. Stempel almost shot Lieutenant Dawes. Instead he shot a lunging Chinese soldier. He saw the man die. In the blaze of the muzzle at point-blank range. The bullet struck his ear below his helmet. Brains sprayed frozen sandbags.

Dawes began firing single shots into the Chinese. A dozen bullets for a dozen bodies. No others made a move. None showed any signs of life before they were shot. All were certainly dead after. The pit was filled with viscera and gore.

The lieutenant made his way over to Harold. He had a large gash running along his jaw that dripped blood. He patted Harold down, finding the wound on his inner biceps. The matching scratch on his chest. By then, Harold's eyes had sunk closed.

'Just a scrape,' Dawes said after probing the wound. The stings of pain were sharp. Hot.

Scraping and sliding sounds drew Harold's rifle. Dawes slapped the barrel down before Stempel killed his squadmates. They piled into the mortar pit one at a time. The 'fighting' in the near distance was now execution-style. Single shots, single grenades, death by ones.

'They ran outa ammo,' the cornet player said as he examined an AKS rifle. He worked the bolt. No bullets came out.

Dawes was pinching Harold's face as if examining pimples. Harold closed his eyes and hissed in pain. 'You got some metal splinters from a grenade,' Dawes reported. 'You'll have to get 'em out at an aid station.' The artillery surveyor held a pressure bandage on Harold's face.

'Hey, man,' the guy said. 'You got *way* outta line, there. We couldn't throw any grenades 'cause you got so far out . . .'

'He fuckin' saved your *ass!*' Lieutenant Dawes snapped. The man fell silent. 'You can't go to *ground* out in the open! When you *attack*, you gotta *take* the Goddamn position! This *private* here is an *infantryman!* You should all spend the rest of your miserable lives thanking God for that!'

The guy said nothing. The lieutenant made him reply with an unequivocal, 'Yes, *sir!*' Harold took over the bandage from him. Dawes told the squad to wait there. He went off. One by one the men thanked Stempel. But all he felt was the prickly, hot feeling that spread across his skin. He grew flushed. His ears rang. The cut along the inside of his bicep and the splinters in his face all burned. His head pounded.

But he was alive. He'd made it. 'Way to go, man,' somebody said. He opened his eyes with each thank-you. He counted. There were five people in the pit – including him. There had been ten men in 1st Squad, 3rd Platoon, 1st Provisional Infantry Company.

'Where're the others?' Stempel asked.

They were slow to respond.

'The Spec Five's dead,' the Multichannel Communications guy

finally offered. He was seated comfortably atop a Chinese soldier in the black, still night. 'Checked him myself. Bullet must've gone right in his mouth 'cause I didn't see no hole. But when I took his hood and helmet off, the back of his head sorta . . . came *with* it.'

'O-o-oh, *gross!*' the cornet player said.

'Where the hell're those *Air* Force fucks?' someone asked.

'I never saw 'em once we left the slit trench,' came the reply. The implication was clear.

'I saw two of 'em get hit,' the Motor Transportation Operator reported.

'Well, what about the third guy?' No one knew. He was, therefore, either a coward or dead.

'Where's that woman?' Stempel asked.

'Dead,' the Motor Transport man said. 'Grenade blew up right in front of her.'

'*Jesus*,' the cornet player said. He rubbed under the obviously itchy cap that he wore under his helmet. 'That's *half* of us . . . dead.'

Lieutenant Dawes returned with a sergeant. Stempel thought it was their new squad leader. But he saw too many rockers and chevrons on the man's black plastic insignia.

'Listen up,' Dawes said. 'We're gonna combine you with 2nd Squad. This lodgement has been reduced. But there're still infiltrators running around loose. We're gonna form a skirmish line and sweep the runway. When we find 'em, just drop, return fire, and wait for orders. Let's go.' Stempel started to rise. 'Not you,' Dawes said. 'You go with the First Sergeant. The line companies need infantry fillers.'

'Well, *shit!*' the Motor Transportation guy said. 'We need him *too*, sir!'

'He's infantry,' Dawes replied. 'This is a provisional company.'

'Yeah, but I don't see *them* out here attackin' Chinese *"lodgements."*'

'*You* wanta go out to the perimeter?' Dawes snapped angrily. He turned to the First Sergeant. 'I *know* it must be a little *slow* up there, Top! But you think you can use one more man?'

The man's slow laugh sounded like a smoker's cough. '*Well*, sir, we *do* have this patrol goin' out come sun-up.' The soldier didn't say another word. Harold parted company with his second unit since the war began. They shook hands and wished each other luck. Dawes led the small group off.

That left Stempel alone with the First Sergeant. 'You were with the 2/263rd?' the senior non-com asked. Stempel nodded. The man looked around at the dead Chinese. Stempel had grown accustomed to their presence. He was safe there. 'We tried to come help,' the man said. 'Ran right into the main force coming in to attack this base. Made it back with the whole People's Liberation Army on our heels.'

The man's voice sounded far away. Stempel didn't know what to say. 'Thank you,' he managed.

The dark profile of the helmet slowly turned Stempel's way. He stared at Stempel in silence before reaching out to Stempel's shoulder. 'You got that the wrong way around, private,' the raspy First Sergeant said softly. His hand gently squeezed.

It was a bad time for introductions. Stempel's new comrades had just survived a major attack.

'Private Stempel, here, is joining First Squad,' the First Sergeant announced. The hollow-eyed men sagged low against the main trench wall. No one rose, or nodded, or extended a hand, or said a word. The First Sergeant took Stempel's new squad leader aside for a few private words. The men sat facing Stempel – their backs to the fighting steps and covered machine-gun revetments. Some looked down at his blood-caked parka. Not in horror, or even curiosity, it seemed to Stempel, but in a daze.

The First Sergeant left. The squad leader stepped back up to Stempel. 'We better get those wounds seen to,' he said – peering at Stempel's face.

'Oh,' Harold remembered – raising his left arm. 'I got grazed here, too,' he said. He showed the sergeant the bloody hole in his sleeve. Harold looked up and caught the man looking at him.

'You were with the 2/263rd?' he asked. Heads turned from among the zombies on the trench floor. Stempel nodded. The sergeant's gaze now fell. Hard, black ice covered the trench floor. 'We tried to back you guys up,' he said. 'We tried to make it out to you.'

'We *barely* made it back *here* alive,' one of the men against the wall said. He snorted.

'Patterson!' the squad leader snapped.

'Well, *shit*, sarge!' Patterson replied – looking around for support. 'We lost *two* on that little, stupid fucking *excursion*. Then we lost Taylor *last* night.' Stempel didn't understand the reason for the men's heated exchange. 'Now they got us goin' out on a Goddamn *combat* patrol?'

'We're not goin' out. We're gettin' fillers like Stempel here.'

Patterson leapt to his feet and shook Harold's hand. 'Welcome, new guy!' He was grinning.

'We're gonna dig instead,' the squad leader said. There were groans. Patterson bitched. 'And yeah, Patterson, we've lost three guys out of ten.' He turned to Stempel. 'How many did *you* lose in *your* squad?'

Stempel's mouth hung open. Patterson's smile disappeared. He quickly released Stempel's hand.

'*Come* on, sarge,' Patterson whispered.

'*How many?*' the squad leader snarled at Stempel.

'Out of *my* squad?' Stempel asked. The man nodded. Stempel's throat was dry. He didn't know any of their names. 'Well . . . *all* of 'em. Except me.' He asked about casualties in Harold's platoon. 'M-my . . . *platoon?*' The squad leader nodded. 'Uhm, everybody. I think I was the only one in my company to . . .'

Gone was the dissension – the back-talk from Patterson. Stempel's answers seemed to roust the men from their well of fatigue and self-pity. 'Let's get you some new gear,' the squad leader said. He came back with a new parka. Stempel quickly changed. The new jacket was freezing cold, but clean. 'Just toss your old one over there,' the sergeant directed him – pointing.

Stempel went over to the heap. When he got there, he realized it was a pile of gear. Webbing. Packs. Wool underclothes. Bloody Arctic whites. He added to it. Tossing the caked-brown parka on top.

Chapter Fourteen

BETHESDA NAVAL HOSPITAL, MARYLAND
January 31, 1300 GMT (0800 Local)

The knock at the door woke Gordon Davis. When he opened his eyes, he saw Daryl Shavers.

Gordon smiled. His old friend approached the bed.

Gordon could hear a faint chant in the distance. Demonstrators shouting, 'Hell no, we won't go!'

'You made it through that all right?' Gordon asked.

Daryl smirked. 'They're pacifists, not anarchists.' He laughed. 'They got these doctors – you know, in those green scrub suits – standing in front of the cameras protesting your drafting them. Haven't seen 'em this mad since that big managed-care legislation. You remember that?' Daryl sat. 'So, what's it like to be president? Is it everything you dreamed it'd be?'

'No jokes, please,' Gordon said. 'It hurts to laugh.'

There was an awkward pause. 'Helluva mess you got yourself into, Gordon. I think you've singlehandedly set the civil rights movement back thirty years.'

'Is it that bad?' Gordon asked. 'Are they bringing up race?'

Daryl shook his head. 'I'm just pulling your leg. About the only thing you've got *going* for you in the polls is that you're black, and you're all shot up.'

Gordon's eyes strayed to the window. The chant had given way to a fiery but unintelligible speech shouted through a bull horn. 'My honeymoon period?' he said.

Daryl smiled. 'Seriously, Gordon, how do you feel?'

'What did that drunk cowboy say down in Dallas?'

'I don't know. I wasn't in Dallas.' Gordon looked at him. 'What *did* he say?' Daryl added quickly.

'"Rode hard and put up wet,"' Gordon replied in a lifeless voice. 'Listen, Daryl. I'd like to talk about what happened.'

'Yeah, well . . . I've moved on, Gordon. Got a job at a company in Chicago that makes biodegradable bags for potato chips. Hires inner-city workers. Donates one percent of its payroll to liberal causes. That kinda shit. You didn't get my card?' Gordon shook his head. 'I guess you don't get to read your own mail any more.'

'Are you . . . wed to this potato chip thing?'

Daryl stared back at Gordon, then spun and began to pace. 'I don't need this shit in my life right now, Gordon! Jesus! I've got a job. I've got a contract on a house in an upscale white neighborhood on the North Shore. I've had *two* offers to join country clubs that are worried about discrimination lawsuits and are willing to waive my initial membership fee, which is like forty *thousand* bucks!'

'Sounds like a good deal,' Gordon said. Daryl was standing at the window. His fingers separated slats at eye level. His back was to Gordon. 'I mean, if this thing has some career potential . . .'

'*"Career potential"!*' Daryl exploded. He spun to face Gordon.

The door opened. Two Secret Service agents stood in the narrow space looking in.

'Could we have some privacy?' Gordon said. The men disappeared. He turned to Daryl. 'I'd like you to be my Chief of Staff.'

Daryl snorted in derision. But he couldn't quite keep the sickly smile from parting his lips. 'You're serious.' He shook his head. 'Man, I thought you had better political sense than that. What's in that IV bag? Demerol? Morphine?'

'I need you, Daryl. I'm all alone. Stuck in this bed. I don't know the people who work for me. They don't tell me things I need to hear. I find out more from listening to *that*,' he said, jabbing his thumb at the window, 'than from talking to my advisers. I need somebody I can trust.'

Daryl snorted again – this time in amusement. 'Running for cover, are they?'

'Like scalded dogs.' They laughed. Gordon cherished the moment despite the pain. 'Daryl, I'm going down in flames, here. I need you.'

'To do what, Gordon?' Daryl asked. He hovered close by Gordon's bed. The hook was in deep.

'Pull up a chair.'

'I wish you'd worn a tie,' Gordon mumbled to Daryl, who stood at the head of his bed. The National Security Council was about to convene their briefing. Entering the now map-filled room were some of the most powerful people in Washington.

Each new political animal to arrive sized up Daryl – the new beast at the watering hole. Each smiled and greeted Gordon and then Daryl – the latter with an abundance of grace and enthusiasm. 'I remember you from the . . . the *Houston* convention, wasn't it?' the Secretary of Defense said. 'You were a *floor* manager, tha-at's right!' He shook Daryl's hand a second time as if Daryl had not yet been properly greeted.

'Daryl's going to be my Chief of Staff,' Gordon lobbed into the gathering.

Good-natured smiles never left the faces of the well-mannered men and women. They descended on Daryl again. Shaking his hand anew. Congratulating him. Even grabbing and squeezing his shoulders with both hands. But by lunchtime, Gordon knew, the long knives would be out. Dirt dug up and leaked to the press. Snide remarks made off the record. Political sabotage of the upstart challenger. Gordon decided to turn the tables on the previously secure Cabinet heads.

'Daryl has agreed to take a look at the staff – from top to bottom – and make recommendations.' The grins now grew slightly more strained. Some even dropped the effort altogether. 'Since I'm laid up here indefinitely, Daryl is going to have carte blanche to trim things up for the rough sailing we've got ahead of us.' *Always good to use sailing metaphors*, Gordon thought. 'Except high-level positions, of course.' Gordon smiled. Everyone smiled back. 'I'll make those calls myself . . . after Daryl's recommendations.'

Their ears were all twitching at that. No longer did they lap at the still pool. They now scoured the terrain for the sound of breaking twigs that announced the approach of a predator. It was probably enough of a charge, Gordon decided, to break up the liaisons and cliques and make it every man for himself. If not, he could up the voltage. Like Daryl had said after Gordon had sold him on the plan but then began to falter – 'Hey, Gordon. *Fuck* them! You're the President of the United States!' The pain from his laughter was still fresh – Gordon had had to work hard to keep the grin off his face.

OUTSIDE KHABAROVSK, SIBERIA
February 2, 0400 GMT (1800 Local)

Chin stopped long enough to look at his new watch. The impressive radium dial glowed in the dark. They had two hours to be in position for a dawn attack. But the going was slow through the thick woods and heavy snow. It was then that the worst happened.

A stunning display of noise and fire tore the forest apart. Chin was so shocked by the violence of the explosions that he didn't dive to the ground as he'd been taught. He sank onto his haunches and sat – his head swimming. In the moment before the second wave of explosions, Chin willed himself down into the powdery snow. A tidal wave of fire passed over him. In the aftermath, he heard the crackling of dry evergreens and the wails of the wounded.

But they weren't through. The ground slammed against him time and time again. He was covered in snow falling from thick branches. He was suffocating. He struggled to rise up for air. But when he got to his knees he still couldn't catch a breath. The searing licks of heat flashed yet again.

Snow fell from the limbs above and bounced from the ground in a fine mist of ice crystals. Chin inhaled them with all his might – breathing ice amid raging fires.

When Chin awoke, he was all alone. The cloak of darkness and silence had again descended on the woods. His head hurt so much the first thing he did was probe his bristly scalp for a wound. There was none.

But his limbs were numb from the cold. When he half rose, his skin tingled like at the onset of a fever. He retched.

Over and over Chin's stomach heaved until it was empty. The effort drained him so completely he collapsed back into the snow. There he lay. Sweating and cold. For how long he couldn't tell. He rested his eyes. Time seemed to slip. He was cold.

The sky was noticeably lighter. The attack should have begun already. But there was no sound of fighting. Chin listened more closely. He'd not yet seen combat. But he'd listened to the sounds. They could hear the attacks on the big American base miles away. For several days they had listened as they waited for their turn to come. But Chin heard nothing at all now. Nothing but the silence of the empty forest.

He struggled to his knees. The world was spinning. He almost blacked out completely when he rose to his feet. A bitter pit of nausea still burned in his stomach. Chin had to support himself with his hands on his thighs. He stood bent half over around the source of the pain. When he finally straightened, he saw immediately what had not been obvious before.

The forest was shattered. Healthy evergreens were cracked in two. Green bristles littered the snowy ground. Huge splinters of shredded white wood protruded from broken trunks like exposed bones.

And there were gaping black craters. Yawning holes blasted out of the earth by huge explosions. The closest lay less than fifty meters from where Chin stood.

Bombs, he realized. They'd been bombed.

He suddenly panicked. What was he doing there? Where was everyone else? Could it be that . . . he was dead? That he had died and his spirit had just risen . . . uncertain what to do next? He looked down at the snow beneath his boots. He saw no corpse. Only the bile he'd spewed from his aching belly.

Where is everybody? He looked all around. At first he saw no one. Then – slowly – the crumpled shapes that had moments before been logs metamorphosed into human form. Half-covered in snow. An elbow. A helmet-covered head. A severed leg. Chin stood there . . . alone among the dead.

He was alive. If they were dead, he must be alive. Chin groped in the snow with numb hands for his rifle. He pulled the weapon from the powder. He shook and brushed it until it might possibly be in good enough condition to fire. Then he listened. Nothing. The attack must have been called off. They'd been discovered. Bombed. They'd never made it to the American guns.

He took one last look at the brightening sky to the east, then headed back in the direction from which they'd come. Away from the American base. When he got back to his platoon that afternoon, his senior sergeant gave him the headcount. Twelve missing. Two wounded. Fifteen present and ready for duty.

His platoon was now down to half strength. They had yet to fire their weapons in combat.

UNRUSFOR HEADQUARTERS, KHABAROVSK
February 3, 1730 GMT (0330 Local)

The French colonel took the radio microphone himself. The interpreter whispered the translation into Clark's ear. 'Do you read me, Firebase Toulon, over?' But Clark had been listening to the repetitive calls for so long that he needed no translation. Two hundred French paratroopers and engineers had been helicoptered into Firebase Toulon. Their mission was to prepare the base for a brigade that had gotten bogged down by a series of minor ambushes dozens of kilometers away. The colonel repeated his call. Clark walked over and put his hand on the man's shoulder.

The officer lowered his chin and continued to call out over the radio. Clark left him alone. But the spell his vigil had cast over the group around the radio was broken. By returning to his desk, Clark had pronounced the unit dead.

Papers lay spread over the working area that he used at one end of the operations center. He had a spacious office upstairs, with oriental rugs and hard, dark wood furniture of vaguely Scandinavian style. But he preferred this spot – in the company of others – to the quiet of the tomb-like room.

The calls in French drowned out the other noise and chatter of the big room. It wasn't that they were any louder. It was the regularity of the man's efforts. First a call, then a pause to listen for a response, then the exact same call again. Clark sat there staring at the paper. Waiting for the next try. It was like water dripping from a leaky faucet. As the man's wait for a reply grew longer, the silence grew more oppressive. Clark listened intently. All that was missing in the din of activity were the few words spoken in French. The silence went on and on. Clark's mind tried to fill the void with what it expected to hear – the words that were now long overdue.

But it was over. Even the colonel had finally given up. There was no one single event that marked the death of a unit, Clark thought. Like the death of a single human, the line was a wavering one. Was it when the heart stopped functioning? Or respiration? Or the brain?

A unit was a living organism too. Its death was also purely definitional. When the last man had been chased down and shot like a dog, the unit was clearly dead. But its death really occurred some time before that. *Was it when the main line of defenses was breached?* he thought. No. The unit still lived. It still fought. Hand-to-hand in trenches and holes. The commander desperately sending his last feeble reserves into the gap. Was it when the command post was overrun? The commander killed? No. The military made its units tough. Resilient. Even after the command post was overrun, the subordinate commanders held their panicked men together for the final phase of every decisive battle – the slaughter.

Clark was tired, but he forced his mind to focus on the question he'd posed. He knew he couldn't sleep now anyway, even if he wanted to. When is it that a unit dies? When would he know to take the marker off the map? To declare its men 'Missing in Action, Presumed Dead or Captured'?

The radio traffic that poured into Clark's nerve center was growing by the minute. The operators' replies formed an ever louder buzz in the background of the windowless shelter. He looked at his watch – the only way to learn the hour in his perpetually darkened world. Dawn was approaching. Each cell of the UNRUSFOR organism was preparing for the inevitable 'contact.' Clark realized just then he had his answer. A unit died when it quit calling him on the radio. It no longer existed when he couldn't talk to it. No matter that the last soldier hadn't yet been tracked down. When a unit's radio goes off the air, it's dead.

Clark pulled out a pad and a pen. He began to write. 'Dear Lydia: By now I know you and the boys must be back in McLean. I understand your desire to return home, and I totally approve. You must also have

309

seen by now the accounts of my visit to Birobidzhan. I must tell you that my actions there were every bit as foolish as was reported in the press, if not more so. I know you must be worried sick about me. And added to those worries, I know, is the already heavy burden of caring for our two sons alone. But I have to write this letter. I have to talk to someone. I have nowhere else to turn. No one with whom I can speak these words that now crush me so completely that I can hardly breathe. I'm sorry. Please forgive me, but I must put them down on paper and know that someone else has read them. I must ask you to help shoulder the weight of these words, because I'm too weak to bear it alone.

'War is the saddest thing I have ever known. In this world, I know, human tragedies abound. Loved ones perish by illness or accident or old age, and their loss is immense. But in war, huge armies of bright, healthy young people are sent out into the field to rip the life from one another. They are our very best. The brightest hopes of a million mothers and a million fathers. They are strong, and brave. They know where they're going. They know what lies ahead. They know what's going to happen to them when they get there. God Almighty, Lydia, how do they do it? What cause could be so great as to bind them to their duty?

'I must confess, Lydia, that at times my strength fails me. At times I cannot remember the cause for which I send those young men and women to their deaths. I know the words. But they're like mental tricks which work sometimes, and fail me at others. They are failing me now, Lydia. At times like these, I feel I owe a duty greater than to my country. A duty to God or to nature or to those hundreds of thousands of men and women whose lives are being wasted. Wasted. I feel an overpowering urge to step out into the middle of no man's land and shout "Stop!" at the top of my lungs. "Nothing matters more than life! None of this will change a thing!"

'It's then I realize that I could no more stop what is happening here than I could alter the drift of the continents. We were always going to fight. Here. In this awful place. Some immutable law of nature bound us to this battlefield as surely as gravity holds our feet to the earth.

'I have been through war before, Lydia, as have you. I know

that my present weakness will pass. I will banish it, because it is defeatist. It goes against what I was taught to think. But what if I'm wrong, Lydia? What if everything I've been led to believe has misguided me? What if the deeds I believe to be heroic prove nothing more than base sins against humanity? Lydia, if I'm dragged down into the fires of Hell to pay for the evil I am committing, I will go without complaint. I will wish nothing more than that I spend eternity paying the price for my corrupted ideals. I will bear all, suffer all, pay whatever toll with a lightness of heart born of the certainty – finally – of knowing what is right and what is wrong. I will gladly accept that fate, Lydia, but only if you will forgive me those sins. If you will know and believe my one excuse that I give only to you, Lydia, only to you – I didn't know what I was doing was wrong. I didn't know, Lydia. I didn't know.'

Clark sensed Major Reed standing patiently beside his desk. He had no idea how long he'd been there. Clark looked up and drew a deep breath with difficulty. 'Yes?' he said.

'J-STARS has positive contact with a five-hundred-plus vehicle convoy. It's crossing the Amur near Madagachi. The Joint Controllers have asked to divert the morning's B-52 raids to hit the convoy. Their targets are a hydroelectric plant and some munitions factories at Harbin that we can hit any time. The convoy is hemmed into a pass between steep hills, waiting to cross. Estimates are that it could be an entire infantry division. The Joint Controllers need your authority to divert and hit those passes.'

Reed stood there, waiting. After a moment, Reed said, 'We could knock out a whole division with one air raid, sir.' Clark forced his eyes to focus on the man. 'We've got three cells – nine B-52s – chock full of five-hundred-pound bombs. They could overlay that box one after the other.' He fell silent. He waited.

He seemed not to understand what he was asking Clark to do. That he was asking Clark to commit his mortal soul to a course that was irreversible. To sign the death warrant of thousands of human beings with no more reflection than one would give the most casual of the day's issues.

Clark nodded, and Reed ran off. Lt General Nate Clark looked down at the letter, which awaited his signature. He crumpled it into a ball and tossed it into the trash.

SMIDOVICH, SIBERIA
February 4, 2100 GMT (0700 Local)

There they are, Chin thought to himself as he peered over the shredded trunk of a tree. He scanned the small dale that separated his ridge from the southern edge of the small Russian town. In the early morning light he could clearly see the American soldiers scurrying around and digging in. He wished that he had binoculars to survey the approaches to their objective. The amazing view given by the pair his training class had passed around had astonished the officer candidates. But in the five months Chin had been in the Army he'd only seen two other pairs. Both were dangling from the necks of colonels like all their other badges of rank.

Chin spotted his platoon's objective – the lower of two stone walls that traversed the gently rising hill opposite him. 'You see the wall, senior sergeant?' Chin asked the man lying next to him. The sergeant was a veteran of several years. He was the only man over the age of twenty in the platoon. 'Yes, sir.'

Chin eyed him for signs of disrespect, but could detect none. 'Do you have any questions?' Chin asked.

The senior sergeant stared out across the dale at the busy Americans. 'Did they tell you how many of them are over there?'

'No.'

The sergeant didn't respond for a few moments. 'Did they say anything about getting a third magazine of ammunition for the men?'

'They said regimental stretcher bearers will bring ammunition up and take wounded back,' Chin replied. He was growing more and more wary of the man's tone.

'Did the company commander give us a second objective?' the senior sergeant asked.

'*No*,' Chin said testily. He looked over at the man. The senior sergeant stared out at the three hundred-odd meters of open space that ran down their hill and back up to the edge of the city. He nodded his head slowly – almost imperceptibly – and fell silent.

Chin rubbed his eyes, which were bleary from lack of sleep. They had been spared the last few days of furious assaults on the American base while their platoon awaited replacements. Then, their commanders changed their plans. They had marched right past the surrounded

Americans. It was a great victory, he'd told his men. The airbase's defenders would wither on the vine. Even as he'd repeated the words passed down to him by the company commander, the air overhead was filled with the sound of huge transport planes. They landed at the base every couple of minutes.

Chin forced his mind back to the present. The enemy lines across the valley didn't look so formidable. The open fields below had only traces of snow and ice. They wouldn't have to slog through knee-deep drifts while exposed to fire.

But the sun was well up now. *We're over three hours late*, Chin saw, looking at his wristwatch. They had intended to take advantage of the darkness for the dash across the open dale. *But now?*

He looked up and down the line of helmets. The men of his battalion lay in the brush – their packs on the ground around them to be left behind per the battalion commander's orders. Twisting around, he caught glimpses of 1st Battalion's line thirty meters behind. They were poised to rush forward and fire at the Americans as Chin's 2nd Battalion advanced. He looked down at the floor of the valley. The distance suddenly seemed far greater than before. He felt ice water course through his veins in place of the warm blood from before.

The lower of the two stone walls – his company's objective – sat about a third of the way up the opposite hill. The route he would take to it seemed smooth and unbroken. There was good footing except for the small clumps of manure whose tiny shadows dotted the valley. The animals which had been penned between the two walls were nowhere in sight. *Sheep and goats*, he reasoned. *Oxen would have wandered right through the loose stones.*

He smiled and felt calmed by the thought. He'd been an ox boy as a youth on his family's farm. He'd seen the animals use their tremendous strength to simply walk through most man-made obstacles. Sheer, brute force – almost nothing could stop the massive beasts.

Chin closed his eyes – feeling bathed by the crisp morning air. He took a deep, refreshing breath. When he opened his eyes, he saw the platoon leader to his left – Lieutenant Hung – staring blankly into the dirt beneath him. *College boy*, Chin thought with disgust. *City puke.*

The sound of shells overhead ripped the fabric of Chin's fragile calm. He cringed and hunched his shoulders in anticipation. But the first explosion burst not over their heads but on the opposite ridge just short of the American positions. The men of his platoon began to

313

cheer. He turned and snapped 'Quiet!' at their stupidity. His hand fell to his rifle – as taught – to reinforce his particularly important order.

Chin heard a whistle from his far left and his heart skipped a beat. A flare shot into the air and burst as whistles sounded on both sides. His skin crawled. A slight shiver shook his body. The last of the Americans leapt into their holes at the town's edge, and then their positions were still. The time for their attack had seemed so far away just minutes ago. A full company of men to his left rose from the low brush and moved forward. The shells now fell randomly amid the Americans.

Another whistle sounded. Two shorts – one long. His company commander's order. Chin reached into his parka and placed the warm whistle to his lips. He blew it with all his might. Chin turned to see his men rise to their feet. The entire platoon moved past him through the light brush. He and the senior sergeant then rose to follow them at the prescribed distance.

The men began to shout as they burst out into the open. Chin felt the slope fall away under his feet. The full-throated roar of the attacking battalion filled the valley. It inspired Chin with its volume and mass. He was not alone.

Down the hill they ran. The only sound in the valley was that of their voices. He felt a part of a great process many thousands of years old. Chin looked across at the American positions. Always the outsiders came. Always this was the way they left.

Chin's whole body flinched as if struck by a blow. A phenomenal burping and cracking roar had erupted from the American lines. The battalion's shouts trailed off to silence as men began to fall. Some stumbled. Others stood straight up, then slid to the ground awkwardly. Still others cartwheeled or spun to the ground with a dramatic flourish. Some men emitted bloodcurdling screams. Some not so much as a grunt. But all had one thing in common. All died from their devastating wounds . . .

'Buzzes' and 'zings' rushed by Chin's ears. An almost electric sense of alertness vibrated every nerve ending. His legs continued to propel him forward. But the rest of his body awaited the impact that would end his life.

Fully half his tightly packed men fell before they reached the valley floor. Small geysers of earth erupted with sharp 'booms' as American mortars dropped in their path. Machine-gun fire came at them in sheets. His platoon's advance slowed as if running against a stiff wind.

The line quickly began to grow ragged. Chin clenched his teeth and ran harder to catch up with his flagging platoon.

'Keep moving!' he yelled as he pulled nearly even with them. 'Faster!' he ordered as he came up behind one man and shoved. But the sound of his voice was lost in the stunning noise from the guns toward which they raced. Looking back to make sure no one lagged, he saw the slope littered with wounded and dead. Behind them appeared 1st Battalion. They charged out of the treeline with their mouths wide with shouts. The first men in their long line began to fall. The ground on the floor of the valley flattened. Chin almost stumbled before turning back toward the enemy. As he regained his balance, he noted that his men were still advancing. But their shoulders were hunched as if a heavy rain beat down upon them. Large gaps had been opened in their line.

A series of explosions suddenly burst up and down the battlefield to each side of Chin. The remaining men from his platoon came to a complete stop. They pressed themselves to the ground. They didn't return fire. They curled themselves into fetal positions and held their helmets or hugged their bodies. It did nothing to ward off the bullets that hailed death from 150 meters ahead.

Chin dropped to the ground. He opened his mouth to yell at the man lying barely five meters away. Great splashes of frothy orange blood erupted from the smooth white parka that was stretched over the soldier's broad back. Chin watched in frozen terror as the helpless man jerked with each devastating blow.

The sod next to Chin's head splattered into his face. The 'whiz-z-z-z' of bullets passing and the thud as they pounded the earth around him grew nearly continuous. Death was mere seconds away. He willed himself up to a low stoop. It was as high as his rebellious body would go. And he ran. He zig-zagged up the hill toward the low wall.

In his path lay a small round object. Its green plastic was meant to blend into grass. But it stood in stark contrast to the gray patch of ice beneath it. Wires like a spider's legs radiated outward in all directions.

They were everywhere. *A minefield!*

But Chin didn't slow down. He couldn't. There was only one way out. High-stepping as if through puddles, Chin wove his way through the web. He was unable to see the sinister tentacles. He simply stayed as far as possible from their explosive center. He concentrated on the ground just before his feet. He completely lost track of his platoon and its fate. His toes dug into the uphill slope. He dodged and weaved. Each second was a game of chance with bullets that sliced through the air all around. Giant explosions burst on both sides of him. He thought nothing. Saw nothing. Felt nothing. He was frozen in motion. Eyes peeled to the ground. Legs pumping. He was neither alive nor dead. He instead walked a tightrope in between – awaiting the outcome.

Suddenly, Chin was confused. He was running, but it was like running in a dream. He wasn't exactly sure what he was doing. A choking smoke made him begin coughing. A wave of great nausea swept over him. He was sure now that he wasn't running. But nothing in Chin's world seemed right. As he sought out reality, the first thing he found was terrible pain emanating from his ears and the center of his head. The pain deluged him. His body hummed with the agony of it.

He opened his eyes and lifted his wobbly head. He saw a smoking hole. Behind it was a hill with trees on top – the ridge from which his battalion had attacked. A ragged collection of men crawled across it or flopped from side-to-side. And in their midst, geysers of dirt erupted into the air in great sprays. He heard jarring sounds – a jumble of very loud noise. In the woods behind the writhing men Chin saw flashes and puffs of smoke from the treeline. *3rd Battalion*, he remembered. *That's 3rd Battalion.*

A pair of jets flew wingtip-to-wingtip. They banked steeply to align themselves with the hill's treeline. He fought to focus his blurred vision. Four canisters – two from each plane – tumbled end over end. They fell into the trees on top of 3rd Battalion.

Billowing flames mushroomed skyward. The heat was searing even at 200 meters. Chin's eyes teared and he jammed them tightly shut. The heat and noise grew more and more painful as the air rumbled and ground shook. Oily fumes filled Chin's nostrils and mouth.

Just as suddenly as it had erupted, the noise was replaced by the crackle of a roaring fire. The valley was quiet. Then the cracks of individual American rifles resumed their methodical killing.

Chin forced his watering eyes to look back across the dale. A huge black cloud rose into the air above the ridge. The entire crest was charred black and flattened. It was broken only by small licks of flame that still found nourishment from unburned wood. A forest of trunks pointed skyward like broken spears. It and everyone in it had been incinerated in seconds.

The pall of thick black smoke drifted in the gentle breeze. The taste of petroleum fouled Chin's mouth. He lowered his head to the ground in great fatigue. Several of his men cowered behind the stone wall, which was being chipped into fragments around their hunched shoulders.

We took it, Chin thought as he lay down to die. *We took it.*

When Chin awoke, it was night. Thick snow fell from the still sky. The noise and the smells of battle were gone. He raised his head. He could make nothing out under the heavy blanket of clouds. He was all alone. And he was alive.

Chin ran his hands over his body. He patted and squeezed in search of pain. But as best he could tell he was uninjured. In the darkness he felt for and found his rifle. All was as he had left it.

He had survived! The Americans hadn't policed the battlefield to kill the wounded. For all Chin could tell from listening, the Americans might even have withdrawn.

Chin rose hesitantly to his knees. Despite the cold, he felt the prickly sensation of sweat rippling across his torso. They could see him in the dark. They had special binoculars that lit up the night, but only for them.

Just in case, he decided to raise his hands in surrender. Both arms rose by his sides, and he knelt on the ground in that pose for almost a minute.

There was no sound.

Without lowering his arms Chin labored to his feet. There he stood – surrendering to the invisible army with their bat-like view from above. His throat was thick with fear. If they were there, their rifles would be aimed at him now. Strangers with the power to kill him with one squeeze of the trigger. With no more care for him than for a stray dog.

Still there was nothing. No indications that life stirred in the village.

His arms were growing tired, so he lowered them. He picked up his rifle and stood there as if to give the Americans one last chance to shoot. The tension of not knowing if he'd live or die gave way to boredom.

He turned and headed down the hill. *The mines!* he remembered, and stopped. The tiny green bombs with their web of deadly legs. Legs Chin would never see in the darkness. He looked back over his shoulder at the Americans. Chin now almost wished they were

317

there. But all was still quiet. He had only one way off that cold field.

Willing himself onward, he began his slow descent. He grimaced with each crunching footfall. Despite the cold he could feel himself sweating. The scene ran over and over in his mind. A blinding flash of light. A wall of fire. Pain everywhere. Then darkness.

But his boots found only the squeaking snow. The land underneath flattened, and his inner sense told him he'd made it. He began to walk at a more natural pace. By the time he reached the far ridge, the terrors of the night had receded.

Until, that is, he approached the charred remains of the treeline. The air was heavy with the stale smells of a long-dead fire. And the ground was littered with heaps of ash-coated debris. He stumbled every other step, finally strapping his rifle over his shoulder and groping through the obstacles using his hands in place of his eyes. It was nearly impossible to tell what he felt through his thick boots and gloves. He tried his best to shut the thoughts from his mind. But in the blackness of the burnt forest Chin's senses were alert and alive. And touch was the most intimate of all the senses. The discoveries made in that fashion were not easily shut from his mind.

Chin just tried his best not to fall in that terrible place . . . among the fallen trees and cratered earth and charred remains.

VLADIVOSTOK-USSURIYSK ROAD, SIBERIA
February 6, 0030 GMT (1030 Local)

It had taken almost three days, but Kate and Woody finally managed to talk their way to the front. Their cramped Humvee cruised along the snow-covered road. Its wipers swished the cold, dry snow back and forth. Ice framed the windshield outside the wipers' reach. Kate searched the endless forests that slid by the fog-coated side windows for some sign that a war was on. She saw nothing. Just a perpetual succession of trees.

'You want to do the interview now?' the scrawny lieutenant asked. He twisted around in his front seat. Kate sat in back between Woody and a young soldier. The sullen private held a large bag in his lap that Kate guessed normally occupied her seat.

'Here?' Kate asked. Woody cleared his throat. 'Yeah!' Kate blurted out. 'Sure! Great idea.'

Woody unzipped his camera bag. Kate reached into her backpack for a stick mike. Kate stole a glance at the soldier beside her. His breath had fogged the side window as he stared off into space.

Woody frowned at Kate. 'Batteries won't last long in the cold,' he reminded her for the hundredth time.

'Then use the special battery *saver*,' she said. Woody squinted – not getting it. 'The battery saver, Woody!' She reached up and turned the camera off. The red taping light went out.

The lieutenant was watching. 'It cuts off all unnecessary electrical . . . things,' Kate said. She flashed him a smile. He blushed and looked away. The soldier beside her was smiling.

She cleared her throat. 'Testing, one, two, three, testing,' she said into the dead stick mike. 'Ready?' The lieutenant quickly combed his hair with his fingers and nodded. She had him state his name, rank, and serial number, and identify the unit that he commanded. She dipped the microphone toward him and back. She then had him go through a brief description of his unit's responsibilities.

'Are you getting all of this?' he asked. Kate realized she'd left the mike beneath her mouth.

'Oh, it's a special, multi-directional microphone. Latest stuff. You getting all this, Woody?'

'Yep.' He squinted into the dark viewfinder. He reeked of pot smoke. His clothes were saturated with the odor.

Kate was still looking for tanks or burning hulks or shell craters or something. 'So, how often do you deliver the mail?'

As the lieutenant went through his spiel, Kate caught the soldier beside her watching them. His head lay against the window. He was onto them.

She realized the officer had finished. 'And you go right up to the battle lines to deliver the mail?'

'If we have to, ma'am. 'Course, the unit we're delivering to today hasn't seen any combat yet.'

'*What*? What do you mean?'

'Well,' he shrugged, 'the Chinese haven't gotten here yet. They're coming, but they're still a ways off. Maybe a few more days.'

'*Shit!*' Kate said. She dropped the mike into her lap.

'I couldn't take you up to the front if there was fighting, ma'am. It wouldn't be safe.'

Woody lowered the camera, replaced all the lens caps and closed up the control panels. '*Fuck!*' Kate cursed. The soldier beside her was grinning. She shook her head at her incredible misfortune.

The reporter and cameraman followed Andre Faulk on his rounds. They interviewed soldiers about their feelings on the eve of battle. The quiet woods were filling with snow. It drifted through the dense trees and piled onto the thick blanket already there. The only sounds were the crunching of their feet and the occasionally profane outburst of the woman reporter.

'I can't fucking believe it!' she went on and on and on. Andre walked in front – lugging the bag which grew lighter with each stop. The woman was short but very pretty, the cameraman older and with a ponytail. They both trailed some paces behind and acted like Andre wasn't there. The lieutenant had gone on to the next battalion to deliver the mail in his own heavy bag. He was doing the job of the private whom he'd displaced to get his face on TV.

Andre saw the round white helmets sticking up out of the snow holes ahead. The woman and the long-haired guy bickered about why they had come there. Whose idea it was. What to do next. He paused to hoist his rifle sling and bag higher on his shoulder. The reporters walked around him, not paying attention to where they were headed. He watched in amazement at their stupidity. 'They's mines up there!' he yelled.

The conversation and the two newspeople both halted. They looked back over their shoulders without turning. Andre headed off in the right direction – approaching the positions from the rear. The two civilians waited till he had passed, and then stayed in his tracks. Andre let the self-satisfied grin curl his mouth. *They ain't so Goddamn smart.*

'Ma-ail call!' he heard shouted – as always well before he arrived. As always, by the time he put the bag on the ground, there were a dozen men gathered around him.

'What platoon is this?' Andre asked. They all looked at the camera crew but kept their places around Andre.

'Third platoon, Charlie Company, 2nd Battalion,' someone called out. Andre remembered them from the barracks. He remembered listening to the sounds of fighting over the radio. He began to call out

320

their names. 'Aguire!' He ran the envelope under his nose. 'Mm-*uhm*! Smell *go-o-od*, Aguire!' The soldier snapped the pink envelope out of Andre's hands. He brushed it with his mittens. 'Alvarez!' Andre pulled the package out of the bag like Santa Claus. He raised and lowered it to judge its heft. 'I delivered one o' these yest'day. It's one o' them inflatable rubber dolls, ain't it?' There was laughter as the package was handed to Alvarez. Each man whose hands touched it took turns looking at the package as if Andre's joke had been something more than pure bullshit.

The woman was already interviewing a soldier at the edge of the semicircle around Andre. They hadn't wasted their precious batteries getting any shots of Andre doing his job. But he knew now that he might get in the picture. Or that his voice might be heard by his family. 'Bej-gro-wicz! You still ain't changed that to English?'

The laughter pleased Andre. He handed the letter over and looked at the camera.

'But don't you normally ride around in Bradley armored vehicles?' the reporter asked. She tilted the microphone toward the soldier's lips.

'Yeah, well, usually. But they ain't got enough to go around. They dropped us off up here and went back to pick up some more people at the airport. We ain't seen 'em since then.'

Andre handed the mail out, but listened to the woman's questions. And the soldier's answers. He had wondered himself where all the armor was.

'So you're just up here by yourself with no support?' she asked. 'Chinese combat troops outnumber UNRUSFOR's by twenty to one. I thought the arrival of "heavy" units like the 2nd Infantry Division was supposed to cut down on the high infantry casualties?'

The guy's face – which moments before had shone with happiness at Andre's arrival – now reflected deep concern. He was greatly relieved when Andre called out his name and gave him his letter.

'Were you told that you would have to fight right here – from these holes – without your armor and other vehicles?' the woman asked another soldier.

The microphone was stuck in his face. He arched his eyebrows and shrugged. 'I dunno. We'll fight when we see any Chinese, I guess.'

'But you've dug holes and put out landmines. And you *do* know that the Chinese have eleven divisions headed down this way to try to take the port at Vladivostok. That's over a hundred thousand men.

They're going to hit these lines, right here, in a few days.' Andre was almost done. He stood there looking at the woman, as did everyone else. 'How does that make you feel, knowing what you've got coming your way?'

The soldier's face said it all. But she held the microphone to his mouth nonetheless. 'Wolfson!' Andre called, and handed over the package. 'That's it!'

The soldier never did reply. Andre hoisted his ever lighter load onto his shoulder. The soldiers who had not gotten any mail still stood there, as always, with a hang-dog look. This time, however, even those who held their cherished letter or package remained there. They all had a look of profound dread on their faces. They'd been robbed of the cheer that Andre felt it was his job to dispense. That pissed him off. A sadness.

They walked on toward the next platoon. Again the news crew trailed him and jabbered.

'*Plus*,' the woman said, 'those poor guys are being sent out here to get slaughtered, and they don't even know it! It's criminal! They take these kids, and they brainwash them so they don't think. They don't question. They just trundle off to their deaths without a care in the world!'

Andre spun around. The woman jumped in surprise. He stared at them – stared at her in particular – his jaw set in anger. The white vapor shot out of his nostrils. They shut the fuck up. He turned and headed on to the next unit.

THE KREMLIN, RUSSIA
February 9, 0200 GMT (1600 Local)

The heavy lunch and warm tea cast a blanket of drowsiness over Valentin Kartsev. His eyes drooped as he reclined in the chair behind his desk. It was time for his nap. Although his mind felt like mush, he tried one last time to come up with the words that eluded him. The concept he was trying to express. They were words to describe a process. Like the complexity of balls' motion on a billiards table. You excite them all into motion. They would begin to strike cushions and each other. Newtonian physics described perfectly the forces at work. A supercomputer could predict the balls' travels for the next thousand years. But to the naked eye their motions would quickly seem impossibly complex. There were so many variables that affected the outcome.

Kartsev had excited all the balls on the world table. He had stirred the political pots of dozens of major powers. He had known that there would be motion. But he still had no idea what the outcome would be. It was all so interesting.

He yawned. The sofa beckoned.

But there were three new messages in the Priority One folder on his computer. Every time he cleared them out, new ones appeared. He clicked on the mailbox icon. The first two messages both contained long lists of names. The previous day, he'd put two men on Schedule A. That sentenced them to death. But he'd had them watched for twenty-four hours. These were lists of people with whom the two had made contact in their last day on earth.

Kartsev's vision blurred with tears as he yawned again. He checked boxes with clicks of the mouse. A check by a name meant death. Short descriptions of the contacts were all Kartsev had to go on. 'Lunch in Kremlin cafeteria.' *Too public*, Kartsev thought. They'd never conspire together there. *Ah, but dinner in a private restaurant*, Kartsev thought. He checked the next box beside the name 'Chapaev, Stepan.' He'd never heard of the man.

Rare was it that he'd heard of anyone whose name he saw on these lists. Such was the price of power. He walled himself off even from his closest aides. Computers helped. These e-mails allowed him to do his work at a distance. It was a distance he imagined his staff greatly appreciated.

Such were his thoughts as he checked or skipped the boxes absentmindedly. Kartsev admitted to himself that the process was arbitrary. But he did try to be fair. He even went back and checked the box by the woman who'd had lunch in the cafeteria. After all, lunch – dinner – what's the difference? Besides, what better place to plot his demise than the middle of the Kremlin cafeteria?

The third e-mail was a refreshing change. There were no tedious lists. No boxes to check or skip. Just a short message and a video attachment. He clicked 'Play' with his mouse. A video window appeared.

'Is there anything you'd like to say to your folks back home?' Kate Dunn asked. In the dim, flickering light, Kartsev smiled. There was

Miss Dunn's freshness – even when she asked tired old questions. She stood in snowy woods.

The soldier struggled with his reply. 'Well . . . Hey, I guess. I'll be all right. Don't worry' The soldier's weak reassurances dimmed Kartsev's smile.

The camera switched to Miss Dunn. The young interviewing the young. 'How's the battery, Woody?' she asked. '*Woody*,' Kartsev wrote on a pad. She turned to the next soldier. 'How about you?' It was a young black soldier with a rifle and heavy bag. 'Where are you from?'

'The Bronx,' he replied.

'Do you know what you're fighting for?' she asked. The question was posed so forthrightly that Kartsev loosed a brief chuckle. The soldier looked at the others gathered around. 'Do you know why you're here?' she persisted.

He shook his head slowly, then shrugged. 'I'm s'posed to deliver the mail.'

All the others laughed, to the kid's embarrassment. The satellite feed was replaced with color test bars. Kartsev drew a deep breath which he let out with a sigh. He lifted the remote and turned off the TV. The office was lit now only by the lamp on the table next to him.

All was still and quiet. He could write, or not. He looked at his watch. It was four in the afternoon. A chain dangled beneath the stained glass lampshade. Kartsev yanked it, and the room fell dark with a click.

He didn't sleep, he sat there – thinking. It was dark. He left the windowless office. His mind was unencumbered by sights or sounds. His thoughts were not of words to go in his increasingly weighty treatise. He roamed the clean beauty of the cold expanses in the east. Of the color that cold put in Miss Dunn's smooth cheeks.

He'd loved the years he'd spent in the east. He'd loved the purity of the cold. His love of the winters there, however, had clearly been in the minority. Most – prisoner and guard alike – had relished the short summers that visited Siberia during which life had bloomed with stunning intensity. Nature had so little time to flourish that it burst forth in a verdant display as if to scream out, 'I'm alive! Look at me!'

The same was true of the people. Prisoners who – from a distance

– had appeared little more than trudging greatcoats. They spent long winters buried under clothing. But they bared their skin to the summer sun. In winter, the guards only left their warm huts for duty after bracing for the cold with vodka. But in the summer, they drank less. They exchanged crude jokes with the prisoners through the wire. Learned the prisoners' names. Let portions of the prisoners' parcels from home slip through. To Kartsev, summers in the camps had meant smells and mosquitos and mud . . . and the discipline that only killing could bring. When nature lifted her firm grip from the men's souls, Moscow had sent Kartsev in to replace it.

The words returned now in a gush. He groped for the lamp and turned it on. He wrote feverishly – longhand, with his pencil. He would type it – refine it – later.

'It is the most oppressed among men that possess the greatest potential energy. In them, life lies coiled to its greatest tension. When the repression is eased, there is a brief and instantaneous flowering. Nature's force is released onto the streets. The populace is invigorated. And if uncontrolled, that release is always violent.'

Kartsev wrote for six hours straight – recording the torrent of new ideas. Then – exhausted – he went to his sofa. He pulled the duvet to his chin and closed his eyes. He was smiling the entire time. In his mind, billiard balls bounded off felt cushions in a deliciously unpredictable manner.

Chapter Fifteen

PHILADELPHIA, PENNSYLVANIA
February 11, 0300 GMT (0800 Local)

From the way the passers-by were bundled up, Pyotr Andreev would've thought it was cold. He jogged down the sidewalk wearing gloves and a towel wrapped around his neck and tucked into his Adidas warm-ups. The walk was icy, but the already bright sun would soon melt it away into a warm winter day.

He rounded the block – startling a woman in a heavy wool coat walking her small dog. When Andreev turned to apologize, the car pulled up to the intersection. Two men in the front seat were looking his way. The driver extinguished his left-turn signal and proceeded straight through the intersection.

The nondescript government car sped away. Andre scanned the streets ahead for the team that would pick him up next. It was too cold for them to leave their heated cars. Plus, their sunglasses and dark suits always gave them away.

BETHESDA NAVAL HOSPITAL, MARYLAND
February 17, 1300 GMT (0800 Local)

The Senate and House leadership gathered in a semicircle of seats pulled up to Gordon's bedside. Their faces were grim. The chants of the demonstrators outside the hospital – now nearly ten thousand strong – were clearly audible in the silence.

Gordon knew that the meeting would surely be contentious. His visitors had all just run the gauntlet of protesters at the gate. But it was the quieter protests which worried Gordon most. The flood of anti-war sentiment evidenced by calls, letters and faxes. It was the collective roar of the politicians' constituents against which Gordon would fight his battle.

Daryl got off the phone in the sitting area to the side of the large room. He stepped up to the head of the bed. 'Thank you all for coming,' he began. 'We've had a couple of people who have been held up, so we're going to go ahead and get started.' He looked at Gordon, who nodded. Gordon marveled at how comfortable Daryl seemed in his new role of consummate insider – White House Chief of Staff. 'First, President Davis would like to thank all of you for coming. These are difficult times, and everyone is under a lot of pressure. President Davis certainly doesn't want a confrontation with Congress, but there are some things he would like to say to you, and then he'll listen.'

Daryl looked at Gordon and winked. The crowd turned their full attention to the President.

'The question has been raised,' Gordon began, 'why are we fighting in Siberia?' He surveyed the room. Almost all of the politicians facing him had voiced strong opposition to the war. 'I called you here to answer that question.'

Daryl handed Gordon a glass of water. The painkillers gave him a cotton mouth, and the words sounded as if they were stuck together. Gordon cleared his throat and looked up at the waiting audience.

'Siberia has a land mass equal to that of the U.S., Western Europe, and India combined. It had a pre-Civil War population, however, of only nine million. That population has now dropped by almost half. And yet Siberia contains the greatest deposits of natural resources on the planet. Cobalt, chromium, iron ore, molybdenum, nickel, vanadium, tungsten. The deposits are still virtually unexploited. Gold, copper,

328

mercury, lead, platinum, tin, and zinc are all buried under Siberia in abundance. As are diamonds, emeralds, graphite, mica. And, of course, the fuels that run the world – oil, natural gas, coal, and uranium. There is not a region on earth that is richer in resources. And those resources are now "in play." They're up for grabs.'

He paused to take another sip. The Congressmen and women waited patiently. 'And there is another factor at work here. It is a struggle between East and West. Between China, and the U.S. and Western Europe. In another era – the era of imperialism – it would be quite correct to say that we were the imperialist exploiters. We were in the wrong, then. But that era is gone, and in this new era we are in the right. We have just passed through a half-century of ideological competition in which our principal foreign policy was to contain the spread of totalitarianism, whether fascist or communist. In that struggle, we expended vast sums from our treasury, and we paid for that policy in blood in war after war. This current war between East and West is, in part, a continuation of that competition. It is not racial. It is ideological. We are not imperialists. We are warring for the side that is just. We are fighting *for* liberal democracy and *against* totalitarian dictatorship.'

His voice had grown weak. He again paused to take a drink. This time, several of the Congressmen glanced at each other. Some even leaned to whisper and nod. The signs were not good. 'And finally,' Gordon resumed, having to clear his throat repeatedly, 'we are fighting for something more important than either natural resources or ideological principles. We are fighting for our soul. Our identity. Many are tempted to cast that identity in terms of how the rest of the world sees America. Whether they see a nation that will show resolve when committed to a cause, or cut and run in the face of adversity. But the more important question is what lies inside us? What is the true character of the people of this country? Do our people see America as a powerful force on the side of right and justice? A nation that, once committed, will not back down even from war if that war is in our national interest and is just? Or will we ignore the call to duty whenever the price we have to pay is high? How many times can we back out, fail to commit, look the other way and still retain our national identity? And what could be more important than our self-image? Americans are not defined by any race or religion. We don't have a single, distinct culture. It is Americans' image of themselves that defines what this country is. We

329

become, over time, who we believe we are. And if we are not today the triumphant United States of 1945, then just how different *have* we become? Who are we? That's the question that this war poses.'

Even before he had finished, Gordon knew his effort had been a failure. It wasn't just his voice – weak and faltering unexpectedly every dozen or so syllables. Daryl had wandered to the back of the semicircle and stood there now shaking his head very slightly. Gordon's attempt to win support had clearly been found lacking.

And he hadn't yet made his strongest argument. He hadn't expressed his deepest fear. What if America's grand social experiment with democracy was losing steam? What if the anarchists were right and liberal democracies were in incipient decay? What if they'd lost their vigor and were on the long, slow slide into decline? Did some immutable physical law make anarchy the eventual result?

The House Democratic Majority Leader on the front row cleared his own throat. It was, Gordon thought, a reaction to listening to the unpleasant tones emanating from Gordon. 'Mr President, I think I can speak for everyone here on at least one matter. I think we all appreciate the considerations that you so eloquently expressed just now. They are surely weighty matters, and I feel certain that all of my colleagues on the Hill have paused to reflect on them in a thoughtful a manner. But I also can tell you,' he looked around the front row at the leadership, 'that I think the issue of continuing this war has been so clearly resolved by the members of Congress as to be a thing decided. We will debate the issue, of course, beginning a few weeks before the final funding vote. But I'm sure your people will tell you the same thing that mine do: that vote won't even be close. I'm sorry, Mr President, but the American people don't want this war. And Congress is listening to their voice. I must respectfully counsel you, sir – as a friend – to listen to that voice as well.'

As if on cue, a faint roar rose up from the protesters on the street.

'Gordon,' the Minority Leader of the Senate and a good friend said, 'you inherited this thing from Tom Marshall. We opposed the deployment on the Hill.' The 'we' was the Republican Party. 'There were ample warnings that the Chinese were spoiling for this fight. It's a war between Russia and China, not China versus the world. It's never too late to start talking to Beijing. We don't have to cede them anything. Just get their agreement to a halt in exchange for a ceasefire. Then we can get the hell out of this awful mess. You were pointing out the great forces at play in the world, and I totally agree with your analysis. But those forces are natural ones. Siberia is Asia, not Europe. It was taken from Asians by Russians in the last couple of hundred years. We are standing in the way of a natural realignment of geopolitical boundaries, and that opposition might well be beyond our capabilities. *And*, Gordon, it is clearly beyond the mandate with which this government has been vested by the American people. I have to agree with my Democratic colleagues on that one.' He nodded at the House Majority Leader – normally a bitter political enemy.

That left Gordon all alone. His own party – the leadership of the Senate in which he had been a member until the election – was closing ranks with the Democrats. The force of their stand seemed insurmountable. It came on the crest of a popular backlash that had left Gordon – who had not even been elected to the office which he now held – at an historic low in public opinion polls. Gordon knew they would not be persuaded. They were consummate politicians, all of them. They were cowed into submission by critical letters, faxes, phone calls, polls, press. But when all that feedback was *on* their side of an issue, they were emboldened and would fight to their political deaths. After all, they had to have some principle to live by. They had to believe in something. And it was those 'voices from the heartland' in which they believed.

'It's one, two, three, what're we fightin' for?' the singer blasted over the loudspeakers outside. The muffled tones of the song drifted through the silent hospital room. No one turned to look at the window. But they all heard the lyrics – the calls from the heartland.

'Do you have a date set for the funding vote?' Gordon asked.

'April 19th,' the House Majority Leader said quietly. 'The Senate will vote in the morning. The House in the afternoon. The cut-off would take effect immediately, Gordon.'

It was a clash of titanic proportions. White House lawyers had made a good case that Congress's authorization of the UN deployment gave Davis the authority to fight the war. But on April 20th, there would be no funds to prosecute it. Any attempt to purchase war materials, to ship them to the Far East, to do any of the million and one things that the executive branch was charged with doing to keep the effort going would be illegal. And it wouldn't be Gordon who would be confronted with violating the law. He had presidential immunity. It would be the tens of thousands of bureaucrats who manned the tens of thousands of offices who would each personally be faced with criminal prosecution. No matter how bravely Gordon stood, he knew, those men and women would falter. All it took was one person in some procurement office to refuse to follow Gordon's unlawful orders. Any one functionary could gum up the machine of government and bring the war effort to a grinding halt. And there would be not just one, but hundreds – thousands – who would hesitate, defer, seek clarification, consult lawyers. The Congressmen there knew that. They knew they held the winning hand. It would cost America the war, but that loss would be blamed on Gordon. And the end they achieved of bringing the troops home would be welcomed by a hair over eighty-eight point two percent of the population.

Gordon took a deep breath. 'Then, if the funding vote is April 19th, I will deliver my State of the Union address on April 18th.'

UNRUSFOR HEADQUARTERS, KHABAROVSK
February 13, 2200 GMT (0800 Local)

Clark could barely bring himself to watch the disgusting spectacle. A closed hearing in an underground briefing room. 'Please state your name,' the Congressman said into the microphone.

'Henry Adams,' the shaken officer replied He faced the committee, the microphones, the cameras that were there for 'historical purposes.' 'Lieutenant Colonel, United States Army.'

'And you were commander of the artillery supporting 2nd Battalion, 263rd Light Infantry?' the committee's chairman asked. His suit jacket was bunched up around his fat neck as he leaned forward.

'Yes, sir. I was.'

'And on the day of that battalion's engagement with the Chinese, how many guns did you field?'

The lieutenant colonel cleared his throat. 'I layed thirty-two 155-mms on the battlefield.'

'And how many rounds did those thirty-two guns fire?'

The ashen man hung his head. 'One hundred and three.'

The Congressman nodded. He already knew the answers to the

questions. They were all in the colonel's after-action report. He asked them only to ruin an officer who already looked shattered by the experience. 'That's a little over three rounds per gun. Is that the amount of fire support your battalion was expected to deliver?'

The colonel shook his head. 'No, sir. The support plan called for concentrated fire once the enemy was massed in the open for their attack. We should've gotten off at least two dozen rounds per tube – seven to eight hundred total.' He couldn't even look his accusers in the eye.

'In your opinion, Colonel Adams, would it have made a difference if those guns had fired eight hundred rounds instead of one hundred?' The officer nodded. 'Please answer for the record.'

'*Yes* . . .' he blurted out. His head dropped. Clark wondered whether he'd thought of anything else since that day. 'The measure of artillery performance is placing as many rounds as possible on target in the shortest amount of time. It would've made a difference . . . yes.'

Clark closed his eyes and shook his head. The man had decided to accept full responsibility. When he opened his eyes, the chairman was nodding. 'Why didn't those guns fire the expected number of rounds, colonel?'

The answer was delivered in a monotone. He knew it by heart. 'The guns' lubricants thickened because of the cold. Some recoil mechanisms didn't bring the guns back into battery for three or four minutes. The guns that *could* fire tried to cover but ran out of ammo. The cold also affected a lot of the rounds that we did get off. Their propellants and fuses were frozen, which resulted in a high percentage of shorts, overs and duds.'

'And why is it, colonel, that you experienced so many problems from the cold weather?'

The man finally raised his head. He looked his inquisitor straight in the eye and said, 'We didn't have time to winterize. To acclimatize. To train in a Siberian winter so we could fix the problems before they . . .' He lost his train of thought. His haunted eyes drifted off.

'Please state your name,' the chairman said into the microphone.

'Clark, Nate, Lieutenant General, United States Army.'

'And you are Commander-in-Chief of U.S. Army Pacific and of United Nations Russian Forces, is that correct?'

'Yes, sir. That's correct.'

'Now general, on January 26th – three days after the Chinese invaded Siberia – they cut the road leading from Birobidzhan to Khabarovsk, is that correct?' Clark confirmed the facts. 'And that resulted in Birobidzhan – which was being evacuated at the time *to* Khabarovsk – being surrounded, is that correct?' Again Clark agreed. 'Can you tell this committee how the Chinese managed to cut that road before the evacuation was complete?'

'The Chinese had been infiltrating Siberia for weeks in force. According to prisoners we've interviewed, they were under strict orders to avoid any contact with UNRUSFOR troops. The enormous size of our theater of operations and the thick forest canopy prevented our discovering where and in what strength they were concentrating.'

'And for some hours *after* the Chinese had cut the road with probably a division-strength unit, the commander at Birobidzhan – the late Brigadier General Merrill – still sent lightly-armed convoys down the road toward Khabarovsk, is that correct?'

'The first word anyone had that the road was blocked came from aerial reconnaissance, which reported abandoned vehicles on the road. General Merrill correctly concluded they'd been ambushed and sent a battalion-strength task force up the road on a clearing operation. He continued to send truck convoys behind the mixed armor-infantry force because of the severe time constraints imposed on the evacuation by the advancing main Chinese force and on the presumption that the road would be cleared.'

'And was the road cleared?' the chairman asked – the answer patently obvious.

'No . . . sir. The clearing operation was turned back with heavy losses. The trucks were ambushed and had to be bulldozed off the road. Very few of the unarmored vehicles made it back to Birobidzhan. And there were approximately five hundred men killed or missing and presumed killed or captured.'

The chairman was nodding. 'How do you personally rate General Merrill's performance at Birobidzhan, General Clark?'

'I firmly believe that Brigadier General Merrill, Lieutenant Colonel Adams, and every other soldier in my command has fought bravely and well under the most difficult circumstances imaginable. None were as prepared as they should have been for what hit them. I also, however, firmly believe it is not the government which sent them here who should be asking *them* "why?" . . . but the other way around.'

BIROBIDZHAN FIREBASE, SIBERIA
February 14, 1200 GMT (2200 Local)

'You sure you're ready for this?' Stempel's new squad leader asked. His voice was already lowered in anticipation of danger.

Stempel nodded, trying to slow his breathing. He nodded again, and the man moved on to check the others in Stempel's new squad. He tugged on equipment to see if it made noise. He asked if they knew their radio call sign and that of the company commander and battalion fire support officer . . . just in case. They each practiced giving the password that would get them back in through the wire. When the sergeant talked to his men, he grasped them firmly by their shoulders and squeezed. Sometimes he used a gentle shake to reinforce his comments. He was only twenty-three, but he was a good NCO.

The waiting left Stempel's stomach all churned up. His mouth was dry, and his nerves sent tremors through his limbs. It was his first combat patrol – his first time outside the wire. It was pitch dark. It seemed colder and colder the closer they came to the time.

'All right, Second Squad,' the sergeant whispered to the men gathered in the trench. 'Let's go. Unsafe your weapons at the top.'

The men began to climb crude ladders made from wood packing crates. Stempel got in line to scale the trench wall. On the ladder he could barely handle one rung at a time. The effort required enormous effort. He was carrying eight magazines in pouches on his belt. Another eight stashed in thigh pockets. But that burden was physical. Far heavier was his psychological load.

Ice and snow covered the sandbags at the top. An alien landscape lay ahead. He'd been out numerous times. To police the battlefield after ritualistic dawn attacks. But never beyond the wire.

Stempel rose to his feet at the most forward line of trenches.

Everything looked different about the terrain. When viewed from just inches above ground level – standing at a fighting post – every undulation rose like a mountain. Like an ant who saw peaks and valleys. But now – in the dim starlight – he saw the killing ground was flat.

They picked up the pace to a trot. They moved quickly. Harold leapt over the first strands of concertina wire. They were half buried in snow. Less an obstacle than a boundary. A border. The limits of relative safety. The beginning of extreme danger.

They slowed. Stempel was breathing hard. His breath turned to clouds of starlit smoke. But he didn't see the crystalline sky. He concentrated on looking for Chinese. He stayed in exactly the same path as the man in front. He placed his feet in the tracks. Maybe those places wouldn't explode.

At the trees they all dropped to the ground. Harold raised his rifle to his shoulder and aimed into the dark woods ahead. He'd followed Patterson, who lay three meters away. At night, the spacing was much closer than during the day. You risked bunching up in order to maintain contact. If you ever got separated from your unit – which happened all the time in firefights – you couldn't exactly call out. You were on your own, and both sides' guns would shoot you on sight.

He glanced over at the man on his right. He was a short and wiry grenadier who carried an M-279 grenade launcher mounted underneath his M-16. He replaced a casualty they'd taken the week before. A guy was blinded when a small mortar landed in front of his fighting position. Stempel knew nothing about the replacement other than what he'd noticed that morning. When they awoke in the trench under a light dusting of snow, he looked as if he'd grown a white beard that stood out starkly against his dark skin. It had taken him several minutes to scrape the ice crystals off his two-day-old beard.

The squad rose. There were twelve in all. Their squad's ten men, plus one of the platoon's two-man machine-gun crews. They followed Chavez – their semi-permanent point man – who wore their only pair of night-vision goggles. Everyone else stumbled forward blindly in the dark. They advanced in a roughly wedge-shaped formation. It was an inverted 'V,' with the point man truly at the 'point.' Four men formed each flank of the 'V.' Stempel was next to last on the left. The squad leader and the machine-gun took their place in the center. Their firepower would be able to refuse contact to either flank.

The only sounds were crunching snow and fabric-covered thighs rubbing together. Through the fog of his breath Stempel saw target after target. The thin trunks of trees constantly appeared from behind other trees. Brush and stumps and fallen trees protruded black and menacing from their white blanket. The night was moonless. But the stars still cast shadows on the snowy floor. When the wind blew, the shadows moved.

The snow was tramped down in places into a slick shine. Masses of Chinese had been canalized by artillery fire into the killing fields at the wire. The platoon leader had told the squad he didn't expect them to find Chinese in any force. There were snipers and observers and men with shoulder-fired SA-7 anti-aircraft missiles all around the base, to be sure. But like a snake they would strike only if the patrol walked right over them. And that was the whole point of the patrol – to sweep those Chinese from the woods. The lieutenant's talk had seemed more comforting half an hour before. Now Stempel concentrated on maintaining his place in formation while looking out for snakes.

.Why they called it a 'combat patrol' Stempel didn't know. They couldn't do much fighting – even with the machine-gun. They had a radio and were supposed to call in the base's mortars. Or – once they were a couple of kilometers out – their 105- and 155-mm howitzers. But combat patrols – as opposed to recon – were supposed to engage the enemy. He couldn't imagine twelve men doing much. Maybe trying to survive. Six kilometers . . . Six kilometers was the planned depth of their patrol.

The man ahead of Stempel went to ground with a crunch. Stempel plopped down into the thick snow. He spat. His heart thudded.

He waited for the night to explode.

He pressed his cheek to the hard stock. He couldn't breathe. The lump in his throat nearly choked him. And he couldn't swallow the obstruction. He tried and tried – panicked that he'd have to call out for help. For some sort of Heimlich maneuver to clear the fear that blocked his windpipe. Finally, he managed a few panting sucks of air.

All across his assigned free-fire zone the woods were still. He scanned the horizon. He spotted the white of the last man on his flank. He saw the Siamese twins lying side-by-side behind the machine-gun. It was that awesome gun that might save them if the worst came. If they ran headlong into an inbound attack. The squad's wedge would collapse. They'd form a ring around the gun. The gun was their only chance. Their only strongpoint.

He remembered the waves that had crashed against the wire in the major attacks. If their patrol ran into a company. A battalion. A regiment.

Stempel shook his head. He rid himself of the dreamlike images. Of the faces of the men from that first engagement. Their features were quickly growing indistinct. But not so their identities. The LT's shouts into the radio that had given way to stunned resignation. The angry bitching of the PFC and sergeant in their last moments of life. The cries of nameless men trying to surrender.

Stempel jammed his eyes shut. Dropped his face till he felt the cold sting of snow. Flooded his head with wildly disassociated thoughts till he scattered the visions like rings of smoke with a wave of his hand.

'Ps-s-s-t!'

Stempel raised his head at the sound. Patterson was on his feet. Stempel quickly rose and labored forward. He got back into the wedge and advanced. It wasn't bravery that kept him moving. It was fear. Demon-filled nightmares. Evil figments of his sleep who eyed him from the dark periphery. The ghosts of men he never knew.

So Harold had decided that the first time didn't count. Next time, he'd die fighting.

ALONG URMI RIVER, SIBERIA
February 16, 0630 GMT (1630 Local)

At four-thirty every afternoon, Chin's war against the Europeans ended. His battle against the cold began. Not that UNRUSFOR was ever really the greater threat. The cold dominated the battlefield completely. It took them till ten in the morning to break camp. They'd march a kilometer. Eat their last rations. March another kilometer. At two they began searching for a bivouac. By four he had to strike camp. By then it was a race to survive. At sunset the temperatures plummeted.

Chin could read the company commander's mind. In the briefings he said nothing. In his choice of campsite he told all. If they'd been worried about contact with the enemy, they would've camped on high ground. But the CO always camped in the open. It was warmer there than in the woods. They slept in ravines. On flat terraces at the bases of hills. Places where snow wouldn't collapse the tent while they slept. Never a valley where the killing cold would settle.

'I'd rather eat reindeer than horses,' Chin overheard one of his men say as they erected their platoon's single tent.

'Me too. But we haven't seen any dead reindeer. And there are plenty of dead pack horses along the supply routes. And their meat is frozen so . . .'

'Quiet!' Chin snapped. He still didn't think it right that his men should discuss their hunger so openly. All they'd had in four days was field rations – frozen sugared blocks of crushed sesame seeds, peanuts and rice.

There was a commotion. All dropped what they were doing – even Chin. Two replacements were returning from their trip to the battalion supply depot. They pulled a sled heavy with supplies. 'Back off!' Chin shouted as everyone ripped at the sled's contents. The two men who'd been pulling it collapsed in the snow sweating.

'There's no food, sir,' one of the new men reported – out of breath.

'*What?*' Chin yelled. 'What the hell is *this?*'

'Ammunition, blankets, soap . . .'

Everyone was incensed. Several kicked the new guys, and Chin didn't stop them. When one of his wounded limped up, he ordered the two men to unload the sled and pull the man back to the aid station. 'And this time don't come back without food! At least some cabbage! I don't care how you get it, understand?'

They understood.

'Back to work on that tent!' Chin ordered. They were supposed to have two tents for thirty men. But they were supposed to have lots of things. They would anchor one side of the tent to a small humpback ridge which would form a natural windbreak. One detail had cleared the snow to the ground – which was warmer – and was laying a bed of spruce twigs for flooring. Larger branches first, then successively smaller and finer twigs for comfort. In the center, men set up the lone wood-burning heater. Another detail built one-meter-high snow walls along the three unprotected sides to block the wind from those directions. The tent's entrance would be placed at forty-five degrees to the prevailing winds, which Chin was still trying to judge.

Men would occupy floor space in the tent according to the duty roster. The first men on sentry duty or tasked to clear drifts from the lee side of the walls would sleep nearest the entrance. Their relief would sleep in the next row so they could be located without waking everyone else. Shift by shift they slept in rows. No one slept more than four hours. If they all fell asleep they'd all die.

Chin cast a nervous eye to the low and anemic sun. 'Let's start driving those tent pins!' he ordered. 'Where the ground's frozen, look for natural anchors! Hurry up!'

In the near distance, more new replacements were completely

stripping a tree of its branches for flooring and camouflage. Chin stormed over to them. 'Don't take *all* the branches! The enemy can see bare trees from the air! Take a few lower branches and move on to the next tree! There are *millions* of trees all *around!*' They dropped their load and moved to comply. 'Well, take *those* branches!' They picked them up. 'Which are upper branches, and which are lower branches?' Chin asked. They clearly had no idea. 'I told you this already! We burn upper branches before dark because their smoke is white! Lower branches have tar and resin! They burn better and are warmer, but give off dark smoke! We switch to them after sunset!'

The men hurried past like frightened rabbits. Chin rolled his eyes and shook his head. *No wonder they don't live long*, he thought. The wind whistled by. But the frigid gust could do nothing to increase his misery. He was already frozen to the bone. Hungry. Dying slowly, along with all his men.

UNRUSFOR HEADQUARTERS, KHABAROVSK
February 17, 0230 GMT (1230 Local)

Clark saw the thick torso of Admiral Ferguson emerge under the still-spinning rotors. He saluted Major Reed, who led him to the waiting Clark.

Ferguson looked out of place amid the Army security team. He wore a Navy blue greatcoat over black boots. Atop it all rested a white Kevlar helmet. A black 9-mm hung from a pistol belt strapped around his vast waist. He was Clark's superior – commander-in-chief of Pacific Command.

Clark saluted, then shook the admiral's hand. 'Welcome to Khabarovsk, sir,' he said loudly over the dying whine of the rotors. They headed toward the heavily sandbagged bunker. At least a dozen aides and well-armed guards had formed around them.

'Not as cold as I thought it'd be,' Ferguson said as they walked briskly from the heated helicopter to the heated bunker.

Clark let the comment pass. He was already pissed at Ferguson's surprise visit, so he was doubly careful what he said. 'How was your trip?' he asked. He fell naturally into step with the the admiral. The senior man strode unmindful of the expected display of respect. Within moments, the entire phalanx of aides and bodyguards marched in near parade-ground unison.

'Flight was smooth as glass,' the admiral replied. 'No thermals coming up from the ground. Must mean it's cold, I suppose.' They reached the bunker's entrance. Two sentries had risen from behind sandbags to stand at attention.

They entered the cold staircase that led down to the operations center.

Ferguson stopped at the bottom of the stairs. Clark almost ran into the mountain of navy blue wool. The admiral waited for one of his aides to enter the operations center first. 'Attention on deck!' the man shouted – calling the room to attention.

'Carry on!' Ferguson boomed as he walked briskly into the room. Businesslike. Purposeful. As if he were on the bridge of a ship. But he clearly had no idea where to head. He instead wandered among the staff. Clark trailed in his wake but outside the scope of his attention. Several times Clark considered abandoning the entourage and heading back to work. But he dutifully tagged along – seemingly unnoticed by the group's leader.

'Where ya from, soldier?' Ferguson asked.

'Lyon,' the French officer replied.

Ferguson seemed surprised. The man wore cold-weather gear from American stocks. 'A-a-h, *comment allez-vous?*' He thus began a conversation in French that brought smiles from the French contingent.

Clark looked away. He didn't speak French. Ferguson slapped the Frenchman on the back – interrupting the man's intended response and moving on. Clark smirked. *Like a politician*, he thought as he followed the four-star admiral. *Is that what it takes?* he wondered.

Ferguson left a broad wake through the center of the room. His visit completely disrupted the harried officers' routines. At the opposite end of the main area, the admiral suddenly turned to Clark and said, 'Let's go to your office.'

It was the first time since entering the operations center that Ferguson had seemed to notice Clark's presence. Clark led his boss not to the desk in the corner of the big room that he used as his working area, but to the office that he used only for sleep. Luckily, someone had turned on the lights and gathered the pillow and blankets from the sofa.

'I like a man with an uncluttered desk!' Ferguson bellowed on entering. 'An uncluttered desk means an uncluttered mind.' He declined Clark's offer to sit and turned instead to his aide. He brushed the air with his fingers. 'Would you . . .?' The blue-clad navy captain held out his arms and cleared the room of Clark's aides. The naval officer turned and noiselessly pulled the door closed. When Clark looked back around, Ferguson was busy taking an inventory of Clark's office. The supplies lay in neat rows on the unused desk.

In the quiet, Ferguson fiddled with the tape dispenser, the letter opener, the Dictaphone. He even opened a stapler to confirm it was loaded. Clark finally opened his mouth to inquire as to the reason for the visit, but Ferguson beat him to the punch.

'I *suppose*,' he began, overly loudly, 'that you're wondering just what the hell I'm doing here?'

The navy man looked directly at Clark, then began suddenly to peel off his heavy coat. Clark took the opportunity to do likewise. Ferguson tossed the pistol belt on Clark's sofa/bed. 'I'll get right to the point.' The enormous overcoat landed on top of the pistol, revealing a man of diminished but still substantial girth. Underneath he wore white fatigues. Ferguson sat with a groan, and Clark took the chair beside him.

Ferguson picked up a staple-remover. He began to toss it in the air and catch it one-handed. 'I've had some misgivings about the strategy you've employed in this war. I want to discuss with you some possible changes.' Clark arched his brow up as if to say that of course he would be receptive to any advice given to him about the conduct of his ground war by the former carrier pilot – a navy man who by historical accident happened to be his immediate superior. 'You're fighting not to lose,' Ferguson said. He leaned forward and rested his elbows on his knees. His back, while not hunched, was large and round in that position. 'This strategy of pulling everybody back into tight groups of mutually supporting firebases cedes the initiative to the Chinese. We sit back and let them do what they will in the field while we hoard our assets here and around Vladivostok. By doing that, we fail to make use of our superior mobility. We could be out there running circles around their infantry. Hitting them *hard*,' he slammed one meaty paw into his palm, 'and then outrunning them to set up another ambush.'

He sat upright now, and Clark gathered that it was his turn to speak. He cleared his throat. 'It is true, Admiral Ferguson . . .'

'Franklin.'

'. . . Franklin,' Clark repeated, 'that UNRUSFOR's nominal tables of organization and equipment provide us with superior mobility. But that advantage has been substantially degraded by a variety of factors, not the least of which was the failure to deploy the service and support units necessary to maintain that equipment in a harsh environment. Most of the allied units were deployed without their heavy equipment. What they did have has deteriorated through lack of maintenance.'

Ferguson was not the most patient of men. Before Clark had finished, he wore an irritated look on his face. He waved Clark off with his hand and said, 'You're talking maintenance. I'm talking about the operational *art*, general! Campaigning. Our fundamental strategic approach to halting the Chinese advance.'

'Sir . . .' Clark began to explain.

'I told you I'm gonna shoot straight with you,' Ferguson continued, 'so here goes. There's been talk by the desk jockeys back at the Pentagon about you being gun shy. About you being our "General McClellan."' Clark set his jaw firmly to mask his anger. Ferguson knew Clark – a West Pointer – would understand the historical reference. Many in the North had accused the Civil War general of cowardice for his tentative use of superior forces against the South. 'They say you were traumatized by that Birobidzhan thing,' Ferguson went on, 'and that you're now afraid to commit.'

Ferguson shrugged and shook his head as if to explain that he was, of course, Clark's great and tireless defender. 'Now I know what you're going to say. You warned everybody who would listen about the risks of this war. You clamored for more men and heavier equipment that you still haven't gotten. Et cetera, et cetera. But the fact is most of the allied units that are in the field right now haven't even fired a shot. There's a perception by many – and that includes the media – that we're just letting them waltz in and take the place. Plus, there are the parallels to Vietnam.'

'Vietnam?' Clark said – incredulous.

'To the firebase strategy. Sure, sure, defense is stronger *tactically* than offense, but assuming the defensive strategically can *lose* this war, general.'

Clark had no idea where to begin. He looked off into space. While one part of his mind tried to compose a response, the other fought vigorously to rein in his temper. Where should he start? With the politics of the shaky U.N. coalition. Clark felt like he'd barely held the alliance together. If he ordered a risky counterattack, it might bust the alliance apart. Or should he begin with the utter nonsense of his detractors' assumptions That large units could hit the Chinese hard, disengage, set up, and hit them again. Every third time a unit tried that, they'd get so tangled they'd be fixed in place and lost to the man. Better to use airpower to punish the Chinese, who were exposed while on their road marches and . . .

'Washington wants you to change your strategy, Nate,' Ferguson said simply. 'That's why I'm here.'

So that was it. Nate didn't move a muscle. He didn't flinch, or nod, or even blink. 'Admiral Ferguson,' he began in as even a voice as he could muster, 'I have the better part of a million Chinese soldiers coming my way and less than two hundred thousand men in the field to oppose them. Five-to-one numerical inferiority. Now, in a couple of months we'll have narrowed that gap to three- or even two-to-one by attriting the Chinese and building up our forces in theater. At three-to-one, I can show the world something. At five-to-one, I'm hanging on by sacrificing men's lives to buy time.'

'That's one strategy,' Ferguson said, 'but it's not the one endorsed by the Joint Chiefs.'

'It's the one endorsed by the joint command of UNRUSFOR.'

The two men stared silently at one other until Ferguson finally burst out, 'God-*damn* but you're a thick-headed son-of-a-bitch!' He rocked back in his seat. His hands gripped his thighs as he sat there rigidly. 'You must think the same about me.' Clark said nothing. 'Listen, Nate, you're not leaving me much wiggle room here. You've been fighting this war out here all by your lonesome for three weeks, and you haven't heard word one out of me but "What can I do to help?" Am I right?' Nate had to nod. 'Now why, all the sudden, do you think I come here and tell you you've got to change your basic strategy?' Nate just squinted and cocked his head. 'The decision has already been made, Nate. It's been made back in Washington.'

'By the Joint Chiefs?' Ferguson nodded. 'Dekker?' The admiral nodded again. Clark was furious. He rose and began to pace the office, grinding his teeth.

'Don't shoot me,' Ferguson said. 'I'm just the messenger.'

'I could lose more than the war! I could lose the war *and* UNRUSFOR – every last man in my command! A complete rout!

What the hell do they think they're doing? I'm hangin' on here by my fuckin' *fingernails!*'

Ferguson heaved a sigh. 'Hate to say this to you, Nate, but the decision is over my pay grade.'

'Over *your* pay grade?' Clark said – rounding on the four-star admiral. Ferguson nodded in reply. Clark spoke in low tones now. 'I'm not ordering those men out of their firebases. It's suicide.'

'Sounds like you've got some talking to do back in D.C.' Nate was again confused. Ferguson was again frustrated. 'Nate, if you don't get your ass back there chop chop, you won't have to issue those orders because you won't have a command. Timmy Stanton'll get it, and he'll order the counterattack on the flight from Seoul.'

Clark was shaking his head. 'I don't believe it. Stanton's a good man. He wouldn't do it either, not after he saw what he's got, and what he's up against.'

'Maybe you're right, but it wouldn't change the fact that you'd be out of a job, general. You've got one move left to you, Nate. That's to hop on a plane and get back to Washington pronto. You know how fast things move in that city. They may already have yanked the rug out from under you. I don't know.'

'What the hell am I going to say to Dekker that could possibly . . .'

'Nobody said anything about you talking to Dekker. You've got a Major Command, general. You've got access right to the top.'

'Are you suggesting what I think you're suggesting?'

Ferguson shrugged. His hulking mass rose. He walked over to the sofa to retrieve his coat and his pistol belt. He put the gear back on, staring off into space as he spoke. 'I didn't say anything. I'm just a dumb country boy from Tennessee. Don't know why I even joined the Navy, seein' as there's no ocean anywhere near Clark County.' He was fully dressed now. 'I'm just going to take a nice, long tour of the battlefront. I'll go all the way over to Chita in the west and then swing back through here on my way to Pearl. I'll have to report that you refuse to change strategies when I get back. But I'll probably be out of direct communications for a day or so. Sat phone's on the fritz, you know.' Ferguson faced Nate squarely. 'He's at Bethesda. Good luck. You're sure gonna need it.'

The admiral turned to leave. 'Thank you, sir,' Clark said.

Ferguson turned back. 'One more thing, Nate. By the time you land in D.C., you'd damn well better have a plan to win this war tucked under your arm. Capisch?'

VLADIVOSTOK-USSURIYSK ROAD, SIBERIA
February 19, 2100 GMT (0700 Local)

Andre Faulk trudged through the snow. The heavy mail bag was slung over his left shoulder. He held it awkwardly – one-handed – so that he could hold his M-16 by the pistol grip with his right hand. Ugly black holes scarred the virgin snow. Tree limbs drooped to the ground. Exposed, fresh wood dotted the pock-marked trunks.

He finally saw a fighting hole. A white helmet protruded only inches above snow level. Andre headed toward the position. When he was a few feet away the head jerked around. The rifle followed.

'Hey!' Andre shouted. 'Be cool, man!'

'Jesus, get down!' On hearing the tone of the man's voice, Andre didn't hesitate. He dropped immediately. He crawled forward into the man's hole. 'God-*damn*, man!' the soldier spat. 'What're you, fuckin' crazy? *Jee*-zus!'

Andre looked out across the snow-covered field ahead. Trees had been felled by great violence. Otherwise all seemed natural.

'You part of the reinforcements?' the guy asked Andre. He was nervously gripping and regripping the forward plastic guard of his rifle. He didn't take his eyes off the woods in front.

'Naw, man. I'm lookin' for 3rd Platoon, C Company, 2nd Battalion.' The soldier glanced at him. He wouldn't quite look Andre in the eye. 'You know where they are?' Andre asked. The guy didn't respond. He just lowered his helmet to the front edge of the hole. 'Say, man.' Andre reached up and shook his shoulder gently. 'Can you at least tell me where Charlie Company is?'

He mumbled something that Andre didn't understand.

'Say what?'

'This *is* Charlie Company!' he snapped.

'Take it easy. Jeeze. Can you point me to 2nd Platoon, then?'

The man looked like he was going to be sick. His head wobbled. His chin was covered in black stubble. Tiny beads of ice dangled from each follicle. His eyes were red. They'd sunken into swollen sockets above black bags. His jaw drooped, leaving his mouth open. Andre looked around the desolate defensive line in search of someone else. The guy seemed to be the lone defender.

The soldier raised his head and looked at Andre. 'You got a truck or somethin', man?' He spoke in a whisper. 'Take me back with you.'

Andre snorted and half-grinned. Then what he was asking sunk in, Andre shook his head. 'Man, you gotta be kiddin'. *Shit.*' He was still shaking his head, but he noticed the change in the man. He grew nervous, almost hyper. He looked back through the woods toward the supply road. Back toward where the Humvee was parked. He held his rifle in both hands as if ready to use it.

'Say,' Andre reasoned, 'man . . . listen! I rode in here with a Spec Four, and . . . you know.' He didn't seem to be listening. 'He'd fuckin' . . . I dunno! He's carryin' a Goddamn grenade launcher. And he's got about eight mags on his skinny-assed chest. He'd pro'bly shoot you or something if you . . .'

'Not if I greased his ass first, man.' The guy turned to Andre. His face changed completely. '*Please*, ma-a-an! Jesus *Christ*! Do you know what this shit is *like* up here? Motherfuckin' goddamn *hell!*' he shouted. There was a faint echo. 'It can't get any worse'n hell, man!'

'Hey . . . get yer shit together, man. Get a fuckin' grip.'

The guy sort of rolled over onto his back. Andre watched his rifle, which he hugged against his chest. The white cloth cover of his helmet rolled through the snow. He just lay there now with his head on its side, staring right at Andre.

'You want Third Platoon, C Company, man?' The abrupt change took Andre by surprise. After a moment, he nodded. 'They're out there,' was all he said. But Andre understood there was 'in,' and there was 'out.' He raised his head to look toward No Man's Land. There were no friendlies beyond this line. This was it. He saw nothing but trees, snow. Here and there he saw . . .

An arm. Frozen at a right angle as if its owner were trying to push the dead torso upright. A helmet half covered in snow. The boot of a soldier fallen face forward that was draped over a log. It was a cemetery, with all the bodies sloppily buried in shallow snow. But they were Chinese soldiers, not American. Andre could tell from the shape of the helmets.

* * *

'What do you mean, you couldn't find them?' the lieutenant asked.

Andre stood in front of his desk – wondering why the lieutenant didn't get it. '3rd Platoon, sir. They're all MIA, HQ included.'

The entire office was silent, listening. 'Jesus,' the lieutenant muttered. 'But you still should've left their parcels with the company headquarters section.'

'Couldn't find them, either.'

The lieutenant again seemed surprised. 'But who was in charge then?'

Andre shrugged. 'I dunno. Nobody I talked to knew either.'

The lieutenant sent Andre off to process the undelivered mail. He sat in a windowless room no bigger than a closet. There was barely room for a small table and a chair. A single bulb still hung from the end of a wire. He pulled out a thick stack of letters, took the rubber band off, and stared at the first letter.

The envelope was pink. It was addressed to 'Aguire, Todd C., Pvt. USA' in a woman's hand. Andre's eyes flooded with moisture, and it angered him. He picked up the red felt-tip pen that the lieutenant had handed him and held it poised over Aguire's name. The tip left a red splotch where it rested against the absorbent paper.

'Return to Sender,' Andre scrawled across the neat hand of some woman named 'Laney Aguire.' He dropped it in the outgoing bag. 'Alvarez.' The return address was a stick-on label – Christmas holly swirling around the corners. Letter by letter the job grew more difficult. Andre ground his teeth, angrily smearing the words he was writing over the cards, envelopes and packages. By the time he was finished, it had come to him. Somewhere between 'Aguire' and 'Wolfson,' he realized he knew each of those men.

He decided what to do then and there. He went to his quarters, got the letter, and marched straight to the LT's office. Andre spent fifteen minutes arguing, holding his ground, not backing down. He waved the letter in the air.

'All right, already!' the lieutenant said finally. 'Jeeze! It's your funeral.' He got on the telephone.

Half an hour later, he emerged from his office. 'Can't get you into airborne school. Classes are all full. But a buddy at Fort Campbell said they got a spot for you in Air Assault School. It lasts ten days, and it's supposed to be absolute hell.' Andre said nothing. 'The next class starts in three days. I'll give you the papers, but you'll have to wrangle your own transport.' He waited. 'Look, Andre, the 101st Airborne is pouring into Vladivostok right now. If you think this is a ticket home or something, I mean . . .' He was shaking his head. 'You're gonna be right back over here, and the shit's gonna be thick. The real thing. Those guys are the fire brigade. They're bein' choppered in when the Chinese punch through. Dropped smack dab in their line of advance and told to hold.'

Andre was trying to imagine what it must be like. The noise. The confusion. Not knowing what to do, where to go, everything fucked up . . .

'Okay!' the frustrated lieutenant said. He called his secretary into his office. 'Andre, here, wants to part company with our happy band. He has a letter from his AIT school commander recommending him for airborne. Type up some travel orders for Fort Campbell and call the Air Assault School. Tell them he's on his way.' Both men were looking at Andre. 'Right, Private Faulk?'

Andre never did answer. The lieutenant shrugged, and the secretary went to his typewriter.

Chapter Sixteen

ABOARD C-141, OVER CENTRAL PACIFIC
February 20, 1000 GMT (2000 Local)

Clark had left his British Deputy Commander in charge of UNRUSFOR. With him he'd brought his J-1, J-2, J-3 and J-4 – all generals – and Lieutenant Colonel Reed. Once again it was Reed's study that had yielded the basis for Nate Clark's plan. 'In 1939, the Japanese Army in China attacked Georgi Zhukov's Russian forces in Mongolia. Zhukov ordered his front-line troops to hold while he marshaled arriving reinforcements for a counterattack. He'd mustered overwhelming force under strict operational security and obtained air superiority. He concentrated his armor and lavishly employed swift-striking forces. When he counterattacked, he drove the Japanese back deep into China.'

The German staff officer nodded. 'He did the same at Moscow, Stalingrad, Kursk-Orel and Berlin.'

'We must use the *Stützpunkt* – the strongpoint. A network of loosely connected defensive positions backed by local reserves. When the Chinese attack, we kill them in huge numbers. When the pressure grows too great, we pull everyone back to the next line. A properly

351

organized time-phased delay path is our only hope of stabilizing the front when we do not have the troops for a continuous line.'

'Hitler tried that last,' the Russian adviser said. The former general spoke in a slow and thickly accented voice. 'The fascists' "hedgehog" defense on the Eastern Front was a tactic of weakness. Hitler said no retreat, so German units tried to make their stands in open fields. When we attacked in morning, we found men frozen in bottom of holes. And so Nazis pulled back into villages and built these strongpoints. They gave open fields to us and we infiltrated between their positions easily. When we attacked in strength, we were able to shoulder our way through.'

'Strongpoints saved the *Wehrmacht*,' the German general replied. He turned to Clark. 'A continuous line across three thousand kilometers would be like paper. We needed elasticity – defense in depth – to stop offensives. Two rows of firebases. The ones in back manned by support troops. Artillery and air bombardment will fill the gaps.'

'But there is no shelter in Siberia,' the French member of Clark's staff pointed out. He spoke directly to his close comrade the German. 'There are no villages like there were in western Russia. How will we protect our troops from the weather?'

'We have engineers. We will make our own shelter.' He turned to Clark. 'And we will push the perimeters out beyond the firebases to interlock.'

One of the American officers was shaking his head. 'Your firebase system sounds too much like Vietnam. It's reactive, defensive, tailored for long security duty. The operational art has come a long way since Vietnam . . . and World War Two. We need to be proactive, aggressive, decisive.'

'This *will* be aggressive,' countered the German. 'We'll use air, indirect fire, and special operations to interdict supplies and reinforcements. If we isolate the battlefield, the tactical commanders can push out their perimeters and win local engagements. These defenses are not static. They can be made very active. The terrain will canalize the Chinese through mountains and valleys. We will be waiting for them with prepared defenses and concentrated fires.'

'But where will we ultimately stop them?' Clark asked.

The German officer's pen traced the northern rail line running across the map from east to west. 'That is our line. That is where we must stiffen and hold.'

'But all they need to do is break that rail line in one place and they win,' the British officer commented. 'They sever the east from the west. How can we be certain we will stop them?'

Without a moment's hesitation, the most junior officer at the table answered. 'Supply,' Reed said. 'That is the one major weakness of the Chinese army.' Clark followed Reed's eyes down to the map of the vast Siberian wilderness. 'Somewhere, they'll reach the "culminating point" – the point beyond which they can't maintain continuous supply of their front-line troops. They have no road/rail grid. Rugged terrain. Brutally cold weather. *We* have total air supremacy. We have to degrade their supply capabilities through air attack. Make sure that they reach their culminating point somewhere south of the rail line.'

'And then what?' the French general asked.

Clark stared back unflinching. 'We hit them as quick as we can, as hard as we can, where it hurts the most, when they aren't looking.'

MCLEAN, VIRGINIA
February 20, 1900 GMT (1400 Local)

The moment Nate Clark arrived home, he knew something was wrong. He had called ahead, and Lydia had picked up the boys from school. They had hugged him, but they were subdued. Lydia, too, seemed different. Tired.

They sat at the dinner table. Nate drank the coffee he'd made while waiting for them to arrive. 'I don't have long. I've got to go see the president.' The boys nodded. Everyone seemed ill at ease. The boys' eyes darted up at Nate's, but didn't linger. 'What the hell's going on?' Nate asked.

They all looked at him. 'I'm sorry, Nate,' Lydia said, forcing a smile. 'It's just . . . you don't realize what it's been like. For the boys, I mean.'

'What *what* has been like?'

'The war. The protests.'

The boys were looking down. Dejected. 'Are you being bothered by someone?' he asked.

'They've picketed our house,' Lydia said softly. 'The police ran them off. But I've been thinking about moving. The owner of the house . . . he's agreed to let us out of the lease.' There was pain in her eyes. Embarrassment at having raised the subject on Nate's brief return home.

Nate was seething. Lack of sleep. Too much coffee. Frustration and set-back and criticism from all sides. And the immense strain of all that was happening. He knew he was on the edge. He ground his teeth and kept quiet.

'I'm sorry, Nate,' Lydia said. 'I wasn't going to tell you.'

Nate turned to his sons. 'Would one of you please just say something to me?'

They looked up at him finally. 'When are we gonna start fighting?' Jeffrey asked.

'*Jeffrey!*' Lydia chastised.

Again his head hung low. But in that instant of candor Nate caught a glimpse of what was being drummed into everyone's heads. The commanding general was too cowardly or inept to put up a fight.

He took Lydia into his study and closed the door. He couldn't bring himself to speak at first. 'What is it, Nate?' she asked.

'I'm considering requesting relief,' he replied in a monotone.

'From your *command*?' she asked. She tried not to sound surprised . . . but failed. 'Nate . . . that's not *like* you.'

'I'm not running *away*! Is *that* what you think?' She eyed the door. The boys were still there. 'I'm sorry,' he said, and they embraced each other. 'I'm going to propose a plan to the president. A plan to win the war. If he rejects it, I'm considering submitting my request for relief. It's a one-shot weapon. But I believe in the plan I'm taking to him.'

She remained pressed against him. 'What if he doesn't grant your request?'

'Then I'm still legally obligated to carry on in command. But he wouldn't reject my request. I'd be out. Out of my command. Out of the Army. Out.'

'Would that be so bad?' she asked. He tried, but couldn't reply. The lump in his throat prevented him from speaking. Lydia squeezed him tight. She understood it would mean defeat, no matter what the outcome of the war. And, inevitably, cowardice. Desertion of his troops during a desperate war. In his own eyes. In the eyes of his sons.

BETHESDA NAVAL HOSPITAL, MARYLAND
February 20, 2100 GMT (1600 Local)

'Mr President?'

Gordon Davis opened his eyes. A man towered over his bedside. Gordon blinked several times before his blurry vision cleared. He didn't recognize the man who stood before him wearing slacks and an open-collar shirt.

'Yes?' Gordon croaked. He struggled to push himself a few inches up his pillow. The man helped.

'My name is General Clark.' Gordon's eyes shot up to him. 'What . . .?' Gordon began, but then coughed. Clark poured some of what used to be ice water into a paper cup. Gordon drank and cleared his throat. 'What are you doing here?'

'I came to talk to you about the war, sir. Nobody knows I'm here.'

The room was empty. Gordon looked Clark up and down. He was shaven and appeared clean, but he looked exhausted. 'I'm listening,' Gordon said.

The general pulled his chair over to the bed and sat. 'I'm sorry to bother you, Mr President. But what I'm about to say may mean the difference between winning and losing this war.'

'Is this about the change in strategy?'

Clark nodded. 'It's a mistake.'

Gordon took as deep a breath as he could risk – just short of the point of pain. 'This is outside my area of expertise, general. The Joint Chiefs have recommended that we take a more aggressive approach.'

'I know, sir. But it's wrong. The coalition will fall apart. The Germans, maybe even the French will withdraw. The casualties will skyrocket on both sides, but *we* can't sustain the losses . . . politically. The American people won't tolerate them. We'll be forced to negotiate a ceasefire and pull out.'

'You're asking me to reject the unanimous advice of the Joint Chiefs of Staff and accept your opinion? General Clark, no offense . . . but I don't even know you. They had charts and maps and quotes from Sun Tzu and von Clausewitz. It was a helluva show. Made it sound like . . . well, maybe you were too hesitant.'

Gordon studied the soldier. He seemed unfazed by the words. He spoke slowly, and with conviction. 'We have the best army in the world. The soldiers and equipment are unequaled anywhere. But there's only so much they can do in the face of five-to-one numerical inferiority. We have to rely for the time being on the inherent tactical advantage of defense over offense. We have to entrench, dig in, and then pummel the attackers with our firepower. We've got air superiority, so we know where they are and can hit them virtually at will. But if we come out of those holes, Mr President, our casualty rates skyrocket. And for what? The territorial gains would be minimal.'

'But what about morale? I thought it was lagging because of the defensive strategy.'

'It's *lagging*, sir, because this is a winter war in Siberia. A land war on the Asian continent against the Chinese army. They're barely holding on, Mr President. To ask those men to crawl out of their holes and attack now would be disastrous.'

Gordon felt a sinking feeling. The man was, it seemed, just as he'd been described – timid. Generals were supposed to say things like, 'All seems lost, so I'm attacking.' But this man wasn't like that.

'I'm sorry, General Clark. I'm not going to bullshit you. I'm not convinced.'

'Would you give me one chance, sir? Would you let me tell you what I propose?' Gordon nodded, waiting. 'The Chinese have given up trying to take Vladivostok in the east, Khabarovsk in the center, and Svobodny in the west. They're pushing instead for our only remaining east-west rail connection in the north. I propose using existing ground forces in-theater to stop the Chinese south of that line. We'll pound their main supply routes from the air round the clock. All the while we're building up war stocks and massing reinforcements along the rail line. We'll mass two more corps – one American arriving from the east by sea and rail; one European arriving by rail from the west – to add to the one we've got in the field.'

Gordon interrupted with a question. 'How will the Chinese not know what we're doing?'

'Sun Tzu said it first, sir. "All war is based on deception." If the Chinese haven't pulled back into defensible positions before we launch our massive, set-piece attack, the war's over. *We* have mobility. *They* don't. And they have no way of seeing the attack coming. With no space-based or aerial reconnaissance assets left, their battlefield intelligence is purely tactical – thirty kilometers beyond their lines, at most.'

'They have CNN,' Gordon noted.

'CNN and all the other media are a major part of our Strategic Deception Plan, Mr President. That plan is to make everyone think we're losing the war. Since the Chinese will know we're staging somewhere, we'll make them think it's for the limited purpose of relieving Khabarovsk and Birobidzhan. While we're staging for the *main* attack farther west, we'll set up decoy bases in Komsomolsk – north of Khabarovsk. Mock fuel dumps, trucks, armored vehicles, multispectoral close-combat decoys. Fake headquarters will broadcast huge volumes of encrypted radio traffic. The western media is an asset we can use to create the impression that the *most* we could be planning is to liberate Birobidzhan.'

'How do we win this war, general?' Gordon asked.

'We invade China,' Clark replied simply. 'Strike straight into Manchuria with a three-corps front.' Clark stared back at him with an unwavering gaze. 'Mr President, when the Chinese invaded, the mission's objective changed. War is simple. War is about extreme commitment. On the individual level, it's about killing or being killed. On the national level, it's about total defeat of your enemy. And nothing short of taking the war to the enemy will win it. We've got to go into northern China. Cut the roads. Take the cities. Rock the Chinese back on their heels so hard that the war is ended on our terms. Decisiveness, Mr President. It's a quality all great leaders possess. Before you take a risk, you must stand to gain something of commensurate importance. Going from defense to offense is to risk everything. Total victory has to result from success.'

Gordon looked the man over one last time. Clark's war-winning counterattack happened to fit perfectly with Gordon's plan. He was also the first military man to propose actually winning. But there was still one more piece that had to fit. 'Just when would this counterattack come?' Gordon asked.

'The timing is tricky, Mr President. The plan requires for the Chinese supply network to be exhausted and for all our stocks and reinforcements to be in place at precisely the same time. Plus, there's the terrain and weather. For ten days when the ice melts the rivers are unbridgeable. And if we wait too long, the rivers flood and the ground turns to mud.'

'When, General Clark?' Gordon tried again.

'Mid- to late April, sir.'

Gordon smiled. The answer struck the mark. 'Then I approve the plan.' Clark looked up in surprise. 'You will launch the counterattack before April 18th.' Clark appeared confused. 'April 18th, General Clark. The day of my State of the Union address. The day before the War Powers Act vote. But let's not tell anyone we've agreed on that date. Understand? It's just between the two of us.'

Clark understood. He nodded slowly. As commander-in-chief of UNRUSFOR he always looked at the big picture. He was beginning to get a feel for an even larger perspective still.

NEW YORK, NEW YORK
February 25, 1300 GMT (0800 Local)

Roger Stempel fumbled with the antacids his doctor had prescribed. He was tired. His head pounded. The metal foil simply wouldn't tear. He quickly grew angry. He stopped himself and leaned heavily on the bathroom's vanity top. Taking deep breaths, he calmed himself. He was a wreck, and the list of medical complications from the stress he was under was growing. His wife was having lunch with her sister. If he had a heart attack now, he'd die alone. *Like Harold*, a voice whispered.

Roger winced and covered his face. He shook his head and dragged his hands down his cheeks. His eyes shone back at him from the mirror, blood-red.

The last weeks had been the worst of his life. 'Missing In Action – Presumed Killed,' the Army had said. First the shock. The agony. The despair. Their only child. Their little boy. Tears flowed down Roger's face. But the sadness had evolved into depression. His son's death had become handling the details. The Army could produce no remains. No remains, no funeral – Gay had said. Graves Registration had only a blood-soaked parka. It had Harold's name printed inside. *Not 'blood-stained,'* Roger thought. The man had clearly said 'blood-soaked.'

The electronic chirp of a telephone sent him running. His heart pounded as he slipped on the hardwoods in his stockinged feet. He snatched the phone from the cradle. The ringing continued. It was on television. A commercial selling voice mail to Nynex customers.

Roger hung up. The mail clapped onto the floor of the foyer. A flood of catalogs, junk mail and the occasional bill. Roger checked the answering machine once again. The red light was not lit.

He picked up the mail. His head swam after having stooped to gather the pile from the floor. He trudged into the study to be near the trash can – the repository of at least half their mail. The television was on. Its sound muted. He could still hear the news report from the media room down the hall. Like most of the apartment's TVs, the set was tuned to CNN around the clock.

Catalog. Catalog. Encyclopedia offer. Magazine subscription offer made to look like a check. Pre-approved credit card. Charitable donation solicitation. The trash can was quickly filled. As Roger lifted another catalog to toss it in the trash, a letter slipped out. It had the rare look of personal correspondence. He turned the envelope over.

It was in Harold's handwriting. A tight grip pinched Roger's throat and stomach. He sunk into the chair behind his desk. A prickly feeling spread across his skin. With trembling hands, he tore the top of the envelope off and yanked the letter out. It was dated less than a week earlier! The first paragraphs were about Harold's unit being overrun. The trouble they had getting back on base. His slight wounds while fighting with the provisionals.

'He's *alive!*' Roger shouted. He looked around the empty apartment. He was standing now – pacing as he read. Reading out loud. Running his hand through his unwashed hair and then over his bristly face. He sat to read the rest. He reveled in the relief it brought from his unrelenting grief. His joy subsided with Harold's every word.

'I know now what "biting" cold means. Your teeth chatter. Your body clenches up so hard that it's exhausting. Your breath freezes into large sheets of ice outside the towel or strip of wool blanket that you wrap around your neck. When you don't shave, tiny little droplets of ice cling to the tips of the hairs. It's very painful to pull them off, especially with wind-burned cheeks. Tears freeze, and the droplets weld your eyelashes together in big clumps. I've seen guys grope their way back into the warming hut from the trench with long, white mustaches of ice hanging from their eyebrows. When we come in from trench duty, our weapons steam for a long time when you put them near the fires. Every square inch of skin is chapped, especially your hands, face and lips. If you leave your nose or cheek exposed even for a few minutes, the skin will turn yellow. That's when you know you've got trouble. Red is okay. Pale yellow means frostbite. The only way to get the color back from yellow is to rub snow as hard as you can on it. Two guys in our platoon who were supposed to be on sentry duty crawled behind a log to get some sleep and froze to death.

'But it's when the wind blows that things are the worst. It's like a bath of cold water being poured onto you no matter how warmly you're dressed. At least when it blows hard, you know the Chinese won't attack. Then, everybody is just trying to survive. The wind feels like it cuts your skin when it hits your face. And when there's snow, it hits you like little darts – like a handful of pebbles that someone throws at your face. Even inside the shelter, the wind whistles and howls through the cracks in the roofing timbers so loudly you can't sleep no matter how exhausted you are. And it's coldest at night, especially out in the open.

'At night, the Chinese try to sneak between our positions. So we have to go out patrolling to find them. The guys in the next battalion down the line swear they patrol their front aggressively. But we always draw fire from their sector. Once we found bunkers the Chinese had lived in for several days, which is kind of impossible if they're actively patrolling. But I understand. Patrols are spooky. In the distance all around the base they fire white phosphorous marker rounds for artillery spotters. The shadows are always moving. The snow squeaks under your boots. The sound carries so far in the cold, especially downwind, it gives your position away. And under the snow, the ice is as slippery as a skating rink. The sunshine at midday will melt the top layer, and it'll freeze again at night. You carry a heavy load in case you're stuck outside the wire till morning. And you're constantly at risk of falling, especially on the roads. They were muddy from the summer rains when they froze, and the deep ruts made by the vehicles are now sharp ridges. When the wind blows the snow off, they look like six-inch-high black marble knives. If you fall on them, you break bones because they're as hard as iron. But we don't use roads much. You can't tell the road from the shoulder. Plus, the Chinese are sure to have ambushes prepared for us, just like we have for them. When we go outside the wire, you can see that they've been there. If you turn your ear to the wind you can hear all kinds of things. The woods are alive at night. They're filled with tracks. Every step anyone has ever taken is recorded in the snow. Your tracks, theirs – they're all mingled together.

'I don't want you two to get scared. Most of the time is spent in the trenches, where we're relatively safe. Our stretch of the perimeter is fairly solid. The Chinese haven't once made it within grenade range of the main trench. And they're in terrible shape. They loot the dead and crawl through piles of our trash for food and clothing. They're hungry and ragged and more frightened than we are. A lot of the corpses we police up are wearing U.S. uniforms. We even found some Christmas packages we think came from the convoys that got overrun on the road to Khabarovsk. I feel sort of sorry for them. One patrol came back after a blizzard and reported they'd found an entire regiment frozen to death. I don't know how the Chinese do it. Especially the second and third waves, which have to pass mounds of the dead and dying.

'Please don't think everything here is horrible. We sometimes get fresh food from the French. It's usually frozen by the time they bring it to the perimeter, but we reheat it and it tastes great. Everything freezes. Even in the warming huts or the bunkers where we sleep, you have to chop the food with a hatchet or an axe to cook it. We usually don't cook in the bunkers, though, because of the smell. They're also our bathrooms. And trench duty is fine when the weather is clear. The skies can be pure as crystal and a pale blue color I've never seen before. And the ground is like a winter wonderland, entirely covered in white. If you don't police up the dead, they're just covered up by the snow. At least until spring. And even the night, which almost always brings an attack if the weather permits, has a beauty of its own. The air is so dry that you can see every star. And when the fighting starts, the tracer rounds fly through the air like fireworks. When long, continuous bursts from each side intermingle, they look almost like bouquets of flowers. And when you're caught in a firefight out on patrol, the woods come alive with tracers like flaming arrows from some old western. Green ribbons of light from the Chinese. Yellow beads on long strings from the good guys.

'So don't worry, mom and dad. I'll be all right. They say if you make it past two weeks, your odds go way up. And I'm past two weeks. So don't get all stressed out over this. I'll make it. Lots of people live through war without anything terrible happening. It's just a job. I'll write again soon. Love, Harold.

'P.S. When you write back, I'd like to ask you to do something. When things get really bad and I have to just shut everything out, there's this poem that I read in prep school that I keep saying over and over to myself. And the thing is, it's driving me crazy because I can't remember the name of the poem. I think it's by T. S. Eliot.

If you can look it up or something and tell me what it is, I'd really appreciate it. The part that I repeat to myself goes like this:

> Footfalls echo in the memory
> Down the passage which we did not take
> Towards the door we never opened
> Into the rose garden.'

The apartment's front door opened. Gay found Roger holding the letter to his chest and crying.

OUTSIDE USSURIYSK, SIBERIA
February 27, 2330 GMT (0930 Local)

Kate Dunn positioned everyone. 'All right, Woody! You get the shot from on top of the trench. Okay, Jurgen. You go about your business.' Woody scampered up to ground level with his minicam. But the German and American paratroopers hesitated.

'Is there a problem?' Kate asked. The sky was perfect. The sun was nicely covered by thin cloud. But soon it would clear. Direct sunlight would change everything. Shades. Shadows. They'd lose this shot.

'What do you want me to do?' the German asked.

'Just do what you were doing,' Kate said. 'I don't *stage* shots.' They didn't understand. They looked at each other. Kate explained by grabbing the man's parka. She moved him to the trench wall just below Woody. 'Now go. Teach the Americans how to fight the Chinese.'

The GIs stirred and snorted. The German shook his head. 'No, no. Not how to fight. How to prepare positions. Winter positions.'

'Right. That's what I meant. Just go back over what you were telling them before you stopped. Only for the camera.' She smiled and pointed up at Woody. He waved from behind his eyepiece.

Kate placed the American paratroopers in a semicircle around the German. She held a boom mike over the group just off-camera. She had the German give his name and rank. He spoke English very well. No on-screen transcripts were needed. Woody gave her the thumbs up. The taping began.

'Okay,' the German advisor said, 'the best cover in the trenches

362

are ice parapets. They are bullet-proof. You make them by taking a poncho . . . like this.' He held the thin fabric up with a rustling noise. 'You roll small sticks inside it like this, ya?' The crinkling of the poncho was far too loud. Plus Kate saw Woody having to shift position. Kate motioned for the Americans to kneel. They did. The adviser held a thick bundle of small sticks. They were rolled into the poncho. He climbed a raised step on the trench wall. Kate's mike followed. He placed the bundle in front of the firing post. 'Now, please, would you hand me the water.'

An American carefully handed him a heavy can. The men all stood back from the liquid. They exchanged it slowly as if it were a vat of acid. Snow was being melted in fires up and down the trench line. The German used a stick to break the thin ice. He raised the can. He poured the water onto the poncho.

The Americans – all in their teens, from their looks – marveled as the water froze. The poncho was slowly covered in translucent layers of ice. They thickened right before their eyes. *Too long*, Kate thought. But the adviser took his time emptying the bucket.

Kate was reminded of high school science projects, the 'gee whiz' experiments meant more to intrigue than inform. Maybe they'd see that angle back in New York. Or maybe she should mention it.

'Pour slowly, *ja*? So the ice will freeze.' When he was done, the bundle of sticks was frozen solidly onto the front lip of the trench. 'An ice parapet,' he said – showmanlike. 'Let the ice set. Then cover it with snow for camouflage. You can bank the snow. Pour water over it. Two of this-size buckets. That will make a "snow-*und*-ice glacis."'

The Americans laughed. 'Snow-*und*-ice' was repeated.

'Okay, *cut*!' Kate shouted. She lowered the mike. 'Great! Did you get that, Woody?' He gave her another thumbs-up. He wasn't talking because of a sore throat he was protecting with scarves and mufflers. 'Okay, I need to do the story's lead-in. I'm going to stand right up there where he is. Everybody down here just go about your business.' She showed with her hands the camera's field of view. They stood there. 'Good. Say, you all have your rifles, don't you?' They showed her. They weren't even loaded.

She climbed up the wall rolling her eyes. Woody held the camera to her face. She took a quick glance at her compact, cleared her throat . . . and looked around.

Soldiers cleared the gentle slope in front. Engineers cut tree trunks with noisy chain saws. When trying to choose her story, they'd told her it was a dangerous job. You could hit an ice core. Break the chain. Maybe send the whole saw flying back at you. White-painted backhoes carried trees and brush to the rear. Other soldiers were sawing logs for ceiling timbers. Kate had chosen to stick with the paratroopers.

Kate had Woody try to get it all. Engineers preparing the killing fields in the background. Troops in the trench below. A close-up of Kate.

Woody counted down with his fingers, then pointed.

'The 82nd Airborne Division was the first major reinforcement to arrive in Siberia after the war began. But this fabled unit has yet to see action. It is traditionally reserved for the ultimate in national emergencies. But now, the "All-American" Division is in the fight. They're bracing for the shock of the main Chinese assault. At night, the wind carries the sounds of approaching combat. The German Army will soon "pass the line" to their American comrades. These paratroopers will learn firsthand the brutality of winter infantry war.

'But lessons are already being learned. They are being passed from ally to ally. German soldiers have been pulled back from the lines. The experience of battle they have had visited upon them is helping fellow UN troops to better prepare their ice-bound positions.' She lowered the mike. 'We'll cut here. Insert the scene we just taped.'

Woody shook his head. 'That form you signed with the public affairs guy is gonna haunt you. It's a pact with the devil, Kate. The censor's gonna hold the tape. They won't let you mention the 82nd till they start fighting.'

Loud gunfire erupted from the hills. It wasn't close. But it was near enough to cause everyone to turn. Even in daylight you could clearly see the flashes. They lit the clouds.

Kate smiled. She had Woody start taping. Scenes of officers shouting. The men on the slopes dropping their logs and saws and coming back up the slope. A sergeant marching down the trench and weapons being loaded with magazines. Kate couldn't believe their luck.

'Hey!' an officer shouted. 'Get down from there!'

'We're from the press,' Kate said.

'*I* know who you are!' The man was a captain. Kate and Woody climbed down. Woody filmed the paratroopers' grim preparations close-up. 'Show's over. Out of my trenches.'

'But we want to get this,' Kate pleaded. She was outraged. Artillery shells cut through the air overhead. They exploded on a ridge a mile away. Kate flinched at the loud booms. '*Besides!*' Kate yelled – stopping the man. 'It's probably too dangerous out there already.'

'What's too dangerous is what's comin' this way! Now lady, there's *no* way – *no* how – you're stayin' here!' He left.

'What an asshole!' she said. Men laughed. They all stood on or near their fighting steps. Woody's camera whirred. More shells rumbled through the sky. She ran out in front of Woody. She stuck her stick mike in a soldier's face. 'Have you been told what is happening? We were told the Chinese were thirty miles from here.'

'One of our patrols ran into one of their patrols,' he said. He kept turning to look at the camera. 'It's just sorta . . . escallatin.'

'But how could they get so close without us knowing? With satellites and spy planes and . . .?'

'There's only one way to know where the enemy is, ma'am. That's to bump into him. That's what patrols do. That's how we know they're comin'.'

Kate glanced to make sure Woody got the sound bite. He wasn't there! 'Snit!' Kate snapped. She found him around a turn in the zig-zagging trench. He was hovering above the German adviser and two kneeling Americans. Their heads bowed. Their eyes closed. One was muttering Hail Marys. One clenched a tiny, homemade cross. Short strips of leather bound by string.

Kate couldn't help herself. She balled up her fist and pumped her arm in the air. *Yes!* she thought. Before they got to the Humvee, she'd composed the words for her voiceover.

UNRUSFOR HEADQUARTERS, KHABAROVSK
February 29, 2000 GMT (1000 Local)

Clark wasn't much for theatrics, but he was playing this for all it was worth. He'd left most of his senior officers out of the planning. He'd been ordered to wait until the last ally had committed. That had occurred the night before. 'Are they all there?' he asked Major Reed, who nodded. Clark took a deep breath, tugged down on his

365

BDU blouse, and straightened his back. He turned to ensure that his aides all stood ready behind him. 'Okay, let's do this.'

He opened the door and entered. Conversations in a half-dozen languages fell quiet as the national commanders of the various UNRUSFOR contingents turned their attention to the procession of American officers. Clark was at its head. As he sat, his aides arrayed easels in a semicircle behind him. The maps remained covered with an opaque plastic sheet.

'Good morning, and thank you all for coming,' Clark began. 'I am fully aware of the internal debates each of you has been having with your capitals ever since I returned from Washington. And I apologize for not consulting with you earlier. But I am also informed that your political leadership and mine have agreed to broad strategic plans for prosecution of this war to its conclusion. Therefore, I am here this morning to issue the operation order. The plan's code name is Winter Harvest.'

Clark could hear the theater map being uncovered behind him. Reed had hit his cue perfectly. Everyone's eyes turned to the map. To the two sweeping blue arrows stabbing deep into the heart of Manchuria.

'To put it simply,' Nate said, 'we will marshal and hold in reserve every soldier and weapon that arrives in theater from this point forward. We will hold our current lines with units currently in the field. And in a little under two months, we'll strike the Chinese with everything we've got.'

He didn't tell them the deadline for the counterattack was April 18th. After all, he reasoned, Davis could be convinced of a better time, if necessary. But he knew he'd made a pact. Davis was issuing statements vigorously defending Nate. Neither Ferguson nor Dekker had interfered much in his planning.

Reed stood at the map wielding a pointer. He'd gotten little sleep the past week. The fatigue prevented Clark from measuring the effects of combat on the man. 'The first column,' Nate began, 'will move west from Vladivostok toward Kirin, China. The second will move south from the Trans-Siberian Railway west of Urgal. Its objective is also Kirin. The objective of Winter Harvest is to pocket the entire offensive threat of the People's Liberation Army between the twin pincers . . . and destroy that threat.'

Heads turned. 'Any questions?' Clark asked.

'How will we maintain operational security?' the British Deputy Commander said. 'The world press is running rampant throughout the theater.'

'Our strategic deception plan,' Clark answered, 'is this – we are defeated. We are barely clinging to our positions. We are reeling under the weight of unstoppable Chinese assaults. Our troops are dispirited and demoralized. In short, they pose *no*,' Clark said slowly, 'offensive threat whatsoever. That shouldn't be too much of a leap for our news media to make.'

There was laughter – a release of pent-up, nervous tension.

'The Chinese will know,' the Dutch commander commented. 'They won't be swayed by news reports.'

'We intend,' Nate replied, 'to begin vigorously demonstrating against China from the sea. We'll sail U.S. Marine amphibious forces up and down the Chinese coast. Put SEAL teams on their beaches. They'll gather intell on beach gradients, sand firmness, minefields, troop dispositions. Only one of those landing ships, however, will be loaded with Marines. It will also carry the press.'

Amid the laughter, a British officer noted, 'The empty ships will ride high in the water.'

'We'll offload the Marines and equipment at Vladivostok. They'll fight with the southern prong of the advance into China. We'll load Russian trucks filled with rocks as ballast.'

'Where will you hold landing exercises for the press?' the grinning German officer asked.

'Korea. It'll be the best-trained amphibious assault battalion in Marine history.' More laughter. 'In addition to achieving strategic surprise, we hope to tie down at least thirty Chinese divisions along the coast.'

'What will the dummy target be?' the French general asked.

'Hong Kong,' Clark replied.

'What about the flanks of the main attack?' the French general asked. It was a far more serious challenge. He waggled his finger at the twin arrows, which extended far into northern China. 'You don't seem to broaden the neck of those advances at all. Once UNRUSFOR crosses the Amur and Ussuri into China – *if* we can cross them – the PLA is going to pull everything back. Those troops will be positioned to attack straight into the flanks of our advances.'

'*We* will make it across the rivers,' Clark replied. 'The Chinese won't.

We will put at least one armored corps across in each prong before the ice breaks. Once the ice breaks, my engineers tell me that no bridging equipment made can stand the flow. The People's Liberation Army will be stranded on the Russian side for ten days. In those ten days, we will win the war.'

THE KREMLIN, RUSSIA
February 29, 0900 GMT (1100 Local)

When Kartsev returned from the bathroom, he froze in the door to his office. Someone had been there. A letter sat in the middle of his desk chair. All was still.

He chided himself for being so anxious and walked around to his desk. He returned to his running, subvocal conversation with himself – half mumbled aloud – but then looked up startled. For a moment, he thought he'd seen the door open a few inches.

He tried to steady himself. Why worry about such things? No force on earth could change the outcome if his complex system of reward and terror failed. *Besides*, whispered a voice, *that end is inevitable.*

Kartsev smiled. It was a voice with which he was well acquainted. It had been his counsel on many a long, cold Siberian night. Most people, he knew, shut out those awful whispers which arose from the dark recesses of their heads. Kartsev, however, listened attentively. They had served him well for they spoke terrible truths. Truths about the nature of man. About himself.

The envelope lay in the seat of his chair. It was thick and unopened. He never opened his own mail. He never received anything personal. At the very least he hoped they'd X-rayed the letter. People could make bombs out of the most innocuous and compact packages.

There was no return address, just Kartsev's typed name. He opened the letter. It was from the President of the United States.

Kartsev settled into his chair with a smile.

After reading and then re-reading the letter, Kartsev slipped out of his shoes and lifted his stockinged feet up onto his desk. *Well argued*, he thought as he reclined. The man has a well-ordered mind. He proceeds logically from point A to point Z, connecting all his arguments in between.

'But, alas . . .' he said to no one. He typed the short reply himself.

'Dear Mr President. Pardon so informal a reply to your letter, but I find e-mail suits my needs best for the moment. With respect to your reasoning as to why I should relinquish my role as ideologue for the 'Anarchist Movement,' I must say that I find your logic to be impeccable. I am certain the world would be a better place if I were to do as you requested . . . from where you sit. However, we do seem to find ourselves with slightly divergent interests, don't we? As for your appeal to my patriotism in reference to the war in Siberia against China, might I remind you of what anarchy stands for?

'The border over which you fight is an arbitrary line demarking the limits of power presently exerted by two competing systems of human tyranny. The concept of a 'nation' is itself what anarchy is meant to abolish. You are the leader of the strongest nation on earth. You may draw whatever conclusions you wish from that about my desire to cooperate with your government.

'Sincerely, Valentin K. Kartsev.'

Without so much as a quick proof, Kartsev hit 'Send.' After a momentary delay, his message was at the White House.

So easy, Kartsev thought. He then resumed his writing with newfound vigor.

BETHESDA NAVAL HOSPITAL, MARYLAND
February 29, 2130 GMT (1630 Local)

'So this is it?' Gordon Davis asked – holding the sheaf of papers.

'That's the execution copy,' the White House counsel said. Gordon and the others looked his way. The young man opened his mouth to amend his awkward reply, but decided in the end to say nothing.

There was a select and oddly diverse gathering for the event. In addition to Davis's personal lawyer, he had invited the Chief Justice of the Supreme Court, the chairmen of the two houses' intelligence oversight committees, and – of course – the Director of the CIA.

Gordon leafed through the pages one after the other. He stopped on the section entitled 'Findings.' Everyone in the dimly-lit hospital room waited. Their eyes bored holes in Gordon as he read. It was a perfunctory act. He knew he would sign the order. He'd directed it be drawn up and these witnesses invited. But to complete the formal act he needed to pay correct attention to the carefully drafted paperwork.

'Based upon the best evidence available,' Gordon read, 'Subject is responsible for planning, training and directing over 147 acts of international terrorism leading to 429 dead and 238 wounded.' The second paragraph levied a new set of charges. 'National intelligence sources estimate that Subject has personally ordered the murder of over 1,200 of his own citizens. In addition, his repressive state security apparatus has summarily executed numbers of persons estimated to be anywhere from 10,000 to 60,000.' On and on the allegations went. 'Subject's crimes against humanity also include instigation of a civil war which left over 100,000 dead and another 160,000 wounded.'

The sheer weight of the numbers was numbing. Were 429 dead from terrorism somehow more heinous a crime than 100,000 Russian dead from war? Why else was it that such a small number warranted anything more than, at most, a footnote? But it would've been a footnote that included heads of state. Members of Marshall's cabinet. Phil Bristol. And – twice – almost Gordon himself. *And Elaine, Janet and Celeste*, Gordon thought – grinding his teeth.

They all watched him. Gordon didn't need to read on, but he did for appearances' sake. And as he read, the grounds for the order grew more shaky. 'Subject personally ordered policies that have led to starvation and disease that have claimed upwards of 30,000 lives.' Gordon would have left out that count. It was weak – sounding like bad economic policy even though Gordon knew it was ethically equivalent to the most loathsome of criminal acts. And then he came to the last paragraph on the single summary page. 'Subject is the motive force behind the spread of an ideology that debases the essence of human institutions and values, and seeks to undermine the moral and ethical tenets and precepts from which all liberal democratic governments derive their legitimacy.'

Gordon looked up at his counsel. 'I want this last paragraph out,' he said. Heads all dropped to read the page to which they had all turned.

'All right, sir,' the lawyer said in an agreeable tone. 'We were just giving you the full menu from which to choose.'

'And you might as well take out the paragraph before it, too,' he said. 'The one about starving his people.'

'Well, that one isn't really legally distinguishable from the paragraph preceding *it*, sir,' White House counsel advised. 'Instigation of a civil war is as accepted a crime against humanity as a war of aggression.'

'All of which,' the Chief Justice intoned, 'are based on *dubious* jurisprudential reasoning.'

Gordon's lawyer didn't reply.

'Why not just stick with the first couple of paragraphs?' Daryl Shavers proposed. 'We got him dead to rights on international terrorism and mass murder of his own people. We've got recorded confessions from some of those poor bastards about the training camps and the orders to carry out attacks. And we've got that computer file we decrypted with that *bizarre* way he orders people killed. "Schedule A" or whatever it was.'

'I agree with Daryl,' Gordon said. He took the pen and struck everything on the page but the first two paragraphs.

'We do have some evidentiary problems with that computer file,' Gordon's lawyer pointed out. 'We don't have a good chain of custody back to a credible source. The disk was delivered to us anonymously.'

Gordon was too busy initialing in the margin beside each of the stricken paragraphs to reply.

'*Look*,' the Director of the CIA said impatiently, 'I *know* this has to be done legally. But does it really matter what the words in that executive order say? Is there anyone who can dispute the fact that the son-of-a-bitch is a mass murderer?'

'Done,' Gordon said to cut the debate short. He flipped to the signature page. 'By order of Gordon Eugene Davis,' Gordon read out loud, 'President of the United States of America, be it hereby resolved and directed that Valentin Konstantinovich Kartsev be apprehended and brought to trial or, failing apprehension, executed by appropriate means and in a manner designed to cause minimal collateral damage.'

'*My* counsel,' the CIA Director interrupted, 'has *real* problems with that phrasing, Mr President.'

Gordon looked up at the drafter. 'What the hell is this?'

'It's . . . What part of it is the problem, sir?' the lawyer asked.

'This is *bullshit*,' Gordon said. 'We have to try to apprehend Kartsev first?'

His lawyer shrugged. 'If the opportunity presents itself . . .'

'There'll *be* no opportunity,' the CIA Director responded tersely. 'The bastard never leaves his *office*! Even his *aides* don't see him. He sends 'em e-mails like that bullshit reply to the President's letter!' He turned to Gordon. 'Hell, sir. I don't even know right now how we're gonna do it.' He raised his own copy of the Executive Order. 'Much less "by *appropriate* means and in a manner designed to cause minimal *collateral* damage." Now what the hell does *that* mean?'

White House counsel finally bristled. 'It means you can't pour hot *lead* down his throat!'

The rotund CIA Director squinted at the young lawyer. 'What in God's name are you *talking* about?'

'I'm just explaining that first *clause*. The "appropriate means" limitation.'

The Director opened his mouth . . . then quite obviously reined in his anger. 'Are bullets "appropriate means"?' The lawyer pursed his lips and nodded – the answer obvious. 'Explosive devices?' Again Gordon's counsel nodded – a little more slowly this time. 'Incendiary devices?' This time the question drew hesitation and the beginnings of a shrug. 'Poison? Garrote? Gas? Ice pick in the ear? Electric charge in a door handle? Prolonged exposure to microwaves? Accumulated doses of iridium? Biological contamination of the Kremlin water supply?'

The man could clearly go on. But his voice had risen to almost a shout. He cut himself short and waited for the reply.

'This is why we went with the generic language "appropriate means." It's impossible for me to sit here right now and say which of the ways that the Subject could be executed would, or would not, be acceptable.'

'You *wrote* the Goddamn language!' the CIA Director burst out. 'If *you* can't tell me what the hell it means, how the *fuck* can *I* figure it out!'

'All right, *cut* this shit out!' Daryl shouted just as Gordon was about to do the same.

'He's trying to hang CIA out to dry,' the Director continued.

'Well, what do you propose we *do*?' Gordon's lawyer shot back. 'Have the President sign this order and have you decide to carry it out by nuking Moscow?'

'Who the fuck *is* this guy?'

'That's enough!' Gordon snapped. He again raised his pen. 'Here's what we're gonna do.' He struck words – drawing a line straight through the middle of them. When he was done, he read what was left. 'What if we say, "By order of me, *et cetera, et cetera*, be it hereby resolved and directed that Valentin Konstantinovich Kartsev be executed" – period.'

Gordon looked at White House counsel. He reluctantly assented. The Director of the CIA said, 'Short, sweet, to-the-point. I love it.'

'Now I want to tell *you*,' Gordon said – waving his finger in the air at the smiling CIA man – 'that I *personally* want to approve every aspect of that operation. When it happens, I don't want to be surprised. Do you read me?'

The Director nodded.

Gordon signed the Executive Order. 'I'll go ahead and sign this marked-up version. You make the changes and I'll sign a new one for the files.' He handed it to the nodding lawyer. 'And good job. I appreciate somebody trying to cover my ass.'

There was polite laughter from around the bed, and a broad grin of relief from the young attorney.

'Now,' Gordon said to the CIA Director, 'what's the plan?'

With apologies the man politely cleared the room. When he, Daryl and Gordon were finally alone, all he said was, 'We have assets.'

Gordon and Daryl waited. 'What the hell does *that* mean?' Daryl asked.

'I mean we have several people we think can get close to Kartsev.'

'Who are these people?' Gordon asked.

'Disaffected ex-military types, mostly. And there's this ex-pat Russian security officer living illegally in Philadelphia.'

Chapter Seventeen

PHILADELPHIA, PENNSYLVANIA
February 29, 0245 GMT (2145 Local)

Olga and Pyotr walked arm-in-arm from the movie theater. It was
one of the few times they'd gotten out for an evening on the town.
The girls, they finally decided, could be trusted not to tell a babysitter
everything. But just in case they hired their neighbor's thirteen-year-old
daughter.

The downside to choosing the oblivious teenager was that she spent
the entire evening on the phone.

'I should try calling again,' Olga said as they stood under the bright
marquee lights.

'Darling, if she's on the telephone it means she's there. Everything's
okay. *Ladno?*'

She wasn't satisfied. But he'd bought enough time to make it to the
restaurant for coffee and dessert. There would be a payphone there.
The busy signal sure to come from it would provide thirty additional
minutes of conversation.

The crowds thinned. The streets darkened. Olga was too busy
silently fretting to notice the subtle change. But Pyotr grew more

and more alert. He hadn't seen the government car which usually shadowed him.

'Pyotr Andreev?' they heard from behind.

Olga gasped. She lowered her head and jammed her eyes shut.

But the accent was distinctly American.

Pyotr turned. Two men in dark overcoats stood behind him. A parked car turned on its headlights. It pulled up beside them. It was unmarked. But to Pyotr it may as well have had 'U.S. government' printed on the door.

'It's all right,' he said quietly to Olga.

'And what is this "business" you're talking about?' Pyotr asked.

The man across the small table in the suburban house flicked his cigarette repeatedly.

'It's an operation,' he said as if he were breaking significant new ground.

But to Pyotr it was stating the obvious. He drew a deep breath and looked around the room. It was dimly lit except for the bright light over the table. The other agents all loitered at a distance.

'What kind of operation?' Pyotr asked.

There was again a long delay. The talker took a drag of the cigarette. He slowly exhaled. 'A foreign operation,' he said – each syllable accompanied by puffs that were lit by the warm overhead bulb.

It was almost midnight. Olga would be home, worried sick. 'Can you be more specific?'

The man had seen too many old movies. He took his time replying. 'No,' he finally said.

It's in Russia, Pyotr surmised. *And it's so dirty they won't talk about it till I sign on.* 'I'd like to help, bu- . . .' he began.

'*Good*,' the man interrupted. 'We thought you'd appreciate your position.'

Pyotr heard the thudding threat. He sat forward. His weight rested heavily on his elbows. He raised his voice for the microphone – wherever it was. Maybe someone out there was listening. 'I have a wife and kids. My first duty is to them. If you're proposing that I take some personal risk, then I cannot help. My wife and children need me . . . *alive.*'

Again there was smoke. Only this time the wait was sheer agony for Pyotr.

'All right,' the man then said. He reached into his pocket. The agent shoved a card across the table. Pyotr began to breathe again. 'If you change your mind, call that number any time.' Pyotr eyed the card without reaching for it. 'We can help . . . with things,' the man said. 'Certain legalities . . . like citizenship.' Pyotr couldn't tell whether the man was dangling a carrot or wielding a stick. Probably both. 'And I wouldn't take too much time thinking it over.'

Pyotr took the card from the table. The agents drove him home. Pyotr was shocked.

Olga wasn't. 'It's *America!*' She clutched him joyfully to her chest. 'Everything is different here!'

Pyotr decided not to tell her about the veiled threat. She was too in love with her new home.

FORT CAMPBELL, KENTUCKY
March 1, 1600 GMT (1000 Local)

'Listen *up*!' the sergeant shouted. His chest heaved under the tight, olive drab T-shirt. They had just come from the obstacle course. Andre and the other trainees were exhausted. Even the instructor was sweating. 'Today we're gonna teach you two methods of heliborne insertion into inaccessible landing zones! Method one is tactical rappeling!'

He turned to the helicopter around which the class sat and picked up a rope. 'You men and women had *better* pay attention to this, 'cause in about one hour you *will* be descending from *this* helicopter to the ground one hundred feet below!'

There was nervous fidgeting and sideways glances among the young trainees. Andre was petrified. He tried to calm himself by imagining doing the same thing, but with people shooting at him.

'The second method – which we'll go over this afternoon – is called "STABO"! That stands for "Stabilized Tactical Airborne Body Operations"! In STABO insertions, four of you will hang side-by-side from hundred-foot ropes! The helicopter will take off, lifting you into the air with it! It will then fly to the drop zone and lower you to the ground!'

There was a snicker.

'*You got a problem with that, soldier?*' shouted another instructor. He stepped into the semicircle.

'No, sergeant!' the man barked back.

'You guys had better realize something, right now! If you get that Air Assault Badge, you're headed for the 101st Airborne Division (Airmobile). You ever heard of the Screaming Eagles? D-Day! Operation Market Garden! The Siege of Bastogne! The Tet Offensive! Hill 937! You ever heard of *Hamburger* Hill? Well, this is the home of the men who fought there! And right now, they're in the shit in Siberia. Right now, they're doin' what we're training *you* to do. I'd pay attention!'

The instructor raised a shiny 'D' ring and returned to the lecture. It went on for almost an hour. Each recruit was again run through the procedures for attaching his personal harness to the ring. They had, all been taught how to rappel on a tall wooden tower. But the instructor went back over how to clamp down on the twin ropes to control their rate of descent. 'All right, then!' the instructor shouted abruptly. 'Everybody *up*!'

The trainees all looked at each other. *Just like that?* Andre thought. The helicopter's flight crew had been quietly checking out the aircraft. They were now strapped into the cockpit. Andre's class rose. The instructors made their way through, tugging on the harnesses the men wore.

The engines began to whine. The rotors turned. 'Mount up!' the instructor shouted. The class of twelve climbed through the open side door. By the time they were all aboard, the wash from the rotors was at gale force. Everything was happening so quickly. The cold wind swirled through the open side doors. With a lurch, the helicopter began to move. Not up, but forward. The grassy field rushed by not five feet beneath them. Andre sat on the hard metal floor. Dozens of aircraft and their trainees filled the open field.

Andre felt the helicopter's rise in his gut. It banked quickly, turned, and pitched nose-up. Andre's insides were all tied in knots. The muscles from his stomach to his shoulders were clenched tight. He had trouble drawing a breath. The helicopter settled into a hover. The noise of the rotors and wind roared through the open doors.

'When you get to the ground,' the instructor shouted, 'clear the LZ and set up a perimeter!' Andre couldn't believe the time had come. He'd listened to the lectures. But he felt like they hadn't told him enough. Maybe the others all understood, but he didn't. He wasn't ready. He was terrified.

'Okay!' the instructor shouted. He clapped a guy hard on the shoulder and jerked his thumb toward the door. The trainee hesitated. The sergeant kicked him. He rose carefully and grabbed onto the bulkhead beside the door.

Andre felt a tap on his shoulder. Another instructor waved him to his feet. Andre's head jerked around. There were two instructors. Two ropes. Two open doors. 'Let's go!' the instructor shouted.

Everyone looked at Andre. They were checking him out, searching his eyes. Andre got the impression that they were hoping he would back out. Say no. If he refused, maybe they could too. Maybe they'd call the whole thing off. Decide it was too dangerous. Land and go back over everything again.

Andre rose. It was a struggle. Gravity tugged at him hard. He stood beside the instructor. The man pressed the spring-closed bar on the 'D' ring and wove the two ropes into Andre's harness. He went back through the principles that would keep Andre from plummeting to his death. Then he said, 'You ready?'

Andre nodded. A shiver quaked through him. The sergeant punched him on the arm. 'You'll love it! It's better'n sex!' He ushered Andre to the edge. The void loomed at the tips of his combat boots. It was a hundred feet down to the green field.

'Turn around!' the instructor ordered. 'Back up to the door!' Andre turned carefully. The instructor held onto the ropes – repositioning them as Andre turned. He held them out to Andre, who gripped them with all his might. 'Lookin' good!' the instructor shouted. 'Now back on up!' There was a cliff behind him. Andre could feel it. The wide-eyed soldier opposite him took baby steps. His heels inched closer to the edge. The instructor shouted in his ear.

He slid his boot back without lifting it, and there it was – the edge. He could feel it through the thick sole of the combat boot. A distinct boundary beyond which lay nothing but air. His heels hung out. His toes still solidly gripped the deck. 'Okay, son! Just lie back!'

No matter how hard he tried, Andre couldn't bring himself to lean backwards out the door. Inside the helicopter were the pallid faces of his sickly class. Outside were spinning rotors. A roaring engine whose hot exhaust heat lapped at his face in gusts amid freezing winter air. And a great drop to the green lawn against which his body would break if he fell.

'We don't have all day, private!' the instructor shouted. Andre saw his counterpart across the cabin at the other open door. He wasn't leaning, but sort of sitting out into space. His knees were bent. He kept almost losing his footing. He managed to struggle back inside and start the process over again with the now livid instructor hounding him loudly.

Andre let the rope slide through his gloved hands and leaned back. It was only a few inches, but he had crossed the imaginary line between inside and out. The noise and the gale were overwhelming. The dark green fuselage framed the open door. The world of his classmates inside the helicopter seemed like a million miles away. His hands cramped from their firm grip. The thought flashed through his head that paratroopers had it easy. They just jumped. No thinking. But he had to will himself out in slow motion.

'You're almost there!' the instructor yelled. His distant voice came from the other side of the gulf. He was motioning for Andre to keep going.

Andre was paying no attention to the man. He had his own plan. He let a few more inches of rope through his fingers. He was at a forty-five degree angle. He looked up at the turning rotor. Down at the two dangling ropes. Back inside the cabin, the guy who'd been opposite him was unhooking. Another trainee – a woman – was taking the guy's place at the door. Andre even saw the pilot, twisted around in his seat and looking back at him from under his large green helmet and black visor.

The instructor was still yelling. Andre let a few more inches of rope through. His heart was pounding hard. He squinted in the downblast of the rotors, which whirred unseen through the crystal blue sky. When he was reclined almost level with the floor, he realized with a start that he was past the point of no return.

The rope shook. Andre saw the instructor shouting at him. Shooing him away from the aircraft. Across the cabin, he saw the jerky nods of the terrified female soldier as she replied to the shouts of her instructor. She winced at the sound of them as the NCO's body quaked from its effort.

Andre let a few more inches through his hands . . . and his feet lost their grip and he fell. He grabbed the ropes hard and stiffened his legs. He stared straight at the wheels – suspended in air. Tentatively he loosed his grip . . . and down he went. He clamped down again to stop his fall. His rate of descent had been dizzying. He looked back up. His instructor was giving him the thumbs-up sign. The woman's butt protruded from the opposite door.

Down he went in five- and ten-foot falls. Every time too fast. Every time stopped by a frantic pinching of the ropes. By the time he was halfway to the ground it was the easiest thing in the world. He even hung for a moment – fifty feet below the helicopter, fifty feet above waiting instructors. The helicopter's engines were still incredibly loud, but it was much more peaceful than the doorway had been. He looked up and saw that the woman was clinging to the rope about even with the wheels.

Andre went on down – a complete master of the process. He even finished with a flourish – zipping the last twenty feet and landing with a springy thud on his feet. He grinned broadly at the instructor.

'You're under fire, asshole!' the man shouted – peppering Andre's chest with backhanded blows.

Still grinning, Andre acted out his part in the pretend battle. He released the ropes from the 'D' ring and ran to the edge of the landing zone. He dropped to the ground, raised his empty M-16, and defended the perimeter. He even lined up imaginary targets. A fire hydrant at the corner of the parking lot

'You're under fire, sweetheart!' Andre heard the instructor shout over the noise from above. He turned to see the female soldier dive to the ground next to Andre with a rustle of fabric from her BDUs. She too raised her rifle to her shoulder. She too had a broad grin on her face.

Andre smiled back. She laughed. 'That was easy as *shit!*' she said. Andre nodded. 'Air Assault, buddy!' she said – raising her hand high to Andre. He slapped it with a flourish – half expecting the instructors to explode in shouts. But the NCOs stood there quietly. They turned their attention to the next to come down.

ABOARD F-117, OVER HARBIN, CHINA
March 7, 1600 GMT (0200 Local)

Major Brian Russell flew the F-117 straight and level. He was ten thousand feet over the sprawling city of Harbin. It was a clear night, but the city lights had been extinguished. But there was no doubt he'd arrived over his target. Global positioning signals were beamed by satellite. They gave him location within five meters of accuracy.

The amber triangle representing his aircraft glowed brightly on his nav/attack screen. It straddled his course line. Up ahead, the line bent. His final turn to target.

Suddenly tracers rose into the air ahead. It took willpower for Russell not to roll the aircraft clear of danger. He stayed the course and watched as balls of fire bloomed in his path.

The 'Triple A' – anti-aircraft artillery – was being fired randomly into the night sky from every quarter. They must have heard his engines as he passed over the outskirts of the industrial city. But Russell knew there was nothing to gain by giving in to the temptation to maneuver. His course had been carefully plotted. It was along the glowing green line on the screen that he would find the safest route.

But that route took him straight through the bursting clusters. Directly through continually erupting orange fireworks. Criss-crossing his path were streaking white tracers. In between were exploding cannon rounds. Larger artillery rounds burst above and below. It was all fused to different altitudes. All around their exploding centers were jagged spheres of expanding shrapnel.

He had to make a choice. And one thing the F-117 gave you was time to think things over. It flew at subsonic speeds. The indicator on his heads-up display read 460 knots. At that speed, there was less reacting and more deliberating. If he'd been flying a Strike Eagle from his old squadron, he'd have been doing twice the speed. That was only half the time for decisions – some of them life-or-death. And he'd have been at treetop altitude. Listening to the blaring tones of threat-warning receivers.

Russell could still hear the radar paints. But their volume had been turned down. They were only a remote threat to the F-117. Maybe if he passed directly overhead Chinese radar might paint its angular fuselage. But even then they couldn't track him. Nor could their remaining fighter-interceptors. He was practically impossible to kill.

But still guns filled Russell's windshield with death. 'Damn,' he muttered. *They must be moving their guns*, he thought. Russell's once clear line of attack had since been filled with several batteries of AAA. The pointed nose led straight into a solid ball of flame.

He knew it was just an illusion. There was nothing solid about the sky in front. It was filled with empty spaces. But he experienced an almost overwhelming desire not to risk it. He was a 'stick-and-rudder' man. And it went against every instinct. He could bank clear of the danger and reacquire the target visually. But years of training for just such a mission bound him to the course.

His grip on the stick grew tight as he approached the fireworks. He glanced down again at the screen. The triangle flew straight down the green line. The darkened cockpit lit with strobes of soundless lightning. He looked up through the flat-paned canopy. Tracers rose from the earth all around. Long glowing strings formed a 'golden BB.' Russell flew straight into it.

His heart skipped with each burst. He cringed as looping chains of tracers swung by him. The gunners slewed their weapons every which way. They fired with wild abandon. A spotter had presumably heard his engines. They threw a thunderstorm into his path.

But he heard nothing but a steady whine and the soft tones of his nav/attack system. They reminded him to begin his descent. To drop to point-blank bombing altitude. Russell cut the throttle and lowered the nose. He made a steady cruising descent while under furious fire from below.

The cockpit was calm. The radio eerily quiet. He was all alone on this mission. Stealth aircraft needed no entourage. No aircraft packages for air defense suppression. No fighter escort. No AWACS controllers with their steady patter of warnings and contacts. Just one plane, one pilot, and two bombs . . . and a thousand Chinese guns all firing blindly into the air.

Flame shot from the ground to the left of the aircraft. Russell's heart pounded as the missile rose. Its astonishing speed put it at altitude in three seconds. But it was no more effective than the artillery. Without a target it went ballistic. It kept rising straight as a bullet into the clear night sky. Russell lost interest – noting only the flash thousands of feet overhead.

A loud knock and a slight roll got Russell's attention. He'd seen no tracers or bright bursts. Just a single rapping sound on his left wing like a rock striking the undercarriage of a speeding car. But the warning lights remained dark. The indicators on his instrument panel were all steady green. He kept his eye on the digital fuel gauge. The fuel ticked off in orderly fashion pound-by-pound.

Russell took a deep breath of oxygen and exhaled slowly. *Must've been a spent round falling back to earth*, he thought. *Or a bird startled to flight by the guns.*

The sky was dark again. He was through the wall of fire. Another tone announced his arrival at five thousand feet. Another shortly thereafter at the last heading change – a thirty-degree turn to the left.

In the dim starlight, the tall smokestacks rolled into view. Russell could've flown by sight and released his bombs visually from there if he'd had to. But the planners had chosen the two release points very carefully. The first was the tailgate of a production line for 155-mm artillery shells. The shells were loaded there onto trucks and carted away. The two-thousand-pounder would fly straight into the loading dock. The explosion should rip into the plant from its one unhardened Achilles Heel. The second bomb would fall straight through an airshaft into an underground explosives bunker.

At two miles, Russell opened the bomb-bay doors. Enemy radars would now have their best chance. The carefully designed lines of the stealth aircraft were now disturbed. Russell shut the thought from his head as he eyed the looming smokestacks. At one mile, his mind and the bomb-release 'pickle' were one.

His thumb flicked open the cover to the buttons atop the thick grip. One would release the first bomb; another the second. Russell's eyes remained fixed on the nav/attack screen. They switched from the triangle and line to the digital readout just beside it. The screen displayed a variety of falling balls and merging circles. But Russell's preferred focus was the range to his bomb-release point.

When it hit zero Russell thumbed the pickle. The aircraft floated upward but remained straight on line. There were no turns on this bombing run. The range numbers to the second target all reset instantly. Almost as soon as Russell digested the new readout, it came time to drop the second bomb.

A brilliant flash lit the instrument panel and dash. Russell hit the pickle and again the F-117 soared. He scanned the instruments for flashing red warning lights. Russell rolled the ship on her side and jammed the throttle to the stop. A second and brighter flash lit the night.

As the plane banked, he saw the blazing display. The entire factory was rapidly being enguled in flame.

He returned the F-117 to straight and level exactly on his egress heading. The sky was lit repeatedly by explosions from his first bomb.

But the target area of his second was dark and still. But in the light from the flames Russell noted jetting black smoke. It came from the air vents with such force that it looked like the exhaust from a revving engine.

Russell blipped the pre-recorded 'Mission Accomplished' message with the press of a button. He then settled peacefully onto the course that led back to the sea. There were more guns firing now than before. But his windshield was dark and clear. He settled into his chair. He craned his neck every so often to watch the flames.

AMUR RIVER, SIBERIA
March 10, 1600 GMT (0200 Local)

The moon was full. The cloudless night was brutally cold. They had lain still and quiet for three hours – buried in thick banks of snow at the river's edge. There had been no sound, no movement, no sign of the Chinese.

Captain John Hadley rose first. One after the other his 'A' detachment of eleven U.S. Army special forces crawled from the snow in rapid succession. The nine NCOs and two officers didn't need to be told what to do. They deployed in a semicircle to give as much defense in depth as a twelve-man unit could. His two lieutenants approached Hadley in the darkness. The only sounds were the squeaking snow.

Hadley and his two officers knelt. 'I want this over with fast,' Hadley said. He spoke in just over a whisper. 'The clock starts when the first man's on the ice. Got that?'

There were two quiet 'Sirs.' Army shorthand omitted the implicit 'Yes.' They were off. The snow was so dry that it reminded Hadley of the beach near his home town in Florida. The saccharine sand there squeaked loudly as you trudged across it.

There was some time spent assembling the equipment. But it was all done under the cloak of strict noise-and-light discipline. Hadley searched the bends of the river in both directions. They had seen nothing of the armored cars that patrolled the flat ice pack. His two Dragon teams would have little trouble knocking them out. But one word by the vehicle's crew over the radio and he and his men were as

385

good as dead. To get in, spend a day and night deep behind enemy lines, and get out depended not on his 'A' team's ample firepower. Their survival relied one hundred percent on stealth.

Four men rose and headed onto the ice. One measured distance by rolling a large wheel at the end of a pole. The two behind him lugged the heavy drill between them. The fourth – a lieutenant – rode shotgun. His M-16 was raised high and at the ready. They all wore night-vision goggles, but Hadley chose not to don his. There was no need. The four figures threw shadows onto the ice from the bright moonlight.

Hadley took another nervous check in both directions. A single man sat hunched over earphones. He'd cleared snow from a patch of ice. He listened to the ice through a flat microphone for the sound of an approaching vehicle.

The man measuring the distance stopped. The distinct whine of an electric motor easily carried the distance. The tone sank nearly instantly as the bit hit ice. The operator kept its motor humming. He was wasting no time standing exposed in the center of the river.

It seemed to take forever.

The whine finally fell silent. The two men extracted the bit and took off running. Their bulky gear and heavy load slowed the men to a lumbering pace.

They were breathing hard when they reached the bank.

'Lemme see it,' Hadley said. Two men hoisted the drill into the air. The stainless steel teeth were covered in white shavings. Hadley brushed the slush clear and saw the four-inch-thick tube of solid ice. That core sample was the sole purpose of their mission.

'All right,' Hadley announced, 'let's get the hell outta Dodge.'

Hadley felt relief at leaving the river behind. But egress was the most dangerous phase of all. They followed their tracks back toward the landing zone. A scar across the virgin snow. If it was snowing hard or blowing briskly, the tracks could be covered in a matter of minutes. But on relatively still nights – like that night – the deep indentations were a dead giveaway. For the only two-legged creatures in the woods were soldiers. If a Chinese patrol found the tracks, they'd either hunt them down or lie in ambush. The twelve-man A detachment was strung out in a line over a hundred meters long. They pulled 200-lb ahkio sleds filled with gear, weapons and ammo.

The soldier in front of Hadley raised his right hand and knelt.

Hadley and the men behind him did the same in rapid succession. Hadley turned to ensure that everyone was still and ready.

Ready for what? he wondered. It wasn't an ambush because they'd never see it coming. The woods would simply erupt in flame and screams of pain. A good number of his men would die in the first frenzied volleys. It would depend from there on reaction times, correct guesses and luck. At ten meters separation Hadley had no chance of issuing orders. It would be every man for himself. Relying on training and instinct.

The man in front of Hadley rose and shoved the heel of his hand toward the sky. Everyone rose, made the same hand signal and moved on. *He must've seen shadows,* Hadley thought. *Or mounds in the snow. Fallen trees. A ghost in his peripheral vision.* Walking point did a number on your head.

BUREYA MOUNTAINS, SIBERIA
March 12, 0000 GMT (1000 Local)

Lieutenant Chin led his eighteen remaining men down a winding path. Snow drifted to the earth amid tall hills. Were it not for the tire ruts, the road would have been indistinguishable from the surrounding landscape. It was a flat gouge out of the flanks of the undulating earth.

At least the wind is down, Chin thought as he pressed his aching legs on. All morning they had lurched forward under heavy direct fire. A hundred meters forward, and three men dead. They lay low for thirty minutes under whizzing machine-gun bullets. One wounded and left for dead as a result. Then another rush toward the shelter of a ledge. It turned out to be no shelter at all as the enemy opened up from a previously silent position. Two dead. The enemy were like ghosts. They fired their weapons from such long range that Chin never even learned who he was fighting, much less brought his platoon's small arms to bear. Rumor was that they were Germans, but they might have been British or French.

The entire time they were under fire, the wind had whistled past Chin's covered face. It had whipped snow and ice off the tops of drifts that stung his eyes and exposed skin. After a while, the blasts of cold had seemed every bit as much a threat as the enemy's bullets . . . until, that is, the airstrike. Then everything had simply come apart. Chin could no longer hear the whistles from over the hill that were his only contact with company headquarters. His men began to rise and flee in bursts of panic timed between dives from enemy bombers. When Chin had risen to chase them – firing into the air over their heads – he was quickly overtaken by the rest of his platoon. Everyone took the opportunity to save their lives . . . Chin included.

And it did save their lives, he had to admit. Most of them, anyway. He had started the day with thirty-one men. Thirteen lay somewhere behind them, either dead or soon to be dead. The enemy never bothered collecting Chinese wounded. They fired from armored vehicles far away, pulled back under covering airstrikes, and set up again a few kilometers to the north.

'Did you see that guy in the tree?' one of his men asked from behind.

Chin didn't turn, but he kept his ears peeled. The unpleasantness of having to fire over his fleeing men's heads hadn't cleared the air between them completely.

'He must've been a sniper,' another soldier ventured. 'Got killed, but his gear kept him from falling.'

'*No*. He wasn't strapped to the *tree*. He was hanging *over* the limb. He got *blown* up there! Did you *see* him? It blew his skin right off his *bones!*'

'Maybe he wasn't even Chinese,' a third guy joined in. 'Maybe he was American.'

Everyone laughed. '*Yeah*, you dumb shit! How many dead Americans have you seen? One? Three? And how many dead Chinese?'

'A thousand,' someone guessed.

'Oh, more than *that*. What about that grave?' Chin remembered the long cut in the earth. Men with white cotton masks had been pouring white powder over mounds of bodies. An army of men with shovels waited by the side of the hole.

'The Americans do it right,' came from one of the men who'd spoken before. 'They don't just piss their men away like last night's beer.'

'Enough!' Chin finally shouted. He wheeled on the loose gaggle of men. They stopped in their tracks and eyed their platoon leader. Chin stood facing eighteen armed and brooding men. Men he'd fired shots toward not three hours earlier. He swallowed the lump of fear before continuing. 'Keep quiet!' he shouted. He then tried to think up some reason they should follow his order. 'The Foreign Enemies might have microphones planted in the woods!'

There was a smattering of chuckles that almost brought the muzzle of Chin's Type 68 assault rifle around. 'Keep quiet!' he shouted. He turned and proceeded down the path.

They walked for almost an hour before they saw another soul. Chin was looking for an alternate route – having decided the road led too far to the east – when shouts rang out from the hill to their right.

'Drop your weapons!' a man ordered. Chin and his men all turned to see an officer waving a pistol from which hung a lanyard. 'Drop them or we'll fire!' he yelled. Chin saw the other guns in the rocks pointed at the trail.

'We're Chinese!' Chin replied.

'You're under arrest by order of the Supreme Commander of the People's Liberation Army!' the pistol-toting officer shouted officiously. 'Now drop your weapons or we'll open fire!'

'But why are we under *arrest?*' Chin challenged. He was suddenly outraged. 'What the hell did we *do?*'

The arresting officer – who looked to be around Chin's age of twenty – seemed hesitant. 'You . . . you are *deserters!* I have orders to arrest all deserters, and to shoot them on the spot if they resist!'

'We're not deserters!' one of Chin's men yelled. The officer turned his pistol and almost fired.

'Shut up!' Chin shouted at his men. Saving his life. Maybe all of their lives, judging from the number of weapons pointed their way. Chin saw too that his men's weapons were generally pointing toward the rocks. A single shot could be the spark that sent flames raging out of control. He turned back to the officer with the pistol. 'We're not deserters. We're loyal soldiers. These are my men. I am their platoon leader. How can you have deserters when I – as their commanding officer – led them down this trail?'

He felt rather than saw his men's heads turn. They were watching Chin now. He felt a sense of pride in that fact.

'The enemy is *that* way!' the officer shouted – pointing back up the path down which they'd come.

'We *know* that,' Chin replied. He was beginning to prevail, he felt, and he pressed home his advantage. 'We've been fighting for the last

three days straight. I lost thirteen of my men this morning.' He raised
his voice to address his real audience – the dozen or so men holding
rifles pointed their way. 'I lose thirteen men to the Americans,' he said
– choosing Americans to create the proper impression. 'And now I'm
going to lose *more* to my comrades in *arms?*'

No orders were issued, but the rifles in the rocks above pointed
away.

The little man with the pistol, however, wouldn't let the matter
drop. 'You are deserting your *unit!*' he screeched. 'The enemy is *that*
way!' he repeated. Again he pointed.

'But didn't you hear?' Chin asked. 'The Americans got around *behind*
us.' He looked down the trail in the direction they were headed. He
hoped that his irreverent men could keep from sniggering. 'They swung
around us and cut off the roads to our rear.' The heads of the men in
the rocks began to swivel. 'Don't you have a radio?' Chin asked. The
now sheepish officer replied that he did not. Chin knew then that he
had won.

'And they have microphones in the woods,' one of his men blurted
out. Chin cringed in anticipation of laughter. But none came.

The man with the pistol suddenly seemed to grow anxious. He no
longer was certain of his position. He looked around warily. And when
he spoke, he did so in lowered tones. 'How did they get behind us?'

Now, Chin thought, *for the capper.* 'Tanks,' he whispered – just
loudly enough for all to hear.

The talking was now among his would-be captor's men. 'Quiet!' the
lieutenant shouted. He quickly checked all around for the enemy.

'Can we go now?' Chin asked.

The distracted man peered in both directions down the road. He
craned his neck to look up the hill above his head. His stern warning to
Chin was whispered. 'Don't come back down this road again without
signed orders! Do you understand?'

There were chuckles from Chin's men. Chin himself had to smile.
He hadn't seen a written order since the war began.

They marched on. The talking and whispering resumed. When a
single shot rolled over the hills from the distance, the grumbling grew
more open. 'Fuck them,' someone said in a tone he obviously didn't
mind being overheard.

At first Chin was incensed. But he reconsidered when he realized
what it meant. They trusted him. They felt that he was one of them.

People didn't openly criticize the government unless they were certain about everyone within earshot. And they certainly didn't say 'Fuck them' about the army after hearing the execution of a deserter.

Chin stopped and turned to his men. They'd grown quiet after the comment. They all watched Chin intently and waited. 'Be careful,' he said in a reasonable tone. Chin turned to lead his platoon on. A grin lit his face that they couldn't see. For the first time, he walked with his back to his men without fear. Without that keen sense of alertness to the danger they posed.

THE BRONX, NEW YORK
March 14, 1400 GMT (0900 Local)

Andre straightened his tie before knocking. He could hear the girls' voices through the door. He could hardly keep the grin off his face. The dot of light through the peephole grew dark. There was a squeal and a metallic jangling of locks and chains. The door flew open.

'*Ba*-by!' Evelyn shouted. She leapt on Andre. Threw her arms around his neck. Her joy was so unrestrained that Andre started to cry even as he laughed. 'My *baby*! My baby! My baby!' She twisted his neck and shook him from side to side.

Andre's sisters came running. They all screamed and screeched and threw their arms around Andre. The family hug was all noise and celebration. When his mom pulled back, her face was soaked. But her smiling eyes shone through the tears. 'Look at you! All dressed up in that *uniform!*' After restraining herself as long as she could, she grabbed and hugged his neck so hard it knocked his hat off his head. She pulled Andre into the apartment. 'Why didn't you *call*? What are you doin' *home*? I thought you were in Ko-rea.'

'I was. I came home for some more trainin'.'

'In New York?'

'Na-a-aw!' Andre said. He put his hat on his sister's head. It covered her face all the way to her eyes. 'In Kentucky. I had a two-day leave after I was done so I caught a flight home to surprise you.'

'Listen to *you!* "Caught a flight!" Aren't you a *world* traveler! My little boy.' She pinched Andre's cheek. He pulled free. 'But you said only two days? That's all you got?'

'Yep.'

'Where you gotta be in two days?'

Andre hesitated. He turned away. 'I gotta go back.'

Andre could tell that his mother was on guard. 'Go back where?'

'To join up with my new unit.' He glanced up at her. She was squinting.

'What kinda trainin' you been up to in Kentucky?'

Andre shrugged. 'It's Army stuff, momma,' he mumbled.

She grabbed his chin and forced his face up. 'What kind of "Army stuff", Andre? You answer me.'

He pulled his chin free. His sisters were silent, listening. 'Air Assault School.'

She didn't shout, as he had expected. She didn't ask him for more details or where he was headed or what his unit was. She pushed through the girls, headed into the kitchen and started cooking.

Andre followed. 'Momma.' She wouldn't turn around. 'I got into the 101st. That's the division.' His sisters trailed behind. 'I wasn't in a good spot before. For me. I mean, I was deliverin' the *mail*, momma!'

'Ain't *nothin'* wrong with deliverin' the mail!' she said. She turned to him in anger. 'Mr High and Mighty! Who are you that deliverin' the mail ain't good enough for you?'

Andre shrugged. 'I'm a *soldier*, momma.'

Her hands went to her hips. 'A *soldier*? A *soldier*? You're *eighteen* years *old!* You ain't a *soldier!* You're a little *boy!* You're playin' Army,' she threw her dishrag onto the counter. It slid all the way to the corner.

'But I'm good at it, momma.'

'At what?'

'At bein' a soldier.'

She was nodding. Her mouth hung open. 'You kilt somebody yet?' Andre shrugged. 'You been shot at?' Andre rolled his eyes. 'Answer me, boy! Have you shot your gun at another human bein' even once? Answer me!'

'No.'

'So what makes you think you're a soldier?'

Her last words hurt Andre more than anything she'd ever said. Her face softened. Her hand rose to his cheek. Her head tilted. Her eyes remained fixed on his. 'It's the only thing I ever been, momma.' She froze. Andre felt the tears welling up. He grabbed his hat and headed for the door. She grabbed his arm and pulled him back. The family hugged again . . . but not in celebration.

NEAR ALDAN, SIBERIA
March 17, 2000 GMT (0600 Local)

'We've gotta drop off this load, Miss Dunn,' the driver said. He turned the wheel of the large truck and pulled to a stop. 'We'll meet you back here in one hour.'

Kate and Woody climbed down to the deserted street of the ramshackle village. The U.S. Army truck rumbled off. When it was gone, all was quiet. There was no sign of life anywhere. The entire town appeared to have been abandoned.

'Well,' Kate said. She raised her arms and slapped them down against her thighs. '*This* is exciting.'

'Hey, you wanted to go somewhere off the beaten path. It doesn't get much farther off than this.'

'Yeah, but . . . The point was to dig up a *story*.' She looked up and down the empty road. Nothing moved, not even a stray dog.

'So let's go *dig*,' Woody said. He took off past buildings whose windows were blackened. By the time Kate caught up with him, he was lighting a joint.

'Wo-o-ody,' she chastised.

'*What?*' he snapped. Kate frowned as he pointedly took a long toke – his cheeks sucked into his face. 'What are you?' he managed to say without leaking too much of his precious smoke. 'My mother?'

'I just don't like being the designated driver in the middle of a Goddamn *war*.'

'Here, then,' Woody said – holding the joint out to Kate.

She sighed and rolled her eyes. She walked up to the small garden in front of a house that was deeply pitted and burned. 'Where are we going?' she asked.

'*I* dunno,' Woody replied. He took a deep breath of the frigid morning air. He wore a large grin on his face.

'There's no story here,' she said, looking all around.

'*Sure* there is, Kate. There's a story *every*where.' He stepped up on

393

a low stone wall – balancing himself with his hands out to the side. The joint was pinched between his gloved thumb and index finger. 'The White Army troops came into town with their guns blazing.' He held his imaginary machine-gun up and trilled out a few rounds with his tongue. 'A-a-ah!' he screeched in mock agony. 'Lots of people died. There was blood everywhere. Two minutes of prime time – guaranteed! But with their black flags flying, the Anarchists beat the White Army back, slaughtering them by the *thousands*.' Again he acted out the massacre. 'Both sides were exhausted, and both tried to surrender to the other. In the end, they decided to simply lay down their arms and go home. Right here, Kate, in this little village. Right here is where the collapse of Russia occurred.'

Kate looked at Woody, then at the meager collection of shacks along the side of the road. They were all burned and shelled out. 'How do you know all that happened here?' she asked.

Woody shrugged and stepped down off the wall. 'How do you know it *didn't*?' He relit the joint.

'*Jesus*, Woody!' She huffed, expelling her breath in a puff of white fog. 'What do you propose we do? Give me the camera while you do a one-man dramatization of the Russian Civil War?'

Just then, they heard the heavy rumbling of a train. They both stared in the direction from which it emanated. Kate wandered through the yard of the abandoned house and to the edge of the snowy woods behind it. Woody followed. The supply truck with which they'd hitched a ride generally followed the rail line to the west from the port of Vanin. They'd seen several long trains hurtle past them on the five-hour ride. But the sounds to which they now listened were different. This train was stopping.

'Come on,' Kate said. She trudged out into the deep snow of the woods.

'Hey, Kate,' Woody called out from behind. She turned. 'I'm not so sure this is a good idea.'

'What? I just wanta go see why that train stopped.'

'Yeah, but . . .' He faltered.

'But what?'

'What if they don't want us to see? I mean, UNRUSFOR put this whole area off limits.'

'So? You mean to tell me you're perfectly happy smoking *pot*,' she said sarcastically, 'but *tre-espassing! Well . . .!*'

'I'm not worried about getting busted, Kate. I'm worried about getting shot.'

She laughed dismissively and turned. 'We'll just be quiet and take a look over this hill.' She labored through the snow with loud squeaks from her boots. Woody followed. She heard the flicking of his lighter and his renewed sucking on the ever-shortening joint.

It was slower going than she'd expected, especially during their ascent of the hill. The snow was up to her knees. Woody had to help her in some spots where she sank particularly deep. Finally, they reached the crest of the hill.

The rail line ran to the east and west for as far as she could see. About a quarter of a mile away, the train they'd heard sat parked in the middle of nowhere. At least seventy cars long, the train was brimming with military vehicles of every size and description. The only uniformity to its cargo appeared to be the two dozen flatbed cars in a row. They each had the same vehicle on top. M-1 main battle tanks – painted white. Car after car was loaded with the monsters. Their thick barrels were all pointed toward the rear.

Several people walked along the train's length. At first Kate surmised that it had broken down. It was the middle of nowhere. The snow was particularly deep on the open fields to the sides of the tracks.

All of a sudden, the snowy ground opened up. Two men peeled back white fabric to reveal the artificial light inside.

'Holy *shit!*' Woody whispered. He raised the minicam to his shoulder on reflex. It began to whir quietly. A large truck emerged from the opening towing a wedge-shaped green ramp. The men and vehicle gave everything a scale. The snowy field was in fact the polyurethane roof to a massive depot of some sort. The thick metal braces that held the fabric aloft attested to the enormity of the subterranean labyrinth.

Soldiers crawled over the tanks. One fired up an engine with a puff of smoke. The engine's growl was audible despite the distance. Still more smoke belched from its tailpipes as the tank pivoted toward the ramp. The driver nudged the tank forward. Its nose dipped and it descended to the ground.

The tank disappeared inside the white cavern. Behind it came other tanks.

The camera fell silent. Woody lowered it from his shoulder.

'Wait,' Kate said – transfixed by the sight of the earth consuming the massive stores of equipment. 'I wanta do a stand-up.'

'Kate . . .' Woody began woodenly.

'I know, I know!' she interrupted. 'But if I look like a camera hog we'll edit it out. I just don't want the network taking the raw footage and doing their own . . .'

'Kate,' Woody said – whispering.

She turned. A team of men moved silently through the trees toward where they stood. Their weapons were raised.

Chapter Eighteen

BIROBIDZHAN FIREBASE, SIBERIA
March 17, 2000 GMT (0600 Local)

'Everybody *up!*' the platoon sergeant barked.

For a moment Stempel thought he couldn't possibly move. He was at the bottom of a deep well of sleep. A ton of fatigue pressed him down. Kept him wrapped inside the womb of his sleeping bag.

He coughed. Pain shot through his head. His sinuses were dry from the frigid air. His throat was raw. His nose bled nearly constantly. Even his eyes were sore from the dryness. Some of the guys slept with towels or mufflers over their faces. But Stempel felt suffocated and left his face uncovered.

The 'Army cough' was epidemic in the sleeping bunker. The men on either side of Stempel's spot on the icy floor bumped and jostled him as they rose. Stempel reached up to grab the bag's zipper before the sergeant landed a boot on his butt, but he couldn't will himself to pull it down. The bladders of the thin air mattress – when warmed by his body heat – softened and provided just enough cushion to be called luxury.

Half the men were kept at their fighting posts every night with weapons in hand. The other half were roused when an attack was under way. That night, Stempel's squad was in the latter group and there had been only one almost perfunctory Chinese assault. Tonight, it would be them on the walls – all night long.

The nights on trench duty were the worst. Bundled up in an extra layer of clothing – with his head and ears covered with a knit liner, helmet, and hood – he felt like he was in a cocoon. He withdrew into his own little world. His mind became sluggish. Three nights earlier, Stempel had been slouched in the fighting post cut out of a wall – his rifle laid on the sandbags – peering out into the open killing ground ahead. He thought nothing. He saw nothing although he was wide awake and his eyes were open. When the flares went up they illuminated a field full of Chinese infantry. Stempel realized that in the back of his mind he'd seen the men advancing. He just hadn't realized what the shadowy figures were. Like the machinery they'd brought with them to Siberia, his mind slowed in the cold.

Stempel steeled himself for his exit into the open. He and the others slept in two layers: briefs and T-shirt underneath, thermal underwear on top. They also wore sock liners, socks and boots, plus glove liners and a knit cap. The only time Stempel took off his boots was to wash his white and wrinkled feet. Twice a week, like clockwork. He unzipped the bag. A freezing gush of cold air followed. Stempel rushed to climb out of the bag. He worked quickly to don his cold-weather gear. He quickly lost the accumulated body heat from four precious hours of sleep.

At the door men lined up with their injuries. Each requested excused duty from the sergeant. First in line was a man showing off his hand. Stempel remembered him from the night before. He'd suffered a terrible 'cold burn' when he'd touched the barrel of a rifle with bare hands. He'd mistakenly thought it was his. But the cold-soaked weapon had just been brought inside after a night in the open trenches. He'd screamed. The burn looked just like the burn from a stove.

When you worked on cold metal, you bummed cotton 'anti-contact' gloves from artillerymen. You *never* touched metal that had been outside in the elements. The sergeant excused the soldier from duty.

Stempel hefted his M-16 and joined the line at the bunker's exit. The opening was covered only by two layers of tarpaulin. It blocked the wind from outside and masked the dim light from within. The tarps did not, however, hold in the paltry heat from the chemical burners. They couldn't seal the bunker off. Eight guys in a maintenance platoon had been found dead the week before. They'd closed off their bunker during a blizzard. The fumes had killed them in their sleep.

'Whatta ya say, sergeant?' someone up ahead asked plaintively.

'I'd say I've cut myself shavin' worse,' he replied.

'It's *shrapnel!*' exploded the outraged soldier. 'I should get a Goddamn Purple Heart and a trip home! All I'm askin' is light duty for a week or so.' The platoon sergeant laughed. The man was ushered out. Stempel stepped up to the platoon sergeant when it was his turn. The NCO tugged roughly at Stempel's parka. 'Feel loose in the armpits?' he asked.

'Yes, sergeant,' Stempel replied.

The platoon sergeant knelt. 'Loosen these Goddamn drawstrings, son!' He jerked at the cord around Stempel's thighs. 'You wanta end up rattlin' a cup on a streetcorner? Gotta keep yer blood flowin'. Blood is warmth, understand?' He handed Stempel a Snickers bar and turned to the next man in line.

Stempel took the candy bar through the two tarps at the entrance. Both sheets were frozen as solid as plywood. It actually felt good to be outside. The heavy gear had grown too warm inside the sleeping bunker. Plus the air outside was always fresher. Pausing in the slit trench, Stempel pulled down his face mask and tore the end of the Snickers' wrapper with his teeth. *High-energy food for cold weather*, Stempel thought as he devoured the candy before it froze. *Snickers for breakfast. Mom would be appalled.*

With the last chewy bites still in his mouth, Stempel reached the main trench line. His squad was loosening the slings on their rifles and hanging the weapons over their shoulders and heads. Without asking, Stempel did the same. They were going out – probably to raise the wire above the latest depths of snowfall.

When he saw the trash bags, Stempel froze stock still. Every third man got one. Trash bags!

Stempel counted as the squad leader neared. A bag was handed to a man just down the wall. Then one, two . . . *Shit!* The sergeant handed Stempel a trash bag. *Shit!*

Stempel climbed over the front lip of the trench wall. The new sun cast an anemic, flat light. Thick mists limited visibility. The first men from the neighboring platoon were returning in pairs – the man in front carrying the head and shoulders, the man in back the feet. Stretched out in between and hard as a board was a dead Chinese soldier.

'We oughta burn the bastards for firewood,' the tall Arkansan next to Stempel said.

'Smell too bad,' a wiry kid from Detroit replied. Both men – one white, one black – looked like twins inside their mound of thick clothing.

'Why don't we just leave 'em out there, for Christ's sake?' asked the boy they called Jumpy. Stempel had never in his life seen anyone so nervous. The mere presence of the kid had a calming effect on Stempel. Jumpy proved to him again and again there was at least someone more scared than he was.

'When the thaw came, they'd rot,' someone suggested.

'Naw, it's on account of wolves,' came another view. 'They'd come lookin' for food.' He loosed a laugh. 'That's just what we need on trench duty. To have to fight fuckin' wolves every fuckin' night!'

'Snow drifts!' they all heard from behind. They slowed up to admit their squad leader – a sergeant at age twenty-one. 'All them bodies out there would gather snow. The drifts would fuck up our firing lanes and give the Chinks cover.'

They passed men probing with long poles. They searched for Chinese snow tunnels. Harold's squad found the first bodies lying in ranks. They'd been mowed down in rows when machine-guns opened up. Ribbons of grayish bowels were strung out for yards. Contorted bodies lay in pools of crimson ice. Other blood still steamed. It had come from men who'd died more recently. They never found anyone alive. The worst were the men who'd been missed for days. They swelled up from decomposition. If you stepped on them, they'd let loose a shout as gases rushed passed their vocal cords.

The dead were frozen forever in the most grotesque and ridiculous of poses. It reminded Stempel of an exhibit on Pompeii to which his parents had taken him as a child. He imagined them being buried in the permafrost and unearthed thousands of years later. Scientists would study their remains and figure out how they had lived and how they had died.

'This one got hit so hard both *eyeballs* popped out,' a squadmate commented. He had a dozen automatic rifles slung over his shoulder. Some were American M-16s. Some were from Stempel's Lost Battalion, he felt sure. 'He's all yours, Stemp,' he said with a laugh. All he had to police up were weapons.

Stempel began to search for his bounty. Men grunted under the strain of their frozen loads. 'Here ya go, Stemp!' another of his squadmates shouted. He pointed at a brown crater before picking up a severed torso. He hauled the light cargo off unaided. Stempel went to the edge of the hole which was rapidly filling with fluffy snow. Blood and viscera were splattered everywhere. Bits and pieces of humans. A frozen hand – its index finger wrapped around an imaginary trigger. He tossed it into the trash bag.

In his mind, he was a scientist – an archeologist – a long, long time in the future.

BETHESDA NAVAL HOSPITAL, MARYLAND
March 17, 2200 GMT (1700 Local)

'Thank you, Mr President, for agreeing to meet with us,' the anchorman said.

CBS, ABC, NBC, CNN – the anchors were almost invisible in the glare of the television lights. A film of perspiration had formed on Gordon's forehead and neck. He didn't want to mop his brow. The dreadful image of a wounded and weak chief executive would be beamed into every set.

Gordon lay in bed wearing a royal blue robe. A gold Presidential seal adorned his left breast pocket. The tubes, wires and other medical paraphernalia had been moved away from the cameras' cruel, unblinking stare. All of the details of the interview had been thoroughly negotiated. The number of cameras. Their positioning. Which could zoom in for close-ups. The format of the questioning. They had even obtained the networks' agreement not to edit the interview or to lead into it with any editorialization about the war.

In fact, the restrictions imposed by the White House had themselves become a story. They had led to yet another onslaught of negative press.

The CBS moderator began. 'By prior agreement, the first question will be from ABC.' He turned to his counterpart from the rival network.

'Mr President, the casualty figures from the war with China just announced by the Department of Defense are horrible. Three thousand, two hundred and twelve U.S. servicemen dead, another seven thousand wounded or missing. The latest CNN/*Wall Street Journal* poll from *before* that announcement revealed that a striking seventy-two percent of Americans polled oppose the war. And reports out of our allies' capitals indicate that the governments there are making contingency plans for a hasty withdrawal from Siberia should the war take a turn for the worse.'

'Is there a question in there somewhere?' Gordon interrupted as Fein had coached when the question turned into a speech.

'Is it your intention to announce the complete and total withdrawal of American forces from Siberia as has been rumored in Washington for days?'

'No,' Gordon replied.

'Then you intend to continue the fighting?'

'That is my intention, yes.'

'To what end?' the ABC anchorman asked.

'To win the war.'

The man shifted in his seat then leaned forward. 'But . . . why? What is the purpose of the war?'

'The Communist Chinese invaded Siberia, leaving us with two options: flee in the face of aggression and cede to China control over whatever territory it can grab by force, or not. It was not a war of our choosing, but once the die was cast those were our options. We chose the latter. We chose not to flee.'

'You say "we," Mr President,' the NBC News anchor joined in, 'but it was really "you." Word out of your Administration is that – almost to a man – no one outside your inner circle agrees with this war. To put it bluntly, sir, your people have been running for the hills. Putting as much distance between themselves and perhaps the most unpopular war in this country's history as they can. Given that, why are you, sir – Gordon Davis – so personally committed to a war that you could very easily have passed off as your predecessor's doing? You were, after all, a vocal opponent of President Marshall's deployment to Siberia in the first place.'

'We're fighting not because we want to, but because we *have* to. We're fighting because we cannot allow rogue nations to gain from aggression. We are the most powerful nation this earth has ever known. Our system of government is the wonder of the world. We do *not* shrink from punishing injustice. We will *not* back down from our duties as world leader. And first and foremost among those duties is to protect the weak from the strong. To punish aggressors who – despite all the lessons of history – still choose the path of blood, and death, and destruction to further their goals of domination over their fellow man.'

For a moment, the four journalists were quiet. It was enough to prove to Gordon that he was right.

Even as the questioning continued, Gordon's optimism rose. The men before him were undeterred. They jabbed over and over – emboldened by the polls. But Gordon rested secure that a principle had been proven to his satisfaction. If you speak the truth boldly, people will listen. They will be forced to think, however briefly, about what it was you said.

UNRUSFOR HEADQUARTERS, KHABAROVSK
March 18, 0100 GMT (1500 Local)

Major Reed handed Clark the large-format videocassette. It was high-quality three-quarter-inch tape.

'They're in there, sir,' Reed said. He opened the door and stood back. Clark entered.

There was a woman at a table complaining nonstop.

'You should put *signs* up or something,' she said to a military policeman. The ponytailed cameraman kept his eyes fixed on Clark.

'Is this the only tape?' Clark asked the man, who nodded.

'You're General Clark, aren't you?' the woman said. She rose and extended her right hand. 'Katherine Dunn, NBC News.' She waited. He stared back at her. She lowered her hand.

'Let's get one thing straight,' Nate said. 'We're not dealing with some petty violation of military security ground rules, here. We're not talking about suspending your press credentials and expelling you from the combat zone. You're both under arrest, if you haven't noticed.'

The ponytailed man understood. But the female reporter challenged him. 'On what charges?'

'Suspicion of espionage.'

'*What?*' Kate exploded. 'We're *journalists*, for God's sake!'

'Kate,' Woody said, putting his hand on her shoulder.

'What?' she snapped at him, then twisted free of his grip.

Woody spoke in a calm voice. 'Just listen to the man, okay?'

In the center of the table was their gear. In one of the pockets, Clark knew, the MPs had found marijuana. He looked first at the cameraman. 'We have a problem, don't we?' Clark asked. He turned to Kate. 'You two now know something. And, as journalists, to conceal is contrary to your every instinct. But to me, to conceal is to gain advantage. To deceive is an art.' He stared straight at Kate now. 'What you know could, if revealed, cost the lives of thousands of my men. I would do anything within my power to save their lives.'

Kate felt Woody looking her way. She returned his look with a shrug. 'Just what is it we know that's so important? That you've got a secret base out in the middle of nowhere?' She shook her head – at a loss. Woody cleared his throat, which annoyed Kate. He was being overly defensive. 'Just what do you want, General Clark?'

The man looked tired. He had a large frame, but it was slouched in the chair opposite her. There were lines in his face around bloodshot eyes.

'I want this tape, first of all,' he said. He handed it to the officer standing next to him. 'Secondly, I want your cooperation. I want your silence.'

Kate listened until it was clear he had nothing more to say. 'So . . . what? Do you mean, like, our *total* silence?' He nodded, and she chuckled. 'Listen, General Clark, I *understand* the need for discretion. And I'd even understand if you just told us flat out what needed to be edited out of our report. But to just tell us to not *do* a report . . .' Kate felt she wouldn't need to complete the thought. But looking at the expression on Clark's face she realized she would. 'General Clark! I have no intention of jeopardizing the lives of your troops. But First Amendment rights still apply even during time of war. You can't just throw us into the *stockade* because we were going to air something you didn't want aired.'

He stared back for a few moments in silence. 'Are you telling me that imprisonment is the only way I can keep you from broadcasting a report on what you saw today?' he asked . . . carefully.

'*Kate,*' Woody whined in a whisper.

'No, General Clark, it is not,' she said – ignoring Woody. 'There's another way.' Both Clark and Woody waited. From their body language, it was clear that Woody waited with the greater interest. 'I'd be *perfectly* willing,' she continued pleasantly, 'to work *with* you and your staff on this story.'

Nate heard the words. But he wasn't sure he had a clue what she was suggesting. 'What "*story*"?' he asked.

She shrugged. 'Whatever it is that's such a big *secret*,' she replied nonchalantly. 'I presume there's a day coming when it'll all become *totally* public. I'll agree that I won't air a word about any of this until that day comes. You can have guys with guns follow me everywhere. In *return*, you give me the *whole* story. Background, interviews, the opportunity to record everything – like your Army *historians* do – so I can do a truly *insightful* piece . . . when the time comes.'

Clark sat there – unblinking – for a moment. 'All right,' he replied quietly.

Woody let loose a loud sigh of relief and relaxed.

'All right . . . what?' Kate asked warily.

'All right, you can do that story. I'll give you the access you need to do it right. And you'll not breathe a word of anything till I give the go-ahead.'

Judging from Woody's obvious relief he was taking the offer at face value. But Kate was determined not to compromise her journalistic integrity. 'I won't do a whitewash,' she said firmly. 'I won't propagandize or sugarcoat.' Clark nodded, but she continued. 'When I make a legitimate request for access, or ask a question to which you or anyone else knows the answer . . .'

'. . . *about*,' Clark interrupted, '*this* operation – no others.'

Kate considered the modification, then replied simply, 'I want my questions answered.'

Clark nodded again.

Kate sat up straight and shrugged. 'Okay, then. Can we have our equipment and tape back now?'

Clark nodded at Major Reed. Their camera and cassette were returned. The cameraman at first protested when the reporter had him hoist the camera to his shoulder. The ponytailed man maneuvered around the table for a shot. 'Go,' he said finally.

'We're here in UNRUSFOR Headquarters with Nate Clark, commanding general of UN troops. General Clark, what was it we saw under that camouflage covering today along the rail siding?'

She stuck the mike in Nate's face. 'Equipment, ammunition, fuel,' he answered.

'So . . . you're saying that those are ordinary supplies?' She felt the first twinge of disappointment at the deal she'd struck.

'Yes.'

'Why, then, the extraordinary security precautions that you've taken around such an ordinary supply depot?'

Again the mike was dipped to Clark's chin. 'Because of where those supplies are. They're much farther to the west than the Chinese expect them to be. And there are much larger stores building there than the Chinese believe there to be.'

Kate didn't even know how to proceed. She considered briefly even abandoning that line of inquiry and just blurting out an unrelated question. But she tried once again. 'Can you explain, General Clark, what those facts would tell a Chinese general that makes them so vitally secret.'

'It would suggest that UNRUSFOR is planning a massive counter-attack. It could be evidence that we are marshaling our supplies far to the west for a major offensive that would threaten to encircle the entire Chinese expeditionary force. It might cause the Chinese to moderate their advance and assume a more defensive posture instead of pressing on into what might be a trap.'

'Are you . . . are you saying that UNRUSFOR is planning a major counteroffensive against the Chinese?' Kate asked, feeling a stir of excitement at the prospect. The stick mike hovered just in front of Clark's face.

'No,' Clark replied. 'I'm simply saying that intelligence would *suggest* those things to the Chinese.'

'But . . . is it true? *Are* you planning a major counteroffensive?'

'Yes.'

Kate regripped the mike, and then regripped it again. 'Cut!' she finally snapped. She looked at Woody. He leaned out around the eyepiece. 'General Clark?' she said, 'are you sure you want to *say* that?'

He shrugged. 'You said you wanted the whole story.'

'Yeah, but . . . All right.' She nodded at Woody and raised the mike. 'What is your plan?'

'To push south from our supply nodes along the Trans-Siberian Railway, outrace the retreating Chinese, and cross the Amur River in force before the ice breaks. We will then use the ten days

406

during which the ice flows and the river is unbridgeable to win the war.'

Kate's mind reeled with questions, but one was first and foremost. 'Do you intend to enter the People's Republic of China?' she asked.

'No,' Clark lied.

'Cut,' Kate said, lowering the microphone. The faint whir of the camera fell silent. 'Jesus,' she murmured.

'Now you know,' Nate said. He turned to Major Reed. 'No calls, no contact with anyone outside our people, nothing. They can film anything they'd like, talk to anyone they'd like, but I want them sealed off tight. Twenty-four-hour armed escorts everywhere they go.' He turned back to Kate and Woody. 'If they attempt to make any unauthorized contacts, the MPs' orders are to stop them. They have my authority to use deadly force.'

Kate looked back at him without flinching – not intimidated by his little show. 'Anything else?' she asked.

'No pot.'

'What?' Kate asked – laughing.

'Nobody smokes pot in my headquarters,' Clark said.

'You think this place is bugged?' Kate asked as she walked through their underground quarters.

Woody was working intently on the camera. 'No-o-o,' he said – disparaging the notion. 'These're military types, not spooks. They'll just shoot us if they don't like what we're doing.'

Kate laughed at Woody's naivete. 'You don't *really* think they'd *shoot* us!'

'The *hell* they wouldn't!' he said, tightening some loose screw with a tiny tool. 'That's what they're in the *business* of doing. It's bugging *rooms* that's not their thing.'

Clark had been generous in every way. They'd been given free run of the former Russian military base. Their 'quarters' consisted of a large conference room off which their choice of four small bedrooms opened. On entering the underground room, Woody had locked the only door into and out of the room and tested the security of the bolts until satisfied. He'd then opened the door briefly and waved at their escorts just outside. They made no move to intrude upon their privacy even after Woody noisily relocked the door.

'We've been had, Woody. Clark suckered us in and then sprung the

407

trap. Now, this is basically over for us. Everything we learn from here on out is classified.'

'Uh-huh.' Woody squinted and tilted his head this way and that – scrutinizing the inner workings of the minicam.

'What are you *doing?*' she asked as he pried open a circuit board with his screw driver. His mouth remained open as he concentrated – his tongue sticking out between parted teeth.

'Got it!' he said finally, removing a small baggy.

'Got what?' Kate headed for the table but ended up following Woody toward the bathroom. 'What *is* that?' Inside the small room, Woody motioned for her to close the door. She finally saw what he was unwrapping. 'Woody!' she shouted.

'Sh-h-h!' he hissed back.

'But that's *pot!*' He opened the plastic to reveal a round bundle of joints held tightly together by a rubber band.

'Like I said, they're soldiers. They're not spies, and they're *sure* not cops!' He was grinning ear-to-ear over his little coup.

'Clark said no getting high!' Kate reminded him.

Woody sat on the commode and flicked his lighter.

'*Wo-o-ody-y!*' Kate whispered through teeth clenched in anger. The tip of the joint glowed. 'You could get us in *real* trouble, *Woody!* This is, like, the most totally *stupid* thing you could ever do!'

'Don't worry,' he said with a grimace – smoke barely drifting from his pinched lips. He stood up on top of the toilet seat and exhaled slowly into a large vent. 'These are air filters,' he said. 'This is a bomb shelter. They'll never smell a thing.'

'Is this really worth it to you?' Kate asked in a plaintive tone. 'Is getting high so Goddamned important?'

'Well . . . *yeah!* Why do you think I go to so much trouble?' Standing there, he flicked the lighter again and drew a deep toke from the joint.

'Why?' Kate asked.

But Woody turned to her with a serious look on his face. He took his time again to exhale – eking out the maximum buzz for his buck despite having what appeared to be ample supplies.

''Cause,' he answered at long last, 'I got a bad feeling.'

'What could you possibly complain about *now?*' she asked. 'We're at UNRUSFOR Headquarters. Sleeping in a bomb shelter. How much safer does covering a war get?'

'And you think you'll stay here?' he asked, suddenly animated. 'For the duration of the war? You'll agree to . . . to sit back and let the *biggest* military operation since I-don't-*know*-when go off while you twiddle your thumbs in this bunker?'

Kate shrugged. They'd only just gotten there. It was hard to say. 'Clark didn't agree to us covering the actual offensive itself,' she said. But already her mind was filling with the arguments she could make to him. She'd have an unprecedented understanding of the operation once it rolled around. She'd know exactly when and where the true drama of the story would play out. If she did a straight-up job on her reporting – maybe documentary-style – she might just earn Clark's trust. *A documentary*, she thought. The goosebumps rippled up her arms. *The* definitive *documentary on the Chinese War!*

What she lost was the immediacy of a scoop. A fleeting few seconds of nightly air time. What she gained, however, was possibly a special. An hour – maybe even *two* – of exclusive, behind-the-scenes coverage of the biggest operation since whenever! It was perfect. Win or lose the battle, there was no need to manufacture the drama.

And the topper, she now realized, would have to be action footage. Not just any fighting, but the most crucial battle of the whole war. The most desperate, the most evenly matched, the most important. She'd remain on the lookout for that battle. Even though she knew nothing about military science, she was confident that one battle would stand out from all the others. She would talk her way into covering it. She just *had* to!

The flick of the lighter and the sucking of the joint drew her attention back to Woody. He watched her through sullen eyes – weighted down under the burden of his worries instead of soaring to the heights of euphoria.

THE KREMLIN, MOSCOW, RUSSIA
March 21, 0830 GMT (1030 Local)

'Vassiliev,' Kartsev read on the screen, 'Lyudmila. Teacher in Kalina. Anonymous denunciation.'

Anonymous denunciation? he thought. That wasn't enough. She was denounced for *what*, this Lyudmila Vassiliev? 'No,' he half-uttered, and clicked 'Down.' Kartsev's eyes and shoulders were both growing sore. He sat hunched just in front of the bright screen.

Another name scrolled into view . . . another box. *To check, or not to check*, he thought in English. *'To suffer the slings and arrows . . . slings and arrows'* bounced through his mind. He'd always wondered what *slings* were. He had to remind himself to refocus on the screen.

'Ivanov,' he said out loud, 'Gri-i-isha.' As nondescript a name as he'd ever seen. 'Mechanic, Central Moscow. Possible conspiracy involving unknown persons.' That was it? What persons? Conspiracy to do what? 'It's unbe*liev*able, these people,' Kartsev slurred. *I really have to get at least* two-*lines*, he thought. He skipped another potentially guilty suspect because of insufficient information. *But they'll come back with more*, he knew. There was really only one way to get off the surveillance list.

The charge levied against the next man was much more useful. 'Andreev, Pyotr. Former commander, Presidential Security Force. Met with CIA in America.' Well, it wasn't actually a charge. Just a status, really. He was potentially dangerous.

And in America, Kartsev thought as he arched his stiff back. He'd totally lost interest in America after the assassination. Three of five missions had been foiled. The two that were successful didn't seem to have any further effects. He'd written an entire chapter on the observation entitled, 'Diminishing Marginal Effects of Terror: an Econometric Analysis.' But maybe those effects would return with the passage of time.

Kartsev clicked on the box next to 'Andreev, Pyotr' – his hand beginning to cramp.

PHILADELPHIA, PENNSYLVANIA
March 24, 2000 GMT (0600 Local)

'Mr Oscar Meyer?' Pyotr Andrew asked.

'Are zey turkey-baloney?' Olga asked. A woman glanced her way on hearing the accent.

'That's what's on the label.' He dropped the package in the basket. 'I don't think shopping is supposed to take hours,' Pyotr grumbled. He brushed the cookie crumbs off Mashenka's sweater.

'It doesn't take hours,' Olga retorted. She stopped at a display filled with cheeses. There were dozens of wax-wrapped brands. Pyotr knew she would study them all.

'I'm going on ahead for the Cheereos,' he informed her. He rounded the end cap into an empty aisle.

'Honey *Nut!*' she called out from behind.

'Honey-*Nut!*-Honey-*Nut!*' the kids began chanting from the basket. Pyotr could detect no trace of an accent.

There were a million brands. *Special K, Kelloggs Corn Flakes, Cap'n Crunch*, Pyotr read.

Pyotr noticed something at the end of the aisle. He looked up. A man with an overcoat raised a machine pistol. Pyotr dove to the floor behind a stand of iced orange juice. The angry roar of the gun splattered sprays of cold liquid onto Pyotr. Boxes of cereal burst and flew to the floor. There were shouts, and then screams . . . and then footsteps.

Four, three, two . . . Shot after shot rang out. The machine pistol clattered to the floor just beside him. He peered around the edge of the display to see two men in dark suits. They were making their way down the aisle toward the gunman. He lay prostrate in a widening pool of crimson blood.

The screams, the screams . . .

Pyotr turned. They were from Olga. She was bloody and clinging to the side of the basket . . . to the limp shapes of his children. *Oh-God-oh-God-oh-God*, he thought as he ran to them. With every step his fears were confirmed. They lay in the basket covered in blood. He quickly found the open artery in Masha's thigh. He pressed it closed with his thumb and index finger. Poor Oksana sat at the back in total shock. She didn't scream like little Mashenka. She didn't move much, or even look around. Her skin was pale with fright. She stared straight at her screaming mother.

The two government agents rushed to their side. The other shoppers were horrified and kept their distance, but the two agents swung into action. One checked under Oksana's coat. The other pinned his thrashing wife to the slippery floor.

'*Shit!*' the man checking Oksana hissed.

Oksana began to cry. She had been shot like her mother and little sister.

The stranger now fought for the life of Pyotr's daughter. The life of

411

his youngest seeped through Pyotr's cramping fingers ounce by ounce. It seemed like hours before the ambulances arrived. By then the two girls had both fallen unconscious.

Olga screamed till she too gave out.

The rest of the night was all plastic tubes and hospital smells. Sweat-soaked doctors coming to see Pyotr with somber words. He lost track of what was being done. Mostly, he just sat. He broke out crying only when he saw the two agents. They were covered head-to-toe in his family's blood. The men stayed with him the whole time like old friends.

Early in the morning the doctors told him they'd all live. Pyotr didn't remember much else from that night.

WEST OF URGAL, SIBERIA
March 27, 0730 GMT (1730 Local)

Chin and his three fellow platoon leaders sat hunched in the small tent.

'Here he comes,' one of the university snots said. He closed the tent flap.

The company commander crawled in and instantly began to bitch. 'What are you *doing*?' he snapped at the four lieutenants. Chin and the others stared back in stunned silence. 'I could see the light from a hundred *meters!*' His voice was hushed. But from the strain showing in his body and face he might as well have been shouting. 'You men are my *officers!* I've got to count on you to use your *heads!*'

Chin didn't dare look at the others. He'd never seen the captain this mad. Plus his fellow platoon leaders were all pricks anyway.

The captain removed his gloves and pulled a beat-up plastic tube from inside his white poncho. He unscrewed it and extracted a rolled-up paper map with care. His fingers were already trembling from the cold. He noisily flattened the map – the paper crackling under his hands and heightening Chin's sense of anticipation. It wasn't often they got a chance to look at the map

The colorful paper coiled back up as the captain tucked his hands under his armpits. 'Okay,' the captain said – his words quaking from a chattering jaw. 'I called this company meeting to pass down word from army group command. These orders are to go no lower than your rank.' He looked each of his four subordinates in the eye.

Chin felt a stirring of his blood at so solemn a charge. It was a privilege to learn so important a secret – whatever it was. He looked around and immediately grew annoyed. The other platoon leaders' faces all showed disrespect. On one man's face you could even call the expression a sneer.

'The People's Republic is engaged in a glorious victory,' the captain recited woodenly. The tone dampened the excitement Chin had felt. 'You are each to be commended for your efforts.' One of the other officers drew an unusually deep breath. He drew a squinting, menacing look from the captain. The company commander then turned his attention to the map. There were a variety of colors and symbols marked with a pencil. 'We have to be ready to repel attacks on our flanks from here, here and here.' He pointed. Everyone now hunched over the map, eclipsing most of the light from the single lantern. 'Get back!' the captain shouted. Everyone sank back onto their haunches but still stared.

'You're pointing at our left, our center and our right,' Lieutenant Hung said. His tone was just this side of insolence.

'*Good*,' the captain said sarcastically. 'You can read a map!' Chin kept his mouth firmly shut.

'If we're in the middle of a glorious victory,' Hung continued, 'why are we worried about our flanks?'

'Those are our orders!'

'And why do we alternate between ridiculously loose dispersion of our units during the day,' Hung pressed, 'and tight defensive groupings at night?'

Chin had never realized it before, but every day and night it was the same. When they broke camp in the morning, the four platoons scattered widely before moving out. But they bivouaced just meters apart.

'Yeah,' came a seconding voice. 'We used to maneuver at night. The *Europeans* curled up into a ball when the sun went down, and *we* hit *them*.'

'Do you *like* patrolling at night?' the captain finally barked. He shot challenging looks at each face in succession. 'Do you *want* to go up against those bases – night after night – *again*? To run into their patrols and wait for the artillery to come raining in?'

Chin remembered those scary nights with a shudder. The only way to survive the artillery was to hug the Americans so tight the big guns couldn't fire on them. But their patrols always had a machine-gun.

'Our *orders*,' the captain shouted, 'are to pull into a defensive mode *every* night and to be prepared to repel advances against three of our four *fronts!*' He was staring the smart-assed platoon leader all the way back against the tent wall.

Lieutenant Hung didn't flinch. He didn't recoil – as Chin would have – expecting blows. He sat there unmoving, and that in itself was almost insubordination.

'Is that clear enough for you?' the captain asked in low tones.

It seemed to be, for Hung nodded.

Chin tried to comprehend what it was that both Hung and the captain understood. He gave up, however, and drew only the most basic facts from the captain's briefing. China was losing the war – not winning, as he had thought – and they should prepare to be attacked from all sides. And he could also tell from the interactions of his comrades that the glue of army discipline was weakening.

But that it was quite possibly being replaced by an even stronger bond. For there was a palpable sense of fear in that tent. From then on the bickering came to an end.

VLADIVOSTOK, SIBERIA
March 30, 1700 GMT (0300 Local)

The snoring kept Andre Faulk awake.

It was his first night with his new unit. He lay in his bunk and his mind raced. The barracks were frigid. They had to be. Everyone was wearing long underwear and boots. Only your hands, face and throat felt the effects of the chill.

It had come as a surprise when he was told the rules. You slept in battle dress like a fireman slept in his clothes. And you did it for the same reason. For you responded to desperate calls. A firebase on the verge of being overrun. A hole in a line to be plugged. A last-ditch effort to stop a breakthrough. Human filler plugged into a dam that was leaking in a hundred places.

Andre's stomach turned and gurgled loudly. He rolled over onto his back in a series of twisting jerks of his body. The metal bunk creaked and squealed. The snores of the man in the bunk above sputtered. Andre stared up at the bulge. It was dimly visible in the light from the duty room. Several metal links were missing from the Russian bed. The mattress poked through like bald spots on an old tire.

He sighed. His breath fogged in front of his face.

There were nine new guys who'd joined the air cavalry platoon with Andre. Nine replacements for a unit of only thirty-three men at full strength. Nine divided by thirty-three was something like one out of three or four. Those were the odds. One out of three or four. In about six weeks' worth of fighting. With no end in sight. And maybe they weren't the first replacements, he hadn't thought of that.

His stomach lining burned. His skin tingled. Shivers ran up his arms to his chest. They were heady thoughts. Fighting. Dying. He wondered what had happened to Stempel. Alive? Dead? He should have called his parents' apartment.

Andre's heart was racing.

What the hell am I doing here?

A telephone rang in the duty room. The muffled sound of the old-fashioned bell penetrating the walls. Andre's senses focused solely on that phone. It was picked up just as the second ring began. Andre stared wide-eyed at the mattress that formed his sky. The distant voice of the duty NCO ended abruptly as the phone was slammed down.

In the terrible few moments of silence that followed, Andre could hear every noise from the two dozen sleeping men. The snores, a sniff, a cough.

The whining wind-up of a helicopter's turbine.

The door burst open, and Andre just about jumped out of his skin. The flickering of the fluorescent lights overhead announced the coming of a man-made dawn.

'Let's *go!* Mission call!'

Everyone groaned and rolled out of bed. They began to climb into their outer gear. No one moved faster than Andre – the petrified eighteen-year-old.

The brutally cold night air at the helipads was astir in the wash of forty helicopters' rotors. In the lights of the base Andre and his squad scrambled single file out of the barracks. They labored under eighty-pound field packs. All around them brilliantly-lit Blackhawks filled with troops rose into the night sky.

'Air assault!' someone shouted over the roar. A smattering of '*a-a-a-air*-borne!' and other similar calls came in reply. But the enthusiasm was not particularly contagious. In fact, no one in Andre's squad said a word as they climbed through the open door of the white-painted helicopter.

Bright landing lights flashed across the pads as Blackhawks banked at low altitude and headed off. The sky was alive with red and green running lights and flashing white tail beacons. It was a full battalion-sized deployment complete with 105-mm artillery slung underneath giant utility helicopters.

Andre stood last in line. He stooped involuntarily under the idling rotors' wash. It was like stepping into a cold shower fully clothed. He could hardly see through his watering eyes. His squad leader – Sergeant Moncreif – stood at the open sliding door. He grabbed Andre's M-16 and checked to ensure it was safed. He returned the rifle and slapped Andre on the back. Two of his new squadmates helped pull Andre aboard. When all twelve men were on board, a crewman closed the door. It shut out the howling gale and swirling Siberian air.

Andre dropped his field pack and dragged it to the rear wall. He sat on the crowded floor. He hugged the pack to his chest. The wall of muscles along his stomach cramped from their tight clench. He arched his back and took a deep breath. His jaw vibrated, and his teeth chattered from the lingering cold. The engines vibrated through the armored pads on the deck and straight into Andre's itching testicles. With a lurching, stomach-crushing jolt Andre felt the aircraft leap into the sky. They hovered there momentarily. The deck rocked in the turbulence caused by the rotors.

They pitched forward suddenly. The acceleration in the odd, nose-down attitude was sickening. Gone were the bright lights of the base. All was black through the frosty windows of the Blackhawk. The cabin lights were a dim red so as not to spoil their night vision.

Andre looked around the troop compartment. The walls were lined with the ten men of his squad plus two medics. The center of the cabin was piled high with their gear. No one talked over the noise. They just stared straight ahead. Thinking. Andre closed his eyes. *Two medics*, he thought.

Time passed. The helicopter hurtled toward the LZ with its engines at full military power. One minute? Two? Ten? The cabin was warm. The initial chill subsided. But Andre couldn't fully rid himself of an exhausting physical tension. It remained balled into a solid inside him. He resolved to learn to deal with it. To function with it impaled through him there. Stifling his breathing. Cramping his stomach. He'd have to deal with it, he knew, to function on the battlefield. To survive.

There were two loud knocks in rapid succession. The helicopter pitched over onto its side. For just a second Andre thought it was their death spiral, but the sickening dive seemed to be controlled. There was another sharp 'thwack' like the sound of a hammer pounded against the helicopter's thin skin. In that terrible moment Andre realized they were taking fire.

The ballistic mats on the deck jumped with still more hammering blows. Andre felt the string of thuds through his butt. Men raised their feet into the air. They shied away from the ground fire. Andre could smell smoke. The helicopter pitched over the other way, then back. Sparks flew up the wall. A window shattered. Air whistled into the cabin. A heavy thud pressed Andre's head toward his chest. Everyone was thrown forward.

The door flew open.

'Everybody *out!*'

A slow but constant rain of bullets struck home. Holes were being punched through the walls. Men leapt into the maelstrom outside. Andre dragged his pack toward the open door. He ducked as each new hole puckered the bulkheads. Death – ruthlessly random – stabbed into the cabin.

Snow peppered his face through the open door. He squinted and bowed his head against the gale. He judged his odds now from the loud smacking sounds. At the door he was fully exposed. In the red glow of the cabin lights the swirling snow looked like fireflies. It was being blown up – not down – by rotors turning at full power. Andre was the last man in line.

A drumroll of thumps hit the aircraft. It sounded like buckshot fired from a shotgun. The air around Andre was filled with whirring sounds. Two men at the door fell backwards onto Andre.

'A-a-a-*a-a-a-H-H!*' came a blood-curdling shriek. There were screams and sobs in rapid howls made at the limits of a human's vocal chords. Andre froze in terror in the doorway.

'Jesus *Christ!* Give me a hand!' one of the crewmen shouted at Andre.

417

Bullets smashed into the metal fuselage like rocks thrown against tin siding. Andre helped the crewmen pull the wounded man back into the helicopter. Blood oozed through the man's hands where his eye had been.

'Get *out!*' the crewman then shouted at Andre.

Andre turned into the snow, closed his eyes and groped blindly for his pack. He dragged the heavy load to the ground with one hand. He held his rifle grasped firmly in his other.

A man appeared out of nowhere to stand in front of Andre. 'I got hit,' he said. He was holding his rib cage just below his left breast. He was pale, and his eyes were glassy. But otherwise he appeared unhurt.

Another 'z-z-z-i-p' of bullets sent Andre to the ground. Andre dragged his pack in front of him. The force of the downdraft redoubled, and Andre lowered his helmet to the snow. The artificial blizzard subsided. Andre looked up to see that the helicopter and the wounded man were gone.

The noise of the helicopter was replaced by booming explosions and rips of gunfire.

Tracers streaked all through the woods ahead. Some ricochetted off trees and shattered into sparks whose short lives reminded Andre of shooting stars. Grenades lit small patches of the thin forest floor in brief pulses – fiery geysers of snow erupting violently from the earth. One illuminated for the briefest of moments a standing human form. Andre couldn't tell in the brief snapshot whether the person died in the blast. He couldn't even tell if he was American or Chinese.

The scene was the same all through the woods that ringed the flat landing zone. *A lake*, Andre realized. The LZ was on a frozen lake. Forested hills rose on all sides.

The last of the helicopters was now gone. The white bowl was a carnival of noise. Booming explosions rattled Andre's insides and scraped at his nerves. But there were no soldiers to be seen anywhere. And no bullets reached out for him there. It was almost peaceful.

Andre struggled to his feet and headed for the violence.

Chapter Nineteen

SOUTH OF LAKE KHANKA, SIBERIA
March 30, 1740 GMT (0340 Local)

Andre ran bent over at the waist. He reached the edge of the lake and knelt behind a tree. He flicked the M-16's selector to 'Burst' – three rounds fired per squeeze of the trigger. He then began his ascent of the slope. The pack was heavy. The snow deep. His thighs burned. He gave up trying to weave through the trees. He just tried to make it to the crest of the ridge.

A hiss cut through the branches high above. Andre looked up and got snow in his eyes. Stray bullets from over the hill. He wiped the snow away with his gloves. They felt like sandpaper across his face.

Half way up he heard voices. English! He turned on a dime and headed toward the source. He smashed through a low branch laden with snow.

The night exploded in flame.

Andre collapsed in the snow. Bullets flew by like the tail of a whip. They pounded into the pack on his back. His eyes were jammed shut. He waited for death to strike home.

The storm ended. The magazine was empty.

Andre raised his head and screamed, '*American so-o-oldier!*' He dropped back into the snow. His heart pounded. He waited for the killing fire.

'Come out so I can see you!' came a shout . . . close by.

Andre gathered his strength, stood up slowly, and waited.

The man lowered his voice to a whisper. 'We're over here!'

Andre joined two men lying at the base of a tree. One clutched a still-smoking rifle. The other clutched his hands to his bloody stomach.

'Jesus, man!' the armed man said. 'I almost *shot* yer ass!'

'Fuckin' *A!*' Andre snapped. '*Jee*-sus!' He felt like vomiting.

'You don't come runnin' *up* on somebody like that! *Christ!*'

A half-dozen explosions burst over the hill. 'Where's 2nd Squad?' Andre asked.

'*Which* 2nd Squad?'

'First Platoon.'

'*Which* First Platoon?' the guy asked. 'What fuckin' company are you in?' The man clearly had no idea where Andre's company was. 'Fuck it, man. It don't matter. The fightin's up there.' He pointed toward the crest. The treetops along the ridge lit up over and over again with flashes. A continuous roar punctuated by huge blasts from the artillery shells.

Andre looked back at the two men. 'What're *you* doin'?' he asked – still pissed.

'I'm fuckin' *wounded*, man!' He pointed down at his calf. It was wrapped in a small bandage. 'Plus, I can't leave the lieutenant.'

An officer – wounded! 'Is he gonna be okay?' Andre asked.

'*How the hell should I know?*' the guy spat out. It sounded like the reply to an accusation. 'I *tried* to find a medic, *okay?* I ain't seen one!' The man lowered his voice. 'He's gutshot.'

'He needs help,' Andre said.

'I *know* he needs help! Didn't I *tell* you I looked for a medic? Didn't I already *say* that?'

Andre wanted nothing to do with the shithead. 'If I see a medic,' he mumbled, 'I'll send him back.'

'Here!' the guy said. He handed Andre a canvas sack. 'They sent me back for these grenades.'

Andre slung the bag over his shoulder. His legs felt like jelly when he rose. He barely made it to the top of the ridge. The sound was much louder. He dropped to a crawl and peered over the top. He saw everything, and nothing. Muzzles spat flame in a saddle between two hills. Artillery burst every few seconds – lighting the arca. Andre saw contours in the land. Trees and gaps that could be ponds or streams. But he couldn't tell which weapons were whose.

He needed to be with other soldiers, even if it meant fighting. He was terrified he'd be left there – lost and alone. He girded himself and rose. He almost fell several times. Each step down the hill was a controlled slide. His boots had to sink to brake his rapid descent.

By the time the ground flattened out, Andre was physically spent. He sank to the ground and sucked in gulps of dry air. His lungs ached. His legs were on fire. He lifted his head long enough to realize that he was inside the battle now. The 'crack' of each rifle and the 'booms' of machine-guns seemed to echo like car horns in a tunnel. The canopy of evergreens formed a ceiling to a world filled with noise and danger and death.

Andre rose and pressed on – ever closer to the thunderous battles. He was stooped so low that he stood barely half his height. He kept his M-16 at the ready – his safety was off. They could be anywhere.

An unnatural chill crawled from his stomach up his arms and across his chest. It felt like the onset of the flu, but it was fear. Palpable, tangible fear. It was taking control of his body. Its progress was measured in body parts seized by the quiver.

Andre almost made the same mistake twice. During a momentary lull in the fighting, he heard the raspy static of a radio. He headed for the sound, but caught himself and dropped to the snow. He listened as bits and pieces of a garbled answer came back over a radio. It was in English.

Andre drew a deep breath and shouted, '*American soldier! American soldier!*'

'Where?' he heard.

'Over here! Don't shoot, okay?'

'Okay! Keep it slow!'

Andre rose in slow motion and walked forward slowly. A bullet smacked into the trunk. Andre winced and ducked. He practically stepped on the man. He immediately dropped into the snow beside him. He was physically and emotionally exhausted.

'Private First Class Faulk,' Andre said – reporting for duty.

'Dundrey, PFC! Glad to see ya.'

'Where's 2nd Squad, First Platoon, Charlie Company?' Andre asked.

The guy laughed. 'How the fuck should *I* know? This is Alpha Company, Third Platoon. You'd best check in with the LT. He's up there.'

The man pointed into the furnace of muzzle blasts and hand grenades. When the radio-telephone operator answered a call over the radio, Andre began to crawl forward. The RTO grabbed Andre's leg. 'Roger that, India Tango. Out.' He looked up at Andre. 'Tell the LT there's a flight of fighter-bombers comin' in any time now. The forward air controller says heads down, pass it along.'

Andre nodded, then headed on. Now he had a job – a mission. He had a purpose in this otherwise insane and seemingly suicidal advance toward the front.

The noise of guns and hand grenades in the valley and artillery shells bursting on the opposite ridge was deafening. Andre's ears rang. Every so often the air-splitting sound of bullets pressed him face down in the snow. He didn't notice the stinging cold now. He was too obsessed by the flash bulbs of muzzle blasts that popped from the darkness ahead.

It occurred to him for the first time that he could shoot back. He even paused and took aim at where he'd last seen a muzzle flash. But something held him back. Maybe it wasn't a Chinese soldier. Maybe it was an American. He crawled on.

'Hey!' somebody yelled from behind him. 'Where the hell you goin'?'

'What?'

'Get back to the line, you crazy motherfucker!'

In a rush of panic Andre realized he'd crawled right past the American lines. He was in No Man's Land in between the two armies. He scampered back as fast as he could. The man who'd called out to him blazed away with an M-60 machine-gun.

Andre rolled over the log behind which the two-man gun crew had set up. The noise of the weapon was so loud that he couldn't yell out to them. He slapped the gunner on the boot.

The man scarcely paid him any attention. He glanced Andre's way then returned to the gun's iron sights. The yellow fire from its heavy muzzle lit the snow and ice-coated brush ahead.

'You got the extra ammo?' the man's helper asked Andre. He lay beside the gun, holding aloft the last few rounds in a belt.

'Naw! I'm lookin' for the LT!'

'*Shit!* Where's our fuckin' ammo?' the man shouted to no one in particular.

'Where's the LT?' Andre asked.

'He headed down that way!' The man jabbed his gloved index finger to their right.

Andre nodded and began to slither through the snow. 'Oh!' he remembered. 'Keep your heads down! There's an air strike comin' in!' Neither man looked his way. The gunner's face was lit in the yellow flame from his gun. '*You hear me?*' Andre shouted.

The man didn't acknowledge his warning. Andre looked into the woods toward which the machine-gun blazed. A phosphorous grenade illuminated the scene. Men were firing at the Americans as they trudged forward through the snow. A solid wall of tightly-packed attackers – maybe a company of Chinese!

Andre's skin crawled. His body clenched up from his shoulders to his crotch like a string was drawn. Dozens of grenades went off almost simultaneously up and down the American lines. Andre was stunned by the violence of their blasts.

The machine-gun fell silent. The ammo bearer opened fire with his rifle. The gunner rolled back into position and tossed a hand grenade all in one motion.

Andre watched the metal pineapple hit a tree squarely not ten feet in front of where he lay. He grabbed his helmet and ducked. His last sight was of the grenade rebounding off the tree. The entire world jumped. The ear-splitting burst left him covered in powdery snow. His head throbbed. He was dizzy and nauseous. A pain like an ice pick pierced both ears deep into his skull.

When his head steadied, however, he registered the image of blazing muzzles not twenty meters away. Andre looked down and saw that he still held his rifle. Swallowing hard, he raised it to his shoulder. A Chinese soldier paused and tossed a grenade. It got caught in the upper branches of a tree. The guy shouted something. His comrades dove to the ground.

It burst in front of them. After a few more shouts they rose again. Andre switched the selector to 'Semi' and lined up his first man. When his aim was perfect, he pulled the trigger. A single round cracked out the end of his rifle. The butt plate jammed hard into Andre's shoulder. The man – his target – fell.

Andre snorted, half smiling. He looked over at the machine-gun crew. They were gone . . . machine-gun and all. He rolled on his back and looked toward the rear. There was nobody. Nobody but Andre and the Chinese.

He began to fire. He squeezed off rounds, one after the other. Just about every shot dropped a target. Up ahead, the muzzles blazed but Andre couldn't imagine who they were shooting at. Until, that is, the underbrush around him began to snap to pieces.

Andre felt himself leave his body. In his mind, he split in two. There was the part of him that winced at every passing bullet. The air grew so thick with them that the wincing became a constant grimace. And then there was Andre the functioning rifleman. Up pops a target. Swing the barrel. Squeeze . . . bull's eye! The two halves were totally distinct. One raged and screamed and cowered, too afraid to flee toward safety. The other counted rounds, put blinders on and aimed straight ahead – focusing on the job of saving his life by taking others.

Low-flying jets screamed by overhead. The atmospheric pressure changed as they passed. Andre's sinuses squealed and ears popped.

A staggering roar shook heaven and earth. Great geysers of flame rose high into the air. Blazing trees fell to the ground. His ears reported not sound, but feeling. They itched and stung from the wave of compressed air as yet another string of bombs exploded in a long snake not two hundred yards away.

Andre saw a target. A kneeling man waved his arm at Chinese soldiers who cowered on the ground. Andre had the man dead to rights. Crack. His rifle recoiled. The man disappeared in the snow.

Three more waves of jets passed. Andre saw from their bright tailpipes they flew two abreast. Then all fell still save the crackling fires.

The Chinese were still out there, Andre realized. Probably less than a hand grenade's throw away. *What they gonna do?* the calculating part of him pondered. Andre fished another thirty-round magazine from his pouch. He pressed the release to drop the nearly empty magazine from his rifle. He seated the full mag with a faint clacking sound.

The noise attracted a spray of fire from a single Kalashnikov. Its aim was wild. Andre laid his sights on the muzzle flash but held his fire. He had the shot. But now that they'd all taken to ground, they would see him if he fired. Their return fire would then be unhurried, calm, straight into the white lump in the snow.

Andre carefully reached into the canvas bag and began to pile the hand grenades in front of him. Several single shots were fired in his direction. Brief bursts of intense gunfire broke out all up and down the line to both sides. Artillery still rained down on the Chinese-held ridge line. But that was another theater of war. Andre's world measured thirty meters by thirty.

There was whispering. They were talking. Discussing. Planning. When they fell silent, Andre pressed himself as low as he could get. Another Chinese gun lit the night. It sprayed the trees all around. *They know I'm here*, he thought. *But they don't know where.*

He was totally calm now. He pulled the pin on his first grenade. It was a game. They were trying to bait him. To draw him out. Once he revealed himself, they'd kill him. Until then, the leaderless unit was paralyzed. *A Mexican standoff*, Andre thought. *Well, let's see if this shakes 'em up.*

He had to rise to his knees. That was the tricky part. But he'd sunk fairly deeply into the snow. And he was partially covered by a thick tree trunk. He slowly raised the grenade to his chin. He let it fly like a football with a rustling of fabric. The handle sprang off. He heard a terse shout. Andre grabbed another grenade and pulled the pin.

The first grenade exploded dead center between the two muzzle flashes from before. A host of new guns opened up. Andre knelt there exposed. He mentally noted the positions of the flashing muzzles. He tossed grenade after grenade at the flaming bursts. The process was rapid and mechanical.

Bullets passed so close he could feel their wake. The gentle kiss of air belied the grievous wounds the supersonic round would cause.

He pulled the pin on his last grenade. The sack had held at least a dozen. Its burst lit several running men in profile, felling two.

Andre dropped and wrapped his index finger around the trigger. He surveyed the woods for a target. The artillery had shifted to some more distant target. The woods all around were still. The only sound that broke the silence was the distant smack of a tree branch.

They were gone.

Andre settled into the snow to wait. To wait for sunrise. To wait for friendly troops. To wait for the Chinese to regroup and come back. An American patrol found him at dawn. He was numb from the cold but alive.

BIROBIDZHAN FIREBASE, SIBERIA
April 2, 1600 GMT (0200 Local)

Harold Stempel cowered against the icy wall. The trenchline was inundated with artillery and mortars. The night glowed with indescribable orange fire. Each of the crushing blasts was a body blow. Each was the end of the world.

'*What's goin' on?*' screamed the unshaven man next to Stempel.

Stempel didn't budge from his fetal position. He held his helmet down on his head with one hand, his knees to his chest with the other. Stempel's hood was drawn tight around his face. The newly issued body armor covered his torso. He watched the orange lightning from behind layers of wool and Kevlar. Each flash opened a wound in Stempel. But it was a wound you couldn't see.

His vision tunneled. His eyes filled so fully with tears that the orange flashes starred. He was acutely aware of his rapid breathing. He tried to slow it, but he couldn't draw enough air. A near miss bounced Stempel off the ground and covered him in snow. Now even the earth lashed out at him.

'*Dear God in Hea-* . . .!' Stempel began. But the trench itself exploded. His voice was swallowed by thunder. '*Please sto-o-o-p!*' he yelled.

A medic picked Stempel up. The man was profiled against the low blanket of white clouds that had socked in their air support. He dropped Stempel and ran off toward the screaming. Everyone was firing. Everyone but Stempel. No one looked at him. Their weapons blazed. Stempel knew he had to get up. He groped frantically for his rifle.

A massive burst shook the earth. A boiling mushroom cloud rose over the rear wall of the trench. The Chinese had blown an ammo bunker. Smaller and closer explosions still rained down. But Stempel saw something more frightening. Their squad leader came down the trench. 'Let's go! Every other man! Come on!' He pulled people from the wall. He sent them off through a communications trench.

A blast from a heavy shell knocked Stempel to his knees. He was senseless for a moment. Sergeant Moncreif stopped in front of him. 'Come on, Stemp! They're inside the wire!'

Stempel rose. He followed the others. Men he now knew better than

426

anybody else in the world. He'd seen them put through every extreme in life. There remained few secrets about their character. They'd been tested. He knew which had passed and which had failed. But as a unit they'd always done their job.

'*They're inside the wire!*' Moncreif shouted to motivate others to their feet. Stempel followed his squadmates down a slit trench. It was so narrow he had to turn sideways. When the men in the lead slowed, the followers collided. They all were slipsliding on the perpetually slick floor. Time was everything now. Every second that Chinese soldiers remained alive inside the main perimeter meant the chances of holding the base fell. If they circled back to hit a section of the trenches from behind, they'd peel open a hole so wide the base's defenses would burst like a balloon.

Someone began a scream that was cut short by an explosion.

Again the only thing that saved Stempel were bodies. Layers of people in front of him absorbed the shrapnel from a grenade. Searing fire burned into Stempel's right arm. He was underneath a man's body. Bullets flew over his spinning head. The dying man on his legs was unable to draw a breath.

Stempel ducked his chin and looked down his body. The flak jacket was ripped ragged. The pain from his upper arm was intense. The air all around him was filled with projectiles. The ice above him was being sheared away in ledges. There wasn't a thing he could do to survive. He was helpless.

Two grenades exploded among the Chinese. Stempel saw them fall in the trench ahead. French soldiers dropped into the trench with their stubby rifles spraying fire wildly. One of the Legionnaires was shot in the back by his own man. Another's helmet flew off as he collapsed backwards. But they killed more than they got killed.

Boots trampled Stempel. Every third or fourth man stomped right on Stempel's head or chest. He yelled to them for help. Some responded in incomprehensible French. They all kept moving. Finally American medics arrived. They cut at the clothing around Stempel's upper arm. Peeling the fabric back caused intense pain. So did the fiery alcohol and the pressure bandages. Stempel cried out and kicked his feet into the dead men. The medic gave Stempel a pill, which he swallowed dry. 'You'll be fine,' he said. He sat Stempel up and ran off toward the firefight, which was intense.

Stempel could hardly remember what had happened. The artillery barrage had stopped. A deep rumble rocked the ground for some time. Steady and deep like the thudding subwoofer in his father's media room. Like five-hundred-pound firecrackers going off hundreds at a time.

He almost felt good. He remembered the main trench. Then in the slit trench. He couldn't remember the attack. He didn't even think he'd fired his rifle, which he was surprised to find at his side. Another herd of men stampeded past. Stepping on him. 'Off to war!' he mumbled – slurring.

They stopped to toss the bodies of the fallen out of the trench. 'Hey!' Stempel yelled, but not loudly enough to get their attention. 'Those are my buddies!' His shout drew glances from the nearest two men.

They tossed the last body in the snow . . . but carefully. They moved on. Stempel was alone again with the dead.

UNRUSFOR HEADQUARTERS, KHABAROVSK
April 3, 0800 GMT (1800 Local)

Clark's J-2 reported to the meeting of joint force commanders. 'The ice has thinned from over sixty centimeters to under ten.' The chief of joint staff intelligence had become an expert on the Amur River ice pack. 'We're already seeing the Chinese have trouble with their heavy vehicles. They're laying pontoons to distribute the weight. Plus they halve the loads on their trucks. And it appears to us they're preparing for the ice flow themselves. They're using all their available transport just to get supplies across. Pack animals move it from there to the front.'

Clark held his J-2's gaze. 'Any guess as to how long we've got before it breaks?' He knew the answer. He was just raising the subject.

'I'd say . . . between two and four weeks from now.'

His answer brought a stir from around the table. The French commander said, 'That means we must attack sometime between right now and two *weeks*.' He held his hands up in mock confusion. 'But *which*? How can we know?'

'I've got a team goin' in tonight,' the commander of Clark's special operations group offered.

'We launch the offensive at zero four hundred local time on April 18th,' Clark announced. There was stunned silence. Everyone knew of the funding showdown. No one directly raised the subject of any connection. The German commander came closest.

'That means the ice must hold for at least three weeks,' the general said. 'What if it does not? Is there any flexibility in that date?' Clark replied that there was not. Although the question 'Why?' hung over the room, no one gave voice to it.

The senior French general asked, 'Has President Davis approved penetration into China to the Jilin-Harbin-Qiqihar line?'

'Yes,' Clark replied. 'He has assured me that no calls for a ceasefire will be entertained until those objectives have been reached. That line is approximately 560 kilometers or 350 miles south of the Amur. It should ensure that the bulk of their invasion forces and mobile reserves are fully enveloped.'

'We can't get tied down in civilian control,' the British general pointed out. 'There could be chaos. Mass rioting. Disorder.'

'We won't,' Clark replied. 'If the diplomats start negotiating the shape of the conference table, we'll reduce those pockets by force and withdraw. Our mission is to destroy the offensive capabilities of the People's Liberation Army. We're getting back across the Amur quickly. We have no time for anything more than operational security. No humanitarian relief. No civil administration. Just war, gentlemen. War that will be prosecuted with the utmost violence and skill that we are collectively able to muster. From the moment we launch this counter-offensive, to the moment the last track rolls back across the Amur, I have only one goal. To destroy the ability of my enemy to fight so completely that he will pose no immediate threat to the security of Siberia.'

There was no dissension. Clark was sure, however, that there were doubts and fears. Most would center on the ice.

BETHESDA NAVAL HOSPITAL, MARYLAND
April 6, 2200 GMT (1700 Local)

'We've been diverting ninety percent of our resources to the staging areas,' General Dekker briefed Gordon Davis. 'That's put a real strain on the troops in contact with the Chinese. Quite frankly, they're all pretty close to the breaking point. And it's not like they're going to be relieved when the counter-offensive kicks off. We plan on using them for flank and rear area security.

'We have, to date, lost over eight thousand killed and twenty thousand wounded. Those numbers could double before the end of the counter-offensive.'

'Will General Clark's planned counter-offensive win this war?' Gordon asked.

He was putting the man on the spot. Clark had not consulted Dekker before approaching Gordon. It left Dekker free to criticize – to second-guess – Clark's warfighting plans. That was good. It gave Gordon a professional check against overreliance on Clark – a man whom he barely knew.

Dekker looked Gordon straight in the eye. 'It has risks. It's aggressive, but it's sound. We're satisfied we've built up the men and materiel to execute the plan. The biggest wild cards are the ice and any counter-attack they may launch out of the Beijing area. If the ice starts to flow before we get at least a corps across the Amur, the Chinese south of the river will regroup. They could also stabilize the front by counter-attacking with their strategic reserve. They'll surely move up from Beijing. How we stop them depends on where they head and what the battlefield situation is at that moment.'

'You didn't answer my question. Will Clark's counter-offensive through northern China so totally demolish the Chinese army that I won't have to cut deals with Beijing?'

The Chairman of the Joint Chiefs took a deep breath. 'If that ice holds up just long enough – but not too long – and we can fend off their counterattack, then yes. We'll not only destroy most of their armor and transport, we'll hack up their extensive military infrastructure in Manchuria in a Sherman's March to Korea Bay.'

'Have you seen General Clark's objectives and timetables?' Gordon asked. Dekker nodded slowly. 'And?' Dekker arched his eyebrows. 'They're aggressive. *Very* aggressive. If the Chinese south of the Amur resist ridge by ridge, stream by stream, then we'll get bloodied like we haven't been since the Ardennes Forest in 1944. And they *will* be fighting for their homeland.'

'They'll be fighting for communist octogenarians in Beijing,' the Chief of Naval Operations countered. 'And those soldiers are all third-rate conscripts. We've already seen the best the Chinese have to offer.'

The room now fell silent. Everyone had said his piece. None of it had done anything to change Gordon's mind. 'All right, I'm ready to authorize the launch of the offensive as planned – on April 18th.' No one raised a voice of objection. No one commented on the rigid timetable.

But Dekker did ask, 'What about the Congressional deadline, sir? We'll just be cracking their lines when the clock runs out on our funding. If Congress doesn't . . .'

'You let me take care of Congress,' Gordon interrupted. 'All you've got to do is win the war.'

The door opened. Celeste entered alone. When Gordon's daughter saw him looking at her, her gaze dropped to the floor. She crossed the large room with her hands clasped in front of her. 'Hi, daddy,' she said. She kissed him.

'Did your mom pick you up at the airport?' Gordon asked. She nodded. 'Where is she?'

'Oh, she had to run some errands,' Celeste replied. She still wouldn't look at him directly.

'You *mean*,' Gordon translated, 'she wanted you to come in here by yourself.' Celeste nodded. 'Honey, is this about that demonstration at school?'

She hugged him. '*Daddy!* I never meant to do anything to hurt you!'

Gordon winced in pain as she squeezed him. 'It's *nothing*, darling. Trust me.'

'But it was supposed to be just, like, a student memorial. And the newspapers and television just blow my picture up like I was . . . Daddy, I left as soon as they started saying all those things about you! The press made it sound like I was *part* of that, but I *wasn't!*'

Gordon just smiled and stroked her hair. He reassured her repeatedly. He soothed her feelings. Elaine had told him how upset Celeste was. When his daughter's tears finally dried up, Gordon said, 'Have I ever told you why we're fighting this war?'

'You don't have to explain yourself to me,' Celeste replied.

'Yes, I do. I've got to explain myself to everybody in this country . . . and I will. And it's all right to be against the war, Celeste. *I'm* against the war – *any* war. But life presents you with a limited selection of options, and you've got to pick one of them. Sometimes you wish you had more or different choices. Only life isn't always fair. You just make the best decision you can under the circumstances.'

'Is this about my weekend trip to Cape Cod?' Celeste asked sheepishly.

'No. This is about the war. What trip to Cape Cod?'

She loosed a high-pitched giggle. 'Oh . . . never mind. I thought maybe – you know – this was some sort of father-daughter advice thing. Like . . . in *code?*'

Gordon was confused. 'You went to Cape Cod for the weekend?'

She waved both hands as if to erase her earlier comment. 'We don't need to go into that now. I told mom all about it . . . when I got back. She's okay with it. Everything's cool.'

Gordon didn't raise the subject again. They chatted about school. About whether she could have friends hang out in the White House that summer. About the limited number of available roles for her in the drama department's productions of Chekhov, Ibsen and Wilde. They talked about anything but the war . . . and whether there'd been boys on this road trip to Cape Cod.

MERCY HOSPITAL, PHILADELPHIA
April 7, 1300 GMT (0800 Local)

'Mommy,' Mashenka said in her girlish pitch, 'could you read this bo-o-ok?'

'I can't reach it, kissa,' Olga Andreev replied. Masha held the book up over the railing. But in the hip-to-toe cast she couldn't put it within reach. Olga was confined to her own bed. She'd been warned not to strain the stitches. She thought about pushing the call button. But she'd already overtaxed the nurses' patience. She resisted making such a petty request.

Oksana lay in the portable bed opposite Masha. As usual she was disturbingly quiet.

'Where's *daddy?*' Masha asked in frustration.

'I don't *know*, kissa,' Olga said for the hundredth time. In Pyotr's brief absences, the girls had been unmanageable. Or – more correctly – three-year-old Masha had been unmanageable. Oksana hadn't said ten words since the shooting. 'Are you all right, sweetheart?' Olga asked the six-year-old for the hundredth time.

'Where's daddy?' she mumbled. She never looked her mother's way.

'I don't know.'

The door opened. It wasn't Pyotr, or a nurse, but one of the policemen. Pyotr regularly talked to the men protecting them. But they rarely came in the room.

'This was left for you, ma'am,' the officer said. It was a letter with no words of address. The man left. Olga opened the envelope.

'Dear Olya,' Pyotr wrote by hand – in Russian. Olga almost choked on the constriction that formed instantly in her throat. 'I have had to go away. I hope you understand, but this is something that I must do. I missed my first opportunity. Now I must take my second.' Olga drew a deep breath and closed her eyes. *No!* she raged silently. She knew without question what Pyotr was saying.

Repeated demands from Masha forced Olga to open her eyes. She explained again that she couldn't read the book. Olga glanced back over at Oksana. The girl was staring attentively at her mother with dark eyes. 'It's okay,' Olga whispered in English. She moved quickly to dry her face. She pressed on Oksana's mattress – the closest she could come to touching her. '*Vsyo* okay. *Ladno?*'

The girl returned to her sad pose. Masha began an incessant repetition of a cereal commercial jingle. Olga returned to Pyotr's letter. This time she reined in her emotions. She bottled them up. She ground her teeth together and read.

'This is not something that I want to do. No, that's not true. I do want to do this. But I would not be so selfish if not for the fact that our life can never be normal until this is done. We can never live the life you dream of living unless we are free from fear. We've tried to ignore the evil, to pretend it didn't exist, but it does. And fate punished you and the girls for a single mistake that I made. I will try to correct that mistake. But I will also try to return home to you. For, you see, I want that more than anything else, Olya. To live in a small house with you on a quiet street. And I swear by God Almighty that I will try. I swear to you that I will, Olya. With all my love to you, Oksana, Mashenka – Pyotr.'

Olga began to sob. She couldn't help it. Now the girls would see! Even the searing pain from her incisions couldn't stop it.

The door burst open. In walked a nurse. 'You need some pain medication, Mrs Andreev?'

Olga looked around. Oksana lay staring – frightened – with both thumbs pressed down on the call button.

OUTSIDE SOFLYSK, SIBERIA
April 8, 0845 GMT (1845 Local)

Chin's ears were still ringing. His head was pounding. He staggered back for a company meeting. Officers only. The other platoon leaders were gathered in the open. Under shelter of a tree. He stumbled, almost fell right in front of them He expected ridicule. But instead Lieutenant Hung asked, 'How many'd you lose?' All three of the others wore visible bandages from light wounds.

'Four,' Chin replied. 'I'm down to sixteen men.'

Hung snorted. Not really a laugh. 'You know how many I have from my original platoon? *Five!*' He was shushed by the others. 'Five out of thirty-two!'

Chin sat in the silence. 'You had some bad luck on that frozen lake,' he sympathized.

The supply platoon leader unexpectedly hissed out a curse. 'Where's our *air support?*' he whispered angrily. He drew cautionary looks and gestures. 'They keep pushing us *on* and *on* and *on!*' the boiling man continued. 'We're doing *our* job. Where's the *air* force?'

Everyone looked around nervously. Platoon leaders were disappearing. People everyone knew. And not from combat, but from security squads. They marched in, read a charge, took a man . . . usually an officer.

'Where's the captain?' Chin asked. A couple of bitter laughs greeted his mention of their commanding officer. 'Is the company meeting still on?' Chin tried. He got shrugs and frowns. 'Because I really need some more ammo,' Chin mentioned to the supply platoon leader.

The man could barely contain his disgust. 'Get in line. The last supplies we got, we stole out of the 1104th's regimental depot.'

Chin's fellow officers all wore concerned looks on their faces. 'Are you saying our supplies are being cut off?' Chin asked.

His question instantly angered the supply platoon leader. 'Why do they *send* us these fucking sodbusters!' he asked the others.

'Our supply lines are stretched too long,' Hung explained.

'Because we're advancing,' Chin protested. 'We're *winning*. We haven't hit anything solid in *weeks!*'

'Until this morning,' another officer commented. 'That artillery wasn't hit-and-run shit. It was a sustained barrage – maybe fifteen minutes. And when we pushed on, we ran right into prepared positions. By the time we crawled back, I'd lost *six* men.'

Heads were nodded in agreement. 'There's something up there,' Hung ventured. 'When we got the orders to move to our night positions, they were four kilometers back from where we made contact. Four kilometers!' He looked from eye to eye – even briefly catching Chin's gaze.

'And those troops you ran into up there,' the supply officer said. 'They're Americans.' The words had an ominous ring. 'Everybody was talking about it at the battalion depot.'

'What the hell are they doing out *here*?' Chin asked. 'We're in the middle of nowhere.'

'This is as far as we go,' Hung said. He had a distant look. 'It's the end of our "glorious victory"!'

Chin looked around to ensure they weren't overheard. 'You think we're gonna *lose*?' Chin asked to make sure he understood.

'Oh, Chin,' Hung replied. He frowned and shook his head. 'I can't decide whether I pity or envy you. You're the perfect citizen. The "everyman." You believe we're winning the war because they tell you so. And when the hammer comes down on the anvil, you'll believe whatever lies they use to explain that, too.' He was being totally unfair, Chin felt, but there was a strange tone of compassion in his voice. 'I'm only gonna say this once.' He twisted to make certain they were alone and then caught the return gaze of each man – ending finally with Chin. 'The real enemy isn't four kilometers to the north,' he said quietly, slowly. 'It's two thousand kilometers to the south.'

A silence descended on the group. It was a chance Chin welcomed, for he had a lot to consider. Hung had suffered the same hardships as Chin. He and his platoon had more than once laid down the fire that had allowed Chin's platoon to withdraw. Chin had done the same for him. They were joined by a bond of common experience despite their dislike of each other. Chin could conclude only one thing from

Hung's comment. He'd just stated that the enemy was not NATO, but the Communist Party. For Beijing was two thousand kilometers to the south.

Lieutenant Hung was a traitor. He'd guessed as much ever since he'd found him reading English in the barracks bathroom. His views were treasonous. He should be shot for them. But he'd shared that most intimate confidence with only three other men. Chin was one of them. A new bond had been established.

UNRUSFOR HEADQUARTERS, KHABAROVSK
April 10, 0300 GMT (1300 Local)

'Cut!' Kate Dunn said to Woody. He lowered the camera from his shoulder. She turned back to the German colonel. 'We've got enough footage of people talking about supplies and logistics. What I need now is someone who'll talk about strategy. How you're gonna beat the Chinese army.'

The man shrugged. 'But this *is* how we are going to beat them,' he replied. 'We are going to keep our vehicles rolling. Our ammunition loads full. Our mobile troops will fight three, four, five engagements in one day. The Chinese may fight only once or twice per week. We open their lines, and we will pour through it at sixty kilometers per hour.'

'Can you show me when and where on the map?'

'If you want maps and pins, Ms Dunn, you should be down with the divisions. Better yet the brigades. We provide heavy weapons and air support. But our job is mainly to build up and move stores.' He shrugged.

Woody flashed a goofy smile. They headed back to their cavernous quarters. Kate looked at her notes. Their coverage was dry as dust. A lot of headquarters shots. The same thing over and over. They rarely got air time. Woody lit another joint in the bathroom. He sat on the toilet with the door open. 'They don't air interviews about building log roads. They *get* pictures of it! And what do we have tomorrow?' She tapped her pad. 'Tagging boxes with bar codes!'

From the bathroom came a loud sucking sound. 'We could use that stuff from the officers' club.'

'*What?*'

'Yeah. It kinda reminded me of that scene in *Star Wars*. You know. From that bar with all the aliens. Everybody speaking different languages.'

'That's a *great* idea, Woody! Just great! I think blazing battlefields and rows of attackers are a bit *derivative* by this point! We could do a two-hour documentary on how people relaxed from all the *stresses*. Maybe viewers are ready for the *entertainment* side of the largest offensive since World War Two!'

Woody didn't respond. After a moment, the hissing sound again filled the room.

Kate threw her pen to the pad. The most dramatic footage they'd shot was of the quiet perimeter thirty miles out. The defenses were so well-manned that the Chinese hadn't challenged them since the early days of the war. There were combat flights lifting off at the airbase. But how many night afterburner shots can you use?

Woody emerged from the bathroom. He sat at the desk beside Kate. 'Go see Clark. Tell him you need to get up to the front. Work your magic on the guy. He's already gotten out of this v.hat he wanted.'

'And what was that?'

'How many stories have we done about outnumbered defenders?' Kate didn't answer. 'And how many have we done about the counter-attack we know is coming?'

'Yeah, but . . .' she began. Woody shrugged. Kate grew incensed. Humiliated. She tried to force out a laugh, without much success. 'And I suppose you've thought this all *along?*' He shrugged again. 'All right!' She rose and nodded. '*Okay!*' She headed for the door.

'Come in!' Clark said from his desk.

'It's a Ms Dunn,' the NCO announced from the doorway to his office. 'She's with NBC News.'

'I know who she is.' Clark covered some of the paper on his desk. 'Bring her in.' He rose.

'General Clark,' Kate said the moment she entered. 'I have a proposition to put to you.'

'Won't you have a seat?'

She hesitated, then said, 'No, thank you. I'd like to stand.' Clark sank into his chair. She began to pace. 'Here's my problem. I've gotten some great background stories. I can truly say that I now appreciate just how dedicated all the people you've got working for you are. And the perspective I've gotten from Khabarovsk . . .! Well! It gives me an excellent understanding of all the behind-the-scenes work that goes into running an army.'

'I'm glad you came by,' Clark interrupted. 'I've seen all your reports. You've done an admirable job. You've kept your part of the bargain. But I was going to ask if you'd be interested in getting some shots of the action? Being there when the balloon goes up. Maybe follow some of the lead elements in the counter-attack. Meeting the men and women at the sharp end of the stick. What do you think?'

'Well . . . That's a *great* idea! Thanks! Yes! I think I'll take you up on it.'

Clark nodded. 'Okay.' She grinned. 'Get your things packed. It's time.' The grin faded.

PART IV

'The micro-social laws control the individual. They define human interaction on the small scale. They tend to restrain, to inhibit, to control. The macro-social laws control the masses. They define human interaction on the large scale. They tend to liberate, to unchain, to unleash. The same person who would cry at the pathetic sight of a wounded animal might chant loudly for war, for death, for the indiscriminate destruction of men, women and children by bomb and by bullet. Civilization has tamed the individual. But in the collective heart of the mob there courses the blood of primitive man. Both the micro- and macro-social laws must be understood for the effective manipulation of human beings.'

Valentin Kartsev (posthumously)
'The Laws of Human History'
Moscow, Russia

Chapter Twenty

THE WHITE HOUSE, WASHINGTON, D.C.
April 11, 1400 GMT (0900 Local)

The steps of the portico were filled with people as Gordon's wheelchair was lowered to the drive. They all applauded politely, which did little to drown out the jeers and bullhorns of protesters in Lafayette Park. Cameras rolled as the orderly wheeled Gordon up the green ramp. Elaine followed and smiled, followed and smiled.

Still more staffers lined the halls of the White House. Although his family was now comfortably ensconced in the ornate mansion, it was Gordon's first visit to his new home.

'Welcome back, sir,' aides called out – aides whom Gordon had never met.

'Give 'em hell!' someone shouted – a line that drew nervous laughter from all around.

Slowly, the crowds thinned until the only people lining the corridor were mute, pinch-lipped Secret Service agents. Daryl waited beside Gordon's desk in the Oval Office.

Gordon had grown somewhat accustomed to making the executive decisions called for by the presidency. But he was totally unprepared to enter the Oval Office. His now familiar national security staff mouthed words of welcome as he was rolled up to the beautiful desk. Gordon grew flushed – overwhelmed by emotion.

For the first time, he truly felt the awesome power which he had assumed. He laid his hands on the surface of the desk. All was neat and carefully arrayed. Pens, writing paper, a single file folder. He opened the drawer and was surprised to find paper clips, clamps and other office supplies. Gordon looked upon the desk as a museum piece, but it was obviously intended for real work.

For my work, he thought – awestruck.

'Let's reconvene this meeting later on,' Daryl said after an extended survey of Gordon's face. 'Say half an hour.' He herded the group out of the office. When the door was closed, Gordon was alone with Daryl and Elaine.

They exchanged inquisitive looks and then all broke out laughing.

'Where's my chair?' Gordon asked with a grin.

'I had them take it out,' Elaine answered. 'I figured until you get out of that wheelchair it'd be . . .'

'No,' Gordon replied, shaking his head. 'Uh-uh. I want the chair.'

Daryl went to the phone. Within seconds a secretary rolled the padded desk chair up to the knee space. Daryl and Elaine helped ease Gordon onto the smooth leather.

Despite the discomfort he felt from the jostling, he sighed on contact with the soft upholstery. 'Now, that's more like it,' he said. His eyes roamed the room in amazement. After the prolonged tour, they landed on the lone folder lying atop the desk. 'Not exactly a crushing workload,' Gordon said as he reached for the thin press-board file. Elaine and Daryl waited in silence.

When he opened the folder, he found a speech printed out in oversized draft type. The first words were 'My fellow Americans . . .'

Gordon looked up.

'I had some speechwriters give it a try,' Daryl explained, 'just to get a first draft on paper for when you got out.'

Gordon shifted his gaze to Elaine.

'The State of the Union is less than a week away, honey,' she said. 'We just didn't want you to exhaust yourself having to start from scratch.'

'I told you both that I was going to write this speech myself,' Gordon said slowly. He looked down at the paper attached to the top of the file with a clip. He turned the pages. Skimmed it. Line after line of total bullshit. It said nothing in a hundred separate sound bites.

He tossed the folder into the trash and began searching the drawers. When he found a leather folder enclosing a legal pad, he pulled a pen out of its desktop holder and wrote 'State of the Union Address' at the top of the page. 'My fellow Americans,' he began – the only words he used from the professionals' first draft.

After a paragraph, Gordon looked up to see Daryl and Elaine still standing there.

'I guess I'll get back to work,' Elaine said pleasantly. She rounded the desk and kissed Gordon on the cheek. 'I'm writing an article for *Good Housekeeping* magazine on what being First Lady means to me. They sent my first try back because it didn't make enough references to the debts I owe to my "predecessors" in the civil rights movement. My *predecessors* – can you believe the gall!' she said with obvious humor. She headed for the door. 'I'm thinking about changing the title to "Why Malcolm X Led Me to the Republican Party."'

Gordon kept writing, but a smile crept onto his face. The door closed. Daryl waited patiently. Gordon wrote for a while longer, and then he flipped back to the first page. Without looking up – without needing to check to confirm that Daryl was still there – Gordon said, 'Okay, I'm done.'

'Done with what?' Daryl asked.

'With the speech.'

Daryl took the pad, thumbed the bottom edge of the paper, and counted the pages. 'Gordon! That's less than ten minutes *long*!'

'I'll speak slowly.'

'But Gordon . . .! This is the State of the *Union*!'

'Lincoln delivered the Gettysburg Address in three minutes.'

'But we've pinned *every*thing on this address!'

'Read it,' Gordon replied. Daryl hesitated. 'Go on. Read it.'

Daryl raised the pad. He read it without saying a word. When he was done, he looked up. He obviously didn't know what to say. 'This is what you wanta do?' he finally asked. Gordon nodded. Daryl pursed his lips and shrugged. 'You don't even want to mention the counter-attack? How we're winning the war even as you speak? There's a pretty dramatic moment there you're taking a pass on.'

'I'll let the military successes speak for themselves.' Gordon leaned forward. 'Daryl, the war is a part of this, but only a part. This speech is about something bigger. I didn't just sit down here and bang that thing out. I've been doing a lot of thinking these last few months. I very intentionally didn't write anything down until I was sure in my mind what I wanted to say. And that's what I want to say, Daryl,' Gordon pointed at the pad. 'That's it.'

Daryl arched his eyebrows and nodded. 'Okay. But let's not let this thing out before you deliver it. Unless, that is, you want a parade of every party notable in the country traipsing through here politely suggesting you cut down on the pain medication.' Daryl re-read the first part of the speech. 'You know, you could toss out just a couple of policy ideas so the pundits would have something to sink their teeth into.'

'No policy ideas, Daryl. No programs. No legislative initiatives. Nothing on the budget or taxes or government or welfare reform. No social issues or doctrines of foreign policy. Not even a mention of the war.'

'You're sticking to the "vision-thing," huh?' Daryl asked. Gordon nodded. '*Oka-ay.* I'll type it myself,' he said as he turned for the door. 'Shouldn't take long.'

AMUR RIVER, SIBERIA
April 12, 1720 GMT (0220 Local)

The overcast sky blanketed Captain Hadley with a sense of security. He'd never felt it on prior trips to the Amur. The clouds held the warmth of the day beneath them. Hadley found himself unzipping his gear during the arduous trek through the deep forest drifts.

But clouds also meant darkness. No moon or starlight penetrated the overcast sky. That was both a blessing and a curse. A blessing in that his men carried night-vision goggles and the Chinese didn't. The point and rear men and machine-gunner wore theirs constantly. But the dim light was also a hazard. Nothing triggered a firefight more certainly than stepping right on an ambusher.

Hadley heard curses from the line up ahead. It was the second time he'd heard noise from his men. It was probably nothing more than a low branch. They were growing too comfortable with these missions. Not once in their five trips had they seen any Chinese. That bred a sense of solitude. Of being all alone in an impossibly big space. *That*, in turn, led to them growing sloppy. All it took was one chance encounter for them to get swallowed up by endless forests.

Four men headed out onto the ice with the drill. The man in front rolled the wheel which measured the distance. The three who followed . . .

A resounding '*crunch*' broke the silence like a gunshot. Hadley scanned the white ice for the source. Three men – he counted only three. Two more men rushed out onto the frozen river. Hadley followed them down the bank. It was his first time out in the open. He hadn't realized just how exposed it felt.

Brief shouts and gasps for air could be heard. Everyone was lying on their bellies and inching forward. 'Help!' came a watery splutter. It was followed by the splashing sounds of a drowning man. Hadley and the two men with him dropped to their stomachs and began to crawl.

The man was flailing. Men held each forearm. They were counting in unison. When they said '*Three!*' they pulled with loud grunts. For an instant they hoisted the soldier from the black river water.

He gasped for air and coughed before being dragged back under. It was as if a great shark held his feet and fought his rescuers. The soldier slowly sank into the ever-expanding hole.

On the next pull the two men got a rope under his armpits. Hadley and the reinforcements went upstream of the hole. They begin a tug-of-war against the powerful current. They sat on the ice and pulled against the raging force of the water.

Hadley got to his feet and dug in his heels. Without saying a word the other men did the same. Hadley could feel the ice almost break underneath him. Several times he repositioned his feet at the last second. Two more men arrived just then from the bank. The five men dragged the fallen man out of the water. The medical officer slipped an oxygen mask over his face. The others stripped their comrade of his clothing in silence. Off came his parka, his liner, his long underwear. Off came his boots and his shell and his insulated leggings. The dark-skinned African-American sergeant lay naked against the white ice.

They put dry clothes on him right there. Everyone carried extra clothing. They dried and dressed the man from head to foot. It was done as quickly as could be expected. Even so he suffered extreme hypothermia.

'Everybody back to the treeline!' Hadley ordered.

'What about the core sample?' asked the lieutenant who led the team with the drill.

'*Fuck* the core sample!' Hadley replied. 'We're outta here! Call for a medevac. Ditch Jeter's wet clothes and the drill in a drift. We'll double-time it to the emergency pick-up zone.'

'But our orders to . . .' the lieutenant began to object.

'*Listen*, West Point!' Hadley shot back. 'They wanta know how thick that ice is? Well, we got 'em their answer! Mission aborted!'

UNRUSFOR HEADQUARTERS, KHABAROVSK
April 12, 2000 GMT (0600 Local)

Clark pinned the new silver oak leaf cluster on Reed's epaulets. He then shook Reed's hand. 'Congratulations, Lieutenant Colonel,' Clark said. 'You've earned that bird.' There was applause from the gathering of staff. Reed was grinning. Clark had a call to make.

He went into his office and shut the door. He picked up the dedicated line, spoke to the Pentagon operator, and waited. 'General Clark?' finally came the voice of the man he was waiting for.

'Mr President, I've given the action order. Operation Winter Harvest will be launched on April 14th – in two days.'

'Wonderful!' Davis said. 'The timing couldn't be any better from where I sit. You give me five days of battlefield successes, and we'll win that vote on the 19th. Then, we win the war.'

When they hung up, there was a knock on the door. It was Reed. He again looked sheepish. 'I have a favor to ask, sir,' he said without looking Clark's way. 'I'd like to get out into the field. Help out where I can. Even if it's a staff position somewhere. I'd just like to . . .'

'I understand,' Clark said. 'But I need you, too.' Reed wasn't going to object. 'We'll keep our eyes open. Maybe something will come along.' Reed nodded. 'Now, let's start issuing unit orders.'

BIROBIDZHAN FIREBASE, SIBERIA
April 13, 2200 GMT (0800 Local)

'Light duty's over, fuck face.' Stempel looked up from his computer. 'Hey!' he shouted at his squadmates, who crowded into the door of the supply bunker. He greeted them like long-lost friends. He'd been to the perimeter to visit his squad several times. But this was their first trip to the rear to see him. They exchanged high fives. Harold's wounds had healed but he winced from habit. 'You guys gettin' some R and R or something?' he asked.

'Knock it off!' an unseen NCO boomed through the open entrance to his office.

McAndrews grabbed his crotch and pulled. He then looked around at the bare sandbagged walls. 'So you got heat in here too, huh?'

'Yeah,' Stempel replied, proudly showing off their electric space heater. 'And they let us sleep here.'

'This is too *fine!*' Patterson said.

The master sergeant emerged. 'What the hell're you doin'?' he shouted.

'We come here to get Stemp,' Patterson replied.

'And who the hell sent you?'

'The CO himself. Said he was takin' Stemp off light duty and that we was to come'n get him.'

'He can't just up and yank one of my people outa here!' the man snarled. 'Shit! Who's gonna log supplies in?'

Stempel's squadmates looked at each other. 'I will!' several said at the same time.

The grumbling master sergeant went out in search of an officer. Stempel scrambled to gather his things. The visitors eyed Stempel's laptop computer. On it glowed an inventory management program. They helped themselves to a six-pack of Diet coke they found in a rucksack.

'Shit, man!' Stempel objected. 'Sarge is gonna tear you a new asshole if you take those!'

'*Fuck* him!' Patterson replied as he slipped two cans in his parka. 'Let him hump his butt outta Club Med here and come find me.'

Music began to play from the sergeant's office.

'Jeeze!' Stempel shouted. He ran toward the cramped room. Two of the guys were dancing to the country music on the master sergeant's boom box. 'What the . . . !' Stempel shouted, then leapt for the 'Stop' button. The bunker fell quiet save for the laughter. 'If he heard you usin' up his batteries like that he'd *kill* you!'

Chavez's M-16 rose instantly to his shoulder. Stempel stared down the 40-mm grenade launcher under its barrel from a distance of two feet. There was a grenade in the launcher's chamber, and thirty rounds in the banana clip. 'Born to Kill' was scrawled on the man's white cloth helmet cover. Chavez relaxed and pointed the weapon away. But the grin on the man's face wasn't reassuring. Everyone in the squad kept their distance from Chavez.

They hurried out of the bunker before the NCO returned. Stempel joined his squadmates in the fresh, cool air. The whine of jet engines was nearly constant. Giant C-17s had been landing for days. Their noise had become a part of the background.

'Ain't that just like a rear-area motherfucker,' Patterson said. He grabbed Stempel's bulging field pack and rocked him from side to side. 'Got so much shit he can't even hump it.' They all descended on the overflowing pack.

'Hey!' Stempel shouted as they began to toss his things into the slush. 'Come on!' When his load was lighter, they headed down the communications trench toward the perimeter. Stempel collected a few of the essentials they'd discarded, but left most of the stuff where it lay. He hurried to catch up with the others, who walked single file down the narrow slit in the earth.

They passed into the wider security trench that ran alongside the runway. Transports offloaded huge crates of supplies. Stempel's squadmates yelled taunts at the newly arrived airmen. 'Welcome to Hell!' one shouted. The Air Force shits wore ear protectors, but they took the oversized headphones off and walked over toward them. 'You got any booze or pot?' Patterson asked.

'Yeah,' one of the airmen replied, laughing. 'Sure! What you got to trade?'

'How 'bout a Chinese SKS? Got blood on it and everything! You can tell the folks back home you killed him yourself!'

The Air Force troops all stood around laughing. They'd obviously just flown in to help unload. In the day or so since Stempel had last been by, the airfield had become jam-packed with crates, fuel bladders, trucks and Humvees.

'If you got a string of Chinese ears or noses or somethin',' came the reply from an airman, 'I'll get you a fifth of Scotch!'

Patterson wheeled to walk backwards and shouted, 'I'll get you a necklace of Chinese *dicks* for a fifth of Scotch, motherfucker!' Everyone laughed. The airmen donned their ear protectors. A giant C-17 lumbered to the edge of the tarmac. 'Who's policin' the wire this morning?' Patterson asked.

'They don't got no fifth of fuckin' *Scotch!*' McAndrews replied derisively.

'You heard the guy!' Patterson shot back. There were snorts from some of the others. 'No, really! They're just lyin' around out there. It's not like they're gonna use 'em again!'

'Patterson, you are one *sick* motherfucker!'

When Patterson finally gave up on the possibility of a trade, Stempel asked, 'Is there any news about reinforcements?'

'Ain't you heard?' McAndrews said. 'Man, Stemp's gonna drop a load in his trousers when he hears this.' There were chuckles.

'What?' Harold asked. The line of men halted. Their momentum bunched them up. Men rested against the walls of the trench. Stempel looked each man in the eye. They all in turn stared back. 'What the hell's goin' on?' Stempel asked again.

'Some fuckin' general back in the Pentagon thinks we've been fuckin' off around here,' Patterson said. 'Thinks maybe Uncle Sam ain't gettin' a fair day's work outta us.'

Stempel shook his head. 'I don't understand.'

'We got "The Word." We're puttin' on our full battle rattle and goin' over the top.'

'What?' Stempel said. 'Like a patrol?' That didn't sound too bad.

But heads were shaking. 'We're goin' on the offensive,' McAndrews said with a faraway look in his eye. 'Tomorrow morning before first light we're packin' up and pushin' south.'

'Toward the *border*?' Stempel asked – incredulous. 'Toward *China?*' No one answered his question. But they didn't need to. The looks on their faces told all.

'Hey!' Patterson said. 'Look at that!' He pointed back toward the Air Force pukes.

A loadmaster was walking backwards down the angled rear ramp of a C-17. He waved his two flashlights like batons. In the dim light of the cavernous cargo bay you could see the metal tracks. Into the sunlight rolled an armored fighting vehicle. A white-painted Bradley with its 25-mm chain gun and four TOW anti-tank launchers.

'Son-of-a-*bitch!*' McAndrews slowly intoned.

A ripple of excitement quickly spread through the small group. 'Guess we're ridin' in *style!*' Patterson chirped. There were high fives of celebration. They hurried toward the perimeter – stopping along the way to pass news of this latest development.

THE KREMLIN, MOSCOW, RUSSIA
April 14, 0100 GMT (0300 Local)

Despite the late hour, Kartsev paced the office nervously. His glowing but muted television was tuned to the National Broadcasting Company, but he'd seen no reports from Miss Dunn. The other reports on the war meant nothing to him. The course of the war was what it was, and it affected him little.

That's the problem, he thought. *I've become disengaged. I'm no longer an actor, but an observer.*

'But that's the whole *point!*' he said out loud. As a scientist, his role was to observe and record. Introducing a catalyst was one thing. You must apply the proper stimulus to propel the system into action. But if you intervene thereafter, you alter the very dynamic you're attempting to analyze. You become a part of the process, not its chronicler.

The entire debate depressed him further. For it was not new, it was stale. They were words he'd already written. He was simply tilling the same soil as before and not plowing any new ground.

Kartsev caught himself standing in the center of the bright red oriental rug. His eyes focused and he looked at his surroundings. He was always alone. But he occasionally got the sense of how he would appear to some omniscient eye. He moved quickly to the bookshelves beside the fireplace and began to idly peruse his eclectic collection of treatises.

But there was nothing new to be gleaned from them. They were as detached from modern-day life as he was. He might as well have lived in the nineteenth century. It was really a time that better suited him. A time when people tackled the broader questions. But if he'd lived back then, his insights would now be collecting dust on some shelf like those of Marx and Malthus did on his. He shook his head and frowned. *Besides, my studies would've been impossible in their time,* he thought. *They didn't have the technology necessary to conduct them.*

Kartsev returned a book to the shelf. 'I've got to . . . !' he began, but he didn't know how to finish. With grinding teeth he grew determined to climb out of his box. He marched over to his desk and hit his intercom button. 'Hello?' he said, and then waited.

Nothing.

'Hel-*lo-o-o!*' he repeated impatiently.

Still nothing.

With eyes darting all about, Kartsev could wait no longer. He stormed toward the door – half terrified at the unknown that lay beyond, half furious that some aide was asleep on the job. As he neared the door . . . it opened.

Kartsev's heart leapt into his throat. But it was only a disheveled aide. *Not yet,* Kartsev thought. 'I want . . .' he began. But he wasn't sure what he wanted. He cocked his head and searched for the elusive thought.

The aide stood there watching him like the omniscient eye. Kartsev looked up so abruptly that the man recoiled noticeably. The reaction was interesting. It was human and involuntary. Kartsev smiled. The man swallowed – his Adam's apple bobbing.

I need more contact like this, Kartsev thought as the words began to fill his head. Words he would write down. Words about the power and purpose of terror. '*Let them hate, so long as they fear,*' he recalled. 'Who said that?' He vaguely remembered the Latin, so he knew the author was Roman.

'Sir?' the ashen aide said out of the blue.

If I can get this kind of material from just one human interaction . . . Kartsev thought. He looked up. 'I want to hold a rally,' he said. The man screwed up his face and cocked his head. '*Sir?*'

'A *rally*. You do speak Russian, don't you?'

'Y-yes, sir, but . . . What sort of rally?'

'A large one. In Red Square. I want Red Square filled from end to end.'

'With people?'

'No, you idiot! With goats and chickens!' The man looked more uncertain than before. More frightened. '*Yes,* with people! I want to address a gathering of our people in Red Square. I will talk to them about the historic times in which we live. The . . . the *fascinating* opportunities we all share in writing the history of the Twenty-first Century!'

The aide was terrible at masking his thoughts. His face was an open book. Kartsev could almost hear him recite a list of practical problems in getting crowds to turn out.

'Offer them bread,' Kartsev said almost dejectedly. 'And vodka.' He turned. It was always so disappointing to come face to face with the undeniable apathy of his people. He walked around to his desk. To his computer on whose screen glowed a waiting, half-written page. *Future historians will write* volumes *about these times,* Kartsev thought in annoyance, *and all those louts are interested in is bread and vodka!*

The aide still stood in the doorway. 'Well?' Kartsev asked.

The man cleared his throat. 'You want me to organize a large rally in Red Square. And offer bread and vodka to draw people there.' Kartsev waited, then nodded at the dimwit. 'And . . . and *you* will address the rally?'

It wasn't really a question. It was an opportunity for Kartsev to change his mind. The impudent son-of-a-bitch was second-guessing him. Kartsev glowered back at the man . . . but he hesitated. He ruled, as he had written in Chapter Twelve, through a complex system whose main underpinning was based upon the 'principle of coincidence of interests.' *This* man – whoever he was – owed all he had to Kartsev. His comfortable apartment, his food and drink and luxury, the girls or boys that amused him sexually. Everything. Therefore any risk to Kartsev was a threat to him as well. That was *why* the system worked as it did with very little maintenance required by Kartsev.

And the man clearly sensed danger. Kartsev had to admit it wasn't risk-free. But he needed something – something big – with which to finish his manuscript, and this had a certain symmetry to it. After all, Chapter One had begun with a rally in Red Square.

'*May* Day!' Kartsev blurted out – instantly grinning with pleasure. 'We'll have a good, old-fashioned May Day Parade, only with no parade – just a rally. All right? Now go! Make all the preparations.'

The man stood there – unmoving.

'I said *go!*' The aide left. Kartsev sat before the keyboard – ready to type. His mind was again brimming with ideas. The late hour didn't matter to him now. With his fingers poised over the keys, one last doubt lingered. The young aide was clearly worried by his plans. Kartsev imagined that the man's preparations for the event would include some of a purely personal nature. Fake passport, cash, airline tickets. Such an escape might still be possible for a junior aide. But no escape was available to Kartsev. His remaining days – however many there were – would be spent in his windowless office. He could never hope to evade the 'justice' of a vengeful world.

So why not take some risk here and there? he asked himself. He looked around the empty room. *What is it that I have to lose?*

He began to type – the keys clacking rapidly as if in a race against time.

'THE FARM', WEST VIRGINIA
April 14, 2300 GMT (1800 Local)

Pyotr Andreev followed the instructor to the range. It was a sunny day. The place looked like a public park. They stopped at a picnic table with bench seats covered by a small shingled roof. On the table there were weapons.

'All right, two fifty-three,' the instructor began – calling Pyotr by his anonymous case number. 'What we have here is your primary weapon – a semi-auto .50 caliber sniper rifle, military issue – and your choice of secondary weapons.' The selection included an Uzi, a Heckler & Koch MP5, and an Ingram MAC-10. The man started to go over the strengths and weaknesses of the lot, but Pyotr picked up the Ingram. It was the .45 caliber version, not the lighter 9-mm. He slapped the magazine in the pistol grip.

The instructor followed him the short distance to the target range. 'The MAC-10 is a helluva weapon for close-in combat,' he said as he stopped beside Pyotr. Three plastic jugs filled with water sat atop a pitted wall of concrete blocks. A thick earthen embankment lay behind. Single shots cracked in the distance. Pyotr held the weapon at his hip. He grasped it firmly with his right hand and wrapped his left in the leather strap that hung from the muzzle. 'It fires standard .45-caliber pistol ammo. The rounds' tremendous stopping power is also the weapons' main drawback. It tends to ride straight up when you . . .'

Pyotr squeezed the trigger. The weapon thundered. It bucked and shook and shot flame a foot out the end of its short barrel. Pyotr fought it for a second and a half, then the weapon fell silent. 'God*damm*it!' the instructor yelled. '*I* give the Goddamn order to fire on this range! You do that one more time and . . .!'

The instructor fell silent. His mouth was still open. He stared down the range toward the targets. There were no jugs on the wall. 'Cease fire,' he said as an afterthought. He took off down the range. Pyotr followed. Shredded pieces of twisted plastic lay on the ground behind the wall. The soil around the targets was dry. The water had been sprayed all over the soggy embankment.

Pyotr had fought the gun's ferocious recoil with his left hand in the leather strap. He'd slewed the weapon from left to right when it wanted to rise toward the sky. The instructor straightened, but never looked his way. '*Don't* fire any weapon on *my* range again without my *go*-ahead! You *got* that?'

Pyotr nodded. They had asked him to say as little as possible. His accent betrayed too many things.

The instructor picked up a new jug of water and put it on the wall. When he turned, he saw Pyotr pouring water from another container down the wall on the end opposite the target. 'We use these gallon milk containers 'cause they're the same density as a human torso when filled with water.' When the light gray blocks turned dark, Pyotr tossed the jug and headed back to the picnic table. 'So,' his trainer said, 'you'll take the MAC. Let's move on to this mother.' He raised the .50-caliber rifle. 'It fires these,' he said, tilting the open top of an enormous black magazine so that Pyotr could see the stack of rounds inside. They were nearly five inches long. The thick, metal-jacketed bullets were propelled by an enormous charge. The cartridges were the width of a man's thumb. 'The magazine holds five rounds.'

'I would prefer a manual bolt,' Pyotr said, 'instead of a semi-auto.'

'I know where you're headed,' the instructor replied, shaking his head. 'But this bolt is rock solid. It gives an excellent, stable base to the chamber. It's every damn bit as accurate as any Springfield ever fired.'

Pyotr just frowned. The other rounds in the magazine were just excess weight. Like the old adage about striking at the king, you had to kill with your first blow.

'Get a feel for the weapon's weight,' the instructor said. Pyotr took the long rifle from his hands. 'Weighs twenty-eight pounds with the scope.' Pyotr took the magazine from him as well. 'Thirty-two fully loaded.' Pyotr slammed the magazine home and yanked the bolt back against the stiff spring. 'No firing till I say, remember?' Pyotr safed the weapon and nodded. 'Let's head back a ways. You don't get any fifty-foot shots with this thing.'

As they walked, the instructor lectured on the principles of sniping. Elementary things like surveillance, concealment, light, wind. An introduction to long-range killing. They reached their destination – 250 meters from the target, according to the sign. The instructor climbed up to the firing position. Pyotr didn't follow. 'My range is 425 meters,' Pyotr replied.

'Well, I know, but this is the first day.'

Pyotr and the man eyed each other. '425 meters,' Pyotr repeated.

The instructor picked up a small sandbag and they continued their walk. They also resumed the lecture. When the man informed Pyotr that the rifle wouldn't break down, Pyotr stopped in surprise. 'It's too delicate a weapon to allow field stripping and reassembly. The sight'll be zeroed in here – on the range. The elevation set for 425 meters. You just need to make sure you don't bang it around too damn much.'

'How the hell am I supposed to . . .?' Pyotr shut himself up. Infiltration was an operational detail. This man wouldn't know anything about it. The remainder of the way, Pyotr fumed over such a ridiculous choice for a weapon. Standing on the ground, it came up almost to his chest. And he was supposed to walk straight into Red Square carrying it.

There were range markers every twenty-five meters like on the driving range of a golf course. At 425, the instructor dropped the sandbag to the ground. Pyotr laid the rifle on its side with the barrel resting atop the bag. He began to stretch his muscles.

'Good, good,' the instructor said. 'A lot of people overlook the importance of good muscular relaxation. Do you have any natural tics or muscle contractions?' Pyotr shook his head. He leaned over to pull up a few sprigs of grass. 'Marksmanship is also a lot about breathing.' Pyotr let the grass fall from eye level. It drifted slightly to his left. 'Deep, regular breaths.' Pyotr lay on his stomach behind the weapon. The instructor lay down beside him, taking the lens covers off his oversized binoculars. 'When you get ready for the pull, switch to shallow, rhythmic breathing.' Pyotr pressed the huge butt plate of the rifle firmly against the hollow of his shoulder. He reached up and turned the windage knob one click to the plus side. 'Then, when you're settling in on the target, fill your lungs halfway and hold it.'

Pyotr peered through the sights with his eye nearly four inches behind the padded rear lens. At that distance, the scope's field of view tunneled to near extreme. But that was preferable to the tell-tale bloody ring around the eyes of rookie shooters. Besides, the water-soaked concrete blocks filled the sight nicely. By feel alone Pyotr switched the selector from 'Safe' to 'Fire.'

'*Hey*, douche bag!' the instructor snapped immediately.

'May I fire?' Pyotr asked.

'Not till I say!'

Pyotr waited. 'May I fire now?' he asked after a few seconds.

'All right, Mr Professional. Mr I-Know-What-The-Fuck-I'm . . .'

The shot rang out. Pyotr would've fired a second round almost instantly had his hand not risen out of habit to work the bolt. As it was, he got another round off in a heartbeat. Then another, and another, and another. Pyotr looked over at the instructor.

The man lowered the powerful binoculars from his eyes. 'You ready to do some listening for a change?' he asked testily.

'I always listen,' Pyotr replied.

'Yeah, well, I know you're on a fast track here, but there are some fundamentals that will help you hit your target next time. "One shot, one kill" – that's our motto.'

'But I hit the target,' Pyotr objected politely.

The CIA man raised his binoculars. 'That jug's still sitting there. If one of those rounds had even nicked the thing it'd be . . .' He froze. He presumably saw now the opposite end of the wall. He lowered the binoculars and got to his feet without looking at Pyotr. 'Safe that weapon,' he said as he headed for the target area. Pyotr followed.

There was a man-sized gap in the wall. The concrete blocks down which Pyotr had poured water were largely gone. Obliterated. Pieces no larger than a fist littered the ground all the way back to the embankment. The instructor – ex-military, judging from his short haircut – said, 'You fucked up our wall.' Pyotr apologized. The guy took a look at the western sky. 'It's gettin' late. Let's go get a beer.'

OUTSIDE SOFLYSK, SIBERIA
April 15, 1600 GMT (0200 Local)

Chin almost didn't see the others in the darkness. 'Where the hell have you been?' the company commander hissed.

'I brought a man back with me to look for an ambulance,' Chin explained.

'And so you go roaming around the countryside while we sit here waiting for you?'

'Where's your man?' Hung asked Chin.

'He died.'

His fellow lieutenants all fell quiet. The company commander let it drop. 'All right,' he said, 'we're pulling back.' That was it. Three months of driving ever northward – three months during which the merest suggestion of retreat could get you shot for treason – and now the orders to withdraw were so casually delivered.

'What's going on?' Hung asked.

'None of your business!' the captain shot back. 'You don't get paid to ask questions! You get paid to follow orders!'

'I haven't been *paid* in two months,' Hung mumbled.

'*What did you say?*' the CO replied. He was so angry his voice rose. Chin could hear the rustle of fabric as he checked the trees all around.

'I said I haven't been paid in two months . . . *sir*. And I haven't eaten in almost two days. And none of us has had a day off from combat in almost three weeks.'

There was silence. Everyone waited. 'Are you looking to get arrested?' the company commander asked in a low and menacing tone. 'Cause if you are, you can *forget* it! And while we're on the subject, orders have come down that if there are *any* more self-inflicted wounds in this regiment, the colonel will personally *finish* the job!'

'My man didn't shoot himself!' Hung objected. 'He was wounded in a firefight!'

'In the *foot*? It just so *happened* that he only lost a *toe* – his *little* toe at that?'

'It *happens!* People get shot all over! I had a man get his *balls* shot clean off! You think he did *that* on purpose? Two of my men lost their lower jaw . . . from the *same bullet!* One man got a flesh wound in his shoulder! Only he *died*, 'cause the bullet didn't ricochet *out* from his bone, like we thought! It tumbled *into* his chest! I lost my senior sergeant when he started complaining about a headache after an artillery barrage! When he passed out, we looked all over his body for the wound! We stripped him naked right in the snow 'cause he was turning white as a sheet! Somebody finally noticed he had a *ti-iny* speck of blood on his temple, and another under his hairline on the opposite side of his head! A metal *splinter* from one of the shell casings had gone *straight* through his brain! He didn't even know he'd been *hurt* till he keeled over dead four hours later!'

Hung had clearly forgotten whatever point he was making. But in his agitated state no one made any attempt to shut him up. When he ran out of steam, the company commander said simply, 'Get your men packed up and ready to pull back in an hour.'

'In the middle of the *night?*' Hung questioned. 'We're heading back toward our own guns in the middle of the *night?*'

'*Everybody's* pulling back!' the captain explained. 'Don't you *understand?* Can't you get what I'm saying through your thick *skulls?* One hour! Listen for the whistle!'

Chin had pulled his platoon in tight around him so as not to get separated in the darkness. In the distance he heard several tentative toots from whistles. He couldn't tell the one meant for his company from any of the others. But he decided it didn't really matter. 'Everybody up!' he ordered.

His men rose. They followed him back over ground they'd fought for the day before. The woods around them were alive with movement. They completely lost contact with their brother platoons. After the first few tense encounters with strangers, Chin and his men let down their guard. They even took comfort from the shadowy figures streaming south alongside them. The thought occurred to Chin that some might be American infiltrators. But he silently just wished the concern away. He was determined to avoid contact at all costs.

The first sign of danger he saw was lightning. At least that's what it looked like. But it lasted too long. And the rumble that arrived seconds later went on and on and on. The unearthly noise of the distant airstrike set his men talking.

'Quiet!' Chin snapped.

The next strike was much, much closer. The 'booms' could each be made out individually, though they still sounded out of time with the flashes. They were loud enough, however, to be jarring. Chin flinched with almost every string. They were brief strobes of a man-made thunderstorm. In the flickering light he could see fear quickly taking hold of his men's faces. Their eyes darted this way and that. Even their pace began to pick up.

Chin found himself being passed by jogging troops. His initial reaction was to command them to slow down. They were supposed to be following him. But on second thought he instead quickened *his* step, as did the other units against whom they brushed in the night.

The dark forests suddenly erupted with fire. Everyone threw themselves to the earth as the screeching jets tore through the sky overhead. They bombed the positions the Chinese had just abandoned. From a distance of almost a kilometer the explosions did little more than shake loose snow from the trees.

At least that was what Chin thought at first. Then – in the first lull in the bombing – men rose to their feet. They didn't jog now, they ran. 'Hold on!' Chin shouted, but they didn't listen. The few men who remained by Chin's side nervously searched the woods. When the bombing began again, someone shouted '*America-a-ans!*' at the top of his lungs.

That began the panic. All Chin could see in the fiery flashes were the moving forms of fleeing Chinese troops. But they were mistaken. Like a herd made anxious by an unfamiliar scent, they fled now from demons only imagined. He rose to run after his men. To collect them as a shepherd might round up his flock. But the 'pum-pum-pum' of a loud cannon to the rear drew his complete attention. Its rapid fire was like nothing he'd ever heard.

He knelt behind a tree and saw a large armored vehicle approaching to his right. As it raced through the woods its gun again opened fire. Glowing tracers shot far into the distance at incredible speed. It was already firing well past where Chin lay. Firing at some target that Chin couldn't even see. But the gunner on the speeding vehicle could see. He was as comfortable as a bat with his special sights.

An identical vehicle raced up on the opposite side of Chin. And there was another even further away. They were barreling at fifty kilometers per hour into the Chinese, who were panicked and offered no resistance. And how could anyone stop such a thing? All Chin had was his rifle and a single hand grenade.

459

ERIC L. HARRY

Just before the armored vehicles pulled even with Chin, he lay behind
the tree and pressed himself flat. The 'pum-pum-pum' of the automatic
cannon filled the woods. He lay there until the sound of the engines
receded. Then he lay there until he could no longer hear the guns
and the bombing runs. Then he waited for the sun to come up.

He didn't rise from that spot, in fact, until ordered at gunpoint.
Then, he rose carefully, slowly, his hands in air as the nervous Americans
shouted orders he didn't understand.

SOUTH OF URGAL, SIBERIA
April 16, 2300 GMT (1800 Local)

The crowded Bradley armored fighting vehicle rocked and bumped
along at high speed. Kate and Woody were thrown every which way,
banging shoulders and knees with the mechanized infantry squad.
Woody had tried at first to shoot the scene, but he'd given up with
mumbled complaints about bad light.

The men sat with their backs to the walls. They were quiet and
wore looks of deep concern. They were new to the war, Kate had
learned, as she did eve-of-battle interviews with several. They'd only
just flown into Siberia, having remained in Japan as part of the 'strategic
deception plan.' They looked little older than high-school boys, and
they had attempted unsuccessfully to hide their fears. All of which,
Kate knew, made for the first good footage in weeks.

The squad leader began talking on the radio. His words were almost
shouted, but Kate could barely hear them over the whining engine. He
traced coordinates on the map with his finger. He repeated, 'Roger
that! Roger that!'

When the sergeant got off the radio, he squatted in the narrow
center aisle. 'Listen up! We're gonna provide flank security to the
main breakthrough! When we dismount, I want everybody to follow
me toward a line of low ridges! We'll set up there and refuse the
east! One of the recon units up ahead sighted dismounted Chicom
infantry moving toward that ridge! We're gonna drop our packs and
double-time it so's we get up that ridge first!'

Even before he'd finished, the Bradley began to slow to a stop. The
engine noise dropped off noticeably. Men scrambled to get a hold of

460

their gear. The sergeant pulled his bulging pack toward the rear and knelt awkwardly amid the press of knees. The double doors opened. Men raced into the darkness outside. Kate and Woody were the last two out.

The doors closed and the Bradley took off. The soldiers all dropped their loads and raced for the dark outline of a hill. She and Woody followed, but very quickly they lost contact with the men. Woody grabbed Kate's arm and pulled her down into the snow.

'Woody!' Kate objected, but he hushed her angrily. 'Woody, we can't just loiter around here in the dark. That's more dangerous than . . .'

He tackled her flat to the ground. She didn't know what possessed him to crush her like that, but she lay there scanning the dark woods for danger. It took her a few moments to see the shadowy figures.

Nearly a dozen men emerged from the treeline. They walked slowly like a wary patrol. At first she thought surely they were Americans. But their differently shaped helmets were a dead giveaway.

Chinese!

Kate and Woody lay absolutely still. But it was no use. The Chinese headed straight for them. Each step of their approach was announced by the crunch and squeak of their boots.

Kate raised her head. The Chinese soldiers stood all around. They had no weapons. Their hands were raised to the tops of their helmets. Woody got to his feet.

'You guys are all under arrest,' Woody said. 'Get down on your knees.' He motioned, and then demonstrated what he wanted.

'Woody!' Kate cautioned. But the Chinese slowly sank to the ground – their hands still atop their heads. They whimpered – pathetically mouthing things in Chinese. Some cried. Their faces were frost-bitten. One man who was missing several teeth held up family photos and begged for his life. By the time the first American soldiers arrived, the number of prisoners had grown to almost a hundred.

Chapter Twenty-One

UNRUSFOR HEADQUARTERS, KHABAROVSK
April 17, 0400 GMT (1400 Local)

The table was abuzz when Clark entered the room. The din quickly dropped to dead silence. The commanders of the various national forces were obviously far too pleased with the results only twelve hours into the campaign. Clark resolved to set that right.

'The ice is already breaking at Luobei,' he announced. The intensity of the men's stares rose a notch. 'Recon overflights report black water visible across forty percent of the surface.' He tossed photos of the Amur River onto the table. The generals all reached for them at once. In moments, they were scrutinizing the black-and-white high-altitude shots. The previously solid white highway of ice was spotted with black like the coat of a Dalmatian. 'That ice could go any minute now, gentlemen,' Clark warned ominously.

'Thank God we're ahead of schedule,' the British commander said. He held his reading glasses at an angle to study a photo.

'We're not ahead of schedule, we're behind,' Clark retorted – drawing quizzical looks from the joint staff. 'I've accelerated the timetable. I want first units across that river in three days.'

A commotion now filled the room. 'That is impossible!' the French commander objected. He drew vigorous nods of support. 'That is demanding too great a price from the troops. And,' he said in a lowered voice and a sweep of his gaze around the table, 'it will leave us exposed to local attacks *all* along our flanks.'

Clark nodded to Major Reed, who began handing out the new timetable. 'The objectives are all the same,' Clark continued. 'On the basis, however, of our initial success in breaching the Chinese lines – and after review of the state of the ice on the Amur – the time to take those objectives has been reduced by half.'

Again there was a stir. But this was decidedly less vocal. What Clark was proposing was a risk-laden change. 'What about the danger to our flanks?' the senior German general inquired.

Clark finally sat. His delay in responding was not simply theater. He too was concerned at advancing so rapidly. Not only were they leaving their flanks largely unguarded, there were foregone opportunities and unforeseeable risks. Field commanders would be ordered to disregard their better judgment. To let pass chances to consolidate their positions by seizing terrain. To bypass hopefully immobilized Chinese formations. To plunge ahead with inadequate reconnaissance.

'We either win this war,' Clark began slowly, 'with *this* operation, or we lose it. Not to win the war here and now *is* to lose. That isn't a military fact, it's a political one. Each of us now knows after seeing Chinese units fold one after another that we can defeat their armies *north* of the Amur. We can kill or capture three hundred thousand men. Destroy all their heavy weapons. Seize their stores of supplies. Retake *all* of the territory they seized from Russia. And still lose the war in the process. Because no matter how successful this operation is *militarily*, our troops are going home within the year. And when we leave Siberia, we cede it to the half-million Chinese troops *south* of the Amur . . . *unless* they too are defeated.'

Clark knew he was stating the obvious. *Re*stating it for the hundredth time. But by their silence the joint staff allowed him to continue. To focus them on the war's bigger picture. For Clark's primary function as commander was to maintain his command's perspective on the war.

To ensure that their missions and plans remained consistent with overall geopolitical objectives.

'In order to attain total victory we have to risk total defeat. We have to put people across the Amur into China even though powerful forces remain operational to their rear. Even though we know that the day will come quite soon when they'll be cut off by the flowing ice. We're going for broke, gentlemen. *All* out. Starting right now, with those timetables before you.'

'Since you broached the subject,' the British commander interrupted – his brow knit as he studied the thick sheaf of papers – 'it appears you've made an error on page four.'

Everyone began flipping pages in their copies . . . except Clark. 'It's not a typo,' he said.

'Pardon me, Nate,' his good friend from the British Army said – departing from his usual crisp, professional tone – 'but this is *suicide*. You are consigning an entire *brigade* of your troops to a mission that . . . that even if we're *successful* in crossing the Amur in accordance with the new timetable could result in their total annihilation! You're sending your 101st into that valley far, far too soon. I'm sorry, Nate, but I must object.'

Clark took a deep breath. 'The Jinan Army Group is already moving up.' There was a stir. 'We just got the intell. If we don't take that valley now, we'll never block the road-rail line. But at this *very* instant there's a gap. I'm inserting that brigade into it. If they succeed in isolating the battlefield from the rest of China, we'll pocket fifty divisions – over six hundred thousand men.'

'But they have to hold off an entire Army Group by themselves,' the French commander noted. He checked the table of organization and equipment. 'Two armored divisions. Ten infantry divisions. Three airborne divisions. Over 175,000 *men*, Nate.'

'I've ordered the air commander to pound every kilometer of those columns with everything they've got round the clock. Fewer than half should arrive in that valley. Those who do make it will be exhausted, terrified and green. The men I'm committing against them are hardened professionals. The terrain is perfect for defense. On-the-ground recon reports it's broken by deep furrows, pointed outcroppings, shallow cuts. The defenders will have good cover. The attackers will be canalized into firing lanes.' Clark felt a heavy weight descend around him. 'They're my troops. I take full responsibility for them.' He felt his throat thicken. 'Those are your orders,' he choked out – rising. 'Meeting adjourned.'

VLADIVOSTOK, SIBERIA
April 18, 0600 GMT (1600 Local)

'Things must be goin' to shit,' one of Andre Faulk's squadmates said.

'Naw, *man!*' another retorted. 'I hear from this jerk-off over in Signal Corps that the Chinese are runnin' like scalded dogs! This war is *over*, man!'

The door burst open. In walked two clerks from battalion headquarters.

'Close the Goddamn door!' came a quick shout as the cold air quickly chilled the room. The clerks extracted a thick bundle from a sack. It reminded Andre of mail call from long, long ago. Of 3rd Platoon, C Company, 2nd Battalion. Of Aguire and the other names

The clerks pulled rubber bands off the bundles with loud snaps.

'What the hell's that?' said the talker.

'What the fuck does it *look* like?'

'It *looks* like a Goddamn map! But you ain't answerin' my *question!*' He had to be restrained by his squadmates. The clerk threatened to bring an end to their hopes.

The headquarters guy smirked. He handed out the new maps. 'There's a battalion meeting at eighteen hundred hours. Hangar B.' They left. The mood in the room turned foul.

'What the fuck is this?' Men opened the fan-folded maps. 'Su-i-bin? Tang-yu-an? That don't sound Russian to me.'

Andre focused not on the towns and streams and mountains. He traced the single salient feature. A river snaked along the top of the map. It was the Amur. The Amur River was to the north.

'What the fuck is *this?*' came the voices of alarm rising from the soldiers.

* * *

466

There was abundant noise in the large hangar. It was like a bitch session on a battalion scale.

'Ten-*shun!*' the booming voice called.

Chairs scraped across the gym floor. Andre Faulk and his entire battalion rose. Nervous chatter died to absolute quiet during the battalion commander's ascent to the stage Andre's eyes fixed on the man's face. 'At ease!' the colonel called out from the podium. His voice was loud. 'Take your seats.'

The noise from all the movement ended quickly as the six hundred men settled in.

He stared down at a single sheet of paper. He shoved it into his breast pocket when the noise subsided. 'I guess you've all been hearing rumors. Some of those rumors are true. We are currently kicking the butts of the Chinese.' There was an eruption of laughter and good cheer. A release of pent-up tension. 'But this war isn't over yet!' The hangar fell silent quickly. 'At least not for us.'

The man next to Andre mumbled, 'Oh, shit.' A chill ran down Andre's spine.

The battalion commander's head was bowed. 'And I know we've taken more than our fair share of casualties.'

Again Andre's neighbor said, 'O-o-oh, shit.'

'But we've got one more mission to execute. One more before we go home.'

'This ain't good at all,' Andre's squadmate commented. That drew a 'Shut-the-fuck-up!' from the guy behind, and a 'Knock-it-off!' from an NCO.

'Four days ago, we launched Operation Winter Harvest. That offensive is about to enter a new phase. We are about to cross the border into the People's Republic of China. And this battalion – you men – are going to be sent in after that.' The disturbance that followed didn't end quickly. But it never got out of control. In part that was because of barking NCOs. In part because men like Andre sat there quietly. Andre found himself shutting his eyes.

The battalion commander waited for the gym to grow quiet. 'We're going on a strike *deep* behind enemy lines.' There wasn't a cough, a whisper, an audible breath. 'A battalion of Rangers will jump to secure the LZ. Our entire brigade will go in heliborne. Wheels up at nineteen hundred . . . tomorrow.'

There were a few mumbled curses. Andre's stomach gurgled.

The colonel continued. 'Altogether, we'll number five thousand men. Our mission will be to sever the main supply route between Manchuria and Beijing.' He strolled out from behind the podium. His head was bowed as if deep in thought. Andre's eyes closed again. 'Our mission is to seize a steep mountain valley. The Chinese will try to push their way through. It will be mountain fighting, gentlemen. Infantry warfare. A battle for the heights. The fighting will be close-in. If we hold key terrain, we win. If we're pushed off, we lose. It's that simple. I'm not going to shit any of you men. They're gonna throw everything they've got at us. They'll envelop us. Fight us for every crevice, every boulder, every log.'

Andre found himself falling asleep. He caught his falling head or got nudged by his neighbor. He half-listened to the remainder of the meeting. Extra loads. Inspections. Last mail call. Details not bravado. And not a word of complaint from the troops. That Andre understood. Sickening dread had a deadening effect. On Andre it caused almost narcotic sleepiness.

SOUTH OF BIROBIDZHAN AIRBASE, SIBERIA
April 18, 0800 GMT (1800 Local)

The two-and-a-quarter-ton truck bumped along the rough track that passed as a road. Harold Stempel was cold and uncomfortable in the cramped, canvas-covered bed. The driver groaned his way through the gears, and everyone stared at each other glumly.

It was a far cry from the Bradleys in which they all assumed they'd be riding. The Bradleys were just as uncomfortable. But the ignominy of riding into battle aboard ordinary diesel trucks was a little too much for the light infantrymen to bear.

'You know this whole thing sucks!' Patterson said – bitching for the hundredth time about their mistreatment by the Army. 'Those bastards fly in here from the States or Japan or wherever, climb right outta them warm planes and into them warm Bradleys, and then *ri-i-ide* on off to win the war.'

McAndrews replied, 'Hey! You wanna be mixin' it up with the fuckin' Chinese? I'm sure a lot of those fuckers'd change places with you round about now.'

'But that ain't the point, is it? The point is respect, and how we don't get none. Ever since that first day when . . .' His eyes shot over to Stempel. He didn't go on. But everybody knew where he was headed. He was alluding to the 'Lost Battalion'. The overrun unit with which Stempel had deployed. They'd all heard the talk. Light infantry wasn't as good as the airborne or airmobile troops. And it wasn't as well equipped as mech or armor. And Stempel had heard other talk as well. If the Lost Battalion had put up a stiffer fight, maybe this or that would've been different.

'Hey, man,' Chavez said with a sneer. 'We're trench troops. They'll pro'bly have us pullin' sentry duty at some supply depot.'

'The *hell* you say!' came one of the several profane responses.

At that the truck slowed. The men at the rear untied the canvas flap of the clunky 'deuce-and-a-quarter.' With a final grinding of the gears, the brakes were set and the engine shut off.

'Everybody *o-o-o*ut!' came the command from outside.

Stempel and the others piled out through the open flap. They were in the middle of nowhere, but the crisp air was invigorating after the carnival-like ride in the back of the truck.

'Let's go, girls!' Stempel's platoon sergeant commanded. Bent under the weight of their packs the men trudged up a low hill. When they reached the crest, they all stood and stared. Thousands and thousands of Chinese sat or squatted in the valley below. A lieutenant with an MP armband ascended the hill to meet them. 'Man, am I glad *you're* here!'

'You had any trouble, sir?' the platoon sergeant asked the much younger officer.

'No. But we got another few thousand on their way, so I hear. And night's falling in a few hours.'

The platoon sergeant turned to his men and ordered, 'Packs off! Lock and load.'

No one said a word as they were led to the prison camp's perimeter. But they all exchanged looks of rage or disgust. They'd been assigned the only duty for which they were fit.

THE WHITE HOUSE, WASHINGTON, D.C.
April 18, 2300 GMT (1800 Local)

Gordon Davis straightened his tie in the mirror. Elaine stepped up behind him. She leaned against the door frame – lost in her reading of his speech. He waited – watching her face for any sign. They'd discussed in detail what he'd say. But he'd refused to let her see the speech till now. Till he'd nipped and tucked and polished it. Till it was ready. She looked up. Concern was written all over her face. Gordon felt his confidence slipping away.

'This is . . . wonderful,' she said in a tone of awe.

Gordon instantly broke into a grin. 'You think so?' She was re-reading it. She nodded distractedly. 'I *thought* you'd like it.' He walked over and gently took hold of her arms. 'I wrote it for you. It really doesn't matter what everyone else says. The media, the Party, the pundits . . .'

'Let me read this again,' Elaine said. She turned away. He waited. She finally turned back. She was smiling. 'You should sit down!'

'I'm all right.'

She ushered Gordon to the vanity's bench seat. 'If you're going to deliver this thing standing up, you've got to rest.'

'I'm *fine*,' Gordon insisted, taking his seat on the upholstered bench. 'Now, tell me how great I am.'

Elaine laughed. 'Gordon . . .' she began. She bent over and put her hands on his thighs. '*Gordon*, honey. You're going to be spec*tacular!*' She hugged him – careful not to get her make-up on his jacket.

He was grinning from ear to ear. 'And?'

'I'm so, so proud of you. Have I ever told you that?'

'Go on.'

'I can't. Your head's gonna swell up and apply for statehood.'

They laughed.

'Mo-*o-om!*' Celeste whined from the sitting room outside. 'This dress makes me look ten years *old!* Can I at *least* take this stupid *bow* off it?'

Their laughter ended with two comfortable smiles.

Elaine whispered, touching her forehead to his and then kissing him softly.

'Mo-*o-om!* Everybody I *know* is going to be watching this stupid thing! I'll never live this down as long as I *live!*'

470

'This isn't *about* you, Celeste!' Elaine finally replied.

'Oh, yeah, well . . . I'm not *going* then!' The door to the sitting room slammed shut.

'You want me to handle this?' Gordon asked.

'Oh, yeah, right! She'd end up wearing a black smock and *hiking* boots!' Elaine left.

Gordon picked up the three-page speech. He felt a rush of anxiety. You could never know how a speech would be received. His dramatic finish could fall flat on its face. He might walk out of the joint session not to thunderous applause and a standing ovation, but to murmurs of shock and surprise. Nobody had any idea, after all, what to expect. The closest anyone had come to predicting the address's contents had been a *New York Times* story. It had hinted that the speech would be short – 'an attempt at a statesmanlike approach' their exact words. But that had been lost in a sea of misinformation. There was speculation that he'd make a public peace offer. Other reports suggested he'd make veiled threats of nuclear attack. Or perhaps even a national referendum on continuation of the war as a face-saving way of exiting the coalition.

Gordon took a deep breath and looked at himself in the mirror. He'd lost fifteen pounds and it showed. His media consultants, however, had been right. The cameras put it all back on for him. He put the paper in his hands on the vanity and headed downstairs to wait. He knew the speech by heart. That's where the speech was from.

'I come before you tonight not to talk of politics, or of policy, or of war,' Gordon began before the joint session of Congress. 'I come to talk to you about the state of our union. I come to talk to you about the character of our people. About something we have lost. Something we must find again. Rudyard Kipling penned words many years ago that still call out to those who will hear them. "There's no sense in going further – it's the edge of cultivation, so they said, and I believed it – broke my land and sowed my crops, built my barns and strung my fences in the little border station tucked away below the foothills where the trails run out and stop. Till a voice, as bad as conscience, rang the interminable changes on one everlasting whisper day and night repeated – so: Something hidden. Go and find it. Go and look beyond the ranges. Something lost . . . behind the ranges, lost, and waiting for you over yonder! Go you there!"'

The House chamber was silent.

'But what sense is there in struggling, in striving, in forging ahead? "It's the edge of cultivation. The trails run out and stop! There's no sense in going further!" Have not we, as Americans, already built a nation as great as any on earth? As great as any nation that ever *rose*? Why should *we*, the prosperous, the advanced, the comfortable, the *leaders* of the *world*, risk *all* and press ahead toward a future whose *only* certainty is of unending *troubles*?'

Gordon felt a sudden rushing sensation – as if a lens had descended before his eyes. Until that moment he'd been someone else. His mind separate from his body. Banished from it had been the sense of actually being there – of finally delivering the speech that would decide the fate of his presidency. He'd been free of the burden of appreciating just how important the moment was in his life. In the life of his country. He'd strolled like a sleepwalker down the ornate carpet and woken up in front of two Teleprompters. Behind them lay the highest rated audience in American television history.

'Something *lost*, go and find it! The *timid*, the *cautious*, the *perplexed* . . . *they* have always halted at the edge of cultivation. But the ambitious, the curious, the daring – the men and women who *built* this thing we call America – *they* have sallied *forth* to carve out the roads down which we now effortlessly travel! They have listened to the whisper, ladies and gentlemen of this Congress. They have heeded its call. "Over yonder – go you there!"'

There was a burst of applause so spontaneous – so filled with unexpected energy – that Gordon felt a tingle ripple up his body and spur him on.

'"But are not the days of discovery now *gone*?" you ask!' His shouts jarred the room into stony silence. The commotion had ended with no chatter. They had no copies of his address to distract them. Everyone looked up and waited for Gordon to continue. '"But does not that whisper merely lead us down a path of fruitless adventurism? There are *fields* to sow. *Fences* to mend. More *barns* to raise right *here*, where we are *now*!"'

Gordon looked up into the gallery. Elaine smiled. The shot was shown, he was sure, worldwide.

'Beyond us lies a vast and untraveled land. The great unknown of tomorrow. You can't see the future, but it's waiting. And like our forebears we have a choice. A choice. Do we venture forth? Do we *explore* those uncharted regions with an aggressive *spirit* and an imaginative *mind?* By *routes* that will at *some* times be true . . . and at *others* lead astray? Or do we *abandon* our courage – *neglect* that urge, that force, those smoldering ambitions that have *fu-ueled* the engines of our progress and unleashed the all-consuming *fires* of human achievement?'

There was an outpouring of cheers from the partisan crowd of veteran Republican speech makers.

'The call beckons,' Gordon continued, 'yet some will never hear it. They will be enslaved forever to the present. Timid, fearful, they will not understand the glories that rise up all around. The commonplace wonders that they take for granted. Those mere ornaments of convenience that were once *triumphs* of ingenuity and drive! They will memorize formulas, paraphrase words, digest books *filled* with the most powerful and brilliant thoughts of humankind! But they will not reach up to grasp the torch! They will not blaze a new trail! They will not *dare* to see what glories there might have been!

'If we are to survive as a nation of *free* men and women – if we are to stoke the *fires* that *must* burn within us to give us the *strength* and the *will* to explore the future in search of its hidden truths – we must first look within ourselves. We must find those beliefs that lie suppressed beneath the weight of convention, and of comfort, and of ease, and we must give them voice! And so to *those* of you who hear the call I sa-ay . . . *speak* out! Shout at the top of your lungs that we are not a people whose time has come and gone! The time has come to *stand*, and be *counted*, or to *forever* hold your peace!'

There was a cacophonous standing ovation for which Gordon was unprepared. He breathed – deeply – as self-assured as he'd ever felt. He unfurrowed his brow and relaxed. He smiled for the first time. The energy surged through him and left him free of the aches and pains of his days. He waited until there was total quiet.

'Ladies and gentlemen of this Congress, I report to you that the state of our union rests in your hands. To one side lies comfort and security; peace and tranquility. To the other, a churning sea of foam and fire through which our storm-tossed ship of state must sail. It is our choice whether we transcend our time! To slough off our current prejudices and ignorance! To break out of the limits that bind us with heavy chains to the dead weight of our certain present! We, my fellow Americans, must survey the rivers of life! We must not let fear of the difficult inhibit us!

For if we do, we may never know the virgin forests of Eden that lie at the river's source. We may never find the rich lowlands into which the fertile water flows. The state of the union, ladies and gentlemen, rests in your hands. Something lost. Go and find it.'

UNRUSFOR HEADQUARTERS, KHABAROVSK
April 19, 0105 GMT (1105 Local)

For a moment, the television's small speaker was silent. President Davis's stirring words had left everyone gathered around transfixed.

When the raucous applause erupted from the joint session of Congress, however, a similar uproar burst forth from the crowded conference room. Officers and soldiers alike seemed ecstatic and exuberant. Nate turned to look at the scene. Even the Europeans were caught up in the emotion, most particularly the British on whose lips Nate caught repeated references to Kipling in an animated discussion.

Nate turned back to the small television. President Davis slowly made his way down the center aisle. Republicans and Democrats alike stood clapping and smiling – the Republicans in a state of complete rapture. They held hands out as if to some passing celebrity. The camera switched to take in Mrs Davis and her lovely daughters, who were about the same age as Nate's two sons.

Memories of home made Nate anxious and impatient. In just a few hours, it would be his face that filled the screens. It would be his show under the bright lights of international television. He longed for that show to be a success. For his boys to see their father standing tall. Describing their country's amazing victory. He felt guilty for so petty a thought. His men were fighting for their lives. But he closed his eyes and reveled in a victory that was still in doubt. He relished the triumph over all who doubted – even to those who resided in his own home.

'Sir?' Major Reed said. Nate opened his eyes. 'Seventh Corps commander is on the line. He's got the latest unit positions.'

Nate felt a tightening of his chest. The previously boisterous room grew quiet. Nate made his way across the large room to the radio. He could already hear the sound of the general's voice. The man was asking the communications officer what he thought of the President's just-completed State of the Union address. Its buoyant tone was a good omen.

'Clark here,' Nate said loudly over the speakerphone.

'General Clark!' came the voice of his corps commander. 'Are you ready for current positions?'

Pads and paper rustled all around.

'Ready on this end,' Nate replied. His heart pounded. His throat constricted. 'Give me your forwardmost unit.'

'2nd Battalion, 173rd Armored Cavalry Regiment,' came the tinny voice over the radio, 'north bank of Amur River.'

The room burst into cheers. 'Pipe down!' Nate shouted, silencing the room.

'Token resistance only,' the radio voice continued. 'The front-line Chinese units are totally spent. Their stocks of ammo must be ridiculously low. A lot of their units are flat running out. But intell is speculating that some units in the interior of the main pockets may be sitting on substantial stocks that they never succeeded in moving forward. I'd like to request a delay in bridging operations so we can secure our flanks north of the Amur. We're so far ahead of schedule that a twenty-four hour pause shouldn't . . .'

'Negative,' Clark interrupted. 'You're "Go" to cross the Amur in strength just as soon as the engineers certify the bridge.' There was a long pause. 'Do you acknowledge?'

'I read you five-by-five, General Clark,' the reluctant corps commander replied. 'Orders are to begin crossing the Amur.'

When they'd signed off, Reed waited on Clark. 'What about the 25th LID?' Reed asked. 'They've encountered light resistance and are at the Amur south of Birobidzhan.'

'Send them across,' Clark said.

'What's their objective?'

Clark turned to Reed. 'To cross the Amur River into China.'

THE KREMLIN, MOSCOW
April 19, 0110 GMT (0310 Local)

'It's too early to get a read on how President Davis did tonight,' one of the American network commentators said. Kartsev shook his head in disgust. 'He needed to be bold given his abysmal approval ratings and the bleak headcount on the impending funding vote on the war. But a speech of this sort is truly unprecedented and, I might add, totally unexpected. We knew the address would be short due to the President's still-fragile health. But we'll really have to wait for the first flash polls.'

Kartsev turned the television off. He moaned in frustration. It was a brilliant speech. The best he'd ever heard live. Davis had managed to rise above the fractious political infighting of which Americans had grown so tired. And he'd also defended a highly unpopular war without mentioning it once.

It was still in Kartsev's dark office. He reflected for a moment on his depression. Was it due to the fact that he was now sitting on the sidelines? Watching events unfold instead of instigating them? But then he reasoned that he *had* instigated them. He took out a pad and jotted down the sequence of events.

First, the collapse of the Russian government – no mean feat. Then, the destruction of Russia's remaining institutions of power in the civil war. Ditto. UNRUSFOR and China had simply been sucked into the vacuum – pure cause and effect – with war the inevitable result. And who would win that war? UNRUSFOR, of course. His pen rested on the blank space at the end of his list. The dividing point between past and future. He wrote. 'What will happen in China?'

Kartsev could no more predict the future than he could have foretold any of the events he'd just listed. Anarchy in Russia had been an end unto itself. The strained tendons and failing tissues of Russian society had created an historic, once-in-a-lifetime opportunity. The serendipity was finding the large-scale social forces his experiment had unleashed. And the scale of those forces could get no greater than China – one-quarter of the human population.

Kartsev looked at the sequence of events he'd jotted down. An excellent summary of all that had happened. A conclusion to his bulging manuscript. He turned to his glowing computer and set to work on his final chapter. All the while loomed the unanswerable question. *What next for China?*

THE WHITE HOUSE, WASHINGTON, D.C.
April 19, 1100 GMT (0600 Local)

'Who's this?' Gordon Davis asked.

'Ralph Stevenson,' Daryl replied. He held the receiver out to Gordon. His finger hovered above the blinking light. 'He's a Democrat from . . .'

Gordon waved impatiently for the phone. Daryl pressed the button. 'Ralph!' Gordon said in a good-natured tone. His fingers massaged his throbbing temples. 'Have you heard the great news?'

The Congressman was uncertain. 'Uhm, about the *war?*'

'You *bet* about the war! We're kickin' their butts all the way back to Bei*jing!* What do the people back in Louisville have to say about that?' Again there was hesitation. 'You *have* been getting faxes and calls, I imagine.' Gordon spoke so loudly it made his head pound.

As the man answered guardedly, Gordon fumbled with his painkillers' childproof cap. Elaine appeared just then with a mug of hot tea. Gordon made an apologetic face, but she quickly nodded and rested her cool hand on his clammy forehead. He gulped the pill down with the minty tea.

'Well, I *know* you've made commitments to your leadership, Ralph,' Gordon said. 'But you've got other commitments to honor too, don't you? To the people from Kentucky who put you in office? To your country?'

'Mr President, we've given you ample time to bring this war to an end, and . . .'

'What about bringing this war to a *victory*, Ralph? That's where we are, you know. Right there on the verge of *winning* this thing! Now what're you gonna tell the people back in Louisville come election time if you help pull the plug on the *single* most successful American military operation since *D*-Day?'

The man laughed nervously and hedged. Elaine dabbed at Gordon's forehead with a handkerchief. Daryl raised a three-by-five card for Gordon to see. 'Jim Berne on 2!' Daryl mouthed.

'Listen, Ralph!' Gordon interrupted. 'Time's short here. There are men and women over there dying trying to win this war. You've got a vote. On behalf of them *and* your country, I'm asking you to cast it in favor of the continuing resolution. Can I count on you?'

He heard a faint sigh, then a tired, 'All right, Mr President.'

'Thank you *very* much, Congressman Stevenson!' Gordon said. Muted cheers rose up from around the Oval Office. A junior aide changed the tallies on a white board. '221' he wrote under the 'For' sign.

Daryl hit line two. 'Jim!' Gordon said in a fake but vibrant voice.

'No,' came the reply of a small child. 'My daddy had to go to the *potty!* His tummy has germs in it 'cause he didn't wash his hands.'

Gordon smiled and said, 'Well, listen, sweetie. I'm the President of the United States. Do you know who that is?'

'Uh-*hu-u*-uh! I saw you on TV. You're the *fool!*'

Gordon sighed. 'Yep. That's me. And let me ask you one other question. Do you know the soldiers who are fighting in the war?'

'Ye-ah. They wear *white* clothes, and it's *cold*.'

'That's *right!* Now I'd like you to do me a favor, okay? I'd like you to tell your daddy he shouldn't be mean to the cold soldiers. Tell him he shouldn't take away their *food* and warm *blankets* and . . .' Elaine slapped Gordon hard on the shoulder. She chastised him sternly under her breath. 'You just go stand outside the potty door and explain that to your dad.' The little girl accepted her mission with an '*O*-kay!'

'Bill Craft on line 4,' Daryl said the instant the girl hung up.

'Bill! This is Gordon Davis.' Senator Craft launched into a two-minute anti-war diatribe.

'Okay,' Gordon finally said, 'I've listened to you. Now will you listen to me?'

'Gordy, it won't do you any good. I'm one of the Goddamn *sponsors* of the War Powers Resolution.'

'Just give me my shot, Bill, that's all I ask. Just let me make my case.'

Senator Craft huffed, but then he replied, 'Of course, Mr President.'

Gordon leaned back in the padded chair behind the historic desk. It was quiet now. The Oval Office was nearly empty. 'Get General Clark on the line,' he said. He slurred the words and didn't look at anyone in particular. He took deep breaths. His eyes sank closed.

An aide handed him the phone. 'Nate?' he said. His voice was tired and raspy. 'You've got thirty days of funding. The continuing resolution passed. Now you go win that war.'

AMUR RIVER, SIBERIA
April 19, 2300 GMT (0900 Local)

Harold Stempel and the others waited on the riverbank. The newly-plowed road that ran to the edge of the Amur River was already rutted. Their legs and backs ached from the weight of the heavy packs that they carried. But they couldn't sit down or they'd never get back up.

Engineers were stringing additional cables to secure the pontoons. The floating bridge looked all right. But every so often the thin ice would shift. The groaning sound of friction would draw anxious looks from the engineers. A man on the center of the bridge shouted, twirled his arm, and pumped his fist in the air.

'All right, let's *go!*' shouted Stempel's platoon leader.

They headed across the bridge in two files – one down each solid metal track meant for vehicles. The lieutenant was in front. His RTO followed with his radio aerial whipping the air. Then came Stempel's squad leader, then Stempel – fourth in line. The men on the opposite side of the bridge followed the platoon sergeant. A quick check of the upstream ice left Harold distinctly unsettled.

From the riverbank the ice looked fairly solid. But from the bridge it was clearly thin and dangerous. Here and there, the ice cover grew thinner and darker in the bright light of the sunny day. It was broken straight through around the gently bobbing pontoons. The water there was black and ominous and foreboding.

They passed a group of the engineers who were struggling to fasten cables to the bridge. Straining to keep the bridge intact. Harold wanted to quicken his pace, but had to maintain his place in line.

There was another loud groan from the river. Everyone's heads turned in search of the ominous sound. But nothing had visibly changed. The long highway of gray ice remained unbroken. Harold felt a trickle of sweat under the warm rays of the sun.

Several times he felt the bridge sway beneath him. Not a jarring blow. Just a gentle drift with the current. He peered out around the bulging pack of his squad leader. The bridge was bowed to the left. Long guy wires from the banks held the pontoons in place. But the bridge still bent to the relentless flow.

When Harold stepped off the metal pad onto dry land he breathed a sigh of relief.

'I never thought I'd get to China,' McAndrews said.

Harold looked down at his boots. At the icy ruts made by a hundred vehicles' passing.

'What's this?' Patterson asked. He took a can. It looked like oversized hairspray.

'Tear gas,' the squad leader said. He handed one to each man. Harold took the cold green can. Chavez followed with gas masks in canvas sacks.

'What *this* for?' an incredulous Patterson persisted. The sergeant looked pissed. He didn't have the patience to put up with Patterson's shit. But Patterson kept at him. 'Why are they issuing us *this* shit?'

The sergeant wheeled on him. 'You know how many people there are in China, shitface? A billion and a half! Figure it out for yourself!'

NORTH OF TANGYUAN, CHINA
April 20, 1100 GMT (2100 Local)

The Blackhawk bucked wildly through the heavy turbulence. Andre Faulk felt sick to his stomach. It had been hours since they'd refueled and headed in. This was the longest flight he'd ever taken in a helicopter. The weight of the external fuel tanks had forced removal of the armored flooring. After reaching the border everyone had sat on their packs. Andre's back and ass ached.

But it wasn't the threat of anti-aircraft fire or the lack of comfort that caused Andre's greatest distress. The entire battalion had flown straight into a raging cold front. They were being tossed about like a small boat on rough seas. The buffeting was so violent in the mountains it almost knocked his breath out. Several in his squad had already vomited into airsick bags. Andre had been on the verge of doing the same numerous times. He'd stopped just short, however – his mouth and nose breathing the stale air of a bag.

'Thirty miles!' the squad leader shouted after getting off the intercom. 'We're thirty miles out!'

He looked sick to his stomach, and he started to buck and buck. He spilled his stomach all over the center of the cabin.

They all listened for the smacking sound of bullets on the metal fuselage. No one said a word as the engines revved to military power. The deceleration of their descent toward the earth crushed everyone to the deck.

There was a jerking thud. The door cracked open. In rushed the rotors' downblast. The door slid wide. The cabin filled with swirling, frigid wind. The sergeant leapt through the door. One by one the blackness outside swallowed men. Andre slid on his butt toward the opening. The weight of his pack prevented him from rising. By the time his legs dangled in the air under the whirring blades, the first men were returning to offload crates of supplies.

'*Move it!*' came a shout – almost totally washed away by the engines' roar. Andre hopped to the ground – misjudging the distance and collapsing to his knees. Two of the returning men hoisted him to his feet. He lumbered into the night across uneven footing. The LZ was filled with dozens of choppers. The sarge shoved Andre in the right direction. He found the other men's gear piled. With a quick motion he released his heavy pack. It fell to the ground with a jangling thud.

He felt light when free of the weight. He and another man returned to the chopper and dragged out a heavy crate. He and his partner dropped the load amid stacks of others – the tiny battalion supply depot. The choppers were all lifting into the air. They had blinking red, green and white lights to avoid collisions. Andre monitored the sky. A good number of airmobile troopers had been killed by their own helicopters.

The downdraft from a low and unseen helicopter forced the two men to their knees. When it was gone, the night was markedly quieter. It grew quieter still with each helicopter's departure. By the time they reached their packs, the Blackhawks were all gone.

'Head up to the 60,' the squad leader said – his voice a whisper. 'Everybody clear the zone! Clear the zone!' Andre and the other man marched into the darkness. There were six hundred men and tons of supplies on the drop zone. But after the departure of the choppers, the night had become still and peaceful. Andre had experienced the disorienting phenomenon on other insertions. Hours of steady noise. A rush into the rotors' downdraft. Then total silence. It was a change for which you were unprepared.

But as soon as your ears adjusted, you had to guard against something else. You couldn't let the roar of a firefight stun you into inaction. You strained to hear even the tiniest sound. But at the same time, you prepared for a cacophony of explosions. You steeled yourself against the fire and death which could spring from the quiet at any moment. For if you froze in the awful first seconds, you would almost certainly die. He'd ambushed deer in the headlights before. The real killing was in those first awful moments.

Andre hooked up with the rest of his squad. By random luck he lay next to the attached machine-gun crew. On the sergeant's command, they unsafed their weapons and headed into Indian country. He hugged tight to the side of the M-60. The big gun would attract enemy fire. But it was the safest place for him to be. Because working machine-guns almost never got overrun. They were back breakers – the rocks against which waves of attackers would crash. They were the decisive weapons of modern infantry combat.

The platoon headed for the tall ridges and jagged rocks that rose all around the LZ. Andre felt tense at facing the great unknown. At stumbling blindly forward with no sense of what to expect. When they left the flats, word was passed from man to man. They were now in a free-fire zone – all 360 degrees.

Chapter Twenty-Two

UNRUSFOR HEADQUARTERS, KHABAROVSK
April 21, 1100 GMT (2100 Local)

There was a knock on Nate Clark's door. It was his secretary. 'Sorry to bother you, sir, but that woman reporter is back.'

Clark looked up, confused. 'What woman reporter?'

'Me, that's who!' Kate Dunn said angrily. She edged her way into his office. 'You said you were sending me to the fighting! But there was hardly a shot fired!' He began to object, but she pressed on. 'And you *used* me! You fed me bullshit stories about how *weak* you were and how powerful the *Chinese* were! And I repeated them like some stooge!'

Clark nodded at his secretary, who left them alone. 'Have you ever heard of a Strategic Deception Plan?'

'I've heard of *deception!* "*Strategic*" just makes it sound *okay* because it's a *military* thing! But my job is to report the *truth!* And you've been *fucking* me over ever since we first met!' Kate was going for maximum effect, but she wondered whether she was laying it on too thick.

'I didn't arrest your friend for possession of marijuana,' Clark replied.

'Possession of *pot* in the middle of *Siberia*? It's *anarchy!* There aren't any laws here!'

'There's military law, and you broke it by sneaking around that supply depot.'

'I wasn't sneaking, I was reporting! That's my job!'

'And *you* doing *your* job would prevent *me* from doing *mine*! And it would've gotten a whole bunch of men and women killed! *Your* countrymen! *Your* army in this war! You and everybody else in the press view yourself as *supra*-national. You follow some ill-conceived *"neutrality* principle"! You think you have to report from a position mid-way between the opposing sides even if one side is *right* and the other is *wrong!* China is trying to grab Siberia in a war of aggression, and we're trying to stop them! Why don't you try keeping *that* in mind when you choose which reports to file!'

Nate knew he'd gone too far. He'd vented months of frustration over the things the press had been saying about him. The disparaging remarks with which his boys had to live. He and the reporter were at a standoff now.

Kate switched tone, but not direction. 'All I'm doing is busting my ass to do a decent story on what this war is *really* like. And you send me to that Mickey Mouse attack. I thought we had a deal. I thought I could rely on you to be a man of your word.'

Her last words seemed to have the desired effect. She imagined the conflict being played out in Clark's head. The honest, straightforward soldier confronted with an uncomfortable example of his deceit.

'Sergeant Scott!' Clark bellowed. They stared at each other across the No Man's Land of Clark's desk. 'Sergeant *Scott!*' he shouted again. His secretary didn't reply. Clark muttered something and went off in search of the man, leaving Kate alone in his office. It was a Spartan room, nearly devoid of interesting sights. The colorful map on Clark's desk was a notable exception. Clark had been hunched over it when she'd entered. Kate glanced at the open door and walked over to the map.

It was upside down from her perspective. But she could make out the familiar track of the Amur River. It was a commanding general's map – showing the whole war in one oversized picture. The blue marks were UNRUSFOR units. The red were Communist Chinese.

484

Dots formed two blue spikes striking deep into the mass of red. In the east, the advance out of Vladivostok was modest, but the direction of the bulge was clear. It was driving straight into China. The far more impressive prong of the offensive was in the west. It was a dagger plunging hundreds of miles from north to south. Its tip barely crossed the Amur River. Kate had seen, however, what it was really like. Starving Chinese kids in search of food, water, shelter. Wanting nothing more than an end to the horror. The offensive looked great on the map. But there was no glory to be found in the field. No desperate struggle on whose outcome the tide of the war would turn.

One tiny pocket of blue caught her attention. It was buried deep in northern China. The dot was far separated from the rest of the allied forces. She half-turned her head to look at the map right side up. '75th/101st' was written beside the island of blue. To have a number, Kate reasoned, they had to be large units.

She heard voices from the outer office.

Kate quickly noted three other things that were readily apparent from the map. The first was the massive red hammer of a Chinese army moving north toward the tiny blue island. The second was that the two prongs seemed destined to converge on that same blue dot in China. And the third was the name on the map closest to the '75th/101st.' *Tangyuan*, she thought over and over.

Clark returned with his secretary and began speaking. She quickly realized he was dictating a memo. 'To: All UNRUSFOR Personnel. From: Lieutenant General Nate Clark, Commanding. Today's date. Re: Ms Kate Dunn.' Kate stared back – waiting. 'Ms Dunn is a correspondent for the National Broadcasting Company. On my authority, she is to be given complete access to all areas under UNRUSFOR control including, without limitation, all theaters of combat and all units engaged with the enemy. You are hereby instructed to cooperate by all means necessary to afford Ms Dunn and her camera crew the access herein specified.'

'Including transportation,' Kate added in almost a whisper.

'. . . including transport,' Clark appended to his memo. The clerk looked up from his notepad. When Kate nodded and smiled, Clark sent the sergeant off to type it up. 'Now,' Clark said, 'if you'll please wait outside for the memo, I have to hold a press conference in half an hour. Then, God willing, I can actually get back to running this war. Okay?'

Kate held out her hand. 'I truly appreciate your assistance, General Clark.' He shook her hand. 'You won't be disappointed with my reports.'

Clark nodded politely and she left. He returned to his notes. The phone rang. It was the president. The clerk brought the memo in. Nate signed it and mouthed, 'Give it to her.'

'Are you ready for your big show?' President Davis asked.

'Yes, sir!' Clark replied. 'But you're a hard act to follow, if I might say. That was one helluva speech you gave.'

Davis laughed. 'I kind of liked it myself.'

'What's the reaction on the Hill?' Clark asked.

'Apparently, the faxes, e-mails and voice mails are running twelve-to-one in favor of winning this thing militarily. That's why I want you to go out there and give 'em hell, General Clark. Don't hold anything back. I want the people to believe we can win. I want *you* to walk out there and convince everyone that it's possible.'

'But, Mr President, there's still a lot that can go wrong. We only have the equivalent of about a division across the Amur – bits and pieces of half a dozen units from as many countries. If that ice breaks now . . .'

'I know all that, Nate. But you have a job to do – a mission. That mission is to rally the country around this war so we can be freed – politically – to win it. You know how to fire your soldiers up to go do the fighting. But what you *and* I need to do now is to convince our countrymen that this counter-attack is *already* a success. Nothing generates support like victory. I want you to get behind the wheel and jam your foot on the gas. The bandwagon may be half-empty now, but I want people chasing it to hop on. Just put your worries aside for thirty minutes, Nate. Enjoy for a moment what you and your men have accomplished out there! And be *sure* to let the press see that enjoyment.'

It all ran against the grain of Nate's character. To shut out his concerns about stranding men deep inside China. To overlook his exposed flanks and rear. To cease fretting over the unexpected cold front that wreaked havoc on air combat and supply. But Clark said, 'Yes, sir,' in reply to the President.

'I'll be watching,' said Davis before he hung up.

*   *   *

'What're *you* doing here?' the CNN correspondent asked Kate as she entered the briefing room. Woody found his acquaintances among the cameramen. 'I thought you were being Rambette out in the field with the great unwashed.'

Kate smiled. The woman had a reputation for dangerous assignments. Kate's smile turned to a grin when she noticed the woman's flak jacket. It always looked more impressive when you wore a bullet-proof vest even if you were safe under reinforced concrete.

Kate spotted the senior NBC correspondent. 'I'm on my way back out,' she said to the CNN reporter. 'I just dropped by for a little talk with General Clark.' Kate headed across the room to her colleague without waiting for the surprised woman's reply. 'Listen,' she whispered to the man, who covered the Pentagon during times of peace. 'I want you to call New York and tell them I'm going to the front – to the hottest action of the war. I should get back in a few days and put the story together.'

He nodded, thinking. 'If I could help . . . If you wanta just send the tapes back, I could do some editing.'

'I'm not talking *footage* here, Frank! I'm talking *story!*'

'*I* understand. But you know the drill. If the story's even a *day* late, it's stale – footage or not. You miss the window and it's a Discovery Channel documentary for all that hard work. It's ten *thousand* viewers instead of ten million.'

'I'll edit the story in the field if I have to!'

'Oka-ay. Jeeze! I was just offering.'

Clark appeared on stage. The reporters quickly headed for their seats. Kate made her way to the back to find Woody. In the process, she passed half a dozen reporters staring into minicams. They were all introducing the momentous briefing. In French, and German, and English, and Dutch – all were wrapping up and turning their attention to the podium.

'Woody!' Kate said. He was whispering something to a man behind a studio-size camera. The man grinned broadly as Woody shoved something into his pocket. It was a bundle of joints wrapped in a rubber band. '*Woody!*' Kate whispered. She drew a 'sh-sh-sh!' from a nearby reporter.

Kate tilted her head toward the door. Woody joined her there.

'Good morning,' Clark's deep voice boomed. Kate and Woody both turned. The briefing room was still. 'I come to report to you a great victory.' Two aides lifted the gray plastic sheet off a wall-sized map. There were gasps and a general disturbance when the map was revealed.

There were the two blue prongs Kate had seen in Clark's office. On this map, however, something was different. One more deception in Clark's plan of disinformation. There was no tiny island of blue near the Chinese city of Tangyuan.

Nate saw Kate Dunn and her cameraman leave. But he was distracted by the stir the map had caused. As he'd expected, the picture was worth a thousand words. And he was under orders to squeeze every ounce of theater out of the briefing.

'UNRUSFOR forces,' he continued loudly, 'have pushed south of the Amur River into China from the west,' again there was a burst of noise, '*and* west into China from the Vladivostok region, making the results of Operation Winter Harvest . . . spectacular. The most dramatic successes lie in the west.' The silver tip of Reed's pointer tapped the map. 'In sixty hours, UNRUSFOR has advanced over three hundred kilometers – almost two hundred miles.' Reed moved the pointer to the large sea of red. 'In the process, they have flanked and enveloped over two hundred thousand Chinese troops.'

The room was filled with excited chatter.

'In the east, the results on the map *appear* less dramatic.' Reed swung his pointer to the bloody fighting around Vladivostok. 'But something equally significant is occurring there. Chinese lines that had stabilized in the first days of the war have crumbled. Field commanders report no fewer than four main belts of defenses have been breached. Elsewhere,' Clark continued as Reed's pointer moved to the center, 'units based here in Khabarovsk and at the long-surrounded airbase at Birobidzhan report break-outs in their individual drives south for the Amur River.' Reed's pointer brushed across the small blue darts to the south. 'Casualties so far have been lighter than expected – on both sides. As of two hours ago, field commanders report over forty thousand Chinese troops taken prisoner.'

That completed the story of widespread success.

'As you must all understand, due to concerns about operational security I must conclude this briefing here. But let me take this opportunity to give you one personal observation.' He leaned over the podium. 'No war should ever be popular. War is a terrible and ugly waste. But when all efforts at peacemaking have failed – when all the diplomats have given it their best but come up short – you ultimately have two choices. You can cut and run – ceding the field to the enemy – or you can fight. Now I know for many months people have voiced noisy opposition to this war. And that's good. It's healthy. It is *precisely* at times such as these that the right to express your opinions is paramount. But now that the truth is finally out – now that all can see what our plans were to win this war – perhaps the debate can reflect the new military reality. Perhaps the dialogue in the public forum can be as informed and enlightened as that in the war's inner councils has been. *This*,' Clark said – wheeling on the map with a sweep of his arm – 'is what we've planned to do all along. And it's been successful beyond our *wildest* dreams!' He had them. Every face was raised to his. Pens were frozen on pads. Cameras rolled. 'There's still more fighting to come. But one fact should be evident from this map. The People's Liberation Army has been defeated in the field. The entire invasion force will be captured and disarmed. We *will* win this war.'

'Why were you giving that cameraman your pot?' Kate whispered.

'What are we doing at the airbase?' Woody countered.

The major on whom they waited was on the phone. He was another of the insufferable 'Public Affairs Officers' with whom members of the press were forced to deal. PAOs acted as if they were on the press's side. They agreed that everything was unfair. But what could they do? They were just a 'spoke in the wheel,' they always said. All information flowed from the 'hub' – the commanding officer.

There were two signs above the PAO's desk. One read, '"Four hostile newspapers are more to be feared than a thousand bayonets." Napoleon.' The other was of a more recent vintage. '"Wherever commanders go, they should plan for CNN. Like the weather, we'll always be there – just another feature on the battlefield terrain." Jamie McIntyre. CNN correspondent.'

The major hung the telephone up. He re-read the already crumpled memorandum from General Clark. He went into another office. Kate realized Woody was looking at her. All their traveling gear – his camera included – lay by their sides. 'What?' she asked.

'You didn't answer my question,' Woody replied.

'And *you* didn't answer *mine*. Why'd you give all your pot away?'

'I didn't give it *all* away. But it was a gift to me, so it was sort of a civic duty to pass it on.'

'But you're like a human *smokestack*. Why would you part with any of the stuff?'

'Where are we *going*, Kate?'

The major returned with a colonel. The senior officer held Clark's memo in both hands. 'What can I do for you?' the man asked.

'I want to go to Tangyuan,' Kate said. Woody's eyes darted her way.

The colonel laughed and looked at the major. The major laughed just as the colonel turned serious. The PAO was out of sync with his boss – the head of army air transport. 'I don't know what the hell you're talking about,' the man lied inexpertly.

Kate leaned forward and whispered. 'I'm talking about the 75th and the 101st.' Nothing registered on the colonel's face. 'I'm doing a story on the 75th and 101st,' she repeated like a mantra. 'General Clark told me to come see *you*.' Kate glanced down at the name stenciled above his breast pocket. 'He said go see Colonel *Wheatley* at the *airbase*.'

'Whah-tley,' the major corrected – pronouncing it like 'what,' not 'wheat.'

'General Clark mentioned me by *name*?' the colonel said. Kate arched her brow and nodded significantly.

'Well, it doesn't matter anyway,' the colonel said. 'All we've got going in there are airdrops. And I don't imagine either of you are airborne-qualified.' He wore a broad, amiable grin.

'What about medevacs?' Woody unexpectedly asked. His voice was wooden and tired.

The colonel looked at the PAO, who shrugged and said, 'Under conditions of open coverage, field commanders are required to permit journalists to ride on military vehicles and aircraft whenever feasible.' Kate looked at the colonel and arched her brow again.

Kate and Woody were taken to a MASF – a Mobile Army Surgical Facility. The wind whipped across the flat tarmac. They were escorted by a nurse in a flight suit to a large helicopter. It was fitted with bulging external fuel tanks. Its engines were already whining. The rotor was beginning to turn. They hoisted their gear up and climbed aboard. Another female medic pulled the sliding door closed with a bang.

Kate and Woody found a place among the litters. The flight was long, but the two nurses remained busy the entire time. There were drip bags to hang on hooks. Oxygen masks to lay on small pillows. Trays filled with small bottles whose caps had to be removed. These women were obviously veterans of previous flights. They thought ahead – even remembering the towels. Stooping to the deck in their one-piece flight suits, they bunched towel after towel underneath each of the litters. Their combat boots squeaked slightly on the bare metal floor.

Kate and Woody watched in silence from their corner. The helicopter began to rock in the increasingly rough weather. Kate's eyes were drawn by the little squeaks down to the towels. *They had to have good footing*, she thought as she watched the nurses. *The towels were there to keep the slick deck dry.*

When she looked over at Woody, his eyes were on her. Sad, tired eyes which sank closed as he laid his head against the bulkhead.

The final few moments of the descent were the worst. The helicopter had flown straight through a cold front which barreled out of Siberia like an avalanche. Now it bucked and rolled as the pilot fought his way down. Each time the deck pitched Kate imagined the rotors smacking the ground and disintegrating.

A hard thud sent pain shooting up her back.

The door slid open. The blizzard flew into the cabin with full force and fury.

Kate and Woody grabbed their gear and headed out. At the door they saw the first bloody body. It was being hoisted aboard through the hellish wind. Soldiers jumped into the helicopter to help the female medics. Kate stood back and watched a parade of the horrible. Men were crying. One screamed for his mother. She leapt to the ground. Woody followed.

The door slid closed and the air filled with snow and dirt. The blast of the rotors forced Kate and Woody to their knees. When the helicopter was gone, the gusts of the storm seemed tame by comparison.

'Who the hell're *you*?' came a loud voice.

Kate looked up to see a large white parka looming over her and Woody like a polar bear. The distant crackle and boom of gunfire was nearly constant.

'Kate Dunn – NBC News!'

The bear looked down at her for a moment in silence. '*What*?' he suddenly shouted.

*   *   *

491

Brigadier General Lawson, the brigade commander, took one look at General Clark's memo and crumpled it into a ball. He threw the wad against a bucking tent wall and cursed. 'You've got some fuckin' balls comin' in here! Do you realize what you've gotten yourselves into?'

'We're war correspondents covering a military operation,' Kate replied. 'We're just doing our job.'

'Oh, is *that* right?' He was so angry he could barely speak. 'Fine! O-okay! You wanna play war correspondent, you've come to the right place! *Come* here!' He led them to a small folding table. A map of the mountainous terrain was laid out under a battery-powered lamp. 'Here *we* are.' He jabbed his finger at the center of the various blue letters and numbers denoting UNRUSFOR positions. 'And everywhere else,' his palm circled the blue-coated ridges, 'is the Chinese. The better part of the Jinan Army Group, intell says. A quarter-million men.'

Kate shook her head in confusion. 'I don't understand. How are you supposed to stop a quarter of a million Chinese soldiers with – what? – a few thousand men?'

'I believe the plan, as expressed to me, was to fight like hell. That – Ms War Correspondent – means living high up on rocky ridges. Moving fast and at night. Hitting 'em hard and gettin' the hell outta Dodge. Goin' days without a hot meal. Sleepin' no more'n two or three hours at a stretch. And, if you get wounded . . . Well, that's not good. Now, that's what you've gotten your sorry asses into. *And* you've made yourselves a Goddamn *pain* in *my* ass to *boot*!'

Kate wasn't rattled by the man's shouts. But she was scared to death if what he was saying was true. 'But surely they wouldn't send you here if you didn't at least have a *chance* of holding this valley.'

The general's eyes sank thoughtfully to the map. 'The interior and exterior walls of the hills are steep. The valley floor down which the road and rail line run is no more than a few hundred meters wide. It channels the attacking Chinese and narrows our front. If we hold the high ground, we can win. We've gotta dig our toenails in and fight for every rock. They'll keep throwing live bodies at our fighting holes till we make 'em dead. It's a simple and brutal calculus. Nothin' pretty about it.'

NORTH OF TANGYUAN, CHINA
April 22, 2200 GMT (0800 Local)

The lean-to angled away from the gale. It blocked the wind, but snow wrapped around inside. It licked at Andre's body with chilling gusts. It was mid-morning, but the sky was gray and dark.

A machine-gun opened fire.

'*Come-on!-Come-on!*' was shouted by almost all the men together. It was as if they were cheering for the embattled home team. Twice already they had done this. Both times with no casualties in their squad.

Andre and the others crawled out into the storm. When he stood upright, the wind rocked him backwards a step. He had to put his shoulder down to get moving forward toward his fighting hole. The line of ten men weaved their way through the thick trees of the valley floor. At first, it was just a grueling jog into the impossibly cold tide of air. Then, the Chinese began to yell. The howls from their lungs rose up. With the wind at their backs their massed voices carried and were amplified by the narrow mountain gorge.

From a distance of a few hundred meters, the two armies rushed toward each other at the dead run. The Americans raced for their fighting positions. Chinese infantry flooded the southern end of the valley like water from a bursting dam. All at once, the heavy crew-served American weapons opened up. Machine-guns growled out .50-caliber bullets from high ridges. Launchers thumped grenades out twelve a second. The crackling fire took a toll measured in voices. The Chinese quieted. They were either killed or too scared to shout.

Andre labored into the stiff breeze. He tried to check his weapon – to eject a round just to make sure the bolt hadn't frozen. But the driving snow stung his eyes so much they watered. He couldn't see, so he abandoned the plan. Above all the noise a heavy rumble filled the valley. Another distant B-52 raid drowned out the sound of the puny infantry weapons. High wind and low visibility foiled most air support. But at fifty thousand feet, the huge bombers merely opened their bellies and gravity did the rest.

They reached their pre-planned defensive line, but Andre panicked when he couldn't find his hole. He'd hurriedly dug it on the eve of the first battle. Up ahead was the cleared field of fire. They'd chopped or torched the low brush and limbs. He was definitely in the right place.

The others were bailing new-fallen powder out of their positions. Andre stumbled around until his boot sunk into his hole. He leaned his rifle against a tree and began to dig. He scraped the snow out using his gloved hands. When his fingers scraped bottom he crawled in. He grabbed his rifle by the stock and looked it over. The bolt looked clear, but still he blew into the mechanism. He brushed it with his glove, but that only put more ice and snow on the black metal.

The platoon sergeant made his way down the line checking the men. Andre saw splinters fly off a thin tree beside him. A bullet left a deep gash in the otherwise pristine bark. The Chinese were firing at extreme range. Andre laid as low in his hole as he could.

'Hold your fire till the guys from the OP pull back!' the platoon sergeant shouted as he knelt beside Andre's hole. 'There are *three* lines! *Three* lines! One battalion in each line! It's a full regimental attack!'

He moved on.

That was it? Andre wondered. No plans for maneuver? No pre-arranged signal to fall back? *Three lines. Three battalions. Three waves.* A full regiment was a lot of men. Maybe fifteen hundred against two hundred – two companies from Andre's battalion in line abreast.

Andre popped open the large pockets on his parka and checked. They were heavy with newly-filled magazines. He had six in his bulging pockets, plus four tucked away inside the jacket. Together with the full magazine in the rifle that made eleven – a hundred and sixty-five rounds.

He couldn't imagine going through that many magazines, but he also had two grenades. He felt for and found one in each breast pocket. *And then there's the ammo from the dead*, he thought guiltily as he looked around. To his left the man had a log for protection. To his right the guy – like Andre – was in the open. If he had to scoot over for more ammo – to loot the corpse of one of the fallen – he hoped it would be the PFC on his left. The log looked at least eight inches thick.

The wind died down a bit. The heavy bombers had finished working over the Chinese. He could again hear the machine-guns and grenade launchers from the high ridges. The breeze calmed even further. Suddenly it was still in the valley. The cracking and deep popping of the .50 calibers and 40-mm grenade launchers still echoed off the mountain walls. But like in the eye of a hurricane the storm seemed to pause. The last mist of snow drifted from tree branches overhead.

'Say, Andre!' the guy to his left called out. 'You got any extra grenades?'

Andre replied with an exaggerated shake of his head. 'Just *two*.'

'I got movement!' someone yelled.

'Hold yer fire!' came an NCO's reply.

GIs raced toward the rear. The men from the observation posts were sprinting through the woods with wild abandon. They crashed through low limbs and sent showers of snow to the ground. They didn't even slow down at the defensive line. One, two, three men passed on the dead run.

'How many were there at your OP?' one of Andre's squadmates asked the fleeing men. They didn't even glance in his direction. 'I count five guys who've passed!' someone shouted. Up ahead, Andre could see more men.

'Hold your fire!' the squad leader barked.

'Hey!' someone replied. 'Those are *Chinese*!'

At twenty meters, the thinly scattered line of Chinese attackers opened fire.

M-60s cut them down. They rattled the air with rapid strings of fire. In a matter of seconds, Andre could see no more targets. But the 60s kept up their industrial killing – meted out six rounds at a time. The machine-gunners squeezed, traversed, and squeezed again. Their full-sized NATO rounds flew through the woods for over a mile. Unless, that is, they hit something. Most likely a tree, or an outcropping, or one of the small ridges that ran like ribs up the hills to each side. But every so often they struck something soft. They ripped through flesh, and organs, and bone.

Six rounds, then a pause, then six more. Their squad had one of the guns. Andre wished he were closer to it. It was twenty meters to his left. And the gun to his right was thirty or more meters away. He was in the middle of the platoon's two strongpoints. In the weak gap between the two big guns. Right where the Chinese would have their greatest chance at a breakthrough.

The wind picked up again. In a few seconds the lull was over. Powdery ice crystals again peppered his eyes. The frigid air seeped through his clothing like cold rain. Each touch sent ripples through his body. The sudden chill threatened to overcome him. His muscles quivered and his breath grew ragged.

Andre tried hard to shut out his many distractions. To concentrate on the hazy woods ahead. The visibility was shit – at times maybe sixty meters, at others no more than twenty. And twenty was way too close. Twenty was hand-grenade range. At twenty, they were mere moments away from being overrun.

He was almost surprised to see the main body of Chinese. Their large parkas were flapping over pumping knees. The snow slowed them down – made them easy shots. But there were hundreds and hundreds of them. The American rifles began to crack. It sounded like the rifle range at boot camp. With his thumb Andre checked the selector. Single shots, not three-round bursts. The cold plastic stock touched his skin beneath his eye. An oversized white form filled the sight.

The rifle kicked. Its flame lit the gray snow. Down went the large parka. A strong gust sent snow into Andre's eyes. It was like the frozen spray of white caps blown off the tips of ocean swells. He had to wipe his face with the back of his hand to resume firing. But even in the haze of drifting snow targets made themselves visible. Flickering muzzles lit the woods with orange flame. The Chinese were firing their AK-47s on full auto. They didn't have orders to conserve ammo like their foes. Andre forced his watering eyes to line up a muzzle flash. When the faint outline of a human being became visible, he squeezed once and dropped the man at forty meters.

The buzz of a bullet through air made Andre flinch. The angry sound was unmistakably lethal. You needn't have seen the effects of a high-powered round to be terrified by it. You didn't even need to know what the hell it was. Anyone hearing air split at the speed of sound would know to fear the object's passage. Any sane man would curl up in the bottom of his hole.

Andre lined up another target and fired. Three-for-fucking-three.

His first miss came on the sudden arrival of a running soldier. The man rushed out of the swirling snow straight at the guy on Andre's left. Andre spun his rifle on the man but hurried the shot. The attacker's rifle was blazing from his hip. Andre and his squadmate both laid the man flat with their next rounds. He collapsed into the snow three steps short of their line.

Directly in front of Andre's hole he saw three men. They ran straight at him. He flicked the selector and squeezed the trigger in one motion. *Cra-a-ack*, came the roar of three rounds. *Cra-a-ack*, came another three. He had to fire again to waste the last guy, but only two rounds came out this time.

Andre cursed and ejected the magazine. He sank down into his hole. He'd dropped the three Chinese soldiers. But the woods were alive with hundreds of others. A constant yell again rose up. It had to be the second wave! The snow all around his hole was sprayed into the air. His shaking glove couldn't guide the magazine home. He cradled his rifle against his body and used both hands. It slid in until metal touched metal.

He was terrified by the steady hail of bullets. Terrified that he'd see all was lost when he raised his head. But he was fighting for his life so he chambered a round. He rose into the singing death.

There must've been a hundred shouting men charging forward. Andre fired and fired and fired. He missed far more than he hit. But it wasn't about marksmanship right then. It was about pouring out as many rounds as he could. It was about turning the ten rifles in his squad into a machine-gun. About spraying the woods with as much lead as they could unleash.

He bent over and reloaded again. As he rose something smashed into his helmet. Andre was stunned by the blow, but he raised the brim. The nearest attacker was twenty meters away. He jogged forward and fired his rifle straight at Andre. Orange fire blazed right in Andre's face. Andre raised his M-16 and fired. The iron sight of the M-16 was laid smack on the man's mid-section. The Kalashnikov's flaming muzzle swept across Andre as its owner fell. He hadn't felt any bullets pound his chest. Still, however, he waited. Perhaps he was hit, but in a state of shock. He watched the battlefield slowly empty of Chinese.

When he finally snapped out of his daze, he saw that they had won!

'*Faulk*!' he heard shouted through numb ears.

He turned to see everyone pulling back from the line. The squad leader was waving for Andre to come over. The man on his left lay draped across his log. He'd been hit despite the fortification. Andre climbed out of his hole despite severely aching muscles. His joints unlimbered slowly as if he'd been curled up in a cramped space for hours.

'Come *on*!' the sergeant shouted.

Andre joined him, taking the sergeant's and the wounded man's rifles. The soldier was moaning. His eyes were unfocused. He'd been hit bad. The squad leader hoisted him onto his shoulder. He was hunched over in a fireman's carry. He began to stagger to the rear with Andre following. Everyone else had already disappeared.

'What's the deal?' Andre asked.

'We're pullin' back,' the huffing man said.

'But why . . .?'

His question was cut short by the roar of a gun. Andre flinched on hearing the sound at his back. A half-dozen bullets sliced through the air and slammed into trees. Andre dropped to fire as the sergeant stumbled onward. The woods were filled with attackers approaching unopposed. Andre fired burst after burst, but it did little good. The few men he felled were just drops in the surging sea. He grabbed the three rifles and quickly rejoined the lumbering sergeant.

The squad leader was sweating profusely. His teeth were set in a painful grimace. Andre had no trouble keeping up with his slow pace. His only trouble, in fact, was to keep from racing ahead. He glanced over his shoulder. The wind was whipping through the woods. He couldn't see the enemy soldiers, but they would be gaining.

The wounded man was flopping limply like a rag doll. When the sergeant stopped to adjust the load, Andre checked the man's face. His eyes were glassy and lifeless.

'Hey, *sarge*. I think he's dead!'

The squad leader didn't respond. He just resumed his trudging flight toward their alternate positions. Andre glanced over his shoulder and saw hazy forms.

'He's *dead*, sarge! Jesus *Christ*, man, he's . . .!'

'*Shut the fuck up!*' came the reply through gasps for breath.

A stupendous roar filled the woods. This time the gunfire came from in front. From the Americans who were firing at the three men's pursuers. Andre cringed and ducked behind a tree. He hid not from the Chinese, but from the blazing line of American fighting holes ahead. When the first volleys didn't kill him, he figured they'd been recognized as friendly troops. He bolted around the tree and rejoined the laboring sergeant.

But now the Chinese were firing also. The volume of guns from the two sides was shocking. It was like racing across a live firing range. The simple act of remaining upright seemed impossibly perilous. Andre's mind blanked out all thoughts but one. He began to sprint and fled out ahead of the struggling squad leader. When he reached the alternate defensive line he dove to the ground. He crawled behind a tree and watched the sergeant struggle on. He'd almost made it when his legs just seemed to fold. He fell to his knees and the dead man's weight crashed down on top of him. The Chinese poured out of the woods fifty meters away. The sergeant squirmed out from under the weight and began to pull the dead man to the rear.

'Leave him *be-e-e*, sarge!' Andre shouted. But his voice was lost in the maelstrom of noise. He raised his rifle and fired repeatedly. But still the Chinese came. '*Come on, sarge*!' Andre shouted. He never took his eye from his rifle's sights. He emptied his magazine in frenzied firing.

'Shit!' Andre cursed. He laid his empty rifle beside the tree and began to crawl forward. Andre couldn't hear the whizzing bullets now. Chinese hand grenades began to fall all around. They were hurled on the dead run and burst everywhere.

He crawled low and as fast as he could. By the time he reached the sergeant he could see the bobbing heads of racing Chinese. The squad leader paid Andre no attention. He just dragged the hood of his man's corpse. A trail of blood through the white snow marked his progress.

'They're too close!' Andre shouted. The sarge heard him but only gritted his teeth and pulled.

Stray rounds skimmed through the snow all around. Andre was amazed he hadn't been hit. The gusting blizzard rose to a howl. He grabbed the wounded man's arm and began to pull with all his might. He kicked at the ground and propelled himself through the thick drifts.

Through the swirling snow he saw several Chinese. He lay back in terror and stared at the attackers, awaiting the inevitable. His rifle was ten meters away.

My grenades! he thought. As the sergeant continued his slow retreat, Andre pulled a pin and slung the heavy frag side-armed. It didn't go far. It didn't go far enough. But it was just right.

The explosion rattled Andre's insides. It lifted two men into the air with their feet still running. He took his last grenade, pulled the pin and rose to his knees. He hurled it football-style into the thickest clump of approaching Chinese.

The air around him was buzzing with bullets thick as buckshot. One caught the dead man's leg and splattered Andre with blood.

The second grenade lit the woods ahead. A brief orange day. It riddled the attackers with the metal knots of the pineapple. Andre scampered back, grabbed the dead man and pulled. He pulled until his elbows landed on his M-16. The sergeant began life-saving CPR. Andre fired up his half-empty magazine. He then fired the sergeant's and his dead squadmate's M-16s. He fired till 'Cease fire!' was shouted.

Flurries of shots rang out on the still-dangerous battlefield. Between the bursts of gunfire, Andre heard the puffing breaths of the hard-working sergeant. The man lowered his mouth onto the dead private's lips and blew. Andre crawled over to him.

'He's dead, sarge,' Andre whispered. Still the man worked frantically.

A medic slid to the ground and pried open the man's sagging eyelids. He then opened his bag and pulled out a pair of scissors. He cut away at the man's clothing. The two men applied bandages and continued CPR. Others joined them in the life-saving effort. Andre slunk away and rested his back against a tree.

The guy was alive. He was alive, but Andre had given up on him to save his own skin. He couldn't believe it, but it was true. The sergeant caught his eye and crawled over to where Andre lay.

Andre braced himself.

'Thanks, 'Dre,' the sergeant said.

The man's words should've eased Andre's guilt. The wretched feeling of having given up on a wounded buddy. His squadmates came by and added their words of praise. They backhanded Andre's leg or said, 'Way to go.' Andre ignored them all.

The man died before they got him off the battlefield. But even that didn't absolve Andre of his sin.

NORTH OF TANGYUAN, CHINA
April 22, 0100 GMT (1100 Local)

Woody framed the shot. Kate in the foreground. Rising smoke from the firefights in the background. Kate held the stick mike to her mouth. Woody rolled the tape. 'The skies have cleared over this narrow mountain valley. What the sunlight has revealed is death, death and more death.'

She stopped and shook her head. 'That's too much, don't you think?'

'Just keep going. We'll edit it out.'

Kate fixed the appropriate expression on her face. 'To reach this valley, Chinese troops must advance along winding mountain roads through a gauntlet of fire from the air. Sources estimate that as many as forty percent are killed or wounded before reaching this valley. What awaits those who make it can only be called murderous fire. Behind every rock and tree, it seems, is an American machine-gun or grenade launcher or rifle. The fire pours down on the valley floor from the steep mountain walls. An estimated ten thousand Chinese soldiers have tried to force their way into this valley since the fighting began two days ago. Their deepest penetration is less than a mile into a valley that is twelve miles long.'

The thrum of engines from another flight of C-130s caused Kate to change the order of her story.

'Now that the weather has lifted, U.S. Air Force C-130s have become a familiar sight in the skies overhead.' Woody shifted positions to take in the stubby transport. Kate could see out of the corner of her eyes the very scene she was describing. 'Rolling down their rear ramps are the tons of supplies that the intense fighting consumes round the clock. The trees are draped in the nylon of hundreds of parachutes. High above are the criss-crossing contrails of air superiority fighters. This may be Chinese real estate, but up above it's UNRUSFOR airspace.'

Woody swung the camera to follow the low and slow transports. They belched supplies into the valley. Parachutes from previous drops were draped over treetops to form an arrow easily seen from the air. More parachutes bloomed out of the backs of the fat planes, pulling heavy pallets filled with boxes or crates down the aircrafts' ramps. The supplies fell in and around the clearing at the tip of the giant nylon arrow.

Woody lowered the camera from his shoulder. Kate sat on a rock. 'Aren't you glad I talked you into hiking up here?' she asked.

'I'm tickled pink,' Woody said. He read the tape counter and made notes on what he'd shot.

'Are they gonna let you recharge the batteries at the hospital?'

'Yep,' Woody replied, not looking up at her. They sat there. The breeze was cold but not gusting. Woody had a scowl on his face.

'Aren't you going to get high?' Kate asked. Woody shrugged. 'Jesus Christ, Woody! What's the *matter* with you?'

'You want me to get high?' he snapped. 'Will that make you happy?'

'No-o! I just wanta know what's *wrong*? You're not acting like yourself.'

He took a deep breath and looked across the rugged landscape. 'Has it ever occurred to you that we're sitting on a ridge in the middle of China?'

She waited for more, but that was it. She snickered. 'Well ... ye-*e*-eah! It *has*, as a matter of *fact*.' He ignored her barbed reply. 'What's your point?'

'My point is that we shouldn't be here. Because sooner or later the Chinese are gonna get real serious about taking this place back.'

Kate laughed at the ridiculous suggestion. 'And you don't think they're *already* serious? I mean, didn't you just listen to my report? Ten thousand troops sounds fairly serious to me.'

'It's a drop in the bucket, Kate. So's a hundred thousand. They've got *millions* of men in their army. They've got a population of a billion and a *half*, for Christ's sake! Sooner or later, Kate, it's gonna get Biblical. They're gonna sweep over these hills and kill everybody and everything in their paths no matter who the hell has air superiority or air supremacy or whatever.'

'Well ... don't you think UNRUSFOR has thought of that? That Clark's got a plan?'

He shrugged. 'Maybe that's part of his plan. Maybe these guys are expendable.'

'Oh, come on! You don't think he'd piss away five thousand men!'

'If it meant victory? What's five thousand men?' Woody frowned and shook his head. 'Maybe he wouldn't, Kate. But shit happens. Things go wrong. He'd take risks. He'd have to take chances to win. And this is bound to be one helluva risk, don't you think? I mean, we're in *China*, Kate. In China!'

At first, there was nothing but the whistling sound of the wind. Then came a buzzing sound – like a chain saw high in the air.

'Look, an AC-130 raid,' Kate said. She got to her feet and pointed at the orbiting black gunship. You could see the tracer rounds streaking out of the sky toward the ground. Woody just sat there. 'Get the *shot*, will you?' Kate said impatiently.

'I've got plenty of AC-130 shots,' he muttered lethargically.

'Not in broad daylight and clear weather,' she argued. The sky was filled now with a second and then a third set of smudgy streaks. The circling Specter gunships pummeled their targets. Nearly always on call, they responded to fire direction from an AWACS, which monitored ground movement detected by an aircraft called a J-STARS. All of it unleashed punishing blows on the Chinese long before they even came near the valley. The buzzing was from 20-mm cannon and 5.56-mm miniguns. Booms resounded from 105-mm artillery pieces firing directly at targets below. All of it was mounted on the sides of the lazily orbiting gunships.

Woody raised the camera to his shoulder and began to tape. Kate kept glancing back and forth between the raid and her cameraman. She was terrified by what he said but tried not to show it.

SOFLYSK POW CAMP, SIBERIA
April 22, 2400 GMT (1000 Local)

'Take your clothes off!' came the female U.S. Army soldier's high-pitched Cantonese. Chin and the others all looked at each other uncertainly. She repeated the command. The dozen or so prisoners just stared at the woman. She looked ethnic Chinese, but her accent was distinctly foreign. And she was a woman.

A large black soldier with a rifle barked something threatening in English. Everyone began to disrobe. The tent was heated, and they were marched into a warm shower. Under the loud urgings in English they washed with soap and then dried with rough cotton towels. When they emerged, a team of doctors and nurses awaited.

Chin covered his genitals and walked sheepishly to the brightly-lit station. The doctor prodded and probed wearing thin, rubbery gloves. He even made Chin bend over and spread the cheeks of his butt. Once the humiliation was over, Chin was issued socks, canvas slippers, and a new uniform. It was a bright orange one-piece with a long number across his breast pocket. Next came an electric razor which clipped off all of Chin's wet hair. They gathered at the far side of the tent.

'We're gonna freeze to death,' someone whispered. The tent was nice and warm. But his teeth were already chattering. Chin's eyes fixed on the closed flap in the tent. Two guards stood there wearing arm bands and holding rifles. Beyond lay sub-zero temperatures. Their fears subsided when heavy blankets were handed out. Everyone wrapped the blankets over their heads and around their shoulders. They were herded onto a green bus just outside. It too was warmed by heaters. They sat in padded seats. Smiles broke out on some of the men. Two armed men stood at the front. The driver sat behind a mesh wire wall. He ground through the gears and they took off down the road.

'Where you think we're going?' the guy next to Chin asked.

Chin shrugged. He just stared out the frost-covered windows. The fresh clothing and warm blanket swaddled him. He was immersed in a rare sense of comfort. Months of aches and pains eased. He didn't care where they were taking him. He didn't imagine it would be bad. It wouldn't make sense to bath a man before killing him. And they weren't dressed for labor out in the elements.

The bus pulled through a barbed wire enclosure. Inside were row after row of barracks. The bus stopped in front of one. The doors opened to admit a chilly blast. Everyone rose and followed a guard to the street. They stumbled inside and were each ushered to a bunk. Half the long, open barracks was already filled. The human cargo from Chin's bus filled the other half. An American with a clipboard pointed Chin to the lower bunk. He wrote the number from Chin's jumper on his pad. On the bunk lay a metal cup. Inside it was a toothbrush and toothpaste. He eyed his new possessions in wonder.

The man in the lower bunk next to his was grinning ear-to-ear. He sat cross-legged and ate rice from a bowl. 'You want some?' he asked. He didn't have much left in the bowl, but Chin was famished. He nodded. 'There's all you can eat down there,' he said. He pointed with his chopsticks toward the end of the barracks.

Chin immediately got up and headed that way. By the time he got to the stove, he was already third in line. A Chinese cook wore an orange prison uniform. He stirred a vat of hot soup and dished out rice. A tall stack of bowls stood along the wall and Chin took one. There were no chopsticks, so he took a package filled with plastic utensils and a paper napkin.

There was chatter and laughter as Chin returned to his bunk. But no Americans were to be seen in the long barracks. Chin sank down with his steaming bowl of white rice. His bunk had a mattress and wool blanket. Plus he had the blanket he'd brought with him. He tried unsuccessfully to open the clear plastic wrapper. The man next to him laughed at his effort. Chin finally just ate the sticky rice with his fingers.

His yellow-toothed neighbor laughed again. He clicked his chopsticks together. 'Never figure those things out. But everything else?' He looked around the barracks. 'Whattaya think? Not bad, eh?' Chin was too busy stuffing his mouth to do more than nod. 'Been here three days, myself. They come through here twice a day to bring food and coal for the furnace and to take a count. They don't say too much.'

'The Americans?' Chin mumbled. He accidentally spilled rice from his mouth.

His bunkmate nodded. 'Strange people. But I've never eaten better in my life.' He flashed a crooked smile.

'So, is this it?' Chin asked. 'No work? Just sitting around here all day?' His neighbor nodded. Chin shoveled more gooey rice into his mouth. 'Any word from the war?' he asked.

The skinny man abruptly lay back on his bunk. He stared up at the mattress above him. He didn't answer Chin's question. He acted as if he hadn't heard it. Conversation over. That was when Chin began to notice the war's effects. He became a student of the sullen and the aching. He flitted around the brooding at a distance but ever-watchful. They gave shape and form – and sometimes a name – to the damage done to him. He felt a kinship – but never shared it – with his fellow survivors.

UNRUSFOR HEADQUARTERS, KHABAROVSK
April 23, 0200 GMT (1200 Local)

'The ice has broken, sir,' Major Reed reported. Nate Clark and several other officers from various UNRUSFOR armies looked up. Reed lowered his eyes to the printout. 'About thirty minutes ago we lost our first bridge. Within about twenty minutes after that we'd lost four others. We've now got reconnaissance both on the ground and in the air indicating that the ice is moving downstream at a rate roughly equivalent to the rate of flow of the water.'

'Just like that?' Nate asked in amazement. It was an event they'd all anticipated for so long, but it had happened so suddenly and without warning. Everyone's eyes were trained on him. He snapped out of his reverie. 'I want a report of exactly what we've got across. Every unit, every vehicle, what their stores are, where they are, where they're headed, what they're facing. I'm calling a full UNRUSFOR Joint Staff Meeting for,' he looked at his watch, 'sixteen hundred local.'

He rose, as did all those gathered around. 'We've got work to do, gentlemen. Let's get at it.'

JIXIAN, CHINA
April 23, 0230 GMT (1230 Local)

The truck groaned and squealed and stopped. Stempel was glad for the end to the bumpy ride. It beat the hell out of a road march. But it took willpower of a different sort to remain seated on that bench. The engine was shut off. They heard the noisy crowd.

The truck's canvas flap was thrown open. Bright daylight poured in. They were on a dusty, empty street lined by two-storey buildings. They appeared to be in a medium-to-large city.

'Everybody *out*!' the platoon sergeant barked. 'Leave your loads in the truck! Bring yer tear gas and gas masks!'

Stempel and his squadmates exchanged glances. They climbed down with their rifles and the large green cans of CS. They now wore only field jackets and BDUs – mottled green and brown woodland camouflage. Some sort of disturbance raged down the street.

'Form up!' the platoon sergeant bellowed.

'*What?*' Patterson whined in a high-pitched voice.

'You heard the man!' their squad leader shouted. 'First squad, fall in!'

The incredulous men formed ranks as if on a parade ground. Stempel's squad was in the front rank. Second and Third Squads were behind them. Their entire company was forming up platoon-by-platoon. 'Ten-*hut*!' the platoon sergeant commanded. 'Dress . . .

right!' Their drill was far less than boot-camp crisp. They held their left arms out to space themselves evenly. Their eyes roamed the windows of the surrounding buildings. 'What ya lookin' at, Patterson?'

'Private Chavez, sarge!'

'Cut the shit!' When they were properly formed, the lieutenant began a formal inspection. The street was filled with shouted commands. But Harold strained to decipher the meaning of the more distant din of massed people. The platoon leader came up to Patterson. 'Where's your bayonet?'

'Shit, I dunno, LT. In my pack, I guess.'

'Go get it.' Patterson took off for the back of the truck. The lieutenant made a cursory check of Harold and moved on. When the inspection was over, their company moved off down the street. Close-order drill commands were barked. 'Right . . . face! Forward . . . march!' No one called cadence, so they looked sloppy. When they rounded a corner, they came face to face with a single Bradley armored fighting vehicle. A thin line of MPs wearing gas masks extended to either side.

Facing them was a sea of Chinese civilians. They shouted and pleaded and gestured angrily.

'Jesus Christ!' Patterson said.

'Shut up!' their squad leader snapped from the head of their rank. The platoons were maneuvered until they were all three abreast. They stretched from sidewalk to sidewalk. They packed in tight. Three ranks deep. Stempel was in the front thirty meters behind the thin line of MPs.

'Get those masks on!' the company commander shouted to the hundred soldiers. The order was echoed by the platoon leaders, who roamed the street in front of the first rank.

'I can't believe this shit.'

'Patterson!' the platoon leader snapped. 'If I hear another Goddamn word outa you . . .!'

'*I didn't say* nothin', LT!' Patterson interrupted.

It had been Chavez. Everybody stole looks at the taciturn guy from LA. He almost never said anything to anybody. Harold took his helmet off and put the mask on. He sucked down on the rubber and sealed the mask tight. He returned the helmet to his head and looked out through the flat plastic lenses. Everything already seemed unreal. The mask only made it more so.

The company commander raised his gas mask. 'Mount . . . *bayonets*!'

507

he shouted. Harold could hear the grumbling and questioning all around. He fumbled with his scabbard. It took him a long time to seat the bayonet at the end of his rifle. 'Port,' came his next preparatory command, '*arms*!' Harold brought the M-16 up to port arms.

There they stood. Instead of the ten-meter spread of late Twentieth Century warfare, they stood shoulder-to-shoulder like in the Eighteenth. A few feet in front of each platoon stood the platoon leaders. The platoon sergeants stood at their sides. At the center a few feet further was the company commander and his attendant – the radio-telephone operator. There had been no radio in the Eighteenth Century. None was needed in the current engagement. The captain simply turned, lifted his mask, and shouted. 'Company-y-y . . .!'

The lieutenants echoed, 'Platoon!'

'Forward . . . *march*!'

Half the men heard the command and stepped off. The other half advanced just to stay in formation. They halted just behind the Bradley. The semi-organized mob of soldiers now faced the totally disorganized civilians. The officers and senior NCOs pulled their tear gas cans out and held them high. Some of the Chinese turned and left. Gaps began to appear in what had been a solid mass. Others shook their fists. Waved official documents of some sort. Hoisted banners across which were scrawled Chinese characters.

An MP shouted something in Chinese through a bullhorn. He repeated it over and over. The last few times he checked with a major who stood at his side before continuing. The major finally called a halt to the effort. He had a word with their company commander. The lieutenants were then summoned for an impromptu meeting.

Harold's platoon leader returned. 'Front ranks listen up! Every other man shoulder your weapon!' Harold's squad leader counted them off. He pointed at Harold, who slung his rifle over his shoulder. 'Men with weapons in hand assume riot stance!' The LT demonstrated with his own rifle. He leveled the weapon. The black bayonet led the way. 'Jab with each step forward! You men with your weapons sling spray gas! Aim at their faces! *Rear ranks*,' he shouted at the top of his lungs, 'lock 'n load!' Magazines were audibly seated behind First Squad.

'Jesus!' Patterson exclaimed. 'Whatta those people want?'

The platoon leader spun on him. 'How the fuck should *I* know? Our orders are to clear this street! So shut the fuck up!'

The dissent from that point on was quiet. 'This sucks!' someone said. 'This *really* sucks!' The sentiment was repeated throughout the ranks. The officers and NCOs still positioned themselves in front. But they pulled back till they were nearly flush. Harold found the button on the top of his spray can. The green metal was replete with scary warnings about which way to point the nozzle. He held his rifle sling to his shoulder with his left hand. In his right he held what looked like insecticide. 'Forward . . . *march*!'

They began their advance taking baby steps. It was what they'd been taught in one brief drill back in boot camp. In the front rank bayonets were jabbed vigorously at the crowd. With each footfall came a stylized lunge. It was meant to clear the front by intimidation. The pace was slow and deliberate by design. But to Harold – carrying his can – it seemed slow. More reluctance than well-ordered drill.

At a dozen meters from contact, most of the civilians had already turned and fled. A solid wall had been reduced to a small group. They dotted the debris-strewn street. Those who remained were either defiant or desperate. Most were seething with anger. Over what, Harold had absolutely no idea. They didn't seem to confront the Americans like enemies. More like an odd assembly of various protesters and petitioners.

'Grunt!' the officers turned and ordered. From the ranks arose a muffled but still sonorous noise. '*Huh*!' chanted over and over. Synchronized motion and sound feeding each other. Step forward – jab and grunt. Step forward – jab and grunt. The two rear ranks jabbed at air with loaded weapons. It organized the entire formation. They were in step. They were one. They were all braced to sink steel into flesh.

Everyone, that was, but the can holders. Patterson, Harold, and of all people Chavez. Harold felt like he was swept forward by the formation. Pushed along by the blade of a bulldozer. His head darted left and right. He tried to grunt with the others. But he gave up because it didn't seem natural without the bayonet. He felt like a bystander instead of a participant in the clash.

The officers sprayed their cans first. The tight squirts of gas jetted across the divide into the crowd. Everyone in the vicinity flinched and recoiled from the awful gas. Harold shook his can and scanned the 'battlefield' for a target. A man with a kerchief tied over his nose brandished a long stick. He boldly stood his ground. Range six meters. Harold decided he'd try to save the brave man.

509

He aimed the can and pressed the button. He adjusted his aim till the spray hit the man's eyes. The man screamed and dropped the stick to the ground. He fell to his knees and clawed and wiped at his eyes. He rolled to the paving stones in hyperactive agony. He writhed, and bucked, and yelped in pain. He scraped at the skin on his face. As his friends dragged him away he vomited. Harold sprayed mostly men, but some women. Mostly young, but some old. Mostly angry, but some plaintive. He had no idea what they were mad at. Or wanted. Or needed.

When it was over the street was filled only with trash. They made no arrests. All those who resisted were simply roughed up and sent away bleeding. They didn't kill anyone, but they didn't treat the injured. Harold couldn't tell where everyone had gone. They simply disappeared behind closed doors and windows.

They rested on a side street after the fifteen-minute confrontation. The entire company looked exhausted. Heads were hung. No one talked. The air was thick with the smell of tear gas. Men spat to rid their mouths of the taste. And they listened. They listened as their commanding officer ranted and raved. First to the major who commanded on the scene. Then over the radio to battalion staff. Then right in the face of the battalion commander, whose Humvee pulled up to the scene.

An endless convoy rolled down the empty street. But you didn't have to strain to hear the captain's enraged shouts. Everyone agreed with the sentiments he expressed. Even the lieutenant colonel, judging from the man's surprising patience. None of the men wanted to fight. They were all exhausted and ready to go home. But there was a war taking place and they were infantrymen.

WHITE HOUSE OVAL OFFICE
April 23, 0300 GMT (2200 Local)

Daryl Shavers was bubbling over with good cheer. Gordon Davis was concerned, but he didn't know why. Elaine's mood was somewhere between the two. Gordon wanted to know exactly where and why.

'We're gonna win, Gordon!' Daryl said. 'For the life of me I can't see any downside in this.' He tossed the single page on Gordon's desk. 'The

Chinese are cracking. This is just their opening bid. Japan's ambassador to Beijing said so himself.'

'Are you considering accepting it?' Elaine asked.

Gordon eyed her before he shook his head. 'They're basically just offering a ceasefire. We've come too far to settle for that.'

Daryl was grinning. 'Hell, if Clark's plan works and those two prongs hook up, we just do our thing and leave.' Gordon nodded slowly. Frowning. '*What*, Gordon? What's gotten into you? Things couldn't have worked out any better.'

'I know. I know.' Gordon looked at Elaine. 'I don't know what it is.'

'Maybe you're just a little blue,' she suggested. 'I mean, now that it's coming to an end. You know. Maybe everything's finally catching up with you. You remember what the doctor said. About people who suffer serious traumas.'

'Maybe,' was all Gordon could manage. He *was* depressed. But he didn't think that was it. It was something. Some risk. Some danger. He couldn't put his finger on it. He looked up at Daryl. 'I'll tell State not to answer. Let 'em stew for a few days while we press on to that valley. But you talk to the people at the Pentagon yourself. I want plans ready to withdraw those troops from China on a moment's notice.' Gordon felt another wave of concern. It baffled him.

PART V

'Power over one's fellow man is the root of all human activity. For what better way to control one's destiny than to bend others to your plans and your will? The urge to amass that power is both irresistible and subliminal. Whether that power is gained by wealth, by beauty, by office, by the muzzle of a gun, or by the moral suasion of one's ideas, its accumulation is the end, in and of itself, of every human alive.'

Valentin Kartsev (posthumously)
'The Laws of Human History'
Moscow, Russia

Chapter Twenty-Three

NORTH OF TANGYUAN, CHINA
April 23, 1500 GMT (0100 Local)

'Miller?' the squad leader said.

'Three full mags. Eight rounds in my fourth.'

'Fifty-three rounds,' the squad leader mumbled as he wrote. 'Faulk?'

'Two full plus eleven,' Andre answered.

'M-m-mph,' the sergeant said, shaking his head and writing. 'Squeeze 'em off, Faulk. Make 'em count.'

Andre nodded in the darkness. He picked at his MRE – chicken teriyaki and asparagus spears. A spasm of gunfire erupted from the south, but no one bothered even to look. The firefights were as regular as clockwork – every ten or fifteen minutes. The sound of fighting rose this time, however, until it was clear that a major attack was under way. Without being told, the eight remaining men of Andre's squad began to gather their gear.

The call came two minutes later.

'Let's *move* out!' the new platoon sergeant barked. Everyone rose slowly to their feet. There were no groans as the men flexed their sore

515

muscles. No words of complaint from Andre's usually vocal squadmates. There was nothing but the clack of magazines. The metallic screech of a charging handle in need of oil. The snapping latch of grenade launchers being closed, locked and loaded. The resignation of the eight teenagers was oppressive.

They advanced through the thick woods in single file – the better to keep together in the darkness. Their lonely march was made in silence. It contrasted sharply with the thunderclap of Chinese artillery. Shells burst along the high ridges every few seconds. They lit the upper branches of the trees like bolts of lightning. Each explosion drew skyward glances from the frightened soldiers. The sporadic fire from the Chinese guns was new. But Andre knew the big guns' absence wasn't an accident. With fighter-bombers patrolling the skies night and day, the life expectancy of artillery crews had to be short.

'It's almost warm tonight,' the guy close behind Andre commented. Andre nodded – not sure his gesture was visible in the flickering light. 'Hope this weather holds,' he said. There was a quiver in his voice. Andre looked up at the clear and starry night. It was a damn sight more pleasant than it had been just a few days before. 'We'll pro'bly get a big airdrop tomorrow with more . . .'

'Knock it off!' came a shout from up front.

They slowly ascended a shallow humpback ridge. Everyone stooped low near the top and raised their weapons. No orders needed to be given. They'd done this countless times before. The increasing volume of the fighting alone warned of the death that lay ahead. When Andre crested the ridge, he saw the well-lit battlefield. The valley's contours were made clearly visible by flashing muzzles and bursting flames.

The knot in Andre's stomach tightened. He followed the others in a stoop toward the streaking fireflies below. The roar of the guns was now so great only a shout would be heard. Andre kept his eyes on the men ahead for signs of danger. The woods grew thick with smoke. The thin needles of the evergreens overhead had no color in the flashing light from the guns. Andre could no longer make out the sounds of individual weapons.

His stomach was cramping. His bowels were churning. His mouth was dry and tasted of steel. His cold-weather gear suddenly seemed too warm. His palms and armpits were damp. The line filed past a waiting man. With his free hand, the man took soldiers and shoved them to their fighting positions. 'We dig in here!' came the foul breath

516

into Andre's face. The platoon sergeant propelled Andre to the right. He walked into the darkness till the squad leader then grabbed his webbing. He pointed down. Andre dropped his fighting load to the ground and began to dig. He nervously confirmed that he was not in too wide a gap. The men on each side dug into the thawing soil six meters away. At night their spacing was reduced by almost half. If truth be told, Andre preferred fighting at night. He was terrified by the isolation of a ten-meter spread.

He spaded the earth with his metal entrenching tool at ninety degrees. He chopped it up and then sunk the blade in deep. Chop and scrape, chop and scrape. His back ached and his lungs burned.

'Delta Company's gonna pass the line to us!' the platoon sergeant informed the men as he walked down the line past Andre. 'We got five minutes! Dig 'em deep, boys. There's a whole lotta hurt comin'!'

The man disappeared. No one said a word as they dug, but Andre could hear their grunts of effort. Sweat poured down his forehead and neck. He debated taking the time to remove his parka. But the shallow hole would be his grave unless he kept on digging. The next few minutes were spent deepening the hole.

Andre didn't know why he looked up but he saw movement. It came as a shocking realization. He dropped his shovel and sank to his knee to grope for his rifle. But it was only two men helping a wounded buddy to the rear.

Andre vowed to pay more attention to their front. If all went well, they'd get plenty of warning. There'd be another visit by the platoon sergeant or platoon leader. Then the retreating D Company would pass. The last man through – usually an NCO – would call out 'Line passed!' Then the order to commence firing would echo from all sides.

But all didn't always go well, Andre knew. He dropped to both knees to scrape the loose dirt with his gloves. If D Company folded or was flat overrun, the first sign they'd get of approaching danger would be a brief glimpse of sprinting Chinese soldiers. They wouldn't stop and fight. They'd try to get to the rear where confusion would be their ally.

When he was satisfied with his position he folded his shovel and returned it to his webbing. In a hasty retreat he didn't want to have to collect his gear. And he definitely didn't want to leave behind his all-important shovel.

Andre placed his two spare magazines on the ground to his left.

His eyes were long adjusted to the dim light. But he took the time to memorize by feel their location. The first thing to go would be his night vision. Now began the worst time of all. Andre peered into the woods ahead through his M-16's sights. He licked his dry lips but couldn't find the moisture to swallow.

'Where the hell is D Comp'ny?' the guy to his left asked.

Andre didn't know if the question was meant for him. But he wasn't in the mood to answer. It was the talker from the line behind him. Andre wasn't willing to trade invisibility for any calming effect of a reply on the guy's nerves. But the question the guy had asked was a good one. Brief strobes of light from large mortars and artillery bursts gave good enough illumination to the front. Andre grew increasingly familiar with his weapon's sights. Nothing moved. Nothing changed. All was still.

His stomach turned over and he felt a cramp in his bowels. The tension had grown steadily into a pounding headache just behind his eyes. He pressed his fingers against his eyelids then rubbed his temples. It provided him little relief. When he looked up he saw running soldiers. The woods were filled with them.

Andre jerked his rifle to his cheek and flicked the selector to 'Semi.' His vision was still blurry from rubbing his eyes. 'Hold your fire!' was shouted up and down the line. Andre's heart was pounding. He'd almost killed a friendly soldier. Delta Company was falling back as fast as they could run. They passed so close Andre could hear their heavy breathing. There were moans and groans of wounded men being carried too roughly by comrades. Long bursts from trailing machine-guns sprayed the woods behind the withdrawing unit. The gunners and their assistants then hustled the weapons past Andre – the new main line of defense.

One crew dropped to their knees between Andre and the guy on his left. 'They're about two hundred meters behind us!' the winded gunner called out. 'Must be about a battalion! Good luck!' With a grunt they rose and he trotted off.

Andre glanced back at the retreating men in envy. They'd put in their time and survived. There'd be a third line setting up behind Andre's. So Delta Company was probably done for the night. Unless, that is, everything broke.

'Free to fire!' echoed back up and down the line. He gritted his teeth and scanned the trees for the first Chinese. A few more muted calls cautioned, 'Don't waste yer ammo!' or other similar warnings. It gave Andre a sense of comfort to hear the voices stretch into the distance to either side.

We'll be all right, he told himself, trying to swallow. The line had been passed in good order. They were braced for the shock and ready. It was the Chinese who would die that night. Andre caught himself grinding his teeth so hard his jaw hurt. He stretched his neck to both sides and it popped. When his eye returned to his sight he took a deep breath.

Guns first opened fire far to the left. They were machine-guns spitting out six-round bursts. Then a cascading volley of rifles. Next their own squad's machine-gun sprayed the woods. Andre took a quick check of where the gun was to his right. Maybe fifteen meters away. Worst case he'd peel back and hook up with the 60.

Any second now, Andre thought.

Mortars whistled overhead and dropped into the trees a hundred meters to their front. They burst in the upper branches, raining shrapnel and wood splinters with surely devastating effects. Grenadiers looking down from the hills plunked 40-mms into the woods even closer. Andre knew the men on the ridges wore night-vision goggles. They could see through gaps in the trees the surging mass of Chinese infantry.

As if straight out of the blazing forest there emerged the forms of running men. They were easy shots at thirty meters.

Andre dropped them one at a time. Slowly. Aim. Squeeze. *Crack!* He concentrated on his breathing as he lined up his targets. *Crack!* The rifle pounded against his shoulder. The rounds it unleashed struck home. *Slow 'n steady*, he told himself as the double-stack in his magazine dwindled toward empty.

But he wasn't able to keep it slow. Despite the devastating fire from three sides the number of Chinese grew. Andre fired, and fired, and fired. His attempt to count ammo gave way to surprise as the trigger froze.

Andre dropped the empty magazine and slapped a new one home. He forced himself to concentrate as the woods remained alive with . . .

Spitting sounds like a striking serpent flew by Andre's face. The attackers were dodging and weaving. He raised his rifle to his shoulder and fired. His finger pulled as fast as it could. The return fire grew thicker still. Once again he was surprised when the trigger wouldn't pull.

'Shit!' Andre cursed. He was down to his last magazine. *Eleven rounds!* the alarm sounded in his head. *Shit! Shit-shit-shit-shit!*

He again raised his M-16. He was reluctant to fire despite the multitude of targets. Only the straight-on approach of three running soldiers – each spewing great volumes of fire – convinced Andre to part with a few precious rounds. Each shot felled a man. When another attacker leapt from the ground unexpectedly, however, Andre hurried and missed his fourth shot. He killed the charging man with his fifth. Chinese wove through the trees ahead. They were framed by bursts large and small.

Five rounds left! Andre thought in near-panic.

It was frustrating not to fire at easy targets. But it was also kind of a relief. If he didn't fire the Chinese couldn't see him. If they didn't see him they wouldn't shoot back. Andre was safe at least in relative terms. But it also bred a sense of detachment. The view of an observer instead of a participant.

The guy on Andre's left pasted his M-16 flat to his cheek. Spent cartridges were methodically ejected. The same sight greeted Andre's check to his right.

Only Andre lay there useless and inactive. And at the critical moment of a pivotal fight for his life. He thought about rushing forward and grabbing an AK. He'd never do such a thing, but he felt compelled to consider the suicidal act. He craned his neck to see if any squadmates had been hit. He could render aid if someone was wounded, or scavenge ammo if the guy was dead.

But everyone appeared engaged in the fight. Everyone, that is, but him.

He remembered his two hand grenades. *Of course!* he thought with relief. He pulled the two grenades from his webbing. Swallowing hard he grimaced and pulled the first ring. He had to twist the bent pin to get it out. Holding the handle firmly pressed in his right hand, he rehearsed the throwing motions in his head. When he was ready, he rose up onto his right knee, jutted his left boot to the front and raised the grenade to his chin. Pointing his left hand toward the Chinese he hurled. The three-pound frag spun in a tight spiral like a football. He distinctly heard the handle clang off. He dropped to press his face flat to the ground. The short fuse burned down the center of the grenade.

There was a hard thump through the ground, then a boom and a flash. The air all around Andre was alive with streaking rounds. They'd seen him rise up and toss the grenade. After a short while of lying low, the fire died down. He grabbed the second grenade and repeated the process.

When he raised up he saw two enemy soldiers. They darted in a crouch from tree to tree not fifteen meters away from where Andre lay. Andre slung the grenade straight at the two men. The smoking trail spiraled through air until sparks flew.

The grenade rebounded back off a tree.

He was sitting up. His skin was clammy and cold.

'You hear me now?' someone was asking.

He smelled strong fumes and felt a sting in his nostrils. He slammed his head back into the tree behind him.

Pain shot through Andre's skull. He leaned over to the side and vomited.

'*Jesus* Christ!' the man said in disgust and stood up. He tossed the stick of smelling salts to the ground beside Andre. Andre was exhausted. He lay on his side. His head on the ground. His head felt like it was split open at the nose. He was sweating profusely. He couldn't find the strength to do the simplest of things. He took no interest in anything.

A small penlight lit his face then quickly shut off.

'Is he *sick*?' Andre heard his platoon leader ask.

'No, sir. I don't think so. Mild concussion, maybe.'

The lieutenant squatted beside Andre. 'You okay, Private Faulk?'

'Yessir,' Andre mumbled weakly.

The platoon leader rose. His boots were next to Andre's head.

'What's the count?'

'Two dead – both in third squad. Five wounded – two bad.'

'*Fuck!*' the lieutenant replied quietly. Andre listened with his eyes closed. His head hurt so bad he couldn't open them. The radio crackled. The platoon leader answered. A map rattled in the air above Andre. When the LT signed off, he said, 'We're headin' back, Sarg' Davis.' Andre knew they must mean to the rear. Away from the savage fighting. Just a few hundred meters back where you could sleep. Andre opened his eyes. He couldn't see the men's faces. Just two sets of dirty white trousers.

'We need some *time*, sir!' the platoon sergeant whispered. 'We got some people that's shook *up*!'

521

'I *know* that, God*dam*mit! What the hell'm I s'posed to *do*? Tell the CO *no*? We're movin' out. The whole comp'ny. Get 'em up.'

The lieutenant took off in anger. With a rustle of fabric the platoon sergeant reached down. Andre felt a firm grip on his upper arm. 'Let's go, Faulk.' He pulled. Andre at first was confused. He then found himself sliding up the tree. With a yank that almost separated his shoulder, he was on his feet. 'Let's get you back to yer squad.'

'But . . .'

But what?' the man snapped.

Andre licked his dry lips. 'I don't have any ammo.'

The platoon sergeant was older. Maybe twenty-six. 'We'll get you an AK. We got stacks and stacks of 'em.'

CAMP DAVID, MARYLAND
April 23, 1500 GMT (1000 Local)

The joint chiefs all wore their uniforms. Gordon Davis had on slacks and a shirt with an open collar. Maps stood on easels amid two fireplaces and dark wood paneling. 'We're having some real problems with civilian unrest in Jixian and Nancha,' General Dekker reported. He indicated two Chinese cities on the map just south of the border. 'Civil order has broken down completely.'

'Has there been bloodshed?' Gordon asked.

'Yes, sir. But not shed by us. People have been ransacking local Communist Party and security ministry offices. We haven't disarmed the constabulary forces, and there have been numerous shootings. So far, we've avoided direct engagement. But the situation is deteriorating.'

Gordon felt a rush of anxiety. 'How about the military situation?'

Dekker glanced at the other chiefs before answering. The disorder must be a serious concern, Gordon thought. 'The Chinese are making contact with our flanks. No hard jabs. They're just probing till we stiffen. Since they don't have any aerial reconnaissance to speak of, they're probably trying to determine where we are and in what strength. The best way to do that is to press and see if you bump into anything hard.'

'What are our casualties?'

'We've lost about two thousand dead in the counter-offensive, and about nine thousand wounded. Half those KIAs are in the Tangyuan Valley. Overall, we're just over ten thousand dead and thirty thousand wounded for the war.'

Gordon held Dekker's gaze. 'How long till we hook up with those troops in the valley, General?'

Dekker frowned. 'It's difficult to say, Mr President. We're on our time line right now. That would put us there in five days.'

Gordon nodded and turned to the head of the Special Operations Command. 'So how goes the rearming of the Russian military?'

UNRUSFOR HEADQUARTERS, KHABAROVSK
April 23, 2200 GMT (0800 Local)

'She's been ferrying them out by medevacs,' Major Reed said. Clark sat in front of the monitor watching video of parachutes blooming behind fat green aircraft. Guns popped and smoke rose from the battlefields beneath the high ridge. It was Clark's first view of the desperate battle.

And the voice was clearly Kate Dunn's. 'Flying low through the valley, transports drop massive loads of supplies, which are consumed at a prodigious rate. Soldiers are engaged in near-constant battle against wave after wave of Chinese infantry. Although the numbers of troops landed deep in China is classified, this is a major operation aimed straight into the heartland. And the People's Liberation Army is pulling out all the stops to throw the foreign invaders from their soil.' There were pictures of men running with stretchers toward aid tents. 'The twenty-year-olds weathering that storm have no great desire to be here. But they're among the best soldiers in the world. They've been hardened by months of winter war.' There were close-ups of sunken, glassy eyes. 'They know that the course of the war and of history may turn on the outcome of this one battle. But more importantly they know that they're fighting for their lives and for the lives of their best friends.' Two soldiers were crammed tightly into a hole – sound asleep. 'And the force of the bonds forged on this anvil of war are so great they can only be broken by death.'

The final shot was of a vinyl tarpaulin covering all but the upturned boots of a dead soldier.

'This is Kate Dunn, NBC News, northern China.'

Clark looked up at Reed and shook his head. 'No way. Confiscate every tape she sends out.' Reed nodded. 'I would like to take a look at them, though,' Clark added. Reed nodded again. 'Now let's go.'

Nate Clark's Blackhawk hovered far upstream from the heli-bridge. Huge U.S. Marine Corps helicopters ferried heavy loads from one bank to the other. But the more impressive sight was what flowed down the river. Jagged patches of ice – sometimes piled high – meandering toward the sea.

'Beautiful, don't you think?' General Cuvier said. Clark looked up at the area's French commander. They sat knee-to-knee beside the large square window. 'Before I came here it was impossible to conceive of the scale.' He stared down at the scene. 'Of the distances. Of the wilderness. How few roads and villages and people. At least on the Russian side of the border.'

Clark still looked out the window. But his mind wandered. They were entering a new country. A new and more populous theater. 'I won't miss it,' Clark said without realizing. He looked up into the stare of his escort.

The man was alert and leaning forward. The helicopter's engine was loud. It allowed for the fiction that the six aides couldn't overhear their private conversation. 'You seem to be afraid of losing,' the general said. His voice was low and his accent thick. 'If I can speak to you about this.' Clark invited him to continue with a spread of his hands. 'What I am saying about you is very *good* for a commanding officer. There was talk, you know. Talk from Paris, which we were told came from Washington.' Clark just listened. 'That you would resign your command,' he explained as if Clark would immediately understand. 'But that never seemed to me to be the man that I saw – the soldier – and I told them this. They just said,' he made a face and waved his hand dismissively, 'a-ah, you just do your job. Fight your battles. *We* will tell *you* about such things.'

He rocked back with a scowl on his face and locked himself stiff-armed with his hands on his knees.

Clark's gaze drifted off. 'At least they didn't leave a pistol on my desk.'

There was laughter from everyone in the helicopter. Nate turned to see a half-dozen smiles. The captains and colonels in their entourage lightened up. An ease settled over the group that had not been there before.

The ear protectors they all wore looked like large headphones. Up and down the riverside heliport giant CH-53Es dropped their loads on mesh pads. Their huge engines were revved to full power. The noise was quite literally deafening.

Clark strained to listen to his guide. The Marine colonel and his French commander walked him onto the bulldozed and matted landing areas. Men on the ground unhooked the cargo. The loads dangled a hundred feet beneath the U.S. military's most powerful helicopter. 'We got a dozen Echos on loan from the Navy!' the colonel yelled.

The ferries didn't have very far to travel. From one side of the river to the other, they shuttled vehicles, nets and fuel tanks. The traffic was exclusively one-way. They picked up on the Russian side, and dropped off in Communist China. As he watched the operation, he experienced a sudden and unexplainable rush. Thoughts and feelings flooded his mind. It was as if he'd awakened to find himself sleepwalking. He looked at the bustling helipad. The crowded truck park. The tent city. The mounds of crates and boxes. The road that hadn't been there two days before. It had been built solely for this crossing. In a month, it would be a sea of mud. But for the next two weeks it would be an artery through which would flow the life's blood of his army.

And it was all in the People's Republic of China.

General Cuvier was pointing out the short turnaround time. How the helicopters never touched the ground. But Clark's mind roamed down the road into Manchuria. Dust rose high into the air behind two-ton trucks. The same dust also filled the air on the Russian bank. In Clark's mind he visualized the huge pipeline. From factories and ports in America and Japan to the troops on the main line of resistance, the entire supply chain ran across the earth's surface. Until it reached the Amur River, that is, and its gravity-defying heli-bridge.

The parade of ice down the waterway was a testament to nature's power. Clark found himself increasingly drawn to the riverbank. He saw there with his own eyes what had previously been dry engineering theory. Comparisons of the maximum force that a span would withstand with the energy unleashed by millions of tons of moving ice. The thick slabs were broken in places and piled atop one another sometimes several layers thick. They were white monuments to crushing force. The phenomenal energy of the river's movement. And even over the constant roar of the helicopters he could occasionally hear the groan of the grinding ice.

'We'll have pontoon bridges in ten days!' the Marine transportation officer said from Clark's side. 'Not here, but about ten miles downriver!' He raised a gloved hand to point. 'Had to cross up here with the helicopters because there wasn't flat land downstream for two LZs – one on each bank!'

Clark caught himself thinking it seemed too easy. The Chinese defenses built up to counter the Soviets had seemed insurmountable on paper months before. Clark knew intellectually all the answers. That those defenses had eroded. That they'd been abandoned by the troops who invaded Siberia. But he knew also that there was nothing easy about it. That men fought and died for every meter of that dirt road. It was a depressing measure of how detached he'd grown from the killing and the dying in the field. How effectively he had shut from his mind all the horror he'd experienced in his youth.

He turned to his French host and said, 'I've decided to make a change in my itinerary.'

The helicopter landed. Clark and his entourage got out. A British colonel saluted the American and French generals bare-handed. He then quickly replaced his gloves and glanced nervously over his shoulder. Over their heads, the helicopter rotors spun slowly to a stop.

'I apologize, General Clark . . .' the colonel began. But everyone ducked when a loud *boom* rang out from the next block. Clark's security troops tightened their ring around the commanding general. Grayish-white smoke rose above the low buildings. Everything seemed to be under control.

'As I was saying,' the British battalion commander said, 'I do apologize that I am not able to put on a better reception for you, sir.'

It was Clark who felt like apologizing. A total of three helicopters had put down unannounced. In the lead were two green Blackhawks – his and the one for his security team. Behind was a Cobra gunship riding shotgun. His half-dozen bodyguards – non-uniformed employees of the Department of Defense – were packed at arm's length around the three officers. And at least a platoon of the colonel's infantrymen had taken up positions around the impromptu helipad.

A machine-gun opened fire from the same direction as the explosion. Clark listened to the steady drumbeat of high-powered rounds.

'It seems it is *I*,' Clark said, 'who have interrupted your day's work, colonel. I won't keep you long. I just wanted to look around.'

'Of course, sir,' the man said. Clark could tell nothing from his tone or manner. Was he pissed off and Clark was missing it? The British colonel turned and looked over his shoulder. 'It's more like unfinished business, actually. A few hold-outs down in the cellars we're trying to clear out. It's a pity to have to blast them out like that. But I don't want to leave them behind our lines. Could get a tad *sticky* once the sun goes down, what with our perimeter set up about five hundred meters in that direction,' he said – pointing down the street past the rattling machine-gun.

'Is the perimeter quiet?' Clark asked.

'For the most part, yes, sir.'

'Can I take a look?' Clark asked.

The colonel arched his eyebrow, looking at the dozen-man entourage. 'As you wish, General Clark.'

Clark understood the field officer this time. He turned and spoke in a loud voice. 'Everyone wait here while General Cuvier and I inspect the perimeter.' The chief of the security detail turned his dark sunglasses Clark's way. 'You wait here,' Clark said to the man, then he pushed his way through the ring of men.

'General Clark,' the security officer said.

Nate set his jaw and ground his teeth. He was, after all, a soldier. He could take care of himself on a battlefield. He turned back. The man held his weapon out to Clark. It was an M-16 shortened to carbine length. Its short sling was meant to hang the weapon at your hip.

Nate took it. He was within five hundred meters of the enemy, and he'd brought no weapon with him at all. He strapped the carbine over his shoulder and took a pistol belt with ammo pouches. He had to loosen the belt for his waistline. Everyone waited patiently by his side. The belt sagged under the weight of six magazines. Clark had forgotten the feel of a fighting load.

'Perhaps I should get something better than *this*, h-u-*uh*?' General Cuvier asked. He smiled as he patted the pistol in his holster. The two generals and the British colonel hooked up with a squad. Riflemen led the way single file down the street.

'There doesn't appear to be much damage from the fighting,' Clark said. The carbine kept sliding off his shoulder, so he held it by the pistol grip and front guard.

'We didn't have to do too much fighting, actually,' the colonel replied. 'We came in with armor and mounted infantry, and the city's militia didn't give it a go.'

The streets seemed strangely desolate. No smoke came from the chimneys. 'Where are all the people?' Nate asked. 'This city had a population of a few hundred thousand.'

'We don't know where they are, really. We get reports that the roads to the south are jammed. Refugee traffic must be wreaking havoc on the Chinese.'

'And they are in our way also,' General Cuvier noted. 'Slowing us down.'

Another loud explosion rocked the street. The infantrymen instinctively dropped to one knee. They quickly resumed their progress toward the perimeter.

'Well, there do seem to be at least *some* militiamen who've chosen to stand and fight,' Nate commented.

The colonel looked back over his shoulder. 'They're not *fighting*, actually. They just won't come out. When we find them hiding, we back off and evacuate the building of any civilians. We waited several hours for an interpreter, but as the day wore on I decided I couldn't wait any longer.'

'Do you mean you're just dropping charges down into those cellars when they don't give up?'

'We *try* to coax them out. But without an interpreter I'm afraid it's no use.' He paused at an intersection and turned. 'As I said, it *is* a pity what one must do.'

The silence was filled only by the steady pounding of a machine-gun. The colonel's men finishing the job.

'We'll get you an interpreter by nightfall,' Clark said.

They crossed the street one at a time at a jog. The lead infantrymen grew increasingly tense at each intersection. Up ahead there were barricades across the broad street. All the talking was now done by hand. By pointed fingers or blunt fists. By parade-field waves and traffic-cop halts. They raced across open spaces – rifles raised to their shoulders. They knelt behind cover with eyes to their sights.

Nate was tense. But that was natural. Sickening activity was the most prominent recollection of the war he'd fought in his youth. The dread of imminent death. If not you, the guy next to you. And it was mixed with interminable stress and inadequate sleep. Numbing fatigue interrupted by shocking danger. Exhaustion from living unprotected in the elements. Aches and pains from a dozen cuts and bruises. Battling extremes of everything all at once.

Nate's turn to cross the intersection came. He was humiliated by the indignity of an escort. A British private crossed the street at his side. He was so angered that he felt no present sense of danger. When he knelt, General Cuvier was smiling. He understood from Nate's frown how Nate felt. 'At least I didn't break a hip,' Nate muttered.

The amiable Frenchman was just beginning to laugh when a shot rang out. The British soldiers all began an agitated search. Lying in the middle of the street a man cursed and shouted. 'God! Ah! Christ!' he yelled. He clutched his bleeding thigh and writhed in pain on the cobblestones.

'I've got movement in the wind*o-o-ow*!' someone shouted. The bull-pup rifles carried by the British opened up. Automatic rifle fire from six men all at once.

'*I need aid!*' the wounded man shouted – his teeth bared. His eyes were shut in a grimace. His red cheeks bulged out and he began to puff. His mouth formed an 'O' and his chest heaved as he gulped air.

Several of his comrades put down their weapons. Clark raised his. He leaned out around the corner and took aim. A second-storey window was being peppered with fire. Thin curtains jerked with each passing round. With his thumb he selected 'Auto.'

'Go!' the lieutenant shouted.

Clark squeezed the trigger. The stubby carbine recoiled with surprising force. He recentered on the window and put five rounds through and two on the wall. Empty shells 'chinged' off the paving stones. He switched to 'Semi' and squeezed them off one round a second.

He released the empty magazine as soldiers dragged the fallen man to the far side. The rest of their platoon was just arriving, adding great amounts of fire.

Two men set a machine-gun down and dropped behind it. As soon as they settled on the ground, the weapon roared. Flame shot two feet from the muzzle. It was a shocking assault on your senses. An elemental eruption of noise made more dramatic by the narrow and curving canyon of walls.

The burst ended.

'*By* twos!' shouted a mustachioed sergeant. 'Go!'

'*ER-H-H-H-H-H-R-R*' roared the gun.

No riflemen even bothered firing now. A column of men sprinted down the street hugging the walls.

'*Cease* fi-i-ire!'

The street was quiet save for the sounds of the front door being kicked in. Then there was no noise till the troops got upstairs. They smashed through the sniper's door. Seconds passed. The room exploded.

Flame shot through two windows at once. Smoke poured out.

'It's all c*le-e*-ear!' shouted a man from the dark window. 'Sniper's dead!'

'Safe your weapo-o-ons!' shouted the platoon leader. It was a command that Clark instinctively followed. He was kneeling amid brass shell casings. The stench of rifles filled the air. He rose slowly. His knee ached from the cobblestone beneath it. Joints popped. He felt no spring in his muscles. Everyone rose. Gathering themselves. Straightening their nerves out after the brief fight.

A lieutenant appeared in the sniper's window.

'Was it a *partisan*?' the British colonel shouted.

'No, sir!' the platoon leader replied. 'PLA regular, sir!'

'Oh, thank God,' the battalion commander muttered from beside Nate.

'Have you gotten any partisan activity?' Nate asked quietly.

'Not yet.'

The two men looked at each other. 'Do you have a contingency plan?'

The colonel took a deep breath. 'Worst case?' he asked. Clark nodded. 'We just get out. We leave the cities. Bivouac in the countryside. If . . . if *you* say, that is, of course.' Clark nodded again. 'In the country we can maintain some distance. Establish clear fields of fire. Even so, there really is no effective defense against . . . against a billion and a half *people*?' He shook his head. 'Not if they're roused, sir. Not if they're roused.'

'There's a happy thought,' Cuvier said to end the conversation.

'Let me know when you hear how bad your man is,' Nate asked the colonel. 'I'll want to visit him at the hospital. Now . . . let's go.'

The squad reformed for the final approach to the perimeter. The 'front' consisted of two wrecked buses lying end to end. The crude tank trap built by Chinese defenders was blackened by fire. It provided excellent cover for their last few meters. The men jogged in a crouch down the sidewalk. After a short distance they turned through a door. The room they entered had been shot to pieces.

Four men lay against the walls. They hardly moved. Their eyes were fixed on the new arrivals. Their weapons were not far away. One clutched his rifle to his chest. Another lay cradled across its owner's thighs. The others leaned against the wall beside them.

The dozen or so new arrivals crowded into the room.

'How were things today, lance corporal?' the battalion commander asked.

'Oh, it was tolerable, sir. Tolerable. And everything is quiet now, sir. Sounded like you had some trouble on the way, though, sir. Anyone hurt?'

'Had a chap catch a bullet – right here,' the colonel said. He jabbed his thigh at the site of the wound.

'They can be bad – leg wounds. *Bleeders.*'

Several heads around the room nodded.

'Yes. Well . . .' The colonel turned to Nate. 'I'd like to introduce you men to Lieutenant General Nathaniel Clark, United States Army, commanding general of UNRUSFOR.'

The soldiers started to get to their feet. Clark motioned energetically for the men not to rise. 'And it's Nate. My given name is Nate, not Nathaniel.'

The four men all nodded and acknowledged him politely. 'How do you *do*, sir?' and 'It's a pleasure, sir.'

'Lance Corporal Sheffield, sir. Edgar, sir. From Spilsby.'

A couple of the others snickered.

Nate shook the man's hand. 'Spilsby? That's . . .?'

'In the north, sir. Near the sea.'

'A-ah.' Clark said, nodding.

He then duck-walked around the room to meet the others. Like a politician he made the rounds. As he did he looked at the deeply pitted walls. The windows and doors that all lay shattered. The pieces of furniture now tossed into one corner.

Upon returning to Sheffield, he asked, 'So how bad was it?'

'Oh,' replied the lance corporal, 'not that bad, sir. Not as bad as this room makes it look. For *us*, that is, sir. *We* did all the damage in here. Killed *seven* of 'em, we did. Found the blokes after we tossed three grenades.'

'Four,' another soldier amended.

'Four. That's right. It was four, I remember now. We found 'em piled up on *top* of each other.' His helmet dropped until Clark could barely see his eyes. 'One at the bottom was . . . was still saying something, he was. Talked for quite a while. We just had time to make sure he wasn't armed, you understand. We were going at it with some of his comrades in the next room. He was dead when we come back through.'

'Every room's different,' one of the other soldiers said. He was reclined almost flat on the floor. His words were slurred from the posture . . . and fatigue. 'Some of them *we* wreck. Others *they* wreck. It goes back and forth, usually. When you're done, the whole building looks like this.'

Sheffield quickly resumed the liaison with Clark. He'd worn a worried look with every word the man had spoken. He clearly thought himself the more polished speaker, and he jumped back in as soon as he could. 'They cut these *holes*, you see, sir. Through all the *walls*, you see, sir. It's a *rabbit* warren, it is. A *maze*. You have to *we-e-eave* your way through every flat. But we cleared 'em out, sir. Used a *sack* full of grenades!'

'A sack-and-a-half.'

'Almost two sacks,' the lance corporal amended. 'Every time you find a door, you toss 'em in.'

'Sometimes they'd come rollin' back out,' another man said. He began scraping his heels noisily – pedaling his boots like on a bicycle. They left trails in the plaster dust that covered everything – even the men. 'They'd *kick* at them. Send 'em right back through the door.'

'Took one of our men's *arms* off,' the lance corporal said – moderating the discussion. He chopped his left hand on his right biceps just under the shoulder.

'Where're the nearest Chinese troops right now?' Clark asked.

Everyone had an opinion.

'I heard some a few *minutes* ago!'

'They've *completely* buggered off! Every last one of 'em.'

'I bet they're lying low, maybe five or six houses down. We cleared about four apartments that way before we pulled back.'

'We've put up listening devices,' the lance corporal said more authoritatively. 'And flexible camera tubes that can bend around corners. They're all low-light. There are people watching and listening. And if they hear or see something, they call us,' he said – patting the radio beside him. 'So the theory goes, anyway.'

'Sounds like a good system,' Clark commented.

'Till you have to change the *batteries*,' someone griped.

'You've gotta change the batt'ries every six hours,' their leader explained.

'Next change is in four hours,' a man said from across the room – staring at the lance corporal. 'It's gonna be dark as night in three.'

'We'll go in *four*,' the lance corporal said sternly. 'If you want to switch, I'll take the first run. You can go in the *morning*.'

The private looked away.

'*Well*,' the colonel said, slapping his thighs and rising to a crouch. 'The general has a busy schedule. And you do make the point about sunset.'

Clark got the hint. But still he wanted to take a look around. He wandered further into the ravaged apartment. The four resting soldiers all scrambled to their feet. A hand grabbed Nate's shoulder firmly as he approached a dark hole in the wall.

Nate looked around behind him to see the lance corporal. The man jabbed his finger toward the hole and shook his head. Clark nodded in understanding. This room was even more bullet-riddled than the first. The hole was a meter high, and about the same width. A dozen wires disappeared through it. They ran to sensing devices nearer the enemy troops.

Clark allowed General Cuvier a look. They then went back and crouched by the building's exit, beginning the unwieldy process of departure. The squad of heavily-armed troops deployed just outside the door. 'Good luck,' Clark said to the men.

'Sir!' Clark heard. He turned. It was the lance corporal. 'You've done a fine job, sir. We'll do the rest. Don't you worry.' There were nods of agreement from the other three men.

'Thanks.' Nate suddenly remembered the purported reason for the visit. 'You've done an outstanding job. All of you. You and your officers should hold your heads high when you get home. And I'll do everything in my power to get you there as soon as I can – I promise.'

There were more subdued nods from the men this time. But more heartfelt, he could tell, as well.

Everyone jogged the whole way to the helicopters. It felt good to get the exercise. No one had given the order to run. They'd all just assumed that pace. The more he ran, however, the more upset at himself he became. He'd put all these men at risk. Grandstanding by going all the way to the line and trying to stick a toe over. As if that in any way compared to the horrors those men faced. And most of all he was disturbed at how weak he'd become. Not physically, but emotionally. So weak that he had to go to the front under the guise of a pep talk. While really the reassurances he sought were to be received, not given.

The sweat began to dampen his clothes. Physically, it felt good just to get it out. Too many days without a sweat – not even once. But what he really needed was to rid his body of the emotional toxins. The thousand new memories of tragedy and despair. He felt buoyed by the British soldier's remark. For his, after all, was the opinion Clark cared about most. But it still didn't purge his mind of the anguish he felt. And into his system was injected the poison of one more wounded man. And of the periodic demolition charge and thumping machine-gun in the distance.

NORTH OF TANGYUAN, CHINA
April 23, 2300 GMT (0900 Local)

Kate and Woody watched fighter-attack aircraft sweep down the valley. They had followed the forward air observer to a high ridge. The aircraft flew below the high ridges to release their loads at low altitude. The jets rose and banked out of harm's way, dropping flares to divert heat-seeking missiles. The jet-black canisters left in their wake spun slowly. Air brakes popped out to slow the falling high explosives. They arced their way to earth along an ever-steepening glide path.

The strings of bombs struck home with devastating force. Rings of white vapor spread from the points of impact at astonishing speed. Trees were flattened as if by the heavy step of an invulnerable giant. The booming sound waves then crashed across the high ridge on which Kate was perched.

She nearly jumped out of her skin. Her eardrums felt like they'd been jabbed with ice picks. The noise left her head aching as if from a physical blow. And the bombs fell over a mile away.

'Okay, Dodger Two, you're next up on deck,' the Air Force captain said calmly over his radio. The forward air controller and his army security team sat huddled around the radio backpack. Its aerial soared ten feet over their heads.

But there was another radio from which excited voices squawked. This one was manned by an army lieutenant. The shouts it emitted were distorted and indecipherable. In the background, however, was the unmistakable roar of battle.

'Say again!' the lieutenant replied. 'I repeat, will you say again?'

Following a hiss there came shouts of 'We've been overrun!' The radio crackled loudly and broke up. '. . . past our . . . and we're . . .! We need *air* – right now!'

The Air Force captain turned to his Army counterpart. 'Get 'em to call in their position.'

'Foxtrot Zulu One Niner, can you say your position?' the lieutenant shouted.

When he got a reply, the two officers quickly found the coordinates.

'Have him throw smoke,' the Air Force officer instructed. The orders were relayed. A few seconds later purple smoke began to mix with the gray and black of the battlefield. 'Tell him to hug the ground. I'm bringin' it in close.'

As the army officer shouted to the beleaguered ground unit, his air force counterpart spoke in calm tones to the pilot. 'Make one orbit and acquire the purple smoke. Call it once you've got it. Then come in from north to south and drop just past the smoke. I say again, north-to-south – drop *past* the smoke. No more than a hundred meters. They've been overrun. Do you copy?'

'Copy that,' came the cool voice over the radio. 'Beginning orbit now.'

Woody tapped Kate on the arm and pointed. A banking jet flew just over the opposite ridge line.

'I've got the smoke,' crackled the Air Force radio. 'Inbound – weapons hot.' The jet disappeared into a thin white cloud. It reappeared on the other side to complete a wide turn.

'Get your heads down now!' the army officer shouted over the radio.

There was a reply of some sort, but no words. Only shouts and blazing gunfire.

As the jet sank lower and lower into the valley, Kate realized how detached you could grow at a distance. From the tops of ridges battles were just loud noise and smoke. What she was missing was the whole point of the story. The real experience of battle could not be acquired by remote observation.

After a final waggle of the streaking jet's wings all six bombs were released. The pilot pulled the nose straight up. Brilliant flashes lit the drifting purple smoke. A burst of static hissed over the army radio. There was no shouting or screaming. No rattling machine-guns or bursting grenades in the background. Nothing at all to indicate whether the bombs had struck bull's eye or fallen short . . . into the Americans.

A pall of black smoke rose into the air in a long curtain.

'Foxtrot Zulu One Niner, do you read me, over?' the Army lieutenant called out. There was no reply. 'Foxtrot Zulu One Niner, do you read me, over?'

The distant gunfire and explosions continued unabated. There was no further word from the desperate unit. The forward air controller went back to his business of pounding the Chinese. The pattern was full and he had a long day of work ahead of him. But the Army lieutenant sat on his haunches holding the mike. He'd been deflated to the point of total exhaustion.

Everyone in fact seemed more subdued. No one spoke, so Kate got no read on their thoughts. But it was clear what preoccupied *her* mind. *Were those men killed by the Chinese? Or by the bombs these men had worked so hard to call in?*

The more she thought, the more she realized it didn't matter. They were killed in the fighting. Why care by whom? 'Friendly fire' only seemed criminal when considered from afar. Up close, it was all killing.

'You want me to get some more shots of the airstrikes?' Woody asked lethargically.

Kate frowned and then shook her head. 'We've got plenty of bombing runs and artillery barrages and supply airdrops.' She knew what they needed to get next. And to tell the truth, the thought frightened her. Out of the corner of her eye she could tell that Woody was watching her. When she looked up, he caught and held her eyes.

She turned away – uncomfortable. 'You think,' she began, 'maybe, they've aired some of the tapes we put on the medevacs?'

Woody took his time in responding. 'Why don't you just come out and say it, Kate?'

'I just hope they got past the *censors*, that's all.' Still, he stared at her. '*What?*' His eyes were no longer bloodshot. They bored straight into her. 'Just one trip down to the fighting in the valley, Woody! Okay? Then we'll get out. Okay?' He said nothing. 'Okay, Woody?'

Chapter Twenty-Four

THE KREMLIN, MOSCOW, RUSSIA
April 24, 0800 GMT (1000 Local)

Kartsev's writing had grown stale and forced. His treatise was almost complete, but it suffered from his cloistered existence in the Kremlin. One week to go before his May Day address and he was completely out of touch with the world. How could one comment on a society one didn't know? He sat back and took a deep breath. He checked the clock and saw that it was morning. Under the clutter on his desk he found the intercom. 'Would someone come in here, please?' he said. There was no reply. A shot of adrenaline tingled Kartsev's spine. 'Hello-o-o?' he said over the intercom.

There was a steady rapping at the door. Kartsev released the electric locks with the press of a button. An ashen young man entered. He couldn't bring himself to look Kartsev in the eye. He stood with his head bowed and hands clasped like a royal servant called into the king's private chambers.

'I want to go out,' Kartsev announced. The man's head shot up in surprise.

*   *   *

Mounds of trash were piled against the drab buildings. They forced pedestrians off the sidewalks and onto the streets. Kartsev's motorcade, in turn, sent them scampering back to the kerbs. Sprays of slush from the melting snow showered the suffering crowd. Kartsev wanted to get a better look. 'Slow down!' he ordered over the intercom. Kartsev's limousine and his guards' two Mercedes slowed. The car in front turned randomly through the endless maze of streets. Many people, Kartsev noted, wore kerchiefs or scarves tied over their faccs. He again used the intercom. 'Do those people cover their faces because of the smell?'

His nervous aide in front looked at the driver before answering. 'The smell, I would imagine, sir. The temperature is up.'

Kartsev nodded, but then sought clarification. 'Is it rotting garbage, or human remains?'

His aide and driver discussed the response. 'Probably both, sir,' he finally replied.

Some trash heaps rose all the way to the second-storey windows. The refuse went uncollected. But it was stacked somewhat neatly. 'Have these people organized in any way since the revolution? Have they formed any sort of self-government or committees or whatnot?'

'I don't imagine anyone has organized, sir. We still have very effective patrols against organizers.'

Kartsev glanced up at the man on his use of the word 'still.' Did he mean the decline had begun? The deterioration in discipline among even his Black Shirts? It was inevitable. But Kartsev hadn't seen any sign of it yet. The thought alarmed him. 'Stop the car!'

The aide turned all the way around to look at Kartsev through the glass. Kartsev repeated his command, and the aide issued the order over the radio. It took a while, but the motorcade slowly pulled to a stop. Men in heavy black overcoats poured onto the street. Astonished pedestrians carrying their empty shopping bags cowered and scattered in fear. Kartsev didn't wait for someone to open his door.

The air was crisp and cool. It was not putrid as he'd expected but refreshing. His security troops were shouting orders and brandishing weapons. The street emptied quickly. Up ahead was a charred and overturned city bus. They'd seen no cars on the road at all. Kartsev passed the lead Mercedes. The dismounted security people surrounded Kartsev. They scanned for threats in every direction. Kartsev came upon a narrow passage through the heaps of garbage. It led to the entrance of an apartment building. A woman hid there. When the armed men turned their weapons on her she dove into the trash. Kartsev walked up to her quivering back. She was sobbing face-down in the mess. Now the smell was overpowering. Kartsev covered his nose with his handkerchief.

'You!' he said. 'You there, in the trash.' One of his men grabbed her collar and pulled. She curled into a fat ball on the pavement. Her teeth were capped in gold. Her head was wrapped in a faded scarf. She was from the country, not the city. 'Who made this passage?' Kartsev asked, waggling his gloved hand at the neat walkway. The woman's eyes were jammed shut. She seemed to be mouthing something like a prayer. A guard kicked the fat wool mound. '*That's* not necessary,' Kartsev chided. He raised his eyes to the building. There were presumably communicative people inside.

He entered the darkened doorway. His surprised security team got jammed in the narrow entrance behind him. Kartsev headed up the dim stairwell in the lead. When they got to the first floor, the stench of urine was almost unbearable. The wider hallway allowed the guards to rush by without jostling Kartsev, although they didn't know exactly where to go. They all stared at Kartsev – waiting. He went to the first door. Its number was stenciled on the flaked plaster wall. He knocked. No one came to the door. He proceeded to the next. Again, there was no one. After he got no response at the third door, his patience wore thin. He looked at his aide and nodded toward the door.

A brutish man in an oversized jacket stepped up. He drew his pistol and aimed at the door knob. He fired repeatedly from close range. The loud 'booms' each gave Kartsev a start. His ears rang. The flame from the gun lit the hallway. The smoke caused Kartsev to again cover his nose. A firm kick opened the door right up. Several men entered the room with weapons drawn. Kartsev followed, totally unconcerned by the possibility of danger. The patient sufferers who lived in these Soviet-era sepulchers were not the sort who would make trouble.

The wails of a woman greeted Kartsev's entry into the cramped living room. She was being dragged by her hair from behind a sofa. '*Stop* that!' Kartsev snapped. The man released the kneeling woman's hair. She crumpled to the floor holding her scalp and sobbing uncontrollably. Barely visible behind the sofa where she'd hidden was a lone boy of five or so – eyes wide.

Guards returned from the bedroom. 'All clear. Just the woman and the boy.'

The lad remained behind the ratty couch. Kartsev walked up to the petrified woman. 'You, what's your name?' When she didn't answer, he thought quickly and restrained the guard whose boot was already raised. 'I won't hurt you. My name is Valentin Kartsev.' The woman froze. Her quiet gasps for air abruptly ended. After a moment of silence, her back bucked once. She vomited over and over. The mess grew on the floor beneath her. 'Oh, *good* lord!' Kartsev said. He turned away and pressed the scented handkerchief back to his nose. The boy stared out with haunted eyes. Kartsev made his way past the disgusting mess and sat on the sofa. The squeaky springs were sharp and uncomfortable through the thin padding, however, and Kartsev rose almost immediately. The quiet boy kept his eyes on Kartsev, not daring even to blink. 'What's your name?' Kartsev asked.

'*No-o-o-o!*' the woman screeched – lurching toward Kartsev's legs.

The guns all rose. But a guard stomped his boot down on her back before they could fire. He pressed her flat and forced a loud grunt from her diaphragm. Her bones showed through the simple print dress. She lay pinned under the man's heavy foot. His pistol was pointed at the back of her head. He wore a detached, disinterested expression. He looked at Kartsev questioningly through red and puffy eyelids.

'Let her *go*,' Kartsev ordered. The man lifted his boot from her back. She lay flat on her stomach. She wasn't fat yet. Kartsev guessed she was young. 'Why don't you get up?' he suggested. Maybe it was the tone in his voice. Or maybe the woman reasoned that calm was her only salvation. Whatever it was, she got to her feet and stood slouching before him – staring at the floor. 'Now, then. Good.' Her eyes dared only take in his shoes. 'What is your name?' he asked.

She tried to speak, but choked. She coughed and wiped at the corner of her mouth with the back of her hand. Her dress was half again too large for her thin frame. 'Tatiana, sir.'

'A-ah, Tatiana! But that's a *beautiful* name.' She looked up through unwashed hair for an instant. She had a pretty face. 'Tell me, Tatiana. Has anyone attempted to organize this building for any purpose? I noticed the tidy walkway through the trash on the street. Is there some system for keeping the walk clear?'

She was already shaking her head vigorously. Her unkempt curls flung across her forehead and eyes. '*No*, sir! I swear it on my life – *no!*'

'Calm *down*. I'm not a policeman. I'm a scholar. A scientist. I just have a few questions.'

542

The woman was swaying. Kartsev thought she'd collapse where she stood. 'Have a seat. Are you all right? Sit down.' The woman looked around as if she couldn't find the couch in her own apartment.

'Sit down!' barked the menacing guard. She stumbled to the sofa and began to sob again. She held her head with one hand and propped her bony frame up with the other. Her son clambered over the arm of the sofa and collided with her roughly. Guns were drawn in reaction to the sudden movement.

'*Stop* this!' Kartsev ordered the guards. Despite the apartment's chill, it was uncomfortably stuffy with so many people in it. 'In fact, why don't you all just clear out,' he ordered as he unbuttoned his overcoat. '*Out!*' he repeated. By the time Kartsev's hat and gloves were off, the room was empty save for him, the woman and the child. Kartsev pulled a chair up to the sofa. 'Go to your room,' the woman whispered to the boy. He clung to her with both arms and legs like an infant chimp. 'Go!' she said, prying him loose.

The boy ran to the kitchen and disappeared into a room the size of a coat closet. The woman straightened her hair. She wore no make-up. Her skin was pale. But no lines creased her youthful face. Kartsev guessed she wasn't even twenty-five.

'Do you have a husband?' he asked. She found the courage to look at him and shake her head. It was Kartsev who turned away. The apartment was small and in what looked to be a poor area of town. But the furnishings were of decent quality. They were of an age between aging junk and incipient antique. 'Were these things from your family?' he asked. She sniffed and nodded. 'Were they in the Party?' She was alert to danger, but she nodded ever so slightly. 'And where are they?'

She swallowed. 'They're dead.'

'How do you make do? Do you have a job?'

'No! I swear to God!'

'But it is all *right* to have a job. There has been a great deal of confusion about the tenets of anarchy. It is all right to have a job so long as it is not coerced. It is *perfectly* all right to *voluntarily* clear the walk out front. The only form of prohibited social behavior is *forced* behavior.' She looked directly at him now. She swallowed so hard he could see the contractions in her thin neck. Her arms were like sticks protruding from the short sleeves. 'How long has it been since you've eaten?'

Her lower lip quivered. 'Two days.'

'And what did you have then?'

She shrugged. 'Some cabbage.'

'And where did you find this cabbage?'

She again dropped her gaze. 'In the trash,' she practically whispered. 'But I *washed* it!'

Kartsev sat back against the hard wood chair. 'Would you say your standard of living is average, below average, or above? Which of the three?' The woman wore a look of confusion despite how simply he'd phrased the question. When she began shaking her head, he tried again. 'You haven't eaten in two days. Do you consider yourself worse off than your neighbors?'

'They're all *pigs*,' she muttered – her lips curling.

'Why do you say that?'

Her eyes sagged closed. She shook her head in clear disgust. 'They . . . they have food, you know? Some of them. And the men . . . For a moldy, hard end of a loaf of bread they expect . . .' She fell quiet.

'They expect what?'

She looked at him, leaning forward. 'I'd do *anything* to get out of here,' she whispered. It took Kartsev a moment to understand her. Her hands straightened her dress primly at her knees. She dried her palms on the fabric. He now wished she would find some object other than him for her gaze. 'I'm clean,' she continued. 'I have no diseases.'

'Yes,' Kartsev said – rising. 'Well . . .' He began to pace the room nervously. There were photos of the woman as a girl at some Black Sea resort with her family.

She grew upset. 'I can clean up. This isn't what I look like! The men at the institute where I worked were always hitting on me. You'll see. You'll like me!'

Kartsev was highly agitated by the suggestion. By the entire situation, in fact. He wandered to the kitchen, keeping his back to the woman and her now pleading brown eyes. 'That's *not* why I'm here.'

From the creaking sound he knew she had risen. He turned to see her approaching with fists clenched at her sides. 'You'll *not* take my *son!*' she screeched with astonishing vigor.

'No!' Kartsev blurted out – appalled. The apartment door opened. Kartsev waved the guards back outside. 'You misunderstood me entirely!' She relaxed into a defeated, exhausted slump. But with what could only have been sheer force of will, she straightened her back. Her small breasts pointed through her dress. 'You don't like me?' she asked.

Kartsev searched the room for something else at which to look. 'Well, you're a very attractive woman, I'm sure.'

She came up to him. She raised her hands but then thought better of it. She stood before him awkwardly. 'I'll do anything you want. Give me a chance. You've never had anyone like me. I'm almost like a virgin. My son . . . it was one time. I was seventeen. I would have had an abortion, but my mother was afraid I could never get pregnant again.' She stepped even closer. 'You'd like me.'

'*Please*,' Kartsev said, slipping away. He was aroused, but that only made it worse. 'I really just came here to ask you a few questions.' When he looked back at the girl, she was crying. Her hands covered her face. She was sobbing silently. Kartsev was exasperated. 'What is it *now*? Because I refuse to *defile* you you're *crying*?'

The woman turned away and struggled to compose herself. She denied that she was crying even as she wiped the tears from her face. When she turned, she flashed a smile his way as if to prove her case. Kartsev had had enough. 'I'm sorry for disturbing you.' Before the girl could say a word, he headed out. The security troops kept their eyes averted as he passed them for the stairs.

At the building's entrance, the chill hit Kartsev. He remembered he'd left his coat in the apartment. Cursing, he returned to the still-open doorway. He didn't know how to read the startled looks of the guards who waited outside the apartment. But when he entered, he saw the reason instantly. The young woman was on her knees. A large brute clenched her hair in his hand as he stood before her. Kartsev walked right up to the man, whose eyes were closed. He seemed to sense someone's presence. When he looked around, his face registered instant terror. The woman sank back onto her haunches, coughing. Her face was invisible behind her curls.

Kartsev left without his things and found his aide on the landing. 'Get the woman and the child and put them up in a Kremlin apartment. Give them everything they need. Take care of them.' He looked the man straight in the eye. 'And I want you to schedule that man in there.' The aide nodded. 'Oh, and get my coat and gloves.'

Kartsev waited in the cold stairwell. They hustled the woman and boy past. She was frightened but not complaining. She dutifully smiled at Kartsev as she got the boy's jacket on. A single shot rang out from upstairs. The woman stopped and looked back toward her apartment. She was clearly perplexed, but seemed otherwise untroubled. 'Your coat, sir,' Kartsev's aide said.

NORTH OF TANGYUAN, CHINA
April 24, 1300 GMT (2300 Local)

'Sappers *i-i-in!*' came the cries over the furor.

Andre Faulk was crammed low in a hole next to a replacement. Bullets chipped off rock around their shallow position, which was dug on the side of a steep ridge. Some of the fire was Chinese. But most was from the three machine-guns above them that raked their platoon's positions. When the 'sappers-in' call was given, they killed everyone who raised his head.

It was the third time in ten minutes they'd been overrun.

Faulk narrowed his focus to just his hole. To the strong stench of the unwashed man next to him. A private from Iowa or Indiana seeing his first action with the 101st. To the rock chips that peppered them both. To the screeching noise and burst of flames and ever-present shouting of massed attackers. Andre jammed his eyes shut. He grimaced as bullets flew by at supersonic speed.

Andre was at the limits of his ability to function. But the replacement was long gone. He was no use at all. He'd been choppered in that day. Said he'd seen action with the Third Infantry. But the facts didn't sound right.

The storm of fire in the air above subsided. 'Heads *u-u-up!*' shouted the NCOs at their heavily depleted platoon. They'd flown in with thirty-eight. But they were down to twenty-nine *including* nine *worthless* replacements! 'Let's *go*, fuckhead!' Andre shouted. He rose.

Through the dim light crept hundreds of men. The slope was steep. They moved as if their legs were stuck in molasses. Andre aimed and killed a man. His muzzle blazed as he killed and killed. It lit the rock on which he lay with flame. The granite was armor. He'd weathered mortars – even artillery – in the rocks.

The only problem was that the Chinese had the same cover.

They advanced and dove behind the impenetrable stone. Then, in celebration of survival, they fired. They seemed perfectly content to set up shop behind good cover. Until, that is, they were prodded on. The shrill whistles of Chinese officers sounded like those of referees in a basketball game. But the sound sent the men to their deaths. It was as if its exhortation was too powerful to ignore. Andre listened for it. He aimed at the men who were flushed out by it.

His rifle slammed into his shoulder with each round. Each blinded him with the flash for a split second. He kicked the replacement hard and then fired. 'Hey! Motherfucker! Get yer ass up here *now!*' There were dark moving figures everywhere. Profiled against fires in the valley below. 'I *mean* it, asshole!' He fired three well-aimed shots – felling two. 'You're gonna get stuck like a pig if you don't!'

Andre heard a loud whistle. A man was turned and facing downhill. Bent over with the effort of blowing. *Pow!* came the blast from Andre's rifle. The man disappeared in the muzzle flash. The bastard from Iowa or Indiana finally joined him. He laid his rifle on the rock and shot up half a magazine in two seconds. It distracted the hell out of Andre. The guy dropped, apparently done for the night. With gritting teeth Andre braved the deep shit. He'd save their fuckin' asses by himself! He killed Chinese to vent anger at his 'squadmate.' *Useless fuckin' bastard*, he cursed silently as he relentlessly killed the enemy.

Searing pain shot through his ear. His eyes watered instantly. '*Shit!*' Andre shouted as the warm liquid ran down his neck. The enemy was fifteen meters away. He fired and fired until his magazine was empty. When he dropped to reload, the guy from Iowa or Indiana rose. But he didn't even fire a fuckin' shot! He jumped right on top of Andre.

'Mother-*fucker*!' Andre screamed. The full weight of the man pinned him. When he pushed the guy away he saw the problem. A bullet had smacked right into his face. '*Shit!*' Andre cursed. On instinct he pushed away from the carnage.

'Sappers i-i-*i-in!*' shouted a half-dozen men.

The machine-guns fired. The air filled with death. Bullets whipped by inches away. Spits of granite stung his face and eyes. *This is it!* Andre thought over and over. He switched his selector to 'Burst.' He didn't risk rising. He held the rifle over the rock. With his arms at full extension he fired. One, two, three quick pulls of the trigger. Nine rounds at what must have been point blank range. The trigger froze on the fourth pull. The mag was empty. He dropped the rifle and grabbed his dead squadmate's M-16. He lay on his back and waited.

Andre fired at the first dark form to blot out the stars. The three-round burst threw the man down the hill. The next man must've assumed Andre was dead. He climbed the hill, stooped low under the machine-guns. Andre laid him out with a shot fired through his knees. He didn't want to have to reload. He flicked the selector to 'Semi.' Two men appeared right over his head. One opened up on full auto from three feet. The rounds pummeled the replacement's lifeless body. Andre's shot stood the man straight up. He tumbled backwards over the rock. The second man kicked Andre's rifle away. He collapsed on top of Andre as machine-guns raked the position repeatedly.

Andre grabbed the man's searing hot AK-47. A flash of white from an elbow stunned him. The man's knee just missed Andre's groin. The Chinese assault rifle was pressed between them. They wrestled and it went off. The Kalashnikov sprayed rocks not two feet away. But the wide-eyed Chinese soldier had made a critical mistake. He was smaller than Andre and he had tried to use his rifle.

Andre summoned all his strength for one spin move. He surprised the man and threw him off. Andre followed him without losing his grip on the rifle. The guy now was underneath Andre. He was at Andre's mercy, and Andre had none. Andre lunged forward and head-butted the man's exposed face. His helmet flew off, but the blow had stunned the man. Blood flowed profusely from his nose.

Andre knew he had to use the knife. He pressed his torso down and let go of the man's rifle with his right hand. He crushed him flat with his chest and shoulders. He jammed his chin sharply into his collarbone. There was panicked breathing in Andre's ear. Then searing pain shot from Andre's neck where the man bit him hard. Andre seized the combat knife by the handle. It slipped out of its leather scabbard with hardly a sound. But the man sensed something.

The AK-47 trapped in between them roared on full auto. The bolt tore back and forth against Andre's chest. Horrible pain shot through Andre's right side in a half-dozen places. Andre rose up and jabbed the knife into his enemy's chest in one motion. But it didn't go in far. It hit something hard – a belt, a pouch, a bone. For a moment the two men were motionless. The man whispered something in Chinese. Andre raised the knife with both hands. The man raised his hands.

With all his might Andre sunk the knife through the feeble defense. It was awful beyond belief. The most sickening sound and feel.

Andre hurled himself backwards to get away. To get down under the machine-gun fire. He lay bareheaded against the frigid rocks. Sweat streamed from every pore. His left ear burned in pain. From it trickled blood whose course changed with his new position. From his thigh to his ribs were agonizing wounds. Andre stared straight up at the night sky. The burning tracers looked like shooting stars. The fire of two M-60s and a .50 caliber overlapped. It went on, and on, and on. In the end it was just American guns. They fired and then fired some more.

Andre awoke while being dragged out of his hole. Someone pulled him roughly by his armpits. Andre grabbed for his rifle and was dropped to the rocks. 'A-ah!' he shouted. The world started spinning with the pain. It built and built until Andre feared it alone would kill him. He moaned and yelped with sickening dizziness.

'*Jesus!*' came the voice of his squad leader. He scampered to Andre's side. Andre opened his eyes. Everything hurt. He'd never felt worse. He saw it was morning. The sun was up. 'I thought you said he was *dead!*' the squad leader snapped at one of the replacements.

'Well, *look* at him! He was lyin' there with his mouth all open! And his freakin' eyes were starin' up at the freakin' *sky!*'

'Never mind,' the sergeant said. He knelt beside Andre. 'You hurt bad?'

'I . . .' The words caught in Andre's bone-dry throat. He coughed. Incredible pain shot from his ribs. '. . . don't know,' he croaked. 'Water.' They gave him a taste. The more alert he became, the more pain he felt. It wasn't a good sign.

'What's goin' on?' barked an NCO Andre had never seen before. Andre raised his pounding head. The man looked all around Andre's hole. Bodies, brass shell casings and equipment littered the hillside. But the two most dramatic sights lay at Andre's feet. Andre's knife stuck straight up from the chest of the Chinese soldier. And the now-faceless guy from Iowa or Indiana.

Everyone was staring at Andre. At the AK-47 whose pistoning bolt had caught in the loose fabric of his parka. It was now stuck to Andre's chest. Andre felt wave after wave of nausea. He couldn't answer their questions. They tried to work the bolt. But it was locked tight and wouldn't come free. They finally cut it loose, leaving a two-inch hole in Andre's parka. The unknown NCO's probing hands elicited yelps from Andre. *Must be another platoon leader*, Andre figured. Command of their platoon had been passed several times. They rolled Andre onto his left side and cut more fabric away.

'You want me to clean this thing up for you, 'Dre?' asked a squadmate, holding Andre's bloody knife.

A pit of burning vomit boiled up. 'I'm gonna puke,' he groaned, and they stood back. Andre emptied his stomach on the ground. 'That's all right,' the new platoon leader said. 'Go ahead and get that bad shit outta there.' When Andre was done, they went back to work. 'Tell 'em six shrapnel punctures,' the platoon leader said, 'plus one wound that looks like a bullet hole.' Andre whimpered as he probed his side. 'It looks like a through-and-through, but they oughta look real good.' They applied pressure bandages.

'There's another hole up here,' said the replacement. He held Andre's right arm in the air. 'But it's little, and it ain't bleedin' any more.'

The air was chilly where they had cut away his clothing.

'Tell the clearing station about it anyway. It looks like fragments from a round that must've hit these rocks. Ain't too deep. I can see a piece right here.' Andre raised his head and watched the man dig a metal sliver from his hip. He used Andre's black combat knife. Its edges were honed and silvery. Andre threw up again. He heaved even though nothing came out. The NCO gave them directions to the aid station.

'You mean, like, it's on the other side of this *hill*? We're clearin' casualties *outside* the valley?'

'Just *go*. This man needs *aid*.'

They hoisted Andre to his feet. He cursed and hissed and gasped. With the squad leader and replacement on either side, he remained standing. For the first time he saw the extent of the battle's devastation. The slope was covered with dead. Nowhere were there more bodies than around his position.

'Did he fight?' his squad leader asked.

'Who?' Andre replied.

'Hansen! The guy from Illinois. Did he fight or was all that talk about the Third Infantry bullshit?'

'He saved my life,' Andre finally answered. *Hansen*, he committed to memory. *From Illinois.*

MOSCOW, RUSSIA
April 24, 2400 GMT (0200 Local)

At first Andreev thought the sound came from a lunatic. A howling, half-human sound emanating from the desolate streets. But then there was laughter and an attempt at imitation. The mimicked howl ended in boisterous glee.

Andreev was crouched in a notch taken out of the sidewalk. He squatted next to a window that opened below street level. When he'd heard the noise he had leapt into it. He risked looking out through a small railing past some dead flowers. His eyes were level with the pavement. There wasn't much light in the street. But what there was streaked across rain-soaked pavement from a single bright lamp on the opposite kerb. The beam skirted a triangular median with trees, a bench and a smallish monument.

Three streets merged at the tiny park. A band of swaggering men strolled down one. The lead held an AK-47 one-handed. It was pointed skyward and casually resting on his shoulder. With his other hand he raised a bottle of vodka. The liquid was sloshing – about half-empty. Andreev felt inside his valise. He'd packed only soft things – quiet things – around the weapon. The Ingram came out without making a noise.

'No-*o-o-o-o*!' wailed a man who fell to his knees. The leash around his neck was yanked. He collapsed. His fall onto the concrete was unbroken. His hands were bound tightly at his back. One of the trailing men kicked him. Pyotr counted four around the prisoner. But a fifth suddenly appeared – straggling behind the rest.

'Oh, look!' shouted the slurring leader. He held his right hand pointed straight at the park. 'Over there!' From the sound of it the man was drunk, bored, tired. The armed men all wore black from head to toe. Their boots scraped across the pavement as they dragged their captive by his neck toward the trees. The man struggled mightily to get to his feet. He never managed to rise above his knees. Pyotr sank slowly into the tight space making sure he made no sudden movements. He listened. All too quickly it became clear what was going on.

'Right here, right *here!*' came the impatient voice of the lead Black Shirt. He'd reached the stage of drunkenness marked by a short fuse and quick temper.

Then there was, '*You* pull the son-of-a-bitch! You think this is *easy?*' *That's the man holding the leash*, Andreev saw in his mind's eye.

'Get up you miserable f-f-*fuck!*' was followed by a hollow thud. And then another thump and grunt. '*Hey!* You *listening* to the man?'

The two kickers, Andreev realized. All were safely some distance away. In the park. But where was the fifth man – the straggler? He'd not said a word. The others bickered but managed to drag their victim to the intended place. 'Up, up, *up!*' the exasperated leader ordered. Andreev grew preoccupied by the mystery of the fifth man's whereabouts. He brought the Ingram up. He was ready to kill any dark shapes that loomed over the narrow slit in the sidewalk.

There was laughter. They took turns pissing on the man. 'Loo's like e's a fuckin' fountain!' the leader crowed. He obviously had a cigarette in his lips. They were all rolling with laughter at that one. But only the four. That's when the begging began. The pleading. The last attempts from the battered man to appeal for mercy. His lungs grew ragged with the effort. He ceased completing his sentences. Sobs consumed what little energy he had left.

'*Hang* his ass up there,' came the command from the now lucid leader. It was as if he'd been sobered by the whole episode.

'Wait a minute!' It was the fifth man. 'Wait. Why hang him?' There was laughter. 'I mean, nobody said to *kill* him. We don't even know what the guy *did!*'

'Don't you *know?*' replied the leader. 'He's a *conformist!* Or a believer in *orthodoxy!* Or an *objectivist!*' The others all laughed. 'Or . . . or – and *this* is my favorite one – maybe he's an establishment*arian!*'

'O-o-*o-u-u!*' came the voices of the chorus in mock disparagement.

'This *thing*,' said the drunk – putting on a show – 'in other words, is a *very, very* bad man! And *we*, don't you see, are very, very *good* men. Yes, we *are!*' he said to stem the raging cackles. 'We are, because we do *this* to bad people.'

A shot rang out – a single shot.

With his eyes closed Andreev listened to the echoes off the buildings. They had done the worst, he thought, till he heard the screams. Their prisoner was screeching at the top of his lungs. He was trying to cry and gasping for breath at the same time.

Another shot stopped everything. The street fell quiet.

'Now *why* the fuck d'you have ta go do *that?*' exclaimed the drunk leader.

'*That's what you wanted!*' cried the fifth – the straggler. 'That's what we were *going* to do!'

'But not *no-o-ow!* We only just *got* here! We can't just drag the son-of-a-bitch one lousy block from his house and *kill* him! What kind of punishment is *that?*'

'Fuck it,' came a voice of reason from one of the others. 'It's late.'

'No! I wanta hear an answer! What's your answer, little boy? Worried what momma'd say if she caught you out with us? Maybe she'd make you stay home and help carry the *shit* out to the *kerb!*'

'Come on, Seryozha. Let's just go home.'

The silence was filled with the sloshing of liquid in a bottle. Next came a tortured exhalation and a burp. The group burst into laughter again. They proceeded down the street as untroubled as before.

Andreev waited for the sound of them to recede. Then he waited longer just in case someone came out of the apartments to check. So far as he could tell, however, no one even opened a window or a door. The night was deathly quiet. The seven million people who remained in Moscow had receded into the safety of the shadows.

Pyotr raised up slowly. When he peered over the kerb he checked out the scene. The street was empty. In the park, a man hung limply from where his bound hands had been hung on the statue. But Andreev's heart skipped a beat when the dark form by the bench took shape. A lone man leaned his back against a tree. It was impossible to tell which one it was or what he was doing. But Andreev had a guess what the answer to both questions was.

The fifth man rose with an audible sigh. He turned and headed back up the street in the direction opposite his comrades. His rifle dangled loosely at his side. He stared at the glistening pavement.

SOFLYSK POW CAMP, SIBERIA
April 25, 2400 GMT (1000 Local)

Lieutenant Hung – one of Chin's fellow platoon leaders – sat on the end of Chin's bunk. He'd been part of the last wave of new arrivals to crowd the barracks. There were now mattresses on the floor between the bunks, and Hung had moved onto one. From there he'd told

Chin everything that had happened in the two days after Chin had been captured. It was a story of total collapse.

'Would you go back if they gave you a choice?' Hung asked.

'Would I go back where if who gave me what choice?' Chin replied. His voice had assumed Hung's quiet tone despite the noise of a hundred conversations.

Hung leaned forward. 'Would you go back to *China* if the Americans said you didn't *have* to?'

Chin arched his eyebrows. 'Well . . . of *course*. Where *else* would I go?'

Hung shrugged. 'If they said you could go anywhere, you mean you'd just say, "Back to China, please"?'

It see med a straightforward question. But Hung's surprise at his first answer prompted Chin to ponder it. *Where else in the world could I go?* he thought. *America?* He looked up at Hung and nodded. His friend rolled his eyes. 'What?' Chin asked. 'My whole *life* is back in China. My family, my friends, our farm. Why would I go anywhere else?'

'*Because*,' Hung whispered testily, 'things are better in other places.'

'Better how?'

'Not as . . .' Hung stopped himself and looked around. There were others within earshot, but they seemed not to be listening. Then again, how could you just come out and discuss such a thing, if it was what Chin was thinking. 'Not as bad . . . politically,' Hung finally said. His eyes again searched the barracks.

Chin just shrugged. 'What are politics to me?'

Hung turned on him now. 'They are *everything!* Those old men keep us down! They try to control us like it was the 1950s! To them, nothing has changed! But everything *has* changed! Have you ever heard of the Internet?' he asked. Chin shook his head. 'It hooks computers from all over the world together. You can talk – exchange ideas – with foreigners. And there's not a damn thing they can do about it.'

Chin thought about it then shrugged. 'Why is that so important?'

'Don't you *get* it? We can read what people write in the *Free* World. All the great ideas are there on the Internet. You just need a computer that's hooked into it.'

Chin shrugged again. 'I don't see why I have to do all that reading.'

Hung snorted. '*You* wouldn't.' He eyed Chin now with open disdain. 'Have you ever read a book cover to cover?' Chin felt his face redden. 'No,' his friend said, but without ridicule, 'of course not. You're the perfect Communist citizen, Chin. Even if you bitch and moan, they'd love to have another billion just like you. God forbid you use any of those brain cells up there for *thinking!*' He reached out and roughly rubbed Chin's stubble-covered head.

There was something in what he said that Chin found troubling. He hadn't chosen not to read after thinking about it. He simply didn't have any idea what the point was. He couldn't imagine what someone could possibly write that could be so important. Not that he hadn't been educated. But that had been by teachers or army instructors who'd mixed lectures with practical, hands-on demonstrations. Books smacked to him of political classes, and they were the most useless exercise of all.

'You want me to teach you?' Hung asked.

'Teach me *what?*' Chin bristled – his face reddening.

'You know,' Hung said, smiling awkwardly. 'Some of the tougher characters . . . just to get you over the hump. They dropped off some old magazines from Hong Kong. It's not nuclear physics, but they're written, you know, for educated people.' Chin started to object – to explain that *he* was educated – but the words stuck in his mouth. He hung his head. 'Hey, it's okay.' Hung laughed. 'Maybe you can get into the university when you get back!' He laughed even more, which rubbed Chin the wrong way. But the offer was meant to be kind, and Chin resolved then and there to take him up on it. What better place to give it a shot?

'What about you?' Chin then asked.

'What about me?'

'Will you go back if they let you . . . if they offer you . . .?'

'Asylum?' his new teacher supplied. Chin nodded. '*Asylum*,' he filed away – his first new word. When there was no answer for several seconds, Chin realized the question was causing Hung great turmoil. He appeared almost sick with worry. He swallowed, his eyes unfocused and his mouth pressed tight in a frown. 'You know what they'd do,' Hung said, rather than asked. His voice was far away. 'To my family.' Chin frowned and nodded. The process of branding families disloyal was fairly straightforward. 'But they may do that anyway,' Hung whispered.

'Do what?'

'Denounce us because we were captured. Strip our families of everything. Even send us to labor farms, or even *camps!*'

'But . . . *why?*' Chin asked, growing instantly outraged. Instantly terrified that what had happened to him might ruin his family. '*We* couldn't do anything about getting captured! The only choice we had was to get killed for no *reason!* The only difference between us and everybody who died is *luck!*'

'No. That's where you're wrong. There's another difference.' He was speaking in even lower tones now. 'The dead didn't spend any time around the foreigners.'

UNRUSFOR HEADQUARTERS, KHABAROVSK
April 26, 0700 GMT (1700 Local)

Nate Clark was taking an early dinner when the news came in. He was ravenous after having missed lunch. He'd taken a tour that morning of an UNRUSFOR hospital. He just hadn't felt like eating after that. But now, he was ready to dig into the steaming plate of risotto with wild mushrooms.

The different contingents of the UN force took their turns cooking at headquarters. It provided variety, but it also led to the nationalities vying to outdo themselves. The British had the temerity to try kidney pie. The Americans hadn't fared much better with hot dogs. It was really a battle between the French and the nominal contingent of Italians, and the Italians routinely won.

Clark's stomach growled as he mixed the rice and sauce thick with cheese into a gooey consistency. He raised a fork and let it cool in the air. There was a knock on his door. Major Reed stuck his head in. Clark waved him over. He put down the fork and read the terse message Reed handed him. Just twenty-two words, Clark saw from the header before re-reading.

He rose and led Reed to the door. 'Get everything we've got in the air. Cancel maintenance, pilot rest, everything. Don't hold anything back.'

'What about the White House?' Reed asked, and Clark stopped. 'He asked that you call if . . .' Reed didn't finish the sentence.

Clark took a deep breath and looked at his watch. 'Go ahead and ring the President.'

WHITE HOUSE RESIDENTIAL QUARTERS
April 26, 0705 GMT (0205 Local)

Gordon Davis was so deep in sleep that it took Elaine shaking his shoulder to rouse him. 'Hm?' he said when he opened his eyes. The first person he saw was the national security staffer.

'There's a call from General Clark, Mr President.'

Gordon nodded and began the slow process of rising. As always it was filled with hisses and groans. The doctor said the pain would linger. That he'd feel worse on cold, wet days. Sure enough, when Gordon padded down the hall to a small office, he saw the steady rain outside. It fell in the new, bright security lights that bathed the White House grounds for the benefit of Secret Service gun crews. The leather chair was cold against his back through his robe. The aide handed him the phone.

'Gordon Davis,' he said, then waited for the satellite delay.

'Mr President, this is General Clark. Sorry to wake you, sir, but we've had a development here.'

'No apologies, General. What's up?'

'It appears we've got a major push under way against our blocking position in the Tangyuan Valley.'

'You mean something more than they've been trying already?' Gordon interrupted.

'Yes, sir. Let me read you the communication I received from Brigadier General Lawson, commander on the ground there. "Major offensive making progress from south. Casualties heavy. Ammunition low. Situation critical. Last reserves have been committed. Cannot guarantee we can hold."'

Gordon closed his eyes and laid his head back. 'What does he mean "Casualties heavy"? I thought casualties were already heavy.'

'They were, sir. We don't get many communications like this, although I've gotten more than I care to count in this war. It's not a good sign. Lawson isn't given to overreaction. He's been wounded pretty bad for days. But he's refused to accept relief. He's a real steady hand.'

'What can we do?' Gordon asked.

'I've ordered everything we can put into the air to head down there. For about twelve hours we can give them a curtain of fire so thick no new reinforcements can move up to the action. But close air support has its limitations and . . . and risks. The terrain is so mountainous that it makes bombing very dangerous. Because of the bombs' trajectories you sometimes have only one angle of approach. And if you're off by even a degree or two on the reverse slope of a hill, a miss of a few meters on flat land could turn into a hundred or more down the hillside.'

'Is there anything more we can do to help?' Gordon asked.

Clark sighed audibly. 'We could drop some airborne troops in there. We've got a German parachute regiment standing by just in case. But we've limited ourselves to ferrying in replacements because our logistics are strained enough with the people we've got there now. Once the new troops run through what they're carrying they'd just be more mouths to feed.'

'Just how bad are their supply problems? Your man there said they were low on ammunition.'

'We've been dropping in supplies around the clock. Our stocks of parachutes are running low, but there's a shipment due in from Belgium today that should get us by. We just don't have the lift to get them much more. We *can* change the mix. Less food, water and medicine and more ammo – that sort of thing. But there's just not much more that we can do. They're fighting for their lives down there, sir. It's up to them now.'

'Do we have any contingency plans?' Gordon asked. 'If the Chinese break through?'

The delay was longer than usual. 'They go on fighting for as long as they can. Take to the hills and split into smaller and smaller groups.'

'What would their chances be?'

Again, a delay. 'Some of the Rangers might fare pretty well. It's no knock on the men of the 101st to say this, because they're some of the finest soldiers in the world. But they're not trained for the same kind of fighting. For evasion and survival behind enemy lines. Plus they're mainly positioned in the lowlands down in that valley. They're the hard plug the Chinese are trying to push through. Most of them won't even get the chance to climb out of the valley. The Rangers, on the other hand, are dug in on the valley's outer slopes or are patrolling the surrounding countryside – calling in airstrikes.'

'General Clark, what effect would loss of control of that valley have on the war?' Gordon felt compelled to ask.

Clark sighed. 'Not a good one, Mr President. The Chinese could move some major part of the Jinan Army Group up the railroad that runs through that valley. Our forces in China would have to assume the strategic defensive all along the front.'

'Could we resume the advance some time later?'

'Not without major reinforcements, Mr President. At least one heavy corps – another hundred thousand men when you include associated supply and support personnel.'

Gordon frowned. Congress and the American people would never go for that. 'I know it's a lot to ask, but is there any chance if the Chinese retake the valley that those remaining men could still shut the railroad down? Harass the Chinese sufficiently from the surrounding hills that they couldn't safely move trucks to the north?'

'For a day or two max, Mr President. After that, it'd be too much to expect from them. We'd have no way to resupply them, and their stocks are already low. They'd be out of ammo very quickly. And it would soon be the *Chinese* who were dug into those hills, not the other way around.'

It all came down to that valley, Gordon realized. Just as he'd been briefed that it would. That and the timing of the ice flow were the two great risks of the operation. Nature had cooperated nicely. An entire Chinese army was stranded on the north bank of the Amur.

'How about the relief column heading down from the Amur toward the valley?' Gordon asked.

The audible puff from Clark's lungs sounded like a roar of air over the telephone. 'We're pushing them pretty hard as it is, Mr President.'

'Well, push them *harder*.'

'There are problems with that, Mr President. Their main hold-up is that the roads are clogged with several million Chinese refugees heading south. The only way to clear the roads, sir . . . Well, I don't think that would be legal . . . or moral.'

'All right. Just keep me informed, General Clark, about anything you hear. No matter how small. I want reports every hour – every *half* hour – whenever you've got anything at all.'

'Yes, sir. Oh, you might be interested in some videotape that we confiscated. It was shot by that NBC News crew that's down there in the valley. They flew it out on a medevac chopper, and the censors pulled it because it showed too much. I'll have it sent to you via military satellite if you'd like.'

'Yes, do that. I'll wait up. I'd like to see what it looks like down there.'

A digital clock counted the time down to the start of the recording, but the screen in the underground Situation Room was otherwise black. Gordon sat in slacks and shirt at a conference table with the head of the White House Military Office.

The picture burst onto the screen first, followed a moment later by the stupendous noise of battle. The camera lay on its side as bullets audibly whizzed by. The scene quickly cut to a different image. It was a wobbly picture of a female reporter. She now wore a helmet and bulletproof vest and sat on the ground beside the banked shoulder of a railroad. *The* railroad, Gordon realized. The air was filled with smoke and the sound of fighting.

'Got it?' she asked the cameraman.

'Go,' came his overly loud reply.

The reporter cleared her throat and looked at her notes. When she straightened, she looked directly into the lens and began. 'The fighting in the Tangyuan Valley last night took a dramatic turn for the worse. I'm reporting to you now from the rail line and dirt road that are at the center of the two armies' confrontation. Up until midnight last night . . .' A huge explosion of indeterminate nature interrupted the report. The camera shook and the woman flinched and ducked her head. The camera steadied. Behind the reporter, a towering black ball of smoke rose into the air above the trees. 'Up until midnight last night, the Chinese had fought and died in huge numbers but made progress measured only in meters. But as the clock struck twelve on an otherwise calm winter evening, the roar of the guns once again filled this deep canyon. This time, however, the guns were Chinese and they were mounted on tanks. The surprise armored attack broke through line after line despite withering anti-tank fire. Missile launchers were fired down from the hills at almost point-blank range. At one point during the dark early-morning hours the hulks of over a hundred vehicles burned furiously in the valley. But still the Chinese tanks came, and hugging tight behind the shields of their armor were masses of dismounted infantry. With each line overrun, the Chinese gulped up significant stretches of this dusty highway. When the sun came up – instead of being driven back by Americans dug in the hillsides above them – the Chinese came back with still more force.'

In the background you could see American soldiers approach. They ran single file along the side of the tracks toward the camera – bent over at the waist to take shelter from the railroad's embankment.

The female reporter turned just as a soldier skidded to a stop. With one hand he held the brim of his helmet. With the other, a rifle. 'You're gonna have to pick up and move, ma'am,' the out-of-breath man said.

'What's the situation on the ground, lieutenant?' the reporter asked as the camera took in the long line of men behind him. The others all lay in the dirt with their weapons and faces pointed toward the rear.

'You don't understand. I mean move *now*. On the double.'

There was an unartful splice of the tape. They had climbed to higher elevation and were taping the battlefield from behind some rocks. Smoke obscured much of the scene. The woman began.

'We've moved now up into the hills where it's safer. Shortly after we left the rail line, British Tornado bombers dropped canisters of napalm onto the onrushing Chinese forces. The heat was so intense we could feel it even through our winter clothes. Despite the certain devastation wrought by the sticky, flaming petroleum, the Chinese now hold that stretch of road and are surging ahead with suicidal fervor.'

The camera zoomed in through a break in the smoke. You could clearly see Chinese soldiers with their guns blazing as they rushed forward. Behind them was the skyrocketing fireworks from a tank whose turret was missing. Flashing through the air above was a missile trailing thin, silvery wires. Gordon watched as first one and then a second infantryman fell. On hearing the roar of a jet, the cameraman zoomed out. It was just in time to catch the fleeting image of a lone fighter-bomber. At an altitude of less than one hundred feet, the jet's shadow bobbed from treetop, to bare ground, back to treetop. In an instant, both shadow and plane were gone. But they left behind a string of bombs – each with their own smaller shadow.

The camera jumped with the concussion of six blasts. When the cameraman recovered, he panned down the length of the road and rail line and took in the rising columns of smoke. Like from miniature atomic bombs there rose six mushroom clouds. They were spaced every hundred meters or so along the road.

'The American casualties have been heavy,' the reporter continued before pausing to swallow – her voice thick as if from nausea or fear – 'with many whole units now missing in action. But the death toll among the Chinese is staggering. Little opportunity has arisen for the Chinese to collect their dead under the direct fire poured on by the Americans. As a consequence, the woods and foothills of this valley are littered with uncollected and now decaying bodies. And those woods are being filled at an ever-increasing rate as a result of the obviously growing sense of desperation felt by the People's Liberation Army. With a callous disregard of human life, unit after unit has charged headlong into the American killing fields. American commanders on the ground here have no good estimates as to the numbers of Chinese killed. But surely, their best guesses go, they run into the many tens of thousands.'

There was yet another jumpy change of scene. When the picture finally steadied, Gordon felt a knot of nausea form in his stomach. Filling the screen was a seemingly unending row of upturned boots. The bodies of the Americans had been laid out side-by-side under a series of green ponchos. All the boots were the same. Their alignment was neat and orderly. As the cameraman walked slowly down the line, Gordon wondered just when he would come to the end.

'But the cost in American lives has been steep as well. And the supply of Americans in this valley will be exhausted far more quickly than the supply of Chinese.' The camera continued its close-up procession of boots. 'These men all died in the fighting just last night, and they cannot be replaced in time to affect the current battle's outcome.'

'Jesus,' the White House Military Officer said in disgust. The Army colonel – wearing a crisp green uniform with a white cord under the epaulet on his shoulder – was in ensed by the reporter's parading of the dead. But to Gordon, it wasn't a question of dishonoring the fallen. It was a scene that at least *he* – as the dead men's commander-in-chief – should see. The consequence of the actions that only *he* had the power to take. The flag-draped coffins arriving at Dover Air Force Base were too sanitary. Dusty boots turned up to blue sky made the point more clearly. And the point, Gordon thought as the reporter concluded her story, was that the war had to end, and end quickly.

'The Lord is my shepherd,' the kneeling soldiers read from their tiny

Bibles, 'I shall not want. He maketh me lie down in green pastures, He leadeth me beside the still waters. He restoreth my soul. He leadeth me in the paths of righteousness for His name's sake.' The Chaplain stood in full battle dress at the front – his vestments hanging from around his neck. 'Yea, though I walk through the valley of the shadow of death, I will fear no evil, for Thou art with me; Thy rod and Thy staff they comfort me. Thou preparest a table before me in the presence of mine enemies. Thou anointest my head with oil; my cup runneth over. Surely goodness and mercy shall follow me all the days of my life, and I will dwell in the house of the Lord . . . forever.'

'Amen' the men concluded, and they rose. Gordon's skin tingled. The camera turned to take in the diminutive reporter. 'This is Kate Dunn,' she said with a quivering voice and moist eyes, 'NBC News, reporting to you from the valley of the shadow of death.'

Chapter Twenty-Five

UNRUSFOR HEADQUARTERS, KHABAROVSK
April 26, 0730 GMT (1730 Local)

The joint staff's operations and planning team hovered over the map as if they'd find something new if they studied it longer. But Nate Clark understood his options exactly. They'd been evident in the first five seconds. 'Okay,' he said loudly. The closed rank of uniformed backs parted. They turned from the brightly lit map to face their commander. 'What does the PLA have along the Songhua between the 25th Light Infantry Division and the Tangyuan Valley?'

The all looked at the Dutch intelligence officer. 'There appear to be two full Chinese divisions and part of a third along that road. They are survivors of the fighting around Birobidzhan that made it across the Amur before the ice broke. When we inserted the 101st into Tangyuan Valley, they were trapped.'

'Will they fight?' Clark asked.

The Dutch colonel shrugged. 'The southernmost unit has applied some pressure against the north end of the Tangyuan Valley. But our airstrikes reduced that to only token attacks mounted once every day

565

or two. The partial division was damaged so severely that they amount to little more than walking wounded. It's the third unit – which we believe to be the 549th Infantry Division – that poses the most serious concern. We just don't know its strength yet.'

Clark pursed his lips. 'Can anybody threaten the flanks or rear of the 25th if we send them south?'

The British planner replied. 'The hills in that area are very rugged. The roads and rivers run north and south. To go east and west you have to cross mountain ranges. In my opinion, the only forces the Chinese can bring to bear on the 25th are the three units that lie along the length of the Songhua River.'

'If the Chinese dig in,' the German operations officer chimed in, 'just like the 101st has in the Tangyuan Valley, the 25th will have to dismount and dislodge them.'

'But we have air superiority,' Major Reed countered. 'That makes for a big difference between our defense of the Tangyuan Valley, and any Chinese defenses along the Songhua.'

The arguments were just building steam. But Clark had already made his mind up so he headed off the debate. 'We drop the German parachute regiment into the valley as soon as possible. And we order the 25th south along that road at maximum possible speed.' The disbelievers looked back and forth at one another. 'In road miles, they're half the distance from Tangyuan as the main force.'

'General Clark,' the British planner began gingerly, 'their mission, if I might say so, was purely in support of the main attack. They have only two heavy battalions attached to them, and the terrain does obviously favor the defenders.'

'We can't drop any more troops into that valley,' Clark reminded him, reviewing their limited options. 'There's no more room to maneuver. They're already pressed into a four-square-mile box. And I will not consign men to a battle in which they're going to run out of ammunition after the second or third firefight. The 25th Light Infantry Division is the closest unit. The fact that they crossed the Amur at all was due solely to the speed with which they broke out of Birobidzhan. We didn't even know what to do with them, if you'll all remember, so we assigned them the flank support role down that two-lane, piece-of-shit highway. But now they're our only real hope of saving those men in the Tangyuan Valley. And I plan on asking them to do just that. Now you go off and come back when you've got a plan.'

*   *   *

Lieutenant Colonel Reed knocked on Nate's office door. 'Come *in*,' Clark said.

'We're ready with an operations plan, sir.'

'Sit down. Walk me through it before we go in to the others.'

Reed gave Clark his private briefing.

'The road tracks the Songhua, which will protect their right flank unless the Chinese put gunboats on the river. The Songhua runs through a fairly wide valley. The road is out of small arms' range of the hills on the opposite bank. The Twenty-Fifth's trucks and Humvees *will* be vulnerable, however, to pre-registered mortars and artillery. We'll fix them with tactical acquisition radars, then suppress and destroy them with helicopter gunships. But the *dominant* terrain all the way down to the 101st are the hill masses to the *left* side of the road. That road's cut through miles and miles of jumbled hills, slopes and meadows. Nothing else is trafficable in the area.'

'Sounds like good country to defend,' Clark commented – worried.

'Well, the risk of them enfilading those soft vehicles on that roadway is huge. We've got to push the Chinese back from the road at least to the skyline – about 700 yards – the whole way down. We'll try to reduce lodgements on commanding ground with intense air attack. But if we want to go fast, there's no way around mounting clearing operations. *Luckily*, the terrain is covered in thick stands of pine. And there are lots of knobs and finger ridges to screen maneuvering. Good tactical commanders will make short work of Chinese bunkers. But it'll be exhausting and bloody work. They'll be fought out in four to six hours. We'll have to rotate those battalions constantly. We'll have to use them up, General Clark.'

Nate nodded slowly. 'What kind of defenses do you expect the Chinese to have waiting?'

'There are a few huts along the road that'll have to be cleared. But our best bet is we'll find hastily constructed, bunker-centered strongpoints on the forward slope protecting mortars on the reverse slope.'

'Do the infantrymen in those trucks have any cover around the road?'

'Where the road's cut into the hill there's cover on the shoulder. They'll be pretty exposed on the river's side, but there are some draws they could use if they're not flooded with run-off.'

Clark nodded – frowning. 'Okay, give me the plan.'

'We've mustered one battalion of armor and one of mechanized infantry,' Reed replied. 'We'll put a company of tanks in the vanguard to blast their way through roadblocks. We'll distribute the remainder down the length of the road column for local direct fire support. They'll have armored bulldozers so they can widen the road, fill in holes, and push vehicle hulks over the side. The mech can be used for attack on level ground. We'll use the light infantry to go up the hills.'

'What about our artillery?'

'We'll disperse it. But we'll make sure the vanguard and rearguard are within range of all active batteries. They'll leapfrog, with half the batteries always ready to fire on calls. We'll have six batteries ready to repulse an attack or prepare an objective at any given time. And we'll sprinkle the division's senior officers around to organize local action if the column gets segmented by a Chinese attack. That's the main risk – segmentation. The Chinese can move along parallel valleys and punch at our flanks. If they break through, they could destroy the column piecemeal.'

Nate took a deep breath. 'What's the Chinese population along that road?' he asked.

'Sparse,' Reed replied. 'Maybe thirty, maybe fifty thousand people.'

Nate nodded. 'I'm going to . . . lift all restrictions on the fire controllers,' he said. Reed looked at the floor. He nodded. Nate could think of nothing to say. Nothing that wouldn't betray the knot of bile he felt rise in his stomach.

ALONG SONGHUA RIVER, SOUTH OF SUIBIN
April 26, 1000 GMT (2000 Local)

Night had just fallen, and Harold Stempel was quickly drifting off to sleep. It had been a quiet day. They had taken the luxury of building a small fire. With their boots to the heat and wearing cold-weather gear, the spring night was reasonably comfortable.

'All right!' came the loud voice of the platoon sergeant. Stempel and several others groaned when they looked up. The NCO arrived with the rest of the platoon in tow.

'Gather *around!*' came the command of their platoon leader. 'Hope you girls don't mind if we crash your campfire.' A new arrival tried to take Stempel's place by the warm fire. Stempel kicked him, and muscled his way to the fireside. There was jostling among the cranky men as the lieutenant took his place in the middle. He held in his hand a sheet of flimsy paper. 'I've called this platoon meeting 'cause we just got The Word.' There were groans and some loud curses, which were followed by threats from the NCOs. 'As many of you may have heard, there are some good guys holed up in a valley about a hundred clicks south of here. It was the mission of Third Corps' main heavy forces across the Songhua to relieve them. The 25th was providing their flank security.'

There was muttering over the subordinate role. This time, the NCOs remained silent.

'I say *was* because we just got *this.*' He raised the piece of paper in the air, then held it up to the campfire to read. '"Today's date. From: Nate Clark, Commanding General of UNRUSFOR. To: Soldiers of the 25th LID. I was with many of you at Birobidzhan in the most awful first days of this war. The battle there was one of the most brilliant displays of defense in all of military history. Now, however, I must ask you to do the same on offense. I must ask you to go win this war."'

The young lieutenant looked up. There was no noise from the thirty men. Stempel looked around to see all eyes raised.

'"A brigade of the 101st and a battalion of the 75th Rangers were inserted into a valley one hundred miles south of you. Their mission is critical. Holding that valley means a successful conclusion to this war. But they have endured a week of ferocious assaults. The worst began late last night. The Chinese launched a full-scale attack from the south and their situation is desperate. They cannot hold much longer. The 25th is the division closest to that valley. The 25th is now the main attack force. I am calling upon you to relieve those troops. UNRUSFOR will support you with everything it has. I have every confidence you will now prove your greatness and I will forever be in your debt. Good luck, and God speed."'

The lieutenant folded the message carefully, and put it into his pocket. 'There are s'posed to be some trucks down on the road.

Gather your gear and prepare to move out.' Stempel rose, packed his gear and shouldered his load. There was no discussion. Nobody commented on the unfairness of the orders. The desire for respect was a powerful force. They each accepted the mission in silence.

TANGYUAN VALLEY, NORTHERN CHINA
April 26, 1700 GMT (0300 Local)

There was a disturbance. Andre Faulk drowsily opened his eyes. Running in pairs along the ceiling of the inflated polyurethane aid station were rows of bare flourescent tubes. Andre looked at the station's entryway. An officer was arguing heatedly with two doctors and a crowd of nurses. The outnumbered man vigorously shook his head. He spun from a doctor, to a nurse, to another doctor. The medical personnel all had their say, but in the end the officer won.

Andre figured it was another hasty move. They'd packed up twice since he'd arrived at the aid station. He'd not been carried on a litter but had used a crutch. Both times the fighting had sounded much closer than it should.

The officer walked to the central aisle and removed his helmet. 'I'd like to have your attention,' he called out politely. 'I'm sorry to have to bother you men, but things have taken a turn for the worse. The Chinese are giving it their all this go around. And I'm afraid we're going to have to do the same if . . . if we're going to pull this thing out. Now I know you've done all your country could ask of any man. But right now we need everyone who can still fire a weapon. All the headquarters, supply and support units have been stripped clean of fillers. The combat units aren't even sending their wounded back any more unless they're critical. So I'm gonna have to ask for some volunteers to rejoin the fight. You won't have to do any moving around. Just use a weapon from a fighting hole. We won't even make you dig it.'

It was intended as humor, but nobody laughed. The doctors and nurses all glared at the staff officer.

Andre lay on his stretcher and watched the captain nervously twirl his helmet. At first no one rose, and the man stood there all alone. Slowly, however, the first men hobbled up and were sent to the exit. Nurses scolded the wounded soldiers and tried sending them back to their beds. The officer interceded, but finally allowed a doctor to check each volunteer out. Only one man was rejected as too seriously hurt.

'Stupid fucks,' the man next to Andre said. But Andre was already swinging his feet to the floor.

He hesitated, but decided not to listen to the guy. 'Hey, man,' he said, 'if nobody stops the motherfuckers, we're *all* dead. They'll just toss a charge through that door and move on.'

His neighbor made a face – unconvinced.

Andre put weight on his feet. Nothing hurt too badly to walk. But he knew it was in part the painkillers. He limped up to the captain and was directed to the doctor. The man stuck a cold stethoscope onto Andre's chest as a nurse took his blood pressure. 'You feel up to this?' the doctor asked while listening to Andre's heart.

'*No-o-o,*' Andre answered.

The exhausted man didn't bother with a reply. 'Nurse, give this man some ampicillin and some Vicodin.' He turned to the next wounded recruit.

The nurse gave Andre two bottles of pills – the larger one the painkillers. 'Take the antibiotic every four hours – the Vicodin as needed,' she said while still holding his hand. Standing close, she whispered, 'You don't have to do this.'

When the next man arrived, she abruptly left Andre there holding his pills. He reconsidered his decision to leave the clean, warm hospital. But men arrived with rifles and outer gear, which were handed out to the volunteers. Although Andre's wounds were impressive enough – large bandages over his left ear and all up and down his right side – other volunteers were much worse off. There were bandaged faces leaving only one eye uncovered. Legs were wrapped so thick they looked like tree trunks. Blood soaked through dressings from all manner of hidden wounds.

Andre donned the gear and took an M-16.

The provisional platoon numbered over twenty wounded men. They had to climb high into the rocks of a steep hill. About a dozen men preceded Andre. They turned the light dusting of snow into slick ice. His slips were painful, but Andre didn't complain about the effort. The higher the better, as far as he was concerned. They all helped

ERIC L. HARRY

each other make the slow trek in the darkness. The more seriously
wounded were lent shoulders by the few healthy soldiers. The sound
of fighting was a now constant and sonorous roar.

The captain who led them there had lied about the fighting holes.
He placed the men among the rocks in unprepared positions. Andre
lay on a ledge behind a jagged outcropping. Andre could see none
of his new comrades. They were hidden – as was he – in the hilltop's
dark crevices. But they were so tightly packed the captain addressed
them all in a conversational tone. 'Your job up here is simple. Don't
go anywhere, and don't let the Chinese take this peak.' The orders
seemed ridiculous. They were as far away from the fighting as they could
possibly be. 'From up here,' the officer said as his men handed out extra
ammunition, 'enemy troops could fire down on our rear areas. We'd
no longer be able to move freely to react to Chinese breakthroughs.'
A soldier handed Andre eight magazines. When added to the one in
his rifle and two others he'd been given outside the hospital, Andre
had over a hundred and fifty rounds. It was the most he'd had at any
one time since the first couple of days in the valley.

He couldn't help but wonder why they were being so generous
with ammo.

'Good luck,' the captain concluded. 'We'll relieve you as soon as
we can . . . hopefully in the morning.'

After he left, the conversations sprung from the dark hiding places
like mushrooms. Andre briefly saw the profile of a helmet about ten
meters to his right. From the sound of the voices there were men on
each side of and above him.

'Anybody got a machine-gun?' someone asked.

After a few moments of silence, they all heard, 'I've got a SAW.'

The answer didn't seem to sit well with the questioner. A Squad
Automatic Weapon had an impressive six-hundred-round box magazine. But it fired 5.56-mm rifle rounds, not the heavier 7.62-mm
NATO rounds of the M-60. And it would overheat quickly with
sustained firing.

'How about grenadiers?' the same voice asked. 'Call it out.'

'I got one,' someone replied. 'Two!' another man said. 'Three.' The
count ended at five.

At least that was good, Andre thought. Five 40-mm grenade launchers
– M-279s mounted underneath M-16s – could do some good at such
a high elevation.

572

A deep whine rose to a fearsome roar as a jet passed low overhead. '*Jeeze!*' someone shouted as the glowing twin exhausts banked steeply. The jet screamed down the valley and exited the far end uneventfully. It seemed odd that it would risk flying so low.

Then the night erupted in a string of sixteen brilliant flashes. The clouds of flame cooled from white to orange to red as the crackling rumble rattled Andre's insides. Moments later another fighter-bomber crested the ridge. They each wrought the same devastation. In all, eight jets dropped 128 500-lb bombs. They fell along the road and the surrounding foothills. Despite the painful ringing in Andre's ears, he found the display of pyrotechnics entrancing. Soon after the fighter-bombers streaked a hundred feet over their ridge line, a ripple of explosions lit the forested valley in brilliant fire. The flashes darkened before their concussion pounded his eardrums. The lightning and thunder were a half-second out of sequence.

But the more Andre watched, the more his sense of dread grew. The strings of bombs fell closer and closer to their hilltop position. They finally pounded the base of the hill where they lay. When the terrible violence came to an end, the nature of men's chatter had changed. It took on an urgency – a sense of purpose – that was new.

'Look alive!' someone called out. Tracers streaked through the woods below. The fighting raged as the Chinese surged forward.

'Let's do this right! My name is Master Sergeant Golden. I'll command for as long as I can. We appear to be in a semicircle! And we got a 16 on the far right at the edge of a cliff. You're number one. Call it out, son!'

'One!' a man said, sounding fit enough.

There was grunting, then a loud, 'Shit!' from the master sergeant. He puffed and hissed his way to the next position. 'About five meters to the left of number one we got a grenadier and some flat ground. He's coverin' the approach we took to get up here, so we might have to react this way. If we're threatened with an overrun from over here, I want you two guys to call out "Right! Right!" We'll organize a reaction team to reinforce this sector. When I get around the perimeter, I'll designate which guys are on the team. You're number two,' he said at a lower volume. 'Call it out.'

'Two!' yelled another voice in the night.

The orientation and shouted orders continued. There was about one grenadier every two or three M-16s. When the count reached number six, the shout came from the guy just to Andre's right. There followed a conversation in a much quieter voice. 'You doin' okay?' asked the senior NCO.

'I'm not feelin' real good,' the guy said. 'I think I'm still bleedin', and my leg really hurts.'

There was a click. Andre could see the beam of a flashlight dimly reflected off overhanging rocks. 'Yeah, you're still bleedin' some,' the older man said. 'You just don't do any movin' around. Try to maybe prop yer foot up on the rocks and keep it elevated.'

'Like . . . *uh*, like this?' The master sergeant approved.

Andre's mouth was dry and he got his canteen. He took a swig of the cool liquid and felt refreshed. 'Take it easy on that water,' ordered the master sergeant. His teeth were bared as he eased himself into the rocks. His rifle was slung over his shoulder and he hopped on one leg. 'You're lucky seven – call it out.'

'Seven!' Andre barked quickly and with decent volume. He didn't sound wounded, and he was pleased by that fact.

The master sergeant looked Andre over with his fading flashlight. 'You're on the reaction team.' Andre didn't object. He saw in the reflected light that the man was clearly in agony. His face was shiny with sweat. He appeared to be at least in his forties. Must've been from battalion staff. 'Listen for the call. "Right" means head over to where we came up,' he said – pointing up the hill through the huge boulders. '"Left" means that way,' he pointed the other direction – also up the hill.

Andre nodded, and the man was off to continue his tour. The count grew past ten as the fight below raged on. It poured from left to right – south to north – as it moved up the valley. Marked by flashing muzzles, bursting grenades and streaking tracers, the beleaguered Americans were clearly in full retreat. Andre pitied the poor bastards far below. But fear took its place as he watched the fiery lines slowly recede. They were leaving Andre's hilltop far behind.

'Where the hell're they *goin'*?' asked the man next to Andre – number six.

The question wasn't directed toward anyone. But when no one else answered, Andre felt obliged to reply. 'They're fallin' back.'

'But how far? I mean, it looks like they pulled right on back past where *we* are.'

The master sergeant's weakening voice came from the distance. 'Last one's a grenadier!'

'Twenty-two!' came a much louder shout.

'And that makes me twenty-three!' the master sergeant managed. His booming voice was failing fast, but he was done. *Twenty-three*, Andre thought. He watched the fighting down below. Thousands and thousands of muzzles spat deadly fire.

The figures looked like stealthy mountaineers as they climbed in complete darkness. Andre kept his rifle trained on the nearest man. He switched from time to time as a more suitable target appeared. The wounded Americans waited in silence as the Chinese approached.

Pebbles trickled down the hill into Andre's position.

The climbers all froze. Words were spoken in hushed Chinese. Moments passed before a short order was given and they resumed their ascent toward the guns.

Everyone waited on the master sergeant to fire the first round. Andre drew a bead on a dark form. The man scaled a steep rock. He stood upright momentarily with his rifle slung over his back. He climbed on – now less than fifteen meters away.

A single M-16 fired. An avalanche of noise thundered down the hill. Andre fired once and knocked a man off the rocks. For the first few moments the fight was totally one-sided. The Chinese were completely exposed. But even so the pace of killing was measured. The Americans squeezed off shots one at a time. At first they were the only ones firing.

That all changed after five or six seconds. The entire hillside came alive with muzzle flashes. Bullets sparked off bare granite all around. The Americans' 40-mm grenades burst almost the instant they were fired. The explosions seemed dangerously close.

Andre lay on a smooth, cold rock. He did his damnedest to aim each shot. But bullets hit the rocks all around. It was unnerving how thick the fire was. Every squeeze of Andre's trigger was followed by an angry swarm of buzzing death. Both sides sprayed the rocks at point-blank range. When one Chinese soldier emptied a magazine on full-auto, every American had a clear fix on him for two seconds. Before Andre could fire, the man was thrown backwards from his perch.

The Chinese soldiers died in such great numbers the battle ended quickly. The Americans occupied a steep uphill position, and had surprise to add to their advantage. Andre's rifle had killed every second or third shot. A company of infantry lay dead after a minute of combat.

'Cease fire!' the master sergeant called out. 'Cease fire! Cease fire!'

The American soldiers quickly ended the killing. The only sounds were now made by the wounded. A lone Chinese gun opened up. Single shots by a dozen Americans sounded like a machine-gun. They all aimed at where the flame had been and there followed silence.

After awhile, Andre slid back onto the dirt. He replaced the half-empty magazine in his rifle with a full one and rose up. He took long looks into the darkness in search of movement. But there were only the moans, bleating calls, and choking gurgles. They would weaken soon and all would be silent.

The wounds along Andre's side began to ache with renewed vigor. He wasn't cold, but he began to shiver till he was quickly exhausted. He got his canteen and took a Vicodin to settle down.

'Anybody wounded?' the master sergeant asked.

At first there was no answer. Then, '*Everybody's* fuckin' wounded!' came a reply. Andre joined in the laughter. That was their brief victory celebration. They rejoiced for a moment at having survived the first encounter.

'Less than eight hours now,' said a jubilant number six.

Andre wondered at the comment, then asked, 'Eight hours till what?'

'Till they're comin' *back* for us. Didn't you *hear?*'

It was the most stupid remark Andre had ever heard. Didn't the guy have eyes? Couldn't he see that their 'relief' was being beaten farther and farther away? The guy chattered on about their impending rescue. Each word grated on Andre, but he held his peace. He let the man go through the night with his dreams intact.

WHITE HOUSE OVAL OFFICE
April 26, 0400 GMT (2300 Local)

Elaine stuck her head in the door. 'Time for bed, sweetie.' Gordon sat at his desk all alone. She came over and asked, 'What's that?' Gordon showed her the letter. It was the original and would probably end up in the Smithsonian. 'Does that thing bother you, Gordon?'

He shrugged. 'Sort of. Plus ordering someone killed doesn't exactly leave you in the best of spirits.'

She snorted. 'That man *Kartsev* sure has ordered plenty of people killed, and I imagine *his* spirits are just fine.'

'I'm not so sure about that.' Gordon looked again at the handwritten text – in English. There were no mistakes in his script. 'I think Kartsev is a very unhappy man.'

'He's also about to be a very *dead* man,' Elaine said. Gordon looked up. 'Oh, *I'm* sorry, honey. That was the wrong thing to say. I know you feel bad about that Executive Order. But you've had too much on your shoulders for too long. You can't dwell on the things this office demands of you. It's the toughest job on earth, Gordon. But in my unbiased opinion, every decision you've made was just and moral.'

'That's what he said in the letter.'

'Well, he's right about that, but that's *all* he's right about. Gordon, he's a *madman*. You can't take what he says *seriously*.' She hugged and kissed him, then parted with an admonition to come to bed.

Gordon read the letter one last time. '"Dear Mr President. I suppose by now you're trying to have me killed. I understand your decision completely. Every choice you've made to date has been correct. And the results of those choices have been extraordinarily good for you and your nation. But the outcome which awaits your next decision will be radically different. You will err at the most fateful turning point in modern man's history, and that which you hold dearest will be placed in imminent danger. What I am talking about now is the worldwide spread of anarchy."'

Gordon felt a rush of anxiety each time he read those words. His mind raced. He was no longer sleepy. '"Northern China now lies in ruins. Ten million refugees cling to life's fringes. Another hundred million people are unemployed. Into that mixture of physical disruption and economic dislocation will soon return a defeated, demoralized army. Hundreds of thousands horribly brutalized by your war machine. Many of those soldiers will be changed psychologically. They'll cast about for a meaning to it all. For some belief system which will explain the horrors of their youth. Their answer will be found in the simple word, 'No.' They will say no to everybody and everything. No to all authority. No to every norm. No to every order, every request, every plea. Why

577

the word 'no'? Because no empowers the powerless. No denies the dominion of the strong over the weak. '*No*!' is the drug which eases the minds of the tortured, the traumatized, the guilt-ridden. 'No' is the hope that what came before will never be again.

"'From that one, simple word, mankind will finally taste the milk of true freedom. Not the freedom of your democratic rhetoric. The lawyerly parsing of rights and privileges, laws and checks and balances. But total freedom from all constraints. Men and women free to do whatever they wish. It is only then that true anarchy will reign.

"'And you are part of that great process. A bead in the necklace of history. Soon your moment of truth will arrive. Soon you will face a choice. You can stay in China. Do the dirty business of controlling a restive population. Maintain the pressure necessary to prevent man's baser instincts from percolating to the surface. But that course will be opposed by all. Your allies, Congress, your adoring public. 'Bring the boys home for a good parade! Leave the mess for them to clean up!' You will, of course, withdraw, leaving a momentary vacuum of power. What will follow is an inexorable chain reaction. A burst of freedom followed by fiery repression. Escalating uprisings and backlashes in cycles. With each atrocity the pendulum will swing wider. The violence will soon grow uncontrollable. And from that combustible brew there will arise a leader. Someone to spark the inevitable explosion. To unleash the suppressed natural behavior of a billion and a half people. Imagine the soaring heights of ingenuity, and the depths and variety of evil. The social fallout from the unprecedented upheaval will wash over your bastion of order and stability. Your ship of state will be rocked, Mr President. Welcome to the post-ideological age.

"'My purpose in writing you, President Davis, is not to wash my hands of any blame. In fact I am proud of my contributions to society. For I believe mankind will emerge triumphant from its darkest horrors. It will, via that catharsis, transcend one order of human development for the next. Imagine a future in which violent coercion by a king or a count is unnecessary. In which man has been freed of the straitjacket of convention. If my optimism about the human spirit proves correct, how then will historians view heretics such as me, who cried out against the injustices of old? And how differently will they view the old engine's protectors such as you? The defenders of the faith who will unleash great death machines in a desperate attempt to preserve, protect and defend?

"'Oh, but I would love to study the time of troubles that is nearing. But I would not trade places with you. I believe you to be a decent man laboring mightily to do an honest job. Your only limitation is that you have not seen what I have seen. You have not been one of the teeth on a cog which slowly ground human flesh in the machine. Such extremes open the eyes and liberate the mind. They strip away the façade of government to reveal the abomination which lies inside. I am sorry, Mr Davis, that at this crucial juncture in history the reins of power happened to fall to you. V. Kartsev.'"

SONGHUA RIVER, NORTH OF TANGYUAN
April 26, 0500 GMT (1500 Local)

Stempel and his squadmates heard fighting as they piled sandbags in the trucks. They built walls and sat back-to-back in the center. They faced out with their weapons at the ready. The truck's canvas top was lashed down tight with cord. They'd raise the canvas and fire out the sides if they had to. Harold had no idea what the woman driving the truck would do.

But as soon as they began to roll, the soldiers confronted the real enemy. An awful cold numbed their skin and chilled their bones. The men's combat-ready poses gave way. Hands that had once gripped rifles now clenched the mountain bags into which all retreated. Without the truck's lone heater, they could never have made five miles. Its warm air wafted by Harold intermittently. He longed for every lukewarm touch. Every groan of the brakes meant relief. When the column stopped completely, it was heaven on earth. Men rose up, stretched, looked around. They rubbed their extremities and shook like dogs emerging from water. The whole convoy was ordered to dismount. Thousands of men descended moaning and bitching. They did jumping jacks and squat thrusts. When they loaded up and pressed on, Harold felt warm for five or ten delicious minutes.

The road wound through valleys along the river's side. It was a rough land. But curled up on the floor of the truck Stempel could only see the top of the hills through a slender gap in the canvas. He sat there pinching his parka over all but his eyes. The guns of the M-1A1s up ahead sounded like thunder. Echoes turned the sharp cracks into a rumble. They were blasting a narrow pathway through the hills. Smoke rose from the slopes and from blackened craters dotting the road. Tanks with bulldozer blades smashed through barriers and filled in traps. The two heavy battalions that had led the way south from Birobidzhan were almost invulnerable to Chinese infantry. They had been the spearhead easily piercing poorly prepared infantry positions.

The air above the column buzzed with Apache gunships and Kiowa scouts. Trucks carried the helicopters' ground crews, fuel and ammo forward, allowing them to be refitted on the shoulders of the narrow highway. Men swarmed over them like pit crews at the Indy 500, and they were quickly returned to the air. Their chopping blades sounded a near-constant *thwack* overhead as they scouted the column's undefended flanks. Calls from forward air controllers sent them heeling over and charging into action. Their rockets and guns made short work of the enemy.

Only once did the Chinese mount an effective ambush. But the attackers received broadsides from over a dozen trucks. Almost two companies fired at point-blank range up the hills. Harold's unit had been too far away to get in the fight. But he'd watched the ambush end with a stupendous, deafening airstrike. For far above the tree-skimming helicopters flew a dedicated flight of heavily-laden fighter-bombers. They and their tankers orbited in holding patterns awaiting the call. When they swooped down, they made clear the enormous difference between forty-pound artillery shells and two-thousand-pound bombs.

The column rolled on, and Harold had been pleased with the victory. He'd been worried about getting caught in that truck during a firefight. And he quickly saw that those worries were justified. They steered around the burning carcass of a Deuce-and-a-Quarter. The outlines of the truck were clearly visible in the flames. Tires, canopy frame, chassis. The heat was so intense as to be painful. Harold and his squadmates shielded themselves from the searing fire of the fully consumed vehicle.

The wind didn't seem so bad afterwards. Cold was slow death, but fire did the job right away. And the breeze helped rid Stempel's clothes of the lingering stench of the burned truck.

TANGYUAN VALLEY, NORTHERN CHINA
April 27, 0700 GMT (1700 Local)

'That's *it!*' Woody shouted over the noise. 'That's as far as we can go!'

Kate looked in disbelief at the line of smoke rising above the woods just ahead. Woody pulled her to the ground behind a large log. With the thick trunk behind her back and a large boulder on her right she sat listening to the sounds of fighting all around. The rattling machine guns and bursting grenades and earth-shattering bombs were so loud that they drowned out ordinary conversation. Added to that was the noise of six howitzers. The air-transportable guns were rapidly expending their remaining shells. Kate and Woody had passed 105-mms in their flight from the onrushing Chinese. The gunners were already preparing to destroy their pieces.

All night and all day they'd retreated from the Chinese. But now they'd come to the end of the road. Up ahead lay the northernmost lines – half a mile from where she and Woody sat. And from behind came an entire Chinese army – less than a mile away and charging hard. Watching the haze rise from the now continuous fighting, Kate felt like she was trapped inside a forest fire. The blazing ring around their unburned patch of woods was tightening. The small oasis of unconsumed earth was shrinking as fiery death drew near.

Bullets cut randomly through the air overhead. The heavy machine-gun bullets would travel for miles. They expended their force only upon striking something solid. They sounded like firecrackers when they smacked into trees. You could see the cloud of dust as they skimmed off granite rocks. In the meat grinder where they sat, bullets sliced through the air in both directions.

'You think they're going to drop any more paratroopers?' Kate asked Woody. She'd been watching the skies for transports.

'They don't have room. Half of 'em would land behind Chinese lines.'

Kate's throat was tightly constricted. 'Still, they wouldn't have, you know, put that whole regiment in here if things were . . .' She heaved a deep sigh. When she'd first seen the parachutes in the blue sky, she'd thought they were more supplies. But the soaring spirits of the soldiers around her had lifted her mood before she'd even realized what was happening. Once she saw that under the chutes hung reinforcements, she and Woody had hurried to meet them. They were a whole regiment of German paratroopers. They were saviors sent to stop the Chinese. They meant more than just a thousand additional defenders. They stood for UNRUSFOR commitment not to lose that valley. They were a sign straight from Clark's Mt Olympus that the defenders in the valley would hold.

The thousand men had quickly joined the ranks. To all appearances, however, they'd done little to stop the Chinese. There were more parachutes in the sky later that morning, but they'd held boxes and crates, not men. After what would've been lunchtime had Kate and Woody stopped running long enough to eat, the skies had been filled again. But this time not with transports. When the Chinese sent masses of infantry, the allies responded with fleets of bombers.

Woody was clearly right. The narrow cage into which they'd been pressed was now almost too small even for resupply. No long strings of parachutes could descend from the sky without falling into the sea of Chinese. 'Okay,' Kate said. 'What do we do?' Her eyes were transfixed by the smoky boundaries. The ring of killing grounds where weapons blazed. The frontiers of their ever-shrinking hold on this part of China.

'We either lie low down here in the valley, or we hightail it up to the hills.'

Kate longed to choose the former. To curl up in a ball right where she sat, close her eyes, and not wake till it was over. She was scared. Every time she thought about getting captured by the Chinese she felt a chill so complete her thoughts froze. She could think about it no further. She couldn't imagine the horrors that might await.

Woody was waiting for her to reply. His usually smiling eyes were sunk deep into their sockets. And he hadn't even gotten high once since they'd arrived in that valley. 'Woody . . . you wanta smoke a joint or something?' Kate asked. He didn't even raise his head. 'I'll . . . I'll get high with you.' He turned to her, staring straight into her eyes. She couldn't take his gaze for long and looked away. 'I guess that wouldn't be smart,' she said, making an attempt at a chuckle. 'Here we'd be stumbling around stoned . . .' she began, but didn't finish. She brought her legs up into a fetal curl and lowered her chin to her knees.

'I'm not worried about getting stoned and losing my shit, Kate,' Woody said slowly. 'After all these years, I'm as competent stoned as I am straight. I quit smoking, Kate, because I didn't want to spend my last hours on earth high. It just didn't seem right. Like I might miss out on something, you know? Fresh air. Blue sky. Maybe even some last-second revelation or insight.'

'I'm sorry,' Kate whispered in a trembling voice. 'Oh, Woody, I'm *so*, so sorry! I got us into this *stupid* . . .!' Tears choked the words off. She dissolved into sobs – incapacitated by spasms of guilt and fear. Woody put his arm around her. The fervor with which she cried and the extreme fatigue from which she suffered brought a quick end to the episode. Her store of emotions was rapidly exhausted. She apologized again in a wooden voice, then sat there in a daze. Spent. Empty. Waiting.

Time passed. The bedlam of war was all around.

Woody finally broke the silence, speaking slowly. 'Have you ever seen what it's like when soldiers crack?' His tone was calm and matter-of-fact. 'At the end, when they break and just run for their lives?'

Kate's throat was so dry she had to swallow twice. 'No.' She buried her hands – suddenly cold – between her knees.

'In Burundi, there was a company of French peacekeepers guarding a Tutsi refugee camp. The Hutus came at them by the thousands with machetes. The French ran out of ammunition, and then they broke.' He was staring off into the distance. Remembering.

'Did the Hutus . . .?' Kate began, but faltered. 'Did they kill the French?'

Woody shook his head as if in a trance. 'They killed the Tutsis. All of them.'

Kate tried to imagine the medieval scene. The hacking slaughter of a thousand innocent people. But it too was beyond her ability to conceive. 'What do you think the Chinese will do?' She meant what did he think they would do to the defeated UNRUSFOR soldiers? But she was also thinking about herself. Apart from the nurses, she was the only woman among the Americans.

'The most dangerous time, Kate, is right at first. Right when they're taking you, and before you're "in the system." You've just got to stay alive. You understand? That's all. Don't try for anything more than that. Just put everything out of your mind but survival. Don't judge anything that happens to you by any other standard than whether you live through it. Time heals most wounds, and life is long. You do whatever it takes. Do you understand what I'm telling you, Kate?'

Until the question at the end, she'd remained calm. But now she hugged her legs as tightly as she could to ward off the chill. She nodded, and drew a noisy breath. 'I vote for the hills,' she blurted out. 'Not the valley.' Woody glanced at the high ground and nodded. 'When should we go?' she asked.

'Soon. If the Chinese force their way through, UNRUSFOR's gonna turn this valley into a cauldron. They're gonna drop everything in their arsenal in here. Napalm. High explosives. Fuel-air munitions. Cluster bombs. Mines and booby traps and whatever other nasty shit they've hidden away for special occasions. And we gotta pick the right hill, 'cause they'll drop 'em up there, too.'

Kate hesitated, but then forced the words out. 'We could . . . could try to squeeze on a medevac helicopter,' she tentatively suggested. The high pitch of her voice betrayed her. Woody looked at her, but said nothing. 'No,' she quickly added. She was ashamed that she'd even suggested displacing seriously wounded soldiers.

A thin limb was suddenly sheared from the upper reaches of a tree. It never really threatened them, but the cutting sound of the passing bullet was menacing. Kate and Woody both flinched and cringed as the leafy branch crashed to the ground ten feet away.

'Let's go,' Kate said – rising to her feet.

TANGYUAN VALLEY, NORTHERN CHINA
April 27, 0830 GMT (1830 Local)

The Chinese had made three concerted attempts to take the hilltop where Andre Faulk lay. The first appeared to have just missed its intended pre-dawn start. In the dim gray light they watched men climb the icy rocks. They slipped and lost one step for each two they took. Many were injured by noisy falls on the sharp crags even before the automatic weapons mowed them down in huge numbers. Before the hand grenades rained onto them by the dozens. Before grenadiers fired canisters of shot that lit the rocks with sparks.

The next two attacks were in broad daylight. They were slaughters on a brilliant blue morning. All three efforts had been repulsed in bloodbaths that did nothing but diminish the defenders' ammunition. In between, allied bombers had pounded the base of the hill. Andre had no idea how many attacks the air raids had foiled. But the bombs' explosions were stunning at five hundred meters. Shrapnel struck the rocks around their position with still-lethal force.

Andre was petrified each time the bombers came in. There was no unit name or number on their hilltop. They were provisionals hastily organized for a single task. A scratch team of wounded men whose lone radio had been holed and was useless. But someone must have remembered them. Some forward observer must have seen them there. For bombs were dropped all around, but always at minimally safe distances. They laid a cordon of fire around their hill. Its choking smoke set everyone coughing. The air stank. The Marine jets came closest of all. And when the last F/A-18 pulled up, it waggled its wings to signal its last bombing run.

It grew quiet. The pop and crackle of fighting was distant. Andre lay back. Daydreaming. Taking a painkiller. No Chinese came for a while. Andre knew why. Everyone in position to attack lay dead amid the still smoking bomb craters. He looked up at the puffy clouds. The moon was bright and clear in the daytime sky.

'There's another one!' croaked the man to Andre's right – number six by the master sergeant's count. His voice was failing him quickly. Andre had lent the man some painkillers, and he'd come back for more an hour later. He seized on any hope for a rescue. This time he said he'd seen a helicopter. Andre looked, but concluded it was just another mirage.

Number thirteen to Andre's left had binoculars. He kept a running count of the Chinese movements. They streamed in great numbers toward the battle down the deeply pitted dirt road far below. They were out of range of the men's light weapons. But the Americans wouldn't have fired even if they'd been closer. The bottom of the valley was a world away. After the third attack of the day – the fourth overall – their stocks of ammo had dwindled to half. All that mattered now lay within a hundred-meter radius of the summit.

Andre caught his head as he nodded off to sleep. It had almost struck the cold boulder beneath him. That rock had kept him alive. During a lull in the fighting, he'd risen to sit atop it. Its downhill face was scarred and pitted. All manner of bullets and random shrapnel

585

had been stopped by the granite. It was like the armor that wrapped a tank crew in its shell. And it had kept friendly casualties to an absolute minimum. Despite four firefights from as close as fifteen meters, they'd suffered only two new wounds – both slight. Grenades had gone off only a few feet away from Andre. The stunning blasts were deafening. But when the debris fell it was little more than a heavy rain. The rocks had spared them from being shredded to pieces.

The only bad news had been announced by the master sergeant. Two of their brethren, he'd informed them, had taken a turn for the worse. Not from new wounds, but from old ones. Andre hadn't seen them to know how sick they were, but it must have been bad. A man had limped by to redistribute their ammo.

'There it is again!' number six called out raggedly.

This time Andre saw the helicopter. Not a long-range Blackhawk like the one they'd rode in on. But a gunship firing a pod full of rockets. That was now the thin tether of hope on which number six felt his life depended. 'What kind of combat range do Apaches have?' Andre's neighbor asked in a voice he tried to make loud. No one answered. 'It's only, like, a hundred miles or something, right?'

More like two or three hundred, Andre thought but didn't say. It was like the old sailors that Andre had read about back in school. They got excited when they saw a bird because it meant land. Only in this case they weren't on a ship searching for shore. Their salvation was coming toward them. It was drifting slowly like an iceberg ever closer. Sliding over the earth like a glacier. So slowly you couldn't tell it was moving. Inch, by inch, by inch, by inch . . .

A loud explosion from near at hand woke Andre. His eyes shot open and he grabbed his rifle. Smoke drifted over his position. He spun his head from side to side. Pain shot through his cramping muscles like hot fire.

He scrambled up onto his rock parapet and peered over. The hill was filled with Chinese as before. But none moved. All were long dead and beginning to smell in the late afternoon sun.

Another shell burst, stinging Andre's face.

He dropped down behind the rock with his eyes watering from the pain. His glove shot up to his left cheek. A small smear of crimson darkened his white glove. 'Sh-h-*hit!*' He dabbed at the tiny wounds with his bare hand and looked at the droplets of blood.

Yet another blast ripped through their positions. It wasn't the crushing blow from a big artillery tube. And it couldn't compare to the unearthly hell of an air raid. But the new threat brought ragged breathing from Andre's chest.

Bam! shook the hilltop a dozen meters away. *Mortars!* Andre realized in horror. He looked up at the wispy red clouds that drifted overhead. The small shells were fired at a high angle and dropped almost straight down.

Another shell exploded. A man started cursing at the top of his lungs. 'Shit! Mother*fucker!* God*damn* this fuckin' *shit*, man!'

'*Are you hit?*' boomed the master sergeant – managing an impressive volume despite his flagging strength.

'. . . *take* any more of this motherfuckin' crap! I quit! That's *it!*'

'Sit the fuck down!' yelled the master sergeant.

Another shell crashed onto the hilltop. Andre was so startled by each blast that he feared death from heart attack. A light rain of rock dust drifted down around him. He curled up in a ball and braced himself while the master sergeant and the screaming man had their fight.

'Put that Goddamn white flag down!' the furious NCO shouted.

'I *quit!* I'm goin' down there and turn my ass *over! Fuck* this shit, man!'

'Nobody surrenders till I give the order!' the master sergeant yelled.

Another mortar dropped without warning. From his fetal position – every muscle hard as the rocks against which he lay – Andre looked up at the sky. That was all he could do. There was nowhere to go. Nowhere to hide. No shelter that would protect him from the random projectiles lobbed onto them. To his horror, he caught a glimpse of a plummeting mortar round.

Bam! It landed on the hill a safe distance away.

'*A-a-a-a-ah-h!*' came the blood-curdling screech. '*Ah! Ah! Ah! Ah!*'

At first Andre thought a man had cracked. It had happened twice to men in his old company during artillery barrages. The terror and helplessness of lying exposed was too much. They just snapped and began to scream as if wounded. But that wasn't the case this time.

'*Shit!* Number sixteen's hit bad!' reported one of the men from Andre's left.

A bursting mortar interrupted his calls for aid.

'*How bad?*' asked the master sergeant over the noise.

'Bad!' the guy shouted over the screams. 'Took off his legs – both of 'em!'

'Oh, shit,' Andre moaned – jamming his eyes shut. *Please, God,* he begged silently. *Please, please, please, ple-e-ease!* He tried his best to shut the present from his mind. There was a thud. No burst. A dud. The screams went on, but Andre was far away. The trip to New Jersey with the Boys Club when he was nine. How strange the memory was to him now. He'd been so excited because they'd slept under the stars. It was a camping trip for a bunch of kids from The Bronx. It was the only time he'd left the city before boot camp.

The next shell that landed burst. Debris fell as Andre focused on that camping trip. But it wasn't the same memory as he'd had before. It didn't seem to have the same effect. He'd always thought back to that camping trip late at night when he couldn't manage to fall asleep. He'd lie in his bed and imagine he was out underneath the stars. Now, however, he spent night after night under those same stars. But they'd lost all the magic – the sense of adventure – that had captivated him and the two dozen other youths. The stars now meant something different. They meant cold, and killing, and screams of pain . . . like those from the legless man.

Crump! came the sound of a burst in the dirt. Whole ledges of earth showered down around him. Andre jammed his eyes shut. The wailing man had fallen silent. '*Hey!* Listen to me! No, no, no! Open your *eyes*, man! Don't go to sleep! *Hey!* No, man! Oh, Jesus, man – *come* on! Hang on! *Don't close your eyes!*'

Bam! Andre felt the thud through the earth.

Give it up, Andre silently advised. He'd seen it before. Men screamed in horror on first seeing their massive wounds. Then they'd grow quiet. Their eyes would get glassy. The sweat that had flooded from every pore gave way to shivering as if from the bitter cold of death's grip. In basic they'd taught them that shock was the body's defense mechanism to help staunch massive bleeding. But it seemed to kill more men than it saved. Sure enough, the soothing words soon came to an end. Shock was silence. Shock was private. Shock was death.

For no reason that was apparent to Andre, the mortars ceased their deadly rain. Out of ammo. Killed by counterbattery. Shifted targets. It didn't matter which. The silence meant death for the man who'd fallen into shock. But it meant life for everyone else.

'All right!' shouted the master sergeant in what sounded like anger. '*Count* off!'

The rightmost man shouted, 'One!' The next guy called out, 'Two!' The next, 'Three!' Andre looked out over the rock – his armor. The hillside wasn't crawling with a swarm of attackers. The Chinese weren't coordinating an attack with the mortar bombardment.

'Six!' Andre's neighbor called out – dissolving into hisses of pain from the effort.

'Seven!' Andre shouted, and the count continued. It went on until it stopped at number eleven. There was silence – a broken length in the chain of positions.

'Eleven!' the master sergeant prompted. There was no reply. 'Somebody check!'

It took a few moments for the obvious truth to be revealed. Andre waited in silence with all the rest.

'U-uhm!' came the distressed voice of number ten – more of a sigh, or an exhalation, than a comment. But it made the rest of his report unnecessary. 'He's . . . he took a mortar! Right where he was layin'! Right in the back, it looks like! I can't tell, really!'

'All right, let's go!' the sergeant said quickly, moving on. 'Number twelve, you're now eleven! Sound off!'

'Eleven,' came the demoralized reply. It was the man who had been surrendering a few moments before. The count moved on, renumbering again from sixteen to account for the legless KIA. After reaching eighteen, the master sergeant shouted, 'Okay! I'm nineteen! Hand out the ammo from the guys who bought it!'

A short while later, a guy appeared and asked Andre how much ammo he had. Andre's magazines were all stacked at the base of his big rock. 'Four full mags, plus seven rounds in a fifth.'

The guy's face was pitted with small wounds. He lowered his bandaged head to look down at two blood-spattered magazines. The bandages made his helmet sit high atop his head. 'You're flush. I'm gonna pass these out further down.'

Andre nodded. The man turned to leave. 'Hey!' Andre called out. The guy stopped. 'Who're you?'

'John,' the guy replied, breaking into a smile. He held his hand out which Andre shook.

'I meant your number,' Andre said – pissed that he now knew the man's name.

'Oh. Ten. I'm right over there where that little tree is growin' out of the crack in the big boulder.' He was pointing. Andre looked out of politeness. 'What's *your* name?' he asked Andre.

'Seven,' Andre replied. After a moment, the guy arched his eyebrows. He turned to leave – not nearly as upbeat as he had been before. 'Name's Andre! Andre Faulk.' The guy turned back with a smile and nodded.

After he left, Andre wondered why the guy wanted to know his name. Or know anything about him, for that matter. Numbers would do fine as far as he was concerned. And he agreed when the master sergeant renumbered. It was far better than reminding them of each death every time they counted off. Andre was even glad he didn't know what had happened to the two men whose earlier wounds had overcome them. He hadn't once left his perch on the hill. He pissed in a far corner. Ate his meals beside a moss-covered rock. Fought from behind the granite boulder. His world was a ledge of dirt bounded by stone. It was barely wide enough for him to lie down. That was the way he wanted it.

He either lived or died right there. While events outside his ledge were important, he chose not to get too involved. Why should he? Why should he take on something more to have to deal with? He was emotionally spent already. As far as he knew, the two wounded men who had weakened in the night were now doing just fine. They could get new numbers and rejoin the others soon. Why look too deeply into it?

'I wonder why those mortars quit firing at us?' a sullen number six asked from over the rocks.

Andre frowned. ''Cause they don't give a shit about us,' he replied. He climbed up on to his granite shield. The sweet-smelling bodies were the only trace of the enemy he could see. *Fermentation*, someone had said back in the barracks. *'When it gets warm, the dead bodies'll start smellin' like spilt beer.'*

'You mean they'll leave us *alone* now?' number six asked – hopeful.

What Andre really meant was that they'd kill them all when convenient. That they were focusing their efforts at breaking through, not mopping up. Every mortar, every tank, every fresh company of Chinese infantry was probably funneled straight through to the front. They knew that the men on the hill were cut off. Like dozens of other stranded units they presumably posed no threat. They were just a waste of resources for now. Better to come back later when they were starving. Half-dead from exhaustion. Low on ammo and medicine. They could come back then with heavy artillery.

'S-so . . . you think they'll leave us alone?' number six asked again.

'Maybe,' Andre said, 'for a while.'

'Oh, thank God, man!' Number six laughed. 'I just about shit in my *pants* when those mortars started droppin'. I mean, not that I don't piss in my shorts every Goddamn time they attack. It's just when they come up the hill, you know, at least then you can *do* something about it. It's not like mortars or . . . or arty, ya know?'

'Yeah,' came Andre's reply. Number six took the hint and fell silent. The guy reminded Andre of Harold Stempel. But Stempel would never have quit talking. Andre would've had to yell, 'Shut the fuck up!' He wondered whether Stemp had made it over. Surely he had, by now, he figured. He'd been assigned to the 25th, which got into the shit real early. He'd probably been processed through Hawaii and flown in to replace the first losses. He probably had even more combat experience than Andre, although that seemed hard to believe. But while Andre was deliverin' mail or in training back in Kentucky, Stemp was probably notching kills in the deep, deep shit.

Unless he's dead, a voice called out. But Andre found that almost unthinkable. Just as unthinkable as Harold Stempel – combat veteran. Andre smiled, imagining the skinny kid with crossed bandoliers rising up out of the water like Rambo with M-60 blazing.

'You got any more Vicodin, number seven?' six asked.

Andre returned to the present. To his hole on the side of a hill. 'Man, you're eatin' an awful lot of that shit.'

'My leg hurts, man. *Real* bad. I think it's, like, infected or something. It's worse than it was this mornin'. And it kind of, you know, smells'

Andre winced. 'Okay, sure,' he said as he struggled to his feet with the plastic bottle. He climbed up into the corner near where he pissed. Number six struggled up on his side of the tall rock. From the sounds, his pain was excruciating. All Andre saw as he handed four pills over was the guy's pale, shaking hand. 'Thank you,' his neighbor hissed.

Chapter Twenty-Six

WHITE HOUSE SITUATION ROOM
April 27, 1200 GMT (0700 Local)

Maps of various scales shone from the room's multiple screens. Gordon Davis ate a cheese danish with waning appetite. 'The 25th is making decent progress down the Songhua,' General Dekker said. He'd risen at the end of the formal briefing to stand next to the screen. 'But the Chinese have figured out what they're up to, and the resistance the 25th is meeting is better and better prepared. In the last four hours, they've had to order the infantry to dismount and clear the surrounding ridges three times. Their progress has slowed to just a few miles per hour.'

'That's the pace of a road march,' the Commandant of the Marine Corps commented. 'Have you given any thought to just dismounting and plowing on?'

'The head of that column is still almost forty miles from the valley,' Dekker replied. 'We don't want to have them reach their objective on their last legs.'

'Well, General Dekker,' the Marine general responded – not backing down – 'it's the fourth quarter and the shot clock is running down. Those men shouldn't save anything for the locker room.'

593

'Those *men*,' Dekker snapped, 'have been fighting for over three months without a break! They've only got two heavy battalions, but they've made better progress than *either* of the two main prongs.'

'That's because the Chinese they're facing are *done!* You can stick a fork in 'em. They aren't trying to stop that advance. They're just not falling back fast enough. They're on foot being chased by men in vehicles. They're caught in a *trap*, General Dekker.'

'So what would you suggest?' the Army general asked. 'Try to talk them into surrendering?'

Gordon like all the rest waited on the Marine commandant's reply.

'I would *suggest* that they get outta those trucks and *advance*. Get down to basics. Block and tackle, General Dekker. This isn't rocket science.'

'And this isn't a game, either,' Dekker replied. Knots bulged from his clenched jaw.

'Is it possible,' Gordon said, 'those men *could* advance more quickly on foot?' Dekker swallowed his pride and nodded once. 'Well, speed is everything at this point. So . . . I'd give the order.'

SONGHUA RIVER, NORTH OF TANGYUAN
April 27, 1430 GMT (0430 Local)

'Everybody *out!*' came the command – waking Harold up. There were groans from the back of the truck. The order was being shouted up and down the road. The trucks had been parked for almost an hour as the fighting ahead raged. Every last man roused himself in the pre-dawn morning from a deep, deep sleep.

'Shoulder your *lo-o-oads!*' shouted the platoon sergeant. That command brought still more bitching and muted chatter.

'Why the fuck we gotta hump our *loads* around?' someone asked from the dark but bustling road.

The passing platoon sergeant heard the question and replied with a shout. 'You can kiss these trucks goodbye! Get all yer shit and fall in on the shoulders! First and Third Squads in line on the left! Second and Fourth on the right! Ten meters separation! Let's *go!* Let's *go!*'

Quiet dissension spread quickly through the ranks. Men knew better than to openly question the platoon sergeant. Lowered voices were instead leveled on the squad leader. 'Why are we leavin' the trucks?' Patterson asked.

'How the fuck should *I* know?' came the reply from the buck sergeant. The three-striper was two grades junior to the platoon sergeant and often knew no more than his men.

''Cause you're our *squad* leader!'

'I've been asleep just like *you*, fuckhead! Get your pack on and shut the fuck up!'

That did nothing to put an end to the complaints. Harold felt like joining in once the heavy pack settled on his raw shoulders. Standing with his back to the tailgate he shouldered the full hundred and ten pounds. It pressed hard against skin made raw from similar abuse.

The same pain was felt by everyone. But the others didn't have the 60 to carry.

'Don't forget this,' Chavez said sadistically. He was standing at the back of the truck, smiling – holding Stempel's brand new M-60. Along with the fighter bombers, gunships and tanks, someone had scrounged up a few extra machine-guns. They'd drawn straws to see who'd carry it. Harold had lost under suspicious circumstances.

Chavez handed Harold the twenty-three-pound weapon. Harold muttered as he strapped the long sling over his neck and shoulder. That drew laughter from the others, who found his plight amusing. 'How much you weigh, Stemp?' Patterson asked. 'One forty? You're like an *ant*, man! Ants can carry ten times their weight, you know.'

'Fuck you,' Harold replied to more laughter. He weighed one sixty-five buck naked. They fell into a single file on the left side of the road. It was the side beneath the steep hills. The side from which all the Chinese ambushes had come. The men on the right – on the river's side – had a bank they could hide behind. The men on the left were a dozen paces from safety.

'For*ward!*' came the command from the front of the line. They moved out. Harold was bent over thirty degrees at the waist. His lungs hurt from the weight of the pack on his back. Sweat popped out in beads along his forehead and neck. It began to trickle from his underarms despite the morning chill. Every footstep had to be carefully placed in the dark. An uneven patch of road threatened an instantly twisted ankle.

'Feelin' good, *troopah?*' Patterson said to Stempel from behind. 'Those little stick legs startin' to wobble on ya any?'

'F-fuck you,' Stempel said – his voice broken by the immense effort of marching.

'Oh, baby, please! Do me, *Ha-arold* – you big studly . . .!'

'Knock it off!' their squad leader barked. They fell quiet. But the chatter would've ended anyway. When they headed up the hill, Stempel's legs and lungs began to burn.

Harold waited as the maneuver team crawled forward under furious fire. The Chinese knew exactly where the Americans were, where they were going, and what they were trying to do . . . which was kill them. Patterson and the others had some cover, but not much. The earth and underbrush around them was being peppered with high-powered rounds. They never raised any part of their bodies even an inch above high ground. Even so, he'd seen several of the men stop to bandage small flesh wounds from ricochets or splattered rock chips or wood splinters. Harold wished he could help, but his orders were to lie low till the squad leader gave the signal.

That signal came when the four men of the maneuver team were twenty feet from the bunker. Now it was time to pour on the fire. Everyone watched the squad leader's silent countdown. He curled his fingers from five, four, three, two, down to one.

Harold raised his M-60 and laid it over the moss-covered rock. The riflemen around him began squeezing off rounds aimed at the black slit in the earth. The grenadiers fired 40-mm grenades which burst all around the single long firing port. Now it was Harold's turn. He lined up the big gun on the earthen bunker's open slit and pulled the trigger. It roared and pounded Harold's shoulder and belched flame two feet from its muzzle. Harold calmly marched the fire into the opening. At seventy meters, he could easily see the dirt kicked up by the large 7.62-mm rounds. Long bursts disappeared into the dark hole where half a dozen men sheltered.

Out of the corner of his eye Harold could see the maneuver team begin their assault. The four men rose and rushed uphill at the bunker from directly beneath it. The men in the bunker were now as good as dead. Anyone who raised his head to fire would be killed by Harold or the five riflemen around him. But if no one stopped the assault team, they would all die in a meatgrinder of hand-grenade shrapnel.

No one stopped the assault team. The four Americans stood straight up and hurled four grenades. It was risky because the toss was uphill. In fact, one of the grenades rolled back down. The four men saw it coming and dove to the ground. It burst safely a few meters away just as the other three grenades lit up the bunker. Bright flame shot out through the slit. Black smoke poured out after it.

'Cease fire!' their squad leader shouted. The fire team's guns all fell silent. The assault team scrambled up the slope. Harold cringed in anticipation, but there were no mines or boobytraps. The men crawled right up to the smoking hole. On silent count they easily slipped all four grenades into the bunker. The four men then slid back down the hill with their ears plugged. Again flame jetted through the firing slit. Harold safed his machine-gun and relaxed. He closed his eyes and massaged his throbbing temples. He was too tired to give a shit about the Chinese soldiers who'd just died.

UNRUSFOR HEADQUARTERS, KHABAROVSK
April 27, 2100 GMT (0700 Local)

'Nate?' Clark heard over the secure long-distance line. He closed his eyes at the sound of his wife's voice. 'Nate, are you all right?'

'I love you, Lydia. And I miss you and the boys.' His voice was thick.

'What's the matter?' she asked – instantly on guard. He couldn't answer just then. 'Everything seems to be going so *well!* We're all so proud of . . .'

'I screwed up, Lydia' he said. He then cleared his throat. 'I sent some brave men too far behind enemy lines, and now they're going to die. I went too far. I rolled the dice and . . .' He couldn't finish.

Lydia sighed. 'Tell me what you think you did wrong – exactly.'

Nate described their original plans for a counter-attack. Then his revisions to accelerate the timetables. All his gambles had paid off . . . except his biggest and last one. 'I should've settled for something more modest. We should've done it in stages. Pocket north of the Amur first, then cross the border.'

'Wouldn't the Chinese have built defenses at the river? Tried to stop you from crossing . . .?'

'If we lose that valley, Lydia, we could lose this war. Everything we've got is heading toward one choke point. The prize would be two whole Army Groups – six hundred thousand men and all their equipment – pocketed in the Amur River basin. But if the Chinese take that valley, we're stuck. We can't encircle them, and our flanks are totally exposed. We'd have to withdraw and consolidate our positions. They'd get out of the trap and then there's no end in sight for this thing militarily.'

Lydia remained quiet for a moment. Nate felt the agony of being trapped in a box. Like there was no escape and he was running out of air. 'You said *if* the Chinese take that valley,' Lydia finally said. 'That means it's not certain yet.'

Nate sighed. He felt exhausted from worry. 'I've done all I can do.'

'No, you haven't. There's always something more! Think! You've always been the best soldier in the world. Now you're the best *general* in the world! You can do it. I *know* you can!'

The Special Forces team had black grease paint on their faces despite the bright morning sun. Clark and the twelve men all sat on the bare metal deck of the pitching helicopter. He'd chosen the Green Berets team over the DOD bodyguards because there was no subtlety to the coming threat. There would be no doubt who and where the enemy was.

Clark and Reed watched the wooded hills of northern China flash by beneath the window. They put down along a narrow dirt road near the head of a column of dismounted infantry. They got out and the helicopter took off. It threw dirt and grit into Nate's eyes. It would fly several miles to the rear, refuel, and return to pick him up.

Even before the roar of the chopper receded Nate heard the sound of fighting up ahead. Exhausted infantrymen lay on both shoulders of the road. Their rifles were raised onto their huge field packs and at the ready. The dozen Green Berets spread out to avoid crowding their charge and making him a target. Clark and Reed strode down the road toward the boom and crackle of the guns.

'How're ya *doin*?' Nate called out to heads raised in surprise. Men woke from their slumber and stared at the strange sight. 'Good *morning!'* Nate said to men who scrambled to get to their feet. He never gave an order. He never said a word other than the polite – but loud – greetings. But all down the road in both directions, soldiers who had previously been resting began to rise and shoulder their loads.

A delegation of astonished officers soon approached from the direction of the fighting. They all waved perfunctory salutes and gathered around Nate on the road. Clark shook a lieutenant colonel's hand. 'What seems to be the problem?' Nate asked.

The battalion commander was obviously taken aback by Nate's unexpected arrival. He looked back over his shoulder and said, 'Well, sir, the road's not clear. There's a platoon of tanks up there working them over. We're waiting on the call to get moving. Meanwhile, we've begun to draw heavy fire from the knob of this hill right on top of us.' He pointed for Nate's benefit.

Nate tried to keep his temper under control. In a low voice meant not to be heard by the nearby troops he said, 'We've got a war to win, colonel. If there's some obstacle up ahead, I'd suggest you march your men up there and destroy it.'

The man stiffened. 'Yes, *sir!*'

'As for the fire from that hill, I'd send a company up there straight at 'em. If they don't *run*, go to ground, grab 'em by the nose, and maneuver against their *flanks*. Fire and maneuver, colonel. That's what the taxpayers pay you to do.'

'Yes, sir,' the visibly miserable man said. He turned and issued the orders. Nate walked on. The volume of noise rose. The men on the sides of the road now didn't leave the shelter of their packs to acknowledge the commanding general's passage. They lay behind their large loads. Their eyes remained near the rear sights of their rifles.

The captain who led the Special Forces 'A' Detachment came up to Nate. 'General Clark,' was all he said.

'All right,' Nate replied. He left the center of the road for the left shoulder. He moved forward in a stoop. Men were firing machine-guns in short bursts from beside the road. As he got closer still, he advanced only in short sprints from cover to cover. M-1A1 tanks further down the road fired their 120-mm guns at extreme elevations. The flame from their tubes and the explosion on the crest of the ridge seemed simultaneous. Their targets were only a few hundred meters away.

Another battalion commander met Clark near the rear fender of a tank. Neither he nor the captains and majors of his staff saluted in such close proximity to the enemy. 'What's the hold-up?' Nate shouted over the roar of battle.

The closest main battle tank fired. Everyone flinched. Dust rose from the road all around its treads. Clark's ears rang loudly. The stupendous noise drew his nervous system taut like after the slamming of a nearby door.

'We got clobbered by about a dozen machine-guns dug in on the crest of that ridge straight ahead!' the colonel finally replied. 'They held their fire till the tanks rounded that blind curve! Then they opened up at the bend in defilade – firing straight down this stretch of road! I've got a whole company pinned down about four hundred meters that way!' he said, pointing toward the south – toward the Tangyuan Valley.

Nate asked for and then looked through the man's binoculars. There was a line of evenly spaced dots on the hill ahead. Puffs of smoke came from some, but not all. The rocks around the Chinese fighting holes exploded in puffs both large and small. Down on the road ahead, there were men lying prone. It was impossible to tell the living from the dead. They all lay still and helpless. Dirt spat from the ground around them. Machine-guns raked back and forth across the road.

Nate lowered the binoculars. 'Well, what the hell are you *doing* about it?' he asked with mounting anger. He could understand someone disregarding Clark's order to advance. Someone unwilling to piss his men's lives away to hurry down a road not yet cleared. But those were *his* men that were pinned down. Those were *his* men in need of relief.

'We've called in an airstrike, but there's been some kind of screw-up. For some reason everything's been diverted.'

Clark was boiling mad. He looked around. All of the other officers were majors and captains. Nate turned to see Reed – the new Lieutenant Colonel Reed – looking on. In the instant before opening his mouth to speak Nate considered the possible consequences of his order. What his decision might mean for the son of the man to whom he owed his life. But the steady pounding by the heavy machine-guns convinced him that now he had to call on every resource. Now he had to use the young colonel up. 'Colonel Reed, you're now in command of this unit!' The battalion staff was stunned. 'Call off that airstrike, get up that hill, and *clear this Goddamn road!*'

Reed stared back at him unblinking for a moment. In Clark's head there was a ticking clock. Despite the sadness he felt, he was still seething. His eyes were locked onto Reed's. If Reed had cast even a sidelong glance at others, Clark swore to himself he would've found another commander. If he'd hesitated even a moment longer Clark would've fired him and picked one of the slack-jawed majors. Not to punish Reed. Not to find a better commander from among the other officers. But to make the point to every soldier in the column – advance means advance.

'Yes, *sir!*' the new battalion commander shouted. His words were pure boot-camp zeal. But his eyes were dreary and lifeless.

By the time Clark's helicopter picked him up twenty minutes later, the road was clear and the column was moving. Reed had personally led a company of 110 men up the hill. They'd cleared the machine-gun nests with bullets and hand grenades. Clark's last glimpse of the young colonel had come from the Blackhawk's window. Reed stood silently among thirteen of the newly-dead Americans.

Clark watched the fighter-attack aircraft make their runs over Tangyuan Valley from the window of his Blackhawk helicopter. He had a perfect view of Marine F/A-18s. They dropped from the hazy sky one at a time, leveling out fifty feet above the trees. The jets' twin engines smudged the air over the forests. Their burning exhausts left a shimmering wake.

They disappeared one after another into the valley. They followed the road which wound its way to the south. Above the surrounding ridges drifted the haze of ground combat. To that was added billowing towers of black smoke. The mushroom clouds from thousand-pounders lost their shapes as they cooled above the rocky crests.

Nate grabbed the extra crewman's headset. It was alive with the co-pilot's tense warnings.

'. . . gun radar. Sounds like a ZSU-24. Pro'bly up on a hill to the south.'

'Call it in,' the pilot instructed. 'Get a mission on it.'

'This is General Clark,' Nate interrupted. 'Can we put down somewhere in that valley?'

There was an information-laden moment of silence. 'Well . . . uh, it's pretty tight in there, sir. The Chinese are bringin' SAMs and triple-A right up to the front lines. Plus the small arms fire is thick as molasses.'

'But flights *are* going in, right?'

'Yessir. Medevacs are, yes, sir.'

'Then let's do it.' Clark hung up the headphones and turned to the Special Forces captain. He and his eleven Green Berets sat on the metal deck – armed to the teeth. They had M-60 machine-guns, Squad Automatic Weapons, and Dragon anti-tank missiles. Their M-16s had all the bells and whistles – M-279 grenade launchers, long sniper scopes, and shortened barrels with side-mounted flashlights.

The helicopter banked steeply and accelerated.

'We're going into the valley!' Clark informed the captain. Without being told, the men all swung into action. They had unloaded their weapons on boarding. They now worked their weapons' bolts. Twelve rifles and machine-guns clacked in unison. Once they were all satisfied that the mechanisms were in order, they extracted black magazines and long belts of brass. All were reverently loaded into chambers by men wearing intense looks. They called out, 'Weapon safed!' and had them checked by their buddy.

Belatedly Clark remembered his own rifle. He hadn't taken the precautions of his security team. It was loaded with a round chambered but on 'Safe.' All he needed was to flick the switch and fire.

They were low now. The Blackhawk's nose was pitched forward and its engine roared at full military power. Only the loudest shouts could be heard at any distance. Most of the talking among the Green Berets was done by hand. Pointing at men. A sentence spoken in gestures. A point, a point, a splitting of fingers. Two hands curled back-to-back in a swimming motion. A curt nod of acknowledgment. A thumbs-up in reply from the machine-gunner. It was quick, efficient and calm. A team in every sense of the word.

Clark felt a growing sense of selfishness at their mission. What could he possibly do to help the men in that valley? They had no slack left in them. They held no reserve upon which he could call. It was the height of arrogance to imagine they'd even give a shit about his visit. He recalled his days in Vietnam as a platoon leader. How much he hated seeing the battalion commander's helicopter. How he'd felt when men in clean uniforms climbed out.

Once he was trying to retake a hill. They were under murderous fire from an old French anti-aircraft gun. The same man who'd ordered him off the hill – and then to take it back – stepped out of his Huey. His backslapping tour of frightened draftees pushed Clark right up to the edge. His helpful suggestions almost brought an end to the exhausted young lieutenant's military career. A rifle butt into the man's double chin was Nate's favorite fantasy. The metal baseplate of the M-16 to the bridge of the man's nose a close second. Clark gritted his teeth at the memory even now.

Nate was on the verge of countermanding his order to land when they eased into an LZ. He could see the rotors' downdraft flatten purple smoke into the rocky clearing. The door slid open twenty feet from the ground. Noise and wind rushed in. They pitched and rolled as their own rotors' turbulence danced off the ground below. A thudding wheels-down left them suddenly still.

The Green Berets quickly poured through the opening. By the time Clark got to the door, the Special Forces captain was shouting at a stretcher bearer. The medic held the front end of a folding litter – stooped under the gale of the rotors. The pilot left the engine revved high and remained strapped in the restraints of his seat.

F/A-18s streaked by overhead. Clark was momentarily stunned into inaction by the concussion of nearby bomb blasts. The stretcher bearers were turned away from the helicopter. The captain grabbed Clark's elbow and led him to the shelter of nearby rocks. Small arms fire crackled a few hundred meters away. Acrid smoke hung low in the valley.

The small cleared area on which Nate's helicopter sat was surrounded by wounded men. More streamed in from both directions and were deposited in the swirling dirt. The less seriously injured helped the outnumbered medics with those clinging to life. They held IV bags in the air. Oxygen masks on the faces of men thrashing wildly about in pain. Large compresses over massive chest wounds which were quickly saturated with dark crimson stains. Some of the walking wounded even lay on the ground giving blood. The tubes in their arms didn't flow into bags. They went straight into the arms of their comrades.

Clark had landed not in the front lines to rally the defenders. But in the rear where the consequences of his decisions were made manifest. His decision to go to the valley, he decided, was equal parts folly and hubris. His visit would do nothing more than distract the frantic efforts of brave men. Clark's chopper even prevented the landing of medevacs.

'All right!' he shouted over the noise to the Special Forces captain. 'Not much I can do here! Let's board that Blackhawk and get back to Khabarovsk!' They rose and took a step or two before the rocks behind them spat dust. Clark looked at the smooth stone where they'd sheltered. There was a scar made by a bullet not yet spent. He'd avoided being maimed or killed by mere fractions of a second.

'Let's *go*, sir!' shouted the captain. He pushed the dazed Nate in the small of the back. They jogged onto the LZ. The boundaries of the clearing looked like a disaster area. Men were laid every which way. Side-to-side, foot-to-head – a jumbled and disorganized mass. The chopper's blades kicked up a steady breeze of dust and dirt. Many men lay propped on elbows watching Clark.

He crawled onto the deck of the Blackhawk. He'd never felt like a coward in his entire life . . . until then. But he knew that he couldn't stay there. It wasn't his fear of reprimand from Dekker. It wasn't even his fear of capture. He had to leave because he could only do harm, not good. These men weren't in need of aggressive leadership. They were fighting with all their might for their lives. Giving the full measure of their courage just in surviving.

Clark waited alone in the door of the helicopter. He felt old and tired. His memories had faded and dimmed. But they came flooding back to him. Helicopters. The dead and the dying. Fucking senseless Goddamn tragedy.

Outside, the Special Forces team shouted at the captain. The highly disciplined soldiers engaged in a heated debate with their leader. The captain reluctantly came up to the door. 'General Clark, are you goin' straight back to Khabarovsk?' The twelve men all faced Nate. Clark nodded. 'Then, sir, my men wanta stay here!' Clark's thoughts just then were muddled. He opened his mouth to ask why. But he stopped himself. He looked over his shoulder at the makeshift aid station.

He remembered. He remembered what bound such men to their fates. To Nate, the ranks of wounded around the LZ were silent accusers. But to the Green Berets they were soldiers who'd kept their bargain. They had honored the pact they'd made with their country, their comrades, and themselves. They had done it – they had fought – and they bore wounds to attest to the fulfillment of their commitment.

The growing lump in Clark's throat prevented him from replying. What special words of encouragement or thanks were due the men gathered at the door of the helicopter? Their only benefit would've been to Nate. 'We'll take wounded back with us!' he finally replied. He sat back against the far wall as medics and Green Berets loaded the litters. He wallowed in the sudden realization that all his beliefs about command were illusions. What he did – what he said – made little difference. His army fought because its soldiers were the finest of men. Its backbone of field officers and veteran NCOs held it all together. His only contribution was to stick pins on a map in places like Birobidzhan airbase and Tangyuan Valley.

The terribly wounded soldiers were laid on the bare metal floor because the stretchers were needed in the valley. Most of the men were dying, that much Clark could quickly tell. A lucky few who were lightly wounded came along to give aid to the seriously injured. The helicopter was quickly crowded with close to twenty moaning, crying men. Clark kept retreating till he was jammed tight into the rear corner of the cabin. Some of the men were barely conscious but were propped in sitting positions along the walls to make more room.

The door finally closed on the unending stream of stretchers lined up just outside. The pilot lifted off almost immediately as Clark watched a young medic take charge. He wore a red cross on a white armband and a red bandage on his face covering one eye.

'That guy's got blood in his IV tube!' he snapped at a man whose head was rocked back in pain. The wounded man roused himself and lifted the bag of clear fluids higher. Gravity sent the precious red liquid back into his legless patient. The medic tore open another pack of white bandages. 'That guy's bleedin' bad!' he shouted at another of his wounded assistants.

Clark rose and stepped gingerly across the bucking deck in small gaps between the bodies. 'Here!' he said, holding out his hand for the fresh dressing. The medic looked up in surprise. 'Give me that!' Clark demanded. The medic complied instinctively. 'Where's the bleeder?' he asked. The medic pointed to a prone man with a thigh wound.

That began Clark's modest effort at atonement. He followed the orders of a Specialist Third with a medic's armband. By the time the long flight was over, three of the twenty were dead. And Clark was intimately familiar with the rest. On the tarmac back at Khabarovsk, he raced alongside the gurneys – shouting reports to startled nurses. 'He's lost most of his foot and a lot of blood! We tried cutting his boot off but it was too intermingled with some open fractures!' He dashed over to another team with another gurney. 'No, no! Don't worry about the chest wound! It's stable! He's got what looks like a bullet or some shrapnel at the base of his spine! I could feel it hard up against a vertebra so I left it alone! Turn him over carefully!'

He was so intent on saving his patients that he chased the wounded men to the ambulance doors. 'Stomach wound!' he shouted to the nodding nurse. The doors to the green truck slammed closed. 'He needs antibiotics!' Clark shouted – fogging the two small windows. The ambulance pulled away. Clark's BDUs were splattered in blood and stained in orange antiseptic cleanser.

The helicopter's engine had been cut. The exhausted crew slogged toward the hangar. All was quiet. The only people left were three men who still lay on the tarmac. Nate sat on the hard concrete next to the three wool blankets and waited for Graves Registration.

SONGHUA RIVER, NORTH OF TANGYUAN
April 28, 0100 GMT (1100 Local)

'No fuckin' way!' Patterson said to the man handing out ammo.

'*Yes* fuckin' way!' the man replied as he handed Stempel two hundred-round belts.

They were all lying low on the side of the road. They were sheltered by a cut carved out of the hill. The company up ahead was engaged in a fearsome firefight. The Chinese they met now were all deeply entrenched. 'General fuckin' Clark *himself*?' Patterson asked.

The ammo bearer duck-walked past Stempel, dragging the large canvas bag behind him. 'The driver of the deuce-and-a-quarter where I got this ammo saw Clark's chopper with his own eyes. It was sittin' right on the shoulder of the road.'

'Wait-wait-wait!' McAndrews jumped in. 'So Clark goes up to the head of the column and does *what* did you say?' From the high pitch of his voice you could hear the extreme disbelief.

'He orders this battalion commander to take a hill, and the son-of-a-bitch says "No" right to Clark's face!'

'*No* wa-a-ay!' came from all corners.

'It's the God's honest truth!' the man insisted. The doubters wavered.

'So you're sayin' Clark *shot* the guy?' Patterson challenged. The ammo bearer nodded. 'Bullshit!' came from several men at once. Chavez kicked at the bastard for lying. But the guy stuck by his story.

'You mean he just up and shot a *colonel?*' an incredulous Patterson persisted.

'The guy's a fuckin' *general!*' the ammo bearer from headquarters company pointed out. 'A colonel's like ... like *whale* shit to him, man!'

'Where?' McAndrews probed. 'Where'd he shoot him?'

'Right in the fuckin' forehead.' The ammo bearer pointed with his finger just below the brim of his helmet.

'*No*, dipshit! I mean, like, did he just haul off and whack the guy right there on the *road?*'

'How the hell should *I* know?'

'So you know all the *rest* of that shit, but you don't know *that?*'

'Look!' the guy shot back as he strapped his sack over his shoulder. 'You got any better explanation for why we been double-timin' down this road for the last few hours? Why they decided to take the high ground with infantry instead of turnin' those hills into holes with F-16s?'

With that parting remark he was gone, leaving Harold's squad to contemplate the news.

'You know,' McAndrews said, 'we *have* been haulin' ass down this road. And how many times have we humped up those hills just to waste five or ten Chinks? Six? Seven times?'

Their squad leader returned from a platoon meeting. He skidded to a stop in the dirt as he stayed low. 'All right, let's *go!*' he said – out of breath. 'Bravo Comp'ny's pinned down. We're gonna clean up that hill right there,' he said – pointing over the embankment behind which they lay. 'The attack'll step off from the crest next to that burned-out hut. As soon as we breast the ridge, we'll start drawing fire.'

'What the hell is Bravo Company's *problem?*' Patterson bitched. '*Shit!* Cain't they take one miserable fuckin' hill without our *help?*'

'Cut the shit, Patterson!' the squad leader snapped. 'Drop your packs on the road. Take your weapons, ammo and sleeping bag. Everybody'll get an 81-mm mortar round to hump up to the line of departure. We'll file past the mortar, hand over the rounds one at a time, and keep on goin'.'

Behind him appeared their ill-tempered platoon sergeant. A thick bandage wrapped his hand, which had been holed clean through his palm. '*Move it!*' he boomed in a no-nonsense voice. The entire squad

607

scrambled to their feet. No one really believed that anyone had been executed – especially a colonel by the commanding general. But one thing was clear in the voices of the sergeants and lieutenants. There'd be no breaks. No fucking off. No rest for weary legs or aching backs. No time to treat the small wounds from ricochets or shrapnel, falls or blisters. Harold couldn't count the number of times someone had shouted 'move' or 'go' in some combination with other orders. And it was always in an irritated tone that expected no reply.

TANGYUAN VALLEY, NORTHERN CHINA
April 28, 0800 GMT (1800 Local)

Kate and Woody first thought their decision was the right one. They'd climbed to the very top of the hills. All the fighting seemed far away. There was fire and roaring noise from below, but at their height they were detached observers. Kate had even shot a report of the battle's final chapter with the smoky valley as a dramatic backdrop.

But then came an artillery barrage from massed Chinese guns. They'd opened fire and blanketed the hills all around and the valley floor beneath. Woody and Kate were forced to make yet another life-or-death decision. To lie low and hope to ride out the storm of high explosives. Or to take their chances and flee the tall hill on which they'd found refuge. And with the barrage still pounding the north slope there was only one way down their hill. It led toward the south and the onrushing Chinese.

Again they made the right call. They climbed down the hill amid the random bursts of artillery without so much as a scratch. But as they caught their breath in a trough between two crests, the bombers had begun to sweep in. These were not Chinese aircraft, of course, but American F-16s. Strangely enough, however, they pounded the same hill as the Chinese. The same hill on which Kate and Woody had sought refuge.

The nearest bombs fell only a few hundred meters away. Kate and Woody flattened themselves on the ground as the hill above burst into boiling flame. The bombs had struck right where they'd just taped the report. The next pass blanketed the north slope they'd just descended. There was no debate this time. As soon as the bomber passed, they both rose and labored up the next hill farther to the south. They saw the next jet bank and begin its final approach. They took cover before the bombs rained down. The explosions' concussions were more stunning than before. When they looked up, they saw the bombs had fallen in the trough where they'd only recently rested. The air controllers were rolling the fire to the south. Kate and Woody were where they shouldn't be – in an American free-fire zone.

They climbed the hill with furiously pumping knees, throwing themselves to the ground as bombs fell ever closer. Thin trees were toppled from the force of the blasts alone. Their dry needles crackled in flame from the fiery bursts. When Woody pulled Kate up to her feet she almost fainted. Her head was swimming from the thundering blasts so near at hand. Kate cursed as Woody pushed and pulled her to the top of the hill.

Streaking toward them at eye level was an F-16 heavily laden with bombs. They cowered in the rocks as the jet screamed over the ridge. Kate's throat was pinched tight with fear and she covered her ears. The bare stone crevice in which she lay thudded against her back repeatedly. The world rocked on its axis with each stunning blast. Dust rose up. Clouds of smoke filled the air. Dirt rained down. Kate gagged and gasped for breath. Her head swam and temples pounded and ears rang.

Again Woody tugged at her arms. '*No-o-o!*' she screamed. It was no use. They were losing the race with the curtain of fire. Kate lay on her back – waiting for the end. She stared up at the blue sky visible in gaps through the passing black clouds. She saw criss-crossing contrails and tried to decide which one would kill them.

Woody yanked at her arm so hard it almost pulled her shoulder out of joint. She staggered to her feet with tears in her eyes. He led her down the south face in what became almost a sprint. Her head was spinning and she stumbled and slipped on the rocks. Woody's steadying grip kept her upright – her feet flying.

The next bomber came too fast for them to react. The air thumped her chest, rattled her insides, popped her ears painfully and shook the earth on which her ankles were planted. Flames shot skyward all around. But miraculously they kept on their feet until they collapsed in exhaustion at the bottom. To the sound of the bombs, Kate slowly realized, was now added the popping gunfire of a nearby firefight. There was no going on, now.

They were ringed in fire with no way out. No hope of survival. Kate buried her face in her knees. Her tears flowed as she sobbed.

'*Now*, Kate! If you wanta live, come with me *now!*'

She had no reserves of energy – physical or emotional. But for Woody's sake she allowed him to drag her up another hill. They passed rocks draped in dead Chinese. Her lungs burned. Her head swam. Sweat poured out of her hair and down her forehead. The sound of fighting had grown louder than the bombs. Finally, they stopped running. Woody climbed up onto a flat rock and said, 'Come here and look!' When he insisted, she crawled up the smooth granite face of the boulder. Twice she had to grab and hold the rock for dear life. Twice her equilibrium took an unexpected spin. Not from new bombs, but from the after-effects of earlier explosions. When she reached Woody's side, she looked out across a relatively flat and rocky ridge line. The crest rose gently toward the summit of their hill's higher twin. There – interspersed among the rocks of the neighboring hilltop – were the flaming muzzles of a battle. Slowly climbing the hill under withering fire looked to be the entire Chinese army.

All of a sudden, the wooded valley paralleling their own erupted in rolling flame. The shock waves from a hundred bombs formed rings of white mist – expanding outward from each of the hundred bursts at supersonic speed. The storm of fire raced down the valley on the opposite side of their hill. 'B-52s,' Woody said with an awestricken voice.

After a brief discussion, the man-made earthquake began again. When it was over, Kate's nerves lay in tatters. She stared at the rising flames and flattened woods. She raised her eyes to the sky and saw the white contrails high above. There were three planes following one after another. The tortured valley erupted in a continuous gush of flame a mile long. It was over in a matter of seconds, but the scene repeated itself a third time. The final bomber of the three-plane cell completed the total devastation of their bomb box. Kate screamed at the top of her lungs. She grabbed her hair and shook her head and clenched her teeth. Fire and smoke drifted over their hill and blotted out the sun. The day grew dark and her stinging eyes watered and teared.

Woody picked her up in his arms and ran. He jostled and shook her with each laboring step. When Woody put her down, she realized she'd drifted off. She looked up at a soldier in an American army helmet. His rifle was cradled against his shoulder. His teeth were parted in a toothy smile in the midst of a thick, graying beard. His hair was bound in a long ponytail.

Another soldier appeared over Kate – this one with short hair and a stubble-covered face. She looked back at the first man and realized it was Woody.

Kate sat up too quickly and almost vomited. She had to lie back down.

'Take it easy, ma'am,' came the gravel voice of the real soldier.

'Where are we?' she asked.

Woody answered. 'We've gone from being lost to being surrounded. I'd say that's an improvement.' He raised a Chinese assault rifle and inspected it closely. 'Oh, and they're all wounded,' Woody added. 'Every last soldier up here.'

SONGHUA VALLEY, NORTH OF TANGYUAN
April 28, 1000 GMT (2000 Local)

Harold Stempel stumbled along the steep slope of the hill more asleep than awake. Battles raged against enemy positions on the other side of a finger ridge near the road below and in the distance in every direction. But they mattered little to Harold. His world was small. His concerns narrow. His depth of thinking and feeling shallow.

His lungs burned from the cold air that he sucked through chapped lips. Just moving his legs without tumbling down the hill took all the effort he could muster. The weight of his ammo, sleeping bag and machine-gun were now familiar. But his legs quivered and shook with every step. His aching knees threatened to buckle each time he called upon them for support. The soles of his feet were a mass of blisters.

When they took to ground under fire, the real pain set in. His joints stiffened so much that bending them caused searing pain. His muscles cooled and tightened. He had to stretch and massage them constantly to ward off the imminent cramps.

He was so exhausted that his movements – even under fire – slowed to a crawl. Despite facing the flaming muzzles of the Chinese weapons, he could only make his sore body move so fast. He'd drop to his knees and then to his belly like an old man. He'd unfasten his pack and drag it to the front in slow motion. Bullets whizzed by but he barely flinched any more. With lethargic motions he'd line up the 60 on the bright orange flames. He'd lay down a base of fire while riflemen with grenades maneuvered. Harold's gun kept the enemy's heads low. Grenades tossed into their holes then snuffed them out like vermin. One by one the Chinese muzzles would fall dark.

Harold would then doze until he heard, 'All clear!' Then he'd sleep some more until the squad leader kicked him. The hoarse man could barely croak out another word. He just shoved and kicked and hissed through teeth bared in unrelenting anger. With the help of his squadmates, Harold would then climb to his feet and shoulder the M-60. They would march on across the sloping landscape toward the next Chinese position. Footslogging up hills and down hills and back up – all the while in the total darkness of heavy forests. The farther they went the stiffer the resistance. The more frequent the ambushes. The more numerous the defenders.

The men in Harold's squad had given up debating how fucked their duty was. Whether they'd rather hump their asses through the hills rolling up flanks, or march down the nice flat road into the teeth of the ambush. They'd grown too tired even to bitch. After nine hours of unrelenting combat, their minds were a total blank. Their glassy eyes sunk deep in their sockets. They'd given up caring about anything.

Harold walked straight into a tree. His helmet and face smashed into its trunk. He was stunned, but it woke him up. He jogged a few steps to catch up with the skirmish line. His entire skeleton now ached. Feet and knees and back and shoulders. He shook all over – not just in his legs – as if palsied. And the quaking came not from muscular fatigue. It came from complete, full-body exhaustion.

'I can't go any further,' he mumbled – hoping someone would hear. But the shadowy figures on either side were insensate. They were zombies stumbling toward enemy guns. *This is insane!* Harold raged silently. They'd been blundering forward for hours. No idea what lay ahead. Served up like human fodder. They just walked straight *into* the shit! Worst of all, however, was how quickly Harold's anger faded. How resigned he'd become to death. How little he cared so long as the marching ended soon – one way or the other.

There was a challenge from up ahead shouted in Chinese. Harold sank to his knees and flopped onto his belly. Searing pain shot through his hip as guns on both sides opened fire. He'd either been shot or he'd landed on his ammo pouch. Harold couldn't find the strength to release the heavy pack. He lay crushed under its weight, sighting down the machine-gun and grinding his teeth as the pain in his hip subsided. The gun rocked back against his shoulder repeatedly. The last round on the belt flicked through the chamber.

Harold cursed and reached for a new belt. He wasn't angry that he had to reload. Or that he had a hundred-and-ten-pound pack on top of him. Or that bullets buzzed through the night past his face. Or that grenades went off in bunches all around. Instead, Harold cursed the bastards who drove them on. The unrelenting, merciless orders to advance. Once, when their legs had tired, they'd unintentionally angled their march downhill toward the road they were supposed to be screening. Some son-of-a-bitch first sergeant had then marched up the hill and shouted, 'You're all yellow, unfit cowards!' at them. *Fucker!* Harold thought – incensed. He cursed his squad leader for the firm kicks with his boot. Cursed his platoon sergeant for all the shouts of '*Up!*' Cursed the pathetic apologies of the pussy who'd commanded the platoon before he was killed in an ambush. Harold cursed everyone right up to General Clark. He would've shot the man – general or not – had he seen the fucker execute anyone in front of him.

He slapped the M-60's cover down. The big gun was so hot he could feel it on his face. He shoved the bolt forward and lowered his cheek to the stock. Then he resumed his pounding of the sparkling muzzles. It was like blowing out trick candles at a kid's birthday party. You'd puff real hard with your 60, and the flickering lights disappeared. But as soon as you moved on to a new target, the muzzle would flash on again. It pissed Harold off so much he'd swing the gun back. He'd fire a long burst. Ten or fifteen rounds aimed at a single point of light. It almost always fell permanently dark.

The moment the 'Cease fire!' came, Harold laid his head down. He closed his eyes and felt a deep sleep coming. He let the narcotic need seize him. He drifted off in a matter of seconds. 'Let's go!' came the command Harold hated most. He set his teeth and clenched his fist – ready to strike out if the bastard kicked him again. But the squad leader moved on down the hill and kicked the next guy instead.

Grunting and growling to shut out the pain, Harold rose to his feet with the pack on his back. The one thing he couldn't do by himself, however, was lift the heavy weapon at his feet. He looked around at the milling men to ask for help.

'What's the matter?' asked a chipper man Harold didn't recognize.

'I can't lift the *f-f-fuckin'* gun!' Stempel cursed, then wiped the string of spittle from his chin. The guy picked it up and helped sling it over his shoulder. Even in the darkness Harold could see the guy's smiling face. 'What's *your* fuckin' problem?' Harold lashed out.

'Me? I don't have any problems, man! Not a *problem* in the world!' The guy was as happy as he could be. He slapped Harold's pack and then trotted off toward the Chinese.

'Hey!' Harold called out, thinking the man had gotten turned around in the dark. He ignored Harold's call and rushed into the unknown that lay beyond their skirmish line. Other men appeared out of the same dark woods. One approached Harold – grinning with eyes bright with tears. He wrapped his arms around Harold's neck.

It was then that Harold realized what had happened. It all came home to him in a rush. Not just the fact they had finally reached the valley. That they had rescued their trapped comrades and won the battle. But as the sobbing man squeezed Harold's neck tight, he realized what they had been fighting for all along.

The guy drew back. '*Ma-a-an* am I glad to see yer ass! I never thought I'd make it, buddy! You know, I thought I was a *dead* man, right up till a few minutes ago! They sent us here, then back to the southern line, then back here!' He was laughing. 'We were spread so thin we wouldn't even have slowed the next Chinese push *down*, man!'

More smelly, grimy men crowded Harold. Some jostled him good-naturedly. Others shook hands or high-fived. They had made it! They were alive! They were saved!

'Let's *go*, Charlie Compan-y-y-y!' came the booming voice of the company's first sergeant.

For a moment Harold wondered, *Go where?* But they formed up and marched through slopes filled with dead Chinese. They passed through still more ecstatic defenders but didn't stop. Every step they took, the sound of the fighting grew louder and louder. The trees overhead were clipped repeatedly by streaking bullets. Everywhere lay the signs of heavy fighting. Bloody bandages, hurriedly opened crates, smoking craters.

The sounds of fighting forced the men lower to the ground. Harold couldn't believe they were headed right from the march into heavy battle. He wasn't sleepy now. He could hardly feel his aching muscles.

Like the cavalry but without horses they'd made it in time. Only at the end of the road lay more Chinese.

'Drop yer packs!' came the command. They moved forward with only their weapons. The storm of bullets grew thick. When they reached the forward-most defensive line, they filled the gaps and opened fire. The massed weapons of the defenders and the reinforcements slaughtered the attacking Chinese. Even as the killing continued, Harold's neighbor crawled out of his hole. He shouted something that was drowned out by Harold's machine-gun. '*What?*' Harold asked the man.

'Who the hell *are* you?' the guy repeated.

'The 25th!'

'*Who?*'

'*The 25th Light Infantry Division!*' Harold shouted. He then fired a long burst at the fleeing figures – chopping them down like dry weeds. The man next to Harold was lying with his face in the crook of his elbow. 'Hey!' Harold shouted. 'Are you hit?' He began to pat the man down for a wound. The guy raised his head. He was crying like a baby but he shook his head then lowered it again to his arms.

'Everybody *u-u-up!*' came the command. Harold rose. He raised his gun and marched forward – continuing the massacre of the fleeing Chinese army.

WHITE HOUSE RESIDENTIAL QUARTERS
April 28, 1100 GMT (0600 Local)

Gordon wasn't really asleep. He was lying still in bed next to Elaine. He'd given up on any hope of drifting off. Pull out? Stay and keep the peace? He had to make a decision. The army had done its job. The nation had rallied around it. *All is well*, he thought. *All is well.*

But what if Kartsev was right? What if China collapsed into anarchy? Would the world build a wall around the country? Would they quarantine the violent ideology like a plague-ridden city in the Middle Ages? Confine the healthy with the sick in a desperate effort to stop the spread of the disease? Consign a quarter of the world's population to funeral pyres and roving bands of cannibals?

Gordon shook his head at the nonsense. Elaine stirred but drifted back off. *What the hell did Kartsev know*, anyway? Gordon thought. But his attempt at easing his mind with the question had exactly the opposite effect. Kartsev clearly knew something others didn't. Something about man's primitive nature.

In the dark room Gordon's thoughts had no anchor. They were carried by the current toward nightmarish visions. *What if anarchy spreads outward from China?* India, Indochina, the Pacific Rim. Half the world's population could be engulfed in madness. Charismatic psychopaths leading followers to violence like warlords with hypnotic power. Human misery on an apocalyptic scale. What would he do? What would he do?

Someone knocked lightly on the door. Gordon realized he must have fallen asleep. The dreams vanished. His mind cleared. He swung his feet to the floor. The motion was a little too rapid. It brought pain from the sites of his old wounds. The doctor had said the aches would always be with him. And that was good, Gordon thought as he wrapped his robe around himself. He'd just spent hours alone with his guilt. The emotional burden of sending thousands of men to their deaths. Of ordering armies to kill hundreds of thousands. He'd spent hours of doubting, questioning and rationalizing. Praying, chastising himself, crying. In the end all that was left were cleansing pains. The pains of absolution. And in the clarity of waking he made his decision. It was really the only thing he could do. And it *was* the right decision! That was all that really mattered. The only measure of himself that counted.

Gordon opened the bedroom door. 'You've got a call from General Clark, sir,' an aide said. He led Gordon down the hall to a phone. The White House Military Officer waited there with a smile, which tipped Gordon off. He could already feel the excitement of victory as he raised the receiver to his ear. 'General Clark?' he said.

'Mr President!' Clark said from a noisy room. 'I've got wonderful news!'

Clark went on – his voice ecstatic. Gordon didn't follow all the details. He got what he needed from the man's tone. He took a breath so deep it felt like the first time since the war he'd filled his lungs. *It's the right thing to do*, he told himself. He repeated it over and over.

Chapter Twenty-Seven

TANGYUAN VALLEY, NORTHERN CHINA
April 28, 1300 GMT (2300 Local)

At first Andre hadn't heard what number six said. Then he hadn't believed it. Hours had passed before he first saw the two civilians. A long-haired freak and a beautiful woman roamed about the killing fields below. They were gathering Chinese rifles and ammunition belts – strapping them over their shoulders.

He stared intently at the petite woman as she returned with half a dozen AKs. The long-haired guy yelled and had her put the rifles down. He flicked the safeties on one by one. The bitch had been carrying the rifles just at they'd been dropped when their owners died.

Andre decided the strange coincidence made sense. She was a war correspondent. He'd volunteered for airmobile. They'd both been sent into the deepest shit of the war. But what *was* truly remarkable, he thought, was that they'd both lived through the disaster. The great train wreck on a global scale. The collision had ground up bodies by the thousands. It had an appetite for healthy men and women. It took the youthful, chewed them up, and spat them out. Of all the countless bullets, he thought, how had *none* maimed or killed *him*?

Some men died in the first minutes of a fight. Others like Andre made it through more or less intact. And he *had* made it, he was near certain. The Chinese hadn't come back in any strength for a while.

A few minutes after the reporters returned, the long-haired guy climbed down onto the ledge beside Andre. '*There* you are!' he said. 'Jeeze! They *said* you were over here, but I couldn't find yer ass.' He handed Andre an AK-47. 'Magazine's full, and here's two others. If you run out, there's plenty more.' Andre waited, but the guy still didn't recognize him. 'Well . . . nice talkin' to ya. I gotta go.'

When he turned to leave, Andre said, 'Better check number six.'

'Who?' the cameraman asked.

Andre pointed. 'The guy right over that rock.'

The man hesitated, then said, 'Oh. He's dead, man. He was lyin' curled in a ball – really peaceful. I thought he was just sleepin' but . . . There was a lotta blood.' Andre just stared back at him. After an awkward silence, he moved on.

Andre had never felt so alone. He'd never laid eyes on number six. But the man had kept Andre company through the most important days of his life. He had been Andre's only constant contact with another human being. But now, he was alone again. Just like always.

TANGYUAN VALLEY, NORTHERN CHINA
April 28, 2100 GMT (0700 Local)

'Stempel!' the platoon sergeant shouted.

It took all the energy Harold could muster just to lift his head from his pack. They were rounding everyone up. The soldiers began to collect their gear in silence. Nobody bitched or moaned in front of the platoon sergeant, who talked for a moment to their squad leader. The buck sergeant turned to his squad and said, 'Don't need to bring your packs. McAndrews, you stay here and guard 'em.' McAndrews lay back down with a smile on his face. '*Guard* 'em, McAn*drews*!' the sarge yelled – his abused vocal cords barely eking out a sound.

'He'll be asleep in three minutes,' Patterson said.

'Two!' someone else snapped – sounding angry.

'*Shut* up and listen!' the sergeant screeched. 'We're gonna go up that hill with First Squad,' he said, pointing, 'and help some guys at the top get down.'

'*What*?' Patterson squawked. '*No*! Now it's *this* kinda shit that *pisses* me off! It ain't right! We been bustin' our asses! Marchin' and fightin'! Lost Chavez last night! Now they want us to go up that tall motherfuckin' hill and help some lazy fuckin' assholes get *down*?'

'They're *wounded*,' the squad leader said. 'We're *evacuating* 'em, fuckhead!'

Patterson wasn't convinced. 'Well . . . it's *down* hill for them. We take care of *our* wounded. Let 'em evacuate their *own*!'

'They're *all* wounded! They came and got 'em out of an aid station! Told 'em to hang on to that hill!'

'*That* hill?' Patterson asked. He looked around to get his bearings. 'But we just *took* this stretch last night.'

'They got left behind,' the sarge said as Harold drifted off to sleep. 'Been cut off for a long time.' Instead of yelling, the squad leader laughed as if at an hilarious joke. Harold opened his eyes and looked at the man. 'Ain't that the fuckin' army! They fuckin' *ran* off under cover of some *wounded* guys!' He gasped for air amid cackles of laughter. He'd cracked. 'Ain't that just the *fuckin'* way, man! God-*damn*! The Army *fuckin'* way of doin' every *fuckin'* thing the most *fucked* up way you can fuckin' *do i-i-it*!'

'Hey, sarge . . .' Patterson began.

'Now, we're *goin'* up that fuckin' hill! We're gonna *get* them off it! And I don't wanta hear another *fuckin'* thing outa *anybody*! Now *move* it!'

Harold jumped to his feet with the others. The two squads headed up the steep hill in single file. The base and lower slopes looked like a moonscape. There were blackened holes. Shattered trees. Severed parts of human bodies thankfully charred beyond recognition.

'Jesus *Christ*!' Patterson said from just ahead of Harold. The dozen men skirted the edge of a half-buried boulder. Before them lay an open slope covered with Chinese dead. It looked as if a plow had tilled a cemetery lawn and disinterred the graves of hundreds. They wove their way in silence past bodies in various states of decay. Some lay twisted into awkward shapes. Others had died on their backs as if resting in bed. Some lay in rows – sheltered behind rocks where the death appeared organized. Others died in the open with arms and legs akimbo.

Stempel looked up and tried to imagine attacking that high ground. The only approaches were wholly exposed to fire. And the summit above was all bare granite rock. It was filled with crevices, hollows and notches. All would've blazed with staccato bursts at point-blank range.

No one said a word till they found the first of the wounded. 'Got one over here!' came a call. 'Another one!' called a man from the other side.

They brought them all up to the flat hilltop. The only guy that Harold found was dead. A white guy lying in a wide pool of dry blood. There must've been three hundred empty cartridges on the ledge. Some were lined up in neat rows of twenty-four. Hours of the day – days of the week – day after day. *Unbelievable*, Harold thought in amazement.

'Need some help here!' Harold shouted. He and another man hauled the dead guy onto the bald, breezy summit. They put him in a line of twelve other corpses. They then waited while the medics treated the wounded. A nurse and a bearded man with a television mini-cam helped out. Nobody said much of anything as they waited. The stench from the killing ground below was overpowering.

'Stem*pel*?' Harold heard. He looked around. None of his squadmates had said a word. '*Stemp*!'

Harold turned to see one of the wounded, who was propped up onto his elbow and staring. Harold rose and walked over to the man. The recognition was slow in coming. The guy struggled to his feet and waited.

'Andre?' Harold tentatively said.

They stood face to face not knowing what to do. Andre laughed. Stempel threw his arms around Andre's neck. Tears instantly flooded Harold's eyes. They hugged each other tight. The only sound was the whirring of the mini-cam held by the long-haired cameraman.

UNRUSFOR HEADQUARTERS, KHABAROVSK
April 29, 1200 GMT (2200 Local)

Outside Nate Clark's office, the mood was exultant. The French opened champagne and toasted the victory. The British solemnly raised their glasses to the fallen. After a respectful silence, there was a gush of laughter when the German commander shouted, 'To the field artillery!' and everyone drank. But it was a different story entirely in Clark's office. Colonel Reed had been summoned and sat on the opposite side of Nate's desk.

Nate struggled to put into words the things that he'd kept bottled up inside for too long. Even thinking them sent his mood spiraling downward. The sinking sensation he felt in his chest was almost physical. 'Chuck,' he said to his young aide, 'no one should ever be asked to command troops in war. The toll it takes on the soul is just too great. The memories of the things you wish you'd done differently grow more and more awful, not less. You forget how exhausted you were. How confused things get in the fog of battle. How limited your options are when your back is pressed to the wall. In my mind almost every night I still see the faces of men who died in the platoon I commanded thirty years ago in Vietnam. And the burden of those memories is cumulative. Sometimes, it just reaches the point where it's too heavy to bear. If that happens, you can no longer be an effective military officer. You've got to get out. Heal your wounds. Rest your psyche.'

Reed stared back blankly. Nate raised and re-read the short letter. 'I hereby tender my resignation from active service with the United States Army. I will finish my tour, complete my duties and provide for an orderly transition, but I wish to remove my name from consideration for any promotion in next year's cycle. My decision is absolutely final.' Nate took a deep breath and handed the letter to Colonel Reed. 'I'd like to take this opportunity, Chuck, to tell you that you're the best staff officer I've ever had. And you're one of the best tactical commanders I've ever seen.'

Reed opened his mouth, but couldn't speak. What at first looked to be a grimace became an oddly misshapen and sickly smile. Reed looked away, set his jaw and clenched his teeth. When he finally spoke, his voice cracked and quivered. 'It has been the greatest honor and privilege of my entire life to have served under your command, General Clark. I know you'll want to stop me saying this, but no soldier did more to win this war than you did. It was your strength, your leadership, that held this command together during its darkest hours. I know it's hush-hush, but I've heard you're going to get your fourth star and succeed Dekker as Chief of Staff. I honestly believe that your promotion to the Joint Chiefs couldn't be more deserved.'

Nate sighed. He was at a loss for words. Nate felt a kinship with

Reed that inspired candor. But he couldn't bring himself to describe the cowardly way in which *he* had coped with the psychological load. The burden that Reed couldn't seem to bear. The terrible, invisible scars left on the young officer by repeatedly ordering men to their death. Nate was simply too embarrassed of the bandage that he still applied to ease his own emotional wounds.

He couldn't tell Reed that his memories of the men who'd died were indistinguishable from his memories of the survivors. That in his mind those men were still alive. Healthy twenty-year-olds in the prime of their youth. Simple denial was all it was. At night – when his mind still raced with a million things left to do – he had silent conversations with his old comrades. The imagined talks had a calming effect. It was a mental trick he used to help himself fall asleep. To ease the rising tide of guilt he felt when his mind roamed. Nate exchanged jokes with them. Small talk. Complaints about army life. Those men – living and dead – were so familiar to him that they seemed like old friends. But Nate was too ashamed to tell Reed any of that. For Clark's closest friend was a young Second Lieutenant named Chuck Reed, Sr.

Nate got up and walked around his desk. Reed rose and the two men shook hands. Nate then grabbed Reed's shoulders and hugged him as he would his own son. Reed shed tears he'd have to learn to live with for the rest of his natural life.

VLADIVOSTOK, RUSSIA
April 30, 1300 GMT (2300 Local)

Kate zipped up her ski jacket as she waited at the door of the smoky coffee house. Woody still sat at the table filled with Dutch journalists. He was taking one last hit off their brass 'traveling' bong. Chilled vodka gurgled in the tube. 'Woody-*y-y-y*!' she called out. 'Come on!'

That began his ridiculous good-byes. There were soul shakes which led to hugs. They stood holding each other locked in tight embrace. She could've sworn they would break out crying after having bonded so completely around the bong. He parted with his fingers making a peace sign. The aging Dutch freaks responded in kind.

When Woody joined Kate at the door, she said, 'What a *truly* moving moment.'

Woody was stoned out of his mind. 'Did you see the size of that *hash* rock?' he asked in a tone of awe.

'Is this like a *religion* to you? Like those Indian tribes who eat those . . . What do they eat?'

She opened the door.

'Peyote!' Woody grinned and shouted.

Kate was grabbed roughly by two men. They pulled her out and shoved Woody back inside. One man pinned the door closed. Kate screamed into the empty street. They pushed her into a van and slammed the door closed. She sat in complete darkness as the van rocked from side to side through the abandoned city.

AMUR RIVER CROSSING, JIAYIN, CHINA
April 30, 0800 GMT (0800 Local)

'I'm glad you changed your mind,' Chin whispered to Lieutenant Hung. His friend said nothing. The bus bumped along the rutted road. 'Listen,' Chin continued. 'You were right about so many *things*. I've learned so much in such a short *time*! The first thing I *do* when I get back is to sign up for college entrance exams. They only take three kids from my home town, but you can't imagine how dim-witted the others are. I know I'll be one of those three!'

Chin's news didn't seem to make Hung happy. It pained Chin because he owed so much to his friend. He'd known the world was filled with variety. But he'd had no concept of the wealth and diversity of ideas. No understanding the way things were everywhere else! Hung had translated English magazines day and night, filling in the details and opening Chin's mind. The crash course was cut short by the end of the war. But Chin was a voracious student. And nothing had intrigued him so much as his taste of the forbidden fruit.

'You've taught me so much!' Chin said. Hung, as always, waved for him to lower his voice. 'I owe you my life,' Chin whispered. Hung rolled his eyes in protest. 'No! I *mean* it! I owe you the life you gave me. The life filled with . . . ideas! I mean, who else could've explained the Renaissance in Europe? The fall of Communism in . . .?'

'Sh-h!' Hung said – casting Chin a fierce look.

'No one will *ever* take those things away from me! Because I know them now. They're up here,' Chin said – tapping his skull with his finger. 'I can never unlearn them. And I have you to thank for that!'

'Be careful with what you know,' was all Hung would say. His chin was buried to his chest. His voice was low.

'What do you mean?' Chin asked. Hung said nothing more, so Chin moved on to his real point. 'There are also things *I* can teach *you*. They're not brilliant things. They're simple.' Chin hesitated before broaching the subject. He knew it was off-limits, but he forged ahead nonetheless. 'I'm sorry about your brother.' Hung's head shot up. 'But you can't change what happened to him!'

'What they *did* to him!' Hung corrected – his teeth clenched. This time, it was Hung who spoke too loudly.

Chin looked around before continuing in a whisper. 'A lot of people have died. Good men. They died in the riots at Beijing University last August. They died before that in Tiananmen Square.'

'My brother didn't die in the riots,' Hung replied.

'I know, but . . .' Chin tried to interrupt.

'He died in the basement of some building in Beijing. I don't even know which one. They never let us see the body. Now why do you think that is?' His eyes rose to challenge Chin.

Chin wilted – his head waggling from side to side. 'I *know* that, but the *point* is . . .'

'*Four* days! They had him for *four* days! We know that much!' There was agony written all over his face. In his mind, Chin knew, he imagined his brother's end. They had been close – just a year apart. They were an oddity, and Hung had been proud of their uniqueness. Two children in one family was rare – *especially* two boys. Almost nobody had a second child after having a boy. Chin couldn't count the number of times the words 'my brother' had slipped out of Hung's mouth when recounting some boyhood adventure. Each time it had cast a pall over the conversation.

Chin's mouth was dry, but he tried again. 'I guess I mean to say that a lot of people have died. Think about the war. Just think about it.' Chin's throat was pinched closed with emotion. 'But the war's over. The riots are over. It's time to go home.' Hung snorted – like the college puke from before. But Chin wasn't angered this time. 'You did the right thing,' Chin said. 'You'll be glad once you're home and everything's back to normal.'

The groaning brakes brought the bus to a stop. Everyone headed out into the cool day. There was a floating bridge across the broad, fast-moving river. 'Remember the last time we saw the Amur?' Chin asked excitedly. Hung walked with his hands jammed in his pockets. His chin was tucked to his chest, but his eyes were raised to the bridge. On the opposite side stood a small party of Chinese soldiers. Green army trucks were presumably their ride home. Four huge tents had been pitched at the small camp. 'The river was frozen solid! Remember?'

The dirt road behind them was filled with buses. Hung said nothing as the Americans ushered them toward the bridge. A crowd of almost a thousand Chinese prisoners formed on the Russian bank. All faced south – toward China – with expectant looks. Few said anything at all. After several minutes, three men appeared on the far end of the bridge. They walked across the metal span shoulder-to-shoulder. As they approached, Chin could see they were European. They wore flight suits and one walked with a limp.

When the fliers were almost on shore, several American officers walked out onto the bridge. They wore dark sunglasses, blue caps and broad smiles. They shook hands and then hugged the returning men. It was a homecoming filled with great emotion and cheer. The returning prisoners were quickly escorted to waiting ambulances.

An ethnic Chinese soldier wearing the uniform of the U.S. Army said, 'Go across the bridge!' in stilted and almost monotone Cantonese. There were titters from the mass but they complied. Just before Chin's and Hung's turn came to cross, American soldiers blocked their way with rifles. The bridge was filled to capacity, Chin presumed, so they waited. Just ahead, a couple of hundred men slowly shuffled toward the far bank.

Hung kept craning his neck to look back. First at the departing American POWs. Then at the buses, which slowly pulled away. When their time finally came, Chin had to backhand Hung to get him moving.

The bridge swayed and sank with the weight of so many men. Across the river the group ahead had entered a tent. 'Must be more medical check-ups,' Chin said to the taciturn Hung. Chin chuckled. 'Gonna stick fingers up our ass again is my bet.'

Hung didn't seem amused by Chin's attempt at humor. When they reached the south bank, they saw that their welcoming committee carried rifles. There were no hugs, or handshakes, or even greetings.

They were simply herded into a tent filled with cloth partitions, which looked like a field hospital. The process seemed simple enough to Chin. Everyone was crowded into one end of the tent and taken – one by one – into the warren. There arose the clacking of typewriter keys. Hung was called by an armed soldier before Chin.

When Hung was gone, Chin squatted to wait. 'Watch your ass,' he heard out of nowhere. Chin turned to see a peasant man from the bunk next to his in the barracks.

Chin smiled on recognizing an acquaintance. 'What did you say?' he asked the man.

'College shits think they rule the world,' came the reply. Chin realized he was talking about Hung. He started to object, but the shout of an armed soldier called him away. Chin was ushered through the maze to a desk. A man sat behind a typewriter smoking a cigarette. He held out his hand to invite Chin to sit.

'Name,' the man asked – the cigarette bobbing. Chin answered. Rank. Place and date of birth. Army serial number. All the requisite information. Chin was cooperative and upbeat with his answers. He was eager to board a truck and head home. 'Have you observed any anti-state behavior?' the man asked in a bored tone. His fingers never left the keyboard. When Chin hesitated, the interviewer squinted and looked up through the rising smoke.

'*No!*' Chin burst out, then smiled. 'All the men in *my* barracks were totally loyal Chinese soldiers.'

'Everyone?' the man asked – his fingers still poised. 'What about the traitors who stayed with the Americans? Were they loyal Chinese soldiers like you?'

'Well . . . *no!* Not *them*, of course.' Chin's eyes darted down to the man's yellow fingertips. They hovered over the keys – still not satisfied.

'Is that your answer?' the man asked. Chin's eyes rose. He could feel beads of sweat forming just beneath his hairline. He nodded.

The clacking keys made their marks on the paper. An official document filled with Chin's vital records. Chin's mouth was dry and he swallowed. That simple act drew the watchful eye of the interviewer. The man hesitated . . . then continued typing. When he was done, he pulled the sheet from the roller. He laid it in front of Chin and handed him a pen. 'Sign that,' he curtly directed.

Chin took the pen. 'What is it?' The man stared at him through narrow slits. His eyes rose to the trickle of sweat that ran down the side of Chin's face. Chin lowered the pen to the paper. While he was signing, he stole glances at the document. It was a statement of some sort. A claim – sworn by Chin – that the deserters were enemy agents. That they'd been planted years before by the CIA. That they'd worked actively to sabotage the defense of their homeland. That they'd each been given one hundred U.S. dollars by the American government.

Chin laid the pen across the paper and stood. His armed escort took him to the opposite end of the tent. Chin breathed a sigh of relief. He saw Hung squatting off to the side and headed over.

Hung's eyes caught Chin's and he shook his head once. He looked away then as if they were strangers. Chin was instantly alert to danger. He felt a prickly fear spread across his skin. He squatted some distance away from Hung. The short hairs on his neck rose up. The men all now avoided eye contact. No one spoke. They were changed – ill at ease – not like before. Chin acted as anonymous as he possibly could. He knew several of the men right around him. But he dared not look their way.

It took half an hour for the last men to be processed. Out of the maze of partitions emerged a bald officer wearing reading glasses. He held a single sheet of paper. Two guards took up posts beside him. More armed soldiers appeared at the tent's exit. In the center of the guns squatted the former POWs.

The officer began to read off names. One by one the men rose and headed outside. Sunlight streamed into the room with each departure. It was almost blinding after so much time in the darkened tent.

'Hung, Wu-shi!' the officer called out.

Hung rose – a fact confirmed out of the corner of Chin's eyes. Hung headed toward the bright sun – toward the trucks waiting outside. Chin gave in to the temptation and looked. Hung hesitated in the door and looked back. A guard pushed him through with a muzzle to his back.

Twenty men departed quietly in that manner. The officer handed the list of names to a senior sergeant and turned to address the remaining men. 'You have all spent time around the imperialist war machine! You have seen their *deceits*, their *cruelties*, their *evil* natures! You may have been shown kindness by individual soldiers, who are themselves victims of their oppressive regimes! But their inhumane system brings out the very worst in men! They plunder Asia's resources to feed the factories of greedy capitalists! They drop bombs, massacring innocent Chinese civilians whose sole crime was to demand a return of Asia to Asians! Whose sole desire was to realign boundaries drawn by hundreds of years of aggression by the West! To make *just* borders – founded on *natural* law! To put an end to the looting, the *raping* of Asia's treasure by Europeans! And worse even than block after block of houses flattened by the criminal UN bombing of our cities has been *your* fate! *Yours* has been the worst of the indignities suffered by the People's Republic! You have had to bear the unbearable! But your nightmare has now come to an end! The People's Liberation Army salutes you! The people of China welcome you home!'

With that, the guns were lowered. The guards parted. They were each given a loaf of bread for the journey. They were led out. There was no sign of Hung's group. No sign of Hung's truck. No sign of Hung. Chin never saw or heard from his friend again.

And that began the great awakening in Chin. Not an enlightenment. Not a birth of ideas or a flowering of social consciousness. Beginning on the cold, dusty road heading south from the Amur, there arose instead a hatred that knew no bounds. It was all-consuming. It grew with Chin's visit to Hung's family. With each furtive stop by Hung's former radical and now cowering university friends. With the one risky trip made to the Defense Ministry where, Chin found, Hung had never even *been* in the Army. He had never even *existed* – a fact the clerk confirmed with confidence after reference to a large book of names. A book which seemed to list the names of nonexistent people.

Chin's anger grew to such proportions that he could express it to no one. No one knew how deep it ran. How Chin's life was consumed by it. How it suffused his every day, his every act, his every thought. How it motivated and inspired him to work hard. To set his goals and excel as never before. For there was no one whom he could trust with such dangerous thoughts but a brother. And his brother no longer existed . . . he never had.

NEAR RED SQUARE, MOSCOW, RUSSIA
April 30, 1600 GMT (1800 Local)

Pyotr Andreev carried the rolled carpet through the perekhod. He used the dark, underground pedestrian tunnel even though the city street above was barren of traffic. The air reeked of urine and of the unwashed men who lined the walls. It looked like the permanent residence of men driven underground by the terrors of the streets.

Pyotr suddenly saw two men framed in the bright sunlight of the exit toward which he headed. They strolled slowly – walking side by side – approaching him from the Red Square exit. They both wore jack boots, and one swung a baton. Against the backlighting, he saw only their shapes . . . and the two machine pistols they carried. The guns dangled from straps hung over their shoulders.

Andreev had to make a choice. To lie down in the filth with the dregs of society? Or stroll calmly past the two men? A man coughed, and Pyotr stole a quick glance at him. His weathered face and matted beard resolved his conflict. Pyotr knew he would stand out among such men.

He shifted his grip on the large roll. In the process, his right hand moved nearer his Ingram. He could hand over the heavy load to the Black Shirts. As they reacted in surprise at its weight, he'd extract the Mac-10, flick the safety, and kill them both.

And his mission would be aborted one day short of completion.

A flashlight shone straight into his eyes. Andreev halted and rested the carpet on its end. When the beam ran down the roll, Pyotr's eyes began to adjust to the darkness. One of the men wore the black garb of the anarchists. The other wore a garrison cap with a shiny brim – a policeman. The incredible rise in street violence had forced a police recall. Pairs like this one were now a common sight in Moscow. But the Black Shirt was there to keep an eye on the cop. He could act with impunity while the cop walked a fine line.

'What's that?' the Black Shirt asked. Pyotr couldn't see the man's face. But he imagined the sneer that he heard in his tone.

'A rug,' Pyotr answered.

'Where are you headed with it?' the other man – the policeman – asked.

'To GUM, to trade it for food.'

The Black Shirt snorted. 'Open it up,' he commanded matter of factly.

'But it'll get grimy on the wet floor,' Pyotr argued – his hand inching closer to his Ingram.

The slapping of the Black Shirt's sling against his gun preceded the sight of a small round muzzle in front of Pyotr's right eye. The clicking sound of the safety was distinct. Cold metal pressed hard against his cheekbone. Pyotr stoically kept every motion to a bare minimum. 'I won't tell you twice,' the Black Shirt said.

The policeman's flashlight flicked on. 'Cover me while I check it,' he said. The Black Shirt stepped back – holding the machine pistol one-handed and aimed straight at Pyotr's face.

Pyotr's heart began to race. It couldn't have been a more impossible situation. The officer raised the flashlight and peered inside the roll. But Pyotr's entire focus was on the Black Shirt with the gun. He didn't dare look at the man, but he saw there was no sway in the large pistol. The man appeared sober. At three meters, he couldn't possibly miss.

The policeman rooted around inside the roll. Pyotr worked on a plan. He could grab the officer as a shield and try to draw the Ingram. But the Black Shirt cared no more for the cop than for Pyotr. He'd gun them both down without a moment's hesitation. Pyotr had no hope of escape from that gloomy tunnel. At best his dying act would be to kill the Black Shirt. It was hardly the great blow for which he was prepared to sacrifice everything. To give up his wonderful new life with Olga and the girls. To never again feel their smooth faces rubbing against his morning beard. To have heard their last squeals of delight at simple things like fresh snow and surprise sweets.

'Turn it over,' the cop ordered.

This is it, Pyotr thought in a daze. He tried not to let his eyes water. Maybe if he grabbed the policeman's pistol instead of drawing his own . . . He slowly rotated the rolled carpet in the air, raising the open end to the prying man's gaze.

The flashlight clicked on. All Pyotr could see was the top of the hat. Fragments of half-formed plans ricochetted through Pyotr's mind. His thoughts remained in pieces, however, because of the shattering effect of one thought. He would never see his family again.

The police officer's movements fell still. Pyotr's every sense was focused and intense. From the depth of the cop's probing hand – from the steady beam of his flashlight – Pyotr knew that the man stared right at the black muzzle of the enormous .50-caliber sniper rifle.

'You see anything?' the Black Shirt asked.

The brim of the cop's hat rose slowly. Pyotr knew the time was *now* – the time was *now!* But something made him hesitate. From under the polished black brim were two close-set eyes. They were gray – very Russian – and fixed on Pyotr's.

'*Well?*' the Black Shirt demanded impatiently.

The flashlight clicked off and the perekhod fell dark.

'He's clean,' the cop replied. With his eyes still fixed on Pyotr he said, 'Better hurry. We're closing GUM early. The big May Day rally is tomorrow morning, you know.'

Pyotr nodded, hoisted the heavy rug, and headed toward the gray light of Red Square.

WHITE HOUSE EAST WING, WASHINGTON
May 1, 1000 GMT (0500 Local)

Elaine took Gordon by the elbow. She'd been up and dressed by four. She led him into their private dining room and closed the door. There were heaped mounds of hot food and no people. Gordon smiled, and Elaine smiled back. They sat beside each other, not across the table. She stayed close. They hugged and kissed and laughed. The companionship and closeness was comforting. Elaine knew he was sick with worry.

She didn't bring it up, he did. 'You know, Elaine . . .' was all he said. No one else would have understood, but she did. After twenty years of marriage he need only to begin a sentence. Sometimes, he only opened his mouth and the words came out of hers.

'What did the State Department say?' she challenged.

He frowned. 'Pull our troops out.'

'And Defense?' The same, he replied. 'And CIA? The UN Ambassador? Your National Security Adviser? Those disgusting, loud-mouthed *sycophants* from Congress?' He screwed up his face. 'All your *allies* say pull out, Gordon . . . and so do I.'

He closed his eyes, sighed, and sank back in his chair. He was relaxed. His guard was down. 'This job is too big for one man. Just look at this decision. I mean, what if I do the thing *everybody* recommends, but it turns out wrong? *Sure*, nobody wants to keep an army in Siberia. It's not like *I* do! And nobody even *considers* occupying *China* like . . .' Gordon stopped himself short.

'Is *that* what it is? That letter from *Kartsev?*' Gordon felt a twinge of nerves on mention out loud of his innermost fear. 'Honey, that man is good at killing defenseless people, that's it! What special insight do you think he has? Do you think he can predict the future? That *anarchy* will spread to China when the Russians *themselves* aren't even anarchists. His whole system of power is failing completely, Gordon. It's rotting from the top down, and it's about to collapse.'

'Isn't that the whole *idea* of anarchy?' Gordon shot back. 'Maybe it's part of Kartsev's plan. The state withers away and then . . . nothing. Or something even more awful.'

'Gordon, you're doing the right thing. You're taking care of the problem.'

'I'm going to kill a man, Elaine. A man I've never seen, or spoken to, or know *anything* about, really . . . except for that letter. Maybe that's why I'm obsessing about the damn thing. It's as if the son-of-a-bitch is taunting me, you know? Because if he turns out to be right, Elaine – if China and Russia both dissolve into true anarchy . . .'

He didn't finish the sentence or complete the thought, but Elaine put her hand on his arm. She lowered her head to his shoulder and squeezed his arm. It's a decision you have to make, Gordon. There really is no other choice.

'My fellow Americans,' Gordon said into the teleprompter – his hands clasped on the desk in front of him as coached – 'I come before you tonight not to talk of victory, but of peace. For this long and horrible war is now over, and the time for a great healing has begun. General Secretary Lin Tso-chang has accepted the Security Council's terms for a ceasefire.' He unclasped his hands and leaned forward for dramatic effect. 'At eighteen hundred hours Greenwich Mean Time today – approximately six hours from now – all UNRUSFOR offensive operations against the People's Liberation Army will be halted. The Chinese will withdraw all forces in contact with UNRUSFOR to a distance of thirty kilometers. A general and complete prisoner exchange will begin immediately.'

Gordon paused as the camera zoomed in. Now, according to the script, the screen framed his head and shoulders. The director's index finger cued him.

'While we have halted offensive operations, let me make this point perfectly clear. All Chinese military equipment and infrastructure within the control of UNRUSFOR will be destroyed. That will include the tanks, armored fighting vehicles, combat aircraft, artillery, trucks, and other equipment used by three-quarters of a million of the PLA's best-armed and best-trained men – over half of their heavy weapons arsenal. Strict limits will be placed on Chinese military deployments into northern Manchuria. Any violation of the demilitarized zone will be punished swiftly and severely. And any future breach of the peace by Chinese forces or violation of the Russian border will be met with immediate and overwhelming counterforce. We have in this war proven our resolve as a nation and as a people to combat Chinese aggression and we will continue to do so, whatever form that aggression should take.'

This time the pause was unscheduled. There was no pre-planned gesture. No zooming or camera switches or stage direction. Just one last nagging deluge of doubt. One last echo of Kartsev's warning.

'Although UNRUSFOR,' Gordon finally resumed, 'will maintain sufficient combat strength in the Far Eastern theater to fulfil its regional obligations, the Security Council has approved a timetable for withdrawal of forces from the Asian continent.'

There, he thought. *It's done.* Somehow, however, he obtained no respite from his worries.

'And so, as of today, this great travail has ended. The sacrifices made by our soldiers, sailors, airmen and Marines have not been for naught. Siberia is under UN auspices. East Asia is at peace once again. Aggression has been punished severely. China's offensive military capacity has been devastated. And we will remain vigilant against any further crimes against the peace. God bless the United States of America. Thank you. And good night.'

THE KREMLIN, MOSCOW, RUSSIA
May 1, 1200 GMT (1400 Local)

The office door opened, and in walked Miss Dunn. Kartsev confirmed with a tug on his jacket that his pistol remained hidden. He then rose with a truly genuine smile on his face and held out his hand. Miss Dunn hugged her arms across her chest. She wouldn't even raise her wind-burned and red face.

Kartsev sneezed loudly and unexpectedly. He turned and extracted his handkerchief. '*I apologize!*' he said. 'Spring allergies, I'm afraid.' She looked up at him defiantly – her lips pursed as she sucked in her cheek on one side, staring. Kartsev had to smile. He hadn't seen such directness since . . . He couldn't remember the last time. 'I hope you weren't treated badly. I gave specific instructions that you not be harmed, but . . . but people are getting a little sloppy these days.' She frowned – still staring. 'I'm sure you'll understand, however, why I brought you here. Why this is such a *momentous* day.'

She snorted like a bratty child. '*Yeah! May Day,*' she said sarcastically. 'Your big speech to an adoring people.' Her smile turned up only one corner of her mouth. She never broke eye contact.

'You've changed,' he said out loud. It was a comment made not to her, but to himself.

She arched her eyebrows – her expression a study in boredom. 'I've been through too much to put up with your bullshit.' Her words were slurred. Her manner nonchalant. She wasn't scared of him anymore.

They stared at each other – Kartsev's mood darkening. He walked over to his desk, but she didn't follow. '*Well,*' he said, trying to snap out of his funk, 'actually I wasn't talking about the rally. Come here. Let me show you.'

Miss Dunn hesitated for a moment before wandering over. She shoved her hands in the back pockets of her blue jeans. Slumped and slouching, she stood beside Kartsev.

'You see the document on the computer screen?' he asked. Her head was tilted and her hair half covered her face. But he saw her gaze rise to the monitor. The blue phosphors were reflected brightly in her eyes. 'It's my life's greatest work. I call it "The Laws of Human History." I'm really quite proud of it, if truth be told.'

Miss Dunn arched her eyebrows and said, 'Hm.' She lifted a paperweight from his desk and turned it from side to side.

Undaunted, Kartsev said, 'I wanted to invite you to my "publishing party."' He held his hands out to the empty office. She said nothing. The anticlimax was now complete. He didn't know what to say, so he just leaned over to the mouse, rolled the cursor to the 'Send' button, and clicked. The blue status bar rose slowly till it read one hundred percent. Kartsev stood back. 'There!'

After a few moments, Miss Dunn asked, 'What?' Her interest was finally piqued.

'It's published.'

'What do you mean, it's published?'

'I sent it via the Internet to a few thousand different servers in about two dozen . . .' Again he sneezed without warning. '*Excuse* me!' he said – dabbing at his nose. 'As I was saying, I had it translated into a couple of dozen major languages and posted it for all to read. I just wanted you to be here . . . when I published it.'

Miss Dunn was alert now – her old self. Her eyes darted to the monitor. 'What's the book about?'

Kartsev smiled. 'It is nothing more than a . . . a work of non-fiction, if you will.' He looked down at the floor. 'Maybe you could call it a treatise if you judge by the number of bold statements I make in it.' He laughed. 'But I did strive to leave a mark.'

'Oh . . . you've left a mark,' Kate said – feeling her teeth grind. 'You'll be remembered for a long time.'

'But I hope for so much *more* than mere notoriety,' Kartsev said. 'Social experimentation is a duty we owe mankind. No system is perfect. Pristine ideologies become sullied by implementation. Exemplary organizations lose their way, are corrupted or hijacked, or simply decay over time. Every human institution evolves in a complex but not indecipherable way.'

'And you've deciphered that process?' Kate asked.

'I have tried to do my part. To describe a piece of the process, perhaps.'

'What piece?'

'Certain . . . *manners* of *translation* of societal forces. Actually, more like currents that . . .' He faltered.

After several moments of silence, Kate said, 'You're having trouble answering the question?'

635

'Well, you're *asking* it in a *rather* rude way!' He calmed down instantly – ready to apologize.

'You are sick, you know?' she said with disdain that had never been more evident.

'So I understand,' he replied with a sigh.

'You think that characterization is *unfair*? After what you've *done*?'

Kartsev ignored the barb and tried again to explain. 'Can you not see the degree of human interconnectivity? The rippling waves of fashion and culture that criss-cross our world? They create such deliciously complex patterns of interference. Behavioral trends aren't linear, you know. They are dissonant fields in multi-dimensional space. Even if they could be plotted mathematically – described by an accurate model – they could not be visualized in the human mind.'

'Then how did you describe the process in your book?'

'Very primitively, I'm sure,' Kartsev said. He smiled and lowered his head. 'I can only hope I've advanced mankind's thinking in some small way.'

'And that justifies what you've *done*?' she shouted – outraged. 'Does that give you license to harm even *one* other human on earth?'

'Who said that I needed license?' Kartsev asked with an innocent expression. 'Why am I not free to do what I please? Because someone wrote a law in a book? I could write *volumes* of rules and regulations. I assume you would find all of them illegitimate.'

'Because you have no mandate from the people to govern.'

'Who said I need a mandate? Empires and monarchies govern quite effectively. Pluralism is simply the dictatorship of the center over the extremes. A distribution of power along the bell curve. Democratic representatives grope for a consensus as if some magical truth lies in that center. What a comical system it is! Who said that conformity to norms is a measure of fitness to govern? Who defines the degree of deviation from the norm that's allowed? Each society draws its own lines. Things acceptable in Amsterdam would get you beheaded in Afghanistan. Where is the sense in that? Who is to judge the right from the wrong? Humans? God? And if God, *which* god? Whose laws and traditions should rule?'

Kate simply shook her head. 'You've debased everything good in the name of evil. You've led a counter-enlightenment. A Renaissance in reverse. You've led your country into the Dark Ages. You've caused a major war. You've killed millions.'

Kartsev smiled. 'Do you believe a man to be responsible for everything that ensues from his actions?' She didn't answer. 'If the action was well-intentioned, do you still blame the agent for the result?'

'Nothing you've done was well-intentioned.'

'I'm not talking about me,' Kartsev replied. He grinned broadly, but not menacingly. 'I'm a very bad man, yes. To you I must be the epitome of Satan. The incarnation of the Antichrist.'

'You flatter yourself. I actually see you as more banal. A petty tyrant with the aspirations of a Nazi doctor.'

Kartsev shrugged and nodded. His smile was long gone. 'I suppose that's an apt description. But perhaps you should read the book.' He turned and patted his pockets distractedly. He found a pen and stuck it in his jacket. 'The Square is full by now, I would imagine.' He suddenly had a wonderful idea. 'Miss Dunn, have you ever seen Red Square from atop Lenin's Mausoleum? As a reporter I should think you would be very curious. It could be an historic moment, you know. Just imagine looking out on a *sea* of faces. I never have been on the reviewing stand before, actually. But I grew up watching from below. It's really more comfortable down there. Always looking up. Being part of the mass . . . not alone.'

When Kartsev thought to look to Kate for an answer, she almost whispered in a thick voice, 'I want to go home.'

There was a knock on the door. An aide stepped in but said nothing. Kartsev nodded, and the aide disappeared. Kartsev tucked his speech into his pocket. 'Of course,' he said. 'My people will see to it. Farewell then, Miss Dunn. Farewell.' He headed for the door, deeply saddened.

'Who were you talking about?' she blurted out. He stopped and turned. 'When you were asking whether someone should be blamed for the results even if his actions were well-intentioned?'

Kartsev beamed. 'Oh! Why, your beloved President Davis, of course. This generation's Abraham Lincoln, I believe your colleagues in the press are calling him. Every indication that I get is that he's an honorable, upstanding man. His actions seem to have been taken with the best of intentions, which makes them – of course – highly predictable. And yet who is more despicable? Valentin Kartsev, who caused the deaths of perhaps a few million people at most? Or Gordon

Davis, who is directly responsible for the deaths of hundreds upon hundreds of millions of human beings?'

Kate stared back at him. Not understanding. 'You mean the war?' His only response was a noncommittal arch of his brow. 'Your question doesn't make any *sense*. Hundreds of millions of people didn't *die*.'

Kartsev straightened his tie. He wiped his palms on his thighs as if nervous, then tugged his jacket, stiffened his back and took a deep, bracing breath. 'But they will.' He turned and left the chilly, dark room.

The breeze across Red Square gusted slightly. Andreev clicked the windage knob to adjust for the added drift. The sky was a brilliant blue. Heat could be felt in the sun's radiance. The captive mass of pathetic souls below was ringed by black-clad thugs.

Pyotr was calm and focused in the tight space between the ancient chimneys on the roof of GUM. It was the site he'd worried about most as head of presidential security. He'd crawled through the wall space years earlier – just as he had the day before. It was a security nightmare. Ingress was concealed behind the hollow walls of the former government department store. The round, rooftop window was easily opened. Lenin's Mausoleum lay directly in front and beneath the site at a thirty-degree angle of elevation. And there was even rapid egress by climbing down criss-crossing wood bracing to a sub-basement. From there you could get into the sewer and out via the subway service tunnels.

He'd written a detailed report and advised how everything should be sealed up tight. But the president himself had interceded. He had rejected the plan without explanation. Pyotr was sufficiently steeped in Kremlin politics not to ask for one. All copies of Pyotr's report were shredded and burned. Thereafter, every gathering in Red Square was preceded by Pyotr's personal check of the site.

A roar rose up, and a waving man ascended to the flat roof of the tomb. Andreev removed the scope's front lens cover from the potentially reflective glass. He twirled his left forearm in the rifle's sling once more, twisting it ever tighter. The sling would limit the circulation in his left forearm – eventually causing shakes from muscles starved of oxygen. But he would be quick. He'd take the first opportunity presented. He wouldn't rush the mechanics of the shot, but there was nothing to be gained by delay.

One shot – one kill, came the words of the American instructor. They were a motto repeated over and over. They were the only words of advice that stuck with Pyotr. He'd never heard them when he went through the Russian Army's special training course twenty years before. The Russians were less concerned with escape, evasion and survival.

Kartsev mounted the Mausoleum. The rifle was firmly seated in Andreev's shoulder. He lowered his right eye to the scope.

Even though Kartsev knew the cheers were a farce, he got a certain rise out of the sheer volume of crowd noise. When he reached the top of the stairs, however, he was angered to see the waiting collection of toadies. They all stood in front of their seats applauding. They wore black suits like undertakers. But as if that wasn't enough, they wore black arm bands and lapel pins in the shape of a black flag. Their fat little hands clapped noiselessly. All turned to fawn over Kartsev.

He'd forgotten that most of them were still alive. Men he'd worked with – organized – in the months leading up to the government's ousting. Their yellowed eyes and pallid complexions reminded him of the living dead. They had feasted on the flesh of their people, and were now reduced to gnawing on the carcass that remained. They held no higher beliefs. Most of the true believers were now rotting in shallow graves dug on the orders of these men. These men were not social scientists. They were bureaucrats of the death machine.

Kartsev greeted no one as he headed for the podium. He weaved his way among the disinterred – the captains and lieutenants of his army of walking dead. Only when Kartsev reached the podium could he truly turn his attention to the crowd. He smiled as he surveyed the pumping fists and bellowing lungs. The streaming black flags. The faces turned expectantly upward – toward him.

What power to summon such numbers. He raised his hand and waved.

The scope wobbled with each beat of Pyotr's heart. At extreme magnification he could see nothing but Kartsev's torso. Always refining – never fighting – Andreev focused all his attention on centering the crosshairs. Nothing existed for him now but the rifle – the scope. His left hand was locked tightly to the grip by the stock. His right hand grasped the pistol grip. His shoulder steadied the rifle stock at the butt. His cheek rested lightly against the cool plastic. The rolled rug lay under the heavy barrel – completing the man-rifle unit.

His index finger held firm pressure on the trigger. A hair more and the weapon would discharge. The crosshairs remained inside Kartsev's torso. It wobbled, but from shoulder to hip to the opposite shoulder. It wasn't Kartsev he aimed at, but a concept. A defined point in imaginary space. And that point was at the intersection of two lines. The vertical line split Kartsev's necktie down the middle. The horizontal one ran from nipple to nipple. Pyotr waited patiently for the scope's crosshairs to line up. For the momentary unity of imaginary and real lines.

There was an explosion of noise. Pyotr couldn't recall even pulling the trigger. The smoke and haze cleared. The podium was empty. Pyotr slid through the window and was gone.

Kartsev sneezed violently and doubled over at the waist. Even so, he heard the booming report of the rifle. There was no doubt in his mind what it was. He remained bent low – shielded behind the thick armored podium. Directly behind him sprawled three dead men. There was gore and shattered bone everywhere. The backs of their chairs each had bloody holes in a descending line. They grew from the size of a melon at the top of the first chair, to a hole the width of a basketball near the seat of the third. The chairs' former occupants had been cored straight through.

Everyone scurried about the rooftop like desperate cockroaches. Some rose, others ducked – all panicked.

But there were no more thunderous blasts from the lone gun. The assassin had missed his target . . . but didn't realize it. The only sound Kartsev heard now was from the crowd. The disturbance and commotion spread quickly through Red Square.

'He's dead!' Kartsev heard someone shout. The words were repeated far and wide. Kartsev realized too late what was happening. By the time he raised up all was lost, and he got a bird's-eye view of the end. An end he had guessed might come that very day. It was an interesting footnote to his study of man's behavior. The surging mass confirmed the laws about which he'd written. Staccato bursts of gunfire from the Black Shirts ended quickly. They had little or no apparent effect. Kartsev half-turned to see the loyal zombies hurling themselves to the ground. Jumping two storeys in a futile attempt to save their skins. But it only hastened their end, he could tell from their inhuman shrieks. From the blood-curdling screams that rose up from the earth.

Nothing would stop the mob once it was loosed. For it was no longer simply a collection of individuals. It was an entity obeying its own merciless laws of behavior. A detached Kartsev watched the hysteria sweep Red Square. Black Shirts killed, were overwhelmed, then died. Sometimes he glimpsed the living as they were lifted into the air over the masses. After brief torment they descended and were consumed by the crowd.

The most wondrous thing of all was the cacophonous noise. The pent-up potential energy of society turning kinetic.

The fat men atop Lenin's Mausoleum fired feeble shots down the stairs. Their pistols blazed till empty and then died. The surging throng devoured their fattened prey like starving beasts. They brutalized some, threw others over the wall, but killed them all.

One by one the gaunt attackers caught sight of Kartsev. He stood all alone to face the wrath of mankind. They hesitated when confronted by so powerful a man. They were still cowed by their primal fear of Kartsev the Terrible. By the last remaining authority figure in Russia.

Kartsev frowned, drew his pistol and blew his brains out.

'A just system of human government is stable. Unless the catalysts are powerful enough, it will tend to right itself and return to its center. But violence resonates in the unjust system. The vibrations of its excited molecules pass the disturbance along with evergrowing levels of energy. It is in such a system that one man can make a difference. All it takes is one man to send the unjust society careening down the road of history.'

Valentin Kartsev (posthumously)
'The Laws of Human History'
Moscow, Russia

Epilogue

BEIJING UNIVERSITY, CHINA
October 27, 1300 GMT (2300 Local)

Late at night, the university library was empty. Chin still had one hour left before it closed. Janitors mopped the floors. But most of the staff were congregated at the main desk, talking.

Chin sat at the computer – one of a few dozen now available to university students. He was logged onto the Internet. He dared not take what might appear to be a suspicious check of his environs. He stared instead at the on-line drawings of a patent application for a water pump. He'd already completed his report on the pump's design. He'd deliver it to his first-year engineering class in the morning. Now, he just waited till he was absolutely certain no one could see his computer screen.

When that moment came, he typed in the long and complex URL. He hit 'Enter' and waited as the server made its connection. Soon enough the familiar title page appeared. He waited as the table of contents and each chapter loaded sequentially. Page after page was beamed electronically into his computer. Until the process was complete he was at the greatest risk. His trigger finger lay poised on the mouse button. The cursor sat atop the 'Exit' icon. But when

643

the 1.6-megabyte document was inbound, the computer was slow to respond. Its windows closed sometimes in unpredictable ways. A small box filled with the dangerous words might linger on the screen. Chin knew that being caught would mean certain death.

The tiny LEDs flickered as the book poured in. He had a back-up plan. You always needed a fall-back. He'd flick the power switch on the computer and flush the RAM. Any trace of what he was downloading would then be erased. But at a minimum such an act would cost him his computer privileges. At worst he'd be sent to re-education camp for years.

Hung had not been so lucky. Chin tried again to imagine who had squealed. Who from POW camp had turned in his friend. It must have been the peasant man Hung had so often and so viciously derided. But he'd never know who it was in the end. It was just one of the mysteries that seemed to abound in the world. Mysteries such as the cause of Russia's now-raging second civil war. Everyone knew that the violence had started in Moscow. At a rally in Red Square, he had read. The anarchist leadership had been literally torn limb from limb. And there were rumors of a sniper that had never been confirmed. Confusion always surrounded events on so large a scale. They were a blurred swirl of action and reaction -- force and counterforce.

But Chin knew now that the chaotic 'dissonance' was caused by 'complex, inter-related social variables' – words he'd never even heard before that now explained so much. He was fascinated by his new world of ideas. Especially those that explained things dear to him. Stealing a foreign patent was certainly a challenge for an aspiring engineer. But water pumps held limited appeal in Chin's new order of things. There was so much more to be gained by study and, increasingly, by action.

The red light at the top of the browser finally went black. Chin rolled the mouse and clicked the 'Back' button. The drawings again flashed onto the screen. *Safe*, he thought, relaxing. He clicked 'Forward' and the banned book reappeared instantly.

He was over a third of the way into the treatise. It was one long and fascinating lesson in the nature of man. It answered questions Chin had never pondered before the war. What drives man to extremes of behavior? How does violence reshape personality? It described the micro- and macro-social models with mathematical precision.

The only way he could find his place in the book for each furtive late-night read was to memorize the last words he'd read and search for them the next day. That wasn't difficult. He'd already committed much of what he'd read to memory. Nothing had ever spoken to him like this book did. He'd found it late one night while browsing the Web. The propaganda about the great victory in the north obviously held no answers to any of Chin's questions. Neither Chin's family nor his friends discussed what it felt like to return home from hell. But Chin had found newsgroup postings by his former enemies in the West. He dared not reply, of course. But he relished their discussion of the great emptiness both he and they felt. From continent to continent, everyone talked about the great void that had been left inside them. About the end of life's most cathartic experience and the beginning of the great nothingness that followed. 'I was in the 1st MEF west of Vladivostok . . .' would begin the heart-wrenching message. The replies would be from Germany, Belgium, Holland, France.

Chin barely held in the surge of emotions when he read what the men had to say. It took the greatest willpower he could muster to keep his facial expression neutral. When he was done, he'd run all the way from the library back to his room. He'd lie in bed and sob. Part in joy on realizing he wasn't alone. Part in sadness on reliving the ordeal. For the experience of the cogs in the machine was universal no matter what the uniform. And he felt a kinship that cut across national boundaries. A closeness that linked brother-to-brother by spilt blood.

He'd learned many things from those postings. That the panicked, sweaty awakenings were quite normal. 'Post-traumatic anxiety attacks' were their name. No one ever talked of them in China. But his brothers described it exactly, just as they did the now-constant pain in his joints. According to a British vet, one in four in the UN army had been medically discharged due to 'cold-induced rheumatism.' The doctors at Beijing University clinic had denied there was any such thing. But he trusted only his brethren, and the news from them wasn't good. The pain Chin felt now would worsen steadily for decades to come.

But his greatest discovery had come ten nights ago. It was a posting by a French combat veteran. One of the war-related sites he listed in his message contained the book Chin now accepted as his bible. It was the Rosetta Stone of his attempt at understanding why his life had changed. It not only answered all his questions, it posed new ones he hadn't thought to ask.

But the most fascinating thing of all was its breadth and scope of subject. It not only answered whys – and the far simpler whens, wheres and whos – but it spent long sections discussing the ever-practical hows. The cause and effect of human behavior – both mass, and individual. The universal truths about man no matter how dark and base.

What had happened in the north after the UN withdrawal was only a precursor. But it was enough of a shock to Beijing that they'd quarantined all of Manchuria. No news or people flowed into or out of the rebellious provinces. But the fighting there still raged, according to reports he'd read on the Internet.

He fantasized late at night in the darkness of his room. In Chin's mind he saw wave after wave of stimuli washing over a seething population. They would unleash violence on a scale never seen before. The destructive potential of a billion and a half people. He imagined the feeble efforts of the decrepit Communist government to stem the tidal forces. He imagined the liberating blows which would topple the weakened state. He went from grinding teeth to smiles to blissful sleep. Then he'd awaken the next morning to aching knees, hips, shoulders and elbows. He took painkillers he'd bought off the black market in ever-increasing doses.

It was, in fact, his first forays in search of drugs that had led to his great breakthrough. He'd thought at first of organizing the students at Beijing University. Of forming 'study' groups which he could carefully lead into social discussion and eventually criticism. But when he ventured into the back alleys of Beijing to find relief from his pain, he realized what a waste of time dealing with students would be. Instead of nudging them warily into subversion, he could step into opium dens filled with hatred. And while university groups were closely watched, commoners were too numerous for scrutiny. There were brutalized veterans like Chin. Angry men like Hung who'd lost loved ones to the basements and camps of the security apparatus. Refugees fresh from bloody reprisals in Manchuria. And a vast sea of the disenfranchised, whose bleary eyes lit up when Chin spoke of a world in which they would be free to say 'No.' For what he offered them was priceless. A relief from dreary existence. A break from incessant boredom. A justification to swing the fist they'd long before balled up in anger. A sense of belonging which was more addictive to society's outcasts than the opium which they smoked around the clock.

Already Chin had gotten them to kill. It was no more difficult than issuing orders to his platoon. Part challenge, part coaxing, part plea –

the result had been three dead policemen. Three slit throats. Three service pistols added to their budding arsenal. But it was discovery of the treatise on the Internet which had given Chin focus, direction and drive. For armed with the tools that the book provided him, he could send masses crashing against the bastards who'd killed Hung. The fucking assholes who'd sent hundreds of thousands to their deaths. Who'd consigned many more men – like Chin – to a life filled with physical and emotional agony.

The clicking heels across the library floor elicited the same reaction from Chin as a boot squeaking in snow. Chin calmly hit the 'Back' button even as the sweat beaded at his forehead. As his heart raced. As his entire body tensed up and he experienced a clarity of vision and of thought he'd never known before the war. The enemy passed uneventfully. He wore the uniform of an ordinary police officer – white belt, white gloves clasped behind his back, white holster with a white lanyard hanging from his black automatic. Nothing but the finest for China's most elite university. But Chin and everyone else knew that he and the others like him were from the Ministry of State Security. You could tell it from the way the real police officers at the university's gates acted. They wore the drab uniforms and bored looks of the low-paid, and they snapped to attention when such men stopped by. Chin couldn't wait to see the blood drip from the fine, white accouterments.

The government kept a watchful eye on Beijing University. After years and years of turmoil, admission was now limited to the trusted few. To the sons of peasants, to war heroes, to the apolitical. They'd done checks in Chin's village and he'd scored high on all three. 'Congratulations!' the admissions officer had said. 'We not only turned up *no* politically insensitive remarks in your past. We apparently turned up no remarks of a political nature whatso*ever*. And *that's* rare.'

But that had been before the war. Before 'The Laws of Human History.' Before Valentin Kartsev.

The cop was flirting with a girl who worked at the main desk of the library. Chin switched back to the book and hit 'Find.' In the small window he typed the last phrase he'd read before being kicked out the night before. 'It is man's most basic nature,' Chin typed, 'to subvert all attempts at control.' When he hit 'Go,' the computer quickly found the passage. As Chin began his night's reading, he had to force himself to remain alert. He got so absorbed in the book that he was at risk of ignoring the danger signs. For the words sparked wildfires of imagination. Streaming banners. Barricades manned by armed and defiant people. 'Creative destruction.'

He set his jaw, and ground his teeth, and clenched his fists. His body was tensed in preparation for action. But now was not the time or the place.

The day will come, he thought – he pledged. *Soon . . .*